Ink and Blood
By Willia...

To

MARGARET

William P...

Thanks to my father-in-law, Alex Struthers, for taking a doodle on a piece of paper and turning it into a superb cover.

Thanks also to my wife, Julie, and my little sister, Janet.

Chapter 1

In a house on the outskirts of a little town called Pormount in Rutherford County, Tennessee.

The meal was over, the table was cleared, the curtains were drawn, the candles were lit, and mood music drifted lazily from the surround sound speaker system. In the middle of their large living room, Ralph and Blair Walden, 53 and 51 respectively, danced slowly in a little circle. Her arms rested on his shoulders, her hands clasped loosely behind his neck. His hands sat comfortably on her waist, stroking up and down every so often, tracing her curves. They were full of good food and wine. They were warm, comfortable and both were looking forward to some gentle lovemaking before bed.

The music changed, the slow song ending and something a little more up tempo taking its place. Ralph took his wife's hand and stepped back so that their arms were fully extended. Blair let out a little "Woo!" as her husband pulled her towards him, spinning her into his arm as he did so. And so they danced some more, this time with more twirling and shaking involved. Just before the song ended, Ralph let his wife's hand go and pressed a hand to his stomach.

"Think I might want to leave it a little while longer before I do any more dancing like that."

"You should know better than to go jiving around like that so soon after a meal," Blair said to him, a note of playful rebuke in her voice.

"Why do you always wait till after I do something dumb to tell me I shouldn't have done it?" asked Ralph. Blair smiled warmly at him and cupped his face with both hands.

"That's how you learn, pumpkin."

Ralph suddenly stepped to the side and swatted his wife's rump. Blair let out a little squeal of surprise.

"Learn to dodge quicker," chuckled Ralph.

Blair slapped him on the shoulder and led her husband to the couch, where they sat side by side, snuggled close together, and listened to some more music.

The pair had met through a mutual friend when Blair had been 21 and Ralph 23. It had pretty much been love at first sight, though it had been almost three months before tall, lanky, bashful Ralph Walden had asked shy, slinky Blair Haspeth to go out with him. It had been a mere month after that that he had asked her to marry him, and a year later the two were wed. There had been some grumbling from their families regarding their ages, particularly from Blair's parents. However, as their daughter had recently reminded her husband, mistakes were how you learned. The Haspeth's had decided that if it was going to work out, it would work out, and if not, then their daughter would learn from the experience.

Many happy years down the road, with several more in the tank (god willing), a paid for house, three kids and four grandkids, even Blair's dear departed mother and father wouldn't have argued that it had worked out beautifully.

"Have we heard from Parker lately?" asked Ralph, referring to their youngest child, who was currently off touring the world. Unlike his parents and his siblings, Jessica and Raymond, Parker did not relish the slow and steady lifestyle. As a child he had devoured book after book on countries far and wide, his determination being to visit each one. When he had turned 21 he had been off, emptying his savings account and heading for the horizon. His parents, who trusted that they had raised their children well enough to let them forge their own paths in life, had asked only that he take care and keep in touch. He had given his word that he would and he had kept it.

"He sent me a text yesterday," Blair replied. "He's in Australia right now. He said he'd text again soon to arrange a video call with us." Ralph grinned.

"Damn, he got far, didn't he? Seems to me that it wasn't so long ago he was just looking at places like that in books and asking me if I'd take him there one day."

"M-hm," nodded Blair. "And you always used to tell him that one day he'd make it there on his own. What you didn't tell him till much later on was that he'd have to go on his own because you were afraid of flying."

"It's a common phobia," Ralph defended himself. "Besides, he got to where he wanted to go. It's not something I could have done, and not just due to the fact the idea of getting on a plane makes me want to puke. I guess I've just never had that wandering spirit."

"Me neither," said Blair. "Makes you wonder where he got it from, doesn't it?"

"It does, but to be honest I'm just happy he used it. Would have been a damn shame if he'd had all those grand ideas of visiting far off places as a kid and then just sat on his ass all the time when he grew up. But he's out there, doing his thing... Bet he's had himself a fair few foreign girls too."

"Ralph!" cried Blair. Ralph chuckled.

"I'm just saying; he's out there on his own without us to tell him what to do. You don't think he's..."

"I don't mind just so long as he's careful," said Blair.

"He'd be totally freaked out if he knew we were talking about this."

"You're talking about our youngest being out there in the big wide world, laying down with who knows who; I'm not that far from freaked out myself."

"Well," began Ralph, grinning devilishly. "If it makes you feel any better, he'd be just as freaked out at the thought of us doing it."

"Any more of this talk and you won't be doing anything, Ralph Walden."

"Oh, you think that at my age you can still use withholding sex as a means of getting your own way?" Blair nodded confidently. Ralph's nod had a defeated quality to it. "Yeah, you're right. I'll drop it." Blair smiled and leaned in to kiss his cheek.

"Right round my little finger, right where you belong," she said.

"Seems to me the decent thing would be to not point that out."

"Oh, Ralph," she said, her voice taking on a tone he knew very well, a tone loaded with promise. The years since they had met had added lines to his face and inches to his waist, but in no way had it dulled his want for her. Ralph looked into his wife's suddenly wicked, smiling eyes as she told him, "As it turns out I'm just not feeling all that decent tonight."

The digital clock on Ralph's bedside table read 03:26. He and Blair were fast asleep, back to back. No dreams troubled their slumber.

But a nightmare cautiously approached their back door.

Meet Andrew Corday.

In late 1984, under the name of David Brannon, Corday had been committed to the care of the doctors at The Berrybeck Centre, though back then it had been known by a different name: The Berrybeck Hospital for the Criminally Insane. The name change came about in the mid 90's, when the hospital had been sold into private ownership, and since then the nature of the work done there had changed, altering over time to something a little more lucrative. The low risk patients had completed their rehabilitation and re-joined society, and the higher risk patients had been shipped out to other institutions, or in some cases prisons. Thereafter, those being admitted to Berrybeck were referred to as guests rather than patients, the place having been turned into a private retreat for those who found modern life a little too stressful or depressing, and who wanted some time away from whatever rat-race or addiction had left them burnt out.

During his time there as a patient, Corday had exasperated every doctor who had ever tried to treat him. Each one had eventually moved on, leaving Berrybeck behind, and leaving Corday to whichever unfortunate decided to tackle his inscrutable mental condition next. Corday would sit in the same spot for days on end, staring at the wall or out of the window into the distance, moving only to go to the bathroom or to the dining room. The vast majority of the time he never said a word to anyone. On those occasions when he did speak, he was never rude, never violent. He was always well mannered, open, even blasé, about the crimes he had committed, and he never showed the slightest remorse. As time passed, the new doctors who came to the hospital had given up on trying to rehabilitate Corday, instead leaving him to while away his minutes, hours, days, weeks, months and years. His status had gradually been down-graded from extremely dangerous to low risk. When the hospital changed hands, he had been due to be shipped out to one of the minimum security institutions along with a few of his fellow inmates, but someone had intervened on his behalf. Not even the head of the company that had bought Berrybeck was aware of this person's identity, but the fees were always paid on time and so Corday had been allowed to stay.

These days no one who had been working at Berrybeck in the winter of 1984 was still there. They had all gone, one way or another, and had taken with them the knowledge of what Corday had done, of what he really was. To those staff working there now, he was just a long term guest, a resident really. Sure, he refused to have his hair cut shorter than the length required for it to reach between his shoulders. Sure, he refused to shave, leaving most of his lower face obscured behind a bushy beard, but he was no one to pay an undue amount of attention to, certainly no one to be afraid of.

It might have been that Corday would never have bothered leaving Berrybeck. However he had slowly come to realise that he might have the means to get everything back on track right at his fingertips. At first he had been angry with himself for playing the part of the mentally absent patient for so long, wasting so much time. Then he had been furious at his associates. Why had they not gotten him out of here? But then he decided that all of this was wasting even more time. A little studying in the library, a few weeks on the computers they made available to guests and his research had been successfully concluded. He had even managed to contact his old associates and arrange a pick up point. All that had been left for him to do was leave, and for that he had decided to go old school.

Gathering together the things he required had been child's play. No one in the place ever gave him a second glance. He was part of the furniture here. If a knife went missing from the kitchen, surely it wasn't that nice Mr Brannon who took it. If some matches were misplaced, who would suspect kindly Mr Brannon? To a one, they had all been oblivious to the monster in their midst.

Not anymore.

Corday's exit from Berrybeck had been accompanied by blood and fire, though now he was wondering if perhaps a quieter exit had been in order. It wasn't inconceivable that he could have affected a much subtler escape. In fact it was entirely possible he could have faked his own death, and walked out of Berrybeck confident in the knowledge that no one would be out looking for him.

But where would have been the fun in that?

Even when everything calmed down at the centre, which would take some time, and it was discovered that he was missing, they might assume he had died in the fire and search for him inside the building before looking farther afield. It was his intention to be well on his way before that happened.

He used a rock to smash one of the small panes of glass on the back door. If it woke anyone up, then so be it; he'd be introducing himself to the occupants soon enough. The back door opened into the kitchen. A few moments spent waiting and listening suggested no one was coming to investigate. A quick - and quiet; he felt no need to push his luck - search of the drawers yielded a nice, sharp kitchen knife. He also found a torch. He switched it on, holding it by the wide end so he could shade the beam with his fingers, and made a quick inspection of the downstairs area. He ended up in the lounge, raising the torch and playing the beam over the pictures on the mantle. There was a wedding photo, and pictures of three other young adults he assumed were the happy couple's children. The largest photo was in the centre, a family shot, dated early last year. Corday stared at it for a few moments, then turned his attention to the photograph next to it, a candid shot which showed the man and wife together, smiling broadly for the camera, their arms around one another.

Corday sneered. What did these fools know of love? There's was nothing more than a pale imitation of the real thing. *However, mine is but a mere memory*, he told himself. No matter; what use did he have for love anyway?

He turned and made his way to the stairs. Up he crept to the landing and from there to the left, going down the corridor, not bothering to listen at the doors; he knew which room they were in. He had seen the light go on earlier, just after all the lights downstairs had been switched off. Pausing outside the room, he wondered how he should approach this. He had never been in such a situation before. Not for him the breaking and entering, sneaking about, bursting into bedrooms and whatnot. However he had to admit that he was getting a bit of a kick out of it. What he didn't want was that good feeling to be brought to an end by bursting into a bedroom to discover one of the occupants slept with a gun under their pillow. He knew that only the two of them lived in the house, but he hadn't been able to find out much about them online. They could be gun nuts, or collectors of bladed weaponry. Hell, for all he knew, they could be flat out fucking psychos and he was about to walk into a room full of rusty bear traps with chunks of rotten human meat clinging to the teeth. As delightful as Corday found the idea of having stumbled upon a house occupied by people whose world view was just as fucked up as his own, he knew that such people didn't play well with others.

Shutting off the torch, he reached out, gripped the handle and opened the door.

He was tensed, ready to pounce should a creak awaken either one of the occupants. If both woke up, he would go for the man first.

The door barely made a sound. Corday opened it far enough to enable him to enter the room, then he closed it again. He approached the bed, going to the man's side; he could see the face, cast in red and black thanks to the light from the digital clock on the bedside table. Ralph was still sleeping when Corday brought the torch down on his head. The noise and movement roused Blair, who didn't even get the chance to open her eyes before she too was struck.

Ralph opened his eyes, only to have the ache in his head intensified by the light being put out by the two lamps that were switched on. He squeezed his eyes shut, which also hurt. After a few moments he slowly and carefully opened them again. Blinking, he looked around his lounge. Slowly he became aware that he was seated on the floor in front of the fireplace. His hands had been tied behind his back, his ankles had been tied together and he had been gagged. The reasons for all this were pushed out of the way for the time being, overtaken by one simple, urgent question: where was Blair?

He forced the panic down, told himself to concentrate, to ignore the pain throbbing through his skull. He took a breath, and realised that there was someone behind him. He looked over his shoulder and saw Blair. Relief flooded through him, but then he spotted the blood matting her hair. The panic began to rise, like a shark swimming to the surface to feed, but Ralph held his breath and listened. She was breathing. He let the breath out again, tears stinging his eyes. She was alive. Injured, but alive. He had to get her out of here, had to get her to a hospital. He started to struggle against his bonds, but whoever had tied them had done a good job.

Minutes passed and he had made no progress, and then he heard a door open upstairs. Ralph froze, his eyes wide. He was facing the stairs and watched as a man, clean shaven and roughly his age, came down, dressed in some of Ralph's own clothes. He was drying his hair with a towel and quickly noticed Ralph staring at him.

"Hello," he said simply, as if their meeting was nothing out of the ordinary. "I'm Andrew. You're Ralph Walden, and the unconscious lady behind you is your wife, Blair. I expect you're wondering exactly what is going on."

Ralph, his eyes still wide, nodded. He had in his time watched a lot of movies and TV shows. They had taught him that if a bastard like this showed you their face or told you their name, they were probably going to kill you. Ralph's pulse quickened and he felt himself begin to sweat. As subtly as he was able, he began working at his bonds again.

"Well, I have broken into your house, and smashed you and your wife over the head with a torch, so I suppose I owe you some sort of explanation. Long story short, I needed a place where I could hole up until some friends of mine come to get me. Yours wasn't the first house on the road from where I was coming from, but of the addresses I found online, yours was the one I picked." Corday made a clucking sound with his tongue. "Bad luck. But you've no need to worry. When my friends arrive, I will leave with them, and you and your lovely wife will never see or hear from me again.

"Now, first of all, do you understand? Have I made everything clear?" Ralph nodded. "Excellent. Second, stop trying to untie your wrists. There's no way you'd manage to undo the knots, and I should also have mentioned that any attempts at escape by you or your wife will result in fatalities. Got that?" Ralph stopped fidgeting, gulped, and nodded his head. "You're doing great, Ralph," Corday told him. "One last thing: are you expecting anyone to visit anytime soon? Before you answer, know that if you lie and someone shows up and surprises me, it will result in their death, your death, and your wife's death. So, again: are you expecting anyone?" Ralph shook his head. "Then we're all set."

Corday walked past the couple on the floor and stood at the window, peering out between the blinds into the darkness. He threw the damp towel onto the nearest chair and ran his fingers through his damp hair, exhaling a long breath through his nose.

He had been surprised to find out, via the internet of course, that she had never moved away from her hometown. This couple had a car. All he had to do was hop in it and drive to her town, just as he had done so many years ago. How wonderful it would be to see her, to catch her, to take her. No. No, he had waited a long damn time to go and see her again, and when he did he wanted it to be done right, not slipshod. Not spur of the moment, as it would be if he went now. He had been patient for years. He could be patient a little while longer.

Feeling some friction south of the border, Corday realised he was becoming erect. He tutted and adjusted himself, turning back into the room, his eyes immediately falling on Blair Walden. He had enjoyed feeling her up as he had brought her downstairs, liking the fact that she slept in nothing but panties and a nightie, but at that point his mind had been on other things. Now he had some time to kill. She was a reasonable looking woman, kept herself in shape, most likely for health reasons or for her hubby. Certainly not for men like him, but that was beside the point. He approached the couple, picking up the torch from where he had put it down when he'd switched on the lamps.

Ralph Walden looked over his shoulder, saw Corday approaching and knew he had been lied to. He started struggling against his bonds and screaming against his gag. Corday clubbed him with the torch, this time hard enough to shatter the lens and bulb. The blow did not kill Ralph, but did, perhaps blessedly, knock him out.

FOUR MONTHS LATER

Chapter 2

Dear Marty

Do you ever feel old? I do, more and more these days. My friends tell me I'm being ridiculous; I'm only 34, but I still can't help feel that some things have passed me by. I mean I have a lot to be thankful for. I have no money worries, my own business, my friends, my health and you, of course, my oldest friend. But there are times, Marty, when I'm sitting at home on my own and I look around and think "Where do I go from here?" My aunt and uncle think maybe I'm bored at work, and that completely redecorating the store might help. Beth thinks I need a holiday. Amanda thinks I need a hobby. Sophie thinks I need another boyfriend. I think Sophie's talking out of her ass! Last thing I need or want right now is someone new in my life. I have to admit the idea of a holiday is nice though. Somewhere sunny and quiet.

What do you think, Marty? Get away from it for a couple of weeks, come back refreshed and ready to get on with things?

In other news from Hannerville USA, my neighbours' cat, Jess, gave birth to kittens. Her owners, Ted and Annette (they own the local laundromat, remember?) have been trying to get me to take one and I've been giving it some thought. It kind of clashes with my holiday idea (can't get a kitten and then put the poor thing in a cattery for two weeks) but the idea of having a pet is starting to grow on me. Might make my house feel a little less empty. It's a dangerous road though, right? I mean, I start with one cat and the next thing I know its 20 years later, I have dozens of them, and kids run as they pass my house!

I honestly don't know why I'm feeling like this, whatever the hell this feeling is. My last relationship broke up a couple of months ago, but I got over that (already had done last time I wrote to you). I have a good life, but I think I might want a little more out of it. Do you ever feel that way? I mentioned it to one of my customers at the store, a nice old guy called Mr Bickerson, and he told me that if I wanted more from life, then I should go out there and take it. But take what? Take a safari in Africa? Take up bungee jumping or bridge swinging or sky diving? Mr Bickerson didn't have a clue, and neither do I.

Perhaps I'm just in a funk and it'll pass. One night I'll have the girls round, we'll have some drinks and snacks, watch a movie or go out dancing, and I'll wonder what all this crap I'm thinking and feeling now was all about. I hope a deep funk is all it is. Or maybe I am in a rut and I need something to get myself out of it. A hobby, like Amanda says. Something nice and simple that can be done at home, or at least in town. I don't really see myself in khaki, or in a harness jumping off a tall structure, or swinging under one. And I sure as hell don't intend to go throwing myself out of a plane!

Enough about me; how are things with you? Everything still going well with Elaine? Work keeping you busy? How's your buddy Stephen?

As always, I look forward to hearing from you. Till next time.

With love

Abigail

Chapter 3

As had become his custom, Martin brought the sheet of handwritten A4 notepaper close to his face and inhaled, catching a very faint whiff of Abigail's perfume. It was a lovely smell, one that always made him feel happy and relaxed. On several occasions over the years he had thought about asking her what brand it was, but he feared that he would sound a little like a creepy stalker, admitting to sniffing the paper she wrote her letters on.

Folding the paper, he placed it back in the envelope and thought about how he might reply. He had a few things to get done today, so he'd have to write the letter either late tonight or sometime tomorrow. He thought tomorrow might be best; he liked to give his letters the consideration his long standing pen-friendship with Abigail deserved. He was a little concerned about this funk she was in.

Before he got caught up in his reply, Martin sat the letter aside and returned to his paper and breakfast. It was a Tuesday morning, just after 10:00am, and his first task of the day was at 11:00am, at the health club. Health club. Christ, it sounded so... *L.A.* It wasn't the kind of thing Martin normally bothered with, but Stephen had decided that he wanted to join a gym. He hadn't wanted to join on his own, so Martin had been roped into it. And he hadn't wanted to join a little local gym or a gym at a sports centre either. No, he had wanted to join the £500 a year, members only gym at the newly refurbished local branch of the Bennington Health Club chain. Martin's eyes had nearly popped out of their sockets when he'd heard how much membership would be, but he'd gone ahead with it, telling himself that maybe joining a gym would be good for him. Keep him fit and healthy for all the other things he enjoyed doing. After all, the constant lifting of the remote controls and all that bending and stretching to peruse the numerous shelves housing his DVD collection would require him to be in tip-top shape.

Abigail's reaction to the news of his joining a gym had been to fill almost half a page of A4 with nothing but "Ha, ha, ha!"

He was hoping Stephen would decide it was all a waste of time, and not bother to renew his membership. No way he would cancel before the year was up because it had been pointed out to them several times upon joining that the fee, once paid, was non-refundable. Stephen could be ridiculously frivolous with his money, but he always made sure he got his money's worth.

With his scrambled eggs eaten, and the more interesting stories in his newspaper read, Martin put the paper in his recycling bin, and his cup, plate and cutlery in the dishwasher, then went for a shower. A short time later, as he got dressed, he ran through a mental list of the work he had to get done before he went out for dinner tonight. There were a few sets of business cards and some promo artwork he had to polish up before meeting with the clients tomorrow. Nothing that should give him any problems.

He went to his bedroom window, and looked out at a bleak morning. The sky promised drizzle, the weather forecast in the paper promised showers later. In all likelihood Stephen would want to go for lunch in the club canteen after they had been to the gym, so it would probably be raining by the time they left. Martin crammed his training gear into a backpack, put on his jacket, grabbed his wallet, keys and mobile, and headed for the door.

He lived on the top floor flat of a very nice private development in the West of Scotland town of Hamilton. He refused to think of the place as exclusive, the way it had been billed on the sign outside the site when the place had been under construction. It had been Stephen who had talked him into visiting the show-home, and Martin had been very impressed. A far cry from the much smaller, but still perfectly serviceable, flat he had been living in at that time, Stephen had gone on and on about how the place would be so much better for him. How it would reflect his new found success in the world of graphic design, as well as his blossoming bank account. Martin hadn't been sure about either of those points, but he had really liked the flat. An examination of his finances had proven he could comfortably afford it, so he had bought himself a flat – though the developer had always referred to them in the more American style of apartments – on the top floor. Stephen got the idea that this was because he liked to be on top, prove to the world he had made it, but the simple truths were that Martin didn't like the idea of someone living above him, and the top flat afforded him a great view.

At least it did on sunny days.

His hand was on the door handle when his mobile rang. He checked the screen and found that it was Stephen calling.

"Don't you dare," he said on answering.

"Sorry, pal," apologised Stephen. Martin could hear the hangover in his voice.

"You're a dick! Why can't you make it?"

"I thought you'd be chuffed about not having to go."

"I would be if I wasn't literally standing at my front door, dressed and ready to leave."

"Sorry, Martin. Met some people for a drink last night and got a bit carried away. If it makes you feel any better, I am really annoyed at myself; I was going to ask that new receptionist for her phone number today," Martin grinned and shook his head. "I can hear you smiling, so you can't stay mad at me."

"You're still a dick."

"I am, and I don't deny it. So what else do you have planned for today?"

"Got some work to get done, then I'm meeting Elaine for dinner tonight."

"Cool. That's nearly three months now, right?"

"Just over three months."

"Excellent. Have to say though, I still have no idea why monogamous relationships are your thing. Young, financially secure, reasonably good looking..."

"What do you mean "reasonably"?"

"Compared to most other guys, you shape up fine; you're painfully ugly compared to me though."

"Big headed twit."

"I'm just telling it like it is, amigo. Seriously though, you should give playing the field a go. Low risk, high reward, and lots of variety. It's the spice of life, Martin."

"Which explains your new car every year, the constant upgrading of your gadgets, your ever changing wardrobe... I'm surprised you don't actually get a new job and move to a new flat every year, just to keep them in line with everything else about your life." Stephen shook his head.

"You know me, Martin; there are some things in my life that are too good to change. I *love* my job; it's brilliant. I also love my apartment. And then there's the one other thing that will never change in my life."

"Which is?" Martin asked, slightly puzzled.

"My inferior looking best friend," Stephen answered with a chuckle.

"Enjoy your hangover, numb nuts."

"Talk to you later."

It was half past six before Martin finished the tasks he had set for himself. The artwork had taken longer to finalise than he had anticipated, as he hadn't been able to get it quite the right way the first nine or ten times he had tried. A perfectionist where his work was concerned, he had kept at it until, finally, he had been able to look at it and say to himself that he was completely happy with it, and hopefully the client would be too.

He was due to meet Elaine at the restaurant at half past seven. By the time he had had shaved, showered and dressed, it was only just after seven, still too early to leave as the restaurant was only ten minutes away. Plus, Elaine was bound to be at least ten minutes late anyway. She was a lovely woman, but her inability to be on time for anything sometimes annoyed him. Still, at least he could be sure of some engaging company when she did arrive.

Martin listened to a few songs on his MP3 player and thought some more about his reply to Abi's letter. It seemed to him that her friends and family were right, that she had to do something to get out of her funk, but to do that first she had to pin down what was causing it.

He left his flat at 7:15pm, and got stopped for a full ten minutes at some road-works. He arrived at the restaurant just after 7:35pm to find that, for once, Elaine had beaten him to it, and was sitting sipping wine, waiting for him. She looked fantastic, as always. Martin smiled as he approached. She noticed him approaching and smiled back.

"Colour me surprised," he said, bending down to give her a kiss. As he sat down he said, "Here's something I've never had to say to you before; I'm sorry I'm late."

"As you would normally say to me: don't worry about it. Just out of curiosity though, why were you late?"

"Bloody road-works. I ended up sitting at a red light for nearly ten minutes before I thought "Sod it!" and just drove on."

"Well, you're here now. I don't know about you, but I am ravenous."

"I was hoping you'd say something like that, but let's have something to eat first."

"Food I can promise you," she said. "Anything else... well, we'll just have to see how good a boy you are tonight."

It didn't take Martin long to realise something wasn't right.

First there was Elaine showing up on time. They bantered back and forth at first, but as the meal progressed her usual loquaciousness became conspicuous by its absence. Also, she was drinking more than she usually did. Also his attempts at starting a conversation were met with one or two word responses before she returned to pushing her food around her plate.

He was just about finished with his main course when it dawned on him what was happening. Though he had been through it many times before, and almost always for the same reason, his heart sank. Martin told himself that perhaps he was wrong, but he didn't believe it. His options now were either to bring it up himself or wait for Elaine to work up the courage to say what she was so anxious about saying.

Martin waited, still hoping he was wrong.

He wasn't.

Halfway through dessert, Elaine put her spoon down, took a long drink of wine and looked up at him. As he looked back at her, Martin tried to deny the idea that the outcome of the evening was a foregone conclusion. She blew his efforts right out of the water with her next sentence.

"Martin, I want to see the letters."

And there it was. Most men dreaded hearing phrases like "We need to talk," or "I need to hear you say you love me," or "I'm breaking up with you". For Martin Muir, any of these phrases, or any of their variations, would be a nice change. Every time a relationship ended, it was always about the letters.

"Elaine, you know I can't do that." He saw the colour rise in her cheeks.

"You mean you won't."

"No, I mean I can't, and I've told you why I can't." He watched as she took a drink, wondering which road she was going to go down: angry or resigned. Elaine sat her glass down and in a low voice said,

"Well maybe I feel that if you were serious about this relationship, Martin, you'd be willing to make a change."

Angry. Martin could relate; he was pretty pissed off himself. He took a drink and decided that this time he wasn't going to sit and ask for a chance to show her it could work, or listen to her question whether he was committed to the relationship, or listen to her tear him to shreds and call him an arsehole. This time he would take a little control over the situation. He sat his glass down, took a deep breath and said,

"Elaine, let me save us both some time and trouble. I've been here before and I really can't be bothered going through it all again, so we're finished. I'm sad to say it, I really am, because you are a great person and I really enjoy being with you, but if that's your attitude then it's obviously not going to work." He reached into his pocket and took out his wallet, watching as shock wiped the anger from her face. He took out enough money to cover the bill, dropped the notes onto the table, then put his wallet away and stood up. He stepped around to her side of the table, bent down, kissed her on the cheek and told her, "Goodbye."

Every time. This was how it ended every damn time. In every relationship he had ever had, Martin had never been less than completely up front about his friendship with Abigail. He always made a point of mentioning that he could never show anyone the letters because they were for his eyes only. Not sleazy or explicit, just private conversations between friends. Martin and Abi had agreed long ago that, though they could share general information with their friends, the deeper and more private aspects of their communications should remain solely between them. No one got to read the letters. He had stuck to that, and he believed she had too.

At first, his girlfriends would be all right with it. They would think it was cute that he had a pen-pal. They thought if he had the ability to maintain a lasting relationship with someone on another continent then surely he would be able to maintain a relationship with someone he could see and speak with on a daily basis. But eventually things would change, and they would decide that they didn't like his relationship with Abi. No matter that he had never tried to hide it from them, they would decide that it was exactly what it was not; sexual and behind their backs. They would start to get jealous, start seeing Abi as the other woman, and would become convinced that they were somehow being cheated on, or they would just decide that they didn't like being in the dark about that aspect of his life.

It always came to a head with them demanding to read the letters. Martin always refused and the relationships always ended, sometimes amicably, sometimes with a whimper, sometimes with shouts and name calling.

He considered not telling Abigail about it this time. He feared that, as down as she was these days, she might make herself worse by blaming herself for the end of another of his relationships. That was exactly what she had done the first time it had ever happened, and he had written three solid pages explaining to her that it was not, in any way, her fault. But Martin knew that he could not keep it from her. They knew one another too well, and she would know that something was wrong just by his writing. Lying to her was not an option; they had always been completely honest with one another. Hell, Martin had been told she had started her period before anyone else, and no one else in the world had been informed when he had had his first wet dream.

Still, he fretted over telling her.

Martin arrived home, got changed into a T-shirt and lounge pants and then went to his office. Switching on the lamp he opened a drawer in his desk and removed a key, which he took to the large metal cabinet at the very back of the room. Inside it were a series of binders, all sat upright with the spines facing outwards. Each one had a year written on the spine, the earliest of these being 1987. Each binder held a series of plastic pockets containing all the letters Abigail had sent Martin during the stated year. Some time ago, Martin had scanned each letter into this computer, which had taken no small amount of time. It had been worth it though, simply to have backups in case something ever happened to the originals. Sometimes, when he was having difficulty with a job, he would open up the files on his PC and read one or two of the letters. They helped relax him, allowed him to get a grip on whatever was giving him bother. But on nights like this, when he was low, it had to be the real thing.

He took out the first binder and sat down at his desk. Sitting the binder on his lap he opened it and looked at the first letter, dated August 1st, 1987. He didn't need to remove it as there was only one page, written in surprisingly neat handwriting for a child of 8. It read:

"Dear Martin

My name is Abigail Morton and I am 8 years old. I live in the town of Hannerville in Tennessee in the United States of America. I live with my Aunt Janine and my Uncle Peter. Hannerville is a really nice place to live. There are places you can go where you can get great views of the Smoky Mountains, and there is a huge lake nearby where my Uncle sometimes takes me out on his boat. Our town even has its own movie theatre.

What is it like where you live?

Abigail"

The pen-pal scheme had been an exercise planned and implemented by Miss Andrea Coyle, Martin's teacher in primary 4, who had decided to broaden her pupils' minds by getting them to communicate with pupils of the corresponding grade in a school in the States. It had lasted only a few months, and most of the pupils involved showed little enthusiasm and so the idea had been abandoned.

Martin himself had been somewhat less than excited at the prospect of receiving a letter. Also the replies had to be written at home, and he hadn't wanted to spend precious play time writing to someone thousands of miles away whose life he had no interest in. However his parents had thought it was a great idea and encouraged him to give it a go. His first letter to Abigail had been sent on August 20th, 1987.

"Dear Abigail

My name is Martin Muir and I am 8 as well. I live in a town called Hamilton. We don't have any mountains around, but there are some hills you can walk up. My Dad took me once. The view at the top was great but the walk there and back left me really tired. We have a dog called Jacob. He's an Alsatian. My Mum says they're also known as German Shepherds. He's not full grown yet, but he's a big dog. Very friendly. But he sometimes wees on the carpet. That makes my parents a bit cross.

Do you have any pets?

Martin"

Writing that much had been something of a push for him, and without doubt the eight year old Martin Muir wouldn't have believed you if you had told him that he would still be writing to Abigail all these years later.

Martin smiled as he closed the binder over and put it back in its place, moving ahead several years and taking down the binder labelled 2012. The fourth plastic wallet in this binder held not only a letter but also a photograph. When they had been around the age of eleven, Martin and Abigail had both become very curious about what the other looked like. Abigail asked for his photo first, and he sent her one. She reciprocated, and every year since they had sent up to date photos to one another. Last year, Martin had sent her a shot of him taken at the gym, just to prove he was actually using the place. Abigail had sent back the picture he now removed from its pocket.

It was an informal portrait, showing a beautiful young woman. Her deep brown eyes perfectly matched the cascade of hair that fell down across her shoulders. She wore no make-up - not that she needed any - and she was smiling, which caused her eyes to scrunch up, putting little wrinkles at their corners.

Seeing that smile always made Martin feel better.

Chapter 4

"Dear Abigail

To get it out of the way, Elaine and I broke up. No biggie. Just got to deal with it and get on with things.

My main concern right now is the way you're feeling. You've got me worried over here, Abi. If I worry any more about it I'm going to end up all wrinkly in the face! I hope you feel suitably guilty about the fact that you are doing severe damage to my youthful(ish) good looks.

In all seriousness, I've thought a lot about what you're going through and, unsurprisingly, I can't come up with any reasons for it. I'm afraid the only thing I can suggest is maybe contacting a doctor. A psychologist or something. I'm not for a moment suggesting there might be anything mentally wrong with you, but it might help for you to outline what's been going on recently to someone with the training and insight to help you overcome whatever it is that's getting you down.

I would understand if you felt this was a bit over the top just because you've been down of late, but I think it might help you.

Anyhow, I'll say no more about it, but let me know what you decide.

Other than that, things are quite quiet here. Stephen is Stephen, and that simply can't be helped! I don't know what the weather's like on your side of The Pond, but it's bloody depressing over here. Grey skies, constant drizzle and cold. Not surprising given the time of year, but a little bit of sunshine would be nice.

Work is going fine, though there has been a bit of a fall off lately. To be honest I'm glad of the slower pace, though hopefully it won't last too long. I'll get by all right though; I'm the fiscally responsible type, which Stephen often berates me for. A friend and a financial adviser: what a guy!

I think that's about it for the time being. Get back to me as soon as you can to let me know what you think of my idea.

With Love

Martin"

Chapter 5

Abigail sat the letter down on her table beside her half eaten plate of nachos and cheese. It wasn't the greatest meal she had ever prepared for herself, but after a long shift at her book store, Pages and Pages, it was all she could be bothered making. Turned out she hadn't really been that hungry. In fact, she hadn't been much of anything these days. She hadn't been very energetic, awake, happy or outgoing. In short, she had not been herself of late. Only once recently had she been close to being her old self without having to force it: the flare of excitement she had felt on coming home to find the envelope with Martin's handwriting on the front. It was difficult to believe that all those years ago writing a letter to, and then receiving a letter from, a Scottish schoolboy was something she hadn't exactly been enthusiastic about. That Scottish schoolboy was now her most trusted friend, and probably knew more intimate details about her life than anyone else.

As she picked up a couple of nachos laden with cheese and moved them slowly to her mouth, her eyes roved over the first line of the letter. How many times had she read something like that from Marty? Impossible to say without going and getting the letters out of the cabinet in the attic, reading through them and taking a tally, but it had to be a fair few. Sometimes Martin ended the relationships for his own reasons, but more often than not either the woman ended them after demanding something of him they knew he wasn't willing to give. It was sad, and his glossing over it in a way that was obviously designed to impart the news without eliciting guilt was wasted.

Abigail always felt guilty about Martin's breakups, even after all this time, even after the wonderful letter he had sent her so long ago after the first time it had happened. She couldn't help it. These women were basically jealous of her relationship with him. Not at first, but it always happened eventually. The hellish thing was that Abigail could see their point of view; she *was* like the other woman. Unseen, unheard, not even in the same country, but someone with a long standing and very deep connection to the man they were seeing. She could well imagine how that would eat away at them. Niggle at them just before they went to sleep. Over time it would build until they would have a burning need to see those letters, as it was the only way they could confront the woman they saw as the third person in their relationship.

But years ago, she and Martin had agreed that their letters, as innocent as they were, were private. She had stuck to that agreement and, to the detriment of most of his adult relationships, so had Martin.

As she chewed on her mouthful of unhealthy food she recalled how, on a suitably dark and stormy night some time ago, she had sat down to write the letter that would be the end of her friendship with Martin. Her tears had soaked into the paper as she had explained to him that it was because of her that his girlfriends always got so upset and broke up with him, and that he shouldn't have to deal with that all the time. She had already mentioned to him in a previous letter that perhaps he should stop telling his girlfriends about her, but he had said that that was tantamount to lying to them, plus he wasn't about to deny a friendship that meant so much to him. Abigail saw his point; she had always mentioned Martin to her boyfriends.

Thus, on that night, she had suggested to Marty that maybe the time had come for them to stop corresponding. It had broken her heart to write it, had taken her three days to work up the courage to send it, and it had been a three week long nightmare waiting for the reply.

When it had been delivered, the envelope had lain on her mantle for a day and a half before she had plucked up the courage to open it and read the letter. Part of her had been hoping that Marty agreed with her because it meant he might have a proper shot at happiness with whoever he went out with next. Another part, one which had regretted writing the letter let alone sending it, had desperately hoped she had not ended the friendship that meant the most to her in the whole world. Certainly she had friends here in Hannerville, and she loved them dearly, but she and Marty had been so close for so long, despite the physical distance between them, that the idea she would never get another letter from him had been almost too painful to face up to.

Never before, and never since, had she received such an obviously incensed letter from him. Seldom had her heart lifted as it had when she read it.

He had raged at her for suggesting that, just because none of the women he had gone out with were willing to trust what he said about his relationship with her, that their relationship should end. He had gone on about how, one day, maybe, he would meet someone willing to put some proper faith in him and his word. Someone who would recognise what his friendship with her meant to him and that that friendship was such a huge part of his life that he simply couldn't function without it. If that person never came along, then that was something he would have to deal with, but under no circumstances would he give up his oldest friend over the paranoia of others. Marty had stated that he would continue to write to her even if he never received another reply.

Abigail had cried for almost half an hour after reading it, and had then written her reply.

Swallowing, she picked up his most recent letter and re-read it. Trust Marty to bring up the one idea her other friends had probably thought of but wouldn't have mentioned for fear of her feeling insulted. A small smile touched her lips, and then vanished as she thought of the one thing she had never told anyone about herself, not even Marty. Without knowing it, he had come so close to hitting the nail on the head, for it was exactly as he had said, though he obviously didn't believe so himself. Why would he? Why would anyone?

Abigail shook her head and dropped the letter onto the table. She binned the rest of her meal and put the dishes in the dishwasher. She then checked that all the doors were locked, that the alarm was set and, taking the letter, went upstairs. She sat for forty-five minutes at her desk, writing in her journal, and then she got ready for bed.

Early the next morning, she stuck an arm out from underneath the duvet, slapping a hand around until it came down on top of the alarm clock, shutting it off. As she sat up she recalled fragments of a dream: a bed, need, want, ecstasy, bliss, fear and love. She thought Martin might have been involved in it at some point, but it was all fading and was soon gone. Abigail blinked a couple of times and the next thought that crossed her mind was: *what if my condition does have something to do with the way I'm feeling?*

She reached out and took the notepad and pen off the bedside table, scribbled down a note for later. Replacing the pad and pen, she threw back the duvet and got out of bed, which she then remade before trudging out of her bedroom and down the hall to the bathroom.

By the time she'd had breakfast, cleaned the dishes, brushed her teeth, showered and gotten ready, it was almost quarter past seven. Abigail checked she had everything in her handbag and headed for the door.

It was a crisp morning, but it was also bright, the sky blue and cloudless. Abigail decided that rain probably wasn't on the cards, so she put her car keys back in her purse and started walking to work. She didn't usually open the shop till half past eight anyway, and the journey by foot only took around twenty-five minutes. Beth probably wouldn't arrive until twenty five past eight, so there was no need to rush on her account.

Abigail had lived in Hannerville her entire life, and was certain she would continue to live there for the rest of her days. It was the kind of small town America few people would have credited with still existing in these cynically minded times, and she loved it. Every memory, good and bad, was tied to a place somewhere in town: seeing her first movie at The Majestic Theatre on Main Street. Her first major accident – falling out of a tree and breaking her leg – had occurred in Beaumont Park, which she would have to walk through to get to the store. Her friends were here, her Aunt Janine and Uncle Peter, her store. She knew a lot of people, most of them really nice people too. The town was clean, tidy and picturesque, with some truly beautiful scenery. It was almost a little slice of a bygone era.

Almost.

Like everywhere else in the world, Hannerville had been unable to completely avoid the perils of modern life. Only a few months ago a local woman named Alisha Fisher had found her 18 year old son, Gary, dead in his room of an accidental drugs overdose. Just last year, Barry Tarrer, 67 years of age and one of the town's most upstanding citizens, had been arrested when the technician at the shop he had put his personal computer into for repairs discovered indecent images and videos of children on the hard drive. That event had led to an angry mob descending on the station. Abigail remembered seeing it on the local news. It had looked like something out of an old horror movie, the residents of the town sallying forth with (battery operated) torches and pitchforks (baseball bats) to take down the monster. They had demanded that the sheriff give them Tarrer. Sheriff Flaghan had refused, and had threatened them all with arrest if they did not disperse, which they did, but only after a tense standoff.

Barry Tarrer was tried, convicted and sentenced to thirty years in prison. Certain that he would not survive, he committed suicide in his cell that night. A week later, Margaret Tarrer left town and no one had seen or heard from her since.

Abigail walked through Beaumont Park, listening to the birds singing and, as always, picking out the tree she had fallen out of. She smiled now, but could easily recall the total terror of hanging from that branch, hearing her friends calling to her to hold on, feeling the bark bite into her skin as her grip slipped. The moments after she had lost her hold on the branch had been very odd. She had been unable to hear the terrified cries of her friends as the fact that there was nothing stopping her from falling registered in her mind. The branch started to get further and further away and Abigail's mind locked onto a single purpose: waiting for the impact she was sure would kill her. That impact seemed to take a ridiculously long time to happen, time during which she felt light headed and strangely free. Eventually, though after only seconds had passed, she hit the ground. It had been sudden and jarring but painless. The pain had started in the minutes afterwards, as her friends crowded round her, their voices a babble of questions, none of which got through. There was only the shock and the incrementally increasing pain in her broken leg.

With that old injury now long healed, she made good time to her store. *Her* store. It still seemed like a slightly weird concept. She had been 25, with no real direction in life. Starting her own business had been an idea that had never occurred to her before, but once the idea got into her head, she hadn't been able to get it out. After a great deal of thought she had decided that she wanted to open a dedicated book store, as it was something the town didn't have. She had looked into what it would mean financially and the dream had died; no way would she be able to get a loan from the bank to finance the endeavour. Her uncle and aunt came to the rescue, writing her a cheque for the money she needed. Abigail had been overjoyed, but also nervous at the thought of actually going through with it.

The official opening of "Pages and Pages" had been a roaring success, and one of the proudest days of her life, each minute of it meticulously noted in her journal. Business had been so good that she had been able to pay her aunt and uncle back within a few years. It had also become apparent very quickly that she would need help with the place, and so she had hired her friend, Beth Hayes. Beth learned fast, was a good worker, had needed a job and Abigail really liked the idea of working with a close friend, though it was something her uncle had warned her against. Abigail had had a little faith though, and the arrangement worked brilliantly, though Beth could be a bit loose as far as breaks and timekeeping were concerned, especially when she had a boyfriend.

She unlocked the front door and stepped inside, and on a small keypad entered the code to disarm the intruder alarm. She closed and locked the door again, and then, as always, she did a quick inspection throughout the store, first the upper level, then downstairs, eventually ending up at the rear of the ground floor at a door marked "Staff Only". This led onto a corridor with four doors, behind which lay the bathroom, the staff room and the stairs down to the basement storeroom. The final door, at the end of the corridor, opened onto the alleyway at the rear of the store.

Abigail went to the staff room, which was furnished with a desk, a coat rack, a table and a small sofa. On the desk sat an old but reliable computer, but on the table sat an even more important piece of equipment: the coffee maker. Abigail hung up her jacket and stowed her bag in the desk drawer, then switched on the computer and the coffee maker, and waited to see which of the two machines would win the race.

The computer triumphed, but Abigail had the feeling that if the coffee maker could talk, it would have told her that good coffee takes time to prepare.

Beth arrived right on time, five minutes before opening. Abigail let her in and this time left the door unlocked, turning round the rectangular "Open/Closed" sign so that the former was displayed to the outside world. As she turned to face her friend, Beth took her headphones out of her ears, peered at her, then smiled and said confidently,

"You got a letter from Marty." Abigail couldn't hide her surprise.

"How did you know?"

"You get this look about you when you've had a letter from him."

"I do not." Beth grinned and nodded.

"Yeah, you do. He cool?"

"Yeah, he's fine." Beth's grin broke into a wide, smug "Told ya!" smile. Abigail smiled and shook her head. "Shut up."

"Is there any coffee? Had a bit of a late night."

"Do I dare ask?"

"Doesn't matter if you ask or not; I'm gonna tell you anyway."

At half past twelve, Amanda and Sophie showed up with lunch: burgers, fries and milkshakes. As they sat in the staff room eating, Beth asked Amanda and Sophie,

"Do you guys think she has the look?"

The two looked at Abigail for a moment, and then both of them nodded.

"There has most definitely been a communication from Marty," said Amanda.

"I do not have a look," protested Abigail.

"Then how would we know?" asked Amanda.

"Easy; Beth text you and set this up."

"You want to check my phone?" asked Beth, taking her mobile from her pocket and offering it to Abigail.

"Oh, you'd have deleted it from your sent messages by now." Beth feigned shock.

"Is that how you see me? Duplicitous and scheming?"

"Hell yes!" Giving a theatrical gasp, Beth threw a balled up napkin at her. Abi batted it away and chuckled. "I've known you to scheme before."

"Never against my friends."

"Everything okay with Marty?" enquired Sophie.

"He's fine. He's concerned about me, about the way I've been feeling lately."

"I swear, Abi," said Amanda. "The only problems in your relationship with that man are the few thousand miles separating you from one another."

"I know," agreed Sophie. "I mean, do you know how lucky you are? The guy listens to your problems, he offers advice and support, and he never asks for anything physical in return. I hate you, you bitch!" The four of them burst out laughing.

"So," began Beth. "We can all agree the guy isn't after only one thing. However, I know someone who would like to get a little physical with her Scottish boy toy." Abigail smiled and shook her head as Sophie and Amanda began jostling her.

"Oh yeah," said Sophie, grinning wickedly. "Little Miss Sleepover and the Case of the Naughty Night-time Thoughts!"

"Seriously, you're going to throw that in my face again?"

"Oh yes," smiled Beth. "Then, now and forever more!"

"Tell it, Beth," said Amanda.

"Well, Abi came over to my house for sleepover when we were seventeen. She was in a sleeping bag on the floor of my bedroom and during the night I woke up because I heard her moaning. At first I thought she was in pain or something, but when I turned on my lamp, I saw that she was still asleep. She was sweating, writhing and then I very clearly heard her moan a name. What was that name, ladies?"

Sophie and Amanda both struck the same pose: heads thrown back, one hand clutching a breast and the other thrust between their thighs.

"Marty!" they chorused in a breathless moan, then they started laughing. Beth laughed with them, as did Abigail, who had seen this little show many times before. She made the same defence as always.

"I'm sure that if such a thing happened it was nothing like that, and that a certain someone embellished for entertainment purposes."

"I reported what I saw and heard," Beth stated solemnly. "Nothing more, nothing less." Abigail wagged a finger at her and told her,

"You're going to have major trouble getting your boss to agree to giving you time off in the future, you know that?"

"I will sue. I will take it to the highest court in the land." She looked at the stern expression on Abigail's face, marred only by the hint of a smile at the corners of her mouth. "I will be a good and conscientious worker who will no longer spread wild stories about her boss's dreamy longings."

The four of them laughed again.

Having been asleep at the time, Abigail had never been able to confirm or deny the story Beth told every once in a while. Yes, they had had sleepovers, many of them, and it was entirely possible that during one her teenage hormones had caused her to have the kind of dream that would have caused her to say and do what Beth took great relish in describing. What had always concerned Abigail was that she believed dreams often contained an element of truth. Consciously you could lie to others and to yourself, but when you slept, your mind was unfettered and told you the stone cold truth. She had always denied that she had feelings for Marty that went anywhere beyond friendship, but her relationship with him was the longest standing relationship she had ever had with a man. It was, as Sophie had suggested, damn near perfect in every way other than they were physically nowhere near one another. Though she believed Beth was exaggerating slightly in her recounting of the state she had been in on that night, Abigail would have been lying if she had said that she had never thought what it would be like to be with Marty. Given the distance between them, she had never seen the harm in fantasising a little. He was her oldest, closest friend, who knew more about her than those around her right now. She loved her friends; they had been there for her for years, supporting her and caring for her, as she had for them. But whenever the grim realities of life had touched Abigail, her thoughts had always turned to the one person who was apart from everything that was happening to her. The one person who could look at it all from the outside, yet who cared deeply about how it affected her.

Her Marty.

On more than one occasion she had chastised herself for thinking of him in that way. On those same occasions she always told herself that such thoughts were the reasons she still had no man here with her. Letters were all well and good, but they didn't welcome you home at night, hug you before you went to sleep, share the good times, the bad times, the bills and the responsibilities. However, although some of her past relationships had ended for the usual reason relationships end, some of them had ended for the same reasons most of Martin's had. She had told him that none of her breakups had anything to do with him, that the men she had dated had never cared about the letters she and Marty exchanged, but that wasn't the whole truth. One or two of her past boyfriends had broken up with her because she would not show them the letters, nor agree to stop corresponding with Marty. These breakups were the ones she had never mentioned to him, the second secret she kept, and possibly the one thing about her life that her friends here in Hannerville knew that Marty didn't. She knew how their relationship had damaged almost all of his relationships, and she also knew how that knowledge made her feel. Abigail had wanted to spare Marty those feelings, and so had chosen to simply state that she had broken up with her latest boyfriend, just as Marty had done in his latest letter.

Thus she was well aware why his relationship with Elaine had ended, and why he had simply glossed over it.

The afternoon passed quickly. Beth asked to leave a few minutes earlier than usual, and Abigail smiled and told her to go and enjoy herself. At six o'clock she locked the door and turned the sign to "Closed". Then she took the days takings out of the till and deposited them in the small floor safe concealed in a corner of the basement. After checking everything was switched off, she left, setting the alarm before closing and locking the door, and heading for home.

Chapter 6

Corday walked through the woods, one hand in his pocket, the other holding a shovel, the blade of which, like his clothes, face and hands, was smeared with dirt. The cold light of the moon speared down through the branches and picked out a small smile on his face. Things had gone absolutely beautifully so far.

After leaving the US, he had returned to his old estate in France to be reunited with his worthless minions. The fear of the older ones had been obvious, as they had all believed they would never see him again. He had demanded that dear old Anthony, once his most trusted lieutenant and the one who had been in charge since Corday's incarceration, bring him up to date. His main question was about Madeleine's whereabouts. Anthony had informed him that the woman had for some reason left not long after Corday had been put away, and no one had seen or heard from her since. An unconvinced Corday had said nothing. He had simply listened as Anthony had told him of how, after the capture of their beloved master, they had been unsure how to proceed. They had thought about breaking him out, but decided to wait until he managed to contact them, as they had been sure he would. When he did not, they decided to wait a little longer. The first contact they'd had had not come not from him, but from someone informing them of the change of management at Berrybeck. There had been excitement, Anthony had told him, as they had believed this would be when he would get in touch with them to come and get him. But they received no word, and so did what they could, which amounted to making sure he was able to stay in the repurposed Berrybeck Hospital. What Anthony didn't tell him, and what was obvious to Corday, was that while they waited, they had all spent a great deal of his money living the good life. The Order, it seemed, had been content to leave them be, and so over time the group of men and women he had chosen to help him wage a war had fallen to excesses of every assortment.

The following day Corday had visited a bank and checked on his finances. The money that had been spent had barely made a dent in the account that Anthony had access too, however this knowledge had done little to mollify him. Returning to the estate, he had chatted to a few of the younger men and women milling about. He had discovered that not one of them knew who he was or where he had been. Likewise they had no idea of the original purpose of the group they had joined. As far as they were concerned, it was just a bunch of rich folk living in a big house where they threw huge parties involving lots of food, drink, drugs and sex. That night, he had managed to discover where Madeleine had gone.

The following day he had gone alone to see her. Her reaction when she had opened the door was the one he told himself he should have received from everyone at the estate upon his return: awe, excitement, reverence and fear. That the fools had managed only one of those was woeful. Of course, in Madeleine's case, there had also been that little spark of lust in her eyes. Not love, they knew one another too well for that, but that it reignited so quickly and was so easily noticed made Corday happy.

What Madeleine had told him had not.

He had gone in, sat down, declined her offer of a drink and asked her for the truth of what had happened after he had been sent to Berrybeck. She had told him that she had begged and pleaded with Anthony to do something, to rescue him from his imprisonment, but Anthony had refused. He had said Corday's plan had brought them to the very brink and it was a sign that he had been caught and put away, a sign that they should leave him where he was and go on with their lives. She had argued, threatened them, but had been outnumbered. She had remained on the estate for a short time before, unable to be among those faithless traitors any longer, she had fled. No one had come looking for her, though she had often expected an attack.

Then Corday had asked about the child.

Madeleine had smiled and told him to wait. She had gone upstairs and returned a few minutes later with a beautiful woman in her mid-twenties in tow. She had only been a baby the last time Corday had seen her, chosen from an orphanage to be his successor, another of his little breaks with tradition. Tradition had played no part in his decision to actually have a successor. It had merely been pragmatism; he had intended to come back, but if something had happened and he had been killed, he would want someone to avenge him. He had entrusted the child's upbringing to Madeleine, who had done well, it seemed, as the girl had sized him up only briefly with her dark green eyes, and then bowed her head. After a brief chat, Corday had told Madeleine to come to the estate the following night, and to bring the girl with her.

Upon his return home, Corday had asked Anthony to organise a party in his honour for the following evening, inviting only those in permanent residence at the estate. It was quite an occasion, and had ended with Corday standing before the crowd with Anthony at his side. He had thanked them all for keeping an eye on things, but expressed his disappointment at having been left to rot in a fucking loony bin for so many years. So much of his life had been wasted. At this there had been a shift in the crowd's mood, the merriment dying down a little as they all tried to work out if he was joking or not. The younger ones were clueless, but when Corday, with a cold smile, had called out for Madeleine to come into the room, the older ones had realised that he was being perfectly serious. As they all turned to watch their old associate enter, an unknown young woman just behind her, Corday had stabbed Anthony in the throat. As the man had dropped to the floor, choking on his own blood, Corday had told the shocked assembly that things were going to change.

"Promise me your loyalty," he had told them. "And you will live. Refuse, and I withhold the antidote to the poison I spiked the punch with."

Needless to say, they fell in line. Corday had smiled warmly at them.

"You young ones, take what you say seriously. Speak to your friends, who brought you here to drink and eat and fuck in the rooms of my house, to spend my money as you pleased. The ones who thought themselves safe from me. Ask them to tell you who and what I am, and then know that if any of you betray me, I will hunt you into your graves."

He had beckoned Madeleine and the girl to the front of the room, and informed the assembly that whenever he was not around, Madeleine's word was law. In her absence, the girl, Michelle, was to be obeyed. He then told them all to get out of his sight, and that this time there had been no poison, but that next time there might be. Or a gun. Or a knife. When there had been only the three of them left in the room, he had discussed with Madeleine and Michelle how they were going to go about weeding out those who might well turn against them, and how they would go about recruiting some slightly worthier acolytes. Corday had informed them of his plans, and left the clean up and running of the estate in their hands.

Later, when he returned to his room, Michelle had been waiting for him, naked, on his bed. He had asked her if Madeleine knew where she was, and the girl had told him no, then asked if it would really have made a difference.

"We could fuck on top of her," she had said. "And the old maid wouldn't say a word about it."

Though tired, and in truth not partial to women who were willing, Corday had stripped and joined the girl on the bed. She had been animalistic, more than a match for his loveless groping, gripping, licking, sucking and thrusting. He had surprised himself by how well he had kept up with her, though when she had gone back to her own room, he had fallen asleep almost immediately.

The next day he had booked himself into a private clinic to have facial reconstructive surgery. A lot of money kept the questions to a minimum. During the three months he had spent recovering, Madeleine and Michelle had done a fine job of getting rid of the less faithful among those on the estate, and of finding them some people who would be loyal. Although Corday had decreed Madeleine his proxy, it was Michelle those living on the estate came to truly fear. This pleased Corday; he had chosen well, and Madeleine had done a wonderful job of raising the girl according to the guidelines he had given her.

Corday's last piece of business was one he had carried out himself. With the proper documents for his new identity procured from someone who did excellent work, he had chartered a plane to take him to Egypt. It had required the spending of some money, and the spilling of some blood, but it had all been more than worth it when he had found the item, exactly where his research had led him to believe it would be.

Corday had returned home and, with everything now up and running again, had made preparations to return to the US. He had booked a flight into Knoxville airport, a drive of an hour or so from Hannerville, and had stayed in a hotel for a few nights whilst he decided whether to rent or to buy. He had looked at a couple of places to rent before deciding to purchase somewhere, as that would provide better cover. Corday didn't know it yet, but one of the places he'd viewed, and information he had picked up whilst there, would come in very handy in the near future.

During the little excursion into the woods from which he was now returning, he had happened upon a ramshackle old cabin which he thought might, with a few repairs here and there, provide a little privacy when the time came.

Chapter 7

Martin sipped at his bottle of beer, his eyes trained on the television but not really seeing the images displayed. His thoughts were not on the action movie Trevor had brought with him, nor had they been on the comedy they had watched previously.

In the ten days since he had split up with Elaine, Martin had attempted to do exactly what he had put in his letter to Abi: he had tried to suck it up and get on with things. As far as his professional life went, he had succeeded. His work had not suffered. In fact he had devoted so much time to it that the designs he had come up with recently had been some of the best he'd ever done. His clients had been very pleased, and that was good for him, good for his business, good for his reputation, and good for his bank account. Regrettably it didn't mean shit to his shattered sense of self-worth, because he had again convinced himself that all these breakups had to be something to do with him. They *had* to be. Yes, the women always said it was the letters, or the idea that there was a third person in the relationship, but why did they always end up thinking that way? It had to be because they did not completely trust him. There was something about him that caused them to deem him not completely trustworthy and so they eventually grew suspicious and jealous. So the question he had been asking himself for days now was: why am I so untrustworthy? He had told himself over and over again that he had always been open about Abigail, and had always made sure his girlfriends knew she was just a friend. But then he had started to wonder if perhaps that was the problem. Maybe he was being too open and honest. Maybe if he didn't mention Abi the next time...

This train of thought inevitably derailed when he decided that he was still not, and never would be, willing to deny his oldest friend for anyone.

Thus, when not working, Martin had taken to moping about his flat, watching, or rather staring at, a lot of films and TV shows, and spending much more time than usual on his video games console. It had not taken Stephen long to detect the shift in his friend's mood and, already aware of the reason, he had organised a night in at Martin's.

The first Martin had known of it was at half past six tonight when Stephen, Trevor, Dougie and James had shown up at his front door, laden with DVD's, booze and snack foods of questionable nutritional value.

That had been almost four hours ago, but despite the company of his friends and several bottles of beer, Martin still felt like crap. He wallowed in thoughts of being destined to spend the rest of his life alone. Of being best man at the weddings of the men gathered around him, who were taking swigs of beer in between cheering on the onscreen hero, who had just blown a helicopter out of the sky. He pictured himself chatting to bridesmaids, getting them to smile, asking them out, and then his mind fast forwarded a few months to the point where they demanded to see the letters and everything went haywire. That was how it would always turn out because the only woman he knew would understand, who would always be there for him no matter what, was...

"Knew it!" yelled Trevor. "Every truly great action film has one somewhere."

"Eh?" mumbled Martin.

"What are you talking about?" asked Stephen.

"Tit shot," said Trevor, looking at them as if his point was something that should be common knowledge. "Every great action movie has to have a tit shot somewhere. Might be brief, but it'll be there."

"Pish!" scoffed Dougie.

"It's not," Trevor said. He paused the DVD and then explained. ""Under Siege" had Erika Eleniak popping up out of a cake topless... Best use of a cake *ever*!"

"Okay, that's one," said James. "Next?"

"Showdown in Little Tokyo". Top flick, plus Tia Carrera topless. Priceless."

"And?" said Stephen, grinning.

"Well, there's... uh..."

"There were no topless chicks in "Die Hard"," said Martin. "And that's just about the best action movie of all time."

"I have to back Trev up on that one," said Dougie. "There were definitely boobs in "Die Hard". When the terrorists are clearing out the offices, they come across a couple who were about to have a quickie, and the woman's blouse is open, and you see her boobs as they pull her out the door."

"There were none in "The Raid"," said James. "And that was an amazing action movie."

"Tell you what," said Stephen, raising his hands. "Since you're among friends, Trev, we will save you the pain of admitting defeat and say that many a good action movie has some boobs in it, but not all of them do. Fair enough?"

"Fair enough," echoed Trevor.

"Good..." Stephen couldn't keep the smile from his face as he added. "Cause you were wrong, son! Dead wrong." He pointed at Trevor with both index fingers. "Completely and utterly wrong!"

"Up yours!" chuckled Trevor, picking up a fallen piece of popcorn and lobbing it at Stephen. Dougie and James laughed as well, and even Martin managed a proper laugh. He quickly became morose again after they settled down to watch the rest of the film.

When they weren't watching something, Martin put on a good show, laughing and joking and drinking. After the action movie ended and they decided to play a few hands of Texas Hold 'Em, he carried on the charade, despite wishing he could just sit and drink till he passed out.

At twenty past midnight, after several hands of poker and another action movie, Trevor, Dougie and James all left. Martin thanked them and said he'd see them again soon. As they made their way to the lift, he looked back expectantly at Stephen, who told him,

"You can shut that door; we need to have a chat."

Martin sighed and closed the door. A pep chat from Stephen, or anyone else, was not what he needed, and certainly not what he wanted. Nonetheless he went into the living room and sat down. He thought about asking Stephen what the matter was, realised there was no point, and so simply waited for his friend to say what he had to say. Stephen said nothing. He just sat staring at him, drinking what was left in his bottle of beer. Eventually Martin had to speak.

"I appreciate you and the boys coming over, but I wasn't in the mood for a night like tonight. You should have asked."

"You'd have said no."

"Exactly; I would have saved you all the time of having to come over here and keep my perilously-close-to-depressed arse company!"

"The boys didn't seem to notice."

"You think so?"

"Even if they did, they're obviously unwilling to say anything about it."

"Stephen, I really don't need to be told about how I need to pull my socks up and get on with things."

"And I wasn't going to say that that was what you had to do. What you need to do is break the cycle."

"What? What cycle?"

"Martin, you and I both know you're not thick enough to not see what's been happening for years now. You just have to admit it to yourself."

"You sound like you're talking to an alcoholic or a junkie."

"That comparison is probably closer to the mark than you might think."

"Now you're making no sense at all. In fact you're coming close to being insulting."

"Not at all," said Stephen. "I'm just trying to get through to you that you need to stop looking for the right woman."

"I know I do. I have to stop looking because none of them understand. None of them are willing to trust me enough to stay with me without me somehow proving to them how I'm committed to them alone by showing them the letters."

"That's not what I meant. You have to stop looking for the right woman because you've already found her. And for some time now you've been using her as an excuse to let your other relationships go wrong because none of them are her." He examined Martin's expression and then said, "You've been drinking. Take a minute or two and work it out. I'll wait." He took another sip of beer and closed his eyes.

Martin stared at his friend, wondering if perhaps he hadn't drank a little too much to get what Stephen was getting at. But then he went back over what Stephen has said, and wondered exactly how long his friend had known. Finally, Martin admitted it to himself, and felt tears sting his eyes.

"Holy crap, Stephen," he muttered. "What am I going to do?"

Without opening his eyes, Stephen smiled. After another sip, he said,

"Say it out loud, Martin. Talk it all out. You've got to get it all straight and out in the open. No going back." Martin nodded.

"It's her. It's Abigail. It's always been Abigail. I've loved her since... as far back as I can remember. I told myself I was being stupid, that she and I were friends and nothing else... We live in different countries, for crying out loud. What the hell was the point of falling for someone I've never met face-to-face? I denied it to myself, until I finally began to believe it had been nothing but a stupid flight of fancy, a teenager's idiocy... But the women I've been with... I did care for them. You remember Carole?" Stephen, his eyes still closed, nodded. "She was the first. We had been together nearly a year and I really did see a future with her, but then she brought up the letters and Abi and it all went to hell... After that, I must have realised it hadn't been puppy love; I wanted Abi. As stupid and pointless as it was to do so, I wanted to be with Abi. That's why I started just giving up on the relationships when the women demanded to read the letters; I was never really that committed to them and their jealousy and frustration were just handy excuses for me to move on and start the whole thing all over again. Start hiding from my feelings all over again.

"Jesus, Stephen, I have been such an arsehole to the women I've been with... to Abi..."

"To yourself," said Stephen, raising his bottle to his mouth. It was empty and he opened his eyes, confirmed as much and made a small "Aw" of disappointment. He sat the bottle down and looked at Martin. "You've tried to hide from what you were really feeling, and yes, you used those other women to hide behind, but I was there for all of those relationships. You were good to them, Martin. You might have been using them to hide from what you didn't want to admit you felt for Abi, but you never treated them badly. You never openly compared them to her."

"No, I led them to do that themselves, which led to the breakups. There's not that much of a difference, man."

"Maybe you're right, but you're still not a bad guy. If you're guilty of anything it's that you were confused about your feelings, and there's not a single person on the planet who, at some point in time, hasn't been guilty of that."

"Yeah, but..."

29

"But nothing. Like I said, I stayed behind tonight because I was bloody well determined to stop this cycle you'd gone and gotten yourself caught in..."

"How long have you known?"

"Ages. You think I never noticed the change in you every time you got a letter from Abigail? And since way back when, the excitement every time you spoke about writing back to her, the dreamy look in your eyes when you spoke about her, have all been plain to see, mate. I never said anything because I thought you had a handle on it. I thought you had come to a point where you had accepted your feelings, had reasoned there was nothing that could be done and so had decided to get on with your life. I was right, sort of; you hadn't accepted your feelings, you were denying them, hiding from them. I couldn't let that go on forever, not after seeing your performance tonight. It convinced the others, but they weren't looking at you during the movies. They didn't see the heartbreak... I've seen it before, too many times now. I'm fed up seeing it; you're uglier than usual when you're heartbroken, Martin. Something's got to be done."

"So what do I do? Hell, the one person I'm closer to than I am to you, and I've lied to her for so long. I never even considered telling her how I felt because it was so..."

"Stupid? Pointless? Creepy?"

"All of the above. I smell her letters, you know. Christ, that sounds so bad when I say it out loud, but I smell her perfume on her letters every time she sends me one. It makes me feel closer to her somehow, as if there is something more tangible between us than just letters."

"Don't discount the letters, Martin. Lots of people would love to have a relationship like the one you have with Abigail. Simple, honest, caring, and in no way based on anything physical."

"But it hasn't been honest; *I* haven't been honest."

"Well, maybe it's time to be." That stopped Martin cold. His mouth dropped open and he stared at his best friend for several seconds before shaking his head.

"No, I can't. I can't risk it."

"Risk what? Being miserable for the rest of your life? Going from one doomed relationship to the next because the woman you really want is in another country? Torturing yourself by always wondering what might have been? No way to live a life, Martin."

"Have you sat a course in psychology or something and haven't told me?"

"No, I've just watched my best pal go round and round to the point where he was obviously sick with it, but wasn't willing to do what he needed to do to stop it. Naturally, I had to stick my oar in. Now, if you're finished trying to change the subject, what are you going to do?"

"I can't just come out and tell her something like that after all this time, Stephen. She'll be furious, and she'd have a right to be. It would be the end of our relationship and I... I couldn't handle that. You're right; I do get this feeling every time she writes to me, even after all these years... I don't think I could live without that. Her letters are as close to Abi as I'm ever going to get."

"Martin, if that's what you really think, I am about to say one word that will blow your mind: aeroplane."

"You mean go to the States and see her?" Stephen nodded. "But I... It's... I couldn't because..."

"Why not, eh? You write to her, tell her you'd like to come over and see her, and if she seems keen, great. If not, then you put it all in writing, but you should at least see if there's any way you can tell her face-to-face first. You never know, she might say yes. Hell, Martin, she might even feel the same bloody way. Either way, you go over, tell her everything, and you find out once and for all. If it all goes south, then at least you'll know you tried and that it wasn't meant to be. You'll be heartbroken, perhaps worse than I've ever seen you before – and god alone knows how ugly that's going to make you – but when you get over that heartbreak, you might actually be able to move on with your love life. On the other hand, if it all works out, you're going to owe me big time for the rest of your days."

They were quiet for a short time, then Martin asked,

"Do you really think there's even the slightest chance she might feel the same way?"

"I have no idea, but she's kept writing all this time, same as you have. Your handwritten letters have stood up to the convenience offered by e-mails, social networking, blogging and micro blogging. After so much time, and with those other, quicker means at your disposal, there's got to be a reason for someone to put such effort into communication. I know what yours is, so who's to say hers isn't the same? I'm not going to be a dick and say she's going to fall into your arms, but I think there's a chance she likes you in a romantic way. You owe it to yourself, and to her, to find out once and for all if there can be anything between the two of you. If finding that there isn't means the end of your written relationship with her, well... It might mean the beginning of another relationship that ticks all the boxes."

"I don't know if I'm willing to risk it."

"You have to be. I mean, think about it: how do you know your relationship with Abi isn't having the same effect on her love life that it's having on yours?"

"She's told me about her breakups; I've never been cited as the cause."

"As far as you know, but what if she chose not to tell you?"

"Why would she do that?"

"I recall you mentioning a while ago that every time you had to tell Abigail about a breakup, you were afraid she might blame herself, because once upon a time that was exactly what she did. Correct?" Martin nodded. "Right, so, what if she, worrying you might feel the same way if the situation was reversed, decided not to tell you?"

"But why?"

"Because when you care about a person, perhaps love them, shielding them from pain is something you always try to do."

Martin thought about how he had considered not telling Abi about his latest breakup, and why. Stephen's words made sense, but did that mean...

"She loves me?"

"Hoi, don't go there. When I used the word "love", I also used the word "perhaps". Don't go getting your hopes up. But there is a way to find out, and you know what it is. You probably always have, but now you know I know, there's no hiding from it, because I will bug you till you do what's necessary."

"I need some time to think, Stephen." Stephen nodded, rising and putting his jacket on.

"Fair enough, but try not to overcomplicate things, because when you come right down to it, it's pretty simple."

No, it fucking well is not!

Martin deeply appreciated his friend's words, but, lying in bed at four in the morning, staring at the ceiling, he could not accept "simple" as the word to describe the situation.

He had known this woman for years, since she was a girl, through her teens, into womanhood. He respected her, cared about her and, yes, damn it, he loved her. Out in the open now, nowhere to hide from it: *Martin Muir, you are in love with Abigail Morton. So where do you go from here?* His thoughts whirled, settled, whirled, settled. Bits and pieces of his conversation with Stephen came back to him. Was it possible that Abi had lied about some of her breakups to protect him? Why not: hadn't he considered doing the same thing? All right, so maybe she did care about him enough to want to protect him. That didn't necessarily mean anything other than she cared about his feelings. Was that enough on which to base a trip across the Atlantic? Perhaps not, but as far as such a trip was concerned, did it matter how Abi felt about him? He loved her; to deny it to himself, and to her, for the rest of their lives seemed wrong, a waste. Martin didn't think he could spend all that time lying by omission. It would eat away at him, plus he'd have Stephen on at him as well. That bugger was going to be like a dog with a bone until this situation was resolved.

But asking her if she would be okay with him visiting?

Odd as it may seem, it was something that had never come up in any of the letters they had sent to one another over the years. Thinking about it, Martin wasn't sure why. Maybe both of them had simply been happy enough with things as they were.

Or maybe both of you were worried about rejection.

He rebuked himself for the thought. Stephen was right; getting his hopes up was not a good idea. But maybe now, after all these years, it was time for him to ask, time to find out if there was any possibility of his relationship with Abi becoming something more. Yes, there would be issues, difficulties, but they had such solid bedrock on which to build something greater that the rewards would be worth their perseverance.

So why not ask her? What harm could it do?

It could ruin said bedrock in an instant, that was what. What if he asked how she would feel about his coming over to see her and she said no? How would he deal with that? To the question of furthering their relationship, only one answer could be interpreted from her rebutting his idea of a visit. Could he go on as before after that? Could she? Or would it all come down around their ears, years and years of friendship gone... Did the possible gains outweigh the risks? Difficult to say. The gains would be incredible. To actually *be* with Abigail, to hold her in his arms and tell her how he felt, to look into those eyes and then breathe in her scent before kissing her... The gains had the possibility of being beyond his wildest dreams. But of course if it all went the other way, he'd find himself in a nightmare. Yes, he might come out of it eventually, but going through it wouldn't be pleasant. Stephen sounded like he had all the answers, but Martin didn't think his friend could really conceive of just how much, how deeply, how profoundly, the loss of Abi's friendship would affect him. To never write to her again? To never read another letter from her again? The thought made him feel slightly sick, particularly the thought that he himself was considering being the one to light the cord that might set off fireworks, or dynamite.

But wasn't their relationship destructive as it was? Hadn't it destroyed almost all of his relationships with other women and, if Stephen was right, some of Abi's with other men? Martin wondered if he could really consider starting another relationship with a woman knowing his heart belonged to someone else.

Should he?

Shouldn't he?

It was another three quarters of an hour of tossing, turning, thinking, fretting and cursing before Martin let out a huge sigh and got out of bed. He went to his office, switched on the light and sat at his desk. After taking a sheet of A4 and a pencil out of the drawer, he sat staring at the sheet of paper for about ten minutes, wondering exactly what the hell he was supposed to say to her. Eventually this gave way to thinking about what he would do if he got the chance to meet her in person. Would he even be able to say anything? He had never heard her speak before; what would hearing her voice for the first time be like? And how would she react to hearing his voice, to seeing him in the flesh? Martin shook his head. He would never have answers to those questions if he couldn't actually think of what to write by way of asking her if she would okay with him visiting.

He wrote one letter, redrafted it, binned, it, wrote another, binned it. He went on like that for almost two hours. He was tired and wanted to sleep, but knew this task would haunt him, so he persevered. It had never taken him so long to finalise a letter to Abigail, especially one that ended up being so brief. At first he tried to make it seem innocent, as if the idea of coming over for a visit after all these years had just come to him and he wondered what she thought of it. It was just a visit after all, just so they could finally meet and shake hands and say hello. Then he remembered she wasn't an idiot and would see through such a ruse in no time.

In the end, he did what he always did with Abi: he told her the truth.

He got a few hours sleep and was up, bleary eyed and still tired, later that morning. Quickly washing and dressing, he grabbed the sealed and addressed envelope containing the letter and left his flat. The drive to the nearest post office was a short one. As he waited in the queue, thoughts bounced around in his head like the balls in a bingo machine: am I doing the right thing? How will I cope if things go wrong? Stephen, you're an arsehole for making me do this! God I hope she says yes. By the time he was in front of a window, behind which sat a smiling, bespectacled old lady, he was sweating profusely and felt extremely queasy. He didn't say anything and so, after a few moments, the cashier said, "Yes?" In that instant he almost bottled it, almost ran for the door, tearing the envelope and the letter inside to pieces as he went. But the last little shards of his courage had him putting the envelope on the counter, and informing the lady that he would like to send it first class to the US.

Chapter 8

"Dear Abigail

I've thought a lot about what to write in this letter. Nothing I came up with sounded any good, so I decided to just come out and ask what I wanted to ask:

What would you think about me coming over to Tennessee to visit you?

I know it might seem like a bolt from the blue after all this time, but I would really like to meet you face to face.

I don't want to say anything else in case it seems like I'm trying to pressure you into saying yes.

With Love

Martin"

Chapter 9

"With love? Ooooooh, the boy has got it bad."

"He's signed off his letters like that for years. We both have."

It was seven thirty at night. Last night Abigail had returned home to find the unexpected envelope. As always she had recognised the handwriting on it straight away, and at first she had been concerned. She could only imagine that something was wrong and that was the reason Marty had written back to her before she had replied to his last letter. She had hurriedly dumped her stuff and opened the envelope, expecting the worst.

What she had read has stunned her. She had re-read the letter time and time again, more times than any other letter he had ever sent her.

A visit? It sounded so simple, so mundane, but of course it wasn't. This was her Marty asking, after all these years, if she would be okay with him coming to see her. The first question she had asked herself was the most obvious: why? He gave no reason other than that he would really like to meet her face to face. Okay, so, maybe that was exactly what it was. Next question: how did she feel about it? Her first instinct was to be wary. Did he think something was going to happen if he came over? No, not Marty. He wasn't that kind of guy. Besides, if he was, he would have made the suggestion a long time ago, but their friendship had been well and truly established long before hormones kicked in. It was better than that, deeper in many ways than a purely physical relationship could be. In her heart she did not believe he would, after all these years, ask to come over just so he could try and get into her panties.

But who's to say you don't want him to?

The thought had popped into her head, and she did not follow her immediate urge to simply discard it. Why shouldn't it be that she wanted to be with him? She had thought about it more than once. Imagined what his voice would be like, how he would smell when he pulled her close, what it would feel like to have his hands running through her hair. As it always had, imagining such things had brought a rush of colour to her cheeks. Abigail had sat on her couch, lost in thought, trying to remember if simply thinking about being with any of her previous boyfriends had caused such sensations as the ones she felt thinking about being with Marty. None of them had.

Abigail had told herself to stop being so damn stupid. The guy had just asked to come over for a visit, for crying out loud. It didn't mean he would want to take her to dinner and then... do other stuff... did it? It was a lot of trouble to go to, and one hell of a long trip to make just to say hello. But why not? They'd been friends forever. Why shouldn't he want to put a voice to the face, and do some of the things that friends did together?

For a few hours she had wrestled with the same two questions: why, and how, did she feel? In the end, she had decided that she needed a little more input on this. This morning she had asked Beth to come round to her house at about seven o'clock, and to ask Amanda and Sophie to come too. Beth had hassled her about the reasons all day, but Abigail had told her she would have to wait till everyone was together.

They had all arrived five minutes early, very clearly excited to hear what she had to say, as an invite to her house without a reason being given was unusual.

She told them about the letter. A stunned silence had followed, which was eventually broken when Beth had made her comment about Marty's sign off.

"I had to ask you guys about this," Abigail went on. "I just don't understand why he's asking now, and I'm not sure how I feel about it. What do you think... and no jokes," she added quickly, seeing Beth grin and open her mouth to say something. "This is big stuff." Beth closed her mouth and nodded.

"I think we can be pretty sure he's not after some nookie," said Sophie. "From what I know of him he doesn't seem the type, plus it's a lot of trouble to go to for sex..."

"There are plenty of men who would go to a lot of trouble for sex," said Beth.

"There aren't that many who would wait all this time to do it," countered Amanda.

"And that's part of what's worrying me," said Abigail. "I don't think for a minute that he's asking to come over so he can see if he can get laid, so why is he asking?"

"Maybe," began Sophie. "It's just as he says: maybe he's decided that, I don't know, he wants to go on holiday and that he could holiday here, and meet you in the process." Beth spoke next.

"I don't think his reasons for wanting to come over here are what's important." She looked at Abigail. "It's how you feel about it that matters."

All three of them were looking at her. Abigail dropped her gaze to the floor for a few seconds, which was the amount of time she managed to keep the smile off her face. She looked up and told them,

"I want to meet him so much it's ridiculous."

The three of them started giggling and joshing her. When they had calmed down she went on.

"I wasn't sure when I read it at first, and after hours thinking about it I still wasn't sure, but when I woke up this morning, I knew I wanted to meet him. I know this man so well, so... intimately, that it seems insane that I've never met him. It's all I've been thinking about all damn day. What would I say to him? What would he say to me? Hell, I don't even know what he sounds like."

"If he sounds like Sean Connery," said Amanda. "I want him to record himself saying some nasty sexual stuff to me!"

"Ditto," cried Beth.

"You're both perverts," said Sophie.

"Yes you are," agreed Abigail. Then she grinned and said, "Besides, if he's going to be saying any nasty sexual stuff, it's going to be to me."

More laughter and tomfoolery followed this comment before Sophie asked,

"What if he wants more, Abigail?"

"More what?" Sophie glanced at Beth and Amanda and said,

"Well, the three of us have often spoken about him and you, which will come as no surprise. It takes a lot of something to keep a long distance relationship going, but you and Marty have managed it with seemingly little effort for years now."

"I don't quite get where you're going." Beth took over.

"Do you remember how long you and Marty have been putting "with love" at the end of your letters?"

Abigail shook her head. She couldn't recall the exact date, but she knew who had done it first: she had. She could remember putting it at the end of a letter one day, not even thinking about it. She had wondered if she should remove it, but in the end had left it. In her journal she had noted how worried she was about it, how Marty would react. He didn't even mention it in his next letter, but he did end it "with love".

"I guess I always thought it was an affectionate thing."

"What do you think love is?" asked Amanda. "It's affection, warmth, caring, wanting... all those and more."

"Yeah, but... it doesn't necessarily mean *love* love... does it?"

"Not always," replied Beth. "But in this case I think it might." Abigail gave her a quizzical look. "The something Sophie mentioned, that keeps a long distance relationship going, was love." She turned to Sophie. "Am I right?"

"You're right." Beth looked back to Abigail.

36

"There is a love between you and Marty that has been there for years, and I think it's the real deal. I think for your relationship to have lasted this long it would have to be. But I also think that because of the distance between you, you decided there could never be anything to it, so you kind of brushed it under the rug. You're feeling muddled now because there's a real chance it could happen, but you're worried that if it does and it's not everything you've ever imagined it would be, it'll mean the end of your relationship with him. What if he's not what you thought or he has bad breath or something? What if he doesn't feel the same way you do? We all know how big a part of you that relationship is, and, honey, I honestly can't imagine, and don't want to imagine, how bad it would be for you if it did come to an end. But I also think the answer to one of your questions lies in the fact that he's finally asked to come see you."

"You think he really... loves me?" Beth nodded, and Sophie and Amanda nodded along with her. "But... why wouldn't he just tell me that?"

"Duh," said Sophie. "Because he's probably had a conversation just like this one with his friends. He's unsure how you're going to react, he's worried about it all going wrong and ending your relationship, because you're just as big a part of his life as he is of yours. I think he's just reached the point where he's admitted to himself that he loves you, and he wants to come see you."

"Plus," added Amanda. "You don't "just" tell someone you love them after all this time. He's the kind of guy for whom saying those words obviously means more than it does to some men, who'll say it if they think it'll get them laid. He feels it and he wants to say it properly, to your face. It's not the kind of thing you tell a person in a letter if you can help it. Say it afterwards all you want, yeah, but you don't declare it in writing in the first instance."

"Totally agree with that," said Sophie.

"Me too," said Beth. "So we know why, and we know how you feel about him, and how you feel about seeing him. That gives us a new question: are you willing to take the risk, Abigail?"

"Yes," she answered instantly. "Yes I am. I've never openly admitted it, even to myself, but every man I've ever been with, I've compared to Marty. Not sexually, obviously, but in terms of personality, and most of them have come up short. Sometimes I don't even think I was aware I was doing it, and when I was I always wondered why. I was comparing them to the man I really wanted to be with. I want to be with him... I want him to hold me and I don't want him to let me go. I'm not even sure if you guys are right about his reasons for coming over, and even if you are it holds the possibility of being a disaster that ends the greatest relationship I've ever had..."

"We'll try not to take offense at that," said Beth dryly as a smile lifted the corners of her mouth.

"You know what I mean. But if he does feel the same... Oh, lord, it could be amazing. It could be..."

"True," said Sophie softly. "In every way."

The four of them fell silent. After about few moments, Amanda said,

"I hate you so much right now, Abigail."

The four of them fell about laughing.

They sat around for a while longer, gossiping and giggling. Amanda, Sophie and Beth all wondered what it would be like to meet the man they had all heard so much about from Abigail. She, obviously, did more wondering than the three of them put together, but at the same time she fretted.

By the time her friends had gone home, she was still fretting. She knew she was going to write the letter, knew she was going to say that she thought it was a wonderful idea that he come over for a visit. Yet as excited as she was by the prospect, and of how things could be if it all went the way she hoped it would, there were still those lingering doubts in the back of her mind. If something went wrong, if for whatever reason this little fairytale she was unconsciously concocting for herself and Marty somehow went sour, she had no doubt that she would be able to get through the aftermath. But that aftermath would be hell, and she would be a very different person on the other side of it. A world where she didn't have any contact with Marty? Abigail didn't even want to consider what that might be like. This wouldn't be a normal break-up, this would be an ending to something that she considered to be as much a part of her as her voice, her eyes, her very personality. Marty, his letters, they were everything that was good in her life. They were just so damn right that the very idea they might cease caused her heart to skip more than a few beats.

She told herself that she might be imagining the worst case scenario. If nothing romantic did come of Marty's visit, then there was no real reason they would part as anything less than what they had always been: friends. That being the case, there was no reason for the letters between them to cease. Abigail managed to fool herself with this for a while, but eventually reasoned that, if things played out that way, the letters would never be the same. It would never feel the same to receive one, or write one.

And so the tide of her thoughts ebbed and flowed between good and bad, hope and worry, until she decided that she had to be strong. She had to be like Marty. If the girls were right and he had written the letter because he harboured some hope that their relationship might become something more, then he must have been as worried as she was over not only the reply, but the possible outcomes. But he'd had the guts to take the first step. Tears pricked the corners of Abigail's eyes as she thought of the state he must be in waiting for her reply.

As she sat down to compose that reply, she wept, hoping that what she was writing would make him feel better. She also hoped that someday soon, if he was feeling blue, she would be able to make him feel better not only by words, softly spoken, but also by simply taking him in her arms and holding him.

Chapter 10

That night four months ago, the night of Alfred Meggin's phone call, had been difficult for Philip Glenster and his wife, Anne.

Glenster had been sitting reading, Anne had been upstairs in bed. The call had been unexpected. Meggin had asked to speak to Doctor Philip Glenster, and Glenster had explained that he was retired now, but that it was he. Meggin had explained that he had once been a doctor at Berrybeck, and that name had caused Glenster's gut to start churning. Meggin had gone on to explain that Berrybeck had been sold off to a private company that had turned it into a dry out clinic and that David Brannon had been allowed to stay on there as at the time of the changeover it had been decided he was no longer a danger to anyone, and also because someone had agreed to pay the required fees. Glenster had been shocked and appalled, and instantly aware of the reason for the phone call. He had asked Meggin to confirm that Brannon had escaped. Meggin had explained that technically Brannon had been a guest there, not a patient, and could have left at any time in the last several years, a right which he had now exercised. However it seemed the determination made as to Brannon's mental state had been wrong; as he left Brannon had murdered three other guests, a member of staff and had started several fires in the building.

It hadn't ended there either. Brannon had then gone to a house not too far away from Berrybeck, a house occupied by a couple called Ralph and Blair Walden. It had been Glenster who had stated that the man had been killed, as had his wife, but she had also been repeatedly raped beforehand. Meggin had confirmed it, and then said that he had recalled Glenster's name from the old case files and had thought he might want to know. Glenster had thanked him, and asked if he knew if there were any leads. There were none; it seemed that after leaving the Walden's house, Brannon had vanished.

For some time after hanging up the phone, Glenster had sat trying to calm himself down, trying to work out what to do. He thought about telling people, but decided that might cause a panic. There were plenty of folk left in town who would remember what happened, not the least of whom was Abigail Morton. It was Abigail he feared for most. The news that Brannon was out might do incalculable damage to a woman who, as a child, had seen her entire world torn apart, and who had made a recovery that had been nothing short of miraculous. Not only that, but if the unthinkable happened, if Brannon came back to Hannerville, it could only be to finish what he had started.

Glenster had decided that this was too damn big for him, that it wasn't his responsibility. The solution was simple: he would visit the sheriff and let him know. After all, protecting the town and its people was the job of the sheriff and his men.

However breaking the news to his wife was his responsibility.

After being told, Anne had been silent for some time before suddenly leaping up from the bed and starting to get dressed. Her husband has asked her what she intended to do, and she had looked at him like he'd just asked what purpose the heart served in the human body. Clearly she thought her intent should have been obvious, but she told him anyway: she was going to let that poor girl know that she may well be in mortal danger. Philip had all but wrestled with her to get her to listen to him, to hear his reasons why that should not be done. At least not right now. He'd asked her if she thought he hadn't already considered doing just that, was still wondering, truth be told, why the hell he wasn't on his way round there himself. Then he had outlined his reasons, and his intention to pay the sheriff a visit. Anne had listened and then argued a little, then she had wept, then she had agreed with him. After that she had cried herself to sleep in her husband's arms.

His breakfast had been waiting for him the following morning, and after clearing his plate and thanking his wife, Glenster had left and made his way on foot to the sheriff's station. The morning was bright and reasonably warm, but what should have been a pleasant morning stroll was marred by his concern over how he was going to explain things to the sheriff. He wasn't worried about breaking any confidences – the incident, and the identities of those involved, were public knowledge after all – but about how to voice his concerns in such a way that he didn't appear to be overreacting. Plus he had to convey to the man the horrendous truth that lay behind all the bullshit he had almost certainly heard. Several of the town residents had probably bent his ear on more than one occasion about that night. Dimmed by time and possibly embellished for whatever reason by the individuals (most likely to give themselves a larger role in things), the sheriff had most likely heard a good few versions of what had happened that night. But the recollections passed on to him from the good people of Hannerville couldn't capture the horror experienced by the four who had actually been in the house on that horrible night, and only two of them had survived. Glenster had spent many years trying to forget it, something which the girl seemed to have accomplished. Glenster often envied her that, but then rebuked himself; if ever a person deserved to forget, it was her.

He had entered the building to find Doreen Spellner at her post behind the reception counter. A nice lady, she was also well known as a ferocious gossip. When she had looked up and saw the man who had delivered one of her two children into the world, she had beamed at him and asked him how he was.

"Just fine, Doreen," he had replied. "How're you?"

"I can't complain, Phil. What can I help you with today?"

"Is Mark in?"

"He is. I'll give him a buzz." Pausing as she lifted the phone, Doreen had looked at him, tilted her head to the side and asked, "You all right, Phil? You look... worried."

"Huh? Well, I'm feeling a touch under the weather." He hadn't liked lying, but had seen no other option. If Doreen had found out why he was really there, word would have gotten around town faster than celebrity scandal got round the internet.

"Should get yourself to bed and rest a little. Rest's the best cure for most things."

She had called through to the sheriff's office and informed Mark he had a visitor, told him who it was. After listening for a moment, she had nodded and hung up.

"You can go right through, Phil."

"Thanks, Doreen. See you on my way out."

He had made his way through to the rear of the building, where Flaghan's office, its frosted glass window bearing his occupation and name, sat at the end of a long corridor. As he reached it, raising his hand to knock, a deep, strong voice from inside had called out,

"Come on in, Phil."

Glenster had opened the door and stepped inside. Plain, tidy and more than up to the task, the room reflected its occupant in every way. Sheriff Mark Flaghan was a tall, reasonably good looking man, slightly reminiscent of John Wayne in fact, something that to Philip's mind couldn't hurt when you were a figure of authority. Tough but fair, Flaghan always had a hello ready if you passed him in the street, was always willing to lend a hand if you needed one, even when he was off duty, and he was one hell of a bowler. Well liked and respected by the townspeople, he had been a resident of Hannerville for many years.

Flaghan had risen from the chair behind his desk as his visitor closed the door. He had given him a smile, exchanged a quick handshake with his visitor, and then offered him a seat.

"How're you and Anne doing?" had been the sheriff's opening question. Seeing a chance to avoid preamble, and also avoid the possibility that his nerve might fail him, Glenster had replied,

"Tell truth, Mark, we're both a little concerned."

"What about?"

"You've heard about David Brannon?" Flaghan had grinned.

"Most definitely. Seems to me that just about everyone in town, or someone they're very close to, was there at that house that night. However, I do believe I'm speaking to the one person who actually was there." Glenster had nodded once. "How come that sicko's on your mind, Phil?"

"Before I tell you that, Mark, I want you to understand something." Sensing this wasn't going to be the social call he had anticipated, Flaghan had sat up a little straighter in his chair, giving his visitor his undivided attention. "I don't know what you've been told about that night, but, as you said yourself, you're talking to one who was there. Someone who survived David Brannon, and I don't phrase it like that merely for effect, Mark. I was damn lucky to get out of there alive, and I've got the scars to prove it. The kind you can see, and the kind you can't. Neither of them usually bother me much these days, but I got a phone call last night that..." He had shaken his head. "I'm not sure I'm getting my point across well here, Mark. The stuff you've heard from everyone, I'm not sure it conveys just how... terrible the things Brannon did were. I'm not even sure if I have it in me to paint the true picture for you, but..."

"Phil," Flaghan had said quietly. "You're one of the most liked and respected men in town. Your reputation is one most politicians don't have the money to buy. I know for a fact that there are still some folks in Hannerville who would, if they didn't think they would be imposing on you, and ever so slightly insulting Caroline, come to you for medical advice. I personally think you're one hell of a nice man, and your wife is one hell of a fine cook. Whatever it is you need to tell me, you should feel free to come right out and say it."

Glenster had felt the weight drop off his shoulders. Taking a deep breath, he had thanked the sheriff, and then told him about the phone call from Meggin. Flaghan had listened, not saying a word until he had been certain his visitor was finished speaking.

"I understand why you might have worried that I wouldn't take this as seriously as you think I should" had been Flaghan's first comment. Glenster had felt himself go red; in addition to his other attributes, it seemed the sheriff was a very insightful man. "All these years later, the distance between here and this Berrybeck place, the fact that people are out looking for him, that this is the town he was caught in... Why would I be worried about him coming back here, right?" Recognising that he owed this man the truth, and couldn't have hidden it even if he had wanted to, Glenster had nodded. "I can appreciate that. But rest assured that I will be taking this very seriously. I have heard a lot of different accounts of that night, but one thing they all agreed on was that Brannon was one sick man. If he's out, and clearly no better than he was when he went in, I will be keeping an eye out. You're right Phil: he may come back, he may not. I'm going to hope for the latter, but my men and I will be prepared for the former. I'll get the word out around town, get people watching for strangers and such. I won't give out a name or anything because I think it would start a panic. Also we don't know what this information is going to do to Abigail Morton's state of mind. I have to admit I was shocked as all hell when I heard it was her house Brannon was at that night. I met her before I heard the stories, and it's remarkable to think that she came through all that as lively and normal as she is. I've never asked her about it because I didn't want her dredging all that stuff up just for the sake of my curiosity. It wouldn't surprise to me to find that she's very fragile on that subject. In case of that, we'll keep the identity of who we're looking for under wraps for as long as it's safe to do so. But if it comes to it..."

He had let the sentence trail off, and Glenster had nodded his agreement.

After thanking Flaghan and again shaking his hand, Glenster had left.

During the ensuing four months, Philip and Anne had been somewhat on edge. Before the call they had taken full advantage of Philip's retirement, spending time together watching sunrises and sunsets, dining out, going to the movies, staying up late to watch TV, or being intimate. Their lovemaking didn't have the fire it had in their younger days, but it was still something they both enjoyed. After the call they had tried to live their lives as normally as possible, but it was a nigh impossible task. Everything seemed forced. They had to be careful to let slip to no one what they knew, but *they* knew.

Brannon might be out there.

Chapter 11

Martin awoke, and then lay in bed for half an hour waiting to see if he would drop off again. When it became apparent that wasn't going to happen, he dragged himself out from under the duvet, got dressed and went to get breakfast. A bowl of cereal was all he felt up to. Like sleep, his appetite had all but deserted him in the last two weeks, ever since he had posted the letter to Abi. It had been a bit of a struggle, and he'd had to concentrate much more than usual to get the same level of quality in his work.

This morning he found that his struggling might be over. Either that or he was about to trade one kind of struggle with another; it all depended on the contents of the only item of post he had received: an envelope with his name and address on the front, written in Abi's instantly recognisable hand. Martin bent down and lifted it off the mat, straightened up, and stared at it.

The moment before. Something everyone will experience at least once. You wait for something, you long for it and fear it in equal measure, you imagine how you will react when it arrives. Every conceivable scenario is played out in your mind as you wait. Sometimes you're giddy with the thought of everything turning out the way you want it to, and dread every so often coils itself around your insides at the thought of what will happen if what you hope for is not what you receive. Someone waiting for a marriage proposal, someone else waiting for the answer; the result of an exam or a job interview; a child waiting to be presented with a brightly wrapped gift at Christmas, hoping the dreamed of toy will be revealed when the paper is torn away...

The moment before, when the need to know or to see collides head on with the wish to avoid possible hurt, humiliation or disappointment.

Martin tore open the envelope and caught the faint scent of Abigail's perfume. He slid out the single sheet of A4 inside and let the envelope fall to the floor.

He read her very short, and utterly amazing, reply to his question.

Stephen blinked once or twice, wondering if the noise he was hearing was an actual sound, or the remnant of a dream he had been having. Rising further from sleep, he realised it was his mobile, ringing and vibrating somewhere on the floor. Smacking his lips together, Stephen slid out of bed, trying to ignore the first signs of a nasty hangover. He wasn't going to get much done today. Scrabbling across the cold, hardwood floor of his bedroom, he found the trousers he had been wearing the night before. Inside the left pocket was his phone. The ringing was just starting to set his teeth on edge when he answered the call.

"Hello," he said, his tongue, feeling like a piece of wood wrapped in felt, barely managing to produce the sound.

"She said yes!" Martin bellowed. Stephen tore his head away from the phone, the resulting dizzy rush meaning it took him several seconds to respond. When he brought the phone back to his ear, Martin was talking up a storm.

"Martin..." No acknowledgement. "Martin, slow down, I missed the start of what you're saying. Go back to the start and, please, slowly and quietly: I'm hungover."

"She said yes," Martin said, much quieter this time. "Stephen, she said she would love for me to come over for a visit. She's excited and looking forward to it, and she thinks I should make it as soon as possible." Stephen smiled broadly.

"All right, Martin. Nice one. Maybe now you'll be able to get some sleep."

"I doubt it; my mind's going a mile a minute here. But she said yes. If nothing else comes of this, I'll at least get to actually meet Abi." There was silence. Then: "Holy shit, Stephen, I'm actually going to meet her."

"Now don't go worrying about that just now. After the last couple of weeks worrying about it, bask in the lovely light of her having said yes." His stomach growled and did a backflip. "Christ, what the hell was I drinking last night?"

"No idea, but you'll cope."

"Thanks for the vote of confidence. My insides disagree. As does my head, which at the moment seems to be building towards a very long, very loud and very uncomfortable drum solo." He paused, burped, excused himself and then said, "So, have you actually thought about when you're going to go?"

"No, but the sooner the better as far as I'm concerned. I'm going to try and relax a little, calm down some, maybe even get a decent sleep, then I'll see about getting the flight booked, accommodation sorted out... Shit, what am I going to say when I see her?"

"You can worry about that on the plane. Martin, I am really, truly happy for you, pal, but I have to go."

"You sound pained. What's..."

"Don't ask; you don't want to know. I'll give you a shout later tonight."

He hung up and ran to the bathroom.

Martin tossed his mobile onto the armchair and re-read the letter for the fifteenth time. He hadn't had the chance to ask Stephen what he thought of the mark on the paper. Small and circular, it looked to Martin like a water droplet that had landed on the paper and been allowed to dry in. His first thought about what it could have been was right on the money: a teardrop. Abigail had been crying, or at least weeping, when she had written her reply. He wondered why, and quickly decided it was perhaps best not to speculate. Such logic would be applied to many things in the coming week.

Happier than he could ever remember being, he went back to bed, taking the letter with him.

Getting things sorted for the trip didn't take as long as Martin had feared it might. Not one for holidays, he asked Stephen to come over to give him a hand booking flights and arranging accommodation. A dab hand at such things, Stephen soon had him booked on a flight to Tennessee that left from Glasgow airport in one week. The accommodation, on the other hand, was a little trickier. Martin had intended to book into a hotel or guest house in Hannerville itself for a couple of weeks. There were two hotels and four guest houses, all fairly small and all fully booked.

"There's a celebration of some sort going on apparently," muttered Stephen, reading from the website of the third guest house. Martin looked towards the ceiling.

"Ah, bollocks!" he hissed. "It's the bloody Hanner Carnival."

"Hanner Carnival?"

"Every year the citizens of Hannerville hold a big party to honour the man who founded the town: Arthur Hanner. It's a big deal: speeches, bunting, a parade with a marching band and floats, and a fun-fair in the park. Then there's the Little Miss Hannerville pageant..."

"How little is this Miss Hannerville?"

"It's a kids pageant."

"Damn. Moving on."

"The hotels and guest houses will be full because it draws a crowd from the neighbouring towns as well, and usually a lot of people who were born there but have moved away come back. Shit! What do I do now?"

"Get a tent and camp out?"

"I'm serious, numb nuts: what do I do now?"

"Well, you could write to Abigail, ask if you could stay with her."

Martin shook his head.

"No. That would be pushing it."

"How so?"

"It just... It wouldn't seem right. I know we know each other, but this will be the first time we've ever met, and I'd feel like I was imposing. Plus Hannerville is a small town, so there will still be gossips, and I don't like the idea of people talking about Abi because she's got some guy she just met staying with her."

"You think she'd give a shit about what they say?"

"Probably not, but I would. I don't stay there; she does. When I leave, I don't want to do so thinking that the legacy of my visit will be her becoming the cud being chewed over by old cows with nothing better to do with their time."

"Fair enough, but it does really only leave you with the tent option."

"There must be something else... What about a hotel in another town? A hotel at the airport?"

"From the airport to the town is a sixty minute drive; that's one hell of a commute on a daily basis."

"Lots of people commute."

"As you say, there must be something else."

He turned and started typing search strings, peering at the screen until he eventually sat back again, a big smile on his face.

"If you wouldn't mind shelling out for extra petrol, you won't mind shelling out for this."

He moved his chair back so Martin could get a look at the screen.

The website referred to the place as a cabin, but the building seemed far too large to be classified as such. Martin read the details: only a five minute drive from the town of Hannerville, situated amidst the majesty of the Smoky Mountains, the cabin boasted five bedrooms (the largest of which, belonging to the owners, was locked and off limits), a large combined kitchen/dining/lounge area, a utility room, a games room and a balcony that gave amazing views out over a lake and the surrounding woods. It was absolutely gorgeous, and far too large for one person.

"Book it," said Martin, stepping back to let Stephen in to the keyboard.

"It's a big place," commented Stephen as he started typing. "You should take someone along to keep you company."

"Any other time, you'd be in the games room beating me at pool, but not this time, pal."

"Aw," Stephen whined. "Why not? Abi's going to have her friends there."

"This is something I need to do on my own."

"Yeah," smiled Stephen. "I know; I'm just fuckin' with you."

With all the arrangements taken care of, he had written to Abigail to let her know when he would be arriving, and where he would be staying. His flight wouldn't get into Knoxville airport until eleven at night, so he wouldn't be reaching the cabin till sometime after midnight. Given that he'd have to pick up the car and then drive on unfamiliar roads to a destination that was, in the owner's own words, "stunning, but reachable only via a real bitch of a road", Martin suspected he wouldn't be getting there until closer to maybe one in the morning. Therefore he had told Abigail that he would visit her at her shop the following morning, around midday.

Writing the words down on paper had given him a little shiver of excitement, and the idea of actually walking into her shop seemed surreal. To open the door of "Pages and Pages" and see her there behind the counter... It was almost unbelievable that it would soon happen.

Martin made a list of what he would need to take with him. At the top of this list was his laptop, not just for contacting Stephen, but also because he had copied to it scans of old photographs of his family and friends. Abi would have heard of most of them, but now she would be able to put faces to the names. He had also copied over all the scans he had made of Abi's letters. These he intended to read on the plane, and show her when he got there, so they could reminisce together, maybe after dinner over a glass of wine or...

Best not to speculate.

Two days before he was due to leave, he asked the boys round for drinks. After a movie, a few hands of Texas Hold 'Em and a lot of beers, Martin told them where he was going and why. They all knew about Abigail, but none of them, with the exception of Stephen, had ever guessed how deep his feelings for her ran.

"So," began Trevor. "Just let me get this straight. You've been pen-pals with this girl for years and now you've realised that you've fallen in love with her. Now you're going to Tennessee to see her and tell her, and find out if there might be a future in it. Is that about right?"

"In a nutshell," replied Martin. Trevor, Dougie and James all looked at one another. Martin knew that regardless of what they said he wasn't going to change his mind, but they were his friends and he wanted to know they didn't think he was nuts. Thus he was aghast when Dougie turned to him and said,

"That's sad."

"What?" blurted Stephen, also shocked. Dougie nodded, trying, and failing, to keep a straight face.

"Sad that he has to go all the way over to America to find a woman who can put up with him!" He laughed and raised his bottle in salute. James and Trevor did the same.

"Martin," said James. "You bloody well go for it, pal. Go over there and sweep her off her feet."

"Here, here," said Trevor. "After all, how could she resist you? All you have to do is show her a picture of the classy, good looking lads you hang about with..."

"And she'll run like hell in the other direction," joked a relieved Martin.

"Probably," quipped James. "But show her a picture anyway."

The following morning, Martin woke up with a monstrous hangover that kept him in bed till almost midday. When he got up he spent the rest of the day just sitting around, trying to convince himself that he didn't need to check anything else and it was all going to go fine. He watched some films, played a video game, listened to some music, but he couldn't relax. He knew himself well enough to know that he wouldn't be able to do so until he arrived at the cabin in Tennessee, and even then he'd be uptight till he finally met Abi.

Met Abi.

He was actually going to meet Abi.

Holy shit!

Stephen picked him up good and early the following morning, getting him to the airport in plenty of time for check-in. The only carry-on luggage he had was his laptop bag. Martin did not relish the idea of spending three hours wandering around the airport waiting to board, but he declined when Stephen offered to wait with him.

"Thanks, but I'll just potter about the shops or something."

"Or worry some more."

"Probably. You doing anything today?"

"Nope. Going home after this, and I'm gonna chill."

"Good. When you get back, boot up your computer and we'll make sure the video calling works okay."

"Will do."

"You've got my spare key?" Stephen nodded. "You'll be okay checking on the flat from time to time?"

"No problem."

They glanced around the terminal for a few seconds, then Stephen said,

"Aw, for fuck's sake, we've known one another too bloody long to be doing this whole "we don't know how to say farewell" dance. Come 'ere, you crazy git."

He reached out, grabbed Martin by the shoulders and pulled him into a hug. When they broke and stepped back, Martin said,

"This probably wouldn't be happening if it hadn't been for you."

"Probably wouldn't? Try definitely wouldn't. I made you face up to your feelings, I booked the flights, I found the cabin..."

"Yes, all right, you've killed the tender moment; you can bugger off home now." Stephen smiled.

"You take care over there, and tell Abi I said hello."

"I will. Remember and put your computer on."

"Yes, mother."

Martin watched him go, a smile on his face. Then he looked around, sighed and went to go browse some shops.

Their check of the video calling was a success, though unfortunately for Martin it only took up ten minutes. Afterwards he had to go back to wandering. An hour before the flight he had something to eat: a ridiculously overpriced cup of tea and a blueberry muffin. Then he made his way to the boarding lounge. Thankfully, the plane boarded right on time, and finally he was sitting in his window seat, his laptop stashed in the overhead compartment, almost jittering with excitement and fear. The elderly lady in the seat next to him misread his inability to settle and smiled at him.

"Are you afraid of flying, son?"

"Hm? Oh, no. It's just that I'm going to see someone I've known for a long time, but I've never met her before. I'm excited, but a bit nervous." The lady smiled again.

"Oh, that's nice. I'm sure it'll all go wonderfully."

"I hope so," he said to her.

After take-off he watched a film, then dozed for a short time. When he awoke, the first thing he thought of was that he was actually on his way, right now, to go and see Abigail. He would see her, and hear her voice, and shake her hand, and... Would he shake her hand? Was that how he should introduce himself? Shouldn't he kiss her cheek or the back of her hand, be all old school and suave? Did he even need to introduce himself? Before he got too caught up in such thoughts, he told himself that planning for something like that was pointless, and that he would just have to wing it. Then, after checking with one of the flight crew that it was okay for him to do so, he took his laptop out of the storage compartment and powered it up.

The letters had their own folder, which was sub-divided into folders for each year. The scans of the letter were named for the date on which they had been written. Martin chose one at random: June 27th, 1993.

"Dear Marty

I get the feeling it should feel weird, telling you what I'm about to tell you. Guess it says a lot about our friendship that I don't feel even slightly weird telling you that I had my first real kiss yesterday.

My friends and I went to The Majestic to see "Jurassic Park". It's an awesome movie. The dinosaurs look so real! I won't tell you about it in case you haven't been to see it yet, but if you haven't you have to go so we can talk about it.

After the movie, we all went for a walk, talking about the movie, and about this and that. We knew the boys were following us, but we didn't mind. I think that despite what we all say sometimes, my friends and I kind of like the attention our new boobs get us from boys. It's something new, kind of fun. I've heard women – teachers mostly, when they think no one's listening - say that with boobs you can get a guy to do anything. Makes me think there should be more female hypnotists. Heck, even I have to admit I find them sort of fascinating. Not so long ago there was nothing there and now *poof*, got me a couple of guy magnets. That's a term I've heard said, by the way, not one I made up myself. Like I said, it's a new feeling, but not a bad one. I have an odd new sense of myself, somewhere between vulnerability and power. I guess it's kind of nuts that I'm already worrying about whether or not my boobs are the only things guys are going to like about me now... Then again, they never showed me much attention before now. But that's you males, right? We girls are only worth talking to once the mounds under the sweater appear.

Leaving the deep discussions about the differences between the genders for another time (you can start coming up with arguments for your side by the way; keep a note of them for future use), my friends and I stopped and sat down in Beaumont Park. The sun was out and it was nice and warm, but a couple of us still had on baggy tops. When I mentioned vulnerability and power, did I throw embarrassed and awkward into the mix? No. I should have. Anyway, we're chatting away and pretending to not notice the guys nearby, talking and pretending not to be looking over at us.

Took the damn fools nearly an hour before one of them worked up the guts to come over and say hello. And that was all it took: hello. I mean, we knew these guys, went to school with them, but had never talked to them outside of the school before. But that hello was the ice breaker. After that we were all laughing and talking together, and it was great. We were there for hours, the guys being dumb and showing off, and us girls just laughing, equal parts with them and at them.

Eventually people started to get up and leave, having to go home for dinner or to do chores or something. After a while there was just me and a boy called Eddie Gifford. He's a really nice guy, and the two of us sat in an uncomfortable silence for a while before he stood up, offered me his hand, and asked me if I would like to go for a walk. It was so nice, the way he did it. I could see he was nervous; probably been trying to build up the guts to ask the whole time we'd been sat there. I actually thought about turning him down because I really should have been getting home myself, and I just about collapsed in on myself with embarrassment, but I said yes and took his hand. He helped me up and we walked across the park, hand in hand. I like the whole hand holding thing, Marty. It's a nice feeling. In fact, given how much I liked the way he asked me if I wanted to go for a walk, the hand holding, the walk itself, and what came at the end of it, I think I might be gearing up to be a romantic fool... or a foolish romantic. Time will tell.

We walked a little ways into the trees that border one side of the park. It was really pretty and... I don't know, Marty. The trees, the birds singing, the sun and the shade, him holding my hand, the newness of it all, the feeling of being on the edge, getting ready to take the next step... When we stopped walking and he asked if he could kiss me, I didn't even bother replying; I just kissed him. I was kind of scared. When he asked me, I knew I wanted to kiss him, but I wanted to be... in control, I guess. I didn't want him to think I was easy or a pushover or a slut or whatever, so I kissed him. God, it was so weird, Marty. For the first few seconds we were both kind of frozen in place. It was horrible, but then we relaxed and it was really, really nice. I'm using the word nice a lot, but it was. I mean, I know I'm not in love with the guy. There were no fireworks and shooting stars and whatnot; it was just... nice. A kiss is a big deal, to a girl anyway (you taking notes for the upcoming battle between the boys and girls, Marty? Better be ready, kiddo), and if it's nice, there's nothing wrong with that.

Perhaps more importantly, his hands went nowhere near my new boobs or my butt. If they had, I'd have kicked him in the nuts and ran home. He just kept them by his sides, and so did I.

When we broke apart, we were both so red in the face we were almost in meltdown! We were gasping for air and grinning, and despite the fact we had kissed it still seemed so awkward! How insane is that? You'd think that would have passed after the kiss, but it seemed to get worse! Life is nuts, man, I'm telling you. Afterwards we both agreed that it had been good, and that we had both better get our backsides home before we got in trouble. We were going in separate directions, and before we split up, Eddie asked me if we were going out now. He was still nervous and awkward and it made me smile. I said yes, we were. He has really nice teeth; I saw most of them when he smiled at me, just before he turned and jogged away.

I came home, and of course I was asked about the movie and what we had done afterwards. I lied by omission. At least I think that's what they call it. Basically I told Aunt Janine and Uncle Peter about the park, but not about the boys, and most definitely not about Eddie. I have no idea how they're going to react to us going out, but I have to say I'm in no hurry to find out. I went upstairs, wrote it all down in my journal, and then I called Beth and told her, so the others all know by now. Soon as I got home from school today, I sat down and wrote this letter to you, buddy.

Boobs, first kiss, first boyfriend. Am I moving too fast? What are your thoughts, Marty? And what's been going on with you over there in bonnie Scotland?

Write back soon; I need an opinion on this stuff from someone who's not going to giggle like... well, like a teenage girl!

Abigail"

Martin closed the file, smiling. He remembered reading that the first time. It had been odd to have had a girl be so open and honest with him. The girls he had known at the time usually just glanced in the direction of him and his friends and giggled. But it had made him feel really special, that Abi had felt so comfortable telling him that stuff. True that Martin had harboured a certain amount of jealousy towards Eddie Gifford. Not because he had kissed Abigail, but because he had kissed a girl. Martin's first lip-lock with a girl had come a few months after reading the letter, and it hadn't been quite as nice as Abi's experience. It hadn't been bad by any means, just in very different circumstances. Abi and Eddie had done the whole holding hands and walking in the sun dappled woods thing, whereas he and Michelle Scallen had been dared to kiss one another by their friends one afternoon behind the technical block of the high school. Needless to say, it hadn't led to a romance of any sort, but it certainly left an impression on Martin.

Abigail's kiss had led to a relationship that lasted for two years. She had eventually told her aunt and uncle, who had handled it well. She had never slept with Eddie Gifford, but they had gone pretty far by the time those two years were up. It had ended in tears: the boy and his family had had to move away because of the father's job. Abigail had been heartbroken. Martin recalled all too well the extreme sadness he had felt when he had read her letter detailing the days leading up to Eddie's departure, the final glimpse of him as the car had turned the corner, the last wave. Had Martin been the uncaring, cynical type, he would have told her that it was the romantic fool in her that had made her watch him leave. She could have said goodbye the night before, and not watched him drive away that morning, but no. They'd had the nice, perfect start to their relationship, and she had wanted the clichéd, teary goodbye. But Martin had been neither cynical nor uncaring. His friend had been in pain, and he had wanted nothing more than to give her a hug and tell her it was going to be all right. Unable to hug her, he had reassured her in his letter that she was going to be fine, that she was strong enough to get over the heartache.

Suddenly feeling tired, Martin powered down the laptop, put it back in the overhead locker, and got some shut eye.

Chapter 12

Tomorrow morning! She was going to meet Marty for the first time ever tomorrow morning!

Time seemed to have rushed by since she had received his letter giving her the details of his trip. Abigail had wondered why, if he hadn't been able to find a room in any of the towns hotels or guest houses, he hadn't asked if he could stay with her. She had guessed correctly at least one of his reasons, and would have been quite peeved had she known the other.

She had taken a drive out to Jackpot Road, had gone all the way to the top where the cabin he would be staying in was. It was a nice drive, but the road was a nightmare, even in broad daylight. She tried not to worry too much about him having to drive up there in the dead of night, on an unfamiliar road, in an unfamiliar car... He would be fine. Marty was the level headed type: he'd drive cautiously, even if it meant the trip would take longer. Looking around the outside of the place, Abigail had had no trouble picturing the two of them going for a walk, or maybe spending an afternoon down by the lake. Uncle Peter still had his boat and he kept it in good condition, though he didn't use it himself much these days, so maybe they could go sailing.

Maybe, while they were out there in the middle of the water, she could tell him her secret.

Abigail decided that out there on the lake, at least he wouldn't be able to run away. There was always the possibility that he could just jump overboard and swim for it, of course, but that might be a bit extreme.

She had resigned herself to some things in the last few days. Her jitters over Marty's visit were not purely the result of excitement; there was a certain amount of fear and anxiety mixed in. Would Marty think she was nuts when she told him her secret? The other thing she had resigned herself to was the fact that, regardless of how impossible it seemed, she wanted her relationship with Marty to go further. Since childhood he had never been far away from her thoughts, but since the visit had been arranged, he was almost all she thought about. It seemed ridiculous: she didn't even know what the man's voice sounded like, for god's sake. But she knew him, knew his heart, his mind, knew that even if he sounded like he'd been sucking helium it wouldn't matter because it was *Marty*. *Her* Marty. If the visit went as she hoped it would, she might never have to rebuke herself for thinking of him that way again. She wanted to hold him, to be held by him, she wanted to wake up and see him lying beside her, and then she wanted to...

Abigail stopped. She felt her face burning red, heard the deep, panting breaths she was taking. Felt the heat building down south. *What the hell?* she thought, because this wasn't like her. She had met men she had been attracted to, been romanced by them, slept with them, enjoyed it, but never before had the mere idea of sex with them had her all but drooling. *You're going too far* she told herself. *You don't know that anything is going to happen. Yes, it's a nice change to be meeting a man who knows your mind* before *he knows your body, and you know it's not just your body he's after, but you don't know if he's looking for anything from this visit other than what he told you. It might just be a friendly visit, curiosity getting the better of him after all this time. He might just want to see where you live, put faces and voices to names.* She told herself all this, but at the same time doubted it. There had to be something deeper to it than idle curiosity. She knew that in thinking that way she might be setting herself up for a fall, but sometimes risks had to be taken.

Finally, there was her secret.

More than anything else it was the thought of having to speak the words she had never spoken to anyone ever before, ever, that caused a cold ball to form in her guts. That it was kind, understanding Marty she would be saying them to didn't make it any easier. But she knew she would have to tell him, and that he would have to accept it, if they were going to go any further. She would tell him; she would know when the time was right, and she would find it in herself to say those words. But as to whether or not Marty would believe her... that was all up to him.

She knew him so well, and the fact that she didn't have the faintest idea what his reaction would be terrified her.

A noise brought her back to herself, and she lifted her head, listening, trying to work out what might have made the sound. That it was one or more of her friends playing a joke was the first possibility that crossed her mind, but she wasn't expecting them tonight, and none of them was the practical joker type anyway. She glanced at the clock: just after 10:00pm. Frowning, Abigail got up from her chair and went to the window, pulled back the curtains and peered out to see nothing but her own front lawn, same as it ever was. She looked left and right and, as she let the curtains drop back, heard the noise again. She realised that it was coming from out back.

Abigail started to feel a little nervous as she went to investigate. Though she was confident of her ability to defend herself should someone break in – she had a spray-can of mace in her handbag, she knew where she kept all the really large, sharp knives, and she was more than willing to stab anyone who defiled her sanctuary by forcing entry – that someone might be out there frightened her. Why shouldn't it? Whatever was causing the noise was unknown, and the unknown, in all its various guises, was frightening. In a neighbourhood where childish pranks were reserved for a Halloween, the possibility of someone on your property in the middle of the night was a scary one.

As she neared the kitchen window, she heard what she thought might have been a sound made by a small animal in pain. Abi stopped in her tracks, staring at the curtains. For a few moments she was frozen. She felt scared, then humiliated that what was probably some idiot from down the street who had gotten drunk and had wound up at the wrong house had her so scared. As it so often does after one feels humiliated – even when, and perhaps especially when, it's only witnessed by one's self - anger surfaced. Shaking herself, Abigail strode over to the window and yanked the curtains apart to reveal her back yard, dark and apparently empty.

In one burst she let out a breath she hadn't even been aware she'd been holding. She pulled the curtains shut and stood back, wanting to forget all about this incident and go back to her chair. But the idea that someone had been toying with her irked her. If she let it slide this time, it might happen again.

"Yeah?" she muttered, heading for the kitchen. "Well fuck that."

She snatched the back door key off the little hook stuck to the corkboard on the wall, which was covered with pictures of the girls, the store, and her aunt and uncle. A quick search of the drawers and she had a flashlight. Click: nice bright light, perfect. She unlocked the back door, pulled it open and stepped out, aiming the flashlight directly ahead. The powerful beam pierced the darkness right the way to the back fence, illuminating nothing but grass and painted wood. She quickly swung the beam left and right, looking to spotlight the joker, but there was no one.

She was about to go back inside when she spotted something over by the fence that separated her back yard from Annette and Ted next door. A small shape... She'd need to get a closer look. Going back inside she took the key out of the door, came back out, closed and locked the door, and then, flashlight leading the way, she walked across the grass towards the shape. She made a quick and sound agreement with herself that if anyone suddenly leapt out at her she would do the smart thing: she'd club the bastard with the flashlight and run for home.

Eventually she made out enough detail to identify the lump as the mutilated corpse of a kitten.

Her heart jumped in her chest and her breath caught in her throat. The hand holding the flashlight began to jitter. A message from her brain to that arm to lower the light, and so hide the horror in darkness once more, went unheeded. Her eyes widened, taking in the details of the blood spatters on the fence, the little internal organs littering the lawn, the poor little creature's wide, glassy eyes. Abigail could only imagine that this was one of the kittens Ted and Annette had been giving away.

The message got through and she lowered her arm, the torch beam now illuminating only her feet. Taking a deep breath, she let it out with the words "Poor little thing", then turned and started walking around the side of the house.

From the shadows at the side of a house across the street from Abigail's, Corday watched her walk across her front lawn to the front door of her neighbours' house. He grinned as he watched the woman answer it, smiled broadly when he heard her shriek and vanish inside, followed by Abigail.

It had been so easy, strolling by that day when they had been giving the kittens away to good homes. Conscientious animal lovers that they were, they had been making a note of the names and addresses of those who had taken one of the little furballs. He had waited till there was a good sized crowd, then strolled up, pushed an arm through the crowd, snatched a little kitty, and had quickly walked off, the mewling little bugger stuffed inside his coat.

He had kept it for a day or two, fed it and such. Earlier tonight he had decided that he wanted to start playing his game with Abigail. He had come here, making just enough noise in her back yard as he had slaughtered the animal to draw her attention, and then he had left it, a gift for her signifying his intentions. Not that she knew that.

But she would soon enough.

As the sounds of a wailing began to drift to his ears from across the street, Corday stuck his hands in his pockets and, sticking to the shadows, walked away.

Chapter 13

Martin yawned and stretched, then had another look at the carousel for his suitcase. The possibility that it had been lost had occurred to him, but it didn't bother him much. All it had in it were his clothes and toiletries, and he could buy more of them. The important stuff, namely his laptop and the printouts relating to his rental of the cabin and the hire of a car, were in the bag slung over his shoulder, and his wallet was in his inside jacket pocket.

Perhaps even more importantly, he was *here*!

Knoxville airport, Tennessee, US of A, a car ride away from Hannerville, from Abi. Yes it was 11:15pm, and that car ride was going to take over an hour of slow, careful driving, and he was completely knackered and rumpled and it looked as though the airline had gone and misplaced his suitcase, but he was here.

Then, finally, so was his suitcase.

Martin reached out, snagged the handle and lugged the case off the carousel, then headed for the exit.

There were no hiccups getting the keys to his car, but finding the thing in the parking garage was a pain in the arse. When he found it, he put the suitcase and laptop bag in the boot and got in. He sat staring at the glove compartment for several seconds, wondering where the hell the steering wheel was, before realising he had got in the wrong door. Looking out of the window, he saw no one around who might have noticed his faux pas. Martin quickly got out, jogged round to the other side, and got back in.

"It's going to be a long, slow drive," he muttered as he started the car, an automatic, and then entered his destination into the on-board satellite navigation system.

Martin had heard some horror stories about satnav systems. People who had followed every instruction their device had given and found themselves in rivers, in fields and, in one case, hanging off a bridge. Thus it was with no small amount of trepidation that he set out on the road, with no choice but to follow the hollow voiced computer as it guided him to the right and left, straight ahead for such and such a distance, then left, right, take the exit ramp and so on. However, with no wrong turns or other such mishaps, it eventually got him to where he wanted to go, the eventually part being due to his cautious driving. The owner had not been exaggerating: Jackpot was one bitch of a road. The turn off onto it was so tight he thought he was going to crash into the rear end of his own damn car! The satnav told him to follow the road, which was easy enough, but it was all uphill, and every single turn seemed to be just as tight as the first. The branches of huge trees dangled over the road. He was concentrating so much on driving that when one branch scraped the roof he jammed on the breaks and let out a cry. Getting out to see what he had hit, he cursed and got back in, slamming the door shut.

The satnav spoke, telling him that his destination was right ahead at the end of the road, and the little map showed no more turns. Martin thanked that most worshipped of deities – fuck – and glanced at the clock to see that it was just after 12:50am. He then stared out of the windscreen as the cabin came into view.

He parked, shut off the ignition and then got out, taking a deep breath and stretching, wincing as various joints popped their disapproval at having been forced to assume a sitting position for so long again so soon after the plane journey. The air was fresh, or to put it another way, it was pretty damn cold. Martin cocked his head to one side, a smile spreading across his face at what he heard: crickets. He had heard crickets in dozens of films and TV shows, had even seen some (live reptile food at the pet shop, yes, but they had still been crickets) but he had never actually heard the chirruping live till now.

He went to the boot, opened it, and rummaged through his laptop bag, which yielded the slip of paper on which he had scribbled the code the owner had given him, the one to unlock the cabin door and unset the alarm. It was then Martin realised there was something he had forgotten to bring after all: a torch. The owner had suggested that if he was going to be arriving at night he should bring a torch along. "Bugger," he muttered under his breath as he shouldered his laptop bag. Lugging his suitcase out, he closed the boot – a noise which sounded impossibly loud to his ears – and started towards the cabin. Halfway there, he stopped, turned, and pressed the button on the key which locked the car doors and activated the anti-theft alarm. As with the boot closing, the twin *beeps* seemed incredibly loud, and the flashing headlights were sudden and painful on eyes that had adjusted to the dark. He turned blinking little stars away from the corners of his vision, and carried on.

After entering the code, Martin opened the front door and stepped inside into more darkness. He put his suitcase and bag down, closed the door, made sure it was locked, and then started slapping the wall looking for the light switch. The first one he hit turned on the light right above his head, the second the lights in the main body of the house.

Martin walked into the kitchen area to find a food hamper waiting for him, a note from the owner welcoming him and giving a number where they could be reached if there were any problems. There was a note on the fridge of the days the rubbish was picked up, and where the tied up bags should be left for collection. The kitchen surfaces, as well as the sink and draining board, were all spick and span. There was a coffee maker, a microwave, everything he would need. He checked the cupboards and drawers, making sure he knew where the cutlery and crockery were kept. Then he moved past the small dining table and into the lounge area: two three-seater sofas aligned along two sides of a large, ornate wooden coffee table, both facing the stonework fireplace. On a ledge above the fireplace sat a reasonably sized flat panel TV, a DVD player, and various remote controls. The curtains were drawn over two doors he knew from the website led out on to the porch. Martin gazed up at the ceiling some 30 feet above his head and wondered how the hell someone got up there to dust.

Back towards the door, investigating the first bedroom, the one he would be using. Nice size for one person. En suite. Good. He brought his bag and suitcase in, and then explored the rest of the cabin.

Going up the staircase just outside his room brought him to a spacious mezzanine which overlooked the lounge. Up here were double doors he had been told would be locked; the owners bedroom. Back down to the area underneath the stairs, where there were four doorways. One led to the utility room, the second to the second bedroom, and the last to a bathroom, as the second bedroom was not en suite. The fourth doorway led to a flight of descending stairs. After switching the light on, Martin went down to find himself in front of another locked door, this one to the garage. From here he could only go right, along the corridor to a T-junction. Directly ahead, another bathroom, to the left the games room – pool table, dart board and a selection of board games stacked in a cupboard. To the right, and at the end of the hall sat a third bedroom. On the right just before that door was the door to the fourth and final bedroom.

Martin made his way back upstairs, checked the front door again, then switched off the lights and went into his bedroom. He went to the bathroom, washed his hands and came back out intending to get changed and lie down. He lay down first, and went out like a light.

"Jeez, Abigail," said Beth. "I've never seen you this... unsettled. Is this because of that poor little kitten you found?"

"It has nothing to do with the kitten," answered Abigail. "It wasn't the most pleasant thing I've ever seen, but it's not like it gave me nightmares."

"Then why... Oh, holy shit, it's *today?* Today's the day Marty's coming here?" Abigail nodded. "What time is he arriving?"

"He got here last night. His last letter said he would be here for around midday." Beth checked her watch and grinned.

"Only two hours away... Why are you so nervous?"

"Are you kidding me? I'm about to meet the man I've known since I thought bows in my hair were pretty, and he thought farting in the tub was funny."

"He's a guy; he still thinks farting in the tub is funny."

"Oh, he does not. But I've known him most of my life. He's been there through so much, helped me through so much... It's only been since he suggested coming over here to see me that I've really thought about how I feel about him and... Beth, you would not believe how afraid I am of how strong those feelings are."

"Isn't that a good thing?"

"Not if his feeling the same way isn't the reason he wanted to visit."

"Oh, Abigail, come on, he has not flown all the way here to say hello. You've been communicating just fine for years; why would he get the urge to say hi in person now, unless there was something more to it? You've realised you've got some deep feelings for him. Trust me when I tell you that he has those same feelings about you, and those are what've brought him here."

"I hope you're right. I just wish I could calm down."

"People are always nervous before a blind date."

"It's not a blind date; it means a lot more to me than a blind date. Damn, I knew I shouldn't have had coffee this morning."

Beth came out from behind the counter and approached her friend and employer with open arms. They hugged, and Beth said,

"You're nervous now, but when you meet him, you won't be, because this is Marty. The one and only, the incredible Marty from Scotland. You know him, and he knows you; there are no secrets between you. If this is a face-to-face relationship starting here today, it's getting off on the best foot possible. Am I right?"

"You're right," Abigail lied quietly. Best foot possible? No secrets? Oh, but there was one, the biggest one, and until she had told Marty what it was their relationship could go no further. Plus there was the possibility that after she had told, their relationship would be over for good. The thought made her feel nauseous.

Beth released her, went back behind the counter, picked up the phone and dialled Amanda, and then Sophie, inviting both of them to come over to the shop at twelve to meet Marty.

"Might help you to have some backup," she said as she hung up.

"Might make Marty feel like he's being ganged up on."

"What? Guy walks into a store to be confronted by four hot chicks, one of whom wants to hump him silly? Dude'll be in seventh heaven." Abigail laughed.

"I do not want to hump him silly..." Beth gave her a raised eyebrow. "The humping is going to be very serious." Both of them laughed.

"All right," said Beth when they had stopped. "Now get your ass in gear; we have inventory to do, and I'm not doing it by myself whilst you're out romancing your pen-pal."

He was awake, but didn't want to open his right eye. His left eye he couldn't open because that side of his face was squashed into the duvet, but he knew that if he opened his right eye it would mean he was officially awake and that he would have to get up. He was still tired and wanted to sleep some more. Martin groaned, turned over, wondered briefly what his workload was like for the day. What day was it anyway? Had he slept through his alarm? These random thoughts edged him closer and closer to wakefulness. As his mind became more active, it dawned on him that he was still wearing his clothes. Puzzled, he opened both eyes and saw above him a strange ceiling. The memory of the previous day became clearer as the fog of sleep thinned, and he sat bolt upright, looking for a clock. None. He grabbed his mobile out of his pocket. He had made a point of re-setting the time after the plane had landed: 10:12am. He was due to meet Abi in less than two hours.

His stomach grumbled, a bad combination of hunger and sudden nerves. He got up, went to the window and threw the curtains open. Sunlight flooded in, blinding him. Squinting, he backed away from the window, calling himself a stupid bastard. He turned away, waiting until his sight recovered before opening his suitcase and quickly unpacking his toiletries. He left everything in his laptop bag, hiding it under the bed, and then undressed and went for a shower.

Ten minutes later, awake, alert, reasonably dry, and with a damp towel wrapped around his waist, he went to the kitchen and worked out how to use the coffee maker. Whilst it was doing its thing, he forced himself to eat some of the cereal the owner had left for him in the hamper. Every spoonful was a challenge he didn't think his stomach was up to, but he finished and then he tried an apple. He got halfway through it, binned what was left and then sat down hard on one of the dining chairs. Martin laid a hand on his gurgling stomach and took a few deep breaths. This was ridiculous. He should have been excited and, yes, maybe a little nervous, but the way his stomach was acting up you would have thought he was about to go skydiving. Martin gave that analogy some thought and decided that it wasn't a bad one: he was about to take a leap in his relationship with Abigail, and if it went wrong and the parachute didn't deploy, he would be a goner. Unfortunately such musing didn't help his stomach.

He got up and walked to the nearest pair of curtains, which he opened to reveal the porch doors. Unlocking them, he stepped out. The morning air was still nice and cool, and he closed his eyes and took a deep breath. Opening them he looked out at a fabulous view of the lake, surrounded on all sides by mountains. He told himself to remember to take a picture from this very spot. Stepping up to the railing, he looked down into the trees that lined the hill below the house, down to where a small area of shingle beach was visible. If he could find the way down to it, it would make a nice spot for a picnic.

The coffee maker buzzed and he went back inside, poured himself a cup. He got through half of it before his stomach started complaining again. He did his best to ignore it and finished his coffee, then went back to the bedroom to get dressed.

Here he was at least able to forget about his stomach problems for a while, because never before had he had so much trouble deciding what to wear. He wasn't exactly a dedicated follower of fashion, but his clothes were casual, comfortable, nice and they suited him. However today everything seemed wrong. After the fifth change, he checked himself out in the mirror and cursed, unbuttoning the shirt again. He tossed it aside and sat down on the bed, glancing at the rest of his clothes, which were now either thrown around the room or spilling out of his suitcase. He wondered if perhaps he should have bought some new stuff for today, but got the impression that even if he were to put on a tuxedo, he would look in the mirror and decide it wasn't right.

She knows you, he told himself. *She knows you're not going to walk in to her store wearing Armani. She probably doesn't have any preconceptions about what you'll be wearing. You think she'll be disappointed if you don't stroll in in a full kilt outfit? Put a shirt on and get going, you dick!*

Finally dressed, Martin checked the time. He had just over an hour to go. That meant he had around forty minutes before he had to get in the car, and he knew there was no way he could potter about the cabin for that length of time, not without driving himself round the twist. He glanced out of the window and saw that it was still sunny, barely a cloud in the bright blue sky. Guessing that it would take around fifty minutes, Martin decided to walk to town instead. He put on his jacket, checked that he had his wallet, and left the cabin. The door locked automatically behind him and a couple of beeps told him the alarm was set. After a quick look around, Martin took a breath and started walking.

The snaking Jackpot Road had not taken long to traverse by car, but on foot was a different story. It took Martin almost forty minutes just to get to the bottom. As he headed towards town, he checked his watch five times in as many minutes, cursing each time, and each time starting to walk a little faster. His fast walk eventually became a brisk jog, and he told himself that this was going to be a great way to make a first impression: late and soaked with sweat. He cursed again, and quickened his pace.

"Something must have happened to him," said Abigail, looking out of the window, which she had been doing on and off for the last hour or so.

"Honey, nothing's happened to him," Beth reassured her. "He probably just overslept. Guy must be jet lagged all to hell and back. He probably should have waited till tomorrow."

Sophie and Amanda both nodded.

"He probably should have," said Amanda. "But he is just so damn hot for Little Miss Sleepover that he couldn't wait to get his ass down here."

The others giggled, but Abigail turned from the window, still wearing a look of concern, and said,

"Well where is he then?" Beth rolled her eyes.

"Abigail, exactly what is it you think has happened to him that is so terrible?"

"You said yourself he'd be jetlagged; what if he crashed on the way here last night?"

"I'm sure we'd have heard something by now," said Sophie.

"Why? The police wouldn't know he was coming here, so they would have no reason to contact me." Sophie walked over to her and took her by the shoulders.

"We're obviously not going to be able to talk you out of this till you see the man, so for crying out loud go up and get him."

"What?"

"You know where he's staying. Go up and get him. Prove to yourself that the three of us are right and that you're worrying over nothing. You never know, if he's tired enough he may even answer the door in his undies."

"Wow, what a perfect first meeting," commented Beth. "Mind you, I agree. You're not going to settle down, so go see what's keeping him."

"He might just be nervous," suggested Amanda. "Could be sitting up there, worrying about how he was going to dress, what he was going to say when he saw you… He might have just lost track of time." Beth looked at her, pointed at her, then looked at Abigail, who shrugged. To emphasise that Amanda might be spot on in her theorising, Beth pointed another finger at her.

"All right," conceded Abigail. "He might not be in hospital, but he's still late and I'm still worried so I'm going up there."

She ran to the break room, grabbed her coat and keys and then ran out, bidding her friends a hasty goodbye. As the door swung shut, Sophie grabbed it, yanked it open, stuck her head out and yelled,

"Drive safe."

Red faced and puffing, Martin came to a bridge that crossed a small river. He walked across, glancing over the side at the clear water running below him, wondering just how out of it he had been last night that he did not recall crossing over the bridge on his way to the cabin. When he reached the opposite side and saw the sign welcoming him to Hannerville, he realised that he had driven right through Abigail's hometown, and had been concentrating so much on driving that he hadn't noticed.

Martin stepped onto the grass verge at the side of the road and took a deep breath in and out. He could feel the heat in his face, knew that he was sweating even though he had resorted to carrying his jacket some time ago. He glanced towards the bottom of the verge, where the bank of a small brook was screened by some bushes. Curious, he made his way down, found a gap in the foliage, and stepped through. The water looked clear and cool and he knelt down, made a bowl with his hands, and scooped some up. He splashed it against his face and smiled, completely unaware of the car that drove across the bridge heading in the direction he had just come from. Shaking his hands dry, he stood up and took out his handkerchief. After drying his face, he unbuttoned his shirt, reached in with the wadded hankie and dabbed at his damp armpits. Stuffing his hankie back in his back trouser pocket, he re-buttoned his shirt as he made his way back to the top of the verge and continued into town.

Hannerville looked so much like every little American town he had ever seen in a film or on TV, Martin felt as though he'd wandered on to a studio back-lot. He walked past a diner and grinned, seeing the stools at the counter, two or three of which were occupied by large trucker looking types shovelling down their food. Behind the counter he spotted a middle aged woman wearing a blue cap, top and skirt with a white apron, looking bored as she went along the counter with a coffee pot in her hand. He came to a crossing, and was halfway to the other side when it struck him that he was a fucking idiot.

The car had sat-nav. He did not. The sat-nav would have known how to get to Abigail's store. He did not. Quickly deciding that he didn't have time to be embarrassed about asking for directions, he approached the first person he saw, a pleasant looking woman in her early forties who was walking her little dog.

"Excuse me, ma'am," he said. "I'm sorry to bother you, but could you give me directions to a book shop called Pages and Pages?"

The little dog started sniffing his feet as its owner looked at him and smiled.

"This is an awful long way to come to buy a book, my Scottish friend," she said. "You could have just used the internet." Martin, knowing how late he was but not wanting to be rude, forced a chuckle.

"I'm over visiting a friend of mine, and I'm running late."

"Say no more." She gave him directions to Pages and Pages.

"Thank you very much, Mrs...?"

"Carborough. Shirley Carborough." Martin extended a hand.

"A pleasure to have met you, Mrs Carborough." The woman smiled warmly at his courteousness and shook his hand, and then he was off again, quickly following her directions before he forgot them.

It was a few minutes later that he found himself approaching the store, and that feeling of unreality intensified. It was no longer as if he were on a set, it was as if he had stepped through the screen into another world entirely. Martin stopped in his tracks and stared at the façade of Pages and Pages. He had a picture of it at home, sent to him by Abigail, taken on the day she had opened the place, but to be here, standing just across the street, looking at it, thinking to himself that she was in there, waiting for him. Possibly a little pissed off at him for being late, it was true, but she was in there.

He experienced the fight or flight moment. Part of his mind told him to get his arse over there and go in, finally meet her face to face and say hello. Another organised a solid ball of ice in his stomach and then told him to turn on his heels and run, get back to the cabin, call Abigail and tell her he had a bug or something. His stomach flipped and he felt himself begin to sweat again. Bunching his fingers into fists, he swallowed, took a breath and took a step forward.

You've done more difficult things than this, he told himself. *Hell, this part should be a breeze. You just walk...*

A horn blared to his left and Martin started, almost tripping on the kerb as he stepped back out of the path of the car. The vehicle rolled by, the driver glowering out at him. Martin gave him an apologetic smile and waved, then regrouped, checked both ways, crossed the street, and entered the store.

Martin found himself confronted by three women, all of whom looked to be in their early thirties. There was a short blonde, who was grinning at him shyly (*Sophie*), another woman next to her, taller, around the same age, lovely raven hair, whose smile was a little more confident (*Amanda*). The last one, standing behind the counter, was the same height and age as the brunette but had long blonde hair that hung down almost to her waist (*Beth*). She had her hands flat on the counter and was flashing him a big smile. Martin smiled and nodded to each of them as he approached.

"Beth?" he enquired when he got to the counter. The woman's smile broadened, exposing perfectly white teeth. She nodded slowly and then said,

"Hello, Martin. Talk to me some more." Martin's nervousness was briefly overridden by puzzlement.

"Talk some more about what?"

"The weather, sports, what you had for breakfast, anything as long as you're saying it in that accent." Martin couldn't help but chuckle.

"Uh, okay... I'm here to see Abigail. I'm a bit late..."

"Did you walk?" asked Sophie. Martin turned to her.

"Yes, I did. I have a rental car, but it was a nice day and I thought I'd walk... I underestimated how long it would take."

"She's gone looking for you," said Amanda. Martin turned, asked her to clarify. "Abigail got worried because you were late, so she drove up to your cabin to look for you."

"Seriously?" All three nodded. "Oh, I am such an arse! I have made a total balls-up of all of this..."

"Even when you're cussing yourself out it sounds good," commented Beth. "You have to record an answering machine message for me before you go back home."

"Might as well do it now then," he told her. "Because I have made a complete mess of this."

"Oh, you have not," Amanda told him. "She went looking for you because she was concerned, not because she was annoyed."

"Didn't she pass you on the road?" asked Beth. Martin shook his head. "Well, listen, Amanda's right, you haven't screwed anything up. I'll go put on some coffee, you guys chat amongst yourself." Martin gave her a weak smile. "You're going to have to put some wattage into that before Abigail gets back, pal. Think about it this way: your first full day in the States and you get to hang out and chat with three gorgeous ladies, and then you get to meet Abigail. That's win-win right there." She went through a door into the back of the store and Martin turned to Sophie and Amanda. He smiled at them, deciding that he was here now so he might as well try and recover from a bad start.

"So, is this the part where you all grill me, trying to suss out if I'm some sort of secret psychopath?"

"It's unlikely that someone with psychopathic tendencies would have spent most of their lives setting up one victim," said Sophie. "Proper psychopathy usually starts to develop early in life and..." She tapered off when she saw the look Martin was giving her. She gave him her shy, but very endearing, grin. "Sorry, I kind of ruined your joke."

"No joke; I've done the whole meeting friends thing before; people size you up, it's as simple as that. But you seem scarily clued-up on the subject of psychopaths." Sophie giggled.

"I just find it interesting is all. Human minds are fascinating, but when something goes wrong in there... look out."

"Sadly enough there are plenty of cases that make your warning one that people should take seriously." He looked to Amanda, saw her finish looking him up and down. "Have you mentally created the pro and con columns in your mind?"

"I have," she said. "You have lateness in your con column, but in your plus you have that accent, and on that subject I have to agree with Beth; it's awesome. Also in your plus column is the fact that I know you've been a really good friend to Abigail for a really long time, and I trust her judgement, maybe not over my own, but certainly over Sophie and Beth's."

"Hey!" Sophie feigned annoyance. She tapped Martin on the arm and, when she had his attention, pointed at Amanda. "You want to talk about judgement calls, she once decided it would be a good idea to go to an all you can eat buffet just to see how much she could eat. She ate plenty, and kept it down for all of five minutes after leaving, at which point she threw up so hard she nearly knocked herself on her ass!" Martin looked at Amanda, who looked back and gave him a slight shrug.

"So, when it comes to food, you're an expensive date, huh?"

The gag drew a laugh from Sophie, and a smile from Amanda. Martin smiled back and then Beth appeared at the door asking what he took in his coffee. Soon the four of them were crowded around the counter, sipping coffee and telling stories. Well, Martin was telling stories: the three of them wanted to know all about Scotland. He told them about how, when the weather was right, there were places that could be more beautiful than anything dreamed up by the mind of an artist. He also said that even when the weather was bad, there were places that possessed a haunting beauty. He had a go at teaching them how to properly pronounce the word "loch", and made some progress, though at first they each found themselves clearing their throats rather than speaking. He mentioned that, like anywhere else in the world, the various urban centres in the country were a mix of the good and the bad. He recounted to them the tale of when he'd been around eleven or twelve and his primary school class had gone to an activity centre in the highlands and had gone hill walking. They had started out in their shorts and T-shirts and walked so high that they reached the summit wearing trousers, jumpers and waterproofs. It was a great feeling to have made it, but then he walked into a bog on the way back down and had to be hauled out by his classmates.

And then the front door opened and the conversation stopped. Martin turned around...
... and there was Abigail.

Chapter 14

Abigail had just reached the cabin when her phone rang. She withdrew it from her pocket, saw Beth's number displayed, and answered the call.

"He's here!" whispered Beth.

"What?"

"Martin's here. He came in not long after you left. He walked from the cabin…"

"He's all right?"

"He's fine; he just screwed up on how long it would take him to walk from there to here."

"I'm on my way back."

"Cool. I'm just making some coffee. I won't say anything; let it be a surprise."

Beth hung up and Abigail tossed her phone onto the passenger seat, started the car, pulled a rather reckless and raggedy turn in the road, and took off back down the hill.

She supposed she should have felt a little disappointed that it all hadn't gone smoother. That it had been Beth, not she, who had been standing behind the counter when Martin first walked in to Pages and Pages. But instead all she felt was relief that he was okay. All sorts of ideas, some of them faintly ridiculous, had gone through her head on the drive up. That he had been so out of it after the flight that he'd crashed into another car on the road, or crashed off this damnable road on his way up the hill. She had also imagined that he'd reached the top, meant to hit the brake, hit the accelerator instead and sent his rental car crashing into the cabin, or off the edge and down the hill to the lake. Seeing the car sitting there, unscathed, as she had pulled up had been a relief, but it had also led to a slew of new ideas about why he had been late. Had he simply overslept? Had he tripped and fallen, injuring himself? Gone for a soak and ended up falling asleep, drowning in the tub?

That he was safe and sound and currently in the company of her friends allowed her to abandon such thoughts, and allow a load of new ones to take their place. What she would do and say when she got to the store. Should she joke with him about being late? Rebuke him for making her worry? Instead of concentrating too much on it, she concentrated instead on making her way back as quickly, and safely (this road was *such* a pain in the ass!) as possible.

She soon found herself outside her place of business, more uncertain about what was going to happen inside than she had ever been before, even on opening day. She walked up, grabbed the door handle, felt the metal slip in her sweaty grasp as she pushed it down, and opened the door.

The conversation around the counter stopped and her friends all looked up, each of them wearing a little half smile. But her attention refocused quickly on the man in their midst, a little taller than herself, with amazing blue eyes and brown hair and a wonderfully boyish grin that spread slowly across his face as he looked at her.

They couldn't take their eyes off one another as they both slowly advanced. Abigail thought about extending her hand for him to shake, Martin thought he should do the same, and that if she took his hand he wouldn't shake it, but would lift it to his lips and gently kiss it. Cheesy as hell, but it seemed proper somehow. In the end it was moot. No hands were offered. They stood a foot or so apart for a few moments and then, as if in unspoken agreement, they hugged. Martin inhaled deeply, getting the full scent of the perfume he had caught only a ghost of before from her letters. Abigail pressed herself against his shoulder, feeling completely comfortable in his embrace. She could think of nothing to say that would complete the moment. Then Martin – her Marty, always with the right words - capped it perfectly.

"Hello, Abi," he whispered to her, his voice a little hoarse with emotion. She smiled, her eyes tearing up, and replied,

"Hi, Marty."

They broke the hug and stepped back, both of them hearing the gentle sniffles from the direction of the counter. Martin and Abigail looked to see Beth, Amanda and Sophie all trying to look like they hadn't been weeping, and failing miserably. Abigail grinned, covertly wiping away a tear herself. Martin smiled, glad he'd managed to reign in his own emotions.

Suddenly, Abigail wanted to be alone with Martin. She wanted him to herself for a while, so they could work out how they should be around one another before having to work out how to be with one another around others.

"Would you like to go for a walk?" she asked him. He turned back to her, smiling and nodding.

"As long as it's with someone who knows where they're going, and how long it takes to get there."

"I'll do it," called Beth. Abigail chuckled.

"You need to watch the store."

"Fine, I'll do that instead, but you suck, boss!"

Martin walked back over to the counter and gave Beth, Amanda and Sophie a hug and a kiss on the cheek.

"It's been a pleasure meeting you all. Work out a time you're all free in the next couple of weeks and we'll all go for dinner. My treat."

"Sold," said Beth. Amanda and Sophie both thanked him and he walked back to Abigail, who opened the door. As Martin exited, she looked towards her friends and mouthed a "Thank you". Beth mouthed "I hate you so much right now", Amanda chose "You lucky bitch" and Sophie went with "If you don't want him, I'll take him." Abigail shot them all a shit-eating grin as she left, closing the door behind her.

They walked for a few minutes before coming to the town square, a large area of flowering gardens and paved walkways with a gazebo in the centre, bordered on all sides by shops and businesses. There were also a few stalls set up, selling flowers and food. It was busy, with people going about their business or sitting on one of the benches eating, either by themselves or in pairs or larger groups.

They walked through the square and continued on. It occurred to Martin that neither of them had spoken since leaving the store, yet it was not an uncomfortable silence. They were just taking a walk on a nice day, and it turned out their destination was…

"Beaumont Park?" said Martin, looking around the vast area of green and making an educated guess.

"Not as busy as the town square right now," Abigail told him. "So I thought it might be a nice place for us to come, stroll around for a while." Martin nodded, unable to keep himself from smiling. "What is it?" Martin saw no reason not to tell the simple truth.

"It's all this," he said. "Hannerville, Beaumont Park, Pages and Pages, Beth and Sophie and Amanda and… you. It all just seems completely unreal right now. That I'm here, with you, walking through the place where you had a big get together with your friends after graduating high school, and got so drunk you nearly had to get your stomach pumped." He looked around and continued. "You broke your leg falling out of a tree somewhere in here when you were… what? Ten?" Martin chuckled. "On the plane on the way over here I read the letter you sent me about your first kiss…" Abigail burst out laughing.

"Eddie Gifford! Oh my god, I remember how upset I was when he left. I might have been a bit melodramatic when I wrote the letter telling you about that. Hold on: you brought all the letters with you?" Martin nodded.

"Well, not the originals: I scanned them all into my computer a while back, just so I'd have backups. I uploaded them onto my laptop before I came over, read a few of them during the plane journey."

"I'm blushing, aren't I?"

"Little bit," he confirmed. "It's understandable, and something I was worried about... Well, *one* of the things I was worried about, when I thought about coming here. It's one thing to have someone know so much about you when you don't have to deal with them face to face, but it becomes a bit different when they're beside you. For instance..." He felt the colour rise in his cheeks. "I am now completely mortified that I'm standing beside a beautiful woman who knows about the first time I ever... well..."

"Got an erection in school?" she suggested. He let out a slightly embarrassed laugh.

"Among many other things I don't want to get into in a public place." Martin shook his head. "It's ridiculous though. I've told you things about myself that literally no one else knows, so why should I be bashful about it just because I'm actually here with you instead of writing it?"

"Human nature, I guess."

"I say we override human nature. I didn't come all this way to spend all my time blushing because of what you know. I told you what you know, and it's too late to regret it now."

"I don't regret telling you any of the stuff I've told you over the years." She put it that simply, and looked him right in the eyes as she said it.

"Well, there we go. No more blushing?"

"Deal." She gave him a mischievous smile. "By the way, did anyone ever find those magazines you used to hide under your bed?"

"Oh, we're playing that game, are we?" She gave him a mischievous smile.

"Hell yes we are!"

They strolled through the park, and more than once Martin had to stop himself from taking her hand. It felt like it was something he should do, but it might have seemed too forward. He listened as Abigail told him about the last few weeks, about how anxious she had been, even though his visit was something she had been looking forward to.

"You weren't the only anxious one," Martin assured her. "I kid you not, I don't think I've ever been as nervous as I was when I got up this morning. I could barely eat... I couldn't even pick out what to bloody wear!"

"All that fuss over coming to see little old me?"

He turned and looked at her, at the way her smile made her eyes scrunch up, the way her hair moved in the breeze. Part of his mind knew that she was wearing a blouse that showed a fair amount of skin and a hint of cleavage, and that same part of his mind knew that normally he would not be able to keep his eyes from dropping. However it seemed these were not normal circumstances; Martin did not want to look away from her cheeky smile.

"You don't get to say that because you've already admitted you were anxious too."

"That doesn't mean I don't get to make fun."

"It does! It totally does."

"Are we going to have to call in a ref on this?"

"We can't because any ref would be biased in your favour; everyone I know is an ocean away." She sighed happily and looked towards the sky.

"Can't beat a stacked deck."

The motion of her head pushed her chest out and now Martin did drop his gaze. He raised it again just as fast; he did not want to have to be hiding an erection. To keep his mind from replaying what he had seen, he said,

"Stacked deck, huh? So board games aren't all you cheat at."

"I do not cheat at board…" She saw the smug smile on his face. "Damn it; forgot who I was talking to."

"Precisely, and any more of this making fun of me for things you yourself have done will result in a few letters being shown to your friends." She gave him a stern look, which quickly changed into a smile.

"We've been talking for about half an hour, and already we're using what we know against one another. We are terrible, terrible people." Martin chuckled.

"We're the dregs of humanity all right." She laughed and, before he knew it, Martin had suddenly said, "Can I hold your hand?"

Abigail stopped laughing and looked at him. Martin couldn't read her expression, and instantly became worried that he had made a mistake.

"I… I'm sorry, that was a stupid thing to ask. I… uh…"

Abigail stopped him by stepping closer, a warm smile on her face, and taking his hand. Martin looked down at their interlaced fingers, felt the warmth of her skin on his, and then looked back up into her eyes. He grinned, and felt his face go red.

"We're setting a terrible example," she told him. "Holding hands like this when we've only just met."

"Are you kidding?" he responded with a dry chuckle. "Stephen usually holds more than a girl's hand before he even knows her name. Besides, we only just met in person; you know me better than anyone."

"Better than Stephen?"

"Most likely. He'd come a close second though."

"What did he think about your coming over here?"

Martin almost told her that it had been Stephen's idea to begin with, but realised in time that that would most likely lead to questions about why Stephen had suggested it. That would lead down a conversational pathway better left for later.

"He was very happy I decided to do it," he told her, salving his conscience by telling himself that this was perfectly true. "Said it was about time you and I met. In fact, if it had been possible he'd have come with me."

"Why wasn't it possible?"

Martin stopped walking. He really didn't want to get into the nuts and bolts of the real reason for his visit so soon, but he realised that her question gave him an opening to lay at least a couple of cards on the table.

"I told him he couldn't come," he said. "Because coming here to meet you… I wanted it to be just for us. I didn't want this trip to be about anything other than us meeting for the first time. I didn't want it to be like a holiday because, well, you mean the world to me, and this trip should be all about spending time with you."

He stopped himself there, afraid that he would go further, afraid that he had already gone too far. The meaning behind Abigail's expression was again a mystery to him and he started walking again, searching his mind for something to bring a bit of levity back to the conversation.

"Besides, if I had brought Stephen, he would just have spent the whole trip trying to get together with your friends." She giggled and said,

"He does have a way with the ladies, doesn't he."

"One that at times is almost uncanny. I've been on holidays with that man where he has met a girl, had sex with her, said goodbye, and then moved on all in the space of half an hour."

"Doesn't everyone have at least one relationship like that under their belt?"

"Not me," he told her. "I at least like to know a girl's name before I have sex with her."

It occurred to him that this might be a somewhat inappropriate conversation to be having, until he remembered who he was talking to.

"And, as you know, it took me a long time to come out of my shell with girls."

"But look at you now: took on conversing with three women, all complete strangers to you, and you charmed the socks off them all."

"Yes," he said, nodding, cocking his head to one side and smirking. "I just let my natural charm take over."

"And you were doing fine with me until that comment."

"Aw, come on, you can't force me to deny my natural charisma. Anyway, as nervous as I was, deep down I'm sure I knew I'd be fine talking to you. When you first meet someone, you're unsure of them and they're unsure of you; everyone holds something back. If you become friends, some of those things are revealed over time. As you get closer, more of those things become known, possibly to the point where someone knows everything there is to know about you. That's how I feel about you. I can be myself around you because there's nothing you don't know about me."

You're getting all mushy again, dummy! said a small voice in his head. But before he could try and say something light hearted, Abigail said,

"I feel the same way about you, Marty."

They stopped walking again and turned to one another. For a few moments they stood there, looking at one another. Birds sang, the leaves on the trees rustled in the breeze, a few children yelled and shouted, their parents calling after them: Martin and Abigail noticed nothing but each other. Martin felt like he could spend all the time between now and when he had to get back on a plane just standing there, looking into her eyes. He wondered if she even suspected the depth of the feelings he had for her, wondered if there was any way he would be fortunate enough for her to feel something for him. There was only one way to find out. Martin took a breath, opened his mouth and said,

"So, what is there to do in Hannerville?"

The moment had been priceless crystal, and he heard it shatter at his words.

Abigail blinked, something changing in her eyes. She recovered quickly.

"Tonight I think it would be a good idea if you caught up on some rest, because you must be jet lagged to hell and back. Right?"

"A lie down is probably in order, yes. But I don't want to waste too much time sleeping."

Yeah, you'd rather waste it by doing that thing where you open your mouth and ask insipid bloody questions, you dickhead! What is there to do in Hannerville? What the fuck was that?

"We can go see a movie at some point. The screen at The Majestic is small but the popcorn is amazing. Drew, the guy who owns and operates the theatre, has his own recipe and has never told anyone what it is. Uh, there are lots of places where we can go for walks, and I'm hoping to be able to take you out on the lake at some point. There's that dinner you promised the girls…"

"I really only suggested that so I would look cool and suave; one guy escorting four women to dinner? My rep in this town will be set." She smiled and shook her head. "And at some point you can come up to the cabin and I'll cook dinner. Better give me a day or two to practise getting it right… And then the number of a good take-out place so I can order something in when I make a mess of it."

"Sounds good," she said, and again he was struck by the brilliance of her smile. The idea of being alone with her in the cabin, having dinner with her, standing on the porch and watching the sun go down. Better yet, standing on the balcony watching the sun come up.

They walked back to the square and sat at a table outside a little café to have some lunch. They chatted about this and that, eventually working out where they had missed one another on the road into town. After their meal – Martin insisted on paying – they strolled slowly back to the shop. When they were approaching it, he admitted,

"This feels so... wrong."

"Wrong? How?"

"We've only just met, and now you're going back to work and I'm going back to the cabin, and I'm not going to see you again till tomorrow."

He was aware that he might be showing his hand a little again, but after his last misstep he had decided that perhaps it would be simpler if she came to the conclusion about his feelings on her own and asked him. It seemed to him that admitting would be easier than confessing.

"I know I can't monopolise your time," he said. "You have a business to run and you can't just dump it all on Beth, but... I've waited a long time to meet you and I don't want to... What? Why are you smiling?

"I understand," she told him. "Twenty-odd years of being friends on separate continents and you're here, in person, for only two weeks; it doesn't seem like enough time. And you're right, I do have a business to run, but Beth knows what it means to me that you're here, and she has already agreed to do the lion's share of the work. Only because she knows it's just for a fortnight and afterwards I'll owe her big time, but I'm willing to suffer that to spend as much time as I can with my Marty." His eyebrows went up and her cheeks flushed red. "And when I am at the store, you're more than welcome to come down and hang around. I can give you a great discount on some quality reading material. And you can treat me to some more lunches. So, how about you come down around midday tomorrow and we'll... have lunch?"

"Sounds good," he said.

"Cool," she concluded. They had reached the shop and she seemed eager to go inside, but before she did she produced a card from her pocket. "This has the store number and my cell number on it, so if you need to get in touch with me you can. Oh, are you going to be okay walking back to the cabin?"

"Yes."

"Then I will see you tomorrow." She paused, seemingly torn between going into the store and something else. Before Martin could ask what it was she reached up, kissed him on the cheek and then darted inside.

With a bemused smile on his face, Martin started the long walk back to the cabin.

Chapter 15

Corday was furious.

He had been watching Pages and Pages all morning, had watched Abigail and Beth show up to work. He had sat in the sun on a bench, sipping coffee and reading his newspaper, surreptitiously watching as Sophie and Amanda had arrived. He had been about to take a break, go for a stroll around the square before coming back to take a seat at a different vantage point, when Abigail came out, got into her car and drove away. Puzzled (normally when she was at work she stayed there till she went home, only occasionally coming out to buy her lunch), Corday had stayed put, sipping his coffee and watching, waiting.

And then another little bit of unfinished business had walked onto the street. Corday had all but dropped his cup. Not a man who was easily shocked, the sight of Martin fucking Muir (far older than he had been the last time Corday had seen him, but he had no doubt who it was; could practically sense it) widened his eyes, and actually caused him to utter a little sound as he choked on a sudden burst of rage. Corday fought to maintain his composure, and only just succeeded. He took another sip of coffee, turned the page of his paper, and kept an eye on Martin as he stood across the street from Pages and Pages. No doubt why he was here, though Corday had been under no illusions since the moment he'd clapped eyes on the son of a bitch. But *how*? How did he and Abigail know one another? How long had they known one another? Had they met before? His mind reeled. He had taken such steps to ensure that this very scenario never occurred (it had all gone wrong in the end, but he had always believed that one part of it had gone right) and yet here it was, playing out before his narrowed, spiteful eyes.

He watched Martin step out in front of the car, couldn't keep from grinning as the driver honked his horn and the idiot jerked backwards out of the way. After he was across the street and in the store, Corday waited for him to come back out. He eventually considered walking past the shop, but waited. Time passed. Muir did not reappear. Abigail, on the other hand, did. She parked and ran into the store and, only a minute or two later, came out with Muir.

Corday's fingers tightened around his cup, squashing it, bursting it, allowing what little liquid was left to escape, run down over his fingers and dribble to the ground. His other hand grabbed and tore a page of his newspaper. It had happened. It had actually gone and fucking happened. Fury and disbelief fought for superiority as he watched them walk out of the square. He started to ask himself how in the hell this had come to be, but decided that was a question for another day. He got up, binned his cup and newspaper and then followed them, drying his hand on his jacket as he went.

He watched them as they strolled through Beaumont Park, watched them go all fucking starry eyed at one another. He punched a tree. Watched them walk to the square, ate lunch only a few tables away as they ate and chatted. It was here Corday noticed the pretty waitress, whom he graced with a warm smile and a large tip before he followed Abigail and Muir back to the store, where their conversation ended on a somewhat awkward note with her giving him a card and a kiss on the cheek.

Corday followed Muir, who visited the grocery store. When he left, now carrying two bags, he headed out of town, going across the bridge and up Jackpot Road. Corday knew then where he must be staying; only one of the places up there was available for rent. He had looked at it himself when he'd come to town. Nonetheless he trailed behind Martin all the way to the top, making sure he knew where the little bastard was staying. This confirmed, he walked back to town, already thinking of later tonight, of the waitress.

Chapter 16

"Have you ever had one of those moments when you're getting ready to say something, you open your mouth, and then something completely different comes out?"

"Everyone has moments like that."

"When they're talking to the woman they've waited most of their life to meet? 'What is there to do in Hannerville?' What the fuck was I thinking?"

"You weren't," Stephen told him. "It's called nerves."

After realising that there were a few things he would need to buy before he returned to the cabin, Martin had visited a grocery store. The check-out operator had recognised his accent and mentioned that he had relatives living in Scotland, though he wasn't entirely sure where. The walk down Jackpot road had been tiring, but the walk back up, laden with his shopping, was exhausting. Reaching the cabin, sweaty and wheezing ever so slightly, he had quickly put away the products that needed to be kept refrigerated or frozen and, leaving the rest, had gone for a long shower. Dressing in a T-shirt and shorts, he had returned to the kitchen to put everything else away, and had then pottered around the cabin for a while. He shot some pool, threw some darts, took a better look around than he had after his arrival, walked around the porch, took a couple of photographs, and then made himself dinner. After that was done he had sat down on one of the couches, delighted to find it extremely comfortable. He had switched on the television, spent fifteen minutes trying to work out which remote control did what, and then had channel hopped until he happened across an old black and white horror movie he liked.

He managed to watch five minutes of it before falling asleep.

Martin slept for two hours. When he awoke, he got his laptop from his bedroom and powered it up. It was just before nine o'clock so, given the time difference, he wasn't certain that Stephen would be at home, but he checked anyway.

No sooner had he logged in than a little window appeared. Stephen grinned and waved at him.

"Open a window, numb nuts; I got nothing here."

Martin made a few clicks, maximising Stephen's window and activating his machine's webcam. In the corner, a little window with what Stephen was seeing appeared.

"Hey, there you are," said his friend. "Right, details, go."

Martin had recounted his mistaking how long it would take to walk to town, and how he'd almost got run over right outside Pages and Pages. He talked about going in and finding out Abi had gone looking for him, then chatting to Beth, Amanda and Sophie and then…

"It was amazing," had been how he'd described turning round to see Abigail standing at the door. "She was just standing there, smiling, looking absolutely beautiful, and I walked over and we hugged… " He had told Stephen about their stroll to the park and the moment. "That once in a lifetime, incredible, perfect moment that I completely and utterly ruined." From this condemnation of his handling of that moment, Martin had then segued into his question about the breakdown in communications between brain and mouth.

"Nerves? No, Stephen, nervous is what you get when you're sitting strapped into a roller coaster waiting for it to go. Nervous is what you get standing at the open door of a plane, parachute on your back, waiting to be told to jump. What I did was take a moment that could have led to everything I came here for and I spat in its face! That's not nerves; that's outright, dumb assed, thick-as-shit stupidity!"

"You're being too hard on yourself," said his friend. "Look, just before this moment you made a mess of, the one you seem to think has killed the possibility of a moment ever happening again, what was it Abigail said?"

"Uh, I had told her that I could be myself around her, could tell her anything because she already knew everything about me. Something along those lines anyway. Then she said she felt the same way about me."

"And that was when you both started star gazing in one another's eyes, right?"

"Yes."

"Well, see, you might have ruined the moment by meaning to spill your guts about how you feel, but I don't think that's what you should be taking from that moment." Before Martin could butt in, Stephen went on. "You said it was intense?"

"Oh yeah. I felt like I could hold her gaze till hell froze over, but I wasn't sure what to do next. I knew what I wanted to do, but I think going in for a kiss might have been pushing it, so I decided to just tell her. Then I opened my mouth and what I said came out."

"Yeah. Nerves. Already mentioned that. Deal with it, and pay attention. Now, two people who have nothing unspoken between them cannot manage that level of intensity in a gaze…"

"Actors and actresses can."

"Are you an actor? Is she an actress? Does she have any reason to act like she has deeper feelings for you? No, so don't be a dipstick. Your little moment happened because both of you are bottling up your feelings for one another. So believe me when I tell you that there will be other moments. Now, I'm sick fed up with the word moment, so what happened afterwards?"

"Uh, she mentioned going to the cinema, going for dinner, going for walks, going out on the lake… Then we walked back to the shop and I mentioned how wrong it all felt, just having met her and now I wasn't going to see her till tomorrow. She said she understood how I felt and that…" He trailed off, a little smile pulling up the corners of his mouth.

"What? What is it?"

"She said she knew Beth would help her out at the shop because Beth knew what my being here meant to her, to Abigail. She said she wanted to spend as much time with me as possible. She called me her Marty."

"Eh?"

"She was speaking about spending time with me and the words she used were 'I want to spend time with my Marty'. Then she seemed to get really flustered, and she's not the getting flustered type. She gave me a card with her number on it, we arranged to meet for lunch tomorrow and then she… kissed me on the cheek and went inside." When he stopped talking, that little smile was back on his face in moments. Stephen was grinning ear to ear.

"You are sorted, my friend. Completely sorted."

"How so?"

"Oh, come on, Martin! She tells you that she wants to spend as much time with you as possible, she refers to you as hers, then she gets flustered when she realises she has revealed that to you. Bet she's never used that term in any of her letters, has she?" Martin shook his head. "And a little kiss before parting. Bingo! I'm telling you, the sooner you tell her why you're really over there, the better it'll be for both of you."

"You think so?"

"Yes, and don't you go overthinking things either. You're doing it right now, aren't you? The wee smile's dropped off your face because you're thinking about what else her words and actions might have meant if not romantic interest. Stop it, you arse!"

"All right, I'll stop it. But I'll probably start again the minute you're gone."

"Nothing I can do about that. So, are you going to tell her tomorrow?"

"I'm not going to think about it," said Martin. "I'm going to see how things go and if it feels right to tell her, then I will. It would need to be something I did off the cuff; if I planned it it'd all go wrong and I'd look like a complete idiot. I did wonder earlier…"

"Stop wondering earlier, and now, and in the future!"

"No, I was wondering if I dropped enough hints if she might pick up on them and ask me outright how I felt. If she's not interested then she won't ask, but if she asks then she's at least curious… What?" he asked, spotting the mystified look on Stephen's face.

"Martin, I want you to listen to my next words very carefully. You listening? Okay. Martin, you are not in fucking primary school! You are a big boy, and big boys do not drop hints in the hope that the girl they like will notice and ask them."

"Of course they do," Martin argued. "A big boy is essentially just a little boy with more hair and a deeper voice." Stephen considered this and then said,

"All right, maybe they do, but not when they're on a strict time schedule. You've got two weeks, Martin, so get a good sleep, then get up nice and refreshed tomorrow, ready to sweep Abigail off her feet. Okay?" Martin smiled.

"Yeah, okay."

"Good. If you're able you can give me a shout around the same time tomorrow."

"Will do. Thanks, Stephen."

Martin logged off, shut his laptop down and then, before he could begin thinking about how he could ever tell Abigail how he felt, he went to bed.

The moment Abigail had entered the store, Beth had insisted she tell her everything that had happened in the most minute detail possible. Abigail had asked after Sophie and Amanda, and Beth had told her they'd had to go, but they were seething that they wouldn't be around to hear about her time with Marty. Abigail disappointed her friend by telling her that she was only going to tell it once, so Beth should contact the others and they should all come to her house tonight around eight.

They had arrived at half past seven.

"I meant what I said earlier," Amanda had said as she threw herself onto the couch. "You're a lucky bitch. That accent alone puts him head and shoulders above most of the guys I've dated."

"Oh," breathed Sophie. "I could listen to that voice recite the phone book."

"And he has a fine ass too," commented Beth. "Plus he's friendly, witty, charming, has his own business… Yeah, I hated you this afternoon, I hate you now, and I'm probably going to hate you later, hon."

Abigail went to the kitchen and came back with some glasses and a bottle of wine. She handed the glasses out, half-filled them, sat down on the armchair and said,

"So he made a good impression?" Beth replied,

"I think it's safe to say that if you vanished tonight, the three of us would be more than happy to help Marty get over you."

"Thanks very much," said Abigail. Beth grinned and raised her glass.

"All right," said Sophie. "He made a good impression on the three of us, but let's cut to the chase: what kind of impression did he make on you, Abigail?"

Her three friends stared intently at her, silently warning her to not even think about trying to conceal the truth from them. Abigail remained silent but was unable to keep the smile and the girlish giggle from happening.

"He's amazing!" she squealed. "His voice, his eyes, and you're right; he does have a really nice butt. We were walking, and he asked to hold my hand. I don't think he meant to; he just blurted it out… He was so cute, and just walking with him was so nice. At one point we were looking into one another's eyes and… I just wanted so much to tell him that I want to try being more than friends, but I kept my mouth shut. When he opened his mouth to speak, I fooled myself into thinking he was going to say it so I wouldn't have to, but instead he just asked what there was to do around town…"

71

"Not what he wanted to say," commented Beth.

"What do you mean?" asked Abigail.

"Aw, honey, come on; he wants to tell you the same damn thing you want to tell him, but he's as nervous and uncertain as you are. Bet when he asked about stuff to do around town he kind of blurted it out, just like he did when he asked to hold your hand. Am I right?" Abigail thought about it, nodded. "There you go. What happened next?"

"I told him about some of the stuff we could do. We walked back to the store and I… I called him my Marty, right to his face. I was so embarrassed. He was too polite to say anything…"

"Too overcome with joy is more like it," said Amanda.

"…and I just handed him my card and kissed him on the cheek."

"What did he do?" asked Sophie.

"I don't know; I ran back into the store. But from tomorrow I want to spend as much time as I can with Marty while he's here. Just walking around town with him today felt so right. A little awkward, but this was the first time we had ever met, so I expected it to be. Hopefully I'll be able to get a sense of how he feels before I say anything too revealing."

"Oh, bullshit," cried Beth. "Get him on the phone right now. In fact, bullshit to that too; get your ass in the car, drive up there, and tell that lucky little… What did he say that stuff was they made out of a sheep's innards?"

"Haggis," answered Sophie, her tone and expression saying everything about what she thought of the traditional Scottish dish Martin had described to them earlier.

"Thank you. You get up there and you tell that lucky little haggis muncher how you feel. I guarantee you you'll be spending the night." Amanda nodded.

"Beth's right, Abigail. I mean, the three of us are hot, but after you walked in, I'll bet that if we had stripped naked and started getting it on with one another right there on the counter, he wouldn't even have noticed." Abigail winced.

"Good lord, I'll never be able to look at that counter the same way again. And thanks for your support, guys, really, but I need a little more time before I say anything to Martin. You are all banned from dropping hints, okay?" No one replied. "Hey! Come on. No hint dropping the next time you see him. Promise me." The three of them, very begrudgingly, promised.

Abigail had no doubts that the three of them were crossing their fingers as they spoke.

After another hour of chat, drinks and snacks – during which Abigail endured no small amount of ribbing over things like how she could work off the calories on her new imported Scottish love machine - Beth, Sophie and Amanda left. When they were gone, Abigail tidied up and then sat down on her couch, her expression pensive, the light-weight feel of the evening having left with her friends.

She couldn't help but think of what she had said to Martin that afternoon, when she had intimated that, just as she knew everything about him, he knew everything about her. It was something she desperately wanted to be so, but it was not quite true. There was that one glaring gap in his knowledge that he was unaware of, that little fact pertaining to her life that absolutely no one other than herself knew.

That little fact she now had two weeks to reveal to him before her chance was gone.

Telling him how she felt about him would be easy compared to telling him her secret, but that had to come first. Abigail had no idea how she would broach the subject. Was it better to try to prepare him for it, or should she just come out with it? What if she dropped some hints and he scoffed at the idea? She didn't think there was any way she would risk telling him after that.

After almost an hour of consideration, she decided that she was not going to be able to make a decision on the issue tonight. Besides, tomorrow certainly wasn't going to be the day she told him. Since the time she had with him before she told him her secret might be the only time she would ever have with him, what she did decide on was that she was going to enjoy it as much as she could.

Abigail went upstairs, got changed into her nightgown, spent an hour writing in her journal, and then went to bed.

Chapter 17

Janice Mallory wiped the last table clean and stood up straight, wincing as her spine popped a few times. For good measure, she lifted her arms over her head and stretched them too. More pops. *I gotta exercise more* she told herself, though at that moment all she wanted to do was go home, shower and then curl up with some trash TV and a pizza, followed by some ice cream.

It had been a long shift, twelve hours in total, and one she hadn't been expecting, nor been prepared for. She had started at ten that morning and had been supposed to finish just after six, but Shirley Tillton had called in sick and Louie, the manager of the Premier Café, had asked her if she would cover, and Janice had said yes. It had been tough, and just about every muscle ached, but the tips had been good. In fact one guy, who'd had a lovely smile, had given her way more than expected.

And she had a day off tomorrow. Sweet as pie.

Some money in my pocket, and a long lie in tomorrow morning. Small pleasures, Janice, honey, but pleasures all the same.

She smiled a big smile as she made her way back through the café to the kitchen, where her boss was just finishing loading up the dishwasher.

"Tables are all done, Louie," she told him. Louie - about five feet seven, getting a little light up top and a little heavy round the middle, but a nice guy and a good boss – pressed a few buttons on the washer and then turned to her.

"Great, Jan. Throw me that cloth." He held his hands out and she did as asked. He caught it and then told her. "Now go home and get some rest. You outdid yourself today; twelve hours and the last thing your last customer saw was your smile. True blue, kiddo, true blue."

"Thanks, Louie. I'll see you day after tomorrow."

"Oh, yeah, right… You doing anything special tomorrow?"

"Nah," she replied, taking her coat down off the hook. "Just catching up on what's on my TiVo, maybe do some reading."

"Do a lot of reading," Louie advised. "Better for you than that bull-crud I know you love watching."

"It's entertaining," she smiled at him.

"No, honey, "The X Files" was entertaining; what you watch is brain rotting."

"Maybe, but that's why I read; to balance things out." Louie chuckled.

"I can't argue with that logic." He gave her a wave as he turned towards the load of linen that was to go into the washing machine. "I'll see you later."

"Take care, Louie."

She walked out to the street, shrugging her jacket on as she went. It wasn't a particularly cold night, but wearing it was easier than carrying it. Janice took a deep breath and began the ten minute walk to her apartment building.

The square was still relatively busy, but as she got further from the centre of town, there were less and less people around. It didn't bother Janice; she had been born and raised here and she knew the town, and, thanks to her job at the café, the people, well. It had its ups and downs, but on the whole it was a great place to live. It was a simple little town and that was what appealed to her; simplicity. She had her apartment, her beat up little car that still started at the first turn of the key, her job, her friends and her folks. She was content with her lot. Not for her the dreams some of her friends had had, like moving to a big city, like New York or some such. Too big, too noisy and too crowded. Her friends had followed their dreams though. One or two had eventually returned home to Hannerville. She still saw them around town, met up every once in a while for drinks or to go to the movies. She had also kept in touch with those who had stayed in whatever bustling metropolis they had moved to, and they seemed happy enough whenever she communicated with them. *As long as they're happy* Janice would tell those others who had found that city life was not for them. That was what mattered to Janice: being happy with your life, and she was.

The collision took her completely by surprise, so lost was she in her thoughts. Someone bumped against her so hard she spun off to the side and almost lost her balance. Gasping, she threw out her arms and managed to regain her balance.

"I'm so sorry," said an unfamiliar voice. "I wasn't looking where I was going... Are you alright?"

"I'm fine," she replied. "No harm done." She looked at the person, a man. An oddly familiar face to go with the voice she didn't recognise. Then it came to her: he was the big tipper from earlier this afternoon. "Are you okay?"

"Oh, yes, I'm fine." he replied.

Janice was about to say something else when she saw the look that had come over his face. Gone was the shock of his having stupidly walked into someone on a well-lit street. Something jarred in Janice's mind and she looked left and right. The street was well-lit, and empty. Looking back to the man, she saw his eyes. Cold, penetrating, frightening. Janice took a step back and stumbled. She was nowhere near the kerb, but she was definitely losing her footing.

The man had something in his raised hand and was waving it at her. As she fell she realised what it was: an empty hypodermic needle.

Corday slipped the hypo into his pocket and reached out for Janice with one hand. He caught her by the upper arm and tightened his grip, pulling her towards him and hugging her, as if they were old friends who had just met on the street. A quick glance up and down the street confirmed they were still alone. He had chosen his place of attack well.

After seeing her at the café that afternoon, Corday had spent an hour or so online, quickly finding out who she was and where she lived. Choosing the likeliest route she would take on her way home from work, and deciding where to ambush her, had been child's play. As had the act itself, pretending to bump into her, the impact distracting her from the slight sting as the needle had punctured her flesh and the drug had been administered. Corday walked backwards across the small stretch of grass, dragging the unconscious Janice with him, towards the shrubs that lined the street. He hid her behind these and then, satisfied she wouldn't be seen by any passers-by, went back to the sidewalk and made his way quickly to where he had parked his car.

Less than two minutes later, he pulled up next to where he had left her. He got out, opened the back door, and quickly ran across to where Janice lay. Heaving her up, he swung one of her arms across his shoulders. Now, instead of old friends embracing, he was helping his drunken girlfriend, who had called him and given him a location before falling asleep in the bushes. He reached the car, bundled the woman inside. He was about to shut the door when he decided that the trunk would be better, in case someone saw him as he was leaving town. He leaned into the driver's side, popped the trunk and, after a quick check up and down the street, transferred Janice into it.

From start to finish, the kidnapping of Janice Mallory took less than five minutes.

Janice opened her eyes and, after only a few seconds, what had happened to her came back. Not fuzzy, as one might have expected given that she had been drugged, but in crystal clear detail. She moaned, the sound so frightened it didn't even dare come much farther than the back of her throat. She tried to move her legs and found she couldn't; her arms likewise. A quick glance was enough to note the restraints over her ankles and wrists, holding her down on the bed. Janice squeezed her eyes shut and fought the urge to scream. Opening her eyes again, she took in her surroundings, a little part of her mind telling her that when she got out of here she would want to be able to give the authorities as much information as possible.

A somewhat more pragmatic voice in her head distracted her, asking who the hell she thought she was kidding with all this bullshit about escape.

But some people do escape situations like this. It's not the usual outcome, but it happens.

She tried to recall if she had glimpsed anyone in those last few moments on the street, someone who might have seen what happened and then contacted the sheriff. When she found herself unable to remember seeing anyone, she told herself that the drug she had been injected with might be messing up her memory.

The way alcohol does.

Alcohol my ass! No one was there.

Obviously whatever he gave me isn't exactly like alcohol; the effects won't be the same.

As she thought about that icy stare he had been giving her before she went under, the way he had been waving that needle in front of her face, she became angry. Who the fuck did this son of a bitch think he was? Little fucking pervert, wandering around drugging women. The idea that she might already have been molested occurred to her and her guts shifted uncomfortably at the idea. She forced herself to concentrate, to try to work out if her clothes looked or felt like they had been removed, or if she was sore down below. Janice took another quick glance down at herself. Her clothes seemed fine, and as far as she could tell there was no pain or discomfort at her crotch. She hadn't been interfered with.

Yet.

Much as she didn't want to admit it, it might be that the little fucker had simply decided to wait until she woke up before... taking her. Maybe he liked to hear his victims yell and beg. A shiver of unadulterated fear coursed through her, prickling the hair at the back of her neck, causing her stomach to sound off again, and making her feet jerk about as much as they could, given that her ankles were tied down. Janice told herself to get a grip.

Take a look around, see what there is. Maybe work out where you are. The more you know the better.

She was in a small room with a wooden floor. Against the far wall was a wooden chair, beside it a small wooden table with a dim electric lantern sitting on it. To her right was a closed door. To her left was a boarded up window. Other than that there was nothing.

Her cursory investigation left her with the idea that she was in one of the old shacks in the hills surrounding Hannerville. The places had a dark history that had been passed down through the generations. In all likelihood the original story had changed greatly from what it had been, embellished and altered with each telling by each story-teller. The version Janice had heard growing up was that anyone who had ever lived in one of the shacks had gone insane not long after moving in. Some had families, some didn't, but all of them found victims before finally doing away with themselves. As kids, Janice and her friends had often scoured the woods looking for the shacks, drawn to these ramshackle constructs with their horrific histories like moths to a flame. That their parents had often warned them away from the shacks, saying that they were dangerous and could fall apart at any time, had only made the children more eager to find them. And they had, though it had always been in the daytime, and even then the places, all quite deep in the woods, far from town, seemed just as unsettling as the stories suggested they should be.

That she was now shackled to a bed in one of the damn things after having been kidnapped off the street was so damn clichéd Janice almost laughed.

She started to wonder how long it would be before she was missed. Assuming she hadn't been out long and today was still today, she was off work tomorrow, so Louis and her co-workers wouldn't find her absence odd. She'd had no plans to go anywhere with anyone tomorrow, and hadn't mentioned to anyone that she would call. This was by design: tomorrow was going to be her first day off in some time, and she had just wanted to potter around her apartment, watch some TV, do some reading, and generally just chill out with no interruptions.

This bastard had at least one whole day to do with her whatever he was going to do.

Janice felt the fear bubbling up, starting as a churning in her gut and rapidly building to a small thunderstorm in her insides that wanted to burst out of her mouth. She prepared to thrash around, shout, scream, cry out for help, try to loosen the restraints holding her down, but then she heard the sound and so stayed still. Even her burbling stomach quietened down.

It had been a footstep somewhere outside.

Friend or foe?

That pragmatic voice in her head piped up again, telling her that of course it had been the footstep of the scumbag who'd brought her here. What were the chances of someone else being out here near one of these decrepit shitholes right when she needed rescuing? She wasn't a gambler, but Janice didn't think she'd have gotten good odds on that one.

The sound came again. Her hands tightened into fists at the thought of what the next few minutes might bring. As her fingers curled in, two of her nails snapped off against the mattress. She hissed in pain as a door opened. Janice listened intently, heard the door close over. Then footsteps, three, and then a protracted creak as the door to the room opened. Janice forced herself to keep staring at the ceiling, to remain calm.

"Hello again"

The door closed over and she whipped her head round as he approached the bed, intending to scream and shout at him, but the maniacal gleam in his eyes, the tight little grin on his face, stopped her cold. Janice felt tears tickle the corners of her eyes. She fought them, determined not to let him see her weaken, but they came nonetheless. As did the small, strangled sob, escaping from between her tightly pressed lips. When she felt his fingers touch her hair, she started screaming. She exhausted herself, took a deep breath, and prepared to scream again.

"We're deep in the woods here," he informed her. "Miles from anyone or anything, so you could go ahead and scream all you wanted, scream until your throat became hoarse and you couldn't make another sound." Janice prepared to take him up on his offer, but then he added, in a lower, more menacing tone, "However it is a very annoying sound, so if you do scream like that again I will be forced to stop you."

Janice screamed, the sound cut short when her captor punched her in the side of the head and knocked her unconscious.

Corday rubbed his knuckles as he walked over to the chair. He quickly undressed, neatly folding his clothes and hanging them over the back of the chair. Naked, he removed the scalpel from the inside pocket of his coat and held it up to the meagre light, which glinted off the wicked cutting edge. He would need to be careful not to nick her as he cut her clothes off. Well, not *that* careful. He turned back towards the bed, and suddenly thought of the perfect place to put her once he was finished with her. Oh, it was perfect. In the gloom, Corday's lips curved into a smile even more wicked than the blade he held.

Chapter 18

Martin stirred, popped one eye open, saw the soft glow of morning light, then closed his eye again and prepared to snooze for a while.

He thought of seeing Abigail, and smiled. Suddenly wary of being late the way he had been yesterday, he checked the time. He was to be at Pages and Pages for midday, and he was definitely taking the car today, so he would have to leave at around 11:40am. Or maybe 11:30, just to be on the safe side. That gave him three hours to kill. He looked out some clothes before going for a shower, taking his time under the hot spray and using up half an hour. Once he was dried and dressed he made himself a nice breakfast – bacon, eggs and a glass of strawberry pouring yoghurt – and sat out on the porch to eat it. He gazed out at the mirror glass smooth surface of the lake, pictured himself way out there in a little boat, just him and Abigail, lying together, dozing in the sunshine.

Martin had just finished eating when a larger-than-average spider dropped down from above him, landing just beside his plate. Unafraid of arachnids, he nonetheless got a bit of a shock and leapt out of his chair, vocally adding a little more blue to the morning. Still muttering under his breath about the spider's questionable parentage, he held out one hand and coaxed the spider onto it with the other. Carrying it to the railing that enclosed the porch, he sat it down and encouraged it to go home. It sat perfectly still. Martin shook his head, and then the little beach caught his attention. Deciding that finding out how to get down there was as good a way to spend his time as any, he loaded the dishes into the washer, grabbed his sunglasses and set off.

As he exited the front door, the spider out on the railing did what Martin had suggested it do, and started making its way back inside the cabin.

He checked that the front door had locked before walking down the steps. Pausing at the bottom he took a deep breath of very fresh air and smiled. Though he was certain he couldn't get used to staying quite this far up in the hills, it was a welcome change from his normal lifestyle. As he made his way towards the back of the house, he wondered how the living arrangements would be sorted out if he and Abigail were to become a couple. Obviously she wouldn't want to leave her hometown, and he wouldn't be particularly thrilled at the idea of leaving his little flat behind, as well as his business, but he admitted to himself that if those were sacrifices being with Abigail required, they would be made.

The rear of the property was somewhat unkempt, the back yard a riot of tall grass and weeds. So concealed was it by the dense undergrowth that Martin almost didn't see the old well. He stopped just short of walking right into it.

"Cool," he observed as he looked down at the grill covering the top. It was bolted down onto the bricks and a quick tug suggested it would take more than gritted teeth and determination to budge it with bare hands. Given that he got the impression the well was quite deep, that was probably a good thing. Martin searched the ground around his feet and found a small stone. He dropped it through the grill, listening for the sound of it hitting water. The splash, when it came, was distant.

He started off through the grass again, heading for the top of the wooden staircase he could see. It was a steep flight, and the steps were narrow and high. Martin practically sidestepped down to where the last step met a small patch of dirt that quickly joined a long tarmacked stretch of road. Martin looked left, saw a long metal gate and walked towards it. There seemed to be nothing beyond but tall grass. Shrugging, he turned and walked the other way. Just beyond where he had first stepped onto it, the road became almost ridiculously steep, so much so he had to lean backwards as he walked. It flattened out a little at the bottom, where a waist high wooden fence separated it from the hillside. To the left was the top of another flight of stairs. Beside this one was a sign that read "Please be careful; they're steep".

The last lot weren't? he thought as he started down. These stairs weren't as steep as the ones leading down from the cabin to the road, but they were much higher and he took them one at a time, eventually reaching a small gate. There was a sign here too: "Danger of slipping". Beyond the gate were more stairs, these ones metal with rubber strips glued to them to aid grip, and at the bottom they joined a metal gangway that sloped down to the shingle beach. Martin opened the gate, stepped through, closed it and descended. The stairs were fine. It was when he was only a few steps along the gangway that his feet shot out from underneath him and he fell, landing heavily on his backside. The hollow *clung* sound he made sounded loud in the quiet morning air. Thankfully no one was around to see his accident and so he was spared embarrassment, but that did little to salve his wounded pride or soothe his bruised rear.

Rather than risk getting to his feet, he crab-walked to where the gangway stopped and the large boulders it sat on, which bordered the beach on three sides, began. Clambering across them to the beach, he felt like a child at the seaside. He jumped down onto the stones, which ran back about one hundred and fifty yards to where they met more boulders, these forming a border between the beach and the foot of the hill. Martin looked up above the densely packed trees to the cabin, and the porch where he had stood some fifteen minutes ago. On the other side of the beach were some large, flat topped rocks that protruded out beyond the beach and into the water. Martin wandered over, leaping over the boulders that littered the beach, and made his way up onto the flat tops. On the other side were more boulders, leading to another small beach like this one. At the far end was a mass of trees and shrubbery. Leaping back down, Martin crossed to the other side to find an almost identical scene on the other side of the boulders there. He dropped down and walked to where the water began lapping at the toes of his shoes and looked out across the lake. It was a stunning view, and he dearly wished Abigail were here to see it. He consoled himself with the thought that, maybe later on during his trip, she would be. And before they came down here they would have had breakfast together, having woken up beside one another, having spent the night…

Calm yourself. Skip a stone or two.

He skipped several, though never managed more than four or five bounces before the stone went under, leaving rippling circles in its wake. He wondered if today was going to be the day he told Abigail. Would the right moment come up? If it did, would he know it? More importantly, would he have the guts to take advantage of it?

The boat came into view from his left, the two occupants sitting with their backs to him. One of them looked over his shoulder, saw Martin, and tapped his friend on the arm. The other man looked over his shoulder and smiled, then brought the boat to a stop. The two men got the boat turned around and waved.

"Good morning, stranger," the first one, a man who looked to be in his sixties, with an unruly mop of white hair and who was wearing a yellow jacket and blue jeans, called out. Martin smiled and waved back.

"Good morning."

"Oh, you ain't from around here," commented the second man, about the same age as his companion, but whose hair was done in a buzz cut. He wore a blue jacket and black trousers.

"No, sir. I'm from…"

"Ireland!" shouted the first man. "Recognise that accent anywhere."

"You're close," Martin informed him. "Scotland."

"Scotland," said the second man. "Had an uncle who moved over there way back in '73. Loved the place. What's your name, if you don't mind me asking?"

"Martin Muir."

"Martin, it's a pleasure to meet you. My name's Jonathan Askew, and my friend here in the glaring yellow jacket is Tommy Tessick."

"Nice to meet you both."

"What are you doing over here, Martin?" asked Tommy. "Holidaying?"

"Not quite; I came over here to visit someone I've been friends with for a very long time."

"Someone you met through that damn social networking site my grandson's always talking about. What do they all it again? Facepage?"

"No, my friendship with this person goes back a long way, to the dark ages of pen and paper."

"Pen-pals?" blurted Jonathan. "Oh, that makes me smile. It's nice to think that in this day and age there are still people who like the more traditional ways of doing things."

"You never upgraded to e-mails?" asked Tommy. Martin shook his head.

"It felt more personal to keep in touch the way we always had."

"And you're over here to meet... he or she?"

"She," confirmed Martin.

"You're over here to meet her for the first time? That's lovely, it really is. My wife'll say the same when I tell her."

"You gents live on the hill?"

"No." Jonathan answered him. "We live in town, but an old friend of ours lives out here, lets us use his boat to go fishing a couple of times a week."

"Not that we ever catch anything," grouched Tommy. "Still, couple of hours out on the lake on a nice morning, shooting the breeze... There are definitely worse ways to spend your time."

"You and your friend are staying in the cabin there?" asked Jonathan.

"Sorry?"

"You and your friend? Staying in the cabin up there? I'm guessing you brought someone with you for a little moral support, huh."

"No, I'm on my own."

"Well then who's that?" asked Tommy, pointing over Martin's head, up the hill to the cabin. Martin turned and saw the man standing at the porch railing, looking down at them. Martin frowned and was about to call out when the man turned and walked away. When he was out of sight, Martin turned back to Tommy and Jonathan.

"Postman, maybe?"

"Not this early in the morning," Tommy informed him, shaking his head. "Not way up at the top of the hill." Martin frowned.

"Then I have no idea. But I think I'll go and find out. Gentleman, it's been a pleasure meeting you both. Hope to see you again before I go."

"Good to have met you, Martin," Jonathan said with a wave.

"If we see you around town, we'll buy you a drink," promised Tommy.

"I'd appreciate that. Have a good day."

The men sat back down and got their boat moving again and Martin made his way as quickly, and safely, as he could back to the stairs. He walked back up as quickly as the awkward steps would allow, wondering who the hell it had been standing on the porch. Would he still be there? What did he want?

At the top of the stairs, Martin jogged up the steep incline. He was out of breath and almost staggering as he reached the bottom of the stairs leading up to the cabin. Wishing he had been a bit more enthusiastic about his visits to the gym, he started the climb.

At the top he looked around but saw no one. Making his way back to the front of the cabin he looked left and right, but there was still no one in evidence. He thought that perhaps it had been someone from one of the houses from down the hill, come to say hello. The people here were very friendly, so it wasn't impossible. However Martin doubted it. Something about the way the person had been watching them, and the way he had quickly left after being noticed suggested it hadn't been someone who wanted to bid him good morning.

He slowed the car down as he approached the bridge, his thoughts split between driving safely and who the mystery visitor could have been.

Martin wondered if it was some sort of joke Abi was playing on him, but decided that wasn't the case; practical jokes weren't her style. Next he wondered if perhaps it was her friends playing the joke. He couldn't recall if Abi had ever mentioned her friends being the practical joking type, but this idea didn't seem quite right either; this just didn't feel like a joke. Martin tried not to be unnerved, but it was difficult. He was in a foreign land, all alone up on that hill, and someone had gotten onto his porch, watched him. It was weird and…

Could it be to do with Abigail?

The question made a great deal of sense. He had never been here before, had been here for only a day so far and he knew next to no one in town, so what other factors might enter into it? Only one: Abigail. Was there perhaps someone in her life, or who had been in her life, that she hadn't told him about? A spurned lover or a jealous ex-boyfriend, someone she was ashamed to have been involved with, or was afraid of? Martin found it difficult to believe that if there were such a person Abigail wouldn't have mentioned them in one of her letters. Plus he could not believe that she would have allowed him to come over to visit her if she had some crazy stalker hanging around. However, despite this very logical conclusion, that his mystery visitor had some link to Abi was a thought that persisted.

Martin gave it further consideration as he cleared the bridge and drove into town, but by the time he parked he had decided the idea was a bit of a stretch. An ex of Abi's disgruntled at his being here trying to unnerve him, make him leave? It seemed so far-fetched. Still, the damnable little thought still circulated in his head as he got out of the car, locked the door, and started walking.

By the time Pages and Pages came into view, Martin had realised he was going to have to speak to Abigail about it.

"I look all right though, right?"

"Abigail, you look great," Beth reassured her. "But I feel like I have to point out that you could be wearing a burlap sack today and Marty would still look at you like you were Cinderella arriving at the ball."

"You really think so?" Beth rolled her eyes.

"What the hell is it going to take to convince you that he is nuts about you?"

"I just don't want to make a fool of myself."

"You're not going to make… Ooh, here he comes. I'll go get the basket and blanket."

"Thanks," said Abigail, turning to see Martin walk in the door. He closed it, turned and stopped. Abigail became worried and looked down at the outfit she had on: a tight, but not too tight, blue blouse, unbuttoned a little at the top, the hem hanging out over the waistband of a loose black skirt that came to just above her knees. No tights, sensible shoes that matched the colour of the blouse. She hadn't spent a lot of time picking it out, but she didn't think there was anything wrong with it. Maybe he had spotted a stain, or maybe one of the buttons on the blouse had come undone.

When she looked back up, ready to ask what the matter was, Martin was wearing a huge grin.

"You look wonderful," he told her. Her heart fluttered a little in a way she had never felt before, though she had been complimented on her appearance many times before. Seldom, however, had it been put so simply and honestly. She smiled and made a play of looking him over. Plain black shoes, dark blue trousers, red shirt, pale blue jacket. Plain and simple, but on him, topped off with that face and that smile and that neatly combed dark brown hair, it looked a million dollars.

At that very moment, she wanted nothing more than to go to him and kiss him. There was every possibility that she would have thrown caution to the wind and done it too, had she not been snapped out of the moment by the sound of Beth returning with the basket. She spun, smiled at Beth, took the picnic basket, the blanket folded up and sitting on top, from her, and turned back to Marty.

"I made us lunch," she announced, hefting the basket for him to see. "Got a few different things in here, so hopefully there will be something you like."

"I'm sure there is," said Beth.

"Hello again, Beth," said Marty, giving her a wave.

"Morning, Marty," she replied. "That accent is still working for you."

"I hope so; it's the only one I've got. How are you today?"

"Looking forward to getting rid of Abigail so I can be my own boss for a while. You?"

"Looking forward to keeping Abi out of your way for as long as possible so you can really enjoy being your own boss." Beth smiled and nodded.

"You rack up points with everything you say. Well, you two want to go, and I want you to go, so go. Enjoy."

"I have my cell phone if…"

"I know, but I'm not going to have to use it. Go."

"I know you're not, but if…"

"Abigail," said Martin, suddenly at her side. He took the basket from her and offered her his free arm. "Beth will be fine, and the shop will still be here when we get back."

She looked at him, smiled and took his arm. They headed for the door.

"Smooth move, Marty," called Beth as they exited. "But I think it sucks you have more faith in me than she does!"

Abigail blew her a raspberry as the door closed.

"Are we going to Beaumont Park?" asked Martin as they walked through the busy square.

"No," replied Abigail. "Do you remember me mentioning a little place out in the woods at all?" Martin thought about it for a few seconds and shook his head. "It's a little clearing beside a pond, about a twenty minute walk from the edge of town. Really lovely on a day like this. My friends and I used to go there a lot when we were kids, sometimes take our bathing suits and go splashing about in the pond."

"A frog in your hair!" blurted Martin. An elderly man walking nearby overheard him and shot him a puzzled look. He saw no such thing in Abigail's hair and, still puzzled, he walked on. Abigail, on the other hand, knew exactly what Martin was talking about. She smiled.

"That's right; I dipped my head under once and when I came up a little frog had gotten tangled in my hair."

"I don't recall about the clearing or the pond, but I do remember laughing a lot about the frog."

"Yeah, smart ass, in your letter back to me you asked if I kissed it." Martin laughed. "Did you?"

"No, I got the little bugger out of my hair and threw him back in the water."

"You might have missed your big chance to nab yourself a prince."

Maybe not, she thought to herself. Then: *Oh, lord, that was corny!*

They chatted, reminiscing about things they recalled from one another's letters. They were quiet as they walked along the barely visible, sun dappled path through the woods. Abigail realised that on other occasions when there had been such silences between her and a man, they had quickly become awkward. However there was not a trace of awkwardness here; the silence between them was perfectly comfortable. So much so that by the time they arrived at the clearing she had, without even being aware of it, laid her head against Martin's shoulder.

Martin was well aware, and loved it.

The air in the clearing was nice and warm after the cooler atmosphere under the trees. Martin took in a deep breath of fresh, flower scented air and smiled.

"When was the last time you were here?" he asked Abigail as she took the basket from him and sat it on the ground. She thought about it as she took the blanket and spread it out.

"You know, I can't even remember."

"Bet it seems a lot smaller now than it did when you caught that frog."

"Yeah," she admitted wistfully. "Lot of things change as you get older." She sat down on the blanket and pulled the basket towards her, then paused, looking up at him. "Except you." As Martin took off his jacket and sat down he asked her what she meant. "You were there when I was a kid and you're still here now, and you haven't changed a bit. You're perhaps the one constant my life has ever had."

They gazed at one another, each thinking the same thing and not knowing it. Again, given the time, Abigail might well have chosen that moment to reveal her feelings for Martin by simply going to him and kissing him, but something interrupted.

Martin's stomach grumbled, very loud and very long. One look at his rapidly reddening face and Abigail burst out laughing.

"Oh, be quiet and feed me," he told her.

Abigail had packed a great deal of food into the basket, including sandwiches, chicken drumsticks, coleslaw, salad, a couple of bottles of cola and two large slices of apple pie. Between the two of them they ate the vast majority of it and, after wiping the pie crumbs off his chin, Martin groaned and lay down. He put one hand behind his head, stretched out on the blanket and smiled.

"That was delicious. Thanks, Abi. I only hope when you come to the cabin for dinner, you'll enjoy it as much."

"I'm sure it will be great," she said as she threw the empty containers into the basket and set it aside. She was lying beside him before she even realised it was what she intended to do. Had she thought about it first she probably wouldn't have done it, but as she laid her head on his shoulder and felt his arm close around her, it felt like the most natural thing in the world.

Martin was just about on cloud nine, the huge smile on his face due only in small part to the meal and the sunshine. He told himself that if there was ever going to be a perfect moment to tell her how he felt then this was it. Unfortunately that thought reminded him of something else he had meant to mention to Abi earlier but had forgotten about. He tried to ignore it, not wanting to spoil things with such a line of questioning, but it wouldn't go away. Soon, instead of enjoying being here with the wonderful woman beside him, Martin was trying to work out a way to broach the subject.

He was still wondering when Abigail asked him,

"What's the matter?" Stunned that his unease had been so apparent, he responded with,

"What makes you think something's the matter?"

"I don't know," she said. "I just get the feeling that you're thinking about something and it's making you… agitated?"

Lying to her was out of the question. Upset to be spoiling the mood, he sighed and asked,

"Abigail, do you have any ex-boyfriends or admirers who don't take kindly to you hanging around with other men?"

She propped herself up on one elbow, her free hand resting on his chest. Her expression was one of open confusion.

"No. I think that's the kind of thing I might have mentioned to you at some point. Why do you ask?"

Martin fought to keep his eyes away from the sight now visible down the neck of her blouse. He looked at her, wanted to tell her that it didn't matter, that he wanted nothing more than for this little clearing to be the first place they kissed, the first place they made love. Instead he nodded and said,

"That's what I thought, but I had to ask."

He told her about his morning, about going down to the beach and meeting Jonathan Askew and Tommy Tessick, and about how they had spotted someone standing on the porch. He finished off his tale by explaining about the thoughts he'd had on who it might have been, and that all he had managed to come up with was either someone playing a joke or someone connected to her.

"A mystery, huh." she said. "Let's go see if we can find any clues."

Martin parked outside the cabin and got out of the car, pocketing the keys as he started towards the door. Abigail was close behind him. She followed him in, stopped just inside and gazed at the large space before her.

"Wow," she breathed. "This place is great."

"Nice, isn't it."

"Bit big for one guy though." Martin nodded.

"Yeah, but I took what I could get." It was Abigail's turn to nod.

"Everywhere else booked up because of the carnival."

"I must admit, I'm really glad that I'm going to be here for that."

"A parade, hot dogs and cotton candy, and funfair rides," Abigail said, smiling. "It's always a blast. Now, where did this person show up?"

"Out here," said Martin, leading her out onto the porch. She glanced over the railing at the shingle beach, then turned and, just as Martin had done that morning after getting back to the cabin, walked to the end of the porch. She leaned over and whistled.

"Getting up onto here from down there is no small feat." She turned and started back towards Martin. "Someone was determined." She stopped in front of him and asked, "Have you considered the possibility that they might have been looking for the owner?" Martin made a "Huh, I never even thought of that" expression and Abigail smiled. "Makes a little more sense than you being stalked by an ex of mine I've never mentioned to you."

"Listen, Miss Smarty Pants, you could have a dozen homicidal admirers out there that you don't know about. I mean look at you: beautiful, funny, single, and with your own business. The loonies might be falling over themselves to get to you, willing to do all sorts of insane things."

"Like flying all the way over here from Scotland?"

"Oh," he said, trying to sound outraged but unable to stop smiling at the way she was grinning. "That was low. Just, so low." She chuckled.

"So, do I get the guided tour of this place, or what?"

"After what you just said to me? No way!"

"Aw, come on. Don't be moody."

"Moody? You insinuated that I am a lunatic; I reserve the right to be completely moody."

"If you don't show me around, Marty," she said, a very convincing tone of menace in her voice. "I will be forced to tickle you."

"Yeah, well you can go ahead because I'm not tickli..." Abigail was grinning from ear to ear and nodding slowly. "Shit! Forgot who I was talking to. You know, that's improper use of personal knowledge, and that is the act of an unfair person."

Without further preamble, Abigail lunged at him, digging her fingers into his sides and wiggling them around. He cried out and backed away but she kept up with him, ignoring his pleas for her to stop, which quickly became laughs. Martin backed into the table and almost toppled backwards, but she pulled him upright and continued with her assault.

"Uncle!" Martin cried out. "I give in! I give in!"

Abigail withdrew and Martin, who had almost managed to get himself into the foetal position whilst standing on one leg, which had done him no good whatsoever, straightened up. Taking a deep breath, and trying to muster some dignity, he gestured with one arm and informed her,

"This is the porch. It runs around two sides of the house. Down there, you can see a wee shingle beach, where this morning I went to skip some stones, met a couple of nice guys, and was watched by someone who in all likelihood mistook me for someone else."

"That was a nice shot at maintaining your pride, Marty, but you caved fast and easy."

"I'll ignore that."

"I'll keep bringing it up. Bet it won't do your hot Scotsman routine much good when the girls find out you can't take being tickled."

"Do you want a tour or not?" Abigail laughed.

"Lead on, MacDweeb!"

He walked her round to where the porch ended at the rear of the cabin, where there was a covered over hot-tub, and another set of sliding glass doors. They re-entered the cabin into the lounge area and Martin showed her the various rooms on the various floors. The tour concluded in the games room.

"Oh, awesome," she exclaimed. "How about we go upstairs, get some drinks and snacks, come back down here and shoot some pool?"

"Sounds like a plan."

A couple of games turned into several. Pool gave way to darts, then back to pool. They took a break at one point, going upstairs for a dinner consisting of some microwave snacks Martin had bought the day before. They ate their meals on the sofa, then sat back and channel surfed as they digested, then they went back downstairs for more pool and darts.

The hours melted away.

Abigail sank the black and smiled. Martin saw her face fall as she glanced out of the window.

"What's wrong?" he asked

"It'll be getting dark soon, and I don't want you to have to drive that damn road in the dark again," she told him, returning her pool cue to the rack. "So I guess you better take me home now."

Martin almost told her that she was more than welcome to stay, but worried it would sound too forward, even if he did point out there were plenty of other rooms for her to use. Instead, he also returned his cue to the rack, nodding sadly.

"You know what I'd like?" she asked. Martin shook his head. "Well, if we stocked up on food, this place would be a one stop shop for everything we'd need. I'd really like to just hang here with you for the rest of your fortnight." She looked at him sheepishly, almost as if she expected him to be shocked at the idea. He looked into her eyes and told her,

"I'd really like that too."

Corday stared daggers up at the cabin. The small motorboat he was in bobbed gently as he hoped silently for a fire, a landslide, an earthquake, anything to bring down the place in which Abigail and that bastard Muir had already spent hours together. He could well imagine them in there, smiling and laughing and kissing and fucking. As the images flitted through his mind, his fingers clenched tighter around the steering wheel. Eventually, when it became apparent that he was not going to be able to bring the building down just with the power of his mind, Corday took one white knuckled hand off the wheel and pushed the throttle forward.

There was nothing else for it: someone else was going to have to die.

Thirty minutes later, he was driving through Hannerville, evaluating every woman he saw. There were a few possible candidates, and Corday had to fight down the urge to simply stop the car, get out and attack. In fact more than once he caught himself putting his foot down and turning the wheel, aiming at a woman who had caught his attention. He told himself this was no good, that he was going to get himself caught, and then the real fun and games would be over before they'd even begun.

Eventually he parked the car, got out, took a deep breath, and started walking. He soon found himself on one of the many pathways that wended through the woods around town. With his hands in his pockets, he strolled along, feeling the anger fade more and more as he went. Not that he had changed his mind about someone having to pay to balance out how badly he felt, but at least he could think clearly. He would come up with a plan and carry it out, instead of just attacking without thinking.

He felt that the time to begin the games proper was near at hand. Yes, Muir's arrival was a thorn in his side, but it really only meant there was one more player for the game, one more eventual loser. As pissed off as it made him, it also seemed to Corday somehow fitting that Muir had come all this way for Abigail, only to die by her side, and at his hands.

His thoughts were interrupted when he heard a voice, faint, but getting louder. Corday paused, listened, and determined two things: the owner of the voice was female, and walking towards him from somewhere up ahead. Not far from where he stood the path curved round, a line of trees shielding whoever was coming from view, but also preventing them from having noticed him. Corday quickly left the path, hiding behind the widest tree he could find. There he waited, listening as the voice got louder. Soon she came into view and Corday grinned. Luck had smiled upon him.

She was perfect.

The simple plan popped into his head fully formed. He would follow her home and tonight, after dark, he would take her. If there happened to be anyone else in the house, well, he enjoyed a challenge. If all went well, he'd have his fun, kill her, and put her with the last one.

He followed the young woman, listening as she moaned to whoever she was talking to about having had to stay late at the office tonight. So late, in fact, that she had opted to take a short cut through the woods. There was a pause as the woman listened, and then she said something about knowing it was almost dark, but it would take twenty minutes off her journey home, plus this was Hannerville, the town where nothing ever happened. Besides, if anything did happen she was capable of defending herself, with or without the taser in her handbag.

Good to know, thought Corday as he tailed her.

He continued eavesdropping on her conversation, listening to her bitch about a couple of her male colleagues who wouldn't stop turning everything she said into something dirty, and a woman who was apparently badly in need of a shower. Talk then moved on to an episode of some reality TV show she and her friend had watched last night. They were shocked at the scandalous goings on and couldn't wait for tonight's episode.

When they exited the woods, he became more cautious. He hung back farther, so far that he was no longer able to hear her side of the conversation, though he didn't classify that as a downside. He watched as she entered an apartment building, then quickly made his way to the security door before it closed. He entered and followed her up the stairs until she stopped at a door, unlocked it and went inside. Corday spent a few minutes walking up and down the stairs, checking this and that, the cogs and wheels in his mind spinning at high speed as he added detail to his sketched out plan. When he had it all worked out, he went back to the woman's front door. Laying a hand on it, he smiled.

"Till later," he whispered.

Chapter 19

Sheriff Mark Flaghan was not a superstitious man. He did not believe in ESP or UFO's, mystics, faith healers, magic or ghosts.

Nevertheless, this morning he had a feeling something bad was coming. As an officer of the law, he was used to paying attention to his hunches, but this feeling was so acute he was almost willing to call it premonition. Almost; it could just as easily have been an after effect of the re-heated chilli he'd had for dinner the night before.

It was 10:45am and the day outside was beautiful, the sun rising towards its zenith in a clear blue sky. The kind of weather that made it difficult for most to believe anything was wrong with the world. But over the years Flaghan had seen many things that proved that no matter how bright and sunny it was, darkness was never far away. After all it had been on a day just like this one, many years ago when he had been a deputy, when he and his colleagues had busted down the front door of their chief suspect in a kidnapping case.

Eleven year old only child Sindy Carlton had been missing for just over a week, taken from her back yard as she was reading a book. The case had shocked the little town of Braskport, and fear had made everyone look at everyone else as though they were the guilty party. That week had seen a surge in violence against perfectly innocent men whose attackers had thought "looked capable of it". Sindy's own mother, Angela, was arrested for attacking someone she'd had a grudge against in high school, someone she believed was trying to get back at her by taking her daughter. Sindy's father, Archie, had been a broken man. He had barely eaten, slept or spoken that week. The parents were the first ones they looked at, but they both had good jobs, were well known in the community, and both had a solid alibi for the time Sindy had been taken. Their backgrounds were checked to see if there was anyone who might wish to see them suffer, but it brought to light no rivalries or, as some suspected it might, jilted lovers who were out for revenge. A week of exhausting nuts and bolts investigation found them a suspect, one George Calvers, who had moved to the area not three months previously. He had left his last home after some of his neighbours had ganged up on him, accusing him of spending too much time hanging around near little kids. With the bit between their teeth, they had run down every little fact they could about the man. It had shown up nothing, not even a parking ticket. But Dwight Ruthby, the sheriff of Braskport and a man Flaghan had looked up to, had not given up. They re-interviewed just about the whole damn town, gradually putting together a picture of Calvers's movements for the day Sindy was taken. Three people confirmed seeing him in the vicinity of her house. Calvers's neighbours described him as a quiet man who kept to himself, but was always pleasant and said hello when they saw him on the street. His boss at the copy shop where he worked said he was always on time and good with the customers. He also confirmed Calvers had been off work the day Sindy had vanished.

When they had approached him and asked if they could ask him a few questions, he had bolted.

The chase had been short lived, concluding with Calvers's arrest on suspicion of kidnapping. Plenty of the guys wanted to have a private word with him, but they were all warned by Ruthby that anyone who laid a finger on him would pay for it. This would be done by the book, so that if it ever went to court Calvers wouldn't get off on a technicality relating to his treatment at the hands of the Braskport Sheriff's Department.

They hit the house half an hour after Calvers had been taken in, Ruthby the first one through the door, which he opened with one kick. The house was neat, orderly and clean. Men were sent upstairs and throughout the ground floor.

Flaghan had been told to check the basement.

The door had been locked. Not only that, but the sturdy key lock had been supplemented by a new looking padlock. Flaghan had motioned for Ruthby to take a look. The sheriff's expression had become grim at the sight of the padlock. He ordered his men to look for a key, but their search, thorough as it was, turned up no key. It did uncover a large box full of indecent images of kids hidden in the back of Calvers's wardrobe. Again it was only because Ruthby ordered them not to that a contingent of men refrained from marching down to the station and beating the bastard to death.

"We have to hope she's still alive," the sheriff had said to Flaghan. "And we don't want to frighten her any more than she's already been frightened. Call out to her, Mark." The future sheriff of Hannerville had been taken aback, and had asked his superior if it shouldn't have been him ascertaining if the girl was down there or not. Ruthby had told him that he had been assigned to check the basement, so he had better get his ass in gear and do it. Flaghan had put his face close to the door and called out Sindy's name, telling her that it was okay, that they were here to help her. Tense moments passed. The house became so silent that the quiet cry from the basement was clearly heard by all present. The men felt like cheering, but instead kept their elation in check, heeding the sheriff's words about not wanting to scare the little girl. Flaghan had called to her, told her they were going to have to kick the door in but that she had nothing to be afraid of; she was going home.

He had personally booted the door open and gone downstairs to find Sindy Carlton sitting on a new mattress. Her wrists and ankles had been bound with rope, which Flaghan had gently untied. Sindy was quiet until she had been freed, at which point she had thrown her arms around her rescuer and bawled.

Mark Flaghan had walked back up those stairs to the low key congratulations of his colleagues, and to a wise smile and a congratulatory nod from Dwight Ruthby. Flaghan had felt capable of kicking the backside of every bastard in the state that day as he had quickly taken Sindy to a waiting car, which had taken her home to her mother and father.

Flaghan hadn't been present at any of the interviews conducted with George Calvers, which was probably just as well as he would have been in great danger of doing something he would have regretted. Not that he'd have regretted beating the son of a bitch senseless, but he would have regretted the effect on his career, and he would most certainly have regretted letting Ruthby down. However he, like every other cop in the station, had heard about the interviews. About how Calvers had been amassing his collection of images for years, those sick and twisted photographs allowing him to stave off his growing desire to "get close", as he put it, to a real child. His will had started to falter in his last town, and people had noticed him hanging around the schoolyard and had been very quick in telling him to watch his step or he'd be in trouble. Their little intervention had him running scared to Braskport, where he had intended to start a new life. But his demons had come with him, he said, and they had gotten stronger. Eventually he had planned and executed the kidnapping of Sindy Carlton. When asked "Why her?" he had replied, "Her name; Sindy." Ruthby would later tell his men that during one interview Calvers had admitted his intention had been to keep Sindy until she trusted him, liked him and actually wanted to become his lover. The sheriff would also admit that it had taken all his willpower not to just draw his piece and shoot the bastard.

George Calvers went to prison and lasted two nights before being beaten to death. No one had thought it any great loss.

Flaghan closed his eyes, took a deep breath in, and then let it out slowly from between pursed lips. Thinking about Calvers hadn't helped him shake the feeling that something was coming today, something bad. His mind switched tracks to Philip Glenster, and the retired doctor's fears about David Brannon perhaps showing up in Hannerville. In the months since Glenster had first come to him about the escaped lunatic, Flaghan had been keeping a close eye on things. One ear had always been open for any little bit of news that might signal something out of the ordinary, but so far there had been nothing. Hannerville had been ticking and tocking just as it always had. The arrangements for the upcoming celebrations were all in place. The carnival was always a slightly more stressful time for the sheriff's department, with a fair few strangers in town and everyone out to have a good time. Most people behaved, but there were always a few who ended up having too good a time and spending a night in the cells.

If Brannon was going to come back, he'd do it during the carnival, Flaghan said to himself. *Big crowd for him to hide in, and that same crowd would make it easy for him to just grab someone and make them disappear.*

Or make just one person in particular disappear.

Going to have a chat with Abigail Morton was something Flaghan had suggested to Glenster a few times, but Phil was always reluctant, fearful of breaking down whatever psychological barriers she had erected against the memories of that night. Flaghan had always argued that it would be a lot worse if the fucker just showed up at her house one night, but Glenster always managed to change his mind. It was an uncanny, and pretty damn annoying, talent the man had. Must have been useful as hell when it came to patients who hadn't wanted to take this medicine or have that examination. Flaghan really didn't think Brannon would come back to Hannerville, but even so he was becoming more and more convinced that Miss Morton should be told about the fact the man was out, that there was a slight chance she might be in danger. Forewarned was forearmed and all that. Deciding that this time he was not going to let up until Glenster saw things his way, Flaghan stood up, grabbed his hat and headed for the door.

On his way out he told Doreen where he was going and how long he expected to be, but that if anything happened she knew how to get a hold of him.

"I do," she smiled at him. "And tell Phil and Anne I said hello."

"Sure thing."

He made his way towards the town square, intending to get himself a nice cup of coffee en route to Glenster's house.

The square was about as quiet as it got for this time in the morning, so he didn't have to wait long to get his coffee. He cut through the square, pausing to remove the cap from his cup, blow on his drink and take a sip. That was when he spotted Louie Follca, owner/manager of the Premier Café, standing outside his establishment looking up and down the street. That feeling Flaghan had been having earlier crept back up behind him and laid a cold hand on his shoulder. Putting the cap back on his cup, he made his way towards the man, who saw him coming and raised a hand in greeting.

"Morning, Sheriff."

"Same to you, Louie. Everything all right?"

Still looking up and down the street, it took Louie a few moments to realise he had been asked a question.

"Uh, yeah, getting along, Sheriff, getting along." He resumed looking up and down the street.

"Once more with feeling, Louie," said Flaghan. Part of him really did not want to ask the question, but he knew he was going to have to. "What's the matter?"

Louie finally stopped looking left and right and shook his head.

"It's probably just me being an idiot," he began. "But Janice was supposed to be back in this morning after having yesterday off. She's a very punctual person, very conscientious, so if she's not going to be in for any reason, she usually calls to tell me. But not this morning."

"When was she due in?"

"Less than an hour ago." Louie shook his head again. "I'm telling you, Sheriff, I'm just being an idiot."

"Worrying about someone doesn't make you an idiot, Louie; makes you a concerned employer, and there's nothing wrong with that."

"I appreciate you saying that, Sheriff, I do. Could be any one of a number of reasons Janice hasn't called. My mind, it always jumps to the worst possible scenarios, you know."

"Mine to," admitted Flaghan. "Comes with the job, I guess. Tell you what, I'll go round to her place, make sure she's okay. I'll stop by to let you know on my way back through." Louie nodded.

"Thanks, Sheriff. I appreciate that."

"Helping out, that comes with the job too. What's Janice's surname?"

"Mallory."

He nodded and clapped Louie on the shoulder with his free hand and then started off, taking his radio out of the pouch on his belt and putting a call in to the station. He asked Doreen to get him an address for Janice Mallory. She responded within a few moments and he thanked her and stopped walking. Turned out Janice's apartment was in the opposite direction, but he decided he wanted some company whilst he ran this particular errand.

The doorbell rang, and Anne Glenster called out that she would get it, but her husband was closer.

"Already on it, honey," he called back. "You just keep doing what you're doing."

When he opened the door and saw Sheriff Flaghan standing on his doorstep, his heart leapt into his throat and his stomach dropped all the way to his slippers. However, Philip Glenster was a man who did not give in easily to fear. Steadying himself, he greeted his visitor and asked what had happened.

"Most likely a busted alarm clock," was Flaghan's odd reply. "I'm just going to check on someone and I wondered if perhaps you might want to go for a walk."

Glenster frowned, examined the Sheriff's face, went back over his words. Flaghan was trying to cover his concern, but he wouldn't be here if he really didn't think something might be wrong. A busted alarm clock? Someone was late for something, and the Sheriff feared the worst.

"Would you like to come in while I get my shoes and jacket?"

"No thanks, Phil, I'll just wait here. Oh, and Doreen asked me to pass on a hello to you and Anne." Glenster nodded and said he would be back in just a minute.

Leaving the door ajar, he went straight to Anne's sewing room, where she was sitting in a rocking chair doing needlepoint. She looked up and smiled as he came in, then she saw his expression. Her smile vanished.

"Philip, what's wrong?" she asked. "Who was at the door?"

"Anne, I know what you're thinking, and like me you're jumping to conclusions."

"Who was at the door, Philip?"

"It's the Sheriff," he told her. Before she could say anything else he went on. "He's asked me to go with him whilst he checks on something. That's probably just an excuse to get me to go with him so he can try and talk me into going to see Abigail Morton again." His wife regarded him for a second or two.

"What aren't you telling me?"

"If there's anything I'm not telling you," he replied. "It's because I don't know myself yet. I won't be too long. I'll take my cell phone with me in case you need to get in touch while I'm gone." He looked at her, saw the worry on her face. "Anne, at the moment it's nothing, so try not to worry." He leaned over and kissed her forehead. "I'll be back soon. Oh, by the way, Doreen Spellner says hello."

He quickly donned his coat, made sure he had his wallet, keys and phone, then swapped his slippers for shoes and exited the house.

The sheriff was standing on the sidewalk waiting, finishing off the last of a cup of coffee. Glenster joined him and the two men walked down the street, the Sheriff throwing his empty cup into the first trash bin they passed.

"So what's this all about, Mark?"

"As I said, it's probably nothing. You know Louie Follca?"

"Yes."

"Employee of his didn't show for work this morning. Louie says that's not like her. I said I'd pop by her place, check if everything was okay."

"And you decided to invite me along because..?"

"I met Louie as I came through the square on my way to your place. I was going to have another go at convincing you to have a word with Abigail Morton. Though to be honest, right now I'm just hoping like hell we find Janice Mallory safe and sound."

"It will probably just be a broken alarm clock, just as you said, Mark."

"I hope so, Phil. I really do." He paused, took a breath, then asked, "I don't suppose you've had a change of heart regarding Miss Morton?"

"Not particularly," answered Glenster. "Although I agree with you that she has a right to know, the girl has built a life for herself. I believe the only way she was able to do that was by blocking the memories of Brannon and what he did. If those memories are brought to the surface it could cause great damage to her psyche, and until I know for certain that that bastard is back in town, I don't want to put her through that."

"That's what I figured," said the Sheriff in a flat tone.

"Responsibility for the wellbeing of others is something I'm used to, Mark," Glenster said quietly. "Or at least I was, and for quite some time. I do understand how you feel. I could also understand why you'd be confused, since it seems that I'm putting others in danger to spare one person, and in doing so may be placing that person in danger also. But that is not the case. I'm not the only one left in town who'll remember the horror Brannon caused. The moment his name is mentioned, it will spread, and there will be panic. People will start seeing him all over the place. Every time a cat knocks over a trashcan, your office will get a call from someone convinced there's a lunatic outside their bedroom window. People will grow more and more afraid, then they'll begin to become paranoid and suspicious, and bad things will start to happen. I don't want to see that happen, Mark, I really don't."

"Me neither, Phil," Flaghan conceded with a sigh. "Me neither."

The walk to Janice Mallory's address was short. The superintendent let them in the security door and both men walked up to Janice's front door, where Flaghan knocked three times. When no one answered, he knocked again. They waited. Still no answer. Eventually the Sheriff looked at Glenster, who shrugged.

"Talk to the super?" he suggested. The Sheriff nodded and they made their way back downstairs to the superintendent's apartment. The man, a short, stocky fellow in his late forties, who earlier had introduced himself as Eric, answered his door within a few seconds.

"I had a feeling it might be you guys again," he said. "Is everything all right with Janice?"

"Can we come in for a minute or two?" asked the Sheriff.

"Yeah, sure," said Eric, standing back and motioning for them to enter.

His apartment smelled of home baking. The smell reminded Glenster of those days when Anne would suddenly get the urge to bake a cake, or some cookies. He smiled, something Eric noticed a moment or two later.

"Great, isn't it?" Glenster nodded.

"Indeed. What are you baking?"

"Me?" blurted Eric, clearly surprised at the suggestion. "Nothing at all, Mr Glenster. Hell, I can barely heat up a can of soup, let alone bake something. No, it's an air freshener."

"Seriously?" asked the Sheriff. Eric nodded.

"It's kind of expensive, but it really is convincing. Nice smell to come home to."

He led them through to the living room, a neat and tidy space containing a couch, an armchair, a TV and, positioned for optimum viewing pleasure, an overstuffed recliner. Eric invited his guests to take a seat, then sat down himself on the recliner. Flaghan was about to speak when Eric opened one arm of the chair, reaching into the refrigerated compartment beneath and bringing out a can of cola. As he closed the arm over, he caught the bemused expressions on the faces of the two men and smiled sheepishly.

"Love watching sport, hate missing parts of the game. This chair represents my one big extravagance in life. Got a fridge in this arm, container for snacks in the other, it reclines until you're lying down, it vibrates, it massages... I love this chair." He popped the can open, took a sip and then said, "Sorry, do you guys want a drink?" Both men declined, and then Flaghan asked,

"When was the last time you saw Janice Mallory?"

"Passed her by a few days ago as she was on her way out and I was on my way in. Nice lady, very polite, never a bother. Most of the tenants here are like that in fact. I have to admit, life may not have gone the way I wanted it to when I was younger, but I could be in worse situations."

"Did she seem uneasy about anything, or did she maybe mention she was planning on going away anywhere?" Eric, who was taking a drink, shook his head. "Have you ever seen her with anybody? A boyfriend maybe, someone she might suddenly decide to go on a trip with? Spur of the moment kind of thing."

"No, sir. I mean, I can't say for sure whether or not she had a boyfriend, but I haven't seen her with anyone. Usually you can tell when one of your tenants is in a new relationship. You'll notice changes in the way they do things, differences in their regular pattern that you didn't even realise you knew until it was suddenly different. But I haven't noticed anything like that with Janice recently." Flaghan nodded and the three men fell quiet. Glenster saw Eric open his mouth to speak, guessing the man was about to ask why they were quizzing him about Janice, when the radio on Flaghan's belt squawked. The retired doctor and the superintendent jumped in their seats. The Sheriff stood, apologised, and went into the hall. When he was gone, Eric asked his question. Glenster had guessed right.

"Is Janice okay? She's not in any trouble or anything?"

"Not at all," said Glenster in a reassuring tone that had been honed on countless patients throughout his career. "She's just a bit late for work and her boss mentioned it to the Sheriff, said it wasn't like her. The sheriff told her boss he would come over and check. Picked me up along the way. Nothing better to do with my retirement than be nosey." He chuckled. "Janice is probably staying with a friend or something and just forgot to call in."

Eric smiled, nodded and took a sip of his drink. Flaghan came back in.

"Eric, thanks very much for your time. We'll be off now."

The Sheriff turned and headed for the door as Glenster got out of his chair. Eric started to do the same, but he was waved back down.

"No need, Eric, we'll see ourselves out. Thank you again for your time."

When they were both back out on the sidewalk, Glenster had to jog to catch up with Flaghan.

"What's going on, Mark?" he asked, seeing the grim expression on the Sheriff's face.

"Another apartment building across town," came the clipped reply. "Door ajar, and drops of blood."

Flaghan hadn't broken his long stride all the way to the apartment building, and having been determined to keep up, Glenster was out of breath by the time they arrived. The superintendent was waiting for them outside, along with one of Flaghan's deputies, a young man Glenster recognised as Jack Parchett. Parchett was clearly surprised to see the town's former chief medical practitioner huffing and puffing his way towards him.

"Sheriff," the deputy greeted his boss. "Doc, what are you doing here?" Before Glenster could answer, Flaghan said,

"I asked him to come by; thought an expert medical opinion might be handy, just in case. Let's get inside." Once they were in the foyer of the building, Flaghan asked Parchett what the story was. The deputy indicated the man beside him.

"Mr Trenter here was upstairs doing some work on a lady's sink. On his way back down the stairs, he noticed that the door to apartment 3A was sitting open just a crack. He took a closer look, spotted some blood on the floor. He called out for the resident but got no answer, and then he called us." Flaghan nodded and turned his attention to the second superintendent of the morning.

"Mr Trenter, did you touch anything? The door, the frame, the blood, anything?" Trenter shook his head emphatically.

"Uh-uh, Sheriff, I didn't touch a thing. I watch a lot of those crime shows, so I know better than that."

"Good. Who lives in 3A?"

"Nice young lady by the name of Charlotte Webster." Flaghan nodded to his deputy, who nodded back and stepped outside.

"When did you see her last?"

"Must have been a couple of days at least." He paused. "Yeah, couple of days; she was having a little trouble with her shower, but I got it fixed."

"No one reported any noises or anything coming from her apartment last night?"

"Not to me, Sheriff." Flaghan nodded.

"Okay, good. Thanks for your help, Mr Trenter. If you could just go back to your apartment and wait, we may have some questions later. And, please, don't discuss this with anyone for the time being."

"Sure thing, Sheriff."

As the man walked off, Flaghan looked at Glenster and raised an eyebrow.

"You know as well as I do how many explanations there could be for both these occurrences," Glenster told him. "Don't be so quick to assume the worst."

"Little coincidental, isn't it? Two girls go missing in such a short space of time."

"They're not missing," the former doctor admonished him. "You've just got the feeling that they're missing because for weeks now we've both been expecting something to happen, and this fits the bill." Flaghan almost mentioned the feeling he'd had earlier, but Parchett came back with some details on Charlotte Webster.

"26, lives alone, her family live a couple of towns away. She works as a clerical assistant at Wennscombe Haulage. No criminal record."

"Thanks, Jack. Doctor Glenster and I will go have a look in the apartment. You go have a look around the outside of the building."

Parchett nodded, spun on his heel, and headed for the door. He turned back when his boss called his name. "If anyone asks, make something up."

"Gotcha, Sheriff."

"Okay," Flaghan said to Glenster. "Let's go take a look."

They went to the front door of apartment 3A, find the door sitting open a crack, and a few drops of blood on the floor, as reported. Flaghan told Glenster to stay behind him, and then nudged the front door open by pressing the toe of his shoe against the bottom of it. It swung open without a sound, revealing a nice, orderly living room. Flaghan entered, Glenster close behind him, both men looking for something they hoped they wouldn't find. They advanced, paying careful attention to where they put their feet, in case they trampled any evidence.

They found nothing in the lounge. The kitchen nook was also tidy and spotless. On a hunch, Flaghan opened the bin lid and saw inside dying flowers, the shards of a vase and a smashed picture frame. The picture that had once been in it was also there. He didn't want to take it out as it would leave a print on the paper, but from what he could see it seemed to show a young woman, possibly Charlotte Webster, with some other people, most likely her family. After he showed Glenster what he'd found, the doctor said,

"People knock things over all the time."

Out through the living room to the short hallway, empty save for a small table on which there was nothing. Flaghan frowned and knelt down beside the table, spotting a small chip in the laminate wood flooring. Someone had knocked the table over. Had the vase and picture frame been on it? It seemed to have been a recent incident, but had Charlotte knocked it over herself, or had it been done by someone else? Had it happened during a struggle? He stood up and turned to Glenster, explaining what he'd found. The doctor nodded. They went towards the nearest door off the hallway.

The door led to the first bedroom, which Charlotte had used to house her computer. The machine sat on a small workstation in the corner. Along the opposite wall was a bookcase full of DVD's. Glenster stood by the door whilst Flaghan took a look around, but he found nothing of interest.

The next room along was Charlotte's bedroom. The bed was made, the curtains were open, the blinds closed. The dresser was replete with all manner of make-up, perfumes, and a silver handled hairbrush. There was also a small jewellery box. Flaghan thought about checking it but decided that, if he was back in Hannerville, Brannon's motive for breaking into a young woman's apartment would not be robbery. He told himself to follow Glenster's advice and stop jumping to conclusions. So far they had nothing that couldn't be explained away. As Glenster had said, people knocked things over all the time. The drops of blood outside the front door might not be Charlotte's, or they might be. Maybe she had a nosebleed just as she got home. Where was she? At a friend's, or maybe at some guy's place. His earlier bad feeling was playing on his fear that a truly evil human being had come back to town, which was wrestling with the fact that there was no solid evidence of foul play here.

The last room they checked was the bathroom. The small window had been left slightly open. There was no extractor fan so there was nothing strange about that, plus it was far too small for someone to fit through, even if they could have reached it from the outside. A quick glance into the tub – a new model designed to look much older, sitting on four large feet - showed it was clean and gleaming.

In the sink were a few small drops of blood.

The Sheriff pursed his lips together and looked back to the bath. Above it was a rail that held the shower curtain, but the curtain was gone. In the bath he spotted more blood, a little red smear. Flaghan hunkered down and looked under the bath. There was a streak of moisture on the tiled floor, and a small shard of glass.

The Sheriff ran over things in his head. Charlotte had been showering and someone had broken in. Hearing the running water they had entered the bathroom and there had been a struggle. Not a lot of noise; someone would have heard a scream, investigated, and he would have become involved a lot sooner. Flaghan looked from the bath to the sink. During the struggle, Charlotte had tried to get out of the tub. She had succeeded but her foot had slipped. She had pitched forward, hit the sink, hurt herself. Things had gotten at least as far as the hallway, where either Charlotte or her attacker had bumped the table. He couldn't say much beyond that, but evidently the intruder had tidied up after themselves, though not thoroughly. He got up and turned to Glenster, reported what he'd found. The man held out his hands, palms towards the sheriff.

"Mark, I know this doesn't look good, but don't go adding two and two and coming up with five. It may very well be that this young woman has been attacked, kidnapped, maybe even killed, but we don't know anything has happened to her yet. And if something has happened to her, we can't yet know who was responsible."

Flaghan suddenly felt incredibly annoyed. Everything Glenster had said was perfectly true, but there was no doubt in his mind that something bad had happened to Charlotte Webster. No, they didn't know who the perpetrator was, but if there was even the slightest chance that it had been Brannon, people had a right to know. Abigail Morton had a right to know. Hell, even if it wasn't Brannon, there was someone going around Hannerville with dangerous intent, and he would be damned if he was going to let this retired doctor's fear prevent him from doing his job.

"Doc, I get that you're frightened, but you need to stop sticking your head in the sand over this. It might be Brannon, it might not, but either way people are going to find out about this because something happened in this apartment last night, and I doubt it was anything good. I can't put off warning people any longer because you're afraid it might turn out that your boogeyman's back."

The moment he stopped talking and took a breath, Flaghan regretted both his tone and his words, but the apology he wanted to make died on his lips as he saw the effects of what he had said. Philip Glenster was a sprightly man with a twinkle in his eyes, but at that moment he looked all his 68 years and then some. His hands dropped to his sides and his shoulders slumped, but he looked the Sheriff right in the eye as he said,

"If you had been there that night, Mark, you'd be afraid too."

Then he turned and walked away.

Corday stood watching the front door of the girl's building. The old doctor came out, staring at the ground. The meddling old fuck turned and started walking away from him. Just as well; had he walked towards him, Corday would have been sorely tempted to shove the old prick in front of an oncoming car.

It wasn't the good doctor – retired now, of course – that he was pissed at, but rather the girl. She had proven to be particularly troublesome. It had given him cause to wonder if the ease with which he had snagged the first girl has been a fluke, if perhaps he wasn't a touch rusty. His skills were unquestionable, honed over several lifetimes, but they hadn't been utilised all the while he'd been languishing in Berrybeck. His mind and body seemed a little slow, and that wouldn't do because the game had started, and he needed to be on top form.

However, being fair to himself, the girl had proven more troublesome than one might have expected. Gaining entrance to her apartment had been easy enough, though he had been surprised to discover she had been taking a shower at such a late hour. Nonetheless, Corday had been convinced that the fact would work in his favour, and for the most part it had. He had been inside the steam filled bathroom, standing right beside the tub, syringe in hand, waiting for her to slide the curtain back when she was done. He had smiled as he listened to her singing to herself, and had briefly wondered if he might get to listen to her pleasure herself before she finished. What had actually happened was that the girl had left something sitting in the sink, and when her hand slid out from behind the curtain, her wet fingers had smacked into his face. As one nail made contact with his eye, Corday had hissed and drawn back, letting go of the syringe and clutching both hands to his face. There had followed a moment during which Corday realised the girl had been taking a breath to scream. Ignoring the pain in his eye he had lunged at the curtain, attempting to gather it round her and knock her down. The move had been what he believed was referred to as an epic fail. Not only had he crushed the syringe underfoot, but he had also slammed his knees into the side of the tub and tripped forward. Instead of wrapping the girl in the curtain, he had used it to try and regain his balance. The rings holding it up had all popped loose and he had fallen into the tub, the curtain falling over him. The girl, rather than stand screaming, had made her escape. He had caught her ankle with one flailing hand as she had climbed out of the tub and she had pitched forward, smacking her head off the sink. Corday could only imagine that it had been a fear induced adrenaline surge that had gotten her to her feet so quickly with blood running freely from the gash on her forehead.

She had staggered to the bathroom door whilst he fought a short but infuriating battle with the shower curtain. By the time he had extricated himself and gone after her, she had reached the hallway, where she had knocked over a small table. He recalled seeing a handbag sitting on it earlier and, sure enough, the bag was now on the floor, its contents spilled out. The girl had also been on the floor, sliding backwards, the damage to her forehead apparently beginning to take its toll. Corday had briefly enjoyed the view before advancing on her.

Obviously forgetting the dangers of mixing electricity and water, the girl had retrieved her taser. When she raised it, an act which had taken tremendous effort on her part, Corday had cursed himself.

He had heard her mention it earlier, had passed by the damn handbag on his way to the bathroom even, but had not had the forethought to remove it. At the time he hadn't expected things to turn out the way they had, but it always made sense to plan for the unexpected, and he hadn't. At that moment he had allowed himself to think that the game might be over before it had properly begun. He made a deal with himself then and there that he would not go to another loony bin, would not go to some stinking prison to spend decades locked away, rotting. If it came to it, he would kill himself. Everything was in place should it come to that.

Thankfully, such measures had not been called for.

The taser had not been of the long range variety, and so the girl had had to wait for him to get in range before trying to use it. But by the time he got in range, the poor dear had hardly the strength to press the trigger. He had batted her arm away and knocked her out cold with one good punch.

He had considered leaving without his prize. Though she hadn't cried out for help, noise had been made, and it had been a definite possibility that someone had heard something and were right now on the phone to the police. However his blood had been up; she needed to pay for the bother she had caused. Besides, the party needed more guests.

So he had proceeded to quickly clean the place up a bit, though he was certain he had left a trace or two behind. Nothing that would give the police any solid clues to his identity or the girl's eventual fate, but clues all the same. He had then wrapped the girl in the shower curtain, gone down to the street to unlock his car, and then brought her down, ever alert for prying eyes. No one raised the alarm as he had bundled her into his car. The street had been empty and silent as he had driven away, thinking of what punishments he could mete out.

Even so, as he continued to watch the building, Corday admitted to himself that the girl had been much more admirable than many. He recalled victims past who had simply screamed and yelled and waited for the end to come, but not this girl. She had saved her breath, made an attempt at escape, had even had the sense to arm herself, and all whilst frightened and bleeding. She had had some guts. Corday smirked at his own sick humour as he recalled removing them last night, after having several hours of fun with her. Then he got up from the bench he was sitting on and walked away, whistling to himself.

Chapter 20

Abigail opened her eyes and looked around. Morning sunlight illuminated her nice, familiar bedroom. Sighing she sat up, rubbing sleep from her eyes, then rubbing her face with both hands, a little disappointed to be waking up in her own bed.

Her mind went back to the moment from yesterday, after Marty had admitted he would like to spend the rest of his time in Hannerville at the cabin with her. In those few seconds it seemed as if all she had to do was simply tell him her secret and everything would be fine, it would all come together and her hopes would become reality. But even as she had looked into his eyes her courage had faltered, her uncertainty that he would accept what she had to tell him taking hold. She had let the moment slip away, turning from him and going back upstairs.

Marty had been awfully quiet on the drive back and Abigail had started to worry that her fears had made her squander what might have been her one and only perfect chance to tell Marty everything. But as they got to the bridge in town, he had asked her if she wanted to join him for dinner at a restaurant. Though still concerned about him driving back to the cabin in the dark, Abigail had been so relieved that she had accepted the invitation and given him the name of a nice cosy eatery she knew on the other side of town.

Their dinner had been quiet, candlelit and delicious. They had arranged to go boating the following day, Abigail telling him she would come up to the cabin and they could walk to where her uncle kept his boat. After coffee, Abigail had offered to pay the cheque and Martin had firmly told her that he would not hear of it. It had been a nice night, unusually warm, and so they had decided to walk to her home. Martin had offered her his arm as they had left the restaurant and she had taken it. The walk had not taken them long and during it neither of them had said a word. It was a little snippet of the life she wanted with him that it ached when she had to let go of him when they had reached her front door. He had looked at her for a couple of seconds, his expression unreadable, and then he had leaned forward. Abigail didn't think of herself as being stupidly romantic, but when she thought he was going to kiss her, her breath had caught in her throat. Alas he had only given her a peck on the cheek, told her he was looking forward to seeing her again, and left.

Half an hour later, alone and angry at herself, Abigail had cried. She asked herself again and again why she couldn't simply tell him, get it of her chest and consequences be damned. But of course the reason was that since she had first laid eyes on him at her store, the feelings she had been so unsure about had solidified. She wanted to be with Martin Muir so much that it made her sick to her stomach to even think that it might never happen. To tell him her secret might be the very thing that made certain it never would. But no relationship between them could exist with him not knowing.

Tired and frustrated, she had written somewhat bitterly in her journal before going to bed.

Yesterday's tomorrow was here and now, and as Abigail got out of bed and prepared to face the day, she told herself that before she went to bed tonight, for good or ill, she would tell Martin her secret.

Ninety minutes later Abigail pulled up outside the cabin, parking beside Martin's rental car. As she was locking her car door, the front door opened and Martin emerged, smiling and waving at her. As they approached one another, she was suddenly struck again by the idea that he was going to kiss her, that during the night he had realised he had feelings for her and was just going to go for broke. What happened was that he took her in his arms and hugged her, planting a gentle kiss on her forehead.

"Good morning," he said, releasing her and stepping back.

"Morning," she replied, as cheerfully as she could as she tried to get over her disappointment that he hadn't gone for a lip lock. However, her spirits were buoyed slightly by the fact that he already felt comfortable enough with her to give her a hug and a kiss, albeit a somewhat chaste one. "You ready to go out on the water?"

"Does it have to be right now?" he asked.

"Not right now," she told him. "My uncle said he wouldn't be using his boat today, so anytime is good. He also said that he and my aunt are looking forward to meeting you."

"I'm looking forward to meeting them too," he said. "Want to go skip some stones?"

"Skip stones?"

"At the little shingle beach you saw yesterday from the porch."

"Oh, right, sure. I warn you though; I was never very good at skipping stones."

"It's not getting them to skip you need to worry about, it's keeping your footing. Once upon a long ago I was skipping stones from the shore of this big lake. At one point I put a bit too much oomph into one of my throws, the stones shifted under me, and I went down square on my arse!" Abigail burst out laughing. She only laughed harder when a grinning Martin added: "Not only that, but the bloody stone didn't even skip once; it just plopped into the water." Getting her giggles under control, Abigail said,

"I remember reading that in one of your letters." He offered her his hand.

"Stop chuckling at the image of a little me yelling because he's bruised his bum and let's go."

Of course his words only induced a fresh burst of laughter from Abigail, who took his hand and was led around to the back of the cabin.

No one fell on their backside during the time they spent slinging stones across the water. Most of Abigail's attempts simply sank beneath the surface. When this happened, Martin would tell her to find another and try again. When she got it right, he would cheer and tell her that that was how it was done.

They sat down for a few minutes on one of the rocks, staring at the clear blue sky. It was bright, but the day had not yet warmed, though Martin mentioned hearing a weather report that said it wasn't going to get particularly warm today anyway.

"Best bring a jacket for the boat," Abigail advised. "It'll be chilly out on the lake."

"Where do your aunt and uncle live?"

"In town, just on the eastern outskirts, but my uncle's boat is kept over there." She pointed out across the lake. "It's maybe a twenty minute drive or so to the boathouse."

They made their way back to the ramp, where he invited Abigail to go first. Unable to help herself, she teased him by saying,

"You just want me to go first so you can look at my butt." She expected him to be flustered, maybe a little embarrassed, but instead he grinned.

"And why wouldn't I? I'm not the kind of man who objectifies women, but I've sneaked a look or two already and it has to be said; you've got a great butt."

"I am just shocked and appalled," she told him, despite being anything but.

"Well, there's no need," he assured her. "My real reason for wanting you to go first is so that if you slip and fall I'll have a shot at catching you."

"Not to mention a shot at copping a feel of the butt you so admire," she joshed. She then sighed theatrically and announced, "There's no such thing as a truly altruistic gesture."

"You really want my backside in your face all the way up the ramp, and all the way up the stairs?"

"Nothing wrong with your backside," Abigail told him as she started up the ramp. "I've sneaked a look or two myself."

For most of the single file journey up the stairs, Martin managed to keep his eyes off of Abigail's shapely rear. His will slipped once or twice, and immediately thereafter so did his gaze, but given that he could quite happily have stared at it until he lost his footing and fell flat on his face, he didn't think he did too badly.

As they reached the cabin, Abigail announced that she would have to use the bathroom before they left. While she did that, Martin went to his bedroom, put on his jacket, and put his wallet in the inside pocket. When Abigail came back, she asked whose car they should take.

"We'll take mine," he replied. "You can navigate; I need all the practise I can get because the road to the airport will be a hell of a lot busier when I'm heading back." He instantly regretted mentioning his eventual return home, but didn't dwell on it. "Then I want to go sailing with you, then I'll bring you back here, you can go home for about a while, and then come back."

"Why can't I just stay here instead of leaving and coming back?"

"Can't tell you that," he said. "Come on; off we go."

Thanks to Martin's careful driving, the journey took a little longer than Abigail had anticipated. As Martin admired the view out across the lake, Abigail went to the doors of the boathouse, digging a small key out of her pocket. She unlocked the padlock, unthreaded the chain from between the door handles, then opened the door and carried both items inside.

A few minutes later, Martin had just decided that the cabin he had picked out across on the other side of the lake was definitely his when Abigail called out his name. He went inside to find that she had opened the lakeside doors of the boathouse, and was now seated behind the wheel of a small four person motorboat. She invited him to come aboard. He did so, his inexperience with boats apparent.

"Not much sailing blood in you, huh?"

"You know there isn't," said Martin, setting both feet on the floor of the boat and steadying himself as it gently rocked to and fro. "Last thing I was in that was anywhere close to this was a pedallo."

"A what?"

" A pedallo. It's a little two-seater boat that you power by pedalling. The stick that controls the rudder is in between the seats." He looked at the dashboard. "This looks a bit more complicated."

"It is," confirmed Abigail as she started the engine. "But, like anything else, once you know what you're doing and you're confident, it's a piece of cake. Do me a favour and cast off that mooring line." After he had done so, she advised him, "You might want to take a seat."

He sat down and Abigail eased the throttle forward. The engine purred softly as the boat moved forward into the open water. Going slowly, she took them out to the centre of the lake and brought them to a stop. Abigail looked over at Martin and grinned.

"See? Easy."

"Once you've had the practice."

"Nah, I was a natural from the start."

"Even if you do say so yourself."

"Not just me; my uncle says so too."

"I'll have to remember to ask him about that."

He stood up carefully and turned through 360 degrees, taking in the fantastic view their vantage point allowed. It truly was stunning, the crystal clear water reflecting the blue sky and the tree lined hills, the green broken here and there by a roof sticking out. Other than the idling engine, there wasn't a sound to be heard. Martin sat back down.

"Wish I'd brought my camera."

"I can always bring you back out at some point," said Abigail. "However, I should point out that if you don't tell me why it is I can't just hang at your place after we get back, then I may be forced to just leave you out here."

"Uh, wouldn't that involve you being here too?"

"Oh, no, I'd just push you into the water."

"That seems a bit harsh. Besides, I would put up a fight, you know."

"Well, you're keeping something from me, Marty, and I don't care to be kept in the dark. And I could take you in a fight."

"Meaning you would exploit my weakness and tickle me till I gave in." Abigail confirmed his words with a sly grin and a nod. "Evil wench," Martin muttered. "But I am resolute; I'm telling you nothing."

Abigail shot him an "Oh, really?" look before turning in her seat and lunging at him. Martin yelped and leaned back, but there was nowhere for him to go. She was on him, her hands searching for a way into his jacket. Martin chuckled and demanded that she stop it.

"You're going to knock me into the water!"

"You can swim."

"It looks cold."

"I'm sure it is."

She got one hand past his defences and started tickling him. Martin laughed out loud and started squirming in his chair. Abigail didn't let up and eventually Martin said,

"Right, your turn."

"You know my underarms aren't ticklish."

"No, but your feet are."

Abigail paused for a moment as she realised what he intended to do. Martin took advantage, reaching down and grabbing her ankle, lifting her foot off the deck and starting to pull at her shoe. Now it was she who yelped, abandoning her tickling efforts and throwing herself back towards her seat. Unfortunately for her this manoeuvre only allowed him easier access to her foot. She began pleading "No!" repeatedly as he yanked at the shoe.

"Marty! No! You know I don't like having my feet touched."

"I know," huffed Martin, still tugging at her shoe. "And I wasn't going to use that information to my advantage, but you leave me no choice."

"Please! I give, I give! I'll wait for the surprise. I'll wait!"

Martin let go of her foot and lifted himself back into his seat, his smile only slightly smug.

"Good. Now, on with the boat trip."

Muttering about him not playing fair, Abigail got them under way again, the route taking them near the shore and then at a relaxed pace counter-clockwise around the circumference of the lake. She slowed down again when they were near the shingle beach below Martin's cabin.

"All right," she said. "Straight line through the middle, but this time I'm gonna open her up, so hold on tight."

She powered the boat forward until the throttle was at maximum, the little craft scudding over the surface of the water. Martin held on, a little uncertain, but then he turned and looked at Abigail and was struck. With her hair billowing out behind her and the sun shining down on her smiling face, Martin didn't think he'd ever seen anyone look so beautiful. He actually thought about saying so out loud, but didn't think he'd be heard over the combined roar of the motor and the wind.

After half an hour or so, Abigail guided the boat back inside the boathouse. Martin climbed out and she threw him the mooring line, which he slid back over the post. He went out and started the car as Abigail locked up the boathouse.

The drive back was comfortably quiet. Sooner than she would have liked, Abigail found herself getting out and preparing to head for her own car. She knew she wouldn't be able to get what her surprise was out of Marty, but she didn't want to have to leave so soon, even though she knew she would be coming back soon. As he had so often managed to do in the past, Marty said just the right thing to cheer her up. After looking at his watch he turned to her and told her,

"This is actually a lot earlier than I was expecting to be back. Do you fancy coming in for a drink and a couple of games of pool before you go?"

Beaming, Abigail headed for the front door.

"I'll have some cola," she announced. "And this time we're playing for cash."

Corday stared at the front door of the cabin, fighting against his wish to burst in and take the two of them apart with his bare hands. But that would end the game too quickly, too easily for them. No, there were other moves to be made before he throttled the life out of both of them. But he would have to get the game moving forward. What had happened after they had left the boathouse was proof of that.

After the police had left the girl's building, he had gone to Abigail's house. Her car gone, he didn't have to spend much time thinking about where she might be. He had actually passed the two of them as they had driven down the hill. A quick turn in the road and he had followed them to the boathouse. Driving a short distance past the turnoff, he had parked his car at the side of the road and then walked back, getting to the lake in time to see them make their circuit. When he realised they were coming back, he had hidden in the bushes and watched them lock up the boathouse, get in the car and drive away.

He had been stepping out from his hiding place when the man had attacked him, if you could call it an attack; it had been one of the clumsiest attempts Corday had ever witnessed, the man announcing his presence before he was anywhere near his target. Corday had actually had the time to turn and face the man, make the determination that the attack hadn't been planned, and prepare to defend himself before the man was within striking distance. His first strike had been ungainly, the man clearly not used to physical confrontation. Corday could not imagine what had caused him to act in such a way, as he had doubtless only been here to watch.

A jab to the throat brought the man to his knees, struggling to draw breath. The colour drained from his face and his eyes went wide. He brought one hand to his throat and raised the other, presumably in an attempt to ward off any other attacks. However Corday had simply knelt down in front of him, both hands raised, and told him,

"I'm not going to hit you again. Just calm yourself down, get your breath back and we'll have a little chat."

As it turned out, the man was not very talkative after he had recovered. Corday had therefore put some theories forward and judged how close he was by the man's reactions, which were easy to read given how shaken he was.

"You were watching me, yes? Yes. Good. Everything I've seen so far doesn't suggest they knew about anything, so you and whoever you're with are probably trying to work out the best way of approaching them." There had been an almost imperceptible shift of the man's eyes. Corday had grinned. "And this would be because of me?" A rhetorical question. "Is that old bitch still running the show?" Another unintentional yes was given. "Excellent. Now, one last thing: why on earth did you try to kill me?"

At this question the man spoke up, lifting his head and glowering at his inquisitor.

"You are a monster. You mean them harm. You must be stopped."

Angered, Corday had lunged forward, seized the man's head and viciously twisted it to one side, snapping his neck. As the man's body had fallen to the dirt, his killer had already been looking for stones to weigh it down in the water.

Afterwards, Corday had driven back to Jackpot Road, where he had parked near someone's driveway before getting out and walking to where he could see the cabin. Both cars were still outside, so they were in there, talking, laughing, kissing, maybe even fucking. He knew now there were other players in the game, hence his having to fight the urge to attack now. But when he thought about it, it didn't seem like these others would pose much of a threat. He didn't believe they would all be as rash and impulsive as the idiot back at the boathouse, but they would be just as ineffectual. They would be frightened, especially now that one of them was dead. They might approach Abigail and Muir sooner now rather than later, but it would have to be handled very carefully. Whoever they were, they had to know that what they had to tell the pair would require a great deal of convincing, assuming they even managed to get them to listen.

They could try to thwart his own plans, perhaps by sending a message to the Sheriff. Presumably they knew where he was staying. Corday cursed this further occurrence of lack of foresight; he should have questioned the man further, gotten as much information as possible by whatever means were required before killing him.

Given that he didn't know and couldn't predict precisely what these other players might do, Corday decided to really kick things off.

Tonight, one of Abigail's friends would be invited to the party.

For the second time today, Abigail parked beside Martin's rental car and got out. She had left only an hour and a half ago, after losing ten dollars at pool. Though she had no idea what Martin had planned, it had taken her most of those ninety minutes to decide what to wear. Never one for obsessing over sartorial decisions, trying on almost every outfit she had was simply a way for her to try and ignore the two voices vying for supremacy in her head. One was telling her that the time was right and she had to go through with her decision to tell Martin her secret. The other made no bones about telling her she would be making a terrible mistake if she told him. No man in his right mind would look at her the same after hearing what she had to say. He would pack his belongings and head for the airport first thing tomorrow morning, it said.

As she approached the front door of the cabin, dressed in a knee length midnight blue dress, the neckline of which revealed more than her usual amount of cleavage, and matching flat shoes (heels sucked), Abigail was still mostly uncertain about whether or not she would be able to reveal, even to Marty, that most sacred piece of information about herself. But the relationship she really wanted with him could never happen if she did not. She would not be able to see him time and time again in a more openly romantic capacity and know that she was keeping something from him. True that she had never seen fit to tell any of her previous boyfriends her secret, but they had been boyfriends; this was *Marty*.

She wondered if keeping things platonic these past few days had been as difficult for him as they had been for her. If he had, upon every meeting, wanted to blurt it all out and kiss her. A warm feeling sparked to life in her at the very thought of his lips on hers. The thought went further; his hands on her, his skin against hers, his flesh inside her…

It was in something of a daze that she pressed the doorbell, and so she got a bit of a surprise when the man who was ravishing her in her thoughts opened the door, smiled at her and told her to close her eyes.

"Excuse me?"

"Close your eyes and take my hand."

Giving him a look of suspicion, she closed her eyes and held out her hand, finding his and grasping it. He pulled her gently forward, telling her to keep her eyes closed, which she did.

She noticed the smell first: lasagne, her favourite. Then under that, the aroma of scented candles: lavender, her favourite scent. Somewhere in the lounge, soft piano music played. Behind her, the door closed and Martin told her to look.

The entire main living area of the cabin and the mezzanine deck were lit solely by lavender scented candles. Dozens of the light purple wax sticks sat in little trays on every surface, bathing the whole place in a warm glow. The dinner table was set for two, the crockery and cutlery all arranged.

"I didn't put on your favourite kind of music because old time rock and roll just didn't seem conducive to the mood I was going for. Oh, and the starters won't be ready for another twenty minutes or so," Martin informed her. "Sorry about that; it took longer than I expected to light all the candles. Speaking of which, if one falls over it'll be everyone for themselves getting out of here before the place burns down."

She turned to look at him. He wore a simple pair of black trousers, black lace ups and a dark blue shirt. Freshly shaved and with his hair neatly combed but still damp, he looked so handsome she felt a little lump form in her throat. Past boyfriends had made romantic gestures like the candles, but none of them had known her well enough to get lavender candles. Nor had any of them tried their hand at making lasagne. Plus there had always been something they hoped to gain, usually sex. Some of them had achieved that goal, but Abigail knew that if things did not work out with Martin tonight, no one would ever again do something like this for her and make it work because she was sure he had done this for no other reason than to make her happy. This was the dictionary definition of special.

"You look... dashing," she told him. He nodded appreciatively, smiling.

"I'd have settled for looked good, but dashing..." He threw his head back and ran a hand through his hair, focussing with an arched eyebrow on a point somewhere off to his right. His eyes swivelled to look at her. "I could get to like being dashing."

Abigail laughed and turned to look back at the room.

"Marty, this is so wonderful. Good lord, how much did all these candles cost?"

"Yes, because I'm going to tell you that," he said dryly. "You don't need to worry about how much anything cost, or anything else for that matter. All you need to do is enjoy the ambiance, and hopefully enjoy the meal and the company. The meal by the way will be breaded mozzarella sticks, followed by lasagne with salad. Dessert will be..."

"Strawberry cheesecake?" she finished the list of her three top menu choices of all time for him.

"Yes," he said, feigning surprise. "How did you know?"

She turned back to him and favoured him with a smile that warmed his heart.

"You are..." she began. He stopped her with a raised hand.

"Please, no further compliments until you've tried the food. The starter and dessert I'm fairly confident about; I bought them at the store. The main course is all my own work, and may therefore be completely inedible. Just in case, I've got the takeaway menu for the local Chinese restaurant standing by." She chuckled.

"I'm sure it will all be fine."

"Optimism; that's what Chef Muir likes in his clientele. Can I get you a drink?"

"Why do I get the feeling you've got some vodka and some lime cordial chilling in the fridge?"

"Because you're a very clever woman," he smiled at her. "Go grab a seat and I'll bring it over."

As he went to the kitchen, she made her way to one of the sofas. She noticed as she went by that the curtains were closed over all the porch doors. A simple sign; this little candlelit world was theirs, if only for tonight, and nothing and no one should be allowed to intrude.

One of the voices in her head was silenced; before she left this place tonight, Martin would know everything there was to know about her.

From the starter to the dessert the meal was delicious. Abigail almost burst out laughing at the look of concern on Martin's face as she tried the lasagne, but the result of his culinary efforts was a complete success. True she had tasted better, but for a first attempt it was superb. Afterwards he had insisted they leave the dishes on the table and adjourn to the sofa, where they sat and chatted as they digested. She had a couple more vodka and limes, whilst Martin had a glass of cider.

"Oh," said Martin suddenly, sitting his glass on the coffee table and getting to his feet." I've got something to show you."

He went to his bedroom and returned with his laptop. He sat it on the table and told her,

"I brought along some photographs for you to have a look at."

"Oh, awesome," she exclaimed, setting her drink down and shuffling over.

They started going through the images. When they came across the first picture of Martin himself, Abigail burst out laughing.

"What are you doing? What are you *wearing*?"

"I'm wearing pyjamas and a wooly hat that belonged to my mum," he replied. "And I'm dancing on the couch and posing like a little male model!"

"You look adorable."

"Obviously, because people always burst out laughing when they see something they think is adorable."

"No, you do; it was just a surprise to see someone who's obviously you posing… in a wooly hat…" The titters threatened to overtake her and she snorted as she tried to hold them in. Martin rolled his eyes, clicked to go to the next photograph and muttered a curse.

"I thought I had deleted that one."

Abigail looked at the picture of a child, aged less than a year, standing up, arms in the air being held by an unseen adult. The child wore a blue T-shirt under a food stained white bib, and nothing else.

Abigail's burst of laughter caused a couple of nearby candle flames to dance wildly.

"That's you!" she cried. "Oh, look at your little weiner!"

"Next photo!"

"Not a chance. Who took this?"

"I have no idea."

"God," she breathed. "How things have changed."

"Well, it did get bigger."

"No," she snickered, playfully slapping him on the shoulder. "Times, Marty, times have changed. People these days wouldn't dream of taking a photo like this for fear they'd be branded a pervert." Martin nodded.

"I don't even know if something like that would have occurred to them back then. Someone just snapped the shot and it went straight into the album, and I eventually scanned it onto my computer." He paused for a moment. "I wonder if those were maybe my first steps, and someone decided the event should be documented for posterity… even if I wasn't wearing a nappy." Abigail nodded and brought up the last photo: a smiling man and woman standing side by side beside a white car. Abigail looked to Martin for confirmation of what she had guessed.

"That's the only picture I have of my biological Mum and Dad," he said.

The letter in which Martin had told her how his mother and father had revealed to him that he was adopted was undoubtedly the most heart breaking he had ever written. Fourteen at the time, Martin's world, though not exactly turned upside down, had nonetheless been dealt a rocking blow. He had poured his heart out to her in that letter. In her reply, Abigail had given all the love and support she had been able to, though at the time she had felt as though it was an insignificant effort: a band-aid over an arterial wound. After writing it, she had cried herself to sleep at the idea that her friend needed more than she was able to provide from where she was. But in his next correspondence, he had thanked her for her words and wishes, and said that it made him feel closer to her in a way, that as it turned out they had both lost their parents at a young age.

"I remember," Martin said wistfully. "Asking Mum and Dad to tell me about them. They didn't know a great deal, of course, but they told me what they could. Most of that was about how they died. Car crash. Dark night, wet road, a momentary lapse in attention or a sudden surprise... No one knew. It was pure dumb luck I survived. Mum and Dad had the forethought to ask for a photograph just in case I ever wanted to know what they looked like. They didn't think they'd get one, but the case worker had a big heart and gave them this."

Abigail, who already knew all of this, simply nodded, bit the inside of her lip, and fought the tears she could feel building. Though her memories of them were sketchy, she had plenty of photographs of her parents, some of which featured her as a baby. They were images that brought forth both happiness and sorrow.

"They were so afraid," Martin went on. "So afraid that I would turn against them when they told me. That hurt more than anything, I think; thinking they had so little faith in me. But part of me, the part that grew up that day, must have understood their fear. I felt so grown up as I stood there and told them that although I was curious about the people in the photograph, *they* were my parents. *They* had raised me, clothed me, fed me, looked after me, done their very best for me... How could I possibly hate them? Never before, and never since, have I seen two people so relieved about something. That image of the two of them is so clear in my mind..."

"And so is the letter you sent me after I told you."

Abigail, who had been staring at the picture, looked up at him. A tear slid from the corner of her eye.

"I have never read anything as beautiful as that letter," Martin told her, his eyes meeting hers. "Something I've never mentioned since is how many times I've gone back and read it when I've felt low. After Mum and Dad died, I slept with that letter under my pillow for a month. I don't think I was even aware of it then, but it's something that seems obvious to me now: I fell in love with you when I read that letter."

Abigail's breath caught in her throat. Her hands began to tremble and she clasped them tightly together. She fought to corral her whirling thoughts, to think of what to say, something, *anything*. Nothing came to mind. How long had it been? Seconds? It felt like ages since Martin had last spoken. He was obviously waiting for a response, and she knew what she wanted to tell him, but should she? Was telling him that such a good idea before he knew? The window was closing. He was going to think she wasn't interested, that he'd made a mistake.

"You're lucky," she said finally, asking herself what was coming next even as she spoke. "I don't remember exactly when I fell in love with you; I just know that I did."

The smile of complete and utter joy that spread across Martin's face was a mental picture she would cherish for the rest of her life. A life that it now seemed very possible would be spent with him, with her Marty. She could scarcely believe what was happening. Was she dizzy, or was he actually getting closer to her? No, he was. His hands were on hers.

She unlocked her hands from one another, locked them instead onto his. She was holding too tight, she knew, but she was afraid to let go. He was so close now she could smell his aftershave over the lavender. It seemed like such a teenage girl thing to think, but Abigail believed this was going to be perhaps the most perfect kiss of her life.

Except, she realised, it wouldn't be because Martin hadn't been told. At the moment this kiss came with one hell of a big string attached.

She unlaced her hands from his and drew back. The look of worry and disappointment on Martin's face stabbed at her heart.

"Did I..." Before he could finish asking the question, she reached out and put a finger to his lips. With her voice only just above a whisper she told him,

"No, you didn't. I need you to listen to me, Marty. Will you do that for me?" He nodded. "Good, because I have something to tell you and I need you to let me get it all out while I've still got the guts to say it. No interruptions, okay?" He nodded again. She removed her finger from his lips, stood up and moved to stand in front of the fireplace. Rather than think of the best way to put it – there was no such thing as far as she was concerned – she got straight to the heart of the matter.

"Marty, there's something about me you don't know, that nobody knows actually. I've never mentioned it to anyone because I always believed they would think I was insane. You know more about me than anyone, and I couldn't even risk telling you because I couldn't risk losing you, but I want more than the relationship we've had up to now. I don't know how we're going to do it, but I know it's what I want, and I'll do whatever it takes to make it happen. But I can't go into that relationship knowing that you don't know the whole truth. And that is what I'm going to tell you Marty; the whole truth. I can only remember things if I write them down."

She saw the look of befuddlement on Martin's face and shook her head.

"Christ, it sounds so stupid when I say it like that. I know some people have bad memories and have to write things down, but my problem is different. Unless I write things down, I have no memory of it ever having happened. Every night I have to record the events of the day in a journal because if I don't, the next day when I wake up I'll have no memory of them whatsoever." She paused but, true to his word, Martin said nothing. "I know what you're thinking: a medical problem, or more likely a mental problem brought on by a traumatic childhood event, like the death of my parents. Or maybe you've just confessed to being in love with a complete lunatic. It's none of those things, Marty, I swear to you. I've researched this time and time again, but I have never come across any reported cases of a condition like mine. Similar conditions, yes, but none exactly like mine. I've even tried an experiment where I set up a video camera, recorded myself throughout the course of an evening. I didn't write in my journal and the following morning I had no memory of what I'd done. The only reason I'm able to tell you about it is because I left a note for myself to play the tape, on which I explained to myself what I was doing, so I was then able to write it down. I still have that tape; I can show it to you. I've even had to transcribe every letter you've ever written to me into my journals so I'll remember what you've written. I kept the originals of course. I still look at them sometimes.

"I... I don't know what else to tell you about it. It's a curse. I do my best every day to write everything down that's happened to me, but I always have this little worry in the back of my mind: have I forgotten anything? If I have, I won't know, but what if I have, and what if it's important? Sometimes I wonder if maybe I am nuts, but after what you said to me tonight, you have the right to know what you might be getting into." She laughed mirthlessly. "On the plus side, if you throw me out right now all I have to do is not bother writing this in my journal tonight and in the morning I won't remember a thing. You will though, so I'll need to write it down so I'll know why you suddenly packed and left without a word. Mind you, if I didn't, it wouldn't take me long to work it out. It's been my greatest fear for the last few weeks."

She felt like she should continue talking, explain it in greater detail, make him understand, assuming making anyone understand her condition was possible. But she knew she would be rambling if she went on, and what she had said so far had sounded faintly ridiculous even to her, so she kept quiet and watched him, trying to divine from his face what was going on in his head. She looked around the room, committing as much detail to memory as she could, bracing herself for the harsh invitation to leave. During her speech she had become so convinced she was going to hear the words, "Get out", she was unsure she was hearing correctly when Martin eventually said one word to her.

"Okay."

"What?"

"I said okay."

She scrutinised his face for signs that he was making fun of her, or being condescending. Even as she looked she told herself that whatever he might think of her now, this was Marty, and Marty was not the kind of dickhead who would do that. Nonetheless it was the second time tonight she had heard exactly what she wanted to hear from this man, and she was having trouble accepting it.

"Okay? What do you mean okay? Okay as in okay, give me a minute and I'll call the men in white coats, or okay as in…"

Martin rose and walked over to her, holding out his hands, which she took as she was almost certain she was about to fall down.

"Okay as in if you say you have to write everything down or else you'll have no recollection of it, I believe you, and heaven help anyone who calls you a liar when I'm around."

There were no words that she could think of to say, which didn't matter because Abigail wasn't sure she would have been able to say them anyway. Also, much like Martin's expression had shown his confusion a short time ago, so Abigail's now expressed how surprised she was. Martin smiled.

"Abi, knowing how difficult it was to come up with a way to confess to you how I feel, which in the end came out in a way that I hadn't planned, I know it can't have been easy telling me what you just did. But you did it because you're strong and you're honest. You're not a joker, and you're not the kind of person who makes up stories to make herself sound more interesting. You know you don't need to; you're interesting enough just being Abigail Morton from Hannerville. So if you tell me anything – the sky is really green, the oceans have dried up, monkeys have spoken and are quoting Shakespeare – then I will, without question, believe every word you say."

Looking into his eyes, hearing the words he spoke, realising that everything was all right, emotion overwhelmed Abigail. The tears flowed and she threw herself into his arms, letting out a huge sob of relief as she locked her arms around him and squeezed. Everything was all right. He believed her. She looked up at him and sniffed, and he smiled and wiped the tears from her eyes.

As she took the lead and started moving her lips towards his, she realised she was trembling. She had never been this nervous about a kiss, not even her first with Eddie Gifford all those years ago. The fact that Martin was trembling too was comforting though. His hands moved down to rest on her waist and hers reached up and gripped his shoulders.

Closer.

She felt his breath on her face.

Closer.

Their chests pressed together and she felt a racing heartbeat that matched her own.

Closer.

Their lips hovered mere millimetres apart, their breaths blowing into one anothers' mouths for a moment that was filled with almost unbearable anticipation.

Contact.

No fireworks ignited. No trumpets blared. Their lips simply came together and two people experienced a pleasure the likes of which they had never known before. Fireworks would have gone unnoticed. The players of any trumpets, or other musical instruments for that matter, would have been told to pack up and go home. The two of them kissed and the world around them fell away. There was nothing else they wanted or needed to know about except each other. The thoughts that had been racing through their minds seconds ago were all gone, replaced by calmness, serenity, comfort. If ever they'd had doubts before, they were erased now as they held one another, realising that they had journeyed far and discovered what many would spend a lifetime searching for but never find.

This very moment.

It ended, as all such moments must, but with a feeling akin to joy, and a burning desire to go further, to experience more. They pulled back and each saw their want reflected in the other's eyes. As Martin opened his mouth to speak again, Abigail went in for another kiss. This one made her intentions plain. Her arms went around him and drew him closer to her. He followed suit, pulling her against him and exploring with his hands the contours of her back. Slowly, in no rush, they made their way down until they rested gently on her buttocks. After a few seconds Martin squeezed and Abi gasped into his mouth, her own hands rising to his head, her fingers running through his hair and then grasping, gently pulling.

She came up for air first, panting, grabbed him by the hand and started leading him towards the bedroom.

"Wait," said Martin, his voice low and gruff with desire. "We can't."

Abigail stopped, turned and quipped,

"I've heard of places that don't allow smoking or pets, but a place that doesn't allow making love is a new one."

"No, we have to go to your place."

"Why?" she asked, dread creeping up her spine. He was going to demand to see the tape she had mentioned, demand to see the journals before he would truly believe her. Like most people he was going to require proof before he could really believe, but that wasn't the way it was supposed to be. Hadn't he told her that her word was good enough? Had that just been bullshit, or was he having second thoughts?

"You have to write all this down," he told her. "And I don't imagine you would have brought your journal with you here tonight."

She again searched his face for signs he was making fun of her, but all she saw was an earnestness that made her want him more. The idea of postponing being with him any longer made her want to scream.

"No," she confirmed. "They never leave the house. I don't know what would happen to me if something ever happened to them." He nodded.

"So, you have to write all this down because, believe me, I cannot abide the idea of you waking up tomorrow and not remembering tonight. I don't know if I'd ever have the balls to tell you again."

"Technically you didn't tell me," she reminded him.

"Now you're just splitting hairs. Come on, help me put out these candles and we'll get going." He went to the nearest candle, blew it out, and proceeded to the next one.

Abigail thought about arguing, but decided that what he said made sense. She did need to record all this, and with what she had in mind for when she got him into bed, neither of the two of them might be in a fit state to do much but sleep afterwards. Almost as if reading her mind, Martin paused and said,

"Besides, giving that I don't think I've ever wanted a woman so badly in my life, you may not be able to get up and write afterwards."

"Huh," she scoffed playfully. "By the time I'm through with you, mister, you're barely going to be able to walk."

"I'll hold you to that. Problem is, what are you going to do about remembering being with me if you're too tired to write it down?"

"I guess I'll need to find the strength from somewhere to scribble down some notes." Martin smiled slyly as he said,

"Or I could refresh your memory in the morning."

Twenty minutes later they stepped over the threshold of Abigail's house. She closed and locked the door, turned to Martin and said,

"Would you like to wait in the living room whilst I write?"

"Uh, yes, that'd be fine." She caught something in his voice and experienced another tremor of uncertainty. During the drive, she had resigned herself to the fact that she was going to experience these for a while after tonight, despite the way things had gone; it still seemed too good to be true.

"What is it?" she asked.

"I feel a little awkward asking this," he admitted. "And you should feel totally free to deny the request if you want to… Uh, can I see your journals?"

"Why?" she asked, the question reflexively confrontational, the idea that he was still looking for proof quickly surfacing in her mind. Martin caught the tone and smiled at her.

"Easy, Abi, I'm not asking because I'm looking for you to back up what you told me. I'm asking because I'm genuinely curious. I mean your… condition? It's not something you hear about every day. Plus it's obviously a huge part of your life that I had no idea about till tonight. I feel like there's a gap in what I know about you and … I don't know… It just seems that now it wouldn't feel right to make love with you without having that one last piece of knowledge. Does that sound stupid?" She smiled and shook her head.

"No, of course it doesn't. I didn't mean to sound snappy; please understand that I had convinced myself that you were going to hear me out and then kick me out. That you're okay with it is going to take a little while to get used to." One side of her mouth lifted and she shook her head, this time in disbelief. "I got exactly what I wanted and now I'm having difficulty accepting it; now who's being stupid?"

He took her by the shoulders and waited until she looked at him.

"You're not stupid, Abigail," he said softly. "Getting what you want after being so uncertain can lead to more uncertainty because you're afraid it's a lie, or that it's going to go away." He smiled. "I'm not lying and I don't intend to go anywhere."

She returned the smile and gave him a kiss before leading him upstairs. On the landing she went into a cupboard to retrieve a long pole with a hook on the end. This she used to snag the metal eyelet screwed into a hatch in the ceiling. She pulled and the hatch came down. Once the edge was within reach, she handed the hook to Martin and pulled the hatch down further, unfolding the ladder as she did so. Martin set the hook down on the floor and followed her up into the attic.

Abigail pressed the light switch and Martin saw that the attic was the length of the house and had floorboards over the joist. The vast majority of the space was taken up by cardboard boxes and black plastic bags, all of them filled with a wide variety of odds and ends that Abigail had collected over the years. As they made their way towards the back wall, Martin saw the top of a plastic Christmas tree protruding from one box, and a couple of legs belonging to a large spider sticking out from another. Almost as if sensing it had been spotted, the arachnid drew its legs back out of sight.

Abigail stopped in front of a tall shape draped with a white sheet. With a nervous grin, she pulled the sheet and it fell away, revealing a seven foot tall cabinet made from a dark wood. The sides and top were decorated with intricately carved leaves and vines. This design continued into the frames of the two doors, and was also etched into the long glass panels in the frames. The little brass lock plate on the right hand door was also in the shape of a little leaf. There was a drawer at the bottom. Abigail saw him looking at it.

"Every letter you've ever sent me is in that drawer," she told him.

Martin glanced at her, smiled and nodded. Though the idea of taking a look at letters he had written years and years ago was a tempting one, it was the contents of the cabinet that held his attention. There were several shelves inside, and all but the bottom one was jam packed with journals, diaries and notebooks. No two were exactly the same, and each had a "from" and "to" date carefully written on the spine. Martin glanced at Abigail, who was watching his reaction closely. He grinned at her.

"Your writer's cramp must be an absolute bitch to deal with." She laughed and said, "It's not too bad."

He looked over the contents of the cabinet again and shook his head.

"It's remarkable," he said. "I've got so many snippets of your life written down in the letters you've sent me, but this is a complete record. I know you regard it as a burden because it's something you have to do, but it's quite an achievement nonetheless."

She put her arms around him and laid her head on his shoulder. Looking at his reflection in the glass, she told him,

"Thank you."

As Martin waited downstairs, Abigail sat in her room at her desk, writing furiously in her journal. More than ever this felt like a chore she could do without; the man she loved was sitting downstairs in her living room, sipping a cola and exploring the cable channels when he should be with her, both of them in bed exploring one another. She held that thought in her mind, eventually reaching the here and now part of her writing. She wrote about how she was anxious in the best way possible, desperate to be with him, to know his body as well as she knew his personality and mind.

Determined to come back later and follow up on what she had just written, she put down her pen, closed the journal, got up and went downstairs.

Despite it being four in the morning, and despite the most delicious sense of satisfaction and fatigue she had ever experienced in her life, Abigail made it back to her desk.

Their first time together was a fifteen minute bout of unbridled lust that had left both of them panting and sweaty on the floor near the foot of the stairs they had been heading for when Abigail had decided they had waited long enough. She had turned and pounced at Martin, from whom there had been no complaint. He had paused only long enough to ask if she had any protection. She had informed him she was on birth control, and that she was sure she had some condoms somewhere. After that there had been nothing holding them back. She was certain she had torn her dress in her haste to get it off, and in the morning she was sure Martin was going to have a hard time finding certain items of clothing, such had been the haste with which they had been discarded. Fingers and hands and lips and mouths had been everywhere, and Abigail had the first of many orgasms mere seconds after Martin entered her.

After getting their breath back they had gone to the kitchen, neither bothering to put anything back on; they were as comfortable in each other's company naked as they were clothed. They had a drink and Abigail had snacked on a piece of chicken from the fridge. Martin had come up behind her while she ate and hugged her, his hands wandering up and down, stroking here, teasing there, all the while his breath hot against the side of her neck. She had felt him pressing against the small of her back, and her appetite had quickly shifted away from food and drink.

They made it to the bedroom for their second time. Their recent coupling having done nothing to dampen their need for each other, they made sure this time lasted longer. They slow danced, gentle and passionate, until they lay side by side, spent. They spoke for a short time, Abigail making Martin promise that if it seemed she was falling asleep he would wake her. Their talk eventually turned dirty and they made love again. As soon as they were done, Abigail, unwilling to chance it any further, got up and went to her desk.

When she finished writing, she turned to find Martin watching her, sitting up in bed. He held out his arms and she ran to join him, snuggling up to his warm body under the covers.

"We good?" he enquired.

"All written down in near pornographic detail," she assured him.

"Did I get a decent review?" She chuckled.

"You did."

She turned out her bedside lamp. Minutes later they were both asleep.

Chapter 21

Several hours earlier, just as the sun was going down, three figures stood beside Abigail's uncle's boathouse. One of them wore a wetsuit and was dripping wet, having recently emerged from the lake. As he removed the breathing apparatus he'd used, sitting it against the side of the boathouse, he shivered, his recent experience not one he had ever thought to have, and one he certainly hadn't signed up for.

The body of the man who had attacked Corday now lay at the edge of the water. The diver did not really want to see it again, but he joined his two female companions and together they stood over the corpse. One of the women shook her head, her face displaying sadness as her manner conveyed quiet rebuke upon the deceased.

"We should have tried to save him," said the diver calmly, his French accent noticeable but not overly so.

"You know as well as we do what the result would have been, Matthew," said the first woman, named Andrea, whose Scottish accent was unmistakeable. The second, Sandra, nodded in agreement.

"We might have succeeded, Andrea," Matthew argued quietly. "We could have ended this before it went any further."

"Possibly," conceded Andrea. "But the greater probability is that we would all have perished."

"I know that, but..."

"I understand you are upset," said Sandra. "Andrea and I are as well; Lucas was a good man. But he acted recklessly, and had we all rushed to his aid the chances are we would all have died. Corday is a killer, pure and simple; forget that at your peril. Let Lucas's death stands as a testament to that."

"Sandra is right, Matthew," said Andrea. "It is my hope that we will be able to avenge his murder soon, but for the time being we must ensure that we are able to do what we came here to do."

"But how do we do that skulking around in the shadows?"

There was a brief silence before Andrea answered him.

"I feel that the time is drawing near when we will have to take more direct action," she said. "It seems as though they are together now; this is in our favour. But we must make sure that when we go to them we do more good than harm. Making sure that happens will require a little more planning. For the time being, we must arrange poor Lucas's burial. Matthew, stow your diving gear and make sure the back of the truck is prepared." Matthew nodded. "Thank you."

As the young man went about his tasks, Sandra quietly said to Andrea,

"Do you think he'll be all right?"

"I hope so," was the reply. "He's a strong young man; I think he's just shaken and scared"

"Corday knows there are others here now, watching him," Sandra said. "I doubt it took him long to work out who we are."

Andrea knew she was right, just as Matthew was; their involvement from the side-lines hadn't exactly proved an effective approach. There were now three dead people to prove it.

"Come on," she said. "Let's give Matthew a hand. The sooner this is all sorted the sooner we can get back to the task at hand.

Two hours later, as a private jet carrying Lucas's body left Knoxville airport, Corday sat watching Beth, Amanda and Sophie enjoying some cocktails at a bar. There was a good crowd in, so it was easy for him to observe them without being noticed himself. Once or twice his attention was drawn by another possible party guest, but he always came back to the three at the bar. He wondered which one meant the most to Abigail. Probably Beth. During the time he had spent watching Abigail, he had decided that the friendship between her and Beth was deepest, the longest standing. The other two, though far from hangers on, definitely occupied the lower rungs of the friendship ladder.

Not that the death of either one of them wouldn't violently rock Abigail's happy little world.

His mind drifted, out from the bar, across town to where Jackpot Road started. Up the winding hill to the cabin at the very top, where even now that fucker Muir was probably balls deep in Abigail! Corday had to fight to stop the thoughts of it; he knew it would make him sloppy, and he needed to be at his best tonight. It was a bit of a risk after last night's escapade, but it needed to be done. No way was he going to let Abigail and Muir enjoy the delights of one another's bodies when it was within his power to plunge them into despair.

One of the girls, Amanda, got up and Corday focussed, though to everyone around him he was an everyday guy having a drink alone in a bar. Just listening to the music and soaking up the ambience. He watched, intending to get up and follow her if she left, but she headed in the direction of the bathroom. He considered following her in there, killing her before he left the bar, but decided it was an unacceptable risk. Not much fun either.

He let his mind drift again, back to this afternoon at the boathouse. He recalled the satisfying snap of the man's neck, the bubbles floating to the surface of the lake as the body had gone down, and the near euphoric feeling of knowing that he had once again exerted his will over the life of another. That feeling was what life was all about. Oh, yes, certainly, with all he had at his command he could have concluded this a long time ago, but where was the fun in that? A knife skilfully used was much more fun than a quick bullet to the head. Life was a gift, and the taking of it a pleasure to be savoured.

Had the man's associates watched him die? Probably. Had Muir's Guardian been one of them? Corday thought it a good possibility. Had someone been watching him whilst he had been in France? Was that how they knew what his new face looked like? Obviously; his supporters had swelled their ranks, so the other side would have done the same. Not to the same degree as before, but in his absence his achievements of some three decades ago had been undone. Corday sipped his beer and pondered.

Had he really been intent on ending it all? Yes, he had. He had been grateful for most of what he had been given by old man Garrett, his direct predecessor, but the baggage that came with the memories and the money was not something he had wanted to cart around for the rest of his life. That was something akin to his life being governed by someone other than himself, and Andrew Corday had not liked that idea at all. Bringing centuries of history to a crashing halt had seemed to him to be the ideal solution. The way to implement that solution had also seemed to him to be quite simple.

Wipe them all out.

So it had been that before he had been locked up in Berrybeck he had been involved in a purge. Ending the game meant wiping out all forces on both sides. His plan had been to use his own people to eradicate Muir and Abigail's, and then he would invite whatever remained of his group to somewhere for a celebration, whereupon he would poison them all. Afterwards his intention had been to live out the rest of his life in comfort and peace knowing that his daring and audacity had allowed him to accomplish what his predecessors had never been able to. But, like all the best laid plans of mice and men, his had gone agley.

Not at first though. At first it had been going brilliantly. Those loyal to The Couple were being felled left and right. True his own forces had also suffered; when they had learned of his intentions, his enemies had stepped up in impressive fashion. Savage skills he would not have believed them capable of came into play when they were called upon to protect the lives of the babies who would eventually be named Martin Muir and Abigail Morton. A great deal of blood was shed on both sides as spies were uncovered and loyalties changed. A great deal of money was spent to obtain information, some of which was utterly useless. The providers of such information had been dealt with in such a way as to ensure that afterwards people checked their facts before they came to him.

It had gone on for almost two years, a true war of attrition. Both sides had been decimated. Not long after having performed the rite, The Couple had died at his hands, as had one of the Guardians. That battle had been a fierce one, leaving many dead and wounded, though the new Bearers had been spirited away. His own wounds had seen him in recovery for several months, and it had taken a lot longer to track his targets down again, but he had been determined to see the thing finished. Eventually Corday, who had no qualms about killing children, had moved in for the endgame.

He had travelled to Scotland where, as one of his few remaining spies had informed him, the boy's Guardian had taken him. The spy had been killed soon after informing him of the child's whereabouts, but the information had been worth his life.

Engineering the car crash had been easy enough, though to his surprise the child had survived. He had only learned of this when he had been on his way to the US, but he had been confident that he would eventually be able to track the boy down again. He had known the girl was somewhere in America, but it was a big fucking country! He had tasked his remaining men with tracking her down and had set himself up in the run down cabin in Rutherford County. Having had to curtail his desires for most of the purge, he had allowed himself to run rampant, raping and slaughtering a dozen young women over the course of the six months it took for his men to locate the girl.

The night he had received the communication he had leapt into his car and headed for Hannerville. He had despatched the parents to the afterlife, and was about to help good old Doc Glenster on his way there too, when the fucking cops had shown up. They had stormed the place, dozens of them, many of whom managed to get a sneaky kick or punch in as he had been handcuffed and led out of the house to the waiting police car. From that night on Berrybeck beckoned, and his dream of being the man who brought the eternal chase to an end was put on hold.

Damn that little fucker Anthony! Years he had sat in Berrybeck, denying himself the simplest of pleasures, wasting his life when he could have been out in the world, living it up and indulging his every desire. But no, that little bastard had left him, had used his money to live in luxury all that time, doing nothing to assist his master. Admittedly it would have raised alarms in the early days had the notorious serial killer received a visitor of any sort, but after a decade or so had gone by and his crimes had been consigned to history, *something* could have been done. Anthony had deserved what had been done to him.

Corday wondered if it might be a good idea to bring in some backup. After all, he didn't know exactly how many enemies he had in Hannerville. He eventually decided that he did not need backup, which was good as he didn't believe that group of arseholes living in the house back in France would be of much use to him. He would win because he was willing to do what his enemies were not. He would torture, mutilate and kill if he had to, just as he had done all those years ago to find Jumaane and Abena, Muir and Abigail's predecessors.

He snapped out of his reverie, noticing Amanda making her way back to her table. She sat back down and she and her friends had another drink before getting up to leave. Corday stood and quickly made his way towards the exit.

Outside a gentle rain had started. He crossed the street and slid into the shadows near the mouth of an alley, where he had a good view of the door to the bar. A few moments later the three friends exited, wailing when they noticed the rain. They said hasty goodbyes and then split, two going one way, the third heading off on her own.

Corday smiled coldly as he slipped from the shadows and began stalking his prey.

Chapter 22

Martin opened his eyes and, after a few seconds, the events of the previous night blossomed to full and vibrant life in his mind before the sheer shock shut his thought processes down.

It had happened! It had really, actually happened. He had told her how he felt, and she had felt the same. They had kissed! They had had sex and it had been, without doubt, the best, most satisfying sex of his life. They had made love and it had been tender, passionate, fulfilling. And now he was lying in bed and she was behind him, one arm draped over him. He could feel her breasts squashed against his back. There was also something that could only be her pubic hair tickling the back of his upper thigh. She had come to bed after writing in her journal...

Her journal. The one she had to write in every night to make sure she remembered things the following day. Her journals: a record of her life that she kept in an ornate cabinet up in her attic. The erection that had sprung to life as he had thought of Abigail naked began to droop as his mind mulled over less arousing thoughts.

Last night he had told her that he believed her completely, but now he asked himself if he had simply been caught up in the moment. Unwilling to see what he wanted slip away over... What? What was this thing with the journals? He had given his reason for believing her as being that he knew she didn't have to make anything up to be more interesting, and that was perfectly true. No, he hadn't been caught up in anything. He had actually given it some thought when she had told him. He had told himself that she might well be a raving lunatic, coming away with such a story, but why would she? She had no reason to tell such a lie, and as she had said herself, she knew how it sounded. If she wanted to be with him, why risk making up such a tale? Simplest answer: she wasn't making it up. She believed everything she was telling him. Someone else might have called into question their entire relationship at that point, told him to do exactly what Abigail had been expecting him to do, but he had such deep faith in their relationship that there was really no question about whether or not he would believe her.

The look on her face when he had told her as much was a memory that would bring peace to his mind in times of trouble for the rest of his life.

Yes, he had questions he wanted to ask her, of course he did; he was curious about her memory problem. However his questions would have to wait because he knew she would still be uncertain. His belief had been something she was not expecting. She had been overjoyed about it, yes, but not expecting it. If he asked questions now it would seem like he was trying to pick holes in her story, and he wanted to do nothing that jeopardised what they had started last night.

He took Abigail's hand and pressed it against his chest. She snuggled tighter against his back, muttered something incomprehensible, and was still. Martin smiled, closed his eyes and went back to sleep.

The first thing he thought when he opened them again? *She's not spooning me anymore.* The second? *We have so little time left together.* Despite being a harsh and undeniable truth, he told himself that he wasn't going to let it taint the rest of his time in Hannerville. They would have to discuss it eventually, but he told himself that when they did he would make damn sure that things ended happily. He'd come back in a month or so, she could come and visit him... He would move here if that was what it took.

Though he had only recently told himself that he would do just that, now that it might be something he had to do, Martin asked himself if he would really be willing to pull up his roots and replant himself here. He supposed he could have a go at rebuilding his business here in the US, maybe even keep some of his existing clients, conduct business with them via e-mail and post, He'd be sad to say goodbye to the boys, but he was also fairly sure they would castigate him if he decided not to make the move if that was what staying with Abigail demanded.

He started to wonder if perhaps Abigail might decide to move to Scotland, but before he got too deep with it he chased the thoughts away. They were for a conversation that was still over a week away as far as he was concerned.

Becoming aware of the pressure in his bladder, he eased himself out of the bed and headed for the door. He glanced at the journal lying on top of Abi's dresser and for a fleeting moment thought about taking a peek. Then he looked over his shoulder at the sleeping form of the woman he loved and knew he could never betray her like that and expect to sleep well again. If she ever chose to show him, fair enough, but until then the journals were off limits.

He went to the bathroom, returning to find Abigail awake. She was still lying down, but was watching the door. As he entered the room she wolf whistled. Grinning, Martin hopped back into bed.

"Nothing to whistle about," he said. "Naked men have got to be the least sexy looking things on the face of the planet."

"I think that's something to be decided on a case by case basis."

"Not for me."

"You may not like to see them, but you are certainly one who doesn't need to be shy in the showers. Nice ass too."

"Is that all I am to you, a piece of meat?"

"Yes," Abigail said smiling. She leaned over gave him a long, deep kiss. When they broke contact she was still smiling.

"That thing I can feel against my leg..." Martin nodded.

"Yeah, sorry. I can't even claim it's a case of morning glory; it's all because of you."

"No apologies necessary," she said, sliding on top of him.

When they were both done, they lay beside one another for a few minutes, staring at the ceiling. Martin, the sweat on his skin cooling rapidly, pulled the cover up over himself. Abigail snuggled under too, pressing herself against him.

"I thought you had gone," she said suddenly. Martin frowned.

"Gone?" He felt her nod.

"When I woke up and you weren't here, I thought you had gone."

"I'm assuming you don't mean you thought I had just gone to the bathroom."

"Before I heard the toilet flush and realised where you were, I was on the verge of tears."

Martin didn't respond straight away. He had a question in mind, and an idea of the answer. He asked anyway.

"Putting aside for the moment the fact that I am terribly hurt you would think I would leave without getting you to make me breakfast first..." She punched him on the shoulder and he laughed. "What reasons did you give yourself for my having absconded?"

"I think you know," she replied in a soft, almost frightened voice. Martin nodded.

"I get the feeling I do, but just for certainty's sake I'll say it out loud: you thought I'd had second thoughts about us, about what you told me last night, and that I'd done a runner."

"That's about it, yeah."

Martin took a deep breath in and held it. She had been honest with him; he was honour-bound to do the same. He let the breath out slowly.

"When I woke up I almost couldn't bring myself to believe where I was, what had happened last night. Then I thought about your journals." He felt her tense up and shifted his position so that he was lying on his side facing her. The worry on her face made him want to hold her, but she deserved to hear this. "I thought about what you had said, and about what I had said about believing you. Everything I said last night still stands this morning, and it'll still stand tonight, and tomorrow morning, and for as long as you need it to stand before you get over the uncertainty you feel. Telling someone you love them is a big deal, but telling me about your memory problem took guts, Abi. You had your ideas about how I would react and I'm very happy that I was able to shoot them all down in flames, and I understand that you might, despite my reassurances, be a little iffy about things for a time. But I am here now, I will be here during that time, and when that time has passed, I will still be here."

She had tears in her eyes, but Abigail did not cry. However Martin was certain that he had never seen so much emotion directed at him by any woman he had ever been with. It lifted his heart.

"I so want to make love to you again right now," Abigail informed him. He chuckled, moving closer to her.

"So what's stopping you?"

An hour or so later, the two of them went downstairs for some breakfast. Abigail was wrapped in her bathrobe and, after finding them, Martin had put on his boxers and T-shirt. He followed her into the kitchen, where she asked him what he wanted to eat. He told her that cereal would be fine and she poured him a bowl of Fruit Loops. After putting milk in the bowl, she returned the carton to the fridge and sat down beside him as he ate a spoonful.

"Mmm," he managed as he chewed. After swallowing he asked, "They give this to kids? In the morning? There's enough sugar in these to put a small child in orbit!" He ate another spoonful. "Mind you, they're really nice." Pausing with his spoon hovering above the bowl, he looked at Abigail and then said, "I could get used to this: being served breakfast every day by a beautiful woman." Abigail raised her eyebrows and lifted her head.

"Oh, I see; a-cook-in-the-kitchen-slut-in-the-bedroom kind of deal?"

"Precisely. Though, to be fair, putting out some cereal isn't really cooking." Abigail narrowed her eyes and said,

"You want to have to suck those loops through a straw, Scotsman?" Martin laughed.

"No, spoon's fine, thanks. You not having anything?"

"I'm hungry, just can't decide what to have."

"Well, you think about it whilst I eat this and then whatever you decide to have I'll make for you. Sound good?"

"Sounds awesome. What can you make?"

"Well, you know I'm not exactly a chef, but…" He looked around the room. "You've got a toaster, so toast is an option. If you have eggs and bacon I can make those. I can do French toast. If you've got the ingredients and you want to take a risk, I can try making pancakes."

"Fried eggs and bacon?"

"I can do that," he assured her, spooning some more cereal into his mouth.

The fried eggs turned out okay, but he was working with an unfamiliar cooker so the bacon ended up a little crispy. Despite this Abigail cleaned her plate. Whilst she ate, Martin made coffee, and when she was done they put their dishes in the dishwasher and went to the living room, each holding a steaming mug; hers of coffee, his of tea. Unfamiliar with the brand, Martin blew on the steaming liquid and sipped it, nodding with approval. Not his usual, but it would do. Abigail sat down on her couch and tried her coffee.

"For a guy who doesn't drink the stuff, you make a mean cup of Joe, Marty."

"The machine made it; I just filled it up and pressed the switch."

He walked to the window, looked out across Abi's well-tended front lawn for a moment, then turned to her and smiled.

"What is it?" she asked.

"I think I'm still suffering from an acute sense of unreality."

"I think I know what you mean. You said exactly what I wanted you to say last night. You slept in my bed after we'd had sex and made love. I woke up beside you this morning and we came down here and ate breakfast and now you're standing there sipping tea. It just seems nuts."

Martin walked over and sat down beside her.

"It seems as if we're both going to have to deal with the fact that we're here and that what's happening between us is actually happening."

"Shouldn't be too hard to deal with."

They smiled at one another and sipped their drinks.

When they were finished they lay down on the couch, Martin at the back, Abigail at the front. His arm was draped over her, holding her tight against him, and her legs intertwined with his. Abigail, who had grabbed the TV remote before lying down, switched the set on and flipped through some channels before settling on an old black and white gangster movie. She asked Martin if this was okay and received a muffled response.

"Did you fall asleep?" she asked.

"Might have," he mumbled. "I'm comfortable."

"This is nice," she agreed, sitting the remote on the floor. "This is the kind of thing I could get used to."

"Me too," said Martin, giving her a squeeze. He nuzzled his face into her hair and kissed the back of her neck. Abigail smiled and clutched his arm.

Inside of five minutes they were both asleep.

Abigail woke up an hour and a half later and found herself almost slipping off the couch. She stuck out a hand to steady herself, inadvertently bending at the waist and pushing her rump into Martin's groin. He woke up with a pained grunt.

"Oh, shit, sorry, Marty." He moaned.

"Just tell me my nuts took a hit for a good cause."

"They did; to stop me falling off the couch."

"Fair enough. What time is it?"

"Uh... It's just after ten."

"If it's all right with you, could I go have a shower?"

"Sure it's okay, but you don't have anything to change into when you come out."

"I'll just put this stuff back on... Or you could take me back up to the cabin and..."

"No way; we're staying put. Today is all about you and me and being alone together in here."

"I like that plan, but I still think I should go for a shower."

"You know where it is," she told him, pushing herself into a sitting position. "Towels are in the closet in the hall, door on your left just before the bathroom." She watched him get up off the couch. "You know, the whole boxers and T-shirt combo isn't really doing it for me. I have an old bathrobe you could wear when you get out of the shower."

"It's your house, and if you don't like what I'm wearing then I will wear what you like."

"Obedience. Good boy."

"Woof, woof," he said, bending down to kiss her. He hesitated halfway there, looking at her puckered up lips. "Uh, on second thought, you might want to hold off till I've used some mouthwash or something."

"My breath smells too; kiss me."

So he did.

In the bathroom, Martin found a bottle of mouthwash and used some. Having done all he could for his teeth, and happy that his breath was now minty fresh, Martin took off his T-shirt and boxers and went to the shower. Turning on the powerful spray, he waited a few moments for it to warm up and then stepped in, closing the frosted glass door behind him.

As the steam quickly began to build up, Martin stuck his head under the cascade and soaked his hair. Then he lifted his head until his face was taking the full force of the spray. After a few seconds he turned around, rubbing his face and letting the water pound against his back. After a few minutes he looked around and discovered that the only shower gel available to him was in a bottle with a picture of a flowery meadow on the front. He lifted the bottle and read the name: Burst of Summer. Opening the cap, he lifted the bottle to his nose and sniffed. Nice. Maybe a little too flowery for him, but it wasn't as though he had a choice. Upending the bottle he squeezed, catching a small dollop of the thick gel in his hand. Sitting the bottle back on the little shelf under the shower head, he began to soap up.

As he washed himself, that feeling of unreality hit him again. He was in Abigail's shower, using Abigail's shower gel. Abigail herself was downstairs, wearing nothing but her bathrobe and willing to kiss him even when he had vile morning-breath. Well, waking-up-after-sleeping-breath anyway. Martin shook his head and chuckled.

Unbelievable, he thought to himself.

Just as he was rinsing the last of the suds from his legs, the door opened. A blast of cool air hit his back and he spun round, almost losing his footing. Abigail's eyes went wide and she gasped as it seemed he was going to fall. He caught his balance and righted himself.

"I'm sorry... again," she said. It was at that point Martin realised she was naked.

"Not a problem," he told her. "But just in case I decide to be nasty about it and sue you for causing me injury, you should probably come in and make sure I'm not hurt."

"For the sake of my own piece of mind," she said with a smile. "I better check." She stepped in beside him. "Good thing my robe fell off just outside the bathroom or it would have gotten all wet." She closed the door. There wasn't a great deal of room and the two were pressed close together. They got a little closer, and the bathroom got a little bit steamier.

Later, Abigail sat on the couch, back in her robe, her hair wrapped up in a towel turban perched precariously on her head. She was watching an infomercial for some new gadget designed to take the sting out of shaving your legs. Being someone who hated it when her legs got too hairy, Abigail was interested, until she saw the price.

"A hundred and fifty bucks? Jeez, I'll stick to waxing; painful but cheaper."

She changed the channel, eventually finding an old sitcom she liked. Sitting the remote on the couch beside her, she tried to watch the programme, but her mind kept wandering. Her thoughts were much the same as Martin's had been earlier in the shower. He was *here!* Upstairs, right now, in her house, putting on one of her old bathrobes. Fifteen minutes ago they had had sex in her shower. She closed her eyes and recalled the feel of the water all around her, her hands against the smooth shower tiles that were slick with moisture, Martin's hands all over her, his nibbling at her ear as he moved in and out of her. Her orgasm building, building...

Abigail squirmed, a shudder running up her spine. *Definitely having more of that later,* she promised herself.

She tried to focus on the show, but again her thoughts drifted. She counted the number of times she and Martin had been intimate so far. She wasn't sure, but she thought it might be around five. Five times in less than twelve hours. She had been in relationships where she hadn't made love to the guy five times the entire time they'd been together. She had been in relationships where she hadn't let the guy near her for weeks, and yet having met Marty only a couple of days ago, she hadn't thought twice about being with him. But, of course, Marty was different. There was no getting to know Marty; the only part of their relationship that had been missing had been the physical part, and it was going wonderfully. *Really* wonderfully. There were a couple of things they were going to have to discuss, but she didn't want them intruding on things right now. They were together – *me and Marty, together... holy shit!* – and they were happy, and here and now that was enough.

But as she tried to return her attention to the TV, the things she didn't want to have to think about right now refused to leave her alone. She tutted and tried to shoo them away, but they were stubborn, hovering at the edges of her mind, distracting her.

Then Martin came downstairs.

"For the record, I am not amused," he said. "And if this is all I have to wear, we have to close the curtains."

He was wearing her old bathrobe, a bright pink affair with white lace frilling the cuffs, which stopped at Martin's forearms, and the hem, which barely covered his knees. The moment after she saw him Abigail let out a squeal of laughter that quickly simmered down to an eye watering belly laugh. Martin stood at the foot of the stairs, trying to look grouchy but smiling slightly; he couldn't really be in a bad mood when he was listening to her laugh.

"Oh, Marty!" gasped Abigail when she had calmed down a little. She wiped tears from the corners of her eyes, still chuckling. "Oh, I haven't laughed like that since god knows when. I think I might even have wet myself a little."

"I'm glad you're amused," he said in a flat voice, walking over and sitting down beside her. "I look like a proper bloody eejit wearing this."

"No, you look cute."

"You can never tell anyone about this."

"Fine, but I get to take a picture."

She lunged for her cell phone, sitting on the coffee table. Martin grabbed her by the hips and yanked her backwards. She squealed and struggled as she landed in his lap.

"Please! Just one photo!"

"Not a chance."

"Just one! I'll never show it to anyone, I promise."

There was a loud tearing sound and they both froze. She looked back over her shoulder at him, watching his face, red with exertion, go redder still.

"Did you just rip my robe?"

"It may require some stitching at the back," he informed her. She started laughing again. "It's not funny; now I have a draft at my back."

Abigail began to laugh harder.

Later, they were watching TV when Martin suddenly asked,

"What's the matter?"

He felt Abigail stiffen slightly in his arms, then she relaxed and asked,

"What makes you ask that?"

"I'm not sure," he answered honestly. "I just get the feeling that you're not... comfortable. Like there's something on your mind and you're focussing on it and it's agitating you."

"Have I been shifting around a lot?"

"No, it's just a feeling. Right or wrong?"

"Right," she sighed, switching off the TV, sitting up and facing him. "There are a couple of elephants in the room I think we need to take notice of."

A slight frown creased his features.

"Don't really think there's anything we need to discuss right away," he said quietly. She made to say something, but he beat her to the punch with: "How about some lunch first. Then, maybe, after, we can talk about what you want to talk about."

"Okay," she said.

Abigail, unable to settle, sat her spoon down when she was barely halfway through her soup.

"We have a finite amount of time here," she declared.

"If we eat too fast we might get heartburn," said Martin.

"You know what I mean, Marty. Everything that's happened has been amazing, and I don't want it to end, but it will. Wishing won't change the fact that in less than a fortnight you have to go home."

Her words killed what little appetite he'd had for his food. He sat the spoon in the half full bowl and pushed it away. His head suddenly felt very heavy, but he made himself look up and meet Abigail's gaze as he said,

"I know. I just didn't want to think about it."

She reached out and took his hands in hers.

"Neither do I particularly, but it's a fact. What are your thoughts on...?"

"I'll move here," he blurted out. "We can research the ins and outs whilst I'm still here. Uh, the forms to fill out, the money involved... I could start looking for somewhere..."

"Marty, slow down. You have a business, a very successful one, that you've spent a long time building. I can't ask you to give that up."

"You didn't; I offered. Besides, I can set up again here. I might even be able to keep some of my old clients using the internet and post..."

"Marty, we're getting way ahead of ourselves. I think what we're experiencing here is the dictionary definition of a whirlwind romance, one that I want to work out just as much as you do. But we can't rush things. We need to give ourselves time to settle, get our heads around the fact that we both got what we wanted. I think we have to face the fact that we might have to do that on opposite sides of the ocean."

He nodded, a heartbroken look on his face. She got out of her seat, stepped over, sat down on his knees and hugged him. His arms locked tightly around her and he pressed his face against her.

"I know I'm coming across like some needy idiot," he told her. "But I know you're right. It's just going to be so difficult."

"Marty, our relationship has been going for years. It's come through so much, and now it's changed into something new, something amazing..."

"That's what's going to make it difficult. It's as if for years I've had the last piece of the puzzle in my hand and I haven't known it, and now it's in place, and soon I'm going to have to take it out of the picture and leave a big gap."

She leaned back and looked at him.

"Wow," she said. "Pink and frills have turned you into one eloquent little man."

"Shut up! I've always been eloquent. Now I'm just putting it to emotionally devastating use."

"Believe me when I tell you that I will be devastated when you have to get on that plane. I promise you, I'm going to be a mess when you leave."

Her voice caught in her throat and she rebuked herself for starting this conversation, but it was done now.

"You're right," she continued when she felt able to keep her voice steady. "Knowing we want to be together and not being able to be is going to be hard. But we can manage,

Marty. The fact that someday we will be together, permanently, will keep me going. The fact that you love me will keep me going."

"The fact that one day we'll be in the same house and I'll have a robe of my own to wear will keep me going. Seriously, my naked bum's actually making contact with the seat of this chair right now."

Abigail let out a noise that was part gentle sob, part barking laugh.

"Guess I'll need to burn that chair then, huh."

"Might be a bit of overkill. Some bleach and a scrub will probably do."

She hugged him again and they held one another for a while. Then Martin said,

"I get the feeling that this conversation is going to rear its ugly head again at some point, but are we good on this subject for now?"

"Yeah, I think we're good."

"So what was the other topic?"

"Other topic?"

"You said earlier there were a couple of elephants in the room. What's the second one?"

"Your questions."

They moved back to the comfort and warmth of the sofa in the lounge, sitting close to one another, but not touching.

"I know you've got some questions you'd like to ask," Abi explained. "I'd be surprised if you didn't. But I'm going to go ahead and guess that you've been holding back on asking them because you're worried I'm going to think you're trying to pick holes in my story. Am I right?" Martin nodded.

"Yes."

"Okay, good. Whatever you've got to ask, ask."

"You don't have a problem with me prying?"

"Marty, now you know about it you've got to be curious. You've told me you believe me and I accept that, so I have no problems answering any questions you have."

"Okay, uh... When did you realise you had this problem with your memory?"

"My parents realised something was wrong when I was a kid. I was always upset in the morning when I woke up and they couldn't work out why. They took me to a doctor and physically I was fine. Then my mom mentioned that it was almost as if I didn't recognise them when I saw them first thing. The doctor said that it might be an idea to get me to write things down, see how that went. My parents started teaching me to read and write and I started making some little notes, starting with who my mom and dad were and where we lived and stuff, and all of a sudden I could remember. They were happy and I was happy and things started going great, but then I realised that if I didn't write stuff down, I didn't remember it. That was when I started keeping it a secret; even at that age I thought I'd caused my parents enough grief, so I let them believe it had been a phase or something and that I'd gotten over it." Martin nodded.

"So you could retain information on how to read and write, but not people, places and events." Abigail nodded.

"There are basically three types of memory. The first is procedural memory, also called muscle memory. This relates to things you do which your brain creates neural pathways for, like riding a bike or even walking. The second is semantic, or generic, memory, which is for information that you've learned, like reading, writing, arithmetic, general knowledge. My problem is with the third one: episodic memory. Any experiences I have on a day to day basis – conversations I've had, movies I've watched – I can't recall unless I write them down. Obviously I've done my research, but I've never come across any cases of a problem like mine."

"How much detail do you write in your journal? Does it have to be written down in minute detail or is just a note enough?"

"The more I put down the clearer the memory. It's like your memory; if you catch a glimpse of something, you have difficulty bringing to mind what it looked like. But, if you see something for a while and concentrate on recording in your mind what it looked like, smelled like, sounded like, then you can remember it in greater detail. Thankfully most of the time I don't have a massive amount to put down, and what I do have to put down isn't very complicated."

"You have to write everything down every night before you go to sleep; what if you doze off during the day?"

"Dozing is fine; I can recall things after a snooze. I was even knocked out once and remembered everything fine after I woke up, but not after sleeping."

"Is it a time factor maybe? I mean, how did you learn to read and write and stuff like that?"

"I honestly don't know. I've looked up a lot of stuff online, and it might have something to do with where in the memory stuff you learn and eventually do automatically is stored, and where you store normal memories. To be honest, reading the hard core medical explanations gave me more headaches than answers. At one point I thought it might have had something to do with the death of my parents, but I had to keep journals when my Mom and Dad were still here."

"And the doctors couldn't give you any idea?"

"I've never been back to a doctor about it," she answered sheepishly. She pre-empted his next question. "I've always been afraid that I'd end up as some laboratory experiment or something. It might sound dumb, but there it is. I've researched I don't know how many memory problems, like short term memory loss, retrograde amnesia and anterograde amnesia. Anterograde amnesia comes close; that's where you can't form new memories after a specific event, but that still doesn't explain how I can recall things if I write them down." She paused a moment and then told him, "I came across a case once of a man who was injured in an accident, spent several months in a coma, and then woke up believing he was eighteen years old? He had no memory of anything that had happened to him after the age of eighteen. Couldn't remember his wife and kids, how to drive a car, nothing. How horrible is that? Hell, I'm lucky by comparison.

"I've also tried several memory strengthening techniques, but none of them have worked. Have you ever heard of the method of loci?" Martin shook his head. "Memory palaces?"

"Those I've heard of. They're to do with building an imaginary structure in your mind and storing memories in the various rooms. To recall something you simply concentrate and walk through the palace till you get to the room containing the memory you're after. Right?"

"Right. I studied for months. Built my memory palace, stored stuff in the rooms, and it all went great, until I tried to store something without writing it down in my journal. You remember I mentioned making a tape? I used that idea again; I wrote a stupid little poem, made a tape telling me what it had been and where I had hidden it, then left the tape out for me to find the next day. I put the memory of the poem and its location in a room in my memory palace and didn't write it down. The next day I couldn't recall anything about it until I watched the tape and went and found the poem exactly where I'd hidden it.

"Anything else?"

"I don't think so." She was clearly surprised. "Well you've already tried this and that, done a lot of research obviously, everything except go to the medical professionals about it…" She gave him a sharp look and he held up his hands. "And I understand your reasons for not wanting to go. But if you've tried all this stuff and none of it has worked, I doubt anything I suggest will be something you haven't already thought of and looked into. I don't see that anything can be gained from badgering you about it."

"You're hardly badgering me, Marty, but I appreciate what you're saying." She moved over and cuddled into him, laying her head on his shoulder. "If you ever think of something you want to ask, you should. I finally have someone I can talk to about this, which is something I never thought I would have. I am so happy that person is you, and you never know; you might think of something I haven't."

"Fair enough," said Martin, stroking her hair.

The afternoon quickly became evening. They ate an early dinner, chatting about this and that as they ate.

The matter of Martin's going home and what would happen afterwards came up during dessert. They kept it light, agreeing that they would have to take things slowly, day by day, see how they played out. Both agreed that being together was their goal, but how to do that in a way that was manageable for both of them would take some planning. No way could it all be hashed out in the time before Martin had to return home, so their being separated for a while was going to happen. Talking about it now wasn't likely to take the sting out of it when the time came, but that they were making plans was something of a comfort to them both.

After dinner they curled up on the couch to watch a movie, though they spent so much time canoodling that they missed much of it. However they managed to settle down towards the end.

"Do you think this is weird?" asked Abigail. Martin nodded.

"Not weird exactly, but since I don't really know what's going on in the film it's a bit difficult to follow the end."

"Not the movie, genius; us. Do you think it's weird that we're sitting here like this, having only met in person a couple of days ago, and now we're talking about things like living together and whatnot? I mean, we know so much about one another; what do we have to talk about?"

"No," he answered immediately. "It's not weird at all. That our relationship had a head start is about the only thing that makes it different from most others. I'd be willing to bet that many a mother would tell you that going into a physical relationship with someone you know so well is the best way to go. No surprises."

"But you could have been lying to me for all these years. I could have been lying to you."

"Were you?"

"No."

"Then there's no problem. As for what we'll talk about, we have lots. Yes, we know just about everything that's happened in one another's lives since we were kids, but reading about it and actually sharing those memories with someone face to face is a totally different thing. Plus we get to make our own memories now. Personally, that's the bit I'm looking forward to the most."

Abigail tilted her head to look up at him. She didn't say anything, just looked into his eyes as he got closer and closer, until they both closed their eyes and their lips met.

By the time the closing credits rolled, neither of them was wearing their bathrobes anymore.

They fell asleep on the couch, wrapped in one another, covered, - just about – by the bathrobes. Martin awoke to find the room in darkness, lit only by the glow from the TV. He got up and switched the lamp on before switching the set off. Turning to look at Abigail he saw that his movements hadn't awakened her. Crouching down beside the couch, he brushed some stray hairs away from her face and gazed at her, smiling.

Eventually he decided to carry her up to her bed rather than wake her. He went upstairs and put on the hall light and the lamp in the bedroom before coming back down, checking that the doors were locked and switching the lamp off. Then, as gently as possible, he scooped Abigail up off the couch and carried her up the stairs.

By the time he laid her down on her bed, still asleep, he was red in the face and out of breath. As he was climbing into bed beside her, Martin decided he'd leave that bit out when he told her about it in the morning.

Chapter 23

Corday glowered at the darkened house for a few minutes, picturing in his head what was going on in the bedroom. His rage boiled and he again had to resist the urge to simply barge into the house and slaughter them. When his rage was at a gentle simmer he walked away, sticking to the shadows.

He walked to his car, got in and started the engine. These roads were quiet, the good citizens of Hannerville either sitting on their fat asses watching the tube or tucked up safe in bed. There would be more traffic nearer the centre of town, but he was heading for the outskirts. Once there he parked his car off the road behind a copse of trees and proceeded into the woods on foot. He had parked some distance from the shack, on the other side of town from it in fact, so if the car was found and he was identified he could claim he had simply been unable to sleep and so had gone for a drive and then a walk.

It took forty-five minutes to reach the ramshackle structure out in the woods. Just inside the front door, which was barely hanging on to the frame, he stooped to lift the electric lantern. Keeping the light dim, he made his way through the shack, checking the empty rooms for signs of visitors. Nothing. Happy, he made his way to the occupied room, where he whipped the cover off the bed to reveal to woman, naked, spread eagled and asleep. Her wrists and ankles were handcuffed to the bedframe, though this wasn't really necessary; he kept her well sedated most of the time. Dropping the blanket he checked his watch and saw that the last dose he had given her should be wearing off anytime now.

Trying to decide if he wanted her awake or asleep tonight, he hung the lantern on a hook suspended from the ceiling. It was positioned in the middle and so cast an even, calm glow throughout most of the room; the corners were still in shadow. Corday went to the shadowy corner furthest from the bed and watched her while he undressed, folding his clothes neatly and hanging them over the back of the chair. Naked, he stepped out into the light and approached the bed, still not sure if he wanted her to wake up or remain asleep.

Crouched down at the end of the bed, he gazed intently at the darkened area between her thighs. He had yet to have her, was holding back for as long as he was able, though he knew when the time came he would tear her apart, front and back. It wouldn't matter; there were plenty of others in town. He gently touched the sole of her foot and she moaned and tried to turn over. Her movements were short lived and by the time they had ceased, Corday had risen slightly, running his fingertips up along her legs to her thighs. Rising further, one knee on the end of the bed now, he brushed his fingers through her pubic hair. Painfully aroused already, he planted a hand on either side of her and lowered his head to her crotch, inhaling deeply. Tonight being the night he took her became a distinct possibility, but he fought the urge. For that he would definitely want her awake and right now – he looked up at her face – she looked so peaceful that he didn't want to wake her. But he needed release.

Sliding back off the end of the bed, Corday stepped around to stand beside the top, looking down at her. He bent forward, reaching down and closing one hand around her breast. With his free hand he began to stroke himself. As he manipulated her flesh gently and his own somewhat more roughly, he kept his eyes on her face. So pretty, so sweet, so innocent... *so damn annoying, such a fucking whore!*

He became lost, his eyes looking at but not seeing the figure on the bed. His ministrations upon himself were so forceful that the motions eventually woke her up.

She opened her eyes just in time to see him loom over her, his throbbing prick in his hand, and hear him groan loudly as he ejaculated all over her face and chest. She already knew better than to make a sound; she simply closed her eyes and hoped he hadn't noticed her waking up.

Panting, Corday stood up straight and looked down at the mess he'd made. He went back to the corner and got dressed, then came out and lifted a towel from the floor beside the bed, which he used to wipe her clean. Tossing the towel back onto the floor, he recovered the blanket and threw it over her before collecting the lantern and leaving.

A few minutes later, as he started the walk back to his car, he decided that tomorrow night he would fuck her, kill her and take her to the party.

Chapter 24

Sheriff Flaghan had been agonising over contacting Philip Glenster since last speaking to him at Charlotte Webster's apartment two days ago. He wanted to apologise to the man for what he'd said, but he wasn't too sure how to go about it. Sometimes he told himself that he should just go to the guy's door and say "I'm sorry for what I said". It was the simplest option, but he wasn't entirely sure Glenster would give a shit about his apology. He hadn't said it in so many words, but he had practically accused the man – a good man, a respected man, a brave man – of being a coward. Glenster's denying the possibility that David Brannon had come back to Hannerville had been irritating, possibly even idiotic given what they'd found in the Webster's woman's apartment, but he hadn't deserved to be insulted.

After assigning men to talk to Charlotte Webster's friends and family, he had gone back to Janice Mallory's place of work and asked Louie if he had heard from her. He hadn't. The man had clearly been very concerned and Flaghan had done his best to reassure him before going to Mallory's building, where he had managed to persuade Eric the superintendent to let him into Janice's apartment. The place was neat and tidy, with none of the signs of a struggle that had been found at Charlotte Webster's place. There had been no note saying she had been called away on an emergency or any such thing. There had just been a quiet, orderly apartment that had felt empty, felt as though its occupant would never return.

As he had left, Flaghan had told himself to knock that shit off. He still had no firm evidence that anything untoward had happened to Janice Mallory. In fact, for all that he'd found in her apartment, there was still no guarantee that foul play was involved in Charlotte Webster's disappearance. No evidence, but he did have a hunch, and not one he could easily dismiss either.

He and his men had been working hard the last two days, building up detailed pictures of the lives of both Janice Mallory and Charlotte Webster. Both lived alone, both had jobs where they were well liked and both of them seemed to be in no financial difficulty. They both had circles of friends and family members, all of whom were not greatly concerned for their wellbeing and who kept pestering Flaghan for updates. There seemed to be no skeletons in their closets, at least none likely to result in them pulling a vanishing act. One of Webster's friends had admitted the missing woman had smoked pot a few times, and Janice Mallory had once got herself a parking ticket. Aside from that they seemed to be model citizens. Never could tell, of course, but it didn't seem likely that they had suddenly changed into women who, at the drop of a hat and leaving no word, might have reason to flee the town.

Given what he had discovered about them, Flaghan was becoming more and more convinced that someone, maybe not Brannon but someone, had made them disappear. He still had no solid evidence, but his instincts were telling him that they weren't going to find either of the missing women alive.

The sheriff wasn't holding out any hope that the evidence collected at Charlotte Webster's apartment would shed any light. No prints of any kind had been found at the scene, but the blood samples and the shard of glass had gone for analysis at the lab in Knoxville. He didn't expect to get the results for a day or two yet.

Sitting back in his chair he closed his eyes and let his mind wander. He thought it reasonable to assume that unless their perp was an overachiever, he hadn't taken both women on the same night. Charlotte Webster had been seen during the day prior to her disappearance, so Flaghan thought it likely that Janice Mallory had been taken the night before. As yet the cases could be unrelated, but Flaghan didn't think so. No further reports of missing women had come in last night or the night before. Did that mean the developing pattern had been disturbed? Or did it mean that the pattern just wasn't as simple as a girl a night? Perhaps one girl one night, another the next, then nothing for two nights. Was it possible that someone would go missing tonight? If so, how did they prevent it? The answer: they couldn't. With no connections between the first two victims (they weren't even similar in appearance) they had nothing to go on as far as potential victims were concerned. As far as *anything* was concerned really.

Pushing his chair away from his desk, Flaghan sat up and stared at his desk drawer. He reached out, yanked it open and withdrew the slim, yellowing folder from it, one he had gone looking for in the records room the afternoon that Charlotte Webster's disappearance had been reported. He had checked their computerised records, but it had turned out that those from the early 80's and earlier had never made it onto the system. He had found it easily enough in the records room, though he had held back on looking at the contents. Sitting now with his chair drawn back up to his desk and the mildew smelling folder unopened in front of him, uncertain of how to proceed and with no leads to speak of, Flaghan decided to take a look.

There were only a few items in the file: a report written by Tim Matty, Hannerville's sheriff back in '84, several newspaper clippings detailing Brannon's killing spree and the night he had brought it to Hannerville, a photo of the house where it had all happened and a picture of a five year old Abigail Morton and her family.

Flaghan looked at the photographs, read through Matty's report and the newspaper articles. By the time he had gone over the material twice, nothing had leapt out at him. From what he could recall, no one had ever found out why Brannon had suddenly widened his hunting ground from Rutherford all the way to Sevier County, or why he had targeted the Morton family. Most just said it was the kind of unpredictable decision the mind of a madman made, but Flaghan had been hoping to find something suggesting Brannon's earlier attacks had formed a pattern. Something that might suggest what he could look for to ascertain if the sick bastard had come back to Hannerville.

He read the newspaper articles a third time. There had been no pattern to the Rutherford murders. Not even the rate at which the women had been taken matched with what was happening now. There had only been one connection between those unfortunate souls and that had been what their killer had done to them. By his own sickeningly gleeful admission, he had mentally and physically tortured them, raped them and then killed them.

Closing the folder, the sheriff slumped in his chair, sighing and rubbing his eyes. He hadn't gotten much sleep over the last couple of nights, unable to switch off from worrying about the possibility of a lunatic stalking the streets of his town. Had he put lives in danger by heeding Glenster's naysaying about Brannon being back? Then there was Glenster himself, a fence that needed mending. He and the good doctor weren't close friends, but Flaghan didn't want to leave things as they were between them.

Even as he sat there he could feel himself beginning to nod off, his tired mind aching to get some rest, if only for a few minutes. Flaghan fought it but knew he would have to get some proper sleep soon. He would be no good to anyone if he let himself get too damn tired, though as he forced his eyes wide open and took a deep breath, he suspected he may already be too damn tired. He had already had a strong cup of coffee this morning, but decided a second might be in order.

He was preparing to get out of his chair when there was a knock at his door. He called out for whoever it was to come in and Jack Parchett opened the door and stepped into the room.

"What's up, Jack?" asked the sheriff.

"We just got another report, sir."

Thanks to the young deputy's tone and expression, Flaghan didn't need to ask what the report was about. His heart sank but he rallied himself and asked,

"Who?"

"Sophie Thomas."

"Who reported her missing?"

Flaghan strode down the corridor towards the front of the station, Parchett walking fast to keep up.

"Uh, her friend, Amanda Cooper. Hasn't heard from her in a day or so, says it isn't like her to not answer either of her phones. She tried the house, didn't get an answer there either. She got worried, called it in. Sheriff?"

"Yeah?"

"Do we have a serial killer on our hands here?"

Flaghan stopped walking and turned, the young deputy stopping just short of colliding with him.

"At present we do not know what we're dealing with," said Flaghan. "We haven't even had a look into what's going on with Sophie Thomas yet, so we have utterly no idea what's going on there." He realised he was sounding a little too harsh; the kid had just been asking a question, one he didn't doubt others had on their minds. "So far we have uncovered nothing that suggests this is the work of a serial killer."

"I get that, sir, it's just…"

"We can't discount the theory, Jack, but until we have something to back it up we should do all we can to stomp down on any rumours that start to go round. They'll only make our jobs more difficult." Parchett straightened up and nodded.

"Yes, sir."

"Good man. All right, did Amanda Cooper leave an address she could be reached at?"

"She's at work. Russo's Pet Store down on Kaspeth Street."

A light rain began to fall as Flaghan got in behind the wheel of his cruiser. As he pulled out of the parking lot it became a downpour. Cursing, he put on his lights and windshield wipers and drove slowly towards downtown.

Not a religious man, the sheriff murmured a quick prayer for the missing women, and then began to wonder how long he had before the stories of a serial killer on the loose started. How long before it was not his men who were asking the question, but members of the public? Probably not long, not in a town like Hannerville. A third woman missing… *Christ!* According to Parchett, Amanda Cooper had said that she hadn't heard from her friend in a day or so. Flaghan was willing to put money on it turning out Sophie Thomas had been taken the night before last, the night after Charlotte Webster. Were they just waiting for the news that a fourth woman had gone missing last night?

An even grimmer possibility was that this could all have been prevented if only he hadn't listened to Glenster. Yes, it had been he who had promised the old man he would be discreet, if only to prevent the spread of panic throughout the town, but Charlotte Webster's apartment should have been enough. It should have been enough for him to warn people of the danger that might be in their midst, and he hadn't. He had listened to Glenster come up with this and that to explain away what should have been utterly obvious to a lawman of his experience: Charlotte Webster had been forcibly removed from the place she called home. Regardless of the possible identity of the perpetrator, he should have started alerting people then. Perhaps it might have been too late for Janice Mallory and Charlotte Webster, but it might have saved Sophie Thomas.

However, he couldn't allow the old doctor to take all of the blame. He was the sheriff, the one with the authority and the training and the experience. He should have done what he felt was right. Perhaps, despite what he had told Glenster when the man had come to him with the news that Brannon was out, the sheriff hadn't really taken it seriously enough. Yes he had mentioned to a few select people around the town to keep an eye out for anything unusual, never revealing exactly what or who it was they should be looking for, but he hadn't really believed Brannon would come back.

Or maybe you hoped he wouldn't come back, thought the sheriff. *Maybe the idea scared you just as much as it scared Philip Glenster. Maybe you thought encountering one monster in your career was enough for a small town sheriff and you didn't want to face up to the idea that you might have to confront another one. Maybe that's why you got so short with Glenster that day, accused him of cowardice; made it a little easier to deal with your own.*

It was perhaps an overly harsh criticism, brought on by his frustration and guilt, but there was some truth in it. A lesser man might have denied it, even to himself, but Flaghan did not. It was something he would need to deal with later because he became determined at that moment to ensure not another foot was put wrong during this situation, whatever the hell this situation turned out to be.

Flaghan took a deep breath and thought about his earlier conversation with Parchett. Really the only things between this being a situation they were unclear on and the hunt for a serial killer were three bodies, and Flaghan couldn't help but think that those bodies were going to be found any day now. He parked the car as close to Russo's as he could, but before he got out he put a call through to the mayor's office and asked to make an appointment to speak to him as soon as possible. Astonishingly he managed to get one for one o'clock that afternoon.

He got out, locked the car and started walking. The rain was lighter now, the air fresh and clean. The grey clouds looked as though they were shifting away, little pieces of blue showing through now. Weather wise it looked as though the day might turn out fine. Flaghan wished the outlook for everything else was as good.

The little brass bell tinkled as he entered, and again as he closed the door. Fresh air was replaced with the smell of wood shavings and small furry animals. Flaghan gazed at the numerous cages containing hamsters and gerbils and guinea pigs. Up above them were cages containing a bright collection of budgerigars, all chirping and cheeping, hopping from perch to perch or preening themselves.

Flaghan made his way down one of the aisles looking for Diane Russo, the owner of the store. He found her in the far corner, where she kept her fish. She was explaining something to a customer. When she noticed him, she excused herself and came over.

"Hey, sheriff. Amanda's in the back." She motioned to a door behind the nearby sales counter. "She's a little upset, but her friend Beth's with her. Go on through."

"Thanks, Diane."

Russo went back to her customer and Flaghan made his way behind the counter and through the door, finding two women seated on a small couch in a little staff room.

"Amanda?" he asked, standing in the doorway. One of the two, an attractive young woman with shoulder length black hair and dark eyes, who looked to be in her late twenties, looked up at him. The skin around her lovely eyes was red from crying and her mascara was smudged a little, but she sniffed, stood up and extended her hand as he stepped inside. He took her hand and introduced himself.

"I'm Amanda Cooper," she said, her voice a little squeaky. She cleared her throat before introducing her friend. "This is Beth Hayes. We're both friends of Sophie's."

Flaghan nodded to Beth and gestured for Amanda to return to her seat. He closed the door and pulled over a chair, sitting down in front of them.

"I won't take up much of your time," he told them. "But would either of you like to get a drink?" They both shook their heads. He took out is notebook and pen. "In your own time, tell me what's happened."

133

"Our friend Sophie," began Beth. "We haven't seen or heard from her since the night before last."

"And that's not like her?"

"No," answered Amanda. "It's not like her not to show up for work either."

"Where does she work?"

"She's the manager of Gowder's Hardware Store, just down the street," Amanda told him. "She worked her ass off to get that job; she wouldn't jeopardise it by just not showing up without so much as calling in."

"We don't live in one another's pockets, sheriff," said Beth. "But we usually text each other at least once a day, see how things are going, make sure everyone's okay, you know?" Flaghan nodded, scribbling notes. "I text Sophie yesterday but didn't get a reply. I didn't think much of it until early last night, when Amanda asked me if I'd heard from Sophie yesterday. I said I hadn't." Amanda took up the story.

"I got worried and tried calling her, but I didn't get an answer. I wanted to call you last night, but Beth said we should wait, try and reach her at work this morning. I couldn't wait; we went round to her house this morning, but couldn't get an answer. We asked at her work and no one there had heard from her since she left the night before last."

"Do either of you know where she went that night after work?" Amanda was dabbing at her eyes with a wadded tissue, so Beth answered.

"She was with us; we went for drinks."

"Where did you go?"

"Tarker's Bar."

"I know it," Flaghan told them. It was a popular place with a good reputation. "Any trouble there that night?" Beth shook her head.

"It was fine. We had a few drinks, talked about stuff. No one bothered us. Eventually we left. I went home."

"I walked with Sophie as far as I could before I had to take a different route to get home," said Amanda. "There was nothing weird, no one hanging around. She didn't have that far to go when I left her…"

She stopped talking and wept, sobbing, turning to her friend and burying her face against Beth's shoulder. Beth put an arm around her, patted her on the back and told her that Sophie was going to be okay. Flaghan gave them a few moments, then asked:

"Did Sophie have any enemies? Old boyfriend with a grudge, something like that?"

"No. I mean, she has old boyfriends, but there were never any weird ones."

"What about family?"

"Not in Hannerville. I think her Mom and Dad live in Florida, and I think she has a brother but I'm not sure where he lives."

Flaghan nodded, scribbled, hoped he'd be able to read the chicken scratches later. When he was finished he asked them for their contact information so he could get in touch if he found anything out. Both women gave him their cell phone numbers and he wrote them down, then closed his notebook and put it away. He got to his feet.

"I won't tell you to try not to worry; you wouldn't be her friends if you weren't worried that you can't get a hold of her. But I'll do my best to find out where she's got to…"

"Sheriff," began Beth hesitantly. "I've heard a couple of rumours about women going missing."

Flaghan all but heard the buzzer signalling that his grace period was over.

"Heard from whom, Beth?"

"Just some people who've come into the bookstore."

"Bookstore?"

"I work at Pages and Pages; I'm running things for a little while to give Abigail some free time."

She continued talking, but Flaghan heard little of what she said. The buzzer in his head shifted tone, got louder and louder until it was a blaring klaxon, one that came with its own spinning red bubble light.

"Uh," he interrupted Beth. "Abigail? Abigail Morton?" Beth nodded. "She's friends with Sophie too?" Another nod. An internal monologue comprised of rapidly spoken curse words rattled off in his head, but he kept his game face on. "You're all close friends?"

"Pretty close, yeah."

"Is Sophie maybe with Abigail then?"

"No," Amanda answered him. "Abigail's with a... friend."

"Does she know that Sophie is missing?" Amanda shook her head.

"We've tried calling, but to be honest we didn't expect an answer."

That they can't get an answer is all the reason I need.

"Okay, well, I'll maybe pop by to ask if Abigail's heard from her. Even if she hasn't it's probably best she be told."

Beth and Amanda both nodded up at him and thanked him. Before Beth could return to the subject of rumours, he told them they knew how to reach him if Sophie contacted them and left.

On his way back to the car, Flaghan lamented that the rumour mill wasn't just gearing up; it was already churning out product. Hell, the kidnappings had happened in such rapid succession that not even the town paper had printed anything about them, but that would change now. The story, or whatever rumours and half-truths the reporter given the story could get between now and when the paper went to press, would be on the front page of The Hannerville Post tomorrow morning. The silver lining was that all this might convince the mayor to agree to an emergency town meeting being organised as soon as possible, so they could set the record straight.

When he got back to his cruiser he radioed the station and asked Parchett to go to Sophie Thomas's place of work and ask some questions. The deputy asked where he was going and was told that he was going to ask Abigail Morton if she had heard from her friend before going to check out the missing woman's house.

He didn't mention he was going to pick someone up first.

Chapter 25

Philip Glenster had heard the rumours slowly circulating around Hannerville as well, and they worried him greatly. He had stood at his telephone several times since the last time he had spoken to Mark Flaghan, thinking about picking it up, dialling his number and apologising.

Glenster had been stung by Flaghan's words that day, mostly because there was an element of truth to them. Glenster did not want to believe that the monster he had confronted all those years ago had come back to town. Indeed, there was as yet nothing to indicate he had. The rumours were of women going missing, not showing up raped and murdered. But nonetheless it had been a possibility, one the townspeople should have been made aware of. Yes it was going to be difficult for poor Abigail, but she had friends who would help her through it.

The rumours, passed along to him by Anne, whom had been told about them by her friend, Tracy Gellet, passing them on from whoever had been the latest link in the chain before her, haunted him. If only he had insisted that the Sheriff inform the town about Brannon being on the loose when it had happened. In truth, the fact that Flaghan seemed to have it all under control had been a relief to him; it meant he could pass things on and not have to worry about them. But Flaghan hadn't been there that night, he didn't know. He hadn't looked into that mad bastard's eyes and noticed the utter lack of anything even remotely resembling a soul or a conscience. He, Philip Glenster, had, and if he hadn't been so damn cowardly then poor Janice Mallory, most likely the first in a new spate of victims, might never have been taken. But other than the fact that she had vanished, they'd had no reason to suspect foul play.

The same could not be said after what they had discovered at Charlotte Webster's apartment. There had been clear signs of a struggle and he had done his best to deny it.

He did not yet know of Sophie's disappearance, and so in the end Glenster came to a similar conclusion to Flaghan: they might not have been able to help Janice Mallory or Charlotte Webster, but if they had acted as soon as they could on what they'd discovered in that apartment, perhaps further vanishings could be avoided.

Or maybe not; Brannon was just the type to go out hunting when he knew lots of people were looking for him. To cut one of them down as he hunted would be a bonus for him.

Seated in his armchair, elbows on the armrests, head down, the apex of the steeple of his index fingers pressed against his lips, Glenster considered going to see the sheriff. This couldn't go on. He should go down there, tell Flaghan that he had been quite right to call him a coward, and then set about helping to catch whoever it was who was stalking the streets of Hannerville. After all there was still no guarantee that it was Brannon, but if it turned out to be then he was just going to have to deal with that as best he could. He owed as much to Janice Mallory and Charlotte Webster.

Anne Glenster entered the room, saw her husband, recognised the pose, the expression: still deliberating. He had talked things over with her, shared his thoughts and feelings, his fears. As always she had listened patiently and counselled wisely. She knew it was only a matter of time before he did the right thing and went to see Mark Flaghan, but he had to come to that decision himself. Philip had never been one of those doctors who felt above everyone else, the way some of them could get. She'd met a few of them in her time, fools who thought their acquired knowledge made them better than everyone, never wrong about anything. Philip quite rightly had faith in his medical training and his abilities, but he knew that in other areas he might not be the font of all knowledge. He could be set in his ways about things, stubborn, aware that how he did things might not be the best way, but it was his way and so that was how he would do it. Like using a knife to open a plug to change the fuse, when there was a toolbox with a screwdriver in it sitting in the garage, or standing on a chair to put a nail in the wall to hang a picture, when right beside the darn toolbox in the garage was a set of stepladders. But when it came to the important things, when it mattered, Philip Glenster knew enough to listen to the thoughts of others, to make a gain from what they knew. She knew what she would have done in his shoes, but he wore those shoes and so when they walked, he had to be the one giving directions. The last time David Brannon had been in Hannerville, Anne had almost lost her husband. She was deathly afraid of what might occur had that insane fiend come back to their town. She had told Philip as much, had seen the relief on his face that he was not alone in his dread. He was a proud man, but he'd never been afraid to admit when he'd been wrong, or when he'd been afraid, at least not to her.

He was her husband and she loved him more than anyone else on the face of the planet, and it pained her to see him still wrangling with himself over this business. But she would endure it, as she had done in the past, even though she knew time may well be a factor. To do anything else would be to break one of the tenets of their relationship. Anne just had to have faith that he would work it out in his head soon and do what needed to be done.

Luckily, faith in her husband was something she had in abundance.

Glenster looked up, saw his wife in the doorway and smiled. He knew she was wondering exactly how long it was going to take him to get his damn fool head together and sort this out. Not that she'd ask him, of course.

Anne returned his smile and walked away towards the kitchen. Philip grabbed the hem of his pullover, along with a wad of the undershirt he was wearing, and pulled. The undergarment pulled free of his waistband and he lifted both, exposing his stomach. Running across his paunch was the scar, faint but still visible after all this time. The lifelong reminder of the night Brannon had opened him up with a kitchen knife, intent on watching his guts spill out. The wound had bled, but hadn't been deep enough to cause what Brannon had wanted to happen. The bastard had been moving in for the kill when the police had burst in the door. Glenster could recall his hands being warm and red, bright lights and harsh voices and then nothing. He had awoken in hospital several hours later to be told that he was going to be fine. He'd lost a lot of blood, but other than the scar he would be fine.

The scar was more than enough.

In the years after that night he had taken to using Anne's make-up to cover it so neither of them would have to see it and be reminded. Eventually he stopped doing that for two reasons: his wife was fed up with him pilfering her cosmetics, and neither of them actually looked at it anymore. It simply became something that they both ignored. Of course he never let anyone else see him with his shirt off, but the scar, and its effect on them both, had faded.

Looking at it now, what with everything that was going on, Glenster could almost see the blood oozing from the wound.

He tucked his undershirt back in, pulled his pullover down and got out of his chair.

No more dicking around, you old asshole, he told himself.

He was in the doorway, about to call to Anne, when the doorbell rang.

Philip answered it, finding Sheriff Flaghan on his doorstep.

"Mark," he blurted in surprise. "I... Aw, hell, you won't believe this but I was just about to come and see you." The sheriff nodded.

"Mind if I come in?"

"Not at all."

137

He opened the door and stood aside and Flaghan entered. As Glenster closed the door, his wife appeared at the end of the hall, asking who it had been. She stopped short when she saw the tall figure of the town sheriff beside her husband.

"Mark," she said in greeting, her eyes quickly flitting from his sombre face to her husband, who nodded and motioned for her to join them as he ushered the sheriff into the living room.

Flaghan declined the offer of a seat, stating that he wouldn't take up much of their time. True to his word, he got straight to the point.

"It was unfair of me to say what I said the last time we spoke, Phil. I hope you'll accept my apology."

Glenster, who had sat down on the couch beside his wife, got up again, approached the sheriff and extended a hand.

"You have nothing to apologise for, Mark; you were quite correct. I was being a damn coward. No more of it, though. As I say, I was on my way to come to tell you just that, and to apologise to you. I put you in a bad position, and I am truly sorry."

"Think it's safe to say we both did ourselves no favours, Phil," said Flaghan, gripping his hand and shaking it.

"Is there anything I can do to help?" asked Glenster.

"Maybe so. Have either of you heard the rumours?" The Glensters both nodded. "Thought so. Well, I don't know what particular rumours are going around, but the facts of the matter are that Janice Mallory still hasn't been heard from and neither has Charlotte Webster. Nothing out of the ordinary was found at Mallory's apartment, but there were the signs in Webster's apartment that… uh…"

"That something had happened and someone had tidied up after themselves," Glenster finished for him. "And I made up all kinds of nonsense when the plain facts were there to be seen. Even if it's not Brannon, I should have been encouraging you to go public, not to…"

"Philip," said Anne softly. "There will be time for self-recrimination later. Let Mark finish." Her husband looked to her, smiled, nodded and then asked their guest to go on.

"We got word this morning that someone else may have gone missing, a woman named Sophie Thomas. A couple of her friends were worried that they hadn't heard from her despite their calls and texts. They went to her house but got no answer, so they called it in. I've got a deputy asking questions at her workplace right now. I've just come from speaking to the two friends who called it in. Phil, they told me that Sophie Thomas is a close friend of Abigail Morton."

"You found nothing to suggest that the others were connected to Abigail in any way?"

"No, but I think it might be time we had a chat with her."

Glenster, grim faced, nodded and then went to get his coat.

Anne saw them both to the door. As the sheriff walked out to his car, her husband turned to her and said,

"If you need me, call me. Otherwise I'll see you when I get back. I don't know how long I'll be."

"I'll be here waiting for you," she told him, then leaned forward and kissed him gently on the lips. "I love you, Philip."

"I love you too, Anne."

He turned, zipped up his coat against the spitting rain, and strode briskly to the sheriff's idling car.

"Do you have any idea what her reaction might be to having all of this brought up again after so long?" asked the sheriff as he drove through town.

"Not really," Glenster answered honestly. "Psychology wasn't my field. Bear in mind though that this is a young woman who went through a horribly traumatic experience. To the best of my knowledge she's never visited a psychiatrist or used any kind of medication."

"How good is the best of your knowledge?"

"Well, I don't know if you'd say we're friends. Perhaps the only thing we have in common is that we both survived something hellish, and both of us managed to get on with our lives. I kept my ear to the ground for news about her. I remember how proud she was the day she opened her bookstore. How she smiled when I went up to the counter. I was her first customer. I remember being so happy for her." The wistful little smile vanished from his lips. "I had to watch him do such awful things to those people, and I was completely unable to do anything about it. I suffered horrible nightmares after that night, Mark, and I had to deal with a lot of guilt over not having been able to help, and over surviving that night. It took a lot of time and support, and more strength and power of will than I ever would have given myself credit for, but I got there. However Abigail managed to get to where she is now, we're about to dig up a past I suspect she has buried very, very deep. She was strong enough to come through it before; I have to hope she'll be strong enough to face what we have to tell her."

"I hope the town is too." The sheriff caught Glenster's confused look and elaborated. "I've got an appointment with the mayor in a little while. I'm going to outline the situation for him and tell him we need to hold an emergency town meeting to let people know. The rumours are already out there, but I'd like to see them stopped before there's a panic."

"You don't imagine the news will cause a panic? Or perhaps disturb whoever has taken the women? What if they're still alive?"

"The main problem is we could tie ourselves in knots asking questions we can't find the answers to, like the ones you just asked. The news might cause a panic, it might make the kidnapper skittish and cause him to hurt his victims, who might well be still alive. But I have to consider those who haven't been taken yet, who might be saved by everyone knowing what the danger is, even if they don't know who it is." He paused. "I don't like saying, or even thinking it, but I don't imagine there's a lot of hope we'll find alive those who've already been taken."

"You mean he took the second because the first one was dead, the third because he killed the second, and so on?" Flaghan nodded, his mouth turned down.

"I'm a strong believer in the idea that assumptions make an ass out of you and me."

"I go by the belief that assumption is the mother of all fuck-ups, but go on." Flaghan smiled briefly.

"All we've got right now are assumptions. Let's assume this bastard is a serial killer, some dickhead out to hunt on the same turf as the notorious David Brannon. Usually they don't go after one victim until the previous one is dead. That means our first two victims are dead and the third one may be as well; to be honest I wouldn't be surprised to get a call informing me that another woman went missing last night. Mind you, it could be that this asshole is just a mad kidnapper, intent on, I don't know, building a harem or something."

"Keeping three women alive together would make things a lot riskier for him."

"We don't know they're together; they might be held in different places, which would also be risky for him. But then such a series of kidnappings isn't something I've ever heard of before." He blew out a harsh breath. "We just don't know anything about this guy, Phil, that's the bottom line. We don't have shit. All we do know is that three women have gone missing, possibly on three consecutive nights, which is a terrible thing. But if those three are the start of a pattern then this is a situation that almost doesn't bear thinking about. But I have to because that's my job. Now it's very possible that I'm wrong in that I don't think it's coincidental that there's a connection between the latest victim and the only other survivor of the last mad bastard who came to Hannerville with murder in mind, however from here on out I am taking no chances. She's got to be warned. Everyone has to be warned."

"Amen to that," murmured Glenster.

Chapter 26

Abigail screamed and thrashed on the bed, the duvet flying up into the air and landing half on/half off the mattress. Her arms flailed and she lashed out with her feet, but Martin hung on and continued tickling her sole.

"There's nothing wrong with my stomach, is there Abigail?"

"Marty!" she wailed. "This isn't fair!"

"I have fantastic washboard abs, don't I, Abigail."

"Oh, you do not! You… Oh, no, don't…" He tickled harder and she shrieked.

"I have fantastic washboard abs, don't I, Abigail."

She held out for another few seconds, but then eventually caved.

"Yes!" she yelled. "You've got the abs of a body builder, now let me go!"

He dropped her foot and got out of the way, giving her a cat-that-got-the-cream grin. She lay on the bed, panting, dragging the cover back over herself. Martin began striking body building poses and she glared at him.

"All I said was you were getting a bit of a paunch, you big pansy." He stopped posing and slapped both hands against his burgeoning paunch.

"Nothing here but pure Scottish beefcake." He narrowed his eyes. "Now I think about it, people often insult the way others look because they're insecure about how they look themselves. I wonder… Might you be getting a saggy bum and that led to your grievous insult?"

"I do not have a saggy bum!"

"Don't believe you. Going to have to check for myself."

He dashed towards the bed, diving under the cover. Abigail laughed as he flipped her over and started drumming on her buttocks.

"I don't know," he said, his voice slightly muffled. "Seems a bit wobbly to me."

"That's it!"

She turned herself over, swatting at the writhing mass under the cover. Martin yelled and started making his way up, nipping and biting at her as he went. She was still swatting as he licked his way over her breasts. She stopped when he was lying on top of her, kissing her. The moment he broke contact she gave him a gentle swat to the crotch. As he let out a low groan, complaining that that was an underhanded and rotten thing to have done, she giggled and pushed him off her, got out of bed and headed for the shower.

Ten minutes later, as she rinsed the suds from her hair, Abigail grinned as she saw the indistinct shape through the misty glass of the shower cubicle.

"You know," came Martin's voice. "If I wanted to be really evil, I could flush the toilet."

"You could," she agreed. "But then I'd have to jump out of here and kick your ass."

There was a brief silence, followed by,

"Come and get me."

Abigail opened her mouth to protest, but she heard the toilet flush and a moment later the water from the showerhead turned from perfectly warm to ice cold. Her protest became a gasp and she shoved open the door, shouting out Martin's name. He was standing in the middle of the bathroom waiting for her. She yelped as she ran into him, her arms going over his shoulders. His hands slid across her wet back down to her buttocks and squeezed. He pulled her to him and kissed her, a deep, hungry kiss. Her first thought was to bring her knee up into his groin, but it got lost amidst the sudden burst of lust she experienced and together they both sank slowly to the floor.

"I'm going to get you back, you know," she told him later as they lay beside one another.

"If it's anything like the way you just got back at me now," he said, the smile on his face evident in his voice. "I can't wait."

They were silent for a short while, and then Abigail spoke.

"It's never been like this for me before."

"Like what?"

"Like… *this.* Waking up to playfulness in bed and sex on the bathroom floor. I should have wanted to kick your ass for freezing me in the shower, but the moment our lips met I just wanted to screw your brains out."

"Mission accomplished."

"I can hear you smiling, you know."

"Why shouldn't I smile?" he asked, sliding his arm out from under her neck and raising himself on one elbow. "I'm lying here with a woman who has been my friend most of my life, a woman I fell in love with before I had even been in the same room with her. Now I'm not only in the same room, I've just had wild, amazing sex with her on her bathroom floor. Why on earth wouldn't I be smiling?" Abigail grinned sheepishly. "Oh, don't go getting shy on me now," he told her, casting an appreciative eye down the length of her damp, naked body. "So this morning isn't the way your other relationships have played out: isn't that a good thing?"

"Yes" she said without hesitation. "I guess I'm just waiting for something to go wrong. For you to confess you have a wife and kids, or you're running from creditors or something. Or for me to make a mess of it…"

"Hey," Martin said sternly. "Enough. I am not married, I have no children, I'm not running from anybody, and you're not going to make a mess of anything."

"But it all just seems to have become so perfect so easily."

"That's because we've spent the last twenty-odd years laying the ground work. There's nothing we don't know about each other, so that period of the relationship where we would have spent time learning all about one another didn't have to happen."

"But doesn't that mean we've skipped over a fairly integral part of the whole relationship process?"

"There's no prescribed route for a relationship to take, Abi. We know everything we need to know, but we've never really shared anything person to person. Now we can. All those memories and stories we've written down over the years, we can actually tell to one another, doing bad impressions of our friends and relatives and all that. Plus we'll be making new memories together. Memories full of good stuff."

"Like you tickling my feet, me hitting your balls, and then you showering me with cold water?"

"Yes!" Martin laughed. "Daft little things like that are the nuts and bolts that hold relationships together. You see an elderly couple walking down the street hand in hand, I guarantee you they started their day with him making her laugh, her touching him in an intimate place and…"

"Getting clean and dirty at the same time?"

"Exactly."

They smiled at one another and then Marty told her,

"I hate to break the moment, but I have to get up; this floor's bloody freezing."

They dried off and got dressed, Abigail in shorts, a T-shirt and her bathrobe, Martin in the clothes from the night before last. He intended to go back to the cabin to get showered and changed after breakfast.

They ate, chatting about what they might do later today, and had just finished cleaning the dishes when there was a knock at the door. Martin began putting the dishes away as

Abigail went to answer it. When she did, and saw the man she would always refer to as Doctor Glenster standing there with Sheriff Flaghan, she recalled her earlier words about something going wrong, and wondered for a second if by saying it she had caused it to happen. When she did not speak, Glenster said,

"Good morning, Abigail. May we come in?"

"Uh, yes, sure."

She opened the door and let them in. Closing the door, she showed them to the living room, invited them to take a seat and asked them to give her a moment. She went back to the kitchen, where Martin was waiting for her.

"What's wrong?" he asked as soon as he saw her.

"Doctor Glenster's here," she told him. "And the sheriff's with him."

"Did they say why?"

"No."

"Do you want me to come in with you?"

"Yes."

"Okay."

He took her hand and she led him back into the living room, where a tall man in uniform and an older man both rose to their feet as they entered.

"Uh, this is my partner: Martin. Martin, this is Sheriff Flaghan and Doctor Glenster."

Martin stepped forward, extending a hand first to the sheriff and then to the doctor, who pointed out as he shook it that he was retired.

"Are you new in town, Mr..?"

"Muir," Martin filled in the blank. "And, uh, no, sheriff, I'm actually just visiting town."

"From across the sea," said Glenster. "Scotland, am I correct?"

"You are, sir."

"Let's sit down," said Abigail. "And you can tell me why you're both here."

The visitors nodded and took their seats. Martin and Abigail sat beside one another on the couch, his arm around her, holding her close. There was an uncomfortable silence, broken when Abigail asked if something had happened to her aunt or uncle.

"No," answered the sheriff. Martin felt Abigail relax slightly. "Abigail, I'm sorry, but it appears your friend Sophie Thomas has gone missing." There was silence for several moments, and when no questions were forthcoming, he continued. "As best we can tell, she was last seen the night before last at Tarker's Bar. She was there with Beth Hayes and Amanda Cooper. Beth walked home alone, Amanda walked as far as she could with Sophie before they parted ways. Neither one of them heard from her yesterday, they grew concerned, went to her house this morning but got no answer, so they called us. Have you heard from Sophie at all, Abigail?"

"Let me check."

She rose from her seat and on stiff legs wandered over to where her handbag sat on the floor. She knelt down, rummaged inside and came out with her cell phone, which she checked. She shook her head as she stood up.

"Can you think of anywhere she might go, or anywhere she said she might be thinking of going that Beth and Amanda may have forgotten?"

Abigail shook her head again as she made her way back to her seat.

"No," she said, sitting back down. "Last minute trips like that aren't her style, and she's really good at keeping in touch." She looked at the sheriff. "Do you have any ideas at all?"

Flaghan glanced over at Glenster, then back to Abigail.

"Have you heard the rumours going around town in the last day or so?"

"About what?"

"I'll take that as a no." He took a deep breath. "Sophie is the third woman to go missing in the last four days. The first two were Janice Mallory and Charlotte Webster. Do those names ring any bell?"

"No. What happened to them?"

"At the moment all we know is that they've gone missing."

"Are you thinking they've been kidnapped, sheriff?" asked Martin.

"That's one possibility. But there is another, which is why Mr Glenster is here with me today."

Abigail and Martin's attention shifted to the former doctor, who sat forward, a serious expression on his face.

"Abigail, it's possible that the man responsible for the missing women is David Brannon." Abigail gasped.

"You mean the serial killer who attacked a family in this town in the early eighties?"

Glenster looked at Flaghan, who looked back at him with utter astonishment on his face. Of all the possible reactions they had each considered to the news they had come to deliver, this had not been among them.

"Uh, yes, Abigail," Glenster went on. "Now, please understand that we have no evidence that Brannon is the one responsible for these missing women, but it is possible that he may have come back to Hannerville. Though we are, as I say, by no means certain it's him, we thought that due to what you went through it would be best to warn you."

Martin frowned, wondering what the elderly gent was talking about. What Abigail went through? He could recall nothing in any of her letters that harked back to an encounter with a serial killer, which seemed to be what the man was alluding to, and that was something he would not have forgotten. Even as these thoughts went through his head, Abigail said,

"What I went through? What are you talking about, Doctor Glenster?"

Glenster was at a complete loss. Possibilities flitted through his mind, but this was neither the time nor the place to try to find out if any of them were correct. He looked to Flaghan, who was staring at Abigail, also clearly dumfounded. Swallowing hard, Glenster decided to call a halt. They had given her their warning and for the time being that would have to do.

"Nothing at all; I must be confusing you with someone else. We'll be calling a town meeting to spread the correct information as widely as possible in one go," he said. "Attend if you can. Also, keep an eye out around town for anyone acting suspiciously." Abigail nodded.

"If you'll all excuse me, I need to go and get dressed; I should go see Amanda and Beth." The three men all rose from their seats as she left the room. An awkward silence descended.

"So," Martin began tentatively, directing his attention the sheriff. "You really think there's a chance this Brannon character has come back?"

"We don't know for certain, Mr Muir. We're not sure of a number of things. You say you're just visiting town?"

"Visiting Abigail. It's a bit of a long story, but I arrived here a couple of days ago. I'm staying for a fortnight."

"You and Miss Morton have a prior relationship."

"We've been pen-friends for years…"

"Oh my," said an astonished Glenster. "You're the young boy she started writing to all those years ago?" Martin nodded. "I remember her coming into my office once; she had a very bad sore throat. During the examination she told me about writing to a kid in Scotland. I never would have believed the two of you would still be communicating all these years later. And now the two of you are together?"

"Yes," smiled Martin.

"And that's why you came to Hannerville?" asked the sheriff. "To meet with Miss Morton again?"

"For the first time," Martin corrected him. "To cut a long story short I realised I wanted to meet her because I'd fallen for her. I asked her if I could come over and she said yes. I finally told her how I felt and she said she felt the same way."

"And when was this?"

"Uh, when we got together? The night before last. I invited her up to the cabin I'm staying at for dinner and…"

"I'm not sure I like you asking my boyfriend all these questions, sheriff," said Abigail from the doorway. "Seems to me you might be suspicious of him."

Martin looked over his shoulder at her as she walked in.

"What? No, he couldn't…" He looked back at Flaghan, held his gaze for a second or two. "Oh, you do."

"Well you can forget it, Sheriff Flaghan," Abigail said sternly as she took her seat. "Marty has nothing to do with this and…"

"Abi, it's okay." She stopped talking and looked at him. He met her gaze and grinned. "Honestly, it is. The man's just doing his job. Women are missing and I'm a stranger in town; his suspicion is perfectly logical." He looked to the sheriff. "All I can tell you is that I had nothing to do with it, sir. I met Sophie very briefly a couple of days ago at Abi's bookshop. That was the first and last time I saw her. I honestly wish I could be of more help."

Flaghan nodded.

"I have to go," said Abigail. "Martin, I'm sorry but I need to go see Amanda and Beth."

"It's all right. Let me just grab my stuff and call a taxi…"

"I'd be more than happy to drive you to wherever you're going, Mr Muir."

"Oh. Thank you, sheriff; that would be great."

With that he went upstairs to collect his wallet and phone. During the time he was absent, Glenster eyed Abigail with concern. The sheriff was the subject of her clearly annoyed stare.

"I know Marty was right in what he said about why you were suspicious, but I can't help being really pissed off about it. It wasn't very hospitable, sheriff."

"I know, Abigail, but three women are missing; I don't have the luxury of being hospitable to anyone right now."

Martin came back down and the four of them left the house. Abigail locked the door and she and Martin hung back as Glenster and Flaghan walked to the sheriff's car.

"I'm so sorry about this," Abigail told Martin, who shook his head.

"I've got a lift back, so don't worry. Go see your friends. I'll go get showered and changed. When you get back give me a call."

"You'll come back?"

"Of course I'll come back."

They shared a brief hug and kiss and then parted company.

Chapter 27

When they were on their way, Flaghan asked Martin,

"How well do you know Abigail Morton?"

"Very well; she and I have been writing letters to one another since we were children."

There was silence for several minutes. Martin caught glances going between the two men in the front seats and realised there was something they wanted to ask him. The sudden twinge of nervousness felt odd, as he knew for a fact that he had nothing to do with what the sheriff and former doctor were investigating. His mind seized on that: why was the elderly doctor assisting the sheriff? His thoughts whirled, coming into focus and presenting him with the image of the two men looking bemused, a snapshot of their expressions in the moments after there had been mention of something Abigail had gone through. Abigail hadn't known what the doctor had been talking about, and this was obviously what had puzzled both men. For all his knowledge of Abigail's past, Martin recalled that he too had been left wondering what event in Abigail's life the doctor had been referring to.

That was when he realised that they didn't want to ask him about the missing women; they wanted to ask him about this event involving Abigail, the one they had referenced but that she had not picked up on. This thought had barely crossed his mind when the sheriff enquired,

"Mr Muir, please don't think I'm prying here, but did Abigail ever mention to you something that happened to her when she was a child?"

"Can you be more specific?"

"I think that answers my question," was the sheriff's cryptic response. He then fell silent. Martin waited and when no further comments were made, he sat forward.

"Doctor Glenster, sheriff, I understand why you might have been, and might still be, suspicious of me. But if something's going on here that has to do with Abigail, something that might put her in danger, then I am asking you to tell me what it is."

The sheriff looked over at Glenster, who stared out of the windshield. Eventually he sighed.

"Before I begin, Mr Muir, know that I have not spoken of this in almost thirty years, and I will do so today because of my concern for Abigail. And please understand that she may not have told you about what I am about to tell you because she has buried the truth deep in her mind. It is not necessarily a reflection on her feelings for you, or whether or not she trusts you."

Confused but intrigued, Martin responded with a nod and a quiet, "Okay."

Glenster took a deep breath, held it for a few seconds and then let it out slowly.

"On the night of June fifteenth, nineteen eighty-four, in a little town called Juller Creek over in Rutherford County, a thirty-one year old woman by the name of Susan Clarky went missing from her apartment. Her body was found a few days later; she had been raped and murdered. Not long after that, another young woman named Clarissa Fielders vanished. Few days later they found her body. She too had been raped and murdered. The night she was found, a third girl went missing. When she was found, the police officially declared that they were looking for a serial killer. Towns all over the county lived in fear for three months. During that time, another ten women went missing, and all of them were later found dead. All of them had been raped, some of them repeatedly, prior to being murdered. The largest manhunt the county has ever seen was mounted, but the perpetrator was not found.

"Then, on the night of October second, nineteen eighty-four, for reasons no one has ever managed to work out, David Brannon came to Hannerville.

"He broke into the Morton house just after eleven o'clock at night. Surprising Ross and Alice Morton in their beds, he knocked them both out, dragged them downstairs and tied them to chairs from around their dining table. He gagged them and then went back upstairs, into their five year old daughter's room; into Abigail's room."

Martin, who had been holding his breath since hearing the names Ross and Alice Morton, breathed out in a quiet gasp.

"He picked up the sleeping child, who stayed sleeping all the way downstairs. She only woke up when he sat her in a chair and started tying her to it. When all three of the Mortons were tied securely to chairs, he went through their house. Later, when he was arrested, nothing was found on him, but he ransacked their cupboards and drawers downstairs, their wardrobes and dressers upstairs. Clothes were ripped and slashed, mirrors shattered, framed photographs torn off walls and smashed, boxes of photographs and all of the family's albums were torn up, spat on... pissed on even. When he came back downstairs, he seemed to be seething with rage, so much so that he picked up a little porcelain figurine off the mantle and threw it through one of the front windows.

"I was on my way home from a house call when that little figurine shattered against the driver's side door of my car.

"I hit my brakes, pulled into the kerb, shut off my engine and got out. There was a small dent, and it didn't take me long to find the cause. I looked up at the Morton house and saw the smashed window. If I had done the smart thing and called the police, maybe things would have turned out differently. But I walked up to the front door, knocked and before I knew it the door had been pulled open and I had been yanked inside. I was released, fell forward and I heard the door close just before something hit me on the back of the head and I was knocked out.

"When I regained consciousness, I was tied to a dining chair. I looked around at the members of the Morton family. I saw the complete terror in their eyes. They were all crying. Then I noticed the blood. Both Alice and Ross had been nicked here and there, not mortal wounds, but they must have hurt like hell. More so when that rat bastard Brannon came back and started literally pouring salt in their wounds. They screamed against their gags, struggled against their bonds, but he had them tied tight. I wept, Mr Muir, wept with fear and frustration. I'm not ashamed to admit my tears were caused more by the former rather than the latter. I watched him hurt those good people, right there in front of their little girl. I closed my eyes, but just listening to them trying to scream, to him laughing and taunting them, was even worse. He went on and on about how they had tried to hide her from him, that that was why he was doing these things to them. That was when he gestured to Abigail with his knife and I realised that he hadn't touched her at all. I actually managed to escape my situation for a brief few moments as I wondered why that might be. I came back to myself when he crossed the room, stuck his face right in Abigail's and started yelling at her, asking her what made her think she could escape from him, *ever* escape from him. He said something about already having met her little boyfriend, about killing his parents and how he was going to go back later and finish the little prince off when he decided he'd suffered enough. Abigail was terrified. So was I. Then Brannon suddenly stopped. He became very calm and he walked back across the room. He slapped me up the side of the head as he passed, called me a meddling prick, and then he walked over to Ross Morton and slit his throat. Abigail bellowed against her gag. I screamed. That son of a bitch smiled at each of us in turn and then stabbed Alice in the heart and twisted the knife.

"He left the handle sticking out of her chest and walked out of the room.

"I started to struggle against the ropes holding me to the chair. Dear god, I had never put that much physical effort into anything before, and I haven't done since. I didn't care if the bastard heard me; I wanted him to come back. I was convinced that the heady combination of my fear and my righteous fury would allow me to despatch him to whatever, hopefully painful, afterlife awaited him. I tugged at ropes, rocked the chair left and right, stood up as far as I could and slammed it down onto the floor. All the time I avoided looking across at the bodies of Ross and Alice. I focussed on Abigail, who did not take her eyes off her parents. She had fallen silent by then, the tears still coursing down her red cheeks. Eventually I snapped the back of the chair, loosened the ropes enough to free myself. I ran over to Abigail and untied her. As I scooped her out of that chair – she was limp in my arms – I heard the sirens. Faint, but getting louder. I headed for the front door, got it open and was ushering Abigail outside when Brannon bellowed. I shoved the girl out, slammed the door shut and turned to see that madman rushing at me. He slashed with the knife he had pulled back out of Alice Morton, catching me right across the belly. He threw me aside and I landed on the floor. When he opened the front door I heard the sirens right outside, could see the red and blue lights flashing. Brannon shouted Abigail's name, and then I heard the officers telling him to drop the knife. He slammed the door shut and ran for the back of the house.

"They caught him. Chased him down and arrested him. I found out later they had received an anonymous call telling them that the Rutherford County Killer was at the Morton's house. They were none too tender with him. By the time they were putting him into the back of the car, they had found me lying bleeding in the hallway, Ross and Alice dead in the living room. Brannon arrived at the station with a few new cuts and bruises.

"After the trial he was committed to the Berrybeck Hospital for the Criminally Insane. There wasn't a peep from him in almost twenty-eight years. About four months ago I found out that Berrybeck had become a rehab centre for people with more money than sense. Someone had paid for Brannon to stay on there after the building had changed hands. The person who told me that also told me that Brannon had vacated the premises, killing several people and setting fire to the place. He vanished. I prayed and prayed that he wouldn't come back to Hannerville, but…"

"We don't know it's him, Phil," said the sheriff softly.

"No, we don't," said Glenster, nodding. "But I have a felling, a bad one. Means nothing of course, but I can't get rid of it." He turned in his seat and looked at Martin, who was in complete shock. "Abigail proved to be very strong, resilient. She got over what happened and made a life for herself, a good one. I owe her an apology; I should have told her about Brannon's escape when I learned of it myself. But I didn't want to bring it up because I was afraid it would damage her, bring it all back after all this time. I was foolish."

"She barely even seemed to recognise the man's name," Martin said quietly, almost to himself.

"She must have buried it deep," said Glenster. "It's going to make it a lot harder for her to deal with when she digs it up, but she has to face it. She must be prepared for the possibility that this nightmare has returned. I hope you're up to helping her through this, young man."

Martin, deep in thought, realised a response was required.

"I am."

Then he was silent, a single sentence from a long ago letter running through his mind over and over.

"My Mommy and Daddy died in a boating accident when I was five."

The sheriff pulled up outside the cabin and put on the parking brake. Martin sat forward and thanked him for the lift. To Glenster he said,

"I'm sorry for what you went through, but thanks for telling me your story."

"You have the facts now, Martin," Glenster responded. "You're closer to Abigail than either of us; you're in a position to help her remember. It must be done gently, and it will hurt her, but she must remember. You'll both have to be very strong."

Martin nodded, got out and watched as the sheriff turned the car and drove away. He jogged to the front door and went inside, heading straight for his bedroom, where he undressed, throwing his clothes on the floor. He took a quick shower, put on fresh clothes, and was on his way out the door when he paused, considering phoning Stephen. Deciding against it, Martin instead booted up his laptop and sent him an e-mail telling him to send him back a time when they could chat. Whilst online, he realised that he had been on his way out without a clue as to how to get to where he wanted to go. A quick search yielded the address of the Hannerville Public Library. He shut the laptop down and left.

He mulled over the idea that had formed in his mind whilst he'd been in the back of the sheriff's cruiser. Glenster had commented that Abigail must have buried the incident deep, but Martin was wondering if it was perhaps more the case that she had destroyed it. Was that even possible? Did her condition work like that? It would explain why she had never mentioned the incident to him. Or, he mused, maybe it was just too painful for her to share with anyone. In any event, if this Brannon really was back in town, Abigail needed to know the possible threat he posed to her. She had to remember. Martin believed himself up to the task, believed that he might well be the only man for the job, but how to go about it was something he wasn't so sure of. Gently, as Glenster had said, though such was a bit of a given. Mind you, Glenster wasn't privy to Abigail's condition. His task would not be simply to help her retrieve a buried memory; he might have to educate her on the whole ordeal. How the hell he was going to manage that he had no idea. What was really troubling him was how Abigail was going to take it.

A sudden anger flared inside and he jammed his foot down on the brake. The car skidded to a halt and Martin slammed his hands against the steering wheel. She had been right; it had all been great, perfect even, and now this. Once again he found himself in the position of needing to tell her something and being unsure of her reaction. But what he had to tell her this time was far different. Dear, sweet Jesus, she had had to endure some lunatic shouting a load of nonsense in her face, and then she had watched him murder her parents in cold blood. That someone had put a child through that was bad enough, but that it had been Abi, the woman he loved, was nigh unbearable. That the man responsible might be back in town made Martin's stomach churn. He was caught between fear and fury, a need to keep Abi safe and a desire to do some serious damage to David Brannon. He swallowed hard, took deep breaths, reminded himself that the authorities weren't sure it was Brannon who had taken the missing women. But of course whether it was or not was moot; that it might be was all the reason required to tell Abi.

The stray thought drifted through his head: *maybe the doctor mentioning it this morning will trigger something, bring it back to her.*

Martin panicked for several seconds, concerned that if she did remember she might have some sort of breakdown. He once again had to calm himself, reminding himself that she had gone to see friends, that if anything happened to her then she would be looked after, cared for. Plus there was the fact that if she didn't recall what had happened to her as a child it was because the memory was simply gone and would not suddenly pop back into her head. However he was not entirely aware of how Abi's memory condition worked.

Martin dug his mobile out of his pocket and dialled Abigail's number. She answered on the third ring.

"Marty? Is everything all right?"

"Yeah, Abi, I… I just wanted to…" He was about to say he wanted to make sure she was okay, but given why she was visiting her friends, that would have sounded bloody stupid. "… hear your voice. And to ask you to tell Beth and Amanda that I'm asking for them."

"Oh, that's sweet, Marty. We're all worried, but we're keeping it together."

"Okay, well if there's anything I can do, let me know. You'll phone me when you get home?"

"You going to come and comfort me?"

"I want to do that now, but I don't want to intrude."

"I'll call you soon."

"I'll be waiting."

He ended the call and put his phone back in his pocket. She was okay. Good. As he started off again, Martin marvelled at Abi's strength and silently promised that he would do whatever it took to keep her safe.

Abigail put her phone back in her bag and turned to Beth and Amanda. Before Marty had called the three of them had been having a good cry.

Abigail had intended to walk in being a tower of strength. She was concerned about her friend and puzzled by the odd visit from Doctor Glenster and Sheriff Flaghan this morning, but the events of the last couple of days with Marty had left her with a wonderful euphoria. She had believed that this natural high would be enough to carry her through whatever might be waiting for her when she walked in to the back room at Russo's Pet Store.

She had been wrong.

The moment she had clapped eyes on the tear streaked faces of her friends, her euphoria had vanished, and her resolve to be upbeat and optimistic had gone with it. A dozen news stories about missing women, heard on the radio and watched on TV, flooded her mind and the tears sprang instantly to her eyes. Beth and Amanda rose to greet her and as they all hugged, they all cried. Abigail had realised then that she had been using her feelings for Marty as a shield, hiding from the reality of what her personal visit from the law the morning her friend was reported missing might mean. She had been offering a silent apology to him for using their foundling relationship that way – and telling herself that Marty would probably tell her it was fine – when her phone had rung. She had been so surprised to see who the caller was that she had stopped crying in an instant. A fact she was glad of; she didn't want to worry him.

She sat down beside her friends and they all dabbed at their eyes with wadded tissues taken from their handbags.

"I don't even know what the hell we're crying about," said Beth. "We don't know that anything's happened to her."

"No," agreed Amanda. "But we're all worried that something has."

"Worrying is fine," commented Abigail. "But we have to be positive. I'm not going to sit here and rhyme off all the ridiculous reasons I can think of that she might have gone missing, but we're going to find her and she's going to be fine." She sniffed, dabbed at her eyes one last time before returning the slightly damp, mascara smudged tissue to her bag. "By the way, you guys, Marty says he's asking for you."

"Oh!" exclaimed Amanda, happy to have something to talk about that was more upbeat than the other subject on their agenda. "Honey, we haven't even asked how it all went."

"You have other things on your mind."

"Today," began Beth. "But not yesterday when we didn't hear a word from you." Abigail tried, and failed, to stop herself smiling. "The jig's up, sweet cheeks. Spill it."

Abigail told them what had happened between her and Marty in the last couple of days.

"Abigail, I am so happy for you," said Beth, in that special tone she reserved for occasions when she was being completely serious. "It all turned out all right... just like I said it would. I totally told you so."

"Shut up," said Abigail, smacking her playfully on the shoulder. "It was all on me."

"From what you've told us, it certainly was," came Amanda's comment, a grin on her lips.

"Oh, that's nasty," chuckled Beth. Abigail was shocked beyond her capacity to respond with words, so she delivered another smack, this time to the back of Amanda's head.

"You're so skanky," Abigail told her friend, but she was only just able to get the words out past the giggles.

Little by little their good humour faded and their minds, untended for just a moment, slipped their respective leashes, all of them going after the subject of Sophie and what had happened to her. Minutes went by. Beth thought of asking Abigail if the distant ringing she could hear might be wedding bells in the near future, but she knew the time for such questions had passed.

"We've got to get on with things," said Abigail eventually. "It'll be difficult, but we can't just sit around worrying."

"You're right," Amanda nodded. "Better that we have something to occupy our minds other than... bad thoughts." The other two nodded, knowing exactly what kind of bad thoughts she meant.

"Okay," Beth breathed out as she got to her feet. "I am going to go to the store and open it up and sell some books so I don't end up bankrupting Abigail."

"I'll ask Diane if there are any deliveries or anything that need to be done," Amanda told them. "Maybe get me out and about for a little while."

"Good. I'll go to the store with Beth and..."

"Nuh-uh. You already have something to occupy your mind... and body."

"Beth, I..."

"No arguments, woman, get your ass back to Marty so he can paint it in latex rubber and spank it, or whatever you two kinky kiddies have been up to."

"Where would you get the idea that *that* is what we've been doing?"

"Shit, I don't know; just popped into my head."

Abigail looked to Amanda, who shrugged and told her,

"Bitch is clearly out of her mind."

"Maybe so, but, Amanda, you are not going to stand there and tell me that you think she should be coming to the store with me to work."

"By no means, but I also don't think she's going to go home and get her ass painted and slapped."

"You make it sound like a college hazing!" She leaned in and kissed Amanda on the cheek. "You need me, you call me. Okay?" Amanda nodded.

"Same to you." She turned to Abigail. "You too."

"Sure thing." Abigail replied, kissing her cheek. "And the same back."

She and Beth left before they could all upset one another again. Outside, they turned to one another.

"You're sure you don't want me to come with?"

"Tell you what, hon," said Beth. "You come over, help me open up, make a pot of coffee, and then I want you out and off home to your new beau. Deal?"

"Deal."

They started walking in the direction of Pages and Pages. Along the way, Abigail asked Beth how she knew about such a thing as latex body paint and Beth fired the question right back at her.

Chapter 28

Martin entered the hushed interior of the town library and stopped just short of the check-out desk, behind which stood a middle-aged woman tapping away at a keyboard. As he approached he heard her utter a curse word and then heard repeated tapping. Martin, knowing without a doubt it was the delete key she was hitting, grinned. How could he be so certain? Simple: he wrote a lot of letters to clients and he never said "shit", fuck it" or "damn it to hell" before hitting the space bar or the caps lock, only the delete key. The librarian's language hadn't been as colourful, but had been a giveaway all the same.

"Excuse me," he said quietly as he reached the desk. The librarian, whose nametag identified her as Dawn, stopped typing, looked up and smiled.

"How can I help you?"

"Uh, well, I have a favour to ask."

"Indeed," she said. "And you also have an absolutely marvellous accent. Scottish?"

"Yes."

"Is this your first trip to the States?" Martin nodded. "Here for a holiday?"

"Visiting a friend."

"How are you liking it so far?"

"It's been an amazing trip," he replied honestly.

"Good. It's always good to know our town has made a good impression. Now, you said you had a favour to ask."

"Yes. Obviously I'm not a member of the library, but I was wondering if it might be possible to do some research?" Dawn's smile was broad and toothy.

"Oh, I don't think that'll be too much of a bother, Mr..?"

"Muir. Martin Muir."

"Mr Muir. What was it specifically that you wanted to look up?"

"Uh, news stories about an incident from October second, nineteen eighty-four."

If Dawn recognised the date and realised what it was he wanted to research, she gave no outward indication. She just pursed her lips as she thought for a few moments.

"You're lucky; we've had copies of the local paper from back then computerised and stored. Any further back and you might have been looking at some time with the microfiche reader."

She showed him to a computer where he could access the information he was after, asking some questions about where he was from. As it turned out she had visited Scotland once when she had been a little girl of nine, taken there by her parents to visit an ailing relative. She couldn't recall much detail, but did recollect being taken to Loch Ness during her stay.

"It was such a wonderful place," she told him. "It was quite dull the day we went, but out on that body of water, with a thin mist hanging just above the surface, it was so easy to believe that there was some ancient creature down there in the depths."

After relaying a quick set of instructions on the use of the machine, and how to do screen prints using the coin operated printer attached to it, Dawn told him, "If you have any trouble, you'll find me at the front desk."

"Thank you very much."

"You're very welcome," she responded as she walked away.

Martin entered the date into the search window and hit the return key.

Brannon's coming to Hannerville had been front page news.

The screen displayed the front page of the Hannerville Post for October third, nineteen eighty-four. "Tragedy In Town" screamed the large, bold headline. Beneath it was a picture of a house, cordoned off with police tape. Underneath the picture: "Full Shocking

Story on Pages 2 and 3". Martin scrolled to the next page. It showed a family photo, two adults and their daughter. Though the picture showed her as she had looked twenty-nine years ago, Martin recognised Abigail instantly. The caption underneath the photograph identified the adults as her parents, Ross and Alice. Martin examined their faces. They looked like nice people, friendly people. As he looked, he picked out the features Abigail had taken from each of them: her mother's nose and lips, her father's ears and eyes. She had been a beautiful child and together the three of them had made a lovely family.

"My Mommy and Daddy died in a boating accident when I was five."

Martin murmured, telling himself that if Abigail had done what he thought she had done, then she hadn't kept anything from him; she had simply told him the truth as she believed it to be.

But the people here in town who knew her - Philip Glenster, her aunt and uncle, her friends - what did they think? Did they all believe that she had hidden the memory away, a terrible truth best locked in a box in her mind and forgotten? Had they never questioned how she had managed to deal with it, or had her aunt and uncle, like Glenster, never been willing to run the risk that mentioning it, questioning Abigail's version of events, might trigger some sort of breakdown in their niece?

He read the story. It contained a watered down, and in some ways slightly inaccurate, version of the story Philip Glenster had told him. Nonetheless he fed the machine some change and printed out the pages. More searching. On October fourth, the story was still front page news, though this time the article focussed on Brannon himself, giving a brief history of his life, about which little was known, and his crimes, about which there was a glut of information. There was also a picture of him. Far from the leering, Halloween mask visage Martin might have expected, Brannon had been a good looking man, the kind who would have had no trouble in getting women to trust him. He would have been able to get close to them and knock them out before they had an inkling of the danger he represented. Martin committed the face to memory and printed out the pages.

The issue published on the fifth of October saw the story move to page four. No new information. A brief mention of Abigail Morton, five years of age, now living with her deceased father's brother and his wife. Martin printed it anyway. He considered looking further, wondering if the paper had charted the trial. But he decided that even if it had, it was information he didn't need. Brannon had been tried, convicted, sent to a loony bin, and nearly three decades later had staged an unexpected and bloody escape. Now it seemed he may have come back to Hannerville.

Martin felt a sudden strong urge to be with Abigail. He folded up the printed pages and stuck them in the back pocket of his jeans, shut down the pages he had been looking at and then made his way to the front desk. Dawn heard him coming and looked up from her monitor, smiling at him.

"Find what you were looking for?"

"Yes. Thanks again for all your help."

"You're very welcome. I hope you enjoy the rest of your stay."

"Thank you," he said as he headed for the exit, digging his mobile from his pocket.

He made a quick phone call to Abigail, who was at her store keeping Beth company for a while. Martin asked if they would like some more company.

"You don't have to drive all the way down here, Marty."

"I'm already in town."

"Oh. What for?"

"Didn't want to spend all my time up at the cabin," he said. He hated not telling her the whole truth, but now was not the time. "How about I pick up some coffee and donuts or something on my way over?"

"Oh, Marty, that's really sweet. Thank you."

"It's no trouble. What'll you have and where can I get it?"

She gave him her order and then he asked what Beth wanted. He heard muffled words, only able to make out what Beth was saying when she called, "You rock, dude!" Martin smiled and Abigail told him what Beth had asked for. He asked her for directions to the place she had given him the name of, then he told her he'd see her soon.

"I'm looking forward to it," she said. "The coffee and donuts that is, not seeing you."

"Oh, very humorous, Abigail, very rib tickling. Remind me, was it spit you wanted in your latte? Or did you ask me to find a dog and get it to lick the sugar off your donut before I got there?" She laughed, then there was a moment of silence after which she said softly,

"Don't be too long."

"I won't."

True to his word, he arrived at Pages and Pages twenty minutes later. Almost the entire journey he had been asking himself if he was perhaps being too presumptuous in his belief that he was the right person to be going through this with Abigail. She had her aunt and uncle, her friends, even Doctor Glenster, not all of whom had known her as long as he had, but all of whom had certainly been close to her for a long time. Would it not be better if one of them tried to help her remember? Was such a thing not the purview of her family? Martin had finally admitted to himself that he was scared, that part of him was unwilling to be the one because he knew it was going to hurt her and he didn't want to be the cause. But he had been the one she had chosen to share her secret with, the only person in her whole life with whom she had shared the knowledge of her condition. That fact alone meant he might not be the best person for the job, but he was the only one.

With that thought in mind, he used his elbow to push down on the handle and shouldered open the door of Pages to Pages.

As he bumped the door shut with his backside, Abigail walked over, smiling from ear to ear. Martin felt his heart kick out an extra thud or three as she approached, one of sudden fear over what he was going to have to do, two of excitement merely at seeing her. She outstretched her arms and he did the same, offering the bag of donuts and the cardboard cup holder with the two lattes in it, but she stepped into his arms, kissed him on the lips and hugged him. He responded in kind, doing his best to not drop or spill anything in the process.

"I missed you," she told him.

"It's only been a couple of hours," he said. "I've barely thought about you at all." She stepped back, feigning shock.

"How'd you like a latte down your drawers?"

"Hmm. Shoving a donut down my drawers might be more fun. For me, not the donut."

She laughed and took the cup holder and bag from him.

"Thanks for this. Come on."

She led him to the back room, where Beth was doing some paperwork. She looked up as they entered, smiling at Martin.

"Thanks for bringing the goodies, man. Appreciate it."

He crossed to her, bent forward and gave her a hug. Abigail smiled at the look of surprise on Beth's face. She felt a tear spring to her eye as Beth visibly relaxed and hugged him back. As they released one another, Martin kissed her gently on the forehead.

"Only the first one's free," he said.

"The hug, the kiss or the coffee?"

"The coffee; hugs and kisses are always free, but if you want something spicier than that you have to pay just like everybody else."

"I bet you didn't say that to Abigail." Martin grinned and shrugged.

"She forced herself upon me. It was all completely against my will."

He ducked as the cardboard cup holder sailed across the room at him.

The three of them sat for a while, Abigail and Beth drinking their lattes and snacking on the donuts. Martin, who felt neither hungry nor thirsty, tried to get into the conversation, which never got anywhere near the subject of Sophie. A few times he succeeded, chuckling along as Beth or Abigail told a story, but always the spectre of what lay ahead of him returned, casting a dark shadow across his thoughts.

Eventually Beth told Martin and Abigail to get lost and go have some fun. Abigail told Beth to call her if she needed anything, and it went without saying that should either of them hear anything about their missing friend they would be in touch. Martin and Abigail hugged Beth in turn and the two of them left. A customer came in, holding the door open for them as they exited. They both thanked him and soon were walking along the street, arm in arm.

"Where do you want to go?" he asked her.

"Home," she replied. "I feel tired. I feel a little freaked out. I feel a lot of things right now and I need to sort them all out, but before I do that I have to get some rest. That okay?"

"Of course it's okay. We'll go get my car and I'll take you home."

"You'll stay."

"Only until you kick me out."

She took her arm out of his and put it round him, hugging him close.

For the entire journey, Martin fretted about whether or not to tell her now or wait until she had rested. He was still wrestling with the decision when they reached her house. He closed the door and followed Abigail into the living room, where she dropped her bag and threw herself face down onto the couch. He took off his jacket and sat down in an armchair. Abigail pushed herself up on her elbows, looked at him and said,

"There are two things bothering me."

"What are they?"

"The first is what Doctor Glenster was talking about this morning, and the second is what's wrong with you."

Martin, simultaneously grateful and nauseated at being presented with an opportunity he could not possibly refuse, breathed in deep and let it out slowly, nodding.

"I thought I'd done a good job of covering it up."

"You did," Abigail confirmed. "I doubt Beth or anyone else would have spotted it, but I had a feeling there was something off the moment I saw you at the store. What is it?"

"What it is ties together the answers to both of the things that are bothering you," he told her. "But it's going to take some explaining."

"The sheriff didn't go gung-ho on you, did he?"

"No, nothing like that. Abigail..."

She saw the way his face contorted, a physical manifestation of the turmoil in his mind. She quickly rose from the couch and went to him, kneeling down on the floor in front of him and taking his head in her hands. She looked into his eyes and told him,

"You know you can tell me anything, don't you?"

"I know," he said, his voice barely above a whisper.

"Martin, honey, what's the matter?"

155

He pulled his head back, cleared his throat and took a breath.

"Abigail, I know what Philip Glenster was talking about this morning when he spoke about what you went through." She opened her mouth to ask the obvious question, but he grasped her hands and stopped her. "Before I tell you I have to ask you something: Abigail, do you know what happens to your memory of something if you destroy what you've written down about it?"

"Of course I do," she replied. "You remember I told you about the experiment I did with the video and not writing in my journal? Well, I did another one, similar to that where I did my usual journal entry one night and, in the morning I remembered everything no problem. Then I recorded a message to myself onto a video tape, detailing what I had done the night before and explaining what I was doing now. I sat the tape in front of me with a post-it on it saying "Play Me Right Now!" and then I destroyed the journal entry. Tore it out and ripped it up. When I woke up I didn't remember any of what I'd done, and still wouldn't if it hadn't been for the tape. It scared me half to death. I re-wrote the journal entry, including the experiment, and vowed never to repeat it."

Martin nodded sadly, his theory one step closer to being proved correct.

"Marty," said Abigail, clearly concerned. "Why would you ask that?"

"Can we go and look at your journals?"

"Not until you tell me why?"

"Please, Abigail. I will tell you, but I want to make sure I'm right before I say anything."

"But how will checking my journals…"

"Abigail, *please.*"

She stared at him for several seconds and thought to herself that she could actually hear his racing heart. Then she realised it was her own thundering pulse she was listening to.

"Okay."

The two of them went upstairs, where he pulled down the hatch so they could get into the attic. The space was warm, almost stifling. Abigail led Martin to the cabinet. She reached up and took a small brass key off the top.

"Which one do you want to look at?" she asked him. The way she sounded, her tone a mix of annoyance and worry, hurt him to hear. She was not stupid; thanks to his question and his request, she had worked out what he thought she had done and how it might tie in with what Glenster had said to her earlier. That was where the annoyance component was coming from. The worry stemmed from something she had told him two nights ago (only two nights ago? Good lord): there was always that little worry in the back of her mind about her having forgotten something.

"The journal that will have an entry for October second, nineteen eighty-four," he told her.

She nodded and unlocked the cabinet. The doors opened soundlessly. Abigail reached up and Martin noticed that her hand was shaking. He reached out and laid a hand on her shoulder, grateful that she didn't shrug it off.

"This is stupid, Marty," she said. "There is no way that I…"

"Abigail, we need to know."

She let out a long, trembling breath and took down the book second from the left on the top shelf. She turned to face him, the book held in both hands. She looked up and their eyes met.

"Whatever happens, I'm here," he reassured her. She nodded and opened the book.

Silent seconds passed, and then Abigail let out an anguished wail that almost tore Martin Muir's heart and soul to shreds. She dropped the journal to the floor and took a step back. Martin stepped forward and caught her as she started to collapse. She slumped against him and he held her up, put his arms under hers and linked his hands together behind her. She got her feet beneath her and resisted him, pushed against him, trying to break free. When that didn't work she beat against him with the heels of her fists, striking his shoulders and chest, weeping and shaking her head. All the while Martin held her, saying nothing. He took the blows, let them serve as his just punishment for causing her so much pain.

Eventually she stopped hitting him and began sobbing deep wracking sobs that made her entire body shudder. Her legs began to give again and Martin lowered her down, going with her until she was sitting on the floor. His embrace could not hold and he released her. Abigail held herself upright, but her head was down, her face hidden by her hair. Martin remained silent, knowing that for the time being there was nothing he could say that would make things any better for her. The pain of her strikes got through and he realised she had landed one or two lucky shots on his jaw. He'd be bruised, but thought he might heal before she did.

He stared at her for several minutes before looking to the side, to where the journal had landed. It had closed over on its way down. Martin gulped, his dry throat smarting, and reached out. He half expected Abigail to suddenly lift her head, to let loose a scream and tell him to leave it alone. She did not move. He lifted the journal and held it in both hands, as she had done, and opened it. He found the entry for October first, nineteen eighty-four, then went to the page headed "October second, nineteen eighty-four". Between the last page of the first entry and the first page of the second were five ragged strips, the remains of five pages torn from the journal.

Martin didn't read the whole entry, but he scanned enough of it to get the gist. Here was the answer Philip Glenster had never uncovered, had never even imagined. The answer to how Abigail had managed to recover from the trauma of watching a madman butcher her mother and father. Here was the lie that Abigail's condition had allowed her to believe all these years, the replacement death she had concocted for her parents to free herself from the hellish reality of what had happened to them, to her, and to Philip Glenster on that long ago night when Abigail had been five. She had written that her parents had gone out of town for the day to go boating on a larger lake in a neighbouring county. They had been out on the water and their boat had capsized somehow. Though strong swimmers, neither of her parents had managed to get to shore and both of them had drowned. A simple but tragic story that she believed with all her heart, that even if she had at any point had to discuss it at length with anyone who knew the truth, they would have nodded and let it go. Even to them it would probably seem better that she believe that than be taken back to that night every time she thought of her mother and father.

Martin closed the journal over and sat it beside him on the floor.

"Marty?"

"Yes?"

"Do you know why I did that? Why I tore those pages out?"

"Yes."

Very slowly she lifted her head. He caught her red, puffy eyes through the veil of hair she didn't bother to move from her face.

"Please tell me."

He told her that he would, but not up there. He put the journal back in its place, closed and locked the doors and put the key back on top. Then he helped Abigail to her feet and all the way back down to the living room. After getting her settled, he went back and closed the attic hatch, then returned to Abigail, who was lying down on the couch, sniffing and dabbing at her eyes and nose with a tissue. He sat down in the armchair again.

"Are you ready?" he asked her. She shook her head and beckoned him. Martin rose and went to her, kneeling down beside the couch. Abigail reached out for him and he leaned across her. She clamped her arms around him.

"Thank you for having the strength to tell me the truth," she whispered. Martin held her as best he could and fought the tears that threatened, knowing that if he gave in right now he'd never be able to tell her the truth. He promised himself that later, if he felt like it, he could have a cry, get it out of his system. For now he inhaled her scent, pulled back far enough to plant a gentle kiss on her lips, and then went back to his chair.

"On the night of October second, nineteen eighty-four, a serial killer named David Brannon came to Hannerville. He had already murdered several women in other towns in another county, and no one knows why he came to this town that night, but he only went to one place: your house. He took your parents by surprise, tied them to chairs from the dining table. Then he got you and brought you downstairs, tied you to a chair too. Then he went upstairs and started trashing your house. At one point he threw something out of the window and it hit Philip Glenster's car. He investigated and got knocked out. When he came to, Brannon was hurting your mother and father. He was ranting and raving and then he... he killed them. Afterwards he left the room and Glenster got free, untied you and made a run for the front door. The police were arriving, alerted by an anonymous caller. You got out and Brannon slashed Glenster and tried to escape. The cops caught him. He was put on trial, ended up in a nuthouse called Berrybeck. It eventually got turned into a swanky rehab clinic and someone paid for Brannon, who hadn't said or done anything out of line for years and years, to stay on there. About four months ago he left the place, killing several people and setting fire to the building. Glenster and the sheriff believe there is a possibility that the women who have gone missing recently have been taken by Brannon. They heard about the escape several weeks ago, but Glenster was reluctant to mention it to you because he has never been sure how you managed to get over what happened; he didn't want to risk unearthing it all in case it caused you to suffer a breakdown or something. He was completely confused by your lack of reaction to the name Brannon."

"He thinks I'm just repressing it?"

"Yes, but when he told me all of this this morning, I had an idea that maybe you had found another way to deal with it." He quickly added. "I didn't say anything to him about it obviously. He feels awful about not telling you sooner, though he doesn't know that even if he had you wouldn't have known what he was talking about. I decided to check out what I'd been told. I went to the library, checked out some old newspapers." He took the folded pages out of his back pocket and put them on the coffee table. "I printed those pages out, if you decide you want to take a look. After I got those I felt the need to be with you, so I called you, and the rest you know."

After a short silence, Abigail sat up and spoke.

"I'm tired. I think I need to sleep for a little while, but before we go upstairs to bed I want you to understand something: there is no one else in the world I would rather have had tell this to me. No one else I'd rather was with me right now."

Martin rose and went to her, gave her his hand and pulled her off the couch and into a quick hug before taking her upstairs.

Chapter 29

Sleep? What a joke!

Half an hour later and Abigail lay on her bed, Martin beside her. He was turned away from her, had somehow managed to actually fall asleep, bless him. She looked at the back of his head and a small smile lifted the corners of her lips. It was gone in a blink as her mind processed thoughts similar to those Martin had had earlier, about how everything had come together relatively quickly and easily, and about how they had gone sour just as fast. Not between the two of them, of course, though she wouldn't blame him for getting up right now and leaving, having convinced himself that he had started a relationship with a complete basket case. That he was still here with her was the silver lining to the dark cloud that had rolled over her life.

How could I? Abigail wondered. She had scrupulously recorded almost her entire life, afraid of missing anything out, even the unhappy and the painful stuff like losing jobs and breakups. Her aunt and uncle had taught her that a person was the sum of all the parts of their life, the good and the bad, and so Abigail had made a point of never leaving anything out, regardless of how painful or depressing it might be to remember. She was completely convinced that there had never been anything that had happened in her life that she had not had the guts to store in her journals, a fact of which she had been immensely proud. Except now of course it turned out there had been something she had left out, something she had apparently written down and then destroyed. Not only that, but she had fabricated a story to replace the truth she had been unable to face, told herself a lie that had allowed her to get on with her life.

Abigail closed her eyes and tried to remember something from the night her parents were murdered, some tiny little flash of memory: a face, a sound, a smell. She thought it might be considered lunacy, trying to recall anything from such an episode in one's life, but now that she knew it had happened, and that she had robbed herself of the memory, it felt like there was something missing. There was a heretofore unknown gap in her life and it did not sit right with her. Even though she now knew the true circumstances surrounding the deaths of her parents, it was third-hand information, filtered through Doctor Glenster and Marty. It wasn't her memory.

For fifteen minutes she tried and tried but, like anything else not written down in those god damn journals, it was simply gone. Abigail felt tears welling up and blinked them away, tried to focus on something else for a while. The first subject her traitorous mind brought up was poor Sophie, something she didn't have the strength to think about just now. She opened her eyes and gazed at the back of Martin's head. Her Marty. She slid across, closing the already small gap between them. Pressing herself gently against his back, she breathed in his scent. At least tonight's journal entry would have a…

The idea came to her fully formed: she had obviously made a conscious decision to destroy the original pages of her journal on which she had recorded the deaths, the murders, of her mother and father. She had also made a decision to not record having done so, so she would never question the version of events she had created to replace the truth. What if tonight, before she wrote about the events of the day, she took that old journal with those missing pages and wrote an entry for October second, nineteen eighty-four? A replacement entry. A replacement memory! Using what Martin had told her she would reconstruct what she had written and destroyed all those years ago, filling in the gap in her memory. She could then write about today without having to mention anything about Martin having had to tell her about her own history.

This was where her sudden elation stalled, where the hastily constructed plan fell apart. If it did work, if she wrote a memory in that old journal and it took, it would be a sudden anomaly in her recollection of her life. Nothing else about her life would make sense as none of it would have happened the way it had if she had known all along how her parents had died. If that memory were to be simply dropped into its proper place and time, it would upset everything that had happened after it. She would begin questioning why she had never thought of it again after the night it happened. Therefore, to make the plan work, she would have to go through every journal and fabricate entries for all the times the ghosts of that night would have risen to haunt her, an impossible task. Of course others would ask questions too. It could be explained away to Philip Glenster simply by telling him his theory about her repressing the memory had been correct, but Martin would know otherwise.

There was also the fact that Abigail was completely unaware if going back and updating an old journal would have the effect of updating her memory in chronological order. In fact it was very possible that it might do her even more damage.

She sighed, breathing in deep and letting it out slowly through her mouth so as not to wake Martin. She closed her eyes again and did her best to let her mind drift, trying to attain the peace of sleep, even if only for a few minutes. She actually did begin to doze, but as she was on the cusp of sleep she wondered what terrors might await her. Abigail had never been prone to nightmares, but was it possible that given everything she had found out today her unconscious mind might well find a few choice images of the night her parents were killed? Bits and pieces her conscious mind was unable to locate? The idea gave her a start and the sandman, startled, fled.

Minutes passed, minutes during which Abigail thought about not making an entry in her journal tonight. She could wake up tomorrow morning feeling the same way she had this morning: happy, carefree and contented. Of course everyone would wonder what the hell was wrong with her that she had to be reminded of the disappearance of her friend. Martin would know, of course, and would have no option but to again remind her of her own past to arm her against the possibility of Brannon's return to Hannerville. That would mean going through all this again a second time, though for her it would be the first again. Her thoughts spiralled out of control as she imagined having no future, simply not recording anything in her journal and waking up every morning to a world where all was well and good. Yes it would all cave in on her every day, but as long as she didn't write it down, it would all go away the next day.

Down this path, madness lies.

She couldn't do such a thing. It would be a terrible waste of the life she had worked hard to build. It would destroy not only her, but those she cared about and those who cared about her. Abigail breathed in Martin's scent again. She couldn't put him through that. She wouldn't. She was going to have to deal with this. It was time to grab the bull by the horns and kick it in the balls. She was a big girl, she…

She was a big girl, but her five year old self hadn't been. Her five year old self had been a little girl who had sat bound to a chair listening to the ravings of a madman before watching him eliminate her parents on a whim. Five year old Abigail had been a child whose family had been torn away from her, and who had probably suffered horrific nightmares afterwards. That Philip Glenster had managed to get on with his life was proof that an adult was capable of making it after going through such an ordeal, but a five year old? A little girl facing a future without her Mommy and Daddy, maybe thinking that every night for the rest of her life she would watch them die, over and over again; could she have dealt with it? Obviously the little girl hadn't thought so, but she had known she had a way out. A way to banish the memories forever, to make things, not all right, but to ease the pain so that getting on with her life was something she might be able to do. And who on earth could blame her for taking the easier path of re-writing her recent past? Certainly not her grown up self, not the adult Abigail, who was only now just finding out about all this, and who had herself considered re-writing her past so she did not have to face the horrors it held.

Abigail closed her eyes and imagined herself standing in the living room of her first home. This was the room in which her parents had died horrific deaths, but right now it is quiet, serene. Behind her she heard a noise and turned to find the five year old version of herself standing there, hands clasped behind her back, rocking on her heels and humming a tune. She is wearing a little red and yellow summer dress, knee length white socks and tan sandals. She has already erased the memory of her loss. Abigail knelt down and beckoned to the child, who stopped humming and approached her, smiling, wide eyed and trusting in a way only children can be. Abigail reached out and embraced the child, who stiffened for a moment before relaxing. Tears formed in Abigail's eyes and she did nothing to stop them when they began running down her face.

"You did the right thing," she whispered. "You did what you had to do. You did exactly what I would have done."

She heard the hitch in the child's breathing and realised she was crying too.

When Abigail opened her eyes, there were very real tears running over the bridge of her nose and down on the bed sheet. She wiped them away with the corner of the quilt and wondered if she wasn't going screwy, imagining encounters with her younger self. Still, she had to admit she felt better, so even if it was a little bit nuts, it had done her some good.

Now it was time to keep going and get through this.

"Marty?" she said softly.

"Yes?" he replied instantly. *Not sleeping after all. Faker.* She smiled.

"I'm going to go downstairs to read the stories you printed. I'd like to do it alone."

"I understand. You know where I am if you need me."

She put a hand on his shoulder and he turned his head to gently kiss the back of it. Abigail got up and went downstairs.

After reading the graphic account of the night of her parents' deaths that had been printed in the local paper, Abigail was convinced more than ever that she had done the right thing in destroying whatever record she had made. For the first time in her life, she considered whatever the hell it was that was wrong with her memory as a blessing rather than a curse.

The strongest emotion she felt at that moment was anger. Earlier she had thought she would be sad and end up crying, but she had, long ago, dealt with the loss of her mother and father. She hadn't been aware of the facts up till now, but she had still felt the emptiness of their passing, their removal, from her life had left behind. She had mourned and she had moved on, cherishing the precious few memories she had of them. The revelations of today had not so much altered the past as shone a new light on it. She felt fury boiling up inside her, a need to inflict extreme pain on the individual who had invaded their lives that night. For a few seconds, Abigail hoped that David Brannon was back in town, and her dearest wish was that they cross paths. So help her god, she'd tear the rat bastard son of a bitch to shreds.

Then she remembered Sophie.

If Brannon was the one kidnapping these women, then the chances of her friend ever being seen alive again was slim to none. And here she sat, hoping this sicko was back in town so she could get her revenge.

Tears threatened again, but she held them back. No sense in getting mad at herself; she was only human. It might be Brannon, it might not. No sense getting upset until she had to. She had to keep hoping that Sophie was all right, that she would be found safe and well and soon.

Abigail sat in the chair, listening to the clock ticking away on the mantle, asking herself what she was going to do now. Eventually, she got up and went back upstairs to her bedroom. As she walked in, Martin sat up, looking at her but saying nothing. She walked over to him, took his hands, pulled him to his feet and hugged him. He hugged her back and they stood there for several minutes. When they released one another, they both sat back down on the edge of the bed.

"I think," she began. "I want to talk to Philip Glenster. Not right away, but I'll have to at some point. I'll have to watch what I'm saying, but it's a conversation that's long overdue."

"Okay."

"Right now, I'd like to go for a walk."

A short time later, hand in hand, they walked through the gates of the Rosecrown Cemetery. They walked along the gravel path until Abigail turned on to one of the aisles formed by the grave markers. Halfway along, she stopped and turned to look at a headstone. It was black, the writing etched in gold.

In Loving Memory of
Ross and Alice Morton
Not Gone
Simply Gone On Ahead

They stood together, Martin reading the inscription, Abigail staring at the ground in front of the stone.

"I don't come here often enough," she said quietly. Martin didn't know if she was talking to him, or to her parents. After several moments of silence had passed, he offered his thoughts.

"You're like me; neither of us finds it very easy to come to a place like this. It's not that they're dark or evil places, it's just we don't really feel the need to be where our parents are buried to pay our respects. I feel far more comfortable sitting at home, looking through a photo album and remembering them that way than standing in reverential silence in a graveyard."

"I know," Abigail said. "It's just that I feel like I somehow cheapened their memory."

"Abi, you did no such thing."

"But for years…"

"No," he said sternly, cutting her off. "For years what you did was believe something you made up as a young girl, something to shield yourself from something you couldn't deal with. There's no shame in that, especially given what it was you were hiding from. Now let's say you hadn't done so. Would your life be what it is? Maybe, maybe not. Maybe some of it would be the same and some of it would be different. The one thing I can promise you would be no different is that your Mum and Dad still wouldn't be here. You would still miss them. Believing what you believed, you *did* miss them. You still had to say goodbye, go through all the grief, grow up without them. None of that would have changed. You changed the circumstances of how you lost them, Abi, that was all. You found a way, not to erase your suffering, but to ease it. I can't imagine any decent parent having an issue with that."

Abigail said nothing. She looked at him and then back to the headstone, and then she nodded and they walked away.

As they exited the gates, they heard a voice. Amplified and distorted, it got louder and louder until the car with the speaker mounted on top turned the corner at the bottom of the street and drove towards them. The message the man behind the wheel was relaying was now clear.

"Citizens of Hannerville," said the speaker. "There will be a meeting held in the town hall tonight at seven pm. All those who are able to attend are urged to do so."

And the message repeated.

"Sheriff Flaghan got his meeting organised then," commented Martin. "I take it we'll be in attendance?"

"I suppose we should," replied Abigail. "Hear what they say, maybe find out of if anything has come to light. I might even get a chance to speak to Philip Glenster."

"Damn nuisance!" came a voice from beside them. They turned to see a man in his early fifties walking towards them, scowling after the slowly departing message mobile. Both got the impression that they had seen him somewhere before, but it was fleeting, and given no further thought. "All that racket," the man griped. "And right here beside a cemetery too." As he passed Martin and Abigail, he turned to them and enquired, "Why the hell couldn't they just send everyone an e-mail?

Chapter 30

After they got back from their walk, Abigail contacted Beth and Amanda to make sure they knew about the meeting. They'd both heard, and they arranged to meet up outside the town hall at 6:40pm. She also called her aunt and uncle, who couldn't make it but who said they would get the news from one of their friends.

After dinner – takeaway, as neither of them felt much like cooking – they got into Martin's car and Abigail directed him to the town hall. A large building taking up one entire side of the town square, Martin had difficulty finding a parking space anywhere near, so parked a few streets away. They walked back and were only a little late in meeting Beth and Amanda. After hellos, kisses, hugs and how are yous had been exchanged, they entered the town hall and made their way to the main auditorium, where they found almost every one of the several hundred chairs that had been laid out taken. They found four chairs together, near the back of the room, which still put them in a better position than those who came in after them, who had to either go upstairs to find a seat or settle for standing.

As they waited, Beth took it upon herself to explain to Martin that the room they were in was also used to hold plays and pageants and the like. Martin already knew this; Abigail had once written him a very excited letter, her enthusiasm linked to her having landed a role in a play which was performed on the very stage at the front of the room, but he didn't mention this to Beth. She had just started telling him about an incident involving her and a guy being caught by her parents necking out back of the town hall when the men and women of the town council began mounting the stairs at the right of the stage. Beth broke off her story and a hush fell over the room as the people, including Sheriff Flaghan, sat down on chairs that had been placed on the stage. One man, average height and build and wearing a very expensive looking suit, bypassed his chair and stepped up to the microphone.

"That's Mayor Ashby," Beth whispered to him. He nodded in acknowledgment.

"Thank you all for coming," said the Mayor, his voice coming from speakers placed around the room. "Before we begin, I would like to point out that this is a town meeting, not a press conference. There will be no questions afterwards as there will be no need; by the end of this meeting, everything we know, you'll know. As many of you will be aware, there have been rumours circulating around the town these last couple of days. Now where there may be some truth to some of these rumours, obviously stories will have gotten around that are ill informed, inaccurate or just plain false. Therefore the main purpose of this meeting is the widespread dissemination of *facts*. I'll hand you over now to Sheriff Flaghan."

He stepped back and went to his chair, nodding at the Sheriff, who returned the nod as he rose from his seat and approached the microphone.

"As Mayor Ashby said, ladies and gentlemen, this meeting is about getting the facts out so that everyone is singing from the same hymn sheet. I'll keep it simple. Over the last few days, three women have gone missing: Janice Mallory, Charlotte Webster and Sophie Thomas. Now at this point all we know is that they have gone missing without cause or explanation. Now the rumours going round suggest kidnapping and murder, but at the present time we have no facts to support those ideas. No ransom demands have been received and no evidence has been uncovered to suggest murder, therefore for the time being they are classed as missing persons.

"Now I would ask anyone in this room to come forward if they know anything, if they suspect anything, if they've heard anything. It might not seem significant, but you never can tell. If you don't feel comfortable coming forward to see me tonight after the meeting, by all means come by my office. After you leave here tonight, if you see or hear anything unusual, out of the ordinary, anyone acting suspiciously, please report it. Again it may be nothing, but it's best that we look into things and make sure they're nothing. Now this advice applies to all; male and female, young and old: if you're going out at night, take someone with you if you can. Make sure someone knows where you're going and who you're going with. Make sure you have your cell phones with you, and make sure they're charged. Be wary of strangers. This is all going to be in the paper tomorrow morning, but if you have any friends or family that couldn't make it to this meeting, call them when you get home, tell them to do what I've told you to do. It may be that our town has someone in it who means our citizens harm, and we have to pull together as a town to find out who it is and stop them."

He took a deep breath and Martin had an idea what was coming next.

"Some of you may have heard another rumour regarding who the someone I just mentioned might be, and it's only fair that I put all the cards on the table. One night, many years ago, a man named David Brannon came to this town and committed a terrible, terrible act. He was caught that very night and ended up in a hospital for the criminally insane. He is now out"

There was an eruption of murmurs from the crowd. Before it got out of control, Flaghan lifted both hands, appealing for calm. When he spoke next, he raised his voice just a little.

"Although we have no reason to believe that this man would come back to town," he told the assembly. "I cannot deny that it is a possibility." More murmuring, louder this time. Before it got out of hand, Flaghan continued. "However, the identity of the perpetrator does not change anything. I still implore each and every one of you to spread the facts of this situation, to keep your eyes and your ears open, report anything out of the ordinary, anything suspicious. Watch out for one another. Thank you."

He strode back to his seat and the Mayor rose again, clapping the taller man on the back as he passed him on his way to the microphone.

"Ladies and gentlemen, that concludes this meeting. Thank you for coming."

He and the others quickly left the stage as the conversation in the room began to rise. Above the rapidly developing clamour, Martin picked out a voice calling on the Mayor and the Sheriff, presumably an eager reporter who either hadn't been listening earlier, or who didn't believe that the no questions rule applied to him.

"That was kind of short," commented Amanda. "I expected it to be longer, more in depth."

"I guess they just don't have a lot of facts to give right now," said Abigail. "Like the Mayor said, the main purpose was to put an end to the speculations." She looked up and around the room, her eyes widening a little as she spotted someone. "Wait here for me, guys, I'll be back in a couple of minutes."

She got out of her seat and started making her way through the throng of people heading for the exit. Martin guessed she had spotted, and was on her way to have a quick chat with, Philip Glenster.

Though many of the citizens who had been in attendance exited the room, many others lagged behind, standing speaking in pairs or small groups. Amanda excused herself to go to the bathroom. Martin and Beth stayed seated.

"So, Beth," said Martin. "What happened with you and the guy around the back of this building then?"

"Actually, before I get into that, there's something I need to say to you."
"Oh?"

"Yeah, and if Abigail knew I'd said this to you, she'd kick my ass, but I feel the need to give you the "Don't hurt my friend" speech, the shortened version since I don't know how long I've got before she comes back." Martin nodded solemnly. "You've got no idea how much she means to me, to us, her friends, Marty. That woman is a rock solid, honest to god, straight up amazing human being and we love her, and we will not stand for someone

165

breaking her heart. Yes she's had other boyfriends, and no I haven't given them this speech, but I have never seen her the way she was when she was waiting for you to get here. She was so excited it was like she had become a little girl again. To be honest, I never gave any of her other boyfriends this speech because, although she liked them, I never really thought they were anything special, but I think you are, Marty. More importantly, Abigail thinks you're wonderful, and that gives you power over her that she has seldom given anyone in her life. I will not stand for you abusing that power, using it to hurt her. If you do, so help me, I will do you damage. You understand?"

Martin felt the need to inject a little levity into the conversation, to jokingly tell Beth that she was just jealous, but he couldn't do it. She had been so honest, put her point across so earnestly, that he couldn't bring himself to belittle it with humour. Martin knew how much Abigail loved and respected this woman, and he himself now admired her enormously because he had no doubt that she was quite correct in what she had said about Abigail's reaction should she ever find out about this little chat.

He leaned forward and planted a gentle kiss on Beth's forehead.

"Everyone should have a friend like you."

Beth smiled wide, revealing her top row of teeth. She nodded and said,

"Good response, Marty, good response." Martin smiled back.

"I know, but there's something even better that's just occurred to me."

"What's that?" He stopped smiling.

"You've given me power over you too." The smiled dropped like a brick from Beth's face. Before she could ask him to explain, Martin continued. "Yeah, you have to do whatever I say because if not, I'll tell Abigail about this little one to one of ours."

A few beats of shocked silence passed and then Martin couldn't hold it back any longer; he giggled. A few snorts at first as the last of his willpower failed, and then a short period where he just shut his eyes and giggled, his shoulders quaking. He opened his eyes and saw Beth realise she had been played.

"Oh, you ass crack!" she said, a smile of relief brightening her face. She punched him, none too lightly, on the shoulder, which just made him giggle harder.

"What's going on?" asked Amanda as she returned to her seat.

"This haggis munching dingbat here got one over on me," said Beth.

"How so?"

Beth briefly explained what had transpired between her and Martin.

"Go Marty," said Amanda when the tale was told.

"Thanks."

"Hey! You're supposed to be on my side."

A group of four or five people walked past the end of their aisle, heading for the exit. The three of them heard a man at the rear of the group say to the woman beside him that that young Thomas girl had served him in the pet store only last week.

The frivolous nature of their conversation suddenly made Martin, Beth and Amanda feel slightly ashamed. Martin felt like he should say something to lighten the mood again, but nothing he came up with sounded right, and so they waited in silence for Abigail to come back.

Walking Beth and Amanda back to their cars was Martin's idea, though it was one Abigail wholeheartedly supported. Martin got the impression that under normal circumstances such an idea would have resulted in some good natured joshing, but tonight both women were thankful for the offer.

Amanda and Beth were parked one in front of the other a few streets away, so the walk didn't take long. When they reached the vehicles, Abigail made her friends promise to text her when they got home safe and they agreed, then they made her promise to do the same. Hugs and kisses were again exchanged, this time followed by goodbyes. Martin and Abigail watched them drive off before heading back to Martin's car.

"So," he began. "You went to talk to Mr Glenster?"

"Yeah."

"How did it go?"

"Fine. I felt a little bad for lying to him, but there was no way I could tell him the whole truth."

"What did you tell him?"

"I told him that I had buried the memory, and then that I had essentially lied to myself my entire life about what had happened that night. I said that I had been surprised by his mention of Brannon's name this morning and so had just blanked it, but as today had gone on I had allowed it to come up, bit by bit. He was concerned, asked me if it had had any ill effects and I told him no. He said he was glad of that and that I had to take care, and if I ever even suspect that Brannon might be around, I should call the Sheriff first and him second."

"Call him? Why?"

"I think he's just as on edge as I am over this. He'd like to know if what we fear most has happened. Personally, I also think he wouldn't mind taking a shot at Brannon."

"He wants payback? Can't blame him for that."

"No, I can't. In fact I know exactly how he feels, but it'd be a stupid move, Marty. Philip's in good health, but he's not a young man, plus Brannon's a certifiable lunatic. Not a good match up. I told him that if he ever wanted to talk to let me know, then I told him to take care and that I'd give him a call in a day or two."

"You're really concerned for him." Abigail nodded.

"The man saved my life, Marty, and for years I didn't even remember. I don't even know if I thanked him back then. Being concerned for him now is the least I can do."

They walked the rest of the way in silence, got into the car and drove off.

"So what did you guys talk about whilst I was talking to Philip?" Martin was silent for a short time, and then made her promise she wouldn't get mad. "No way; someone asks you to make that promise, it's a sure bet what they're going to say is going to piss you off. What happened?"

"Uh, Beth gave me the speech."

"The speech?"

"The don't-hurt-my-friend-or-I'll-hurt-you speech."

"Oh, that speech."

"Now don't be annoyed at her…"

"I'm not. In fact if she met someone she thought was the one, I'd probably give him the speech too." Martin gave her a questioning look. "What? You thought I'd be pissed off?"

"Yes, and so did she." Abigail shook her head.

"If she had given that speech to any other guy, I might have been, but not to you."

"She did say that she had never felt the need to give the speech to your other boyfriends, but she thought I was special." He paused. "She also said that you were as giddy as a schoolgirl waiting for me to arrive."

"I may have to reassess my decision to not kick her ass," Abigail said drolly. Martin chuckled.

"She cares about you. It's something she and I have in common."

"And Beth has seen my boobs; something else you both have in common."

"What? When did she see..?" It was Abigail's turn to chuckle.

"Us girls, Marty, we're not too shy around our friends. Not like you boys, always hiding your wangs in the locker room."

"Hey, I am happy to say that I have never seen my best friend's wang."

"You're not even a little bit curious?"

"No!" Abigail laughed out loud. "I am however a little aroused thinking about you and Beth strutting around nude." Abigail's laugh sputtered and died and she shot him a look, which he responded to with a wide, smug grin. "You want to play, I can play."

"I'm not playing when I tell you that I will hit you, Muir."

"I'm driving."

"I'll risk it."

They looked at one another, held each other's gaze for a few seconds, and then laughed.

It was as Abigail got out of the car and looked at her house that she remembered the kitten.

Her mind had wandered during the meeting, mostly to thoughts of her missing friend, but she vaguely recalled the Sheriff saying something about keeping an eye out for anything unusual. Had she been paying complete attention her discovery a couple of weeks ago of the mauled kitten might have occurred to her sooner, but she had thought of it now and it seemed to qualify. At the time she had wondered if the poor little thing had been attacked by a savage animal, one that had been responsible for several missing pet posters she had seen around town, but what if the savage animal in question was of the sort that walked on two legs?

Given everything else that had happened, it wasn't that much of a stretch.

"Abi? What's wrong?"

"I'll tell you inside."

They entered the house and Abigail asked Martin to help her check all the doors and windows. He agreed without asking why she wanted to do so and together they went through the house, Abigail also watchful for anything that was out of place or missing. It took only five minutes to check the whole house and nothing was amiss. When they were back in the living room, they sat down and Abigail explained about the kitten.

"I mean, it doesn't add up to much at all," she said when she had finished. "But... I don't know. Given what's going on, who it might be, it just adds that sense of creepiness to it."

"Finding a dead and mutilated kitten in your back garden would be creepy at any time but, as you say, everything that's going on adds an extra dimension to it." He paused. "Do you want me to stay tonight?"

"You and I will be together every night till you have to leave," she clarified. "Including tonight. However, I'm a big enough girl to admit that I'm a little freaked out. It pisses me off to feel that way, even more so to admit it, but there it is. This is my home and I feel unsettled in it. I haven't felt that way since I moved in. I'm hoping it's a passing thing, but for tonight, do you think we could stay at the cabin?"

"Course we can. If it makes you feel any better, you could always tell yourself that you're spending the night there not because you feel creeped out here, but that since I'm paying for the place we might as well get some use out of it." She smiled sadly.

"It doesn't, but thanks for trying." She kissed him. "I'll go throw some things in an overnight bag."

Ten minutes later they were getting back into the car and heading for the cabin. Five minutes later, Martin asked,

"Do you think you'll ever tell Amanda or Beth about your memory problem?"

Abigail gave it some thought.

"I honestly don't know," she said at last. "It took a lot to tell you, and the main reason I did was that I wanted to be with you and didn't think that a secret that big should be between us. Trying to keep up the journals and not have them find out has been a problem over the years, mostly during sleepovers, but I think they just got the impression I was really fanatical about my journal, and I never said or did anything to dispel the notion. I don't really think they would make a big fuss about it, and I doubt it would change anything between us. I wonder if maybe I've kept it a secret so long that they might be hurt I had never felt able to tell before." She sighed. "And I can never fully get rid of the idea that maybe they'll make fun of me." Martin made to speak. "I know, I know, they're my friends and I should trust them, and I do." She sighed. "My relationships with my friends are fine as they are and they have been that way for years; to be perfectly honest, I don't see any reason to rock the boat. Maybe not in the future, certainly not right now."

Martin nodded and concentrated on once again navigating the twists of Jackpot Road, illuminated only by his headlights. He made it without incident. Slowly, but without incident. He parked, let out a long breath, and then got out and waited for Abigail. The two of them went inside, had something to eat and watched a little TV. Abigail was understandably tired. Martin sat beside her whilst she recorded the day's events in her journal, and afterward they went to bed.

6:45pm. As the town hall had been starting to get packed, Corday had parked outside the party venue, preparing to escort the last guest inside. As he had dragged the covered body out of the back seat, he'd had a huge grin on his face at the thought that tomorrow morning he would get to royally fuck Abigail and Muir's little whirlwind romance right into the air. His only hope was that the bastard didn't stay at Abigail's tonight again; he wanted him to be there when it all kicked off. He wanted him stunned, squirming, and neck deep in shit right from the very start.

Now, only an hour or so later, Corday felt like Christmas had come early.

He had driven up Jackpot Road even slower than Martin, having been driving behind him with his lights off to avoid being spotted. He had scarcely allowed himself to believe what might be in the offing when the two had come back out of Abigail's house - she with a bag over her shoulder - got into his car and driven out this way. But the lights were out, it was true! She was staying over!

Now all he had to do was wait until morning and then call the party crashers.

Chapter 31

Martin didn't so much wake up the following morning as just decide that he was just going to stop trying to go to sleep.

Last night, before trying to sleep, they had lain in one another's arms, both quiet. It had been well into the wee small hours when Abigail had finally managed to drop off. He had looked over at her. She had been facing him, strands of hair falling over her face. He'd resisted the temptation to reach over and move them for fear of waking her. He had wanted her to sleep a while longer. After the day she'd had, she needed the rest.

Martin sighed quietly, comparing this morning with yesterday morning. There was one commonality though. Yesterday morning he had scarcely been able to believe who he had woken up beside. This morning he was in a state of disbelief again, this time at how different things would be this morning when Abigail woke up. Yesterday it had been laughing and horseplay and making love, and today, well, he didn't have a clue. Abigail had discovered a terrible event she had hidden from herself, and that the bastard responsible for said event might well be back in town. Not only that, but her friend was missing, possibly kidnapped by said bastard. How she was managing to deal with it all was beyond him. What he did know for certain was that whatever today brought, be it good or bad, he would be by her side.

Martin got up and tiptoed out of the room. He eased the bedroom door open, slid out, eased the bedroom door shut, went to the lounge, sat down on one of the couches and tried not to think about what today might bring. A wasted effort; he imagined the police showing up at his door, looking for Abigail to inform her that Sophie's body had been found.

As it would turn out, he wasn't that far off the mark.

Fifteen minutes passed, among other things, Martin thought about poor Sophie. He hadn't known her very well, had only met her once in fact, but she had seemed like a really nice person. He recalled snippets from some of Abigail's letters, times when Sophie had given her a shoulder to cry on or bought her a really thoughtful birthday gift. No, he didn't know Sophie well, but she meant a lot to Abigail, so she was important to him too. He hoped that she was all right, but, much as he didn't want to admit it, he could not see it ending well.

This morning, Martin Muir was close to being a prophet.

There was a harsh knock at the door. Martin, who had finally been close to nodding off, snapped his head up, his eyes going wide. He blinked, looked at the clock: 8:23am. *Who the hell could that be?* He got up and headed for the door, wondering if maybe he should get a nice big knife from the kitchen drawer. He decided against it. Just as he passed the bedroom door, it opened and a worried looking Abigail stepped out. Her look asked the obvious and he shrugged and stepped up to the door, just as there were another few harsh thumps. Not knocking this time; Martin imagined someone hammering the bottom of their fist against the wood. He looked over his shoulder and motioned for Abigail to stay where she was. Martin moved his head closer to the door, keeping as quiet as possible, until he could look through the peephole.

A grim faced Sheriff Mark Flaghan stood outside. Martin blinked hard, looked again. The sheriff was still there. Feeling suddenly nauseous, he looked at Abigail and mouthed the name of their visitor. She visibly paled and, after a slight pause, nodded for him to open the door. He did.

The moment it was open a crack, it burst open and the sheriff filled the doorway. Martin leapt back to avoid being hit.

"What the hell?" he asked, then noticed, over the sheriff's shoulder, the other officer standing at the top of the steps. Part of him was relieved. After all, it didn't take two men to deliver bad news. But if not the bearers of bad news, why where they here?

"Sheriff?" said Abigail.

"Miss Morton, I'm going to ask you and Mr Muir to wait outside with Deputy Parchett." He glanced over his shoulder and the deputy stepped inside.

"Hold on," began Martin. "What's all this about, sheriff? Why are you here?"

Flaghan looked him straight in the eye for several, very uncomfortable, seconds. Martin held his gaze. This wasn't his house exactly, but it was where he was staying, and he wanted to know what the intrusion was all about, and why he and his girlfriend were being bossed around.

"Sheriff?" he said. Flaghan dropped his gaze for a moment and then reached a decision. He looked Martin in the eye as he told him,

"We received a call this morning stating that you were responsible for the missing women, and that if we checked this cabin we would find them."

Martin felt like he'd just been sucker-punched in the gut. Goosebumps exploded all over his arms as a chill ran through his entire body. His breath fled his lungs in a single sharp exhalation. It took so long for him to draw another breath that for a moment he thought he'd forgotten how to. His mind stalled, all thoughts dropping like moths that had flown too close to the flame. He looked at the floor, his brow furrowing as he tried to think of something, preferably a way to respond to the insane accusation that had been made against him. He came up with nothing.

"Are you out of your damn mind?" asked Abigail, her voice low and angry. "Who in the hell told you this?"

"I'm not at liberty to give you that information."

"Oh cut the crap, sheriff," she scalded him. "Someone, I'm guessing an anonymous someone, calls you up and tells you Marty, who's been in town for only a few days, has kidnapped three women and you show up here with your deputy, and almost break the damn door down. Did your source give you *any* kind of reason as to why they suspected Marty?" She heard a small noise that sounded like her name, but ignored it. "Huh? I know the mayor must be on your back to get something done, but this is…" She heard the noise again, clearer now, definitely her name. She realised Martin was speaking to her. "Marty, don't tell me that this is all right." He shook his head.

"It's not," he assured her. "But it is a lie." He looked to Flaghan "Whoever told you this was lying to you. I don't know why they did it, but they were lying. If you want to check this house, you go ahead and check it, top to bottom. I've got nothing to hide." Flaghan turned to his deputy. "But," Martin continued before the sheriff could issue instructions. "Abigail and I will not be waiting outside, and when you're finished in here, I want to know exactly how you're going to go about finding the arsehole who called you this morning, because this is not on."

Flaghan looked at him, saw his resolve and nodded. He then told his deputy to come in and start searching the house. He directed Parchett to check the lower floor first, then the ground floor. Whilst that was being done, he stayed with Martin and Abigail, who stood side by side, hand in hand. After ten minutes, Parchett came back and reported that he had found nothing suspicious. Flaghan got him to go outside and look around the outside of the house.

"There's nothing much but an old well," said Martin, words which earned him arched eyebrows from both officers, the meaning of which sank in immediately. "There's a grate bolted down onto the top of it."

Flaghan nodded to Parchett, who jogged, returning minutes later.

"Nothing. Found the well, just as he said. The grate's rusty and hasn't been moved in a long time. No smell coming out of it either." Flaghan nodded and looked around.

"What's up there?" he asked, nodding in the direction of the staircase.

"Mezzanine," said Martin. "Looks out over the lounge. And the master bedroom is up there too."

"Wait here," the sheriff said to his deputy, stepping towards the stairs.

"You can't," said Martin. Flaghan gave him a narrow-eyed look. Martin sighed and shook his head. "Guests aren't allowed in the master bedroom; the owners have it locked, and they have the keys."

Flaghan looked up the stairs, nodded, then turned back to Martin.

"They can bill me for any damage."

Abigail had been quite right in what she had said about the mayor being on his back to get something done about the disappearances. Flaghan could understand her anger; to be honest he didn't think her visiting Scottish boyfriend was guilty either. Guy had only been in town a few days, and also, assuming she wasn't just covering for him, she had been with him when her friend Sophie had been abducted.

But his opinions on the matter took a back seat when someone called in and gave a name and a location. After all, the really bad ones often wore a mask of friendliness, hid behind a shield of apparent respectability. But he didn't believe that about Muir. That said, he was an officer of the law and he had received information regarding a crime, and the only way to determine if that lead was solid or if someone was, for whatever reason, wasting his time was to check it out. If it turned out someone was wasting his time, he would do his utmost to track that someone down and make damn sure they paid for it somehow.

He reached the top of the stairs. The mezzanine deck was large, with a chaise lounge sitting against one wall and a large, deep pile royal blue rug on the floor. The place was brightly lit by the early morning light pouring in through the huge windows. Flaghan paused for a moment to appreciate the view and then looked out and down over the railing, into the lounge. He glanced up and saw the cobwebs in the corners of the high ceiling and the apex of the roof. Just as Martin had done the night he had arrived at the cabin, the sheriff briefly wondered how the hell anyone got up there to dust. Then he turned to the only other thing of interest on the deck: the door to the cabin's master bedroom.

The two doors looked solid. Flaghan tried the handle and found them to be locked tight. He stood wondering what the best course of action was. He could try kicking the doors in, but the idea that a strong, well-placed kick could bust a lock open was movie bullshit. If he kicked the door with everything he had, the only thing that would end up damaged was his leg. He had no idea how to pick a lock, so that was out. He could shoot the lock out, but given he was here on the strength of an anonymous lead – Miss Morton had been right on the money there too - putting holes in someone's home didn't seem like a good idea.

Flaghan considered putting a call through to the station and organising for a locksmith to come up and open the doors, but he wanted this checked out now. He was very aware that either Abigail or Muir might decide to put in a complaint. Technically he had done nothing wrong in coming out here, but the basis for the visit was pretty damn flimsy to keep them waiting for the hour or so it might take to get a professional out here to deal with this.

"Damn it to hell," he muttered.

Stepping over to the head of the stairs, he called down,

"Everyone cover your ears; I'm going to have to shoot the lock."

"What?" yelled Martin.

"It's the only way I can gain access."

"I have my crowbar in the trunk, sheriff," Parchett informed him

"Why?"

"Bradley borrowed it last week because he was taking apart his old shed. He gave me it back over the weekend at the station and I tossed it in the trunk. Been meaning to take it out of there, but I haven't gotten round to it yet. It'll still cause a bit of damage, but far less than using your sidearm. Little less risk too."

"Works for me," said Flaghan. Parchett nodded and the sheriff stayed where he was as his deputy ran out to the cruiser, coming back in and jogging upstairs to hand him the heavy implement. As Parchett went back downstairs, he returned to the doors. It took some effort, some sweat and some swearing before they finally gave, but eventually he got them open.

He sat the crowbar on the chaise lounge and stepped inside the master bedroom.

During his time in law enforcement, Mark Flaghan hadn't had much call to be around the items which immediately caught his attention, but he recognised body bags when he saw them.

There were three of them: one on the king sized bed, one propped up in a chair by the window, and one on the floor near the door. A cold dread seized him. It was perhaps the last thing he wanted to do at that moment, but he had to make sure. He walked over and knelt down beside the body-bag on the floor. Using a handkerchief to cover his fingers, he gripped the tab of the zipper and pulled it down. The smell that rose from the bag caused him to recoil, and his gorge rose in his throat. Swallowing hard, he started breathing through his mouth as he gripped one side of the zipper between thumb and forefinger and peeled back the bag to reveal the pale, cut and bruised face of Janice Mallory. She was naked, and at first glance it was clear that she had been badly beaten prior to death.

Hot anger flooded through him, bordering on fury. That bastard! He imagined himself striding downstairs and putting a bullet in that foreign fucker's forehead, but he shook the images away. Flaghan got to his feet and checked the other two bags. In the second he found Sophie Thomas, in the third Charlotte Webster, both of them in similar states to Janice. Sophie was fresher – a term that made him shudder to think of, but it was the first word that came to mind – since she had died most recently. She had a little more colour than the others, and there was still a trace of her scent on the air that escaped the bag.

The sheriff straightened up, shaking his head. Why had Muir done this? Did Miss Morton know? Her story was that Muir had been with her when her friend had gone missing, but here her friend lay, beaten and murdered, in her beau's rented cabin. Was Morton perhaps in on it? Why would she do that? Who the hell knew why people who did things like this did it. Shrinks and specialists and experts could debate it all till hell froze over and still never pin down any one thing that triggered such actions. Each one of these monsters was different, if only slightly, and there was usually no way of knowing till it was too late, and for these three poor women it was most certainly too late.

Flaghan's mind shifted tracks, back to asking questions: how had Muir managed to get into this room? There was a large window to his left. Flaghan stepped over and looked out, seeing no obvious way of reaching this level from outside. That he had used a ladder seemed unlikely; climbing a ladder carrying a dead body would be difficult. Maybe he had picked the lock. Where had he gotten the body bags from? Nowhere in town except his own office and the coroner's would have them, and he was sure Muir hadn't gotten them from either of those sources. Online maybe? But to this address inside the couple of days since he arrived? Then again the bastard had known he was coming here for some time. He could have had the stuff delivered in advance, or he might even have arrived before he said he had, gone somewhere else to buy the stuff he'd need. A check with the owners of the cabin and a look at his flight booking would shed some light on that.

He looked around the room. No way they had been killed in here; the place looked spotless. Judging by the wounds he had seen on the bodies there would have been a lot of blood spilled. Somewhere else in the cabin maybe? A room Muir had wiped down so that it looked clean to the naked eye but would yield the truth when subjected to a forensic examination? Somewhere outside?

The sheriff stopped, mentally filing away all the questions that would need to be asked. Flaghan felt a deep sadness creep across his shoulders as he regarded the three faces, their eyes closed, peeking out from the body bags. What a waste. What a god damn pointless waste. He clasped his hands together in front of him, bowed his head, closed his eyes and hoped that the three of them rested in peace.

There was one thing he was glad of: at least it hadn't been David Brannon who'd come back to town, although it seemed they had someone just as sick and twisted on their hands. A copycat maybe? Came here on the pretence that he was visiting his sweetheart but his real motivation was to pay homage to his hero, in the town where said hero had once killed?

Just another question to be asked down at the station.

Martin heard the sounds of the master bedroom doors being forced and wondered exactly what the hell he was going to say to the owners. How did you nonchalantly tell someone the doors to their private bedroom had been burst open because you had been accused of kidnapping three women and keeping them in there? He didn't relish the idea of the conversation. What he did relish was Flaghan coming back down here so they could get to work finding the liar who had caused this. As if Abigail didn't have enough to contend with, someone was accusing her boyfriend of kidnapping her friend. It was ridiculous. Again Martin wondered if this was an old flame he hadn't been told about being vindictive, but Abigail had told him there was no one in her past like that and he believed her. But who the hell could it be? Who in Hannerville could bear him such a grudge that they would accuse him of the recent kidnappings? He only knew one person here, and currently she was standing beside him, holding his hand.

He turned to Abigail and forced a smile, doubting she would be fooled by it. After all, he wasn't fooled by the smile she gave him in return. He glanced at the deputy – Parched? Was that what Flaghan had said the man's name was? – and considered making a comment on how bizarre this all was, but the look on the man's face suggested he was not in a jocular mood. Instead Martin returned his gaze to the head of the stairs. Exactly how long was it going to take the sheriff to satisfy himself that there was nothing in the room? Martin frowned, realising that the owners of this place could be heavily into bondage, or using toys during sex. Shit, Flaghan might have walked into a room with highly polished chains dangling from the ceiling, and black vinyl sheets on the king size bed, at the head of which sat a teddy bear wearing a strap on! Martin mused that such a bedroom might well be the reason that room and only that room was locked. Of course the proclivities of the owners should in no way cast a bad light on anyone who rented the cabin.

One of the longest minutes of Martin's life passed and then Flaghan appeared at the head of the stairs, his face grim. He descended the stairs two at a time and then stopped in front of Martin. The sheriff's eyes were wide, showing a lot of white, and his nostrils were flaring a little. Martin noticed the man's hand was clenched into a fist and it dawned on him that right at that moment, more than anything else in the world, Sheriff Mark Flaghan wanted to punch him square in the face. Baffled, he opened his mouth to ask what the sheriff had found, but as soon as his lips parted Flaghan moved, grabbing his arm and wrenching his hand from Abigail's. Martin was spun round and had both his arms pulled behind his back. He felt something cold touch his wrists and realised he was being handcuffed! For an odd moment – during which time Flaghan's decree that he was being arrested on suspicion of murder went unnoticed - Martin thought he had been right about the bedtime habits of the cabin's owners and that the sheriff was having a laugh at his expense, coming down and putting him in cuffs that he'd found in the master bedroom. Then he realised he was once

174

again hearing in real life something he had only ever heard in films and on TV: he was being read his rights.

"What?" he began. "What's going on? What did you find? Sheriff? What was in that room?" His mind reeled. He felt sick and feared that he was actually going to throw up. He heard Abigail speaking over the sheriff as Flaghan asked him if he understood his rights as they had been explained to him.

"Sheriff?" Abigail was almost shouting. "What the hell do you think you're doing?"

The sheriff jerked Martin's arm and asked him again if he understood his rights. Martin found that he could not speak. He nodded.

"Deputy Parchett, take him out and put him in your car... No!"

Martin felt the sheriff release him and he turned to see the man running upstairs after Abigail. Parchett moved in, his grasp replacing the sheriff's. Martin looked to the man.

"What did he find? What's going..."

Before he could finish the question, there was a loud thud from upstairs. Martin shouted Abigail's name and tried to go up, but the deputy held him fast and told him to stay put. Flaghan appeared at the top of the stairs.

"She's fainted," he reported. "Jack, get him down to the station and get him booked in. I'll bring her round, take her home and then come in."

Parchett nodded. Martin again opened his mouth to speak, but no words came. He allowed himself to be led to the car and he was put in the back. In a state of utter shock, he couldn't even formulate a worried thought for Abigail. Deputy Parchett got behind the wheel, started the engine and pulled away. Then a single devastating thought came to Martin.

It's all over.

Chapter 32

Abigail opened her eyes. In her mind she saw herself run into the master bedroom of the cabin Martin had rented to find the three body bags. Saw herself fighting the urge to look and failing, peeking into the bag and seeing poor Sophie's face, then a scream and nothing. For a few blessed moments she believed it had just been a dream, until she remembered the smell from that room. No, it had happened; she had found her friend's dead body upstairs in Martin's cabin.

She sat upright, a move which brought on an immediate wave of dizziness. Putting a hand to her forehead, she closed her eyes and took a deep breath.

"You weren't out long," said a familiar voice. Abigail opened her eyes and saw Sheriff Flaghan standing behind the couch in the lounge of Martin's rented cabin. "Here," said the sheriff, holding out a glass of water. She took it without a word and took a sip, then held the glass to her forehead to cool it. She began to ask a question, but Flaghan answered it before she got the chance. "You ran upstairs, into the room, saw what you saw, and passed out. I brought you down here, and now that you're up I'm going to take you home."

"Where's Marty?" she asked.

"He's been put under arrest and taken to the station." Abigail made to ask something else, but Flaghan held up a hand. "That's all I can tell you right now. Come on."

She took another drink and then handed the glass back to him. He went to the kitchen, sloshed the rest of the contents down the sink and sat the glass upside down on the draining board. Abigail got to her feet and was led to the front door. As Flaghan opened it for her, she looked over her shoulder, up the stairs. The sheriff laid a hand on her shoulder and she turned and walked out.

They drove back to town in silence. Only when Flaghan pulled up outside her house did she speak.

"You're going to contact her family?"

"I'll be contacting the families of all three women as soon as I get back to the station."

"What will you tell them?"

"What they need to know: that their loved ones have been found, and that we have a suspect in custody."

Abigail felt her insides contract at the fact that the suspect he was talking about was Marty. She felt as though she should say something in his defence, but she did not. Those bodies had been up there in that room. She had spent the night in that cabin with her friend's dead body in the room right above her and…

"Is it all right if I let Amanda and Beth know?" she asked.

"Yes, that's fine. Better they hear it from you."

"What do you mean?"

"You know how this town, and every town like it, works, Abigail. It won't take long for word of the discovery, and the arrest, to spread."

Abigail nodded.

"Thank you for bringing me home."

She unbuckled her seatbelt, got out and walked to her front door.

Once inside, she collapsed onto her couch and cried. She had to; for the moment there was nothing else she could do. The giddy heights of the beginning of her relationship with Marty seemed so long ago. First Sophie had gone missing, then she had discovered the truth behind her parent's deaths, and now Sophie had been found murdered in a room in the cabin being rented by the man she had been imagining spending the rest of her life with. It was all just too much. To have been so high and then to be brought down, not to earth, but what felt like all the way down to hell itself, was simply too much. She had to unburden herself and so she cried. After a while, with her eyes red and swollen and her throat sore from sobbing, Abigail sat up, sniffing, wiping at the corners of her eyes with the backs of her hands.

She needed to call Amanda and Beth and get them round here. She needed to tell them before they heard it from somewhere else. But how, and what, was she going to tell them? That their friend had apparently been kidnapped and murdered by Marty, by her Marty? It seemed absurd, and yet she had seen the bodies in that room with her own eyes. She had smelled that cloying reek emanating from those bags. Even the memory of it made her want to gag. How did she explain that the man she had brought into their lives had…

Abigail squeezed her eyes tightly shut and viciously shook her head. It couldn't be, it just couldn't. She had known him almost all her life and he wasn't a killer, for god's sake, he was *Marty*. But if the sheriff was right, then the women had started going missing when Marty had arrived in town. Had he had his eye on Sophie from the moment he had met her at Pages and Pages? Abigail had read stories about such things, watched news reports and documentaries about them too: someone had started a relationship with a seemingly lovely person over the internet and had arranged to meet them only to end up missing, or dead, or to find out that the person had misrepresented themselves and was an ill-mannered prick or liked to hit women, or at least looked nothing like the pictures they had sent. Abigail shook her head. What she had with Marty was no whirlwind cyberspace romance; it went back to when they had been kids. They had been friends, they had fallen for one another, and now they were lovers. It was an age old story. That they had never actually met until a few days ago made no difference. She *knew* him.

Didn't she?

Just because she had known him for so long didn't mean that he was who he said he was. If he had developed into the kind of person responsible for what had been done to Sophie and those other women, obviously he wasn't going to shout about it. What if his entire life back in Scotland was bogus? What if everything from way back when had all been lies? What if his friends and his business didn't really exist? What if he had been planning all this for years?

So why pick now to do it? Why not years ago if that was why he was coming here? Don't these sick bastards have some need that compels them to do what they do? How did he go so long before putting his plan into action? How come he was never caught back in Scotland?

Taking a deep breath and letting it back out again, Abigail got up, got her bag and rooted around in it until she found her mobile phone. Not willing to trust her voice just yet, she sent a text message to Beth and Amanda asking them to come round as soon as possible. No sooner had the messages been sent than she received a reply from each of them saying they were on their way. Abigail sat her phone aside and went upstairs to prepare herself as much as possible for what she had to do.

Her friends shamed her.

They arrived together, both looking worried when she answered the door. Obviously upon receiving her texts they had imagined something was wrong with her. Of course there was, but that wasn't why she had asked them here. Having said that, given what had happened, she could use a little support. She told them to come in, skirted round their queries about her health and wellbeing, and asked if she could get them a drink. Both refused and she sat down on the couch and asked them to join her.

As calmly as she was able, Abigail told her friends about what had happened earlier at the cabin. The shocked silence that filled the room after she finished was broken by Amanda's wail. Soon the three of them were huddled together, crying.

Once they had cried themselves out - for the time being at least - the trio sat slumped on the couch, dabbing at their eyes with tissues. Abigail was waiting for the recriminations to begin, for the hurt either one of her friends was feeling to turn to anger and be aimed at her. She believed the time had come when, from the corner of her eye, she noticed Beth staring at her. She wondered how she would defend herself, then decided that perhaps part of her penance should be that she did not, that she simply accept what was coming as her due.

"It's not right," said Beth quietly.

I know. If Marty was going to kill anyone it should have been me. That was her immediate thought. It was left unsaid and she nodded.

"I mean," Beth went on. "There's just no way in hell that Marty did this."

As she looked up at her friend, Abigail hid her surprise well.

"Yeah," agreed Amanda. "There is something really off going on here. You told the sheriff that, right, Abigail?"

No, she had not. She should have, she realised now. In fact she had started to, until it had occurred to her what the sheriff had discovered and she had charged upstairs and into that room. But she had said nothing in Marty's defence the entire time she'd been in the sheriff's company. Had, in fact, practically condemned the man she loved for the murder of her friend and two other women. Now her other friends, who had more right than most to hate the man the town would soon believe was the killer in their midst, were telling her something was amiss. What was most amiss, what she honestly thought she'd have a hard time forgiving herself for later, was that she had not seen the glaring truth of it herself.

"I didn't mention," she admitted, adding, "I was in shock," quickly after. "But you guys saw Sophie the night she was taken, and Marty had been with me that entire day, was with me all that night. He never left me. He couldn't have taken Sophie."

Oh, Marty, I'm so sorry.

Abigail wondered if she would ever be able to look him in the eye again after having displayed such a lack of faith. It was something she knew she wouldn't be able to keep from him, so she could only hope that he found some way to understand.

"No, he couldn't have taken her," agreed Amanda. "Plus, you've known this guy forever; you know he's no serial killer."

Stomach roiling, Abigail feared her cheeks would flush, telegraphing her guilt about her earlier thoughts. She nodded.

"No, he is not." Amanda nodded.

"Plus there are the body bags. You don't bring things like that through customs without somebody noticing. How would he have known where to get it once he got here?"

"Internet," said Beth. Amanda and Abigail looked at her sharply. Beth held up her hands. "Hey, it's what the cops are going to think. They'll say that he found a supplier online and had the stuff delivered before or after he got here. Hell, you can buy anything online these days: cars, pets, collectibles, even virginities." She took a breath. "But we know Marty couldn't have been the one who took Sophie…" She paused and her bottom lip began trembling ever so slightly. The others feared she was going to break down, that their impromptu confab of the deductive processes was going to end, leaving them to deal with the fact that their friend was dead. They'd have to eventually, but they were in no hurry. Beth regrouped, bit her bottom lip briefly as if warning it to behave itself, and continued.

"That being the case, what are the chances of him being responsible for the other two? Next door to non-existent in my opinion."

"It makes no sense that the bodies would all have been found in the same place if they had been murdered by different men," mused Amanda.

"An accomplice," Abigail said quietly. "They'll say he has an accomplice."

"They can suggest it, but they've got no way of proving it," stated Beth. "When he was with you, Abigail, did he ever get a text message or a phone call?" Abigail thought about it and shook her head. "Did he ever make any calls himself?" Another shake from Abigail, who then said,

"So say I, but they'll be looking at all the angles, and one of those angles is that I might have been helping him." Beth's face coloured.

"So help me," she said, her voice taking on a tone neither of her friends had ever heard before. "I will personally fuck up whoever is dumb enough to suggest that." Abigail smiled at her.

"They'll be able to check Martin's phone anyway," said Amanda. "See who he called and who called him. The phone records will back you up."

Abigail felt a powerful wave of emotion wash over her. Her love for the two women with her had never been greater, and she swore to herself that if she ever came face to face with the man who had taken Sophie from them, she would hurt him, damage him. She might even kill the bastard.

Knowing that it was an act that might again put their little pow-wow in jeopardy, she threw her arms wide. Beth and Amanda closed in around her. After a few minutes, Amanda spoke, her tears evident in her voice.

"I'm going to miss her so much." Abigail, crying again herself, kissed the top of her head and told her,

"We all will, honey."

They all sat together until the doorbell rang.

Releasing one another, they sat up and pawed at their eyes, each of them thinking that it was an odd thing to do as whoever was at the door was just going to have to deal with the fact that they were grieving. Abigail got to her feet and went to answer the door. It wasn't something she did usually, but today she looked through the peephole to see who was calling. Her Aunt Janine and Uncle Peter stood on the doorstep. Abigail swept her hair back from her face and opened the door.

"Hi, you guys," she said as cheerily as she could.

Her aunt said nothing as she stepped inside and embraced her niece in a fierce hug. Abigail hugged her back and looked to her uncle, who looked at his feet. Abigail released her aunt, pulled back and saw the tears in the woman's eyes. She gestured for them to come in.

"Word has started to get around?" she ventured as she closed the door. Aunt Janine nodded and then walked over to where Amanda and Beth stood, giving each of them a hug and a kiss on the cheek. Abigail and her Uncle Peter joined them.

"How are you girls doing?" asked Uncle Peter.

"Don't really think it's sunk in yet," replied Beth. Aunt Janine nodded in understanding, tears in her eyes. There was an awkward moment and then Beth and Amanda looked at one another. "Uh, listen, we'll head off and..."

"There's no need, dears, really," Aunt Janine told them, fishing in her handbag for a tissue.

"No, honestly, we need to be going anyway," said Amanda. She looked to Abigail. "Call us later?"

"I will."

She walked them to the door, hugged them and then came back to the living room, where the man and woman who had raised her sat side by side. Her aunt was still teary eyed and her uncle had an arm around her. Uncle Peter, the kind of man who was not given to public displays of emotion, was also somewhat watery eyed. Abigail was puzzled. Terrible things had happened, certainly, and her aunt and uncle had known her friends for years, but...

It hit her.

On the phone last night, when they had told her they wouldn't be able to make the town meeting, Uncle Peter had mentioned that they would get whatever news there was from someone. That news, probably delivered by one of their neighbours, would have been about the missing women and the possible return of the man who had murdered Peter Morton's brother and his sister-in-law. The same man who would have killed Abigail that night if not for the actions of Philip Glenster.

Abigail jerked her head to the side, her eyes zeroing in on the digital counter on her answering machine. It was flashing the number six. Her heart sank. She wanted to check her mobile phone, but knew what she would find: missed calls and voicemail messages, several of them, the notifications of which hadn't even registered when she had used it earlier. She took a deep breath and asked herself if there was the possibility of getting through the rest of the day without wronging anyone else she cared about.

"I am so sorry," she said, her apology sounding lame even to her. "I didn't even think... I was so shocked earlier when I got home that I didn't even check my machine." She opened her mouth, but said nothing further. Uncle Peter was shaking his head.

"I want to tell you that it's all right, Abigail," he said. "I do, but do you have any idea how frantic we've been? We hear from one of our friends that women have gone missing. We'd heard the rumours, so that it had been confirmed wasn't much of a surprise, but to then be told that that *monster* might be back in town, and then we can't reach you. We can't get a hold of you anywhere. We've barely slept. Then this morning we hear that the women have been found dead and the killer has been caught. As if that weren't enough, we then discover that the killer is some foreign guy who was supposedly here to visit his girlfriend, who was there when the bodies were found upstairs in the place this guy has been staying. It seemed a little too coincidental. Rather than try calling again, we just came over."

Holy shit, thought Abigail. *Not only did it go round quick, it's also pretty damn accurate. Someone at the sheriff's department has a big mouth.*

"He was arrested on suspicion of murder," she said, realising in the moments afterwards that it might be an odd defence, but it was nonetheless true.

"Because the bodies were found in the room above where you spent last night with him," was her aunt's retort. "Fairly damning evidence, Abigail."

"Not if there's nothing else that links Marty to the murders," she said. "Which there won't be because he didn't kill them. Here's something the rumour mill might not have clued you in on, something that will really screw up the cases of all those back yard and armchair prosecutors out there: Marty was with me the night Sophie went missing. The only way it would have been possible for him to have had anything to do with it would have been if he had left my side, which he did not. Mind you, when that gets out people will probably just say I was in on it with him."

"Abigail, they will not," said Peter, somewhat half-heartedly. "But you have to understand how this looks."

"I know how it looks, and it looks bad, but I also know Marty. I've known him nearly all my life. Over the years I've shared things with him that no one else knows, asked him for advice about things I didn't feel comfortable asking anyone else. That man knows me better than anyone else in my life. I don't even have the words to describe how happy, how lucky, I felt when he and I got together."

"A couple of days ago," said Janine. "It's not like the two of you have some sort of long lasting relationship."

"But we *do*, don't you see? My relationship with Marty has outlasted every other relationship I've ever had with a guy. It's deeper and more meaningful than any other relationship I could ever have with someone else because he knows me. Inside out and back to front, he knows me."

"But how can you know him?" asked her uncle. "What if everything he's ever written to you about himself is a complete pile of bull?"

"How can you know anyone? Anybody can lie to you about who they are, Uncle Peter. Besides, I've thought of that and I can't believe it. If I did then it would destroy me, because it would mean a relationship that has played a huge part in defining me all these years would be a lie, and I couldn't handle that." She shook her head. "I just couldn't. Marty is not a killer. He is innocent, and I am going to do everything I can to help prove that."

"Like what?" asked her uncle.

"I have no idea. Maybe there is nothing I can do from a legal or investigative standpoint, but if that's the case then I will do the one thing I know I can do; I will stand by Marty."

Her aunt and uncle looked at one another. Eventually, they both looked back to Abigail.

"We can't tell you what to do, Abigail," he said quietly. "But one thing we have always been able to do is trust your judgement. Trust your judgement, and trust your decisions. On that score nothing has changed." Abigail opened her mouth but he raised a hand. "I'm not going to tell you that I'm overly happy with you being willing to go up to bat for a man who may, or may not, be a killer, but a lifetime of keeping your word, being trustworthy and always thinking things out to the fullest has to count for something. Am I right?"

She knew there was no point in fighting the tears. Nodding emphatically, she stepped forward, knelt down and put an arm around each of them. She felt her uncle's arm go round her shoulders and her aunt clutched her arm with both hands.

"You just have to make us one promise," said her uncle, his voice suggesting he was having a difficult time doing the guy thing and holding in his emotions. Abigail released them and looked at him. "You have to promise us you'll be careful."

"I will," she said, nodding and sniffing and wiping her face on her sleeve. "I promise."

"What are you going to do now?"

"I'm going to get changed and head down to the sheriff's office. I need to see Marty."

"I don't know if they'll let you in, honey," her aunt said.

"I don't either, but I'll find out."

She almost added that she had to confess to him about her earlier crisis of faith, something which may well make her aunt and uncle's fears over her standing by Marty moot. She didn't say anything, unwilling to admit to anyone other than herself and Marty what she had thought.

She promised to call them later and her aunt and uncle left. Abigail took a shower. She got dried and got dressed and then grabbed her jacket and bag. A quick check showed that it contained everything she needed. She was just closing the bag when there was a knock at her door. She walked to it and again used the peephole. Sighing in slight annoyance at being held up, she opened the door and invited Philip Glenster inside. The former physician saw what she was wearing and asked,

"Just coming in or just going out?"

"Going out. Sorry."

"Not at all," he said. "I just wanted to come over and see how you were doing."

"You've heard too?"

"From a very reliable source; Sheriff Flaghan called me to let me know what had happened. I must say it shocked me."

"It's not true," Abigail stated. Glenster frowned.

"They didn't find...?"

"They did, but Marty is not the killer." Glenster gave her words some thought.

"I understand that you wouldn't want to believe such a thing of your friend, Abigail, but..."

"I don't believe it, not for a second."

"He seemed like a perfectly nice man to me too, but you have to understand that sometimes people hide who they truly are. Monsters can wear the most innocent of masks."

"Doctor, no offense, but there's nothing that you, or anyone else, could say to me to make me believe that Marty is responsible for what Sheriff Flaghan found in that cabin this morning. Beyond the fact that I trust Marty implicitly, there's the fact that he was with me the night Sophie went missing. Whoever is responsible is still out there, so that collective sigh of relief I can hear everyone breathing is, unfortunately, premature."

Glenster looked down at his feet. Abigail could sympathise with him. When he had heard that the killer had been caught, and who it was, it must have been a weight off his mind. Now here she was telling him that he had it wrong.

"Doctor... Philip." He slowly raised his head. "I am sorry, I really am, but Marty did not do this. As far as I'm concerned nothing has changed from what was said last night at the town meeting. I can't expect anyone else to simply believe that, but I am begging you to not let your guard down. I know it's not what you want to hear, but he..." She didn't need to mention his name; she trusted that Glenster would know exactly who she was talking about. "... might still be back."

She walked out with him, locking her door and walking him to his car. Just before he got in, she said to him,

"I want you to bear one thing in mind."

"Yes?"

"If it does turn out to be who we really don't want it to be, remember that we survived the fucker before, and we can survive him again."

Glenster gave her a small smile, got into his car and drove away.

As Abigail walked to her own vehicle, she wondered if she believed what she had just told the man.

Though she had passed by it many times in her life, Abigail had never actually been inside the sheriff's department before. As she walked through the front doors, she discovered that she hadn't been missing much: a reception desk, several chairs, a small table with a selection of magazines, a water cooler and a coffee machine. The black and white linoleum tiled floor was spotless and the air smelled of pine. This could have been the reception area of just about anywhere. In fact Abigail's dentist's waiting area looked a lot like this.

She walked up to the desk and spotted the small button on it. Pressing it, she heard the bell chime somewhere in the office beyond the desk. A few seconds later, the door opened and a smiling Doreen Spellner appeared.

"Good afternoon," she said pleasantly. "How can I help you?"

Abigail did not know Doreen Spellner, and so had no idea that the woman was a rampant gossip. The ultra-fast broadcasting of the news that the man responsible for the disappearances and deaths of three local women had been captured had started with Doreen. She held a high position among her friends, all of whom were notorious gossips more than willing to spread stories about one another, for her job placed her right at the centre of any happenings in town. Often they would call her to see if she had any juicy titbits for them. It was a habit that had become a pastime, which in the past had cost her friends, and once had almost resulted in her losing her job. That she had promised to behave, and that her work was excellent, were the only reasons she still worked for the sheriff. However she was very careful these days to make sure she didn't push things too far. Her radar had been in high gear since the tip-off that had come in that morning. The sheriff hadn't mentioned where he and Deputy Parchett had been headed right after the call had been received, but as soon as she had discovered the reason why the man the deputy had brought in had been arrested, caution had been thrown to the winds and she had been on the phone immediately to her friends. It had snowballed from there.

It was just as well Abigail did not know Doreen and her habits. If she had it was possible that she might have leapt over the desk and flattened the woman.

"I'd like to talk to the sheriff."

"I'm sorry, but he's rather busy at the moment."

"I know, but if you could please let him know I'm here, I think he'll see me. It's very important."

"I can try. Your name?" Abigail gave her name and Doreen picked up the phone. Deputy Parchett, well-schooled in the habits of the stations receptionist, had revealed no details to her when he had brought Martin in earlier, therefore Doreen did not recognise Abigail's name and put two and two together. Unfortunately she asked the next obvious question as she dialled the sheriff's extension. "What's this in connection with?"

"I just need to speak to him about something."

It was more a case of Abigail not wanting to have to fill the receptionist in on the details than being purposefully evasive, but her answer was enough to start the wheels of Doreen Spellner's mind spinning faster.

The sheriff answered after only one ring

"Yes?"

"There's an Abigail Morton here asking to speak with you, sheriff."

"I'll be right out."

When he had come back to the station, Flaghan had also not mentioned any specifics to his receptionist. All he had told her was that he would probably be very busy for a good while. That he saw fit to come right out to speak to this young woman also told Doreen a great deal. It was all conjecture and supposition of course, but such things didn't stop a good gossip, and Doreen Spellner wasn't a good gossip; she was an *amazing* gossip.

She told Abigail that the sheriff would be right out, and then busied herself at her computer. Though to the untrained eye she looked as though she was engrossed on whatever was on the screen, she was taking everything in. She heard the door at the end of the corridor open and close, then footsteps and then Sheriff Flaghan walked into the reception area. He greeted the woman who had come to see him by name, and then motioned for her to follow him, which she did.

When she heard the door at the far end of the corridor close again, her hand was out and lifting the phone with the kind of speed that won high noon shoot-outs.

Abigail sat down in the chair the sheriff indicated. He closed the door and walked around to take his seat on the other side of the desk. Sitting down, he sat forward, leaning on the desk.

"I guess I don't have to ask why you're here."

"I want to see him."

"I'm not sure I can allow that, Miss Morton."

"Why?"

"Why? Because the man you want to see is sitting in a cell right now, under arrest on suspicion of murder."

"Thank you for maintaining the suspicion part, sheriff; I get the feeling a lot of other people have already convicted him."

"As far as I know the law still states that he's innocent until proven guilty, but I have to add that it's a damn strong suspicion, Miss Morton."

"There will be nothing else to link him to the crimes. I know there won't. Besides, I can't believe that you don't think there's anything off about what happened this morning."

"Meaning?"

"Oh come on, sheriff, you can't tell me you don't have your doubts. You get an anonymous phone call telling you where to find three missing women, and it pans out. Are you going to sit there and tell me that you don't find it odd that someone should be able to provide such accurate information? How the hell would they know? Why wouldn't they come forward with the information instead of calling in without giving their name?"

"Maybe he had an accomplice who turned against him, decided to drop him in it without giving himself up."

Abigail noted that the anonymous caller had apparently been male, a little titbit Doreen Spellner had already stored away in her mental filing cabinet of interesting information.

"That's a stretch and you know it, sheriff. This mysterious accomplice could also be used to keep Marty in the frame by saying that they kidnapped Sophie while Marty spent the night with me. There is no accomplice and Marty is not your man. For whatever reason, he is being set up."

"Mr Muir was with you the night your friend was kidnapped?"

"He was." Flaghan took this in, nodding slowly. Then he went on.

"You can't argue with the fact of what we found in that room. You saw it yourself."

"I wish to god I hadn't," she said quietly. She took a breath and looked at the sheriff, meeting his eyes. "It looks bad, I'll admit that, but I know Marty didn't kill anyone. My words alone will not convince you of that. At this point I'm resigned to the fact that only an investigation into things will clear his name. So please, can you just let me talk to him for a few minutes? The man poses no threat to me whatsoever. Do you think I would want to go and talk to him if I believed I'd be putting myself in danger?"

Flaghan didn't answer her right away. He regarded her for a short time and she held his gaze.

"I'll give you five minutes," he said at last.

Flaghan escorted her through to the cells. As he opened the security door, she saw the grey corridor beyond. Lit by three bare bulbs, it ended in a blank wall, and on either side were three cells. The sheriff held the door open for her and asked her to surrender her bag. She gave it to him and he told her,

"Last on the left. Five minutes, Miss Morton, no longer."

"Thank you."

He closed the door behind her and she heard him lock the door. Abigail walked quickly to the end of the corridor and turned left.

The cell contained a toilet, a sink and a low cot with a very thin and uncomfortable looking mattress, on the edge of which sat Martin. His head was bowed, his hands covering his face.

"Marty?" she said softly. Getting no response, she repeated herself in a louder voice. He looked up and Abigail felt a cold hand tighten its fingers around her heart. Gone was the open, friendly face she knew and adored. The brightness that always seemed to be in his eyes, which now had large dark marks under them, had been replaced by a dull apathy. His lips were turned down at the corners, his hair was a mess, and his jawline was darkened by stubble. She wondered if perhaps the dim lighting in the cell was contributing to how badly he looked, but reasoned that if it was, then it was only a minor factor.

What did you expect? That he'd be dressed in a tux and ready for the opera? He's in a holding cell, arrested for crimes he didn't commit. Of course he looks like hell.

"Abigail?" he replied in a hoarse whisper. He cleared his throat, swallowed and paused. "I don't know what to say to you."

"You don't have to say anything. I only have five minutes, so the best thing you can do right now is listen." She took a deep breath. "I had a weak moment, Marty."

"What do you mean?"

"I was so shaken this morning that the fact you and I were together the night Sophie went missing didn't even occur to me. When I got back home after you were brought here, I wondered if you had done it, if you had killed them."

The words left a sour taste in her mouth. She ran her tongue over her front teeth and held back the torrent of words that wanted to come out. Apologies and excuses and the fact that she now believed, without doubt, that he was innocent all went unsaid. Instead she stood and waited to find out if the love affair she had so recently embarked on was about to come to an end.

Martin nodded slowly a few times, then rose to his feet. He stepped over to the bars, moving into the better light. Abigail saw that she had been right about the illumination playing a small role in his appearance. All she wanted to do was hold him. Instead she stood wringing her hands and trying to avoid his eyes for fear of the condemnation she might see in them.

"Abi," he said softly. "Please look at me." Tears stung her eyes and she shook her head.

"I can't."

"Please."

She shook her head again and then, telling herself that she owed him that much at least, she lifted her head and looked at him. He was smiling at her. The effect this had on him was astonishing. His hair was still all over the place and he still needed a shave, but that smile, and the little glint it put in his eyes, made her want to cry. He put a hand out between the bars and she grasped it and squeezed.

"I was so shocked this morning it didn't occur to me to point out that we were together that night. I can't blame you for thinking the worst; Sophie, those poor women, they were found in the cabin I'm renting. I was so afraid you would never want to see me again." Her words would be denied no longer and came out in a rush.

"I'm so sorry, Marty. I don't think you had anything to do with it. Amanda and Beth don't either. There are people who will but I'll set them straight. I've already told my aunt and uncle, and Philip Glenster, and the sheriff..."

"Abi, Abi, shh, it's okay. It's okay."

"It's not," she contradicted him. "People will think you did it, but they don't know you like I do, they don't..."

"People will think what they're going to think, and nothing can be done about that until I am proven innocent. I know I didn't do it, and I'm glad that you and your friends think the same." He drew in a short breath. "Abi, I'm so sorry about Sophie." Abigail only trusted herself to nod. "You saw her?" Another nod. "Oh, Christ." He shook his head. "I take it that since they've seemingly got me bang to rights they won't be investigating any further."

"They will; I'll make sure they do. What they found might appear pretty damning at first glance, but how they found out about it stinks to high heaven, and there's also the fact that they'll find nothing else to link you to the murders. Eventually they'll have to see reason."

"I wonder how long eventually might be."

"They'll appoint you a lawyer who'll make sure they don't hold on to you without finding anything that they can charge you with."

"What if they do?" She looked puzzled. "Find something," he clarified.

"How could they?"

"I've been set up, Abi. I don't know who by or why, but someone put those women there and told the police where to find them. Whoever did it must have known I was staying there, and how it would look. If they were willing to go to those lengths to put me in the frame, what else wouldn't they do to incriminate me?"

She didn't have an answer for him, and even if she had she wouldn't have been able to give it. The door at the top of the corridor opened and the sheriff appeared, saying nothing but making his meaning clear: her time was up.

"I have to go," she told Martin. "I don't know if I'll be allowed back in to see you again, but I'll be waiting for you when you're released."

He smiled and nodded, then his expression became grave.

"Promise me that you'll be careful."

"I promise."

She leaned forward and put her face up to the bars. Martin did the same and they shared a brief kiss. Before her emotions could overwhelm her, Abigail walked quickly back to the door where Sheriff Flaghan stood waiting for her.

As she collected her bag from him and prepared to leave, she decided to share something with him. Chances were it would make no difference at all, but given what had happened she felt it was something he should know. Besides, any little thing that might help Marty was worth mentioning.

"Sheriff, I found a dead kitten." Flaghan frowned. "A few weeks ago," she explained. "In my back yard. I heard a noise and went out to see what had caused it and I found the mauled body of a little kitten. At the time I assumed the culprit was perhaps a wild animal. But the kitten hadn't been killed in my yard; its body had been placed there. I didn't think any more about it until last night, after the town meeting." She slung her bag over her shoulder. "It might be something, might be nothing, I don't know, just as I don't know who killed my friend and those other women. What I do know is that it wasn't the man you have in that cell. I also know you have your own doubts, so for everyone's sake I'll tell you what I told Philip Glenster: don't let your guard down."

With that, she turned and left.

Chapter 33

As Abigail walked away, Martin retreated to the dimness of the corner, to his cot. He lay down, closed his eyes and took a deep, shuddering breath.

It had all been close to too much.

First the arrest and his belief that his entire life was about to come crashing down around his ears, then his being brought here, booked in and having the reasons for his arrest made plain to him. That was when Sophie's name had been mentioned as one of the victims discovered in the master bedroom of the cabin. That had been another shock, the realisation that Abigail hadn't just found the bodies of two strangers, she had also found her friend. The probability that Abigail would want nothing more to do with him had quickly become a rock solid certainty, and the weight of it had carried his heart down to his heels. That she had been there, that she had come to see him, and that she had without preamble told him something it clearly distressed her to admit, possibly even to herself, brought him the kind of joy that only minutes before he had believed to be gone from his life forever. That Beth and Amanda also believed he had nothing to do with the death of their friend pulled him back from the brink a little more.

But there was still the fact that he was sitting in a holding cell in a small town many miles from his home, under arrest for three murders he knew he had not committed. As he considered his words to Abigail regarding someone having orchestrated all of this, a little angry fire sparked to life inside him. Some sick, twisted bastard had taken those women, killed them, and then somehow got into his cabin and left them inside a locked room, and then had called the authorities to reveal their whereabouts. Who the hell would do something like that? Martin wanted to believe that his being selected as the patsy was a random choice, that the killer had clapped eyes on him and followed him and decided that he would do. But this all felt far more personal. This all felt like someone was getting at him, not just using him to divert suspicion or having a cruel laugh at his expense. Martin Muir was not a violent man, but he vowed that if he got the chance, he was going to do some severe damage to whoever was responsible.

Would that chance ever come about? Had the fucker in question been clever enough to plant evidence that would confirm what many would believe, that he really was the killer? At this point, did they really need much more in the way of confirmation? The bodies alone might not be enough to convict him in the eyes of the law, but in the eyes of everyone else it marked him out as a maniac. True that, unless the real killer had been incredibly thorough, he would be released due to no other evidence being uncovered that tied him to the crimes, but there were some kinds of shit that just stuck. Martin imagined meeting again those few Hannerville citizens he had spoken to recently, imagined how they would react to him now. Little doubt that their smiles and welcoming nature would be gone, replaced by accusatory glances and mistrust they had no one to aim at save him. The idea stung, but not because of what effects such a situation would have on him. This was Abigail's home. She worked here, had friends here. Friends who believed in his innocence, but what real good would that do against the weight of the town's belief? Martin had images of the front of Pages and Pages being covered in threatening or insulting graffiti, of Abigail saying hello to people in the street only to be shunned and scowled at.

Yet she had come here to see him, had sided with him, when surely she herself must have realised the potential outcome. Or maybe she hadn't gotten that far yet. After all, he was the one with plenty of time to think.

When he had been given his phone call, Martin had realised there was only one person he could call. He felt a little guilty about it, not having contacted his friend for a while, and when he did get around to calling him it was from a police station to say "Guess what; I've been arrested!" He hadn't quite put it like that, of course. Stephen had been bursting with questions and rebukes about the length of time he had been kept waiting. Martin had had to use a tone much sterner than his usual to get him to shut up and listen. It was more than likely that tone which meant Stephen had not even suggested that Martin might be joking when he had been filled in on the situation. He had asked if there was anything he could do and Martin had told him that he honestly didn't know, but there was no one else he needed to contact. Stephen had then offered to get the next available flight over, but Martin had told him to stay put. Though the presence of another friendly face would be welcomed, there was really nothing that could be gained from his friend coming here. Martin didn't come out and say it, but his chief fear was that his best friend might somehow become implicated in the murders. The short conversation had ended with Stephen eliciting a solemn promise that Martin contact him as soon as he got out. Martin had ended the conversation by telling his friend not to worry, which, now he thought about it, was perhaps the stupidest thing he could have said. Of course the man was going to worry; if their roles were reversed, Martin would have been climbing the walls worrying about what was going to happen. He knew the only thing that would do Stephen any good was the phone call that told him his friend had been freed. Martin was clinging to the hope that he would be able to make that call soon, in time to prevent anything happening to Abigail.

This was the other idea that preyed on his mind, that whoever had killed poor Sophie and those other women was still out there, possibly stalking others, possibly stalking Abigail. Over the course of a couple of hours, Martin became more and more unsettled. As his traitorous imagination showed him clips of Abigail going about the most mundane of tasks, seen from the point of view of someone conducting covert observation, he rose and began pacing the cell. There was nothing he could do. Someone was out there, Brannon or someone else for whom the taking of a human life was an act performed with less thought than the swatting of a fly, and they had put him in here. The more Martin thought about it, the more he became convinced that the most obvious reason for this was that someone wanted him away from Abigail. Having succeeded brilliantly in their endeavour to have him placed under lock and key, what would they do now? Would they toy with Abigail, or would they simply move in for the kill?

Before his intention had really registered, Martin found himself clutching the bars of his cell, pressing his face between two of the cold iron rods and bellowing for the sheriff, the deputy, anybody. He didn't have to wait long for a response. After only a few minutes, the door at the top of the corridor opened and Sheriff Flaghan came striding down. Martin gave him no opportunity to talk.

"You have to watch out for her. Don't ask me who because you know who I'm talking about. I was framed for a reason and the only reason anyone would have to do that is to get me away from Abigail." He paused and drew in a quick breath. "You think you've got your man, and nothing I say right now is going to change that, so I am begging you to watch out for her."

The sheriff regarded him for a few moments. Martin couldn't have known, but Flaghan was debating with himself about whether or not to reveal his own doubts about his prisoner's guilt. In the end he did not. He simply nodded once and walked away.

Ninety minutes later, Martin, lying dozing on his cot, heard the door at the top of the corridor open again. His eyes popped open as he told himself that perhaps it was over, that maybe they were bringing in the real killer and he would be released. Then again, it was just as possible they were bringing someone in for some other reason. His hopes diminished, only to be rekindled moments later when the sheriff stopped outside his cell and inserted a key in the lock. Martin sat up as the sheriff gave him some unexpected news.

"You've got another visitor."

"What? Who?" Flaghan slid the cell door open. As he motioned for Martin to approach with one hand, he removed the handcuffs from the loop on his belt with the other.

"Over here, turn round, hands behind your back."

Martin did as he was told, not bothering to ask any further questions, assuming no answers would be forthcoming. The sheriff cuffed him and then escorted him to the room where he had been interviewed and his statement taken upon arriving at the station.

"Why am I back in here?"

"Because we don't have a visitors lounge," was the sheriff's droll reply. "Now," he began as he unlocked the cuffs. "I'm trusting you to be nice." He relocked the cuffs with Martin's hands in front of him. "But if your visitor has cause to call for help, I will come in here and you will end up with a sore spot somewhere on your person. Understood?" Martin nodded. "Good. Take a seat and I'll show your visitor in in a minute."

Martin plonked himself down in the chair and wondered who else might be visiting him, and why the visit was to be conducted here and not in his cell, as Abigail's visit had been. Was this a more formal visit? Was it maybe his state appointed lawyer?

It was not, though as the woman wearing the dark blue skirt and jacket over a white blouse was shown in, Martin believed he had been correct; she certainly looked like a lawyer. She gave Flaghan a nod as she sat down and as the sheriff closed the door, Martin took a look at his visitor. From the lines across her forehead and at the corners of her eyes and mouth, he took her to be in her mid-fifties. She had green eyes and her shoulder length dark hair was shot through with streaks of grey. Rather than making her look old, it suited her. She gave him a small smile and said, in a low, pleasant voice,

"We have a lot to discuss, Martin."

"I'm innocent," he said immediately, not even noticing the woman's Scottish accent. "First and foremost I want you to understand that I will not be pleading guilty to those murders. I know it looks bad, but I am innocent."

"I know you are," she told him. Martin stopped talking. He gathered that it might be considered good form for a lawyer to state that they believed their client, but there was something in the way she had said it that sounded to him far more sincere than someone saying it merely because they were trying to reassure someone they would be defending. She gave him that small smile again. "You don't recognise me, do you?"

Martin frowned, wondering if perhaps he had passed her on the streets on Hannerville at some point during his stay. He searched his memory but got nothing. He shook his head and she nodded before saying,

"You're a special boy, Martin Muir."

The words propelled his thoughts back some twenty-five years and he saw his nine year old self in an empty classroom, standing beside his teacher's desk. She had asked him to help her out that day. Suffering from a sore throat, she had started reading out aloud to the class from a book. When she could read no further, she had asked Martin to take the book and continue. Though he had been nervous, he had managed it, and when the other children left after the home-time bell, he had been asked to stay behind.

"Well done, Martin," she had said to him. "You read very well today. You were nervous?" He had nodded and she had smiled warmly at him. "Understandable, but you did it." Pulling open a drawer she had reached in and taken out an open bag of toffees and offered him one. Smiling, he had stuck his hand in the bag and withdrawn a sweet. It had been halfway to his mouth, his thumb and forefingers pulling at the twisted ends of the little package to undo them, when he had stopped and put the sweet in his pocket instead. His teacher had smiled and looked at him in a strange way. She had seemed to him to be almost sad. A few weeks later she would set the students in her class the task of writing a letter to a student in a school in Tennessee in the United States, but that day she had given him that sad look and told him, "You're a special boy, Martin Muir."

He came back to himself and stared at the woman for several seconds before speaking her name out loud, though he was unable to keep the note of disbelief out of his voice.

"Miss Coyle?"

Andrea Coyle's smile widened.

"Surprised?"

"Surprised doesn't even come close," he informed her. "What are you doing here?"

"I came to see you."

"What? How did you know I was here?"

Her smile faded a little.

"As I said, Martin, there are a lot of things you and I have to talk about, but this is not the time or place for an in-depth discussion, so I'll stick to the basics for now. I know you didn't murder those women, and I also know who did. The people of this town would call him David Brannon, but his real name is Andrew Corday. Now," she reached into her jacket pocket and removed a piece of paper which she passed to him. "This is a description of him."

Martin, still shocked and confused, read what was written and shook his head.

"No it isn't. I saw a picture of David Brannon, or whatever his name is, and this doesn't describe him."

"He's had surgery to alter his appearance," Coyle explained. "We've been keeping an eye on him, and we believe that what he's done to you is just another part of his game. As long as he's still playing that game we have some breathing space."

"What happens when he stops playing his game?" Coyle's face darkened.

"He'll come after you and Abigail."

The colour drained from Martin's face. He sat up and leaned forward.

"Why? What the hell did Abigail or I ever do to him?"

"That's a subject for another time..."

"It's about Abigail's safety; now is the perfect time to talk about it." She shook her head.

"You've got enough to be going on with for the time being. Please believe me that my associates and I will not let anything happen to Abigail. She is just as important to us as you are."

"What?" he asked, now completely flummoxed. "Why?"

"I sympathise, Martin; this cannot be easy for you, and I am sorry to have to lay so much on you at one time. I hope you can forgive me for that, and understand why I don't want to go into too much detail just now."

"You said you've been watching Brannon, Corday, whoever the hell he is. You knew it was him who had kidnapped those women. Why didn't you do anything? Why did you let them die?" Coyle's face coloured.

"We're not mind readers, Martin. We didn't know where or when he would strike, and we couldn't watch him all day and night; we had to keep watch over you and Abigail too. Yes, we knew who had taken those women, but there was nothing we could do about it. Our priorities were you and Abigail."

"Really? Then why the hell didn't you just deal with this guy when you got here? Why all this cloak and dagger bullshit?"

"The people I have with me are not killers, Martin, and neither am I. However, we could have attacked Corday, but if we had been unsuccessful then Abigail would have been on her own. We had a plan in place to get her out of town if it appeared that Corday was preparing to strike, but I was reluctant to approach her before it was necessary. She was happy and content in her life, and my preference was to find a way for us to deal with him without ever alerting Abigail to his presence. Not one of my better ideas, it has to be said. Then you showed up, Martin, and it dawned on me that you and Abigail might well become a couple. I can't tell you how happy that made me. I was torn between my desire to keep you safe, and my desire to see you both together. I decided to wait, to give you both time, but then Corday went and framed you and now we can't get you out of town without ending up with the police on our tail."

"You've been following him, so obviously you know what he looks like. You could have called the police, let them know who they were looking for, given them a description."

"Doing so would have given away our presence in town," she told him. "He would have realised the police had received information and he would have quickly worked out the only source that information could have come from. He's a lunatic, but he is far from stupid, a fact you would do well not to forget." She sighed and let her head drop forward. "Our intention was not to alert Corday to our presence in Hannerville for as long as possible. We had been following him, and though he had been cautious we have discovered one of his locations, though unfortunately not the one where he takes his victims. As long as he was unaware of our presence we had a slight advantage, one which a foolish young man threw away. Corday knows we're here now and although he has become even cagier, I don't believe he's particularly worried about us."

"Apparently he doesn't have reason to be," Martin said coldly. "You say you won't let anything happen to Abigail, but from what I've heard there's not a damn thing you can do to stop him going after her."

Coyle raised her head and Martin was struck by the steel in her gaze.

"We will die protecting you an Abigail from him, if that's what it takes. However I don't believe it will come to that. Getting the two of you will be his big win, but he's not finished playing just yet. That is why you will be released in a day or two."

Martin thought he knew what she was getting at, and he did not like it. His stomach tightened as he asked for clarification.

"You being put in here was a bonus for him. His amusement at the way he's making you and Abigail suffer might last a day or two, but eventually he'll murder someone else and the police will have no choice but to release you." Martin was appalled.

"You can't let that happen."

"What do you suggest I do to stop it? I think I mentioned that I'm not clairvoyant and so don't know who he will attack. The only good that will come out of it is that it will provide the authorities with conclusive proof that you are innocent."

"They'll say it was my accomplice or something."

"No," Coyle said, giving a slight shake of her head. "If it was an accomplice of yours then they would take someone tonight to expedite your release, but that's not going to happen. Besides I think the sheriff already has enough doubts about your guilt."

"Why do you say that?" She nodded towards his cuffed wrists.

"He cuffed your hands in front of you, and he mentioned allowing Abigail in to see you. I would imagine that dedicated men like Sheriff Flaghan wouldn't be so quick to show such consideration for someone they truly believed guilty of three counts of kidnapping, rape and cold blooded murder."

That brought Martin back to the subject of Corday going after someone else. The idea of another murder, another innocent life lost, whether it meant his being released or not, made him want to vomit. He had been told that this bastard enjoyed his and Abigail's suffering. That being so, the best way to cause even more of it was to go after another of Abigail's friends, or her aunt or uncle. His stomach churned at the thought of Beth or Amanda going missing, only to be found dead a few days later. Martin only just managed to hold down the rising bile.

191

"Damn it! My freedom is not worth someone's life."

"I agree," stated Coyle. "And if I knew who Corday was going to attack, I would do what I could to stop him, but I don't and so I can't."

Martin clenched his hands into fists. Then suddenly it hit him.

"Yes, you can. You say you've been keeping an eye on Abigail and me. Well, I don't need anyone keeping an eye on me anymore because by now the whole town knows exactly where I am. So whoever was watching me is free to tail Corday everywhere he goes. When he attacks someone, have whoever's watching him raise the alarm. Interrupt him in any way possible, just save whoever he attacks. If you're right about the sheriff then the attack alone should raise enough doubt in his mind to release me." He saw doubt in her eyes. "You said Corday already knows you're here, so what do you have to lose by playing the passer-by who stumbles onto an attack and unwittingly foils it?"

Coyle was silent for several minutes as she weighed up the pros and cons of Martin's idea. Finally she said,

"I said if I had any way of preventing another death, I'd do so, and you've given me a way. It will be done."

"Thank you."

"No, Martin, thank you," his old teacher said solemnly. "I fear I may have become far too cold a person, and such a person is not who you need now and not who you will need in the future. Perhaps it is better that I set a good example and perish, rather than live and be someone you would not listen to or seek guidance from. Someone whose explanations for this entire situation you would not believe."

"You'd be surprised at what I'm willing to believe," Martin told her, thinking of Abigail and her journals. The inscrutable smile that curved Coyle's lips upwards brought to his mind a barrage of questions he did not get the opportunity to ask. As he opened his mouth the woman got to her feet and said,

"Hopefully the next time we meet, Martin, it will be in nicer surroundings. I know that advising you to not worry would be utterly pointless. What I will suggest is that, where you will be unable to prepare yourself for what might well be coming when you do get out of here, try to prepare yourself for the town. Even with proof of another attack happening whilst you are incarcerated, they will eye you with suspicion and it will be difficult for you." She paused, frowning. "Perhaps you being put in here for murder was not merely a bonus after all."

"What do you mean?"

"Though I wanted to give you and Abigail time, my intention had still been to get you both out of Hannerville as soon as possible, but as I said that cannot be done now, not without making you a fugitive. Even when you're released from here, you'll still be a suspect, and as such you will be cautioned against leaving the town. Damn him," she breathed. "He wants it all to end here, where he's had time to blend in and get the lay of the land."

She fell silent. Martin waited to hear what she would say next, which he hoped was something that would explain some of this madness.

"I'll see you again soon," she concluded, favouring him with a final brief but warm smile before opening the door and stepping out into the corridor.

A few hours later, after getting some unexpected sleep, Martin lay on his bunk, his hands clasped behind his head, the things he had been told by Miss Coyle running through his mind.

David Brannon is not the killer's name, his name is Andrew Corday, and for some insane reason he has a major grudge again Abigail and I. But my old primary school teacher and her associates are looking out for us for some reason. Willing to die to protect us apparently.

What the bloody hell is going on?

That Miss Coyle was here at all was weird enough, and the things she had told him were even weirder. Had it not been for the fact that she had mentioned Abigail's being in danger, Martin might well have told her to piss off, that her lunacy was something he didn't need right now. But if there was a possibility that whoever had murdered those women was simply working his way up to Abigail, then it could not be ignored. Martin closed his eyes and sighed, trying to ignore the possibility that David Brannon or Andrew Corday or whatever the hell the bastard's name was, was someone Abigail might have come into contact with already. He had gotten the impression from Miss Coyle that Corday had been in town a while. Had the son of a bitch walked past Abigail in the street, or brazenly strolled into her shop and bought a book?

Had Corday been someone that he himself had passed by and smiled a hello at on the street during his brief stay?

Chapter 34

Andrea Coyle went straight to Sandra's house to discuss Martin's idea with her colleagues. Both of them were understandably dubious.

"Who protects Martin and Abigail if we get killed?" asked Matthew.

"If we thought we stood a chance of capturing him," Sandra added. "We could simply storm the house we know he's living in."

"Capturing him is not what this plan is about," Coyle clarified for them. "The plan is to save a life whilst at the same time getting Martin out of prison."

"How do we go about doing that?"

"As Martin said to me, we have no need to follow him at this point because we know where he is and that he's not going anywhere. Only one of us is needed to watch Abigail. Matthew, that'll be you." She turned to face Sandra. "You and I will follow Corday everywhere he goes, as covertly as we are able. Eventually he'll strike, and when he does we will intervene, running towards him yelling and shouting and making as much commotion as we possibly can, drawing as much attention to what's going on as we are able."

"What if he realises he's being followed?"

"Corday only knows for sure that we're in town because of what Lucas did," said Sandra. "He'll be on the lookout, but he won't spot us." Coyle nodded.

"As we have been doing, we'll use walkie-talkies to keep in touch, and we'll carry weapons just in case."

Matthew, who had become increasingly perturbed since Lucas's death, clasped his hands together tightly.

"What the hell are we really doing here? We can't catch this man, can't kill him, can't go to the police about him... We're supposed to be protecting two people and yet there's not a damn thing we can do about the single greatest threat to them. It's all damn well pointless."

"Matthew," Coyle barked sharply. Her voice sobered him somewhat. She let a moment pass and then said, "Though I cannot argue that our original plan cannot be implemented thanks to steps Corday has taken, our purpose nonetheless remains as it always has: we protect our charges." She stared at him until he nodded. "Now, Corday has made sure we cannot simply leave town with Martin and Abigail, not without landing Martin in even deeper trouble with the law. He wants to end this, and we have no way of knowing how long he will play this damn cat-and-mouse game before bringing it to a conclusion." Pausing, she let her head drop forward and stared at the floor. Her eyes glazed over and she spoke, more to herself than the other two.

"Corday attacks someone and we raise a ruckus, even though he'll attack somewhere dark, somewhere secluded. One of us should call the police to let them know what's happened. They obviously don't have a problem acting on information from anonymous sources, so that'll work nicely. It also means they'll be aware of what happened even if the intended victim isn't keen on reporting it. If they aren't, we need to get the story out; this town's got one hell of a gossip network, so we can start spreading the news that there was another attack despite someone being in jail for the murders."

The trio were silent for some time, each mulling over what had been said and what had to be done. When Coyle eventually rose, the others followed her without speaking, knowing that the time had come to put their hastily conceived plan into action.

It took three days.

Few had been affected by the recent kidnappings until the night of the town meeting. That night some rumours had been confirmed as facts, and those facts had cast a shadow over the town. The following morning had brought a light that shone on that shadow, banishing it.

Those connected to the victims still mourned, but everyone else breathed a sigh of relief and got on with their lives, believing the monster responsible for the crimes to be behind bars. The story of Martin's arrest was spread via various methods, with the most accurate version being printed in the local paper. However Doreen Spellner enjoyed heretofore unknown levels of popularity within her social group, and hers was not the only tongue wagging. As is always the case with such things, some details were missed out (the anonymous telephone call featured in very few of the stories passed around), some were altered by certain storytellers for dramatic effect (the sheriff and his deputy kicking down the door of the cabin and going in guns blazing) and some were just made up (one ten year old boy related to his awestruck friends the dark tale of the killer who had been caught doing it with a dead chick whilst simultaneously sucking blood out of her neck).

Regardless what version of the story they heard, most of the good people of Hannerville spent those three days getting on with their lives. Teachers at the schools taught, cab drivers drove their fares here and there, and the coffee shop dished out caffeine in all its various modern day guises. Those involved with the preparations for the Hanner Carnival put in some overtime as the date for the event drew ever nearer. Despite the grip that the recent grim situation had managed to get on the town, everyone went about their business with a sense of relief and a smile on their face.

Well, almost everyone.

There were the families and friends of the victims. Though those who had worked with Charlotte Webster did not count themselves among her friends, they were nonetheless upset as they had all liked the bright young woman with the sunny disposition. The manager of the office was suitably grim as he composed a job advertisement to go in the local press to find her replacement.

Ditto Janice Mallory's colleagues at the Premier Café. Louie Follca, who had been very fond of Janice, had tears in his eyes as he placed a card in the window looking for someone to replace her. One – for there is always one - cold hearted member of his staff, risking possible unemployment should it ever get back to her boss, had snidely commented to one of her friends that she suspected Louie had been banging Janice.

A very relieved Mayor Ashby called Sheriff Flaghan to commend him on a job well done. The sheriff, thinking that such praise was not entirely his due, explained how things had happened that morning. The mayor however did not seem to think that the anonymous phone call was of any great importance, particularly given the result it had brought them. He also dismissed Abigail Morton's claim about being with the suspect the night her friend had gone missing as her covering for her boyfriend. Anxious to discuss his nagging doubts with someone, Flaghan went to see Philip Glenster. He had laid out his doubts about the Scottish guy's guilt. It turned out there had been much discussion on the same subject in the Glenster house, and both Philip and Anne found the fact of the mysterious phone call quite disconcerting.

"Why make an anonymous call?" Anne asked of the two men. To the sheriff she said, "If they had that kind of information, and they were innocent, what stopped them coming to you direct?"

Flaghan was unable to give her an answer.

Abigail, Beth and Amanda all spoke to Sophie's parents over the phone. They had all managed, if only just, to keep it together during the brief conversation. They learned that when Sophie's body was released her parents would be coming to Hannerville to collect it. She was to be taken back to Florida where she would be cremated. After the call, not crying was not an option.

Though she had expected a drop off in customers at Pages and Pages, Abigail found that in the days following Martin's arrest there were actually more people in the store than usual. Unfortunately few of them were there to buy books. It didn't take long for Abigail to notice that several people who appeared to be browsing for something to read were actually making a ham-fisted job of surreptitiously watching her. It led to her standing behind the counter, raising her voice to make sure she was heard as she announced that she would be very grateful if everyone not intending to purchase some reading material would get the hell out. This resulted in a hasty departure of several people, all of whom muttered under their breaths on the way out as though they were the wronged party.

The store was not the only place she received unwanted glances, both furtive and overt, the latter falling into one of two categories: suspicious and distasteful. On the afternoon of the second day, when they were out for lunch, Beth heard her friend sigh and turned in time to see her shake her head. She had asked, Abigail had explained and Beth had offered to slap the next fucker who gave her a dirty look. Abigail had laughed, a sound with a bitter edge to it, thanked her and told her it wasn't necessary.

"They can look at me and talk behind my back all they want," she had said. "They think they're all safe now that the big bad killer has been caught and put away, but they're wrong. It'll happen again, Beth, and it pains me to think that that's the only way any of them will be convinced Marty is innocent. He knows it too, and he feels the same way; I know he does."

Then, of course, there was Andrew Corday.

For hours every day he paced the floors of the various rooms in the house he had bought and furnished, more for appearances sake than anything else. The furniture, floor coverings and decorating were all very tasteful and modern, the kind of stuff that would make any nosey parker who glanced through the windows jealous that their houses didn't look as nice. Though Corday couldn't deny he sometimes enjoyed the comfort and warmth of the place, it did not inspire in him the same feelings of joy that his little shack did. In fact the only way he was able to suppress his desire to find himself a new playmate for as long was because he visited the shack every day, reminiscing. Being there also made him think of where that bastard Muir was, and how much pain he and Abigail must be experiencing.

But as the days went by, he found his amusement at such thoughts lessening. To Corday's mind they would by now have had time to adjust, to get over the initial shock and upset and to start to think of ways to clear Muir's name. Plus the prick's Guardian was obviously in town. She and whoever else she had left with her had probably revealed themselves by now, explained the game. Such would only add to the small reserves of hope Abigail and her beau had built up, maybe even have fostered the idea that they might get out of this.

His displeasure at this was compounded by the fact that he dearly wanted to get himself a new playmate. The hours he did not spend pacing around the house were spent weighing the pros and cons of such an endeavour. For instance on one hand he was sure that if another woman went missing then it would almost surely result in Muir being released. This would have to happen eventually anyway, but Corday liked him being where he was, brought low from such lofty heights as the start of a fantastic new romance. On the other hand he wanted once again to feel supple flesh quiver at his touch, to see fear and pain in a lover's eyes, and he knew those desires would build and build, possibly causing him to do something foolish if not satisfied.

So it was that on the night of Martin's third full day in jail, Corday went hunting on the streets of Hannerville.

Chapter 35

Since she had been a little girl, Cassandra Church's mother and father had always said of their daughter that she was properly pretty, and that she would grow up to be simply beautiful. When she had been in her early teens, Cassandra had asked her parents what they had meant and she had been told that they meant all she had to do to make the world a prettier place was wake up in the morning and smile.

Therefore they would have been upset to see the twist of her lips right now, as she fought to hold back her emotions.

Fucking Derrick, she fumed as she walked, her hands jammed into her pockets. *Fucking asshole, had to go and ruin everything, and then had the audacity to blame me for it! Son of a bitch!*

She and Derrick Gillern had been going steady for a few months now and things had, so Cassandra thought, been going very well. They enjoyed each other's company, could make one another laugh, shared a few of the same friends, and just enjoyed being together. For the last few weeks, however, Derrick had made it plain that he wanted to take things a step further than the heavy petting that had so far been the limit of their physical intimacy.

Cassandra was far from being a prude, and was not a virgin. That ship had sailed when she had been sixteen. A not unpleasant experience, at least not physically. She had been with the boy, Matt Doberson, for almost a year by the time she consented to have sex with him. Less than a week afterwards he had dumped her. No concrete reason was ever given, but the fact that he had hooked up very quickly with a new girl at school, a rumoured virgin, had seemed to provide all the answer she needed. After that, Cassandra had gone out with a few boys, but had never consented to sex with any of them, which was usually the reason for the breakdown of the relationship. Her friends, who slept with their boyfriends seemingly as a matter of course, always told her they were proud and that she should stick to her guns, and she had. Derrick had always seemed so nice, so mature, never forcing her too fast or too far, apparently happy to let things develop as they were going to.

Not so.

As far as Cassandra had been aware, the sleepover at his house tonight would have been different from all the others in one regard: his parents were away from home visiting relatives. Derrick had made arrangements for his little brother, Christopher, to be staying at a friend's house so they would have the place all to themselves. On being told this, her friends had cautioned her, saying that it was obvious he expected something to happen in the bedroom department. Cassandra had laughed off their concerns, telling them that she and Derrick had discussed that a while ago and he was willing to wait for her to be ready. One of them, Deirdra, had told her that as far as Derrick was concerned they had been dating for months, tonight they had a house to themselves, and if she wasn't ready with that going for them then she never would be. Still Cassandra had refused to contemplate the possibility that Derrick was looking to get laid tonight.

Which had turned out to be exactly what Derrick had been looking to get tonight.

Things had been fine at first. He had picked her up from her house, where she had been waiting with her overnight bag. She had kissed her mother and father goodbye and jogged to his car, got in, kissed him and then settled back in the passenger seat as he drove to his house. They chatted about this and that, and when they arrived they had ordered in some pizza for dinner. After that they had sat down on the couch in the living room to watch a couple of movies. Then, at around half past ten, they had switched everything off and gone upstairs.

She had used the bathroom first, brushing her teeth and getting changed. When Derrick had gone in after her, she had got into bed, expecting him to come back fairly quickly so they could kiss and cuddle for a while.

He had come back very quickly, sans clothing.

She had been leaning over the side of the bed, facing away from the door, rummaging for something in her overnight bag when he had walked in. Cassandra had sat up straight and turned to find him presenting himself in the doorway, arms stretched out, cock and balls dangling, an expectant grin on his face. For a moment a giggle had threatened to burst from Cassandra's mouth, but a cold sensation that had flooded through her stalled it. Frowning, she had asked him what he thought he was doing. His grin had stayed in place as he had told her that he was showing her what was in store. She had asked what he meant and only then did the grin falter, replaced by a look of mild annoyance.

"What do you mean?" he had asked, lowering his arms to his sides.

"Just what did you imagine was going to happen tonight?" she had put to him. "Because I don't recall discussing anything like this." She had waved a hand in his direction, indicating his nakedness. Derrick had grunted out a laugh and shook his head.

"I don't fucking believe Arron was right," he had said, talking about one of his friends. "You're really not going to have sex with me tonight, are you?"

"What the hell gave you the idea that I was?" she had asked him, not really caring what it had been, already knowing that it was all over and wondering how her father would react when she called him to come and get her.

"What?" he had sputtered. "We're here, alone, the house is ours for the night. I thought when I told you that I had made sure Chris would be gone that you got it."

"What, because we're the only ones here that means it's nookie time? You didn't think you might want to ask me first, find out how I felt about it? You just thought you'd walk in here naked and I'd see your dick and jump on it!"

"We've been dating for months now…"

"So what? Where did you find the book that said if a couple have been dating for a certain length of time then sex automatically became an option? Where, Derrick? Huh? What the hell happened to letting things happen of their own accord?"

"Things were taking too fucking long," he had spat at her. "Jesus, Cassandra, it's not like you're a virgin. It's not like we're going to be together forever or anything. It's just sex."

Cassandra had turned, grabbed the bedside lamp and lobbed it at his head before she had even given herself time to think about it. Derrick leapt out of the way and the lamp shattered against the doorframe. By that point Cassandra had already been out of bed, pulling on her jeans. Derrick had regarded the broken pieces of lamp with an open mouth and wide eyes.

"Are you out of your mind?" he had asked when he'd looked at her. Without pausing in buttoning up her blouse, Cassandra had raged,

"No, I'm angry, you dumb ass. In fact I'm furious."

"Well it's your own fault; plenty of other girls would be happy to do it."

Such had been her shock at his words, at how she could have been so utterly wrong about someone, prevented her from replying for a few seconds.

"Well trust me, you son of a bitch, my loss sure as hell won't be their gain." She nodded towards his crotch as she finished speaking, then made to bend down to lift one of her shoes. She saw him advancing across the room and looked up to see his anger reddened face, his arms reaching out. Curiously she had felt no fear, only calm and a clear sense of exactly what she had to do.

She had straightened up, reached out, grabbed both his wrists, pulled him towards her and brought her knee up into his groin. His face had been only inches from hers and she had watched in mild amusement as the colour had drained from it. His knees had buckled and she had released his wrists as he had crumpled to the floor, where he curled into a ball.

"You wanted me to touch your dick," she had spat at him. "Well now I have."

Cassandra had then proceeded to finish dressing. Once she had all of her stuff packed into her bag, she had paused beside her ex-boyfriend. She thought of what she wanted to say, what she intended to do, and then decided to get some insurance. Removing her phone from her pocket, she switched it to video camera mode and aimed it at Derrick.

"This is what happened to this asshole when he tried to lay his hands on me." She bent down, making sure she got a shot of his face. Standing back up she reached out with her toe and nudged his shoulder, rolling him onto his back. Derrick, realising too late what she was doing, raised his hands to hide his face. He also realised too late what he had done, and by the time he had cupped his hands around his shrivelled manhood and scrotum, Cassandra already had a good few seconds of footage. She stopped filming and dropped the phone into her bag.

"When I go home, I'm going to hit the web and tell every single person I know what a loser you are. Also, If I ever find out that you've said anything to anyone about something happening here tonight that didn't happen, I will show those same people what I just shot. Oh, and don't you so much as look at me ever again, or I'll get a hold of you and tear that thing right off."

With that parting shot delivered, she had left his house, deciding once she was outside that she needed some air. It wasn't a long walk home, and it would be even shorter if she took a shortcut through Beaumont Park.

So, here she was, finally losing the battle with the emotions that had threatened to overwhelm her since slamming shut the front door of the house of he who would forevermore be known as Derrick the Dickhead.

How the hell could he think like that? How could he let himself believe, after I told him why I wanted to wait, that just waving his dick at me would get me to screw him?

She stopped walking and put her hands to her face as she started crying. As she let the tears flow, Cassandra wondered how she was going to tell her parents. When she walked in the front door and her parents saw her, her eyes red and puffy, who knew what they would think. She would have to be quick in telling them the truth; she didn't want Derrick the Dickhead getting into trouble for something he hadn't done.

But he almost did, she thought. *If I hadn't stopped the fucker in his tracks, who knows what he would have done.*

Deeply unpleasant thoughts filled her head, making her cry harder. No, he hadn't done anything to her, but that didn't mean he wouldn't try it on someone else in the future, maybe on one of those girls he mentioned, one who turned out to be not as easy as he had hoped. Cassandra intended to make sure everyone knew what he was really like.

But he was angry, and you really don't know what his intentions were when he was coming towards you.

Her mind's whispered words; last fleeting shadows of consideration for her ex. Yes, he had been angry. Wasn't it said that men simply couldn't take any negative comments about their equipment? Maybe so, but just because they heard something said about themselves that they didn't like didn't give them the right to come at a woman the way he had come at her, eyes full of anger, his reaching out signalling malicious intent.

Only as her crying subsided did Cassandra realise just how dark an area of the park she was in. She could see next to nothing around her. She looked up and turned in a slow circle, seeing the tree line only as an indistinct shadow against the sky. Wiping at her face with the heel of her hand, she resolved to pull herself together and get the hell out of the park. It was a place she had spent many hours in as a kid and as a teenager, but never this late at night. Cassandra didn't want to admit it to herself but she was a little frightened. Stupidly so in her opinion; nothing had happened to give her any reason to be afraid. Well, there were those women who had been killed, but the guy responsible was locked up. She took a deep breath, told herself she was being silly, and took a step in the direction of the nearest source of light, the street beyond the large fenced off area where they were putting up the carnival rides and attractions.

As she walked along she thought about the last few festivals. She and her friends had all had lots of fun, going on the rides, getting their boyfriends to win them huge teddy bears and whatnot. Afterwards they'd go for a walk in the woods, maybe down to the lakeside, drink a little, maybe smoke some weed (which Cassandra herself had never touched. She didn't judge those who did, she just didn't want to try it herself). Good times. She doubted she would go this year though.

The light seemed far away still and she stepped up her pace, though she was still unwilling to admit to herself that she was afraid of the dark and the quiet. Though the park was not quite as quiet as before. Her fear started her breathing heavily, something she now got under control, and that was when she heard what sounded like someone else breathing. Not heavily, the way she had been, or quietly the way she was now, but slowly, calmly, open mouthed: in and out, in and out. Cassandra stopped and listened. After a few seconds she held her breath. Nothing. A confusion of thoughts vied for her attention: *turn in a circle and see if you can spot someone; stop holding your breath and tell whoever it is to fuck off; run like hell until you're at your own front door.*

When her phone rang out loudly, shattering the silence, she yelled out the breath she'd been holding. Slapping her hands against her pockets, she remembered that her phone was in her bag. She opened it, rummaged around inside but couldn't find her phone. Cursing, she sat the bag on the ground, eventually finding her phone and taking it out. She stood back up as she looked at the screen. Derrick the Dickhead. She made a sound of disgust and rejected the call.

Somewhere behind her there was a sound. Short and sharp, possibly a twig breaking underfoot. The fear came rushing back and she bent down to pick up her bag. Her phone rang again and she glanced at the screen long enough to see that it was The Dickhead again. Was it him out there in the dark, fucking with her? Maybe scaring her as a way of getting back at her, or was his plan for revenge darker than that? Was he capable of that? Only half an hour ago she would have said no, but he had already proven tonight that she hadn't known him as well as she thought. Cassandra thumbed the reject button as she reached out for the handle of her bag.

Footsteps. Fast. Getting closer. Her heart leapt into her throat and every muscle in her legs locked even as she commanded herself to run.

Someone rushed past her in the dark, bumping against her. Cassandra recoiled with a yelp of alarm, breathing in through her nose. She inhaled the scent of cologne, something with a hint of citrus to it.

Never mind what's in it, you idiot! Get your shit together and run!

She continued the motion of reaching for her bag, and realised it was taking too long. Her fingers should have found the handle by now, but it was gone. Gasping, Cassandra dropped into a crouch and started patting the ground with both hands, thinking she had maybe kicked it away and not noticed. It took mere seconds for her to come to the conclusion that it was gone.

Seconds after that she realised that one of the hands currently pressed to the cold grass should have been holding her phone.

Cassandra wasted no more time. She rose to her feet and took off towards the light, stopping only a few steps later when she heard her phone ringing again. She was perfectly prepared to ignore it, to just keep running. It was a phone, it could be replaced. What stopped her in her tracks was that she could see the pale glow cast by the touchscreen display on her peripheral vision. The device floated in the darkness, held horizontally, its light being thrown upwards, illuminating the devilish grin of the man holding it.

As she turned and ran, she almost lost control of her bladder. She thought about screaming out for help, but decided to save her breath for running. She pumped her arms and legs, wishing she had exercised more. Already she could feel herself starting to tire, to lose speed. Over her harshening breath she heard the rapid footfalls behind her and did her best to ignore her body's red alerts and keep going. Just over three quarters of the way towards the fenced off area, some distance to go after that to the street, and Cassandra knew she wasn't going to make it. She could feel herself losing more speed, waited to feel a hand clamp down on her shoulder or grab hold of her hair. But how could this be happening? The killer was behind bars, unable to harm anyone. The obvious answer was that the wrong man had been arrested. *But the bodies,* she thought. *They were in his cabin. Oh god, there's more than one of them! Sweet Jesus, is it a cult or something?*

Fingers swiped through her hair and Cassandra screamed "No!" and gave it everything she had left, aiming straight for one of the fences bordering the carnival area. A few feet from it she leapt, her hands grabbing onto the cold steel of the section's top edge. The construct swayed as her weight fell against it, but stayed up. Cassandra scrambled, seeking toeholds and pushing every muscle in her arms to its limit as she tried to pull herself over the fence. Those fingers slid across her shin and she squealed, the tips of her shoes finding purchase. Pushing with her legs and pulling with her arms, Cassandra flew over the top of the swaying fence and fell into darkness.

Even if she'd had her eyes open, she would have been hard pressed to determine the moment she was going to land. She hit hard, a pained sound escaping her mouth, borne on a harshly ejected breath. Luckily her arms had been in the right place to prevent serious injury to her face, and nothing else was badly injured. Even so, when she remembered where she was and why, she flipped over and a dozen different points of pain made themselves known. Her fingers stung, her knee hurt, her chest felt like she'd just been punched, one elbow stung like a bitch. Her ears heard only the rush of blood, but her wide and watery eyes were working just fine, seeing nothing but inky blackness beyond the fence.

Move!

Heeding the order, Cassandra got to her feet as quickly as her overtaxed and bruised limbs allowed. She lumbered away from the fence, finding herself amidst the darkened shapes of the carnival booths and rides.

Almost everything was covered by tarpaulins to protect it against inclement weather until the day of the celebrations, so the area had no shortage of places to hide. Cassandra, as alone and scared and spent as she was, did not like the idea of staying put. She didn't doubt that the bastard who had chased her in here would find his own way over the fence, and once he did she didn't want to be stuck in one place. All it would take was one stray sound – and she suspected that if she holed up somewhere and focussed on what was happening to her she would surely end up crying - and her hidey hole would be discovered and then she would have nowhere left to run to. So, ears alert for the tell-tale sound of someone coming over the fence, she kept moving, past shrouded booths and large tented shapes that could only be the carousel, the dark edifices for the ghost train and the video games arcade, till she came to the big wheel. This was the sign that she was in the very centre of the carnival area, as that was where this particular ride was always situated. Cassandra stood still and listened. She hadn't detected any sounds suggesting anyone else had scaled the fence, but now that she thought about it that didn't count for much. Though only a small part of Beaumont Park, this fenced off area was still sizeable; if someone had been careful enough they could have gotten over the fence whilst making the minimum of noise. Or they could have taken their time and slipped between fence sections. Cassandra shivered and started off again.

It was only a minute later that the attack came.

Apparently having decided that a sneak attack would not work, the figure charged at her from behind a covered stall, a rushing shadow growling as it came at her. The tactic had exactly the intended effect: Cassandra, petrified, froze on the spot, her head whipping round to gawp as the shadow barrelled into her. The two of them toppled together, slamming into the ground. The impact shook Cassandra from her paralysis and she prepared to cry out, not managing to make a sound before a hand clamped over her mouth. She kicked and struggled, throwing several wild swings with her fists at her attacker's sides, shoulders and face. With his – she was sure now it was a he as she could feel his erection pushing against her through his trousers, a sensation that made her want to throw up – free hand he tried to ward off her blows. As he did he spoke to her, his voice low and easy.

"Stop struggling," he said. "Stop fighting me or I'll hurt you."

She started to bat at the hand across her face, but it was like swatting a steel beam with a feather duster; the man was strong, and her fear was eroding what little strength she had left. Her struggles began to get weaker and weaker and she heard the bastard coo,

"That's good. Just let this happen."

Cassandra had two ideas about what "this" was, and did not care to find out if either, or perhaps both, were correct. After one final futile attempt to get him to relinquish his hold on her face, she stopped moving for a few seconds, took a couple of deep breaths through her nose, and then employed the technique that had worked so well on The Dickhead earlier.

The breath rushed out of her attacker and into her face and the hand covering her mouth finally eased up. The first thing that escaped her lips was a feral growl as Cassandra brought her right hand up and slapped her attacker right across the face. With his mind on other pains, the strike knocked him off balance and Cassandra rolled to her right, got her legs under her and scrambled forward and up into a stumbling run.

"Damn you," she heard behind her. It wasn't long before she realised he was giving chase, and it wasn't long before he caught up to her, throwing himself into her back, forcing her down with him on top of her. Spitting insults and abuse, he got to his knees, straddling her lower back, and flipped her over. Cassandra thrashed beneath him, her eyes closed, and so did not see the sudden movement as he drew back his arm and slammed a fist into her face. Her head bounced off the ground and her movements ceased. The man grabbed her arms, put them at her sides and pinned them there with his thighs. Cassandra was dimly aware of him talking to her as he ran his hands over her upper body, starting at her stomach and working his way up over her breasts, which he squeezed roughly. He stopped with both hands at her throat.

"I'd love to just choke you here and now for what you did," he admitted. "But you deserve to suffer more." One hand made its way back down her torso and he lifted himself, shoving the hand between their bodies and then between her legs, cupping her crotch. "Maybe you'll get a little of your fight back later. That'll make things so much more fun."

At first Cassandra thought the noise she could hear, which sounded like a distant siren, was in her head, a result of the earlier blow. Then she felt the man tense and realised that it was actually a distant siren, and that he could hear it too. There were no guarantees that it was coming their way, but her attacker spat out a vehement "Fuck!" nonetheless. Cassandra told herself not to get her hopes up, that even if the authorities had somehow been notified of what was happening to her, there was no way they could get to her in time. Instead of making off with his prize, this bastard would decide that there was no way to get her out of here as he had planned with the cops on route, and so would just kill her as he had said he would like to.

The sirens got louder and louder and it soon became apparent that they were coming towards Beaumont Park. Cursing again, Cassandra felt the man move and then heard an odd sound she couldn't identify. Moments later she worked out what it was – a knife being unsheathed – when she felt the cold blade press against her throat.

Running feet. Though her head was clearing a little, Cassandra decided that the sound of running feet was another aural ghost, but the sound got louder and louder. The coldness of the blade moved away from her throat and then there was a commotion atop her and the weight of the man was suddenly gone. In his absence was a cold feeling on the left hand side of her face, which quickly began to get warmer and warmer and eventually began to burn. She lifted one hand to her cheek, and as her fingers came into contact with the smooth edges of the cut a bolt of pain made her wince and cry out. She had time to register the warm, sticky feeling of blood on her fingertips before her attention was caught by the duelling shadows – three of them? - not far from her. She heard questions being asked and curses being exchanged, and was sure she heard a woman's voice call someone a bastard. Her attention was then diverted again. The sirens had stopped, but she could now see the flashing red and blue lights. Cassandra gathered together everything she had left and bellowed,

"Please help me!"

Her words caused the tussling figures to pause. Then she heard an angry voice hiss "You're both going to pay for this, you interfering cunts," and one of the figures took off. Not long after, the other two ran away in the opposite direction.

"Hello?" came a deep male voice from the direction of the lights. "Where are you?"

Cassandra tried to shout out again, but didn't manage it. Her strength gone, her mind whirling, the poor young woman passed out.

Chapter 36

After having been denied his prize by the two Guardians, Corday went to his house. Seething with resentment, he had tried to think of a way to calm down before he did something that would draw unwanted attention to him.

He did not succeed.

With no other outlet, he went through every room of his nice house and trashed it. Curtains were torn down, lamps smashed, and tables and chairs broken. He took an eight inch stainless steel kitchen knife to every upholstered item in the place, cursing them as he did so, disappointed that stabbing through material did not feel as much like stabbing through flesh as he had expected. He took a hammer to some of the walls, shattering the framed prints that hung around the house. Corday almost took this same hammer to the fifty inch plasma television mounted on the living room wall, but instead he tore it from its bracket, threw it to the floor and stomped on it. He considered throwing various objects through the windows, but decided against it. He might as well have gone ahead; by four in the morning, with the interior of his pleasant little dwelling comprehensively ruined, he had inevitably attracted some attention.

Corday was standing amidst the cyclonic destruction he had wrought upon his living room when he saw the blue and red lights flash through the slashes in the curtains on the front windows. He flashed back to earlier, to Beaumont Park, and his anger began to rise again, but it did not reach a dangerous level. His scorn at his own stupidity prevented it from doing so. Some, though by no means all, of the rage in him abated and he cursed himself, then he began thinking.

He reasoned that his adversaries wouldn't be able to go to the police, not with the truth at least. Would they concoct some fiction to get the law on their side? Possibly, though they certainly wouldn't be able to leave town with Muir. He would very likely be released since there had been another attack committed whilst he was in prison, but he would still be a suspect and so would be told to stay in town for the time being. The little prick was going nowhere, and although he would probably tell Abigail to get out of town, it was doubtful she would go without her one true love.

To hate takes far more than to love. Love is easy. Oh, you'll get plenty telling you different, but to maintain love is simple. Love wants to live, that's why so many make complete fools of themselves over it, why they make excuses for mistakes their loved ones have made, why they overlook obvious faults. Hatred is a sickly thing. To nourish it and maintain it over time is a task that takes determination, fortitude and the kind of strength that love simply does not imbue in someone. Yes, she loves him and so she'll stay, when a smart person would get the fuck out of town as quickly as they could. That's another side effect of love; it does horrible fucking things to your IQ. Hatred, on the other hand, that makes you smart, makes you think things out more, plan in better detail.

And then some bastards waltz in and screw up all your plans.

His thoughts were interrupted by the sound of a car door closing. Corday went to the window to see a sheriff's deputy walking towards his front door. His first thought was that his address had been given to the authorities by his enemies, but he reasoned that if that were the case they would have arrived in greater numbers. No, it was more likely that his neighbours had heard and reported the uproar that had come from his house. In the seconds before the doorbell rang Corday went into the hall and looked himself over in what shards of glass remained in the frame of a mirror. What he saw was not promising if he wished to somehow convince the cop to leave him be: smears of dirt and grime on his face and hands, a small weeping slit under his right eye, most likely caused by a flying sliver of glass, and his clothes were dishevelled, dirt streaked and slightly torn.

Corday stripped naked. Opening a cupboard door he tossed the garments inside, closed it over and then went to answer the door. As he neared it, he started to shuffle, dragging his feet across the carpet. He worked up some tears and thought about how badly to slur his speech.

Looking to the floor, Corday opened the door, exposing himself to a stunned Deputy Jack Parchett. The young man opened his mouth but could make no sound as he took in the sight of the naked, crying man before him.

"Uh, sir," were his first words when he got his voice back. "We received reports of a disturbance at this address. Are you okay?" Corday didn't lift his head, but shook it in response, wide, loose necked shakes. "Can you tell me your name, sir?"

Corday thought about using the name Ralph Walden, just for shits and giggles, but just before he did he remembered that the town of Pormount, though in another state, was not a million miles away from Hannerville. It was entirely possible that news of his murder of the Waldens had reached here, and the name might ring a bell with his unwanted visitor. Instead he used the name under which he had bought this house, the name on all of the forged documents he'd purchased in France. He also realised that name would be the one the deputy here would have found when he checked the address. His asking for Corday's name had merely been procedure. *Lucky,* he told himself. *That could have led to some difficult questions.* Sniffing loudly, he raised his head and said,

"My name's Richard Ganthorpe."

"What's happened, Mr Ganthorpe?"

"Bitch left me!" Corday wailed. "Took all my money and ran off with her fucking gym instructor. You believe that shit? Her fucking gym instructor. Heartless cow didn't even tell me to my face; I got home from a conference and found a note. Twenty years and she leaves me with a note left on the coffee table. Ah!"

He spun away from the door and wandered inside. After a moment's hesitation, the deputy followed, finding the man he believed was called Ganthorpe amidst the wreckage of the living room.

Corday, eager to put it all on a plate quickly so this dumb hick fuzzball would eat it, swallow it and leave, continued his tale.

"This was our perfect house," he whined. "I was determined to make it special for her, so I had decided to fix up and decorate the whole place myself before she moved in from our old place. I've been sleeping on a mattress on the floor upstairs for weeks, going to and from work from here, spending all my spare time and money on the place." He threw his arms out to the sides. "This is what that evil slut made me do it."

Parchett glanced around the room and then back to the man sitting cross legged on the floor. Thankfully the man had put his hands back in his lap, hiding his crotch. His slightly dirty hands. Dirty knees. Was that also a shallow cut beneath the man's eye?

"Mr Ganthorpe, how did you get your hands and knees dirty?"

Corday made a show of trying to pull himself together, clearing his throat and shaking his head as if to jumble his thoughts into order.

"I read the note, realised I had been taken for a damn fool and I got drunk. After that, tearing this place to pieces seemed like a good idea. After that, going out to the back yard to rip up the rose bushes I had planted for that bitch seemed like a great idea. I tore the knees out of my pants scrabbling around out there in the dark. Hurt my hands, got myself all dirty... Fucking rose thorn nearly took my eye out. Came in, took off my dirty clothes, drank a little more. Then you arrived."

The deputy, believing Corday's nicely put together piece of fiction, asked if he could take a look around. Corday nodded and waved a hand around, drunken sign language for "Go ahead, I don't give a fuck." He did not venture outside to the back yard and so did not see that there had been no rosebushes planted and then torn up. Everything he did see fit with what he had been told, which he had no reason to disbelieve. Back in the living room, he said to Corday,

"Sir, I sympathise, but I need to know that you're not going to be doing any more damage to this house or yourself, or anyone else, tonight. I wonder if maybe it would be an idea if you came down and slept it off in a cell tonight."

Oh fuck! thought Corday, who kept his head down, pretending he hadn't quite heard the deputy. His mind raced to come up with something, some reason that he couldn't leave here. Suddenly he snapped his head up as if his visitor's words had only just sunk in.

"Oh, no, officer, please," he pleaded. "If anyone at where I work finds out I've spent the night in jail I'll be fired. I can't be fired," he went on, allowing his voice to break. "Please. I'll go upstairs, sleep it off. I won't cause any more trouble, I swear."

He aimed wide, teary and pathetic eyes at the deputy, who thought about it briefly and then nodded.

"Okay, but I want you to go straight to bed."

Corday nodded, making his lip quiver, and the deputy took his leave. When he heard the front door close, Corday stopped weeping, sat up straight and dried his cheeks with the heel of one hand. He smiled. He did have a use for love after all. What better excuse to use for looking like your life had gone straight down the toilet?

He yawned and decided to get some sleep. As he trudged upstairs, he realised that, mentally at least, he felt quite refreshed.

Chapter 37

Martin didn't know it, but it was just after six o'clock in the morning when he was roused from his troubled sleep by the sound of the door to the cells opening.

Since his arrest Martin's thoughts had, for the most part, been about Abigail. Was she safe? Had something happened to her? Was she being given a hard time by people for being loyal to a man they all believed was a killer? Even on those occasions when his thoughts turned to the enigma of Andrea Coyle's visit, it was never too long before they returned to Abigail. Those few hours when he managed to fall asleep, his mind played little movies, showing him all the horrible things he feared might befall her whilst he was locked up in here. Mercifully he always woke before the end, which was sure to be gruesome and unpleasant. He had little doubt that by now he looked exactly as he felt. His only consolation was that he truly believed the sheriff would have informed him if anything had happened to Abigail. Though he was still unsure of Coyle's assertion that Flaghan had his doubts about the guilt of the man he had arrested, Martin believed the sheriff was a good man. This was a notion reinforced during Martin's second day in jail, when the sheriff had delivered to him a change of clothes that could only have come from the cabin. Flaghan had passed the garments between the bars and Martin had taken them and thanked him, fighting the urge to ask for confirmation that nothing that further linked him to the killings had been found. Though unsure if he hadn't asked in case it made him seem guilty somehow, or because he didn't believe the sheriff would tell him even if it were so, Martin was sure he had done the right thing by staying silent. He had purposefully not read too much into the gesture. It would have been easy to assume Coyle was correct and that Flaghan had brought him clothes because he believed Martin was innocent and was treating him as such. It was just as easy to imagine that the sheriff knew he'd been wearing the same clothes for a while and didn't want him stinking the place out, or simply that he believed in people being innocent until proven guilty.

Realising he was awake, Martin opened his eyes and stared at the ceiling for a few moments, then asked himself why the door at the end of the corridor had opened. A new prisoner? He listened, hearing no voices. Someone on their own? Flaghan? A deputy? Martin had the terrible idea that he had been completely wrong about the sheriff, who was at the very moment leading a group of deputies to his cell, from which they would drag him, bound and gagged, taking him into the street. There he would be hung from a lamp post, either by the neck or by the wrists, both options coming with his being pelted with rocks as standard. He pushed away the images of his jerking body dangling from a street light.

The corridor lights blinked once, twice, then came on full strength with a quiet humming. Martin squinted in the sudden harsh glare and heard the slow footsteps begin. He decided to just get up and see what was going on.

Still blinking, he reached the cell door at the same time as Mark Flaghan. The sheriff wore a grave expression and Martin's heart dropped into his shoes. The last vestiges of sleep were scattered by the howling winds of worry.

"Is it Abigail?" he asked, gripping two of the bars.

"No," said the sheriff. "It was a girl called Cassandra Church."

"Oh, Christ," muttered Martin. "What happened?"

"She was attacked in Beaumont Park late last night," Flaghan explained. "Bastard stalked her, chased her into the area that's being prepped for the carnival. He knocked her down, pulled a knife on her." Martin shook his head and lowered it, putting his forehead against the cold bars. "Poor girl was sure she was going to die, but then someone, two someone's actually, wrestled the guy off of her and fought with him. The three of them ran away when they heard the sirens." Martin looked up, puzzled. "Someone had called us to say they had seen a young woman being chased into the park. I went to check it out. I heard her call out, went in and found her."

"How is she?"

"Badly shaken up, as you can imagine, but other than a cut to her face, she's physically fine. Doctor says there won't even be a scar."

Martin closed his eyes and blew out a breath, nodding as he released the bars and started backing up towards his cot. He opened his eyes in time to see the sheriff slide the key into the lock and open the cell door. The tall man stepped forward, blocking the doorway. Martin met his gaze.

"I'm going to level with you, Mr Muir. You were arrested purely on the basis of what was found at your cabin, which I think even you would have to admit was incriminating. However, an extensive search of that property has yielded nothing else to connect you with the deaths of those women, and I find that very odd. God alone knows how many people we've spoken to and not one of them could place your accent, your name, your face or put you anywhere near any of the victims, except Sophie Thomas, and you have an alibi I believe for the night she was abducted. There's also the anonymous phone call and now this latest attack, which I know you did not commit. Also, having interviewed you myself, I just get the gut feeling you're not capable of it." He backed up a step. "I've already notified the mayor that you're being released and he sees the sense in it. An article about it is almost sure to run right beside the story of the attack on Cassandra Church in today's paper. Bear in mind however that until this bastard is caught, you are not to leave town. Despite what I think, you are still a suspect. Do you understand?"

"I… Yes. Yes, I do."

"Good." Flaghan stepped back. "Now get out of here so I can lock this cell up and go get some breakfast; it's been a long morning already."

Martin smiled, nodded and walked quickly out of the cell, pausing beside the broad shouldered sheriff. He frowned, trying to think of something to say. He wanted to tell the man that if he could be of any help, the sheriff need only ask. But what good could he possibly do the investigation?

You know the name of the killer, that's what good! Coyle might even be able to give you a description of the fucker. Of course you have no way of explaining any of this to the sheriff, so that's a brick wall hit right there.

Time was moving along and he was starting to look stupid, so he settled for a simple, "Thank you."

Martin offered his hand, and after a moment's hesitation, Flaghan took it, shook it and then, when Martin tried to pull away, he held it. Staring into Martin's eyes he said,

"Know this, Mr Muir: if it turns out I'm wrong, if you are involved in this in any way, I will not rest till I get you."

Martin held the man's gaze and, in a calm voice born of the knowledge of his own innocence, replied,

"Sheriff, I don't doubt you."

Flaghan escorted Martin from the building. On the way he explained that Martin could not go back to the cabin as yet, and that if he wanted to collect his belongings then he would have to contact the sheriff's office so he could be escorted. At the front door he gave Martin his card and a brown bag with Martin's other set of clothes in it, and bid him goodbye for now.

Martin took in a couple of lungfuls of what might have been the freshest air he had ever inhaled, and then set off.

The streets were still dark, a fact Martin was thankful for as he was painfully aware of how shabby he looked. He only spotted one or two people, and they either nodded a good morning, which he returned, or kept to themselves. Martin wondered why it was none of them gave him a second look, and at first decided that it was too dark for them to see him properly. A little time later, he realised something that caused him to revise that decision.

They didn't know who he was.

Hannerville was a small town, but not small enough that everyone knew who everyone else was. It was still a large enough place to have strangers. Yes, his name had been in the papers and banded about by every gossip in town, but it wasn't as if there had been a picture of him in the paper. No one had been around to take one when he had been arrested, and certainly no one had come anywhere near his cell with a camera. He wondered how far a reporter would have gone to get a photo of him. None would have been readily available online; Martin didn't have a social networking page or anything like that. His business website did not carry his picture. Would an enterprising newshound have contacted his friends or family for a snapshot? He doubted it. So everyone in town knew his name, but really his only distinguishable feature was his accent, so if he kept his mouth shut in public then hopefully he might just be able to get through the rest of this nightmare. Martin just wished he knew how much longer it was going to go on.

He reached his destination. Martin stood at Abigail's gate wondering if she would be up. There were no lights on. Would she even answer the door at this time? Should he perhaps go somewhere for a while, wait until she was up and about? Where would he go? He was barred from the cabin, and a stroll around Beaumont Park did not seem like the best idea. What would he say when she opened the door?

Opening the gate he stepped inside, closed the gate again, and then made his way to the front door. He rang the bell and waited. A minute passed. Two. He began to wonder if she was even at home when the hall light came on, shining through the little stained glass window set into the door. Moments later the little porch-light came on. Martin scrunched up the right side of his face and turned away from the glare.

"Marty?" came Abigail's voice from the other side of the door. Unscrunching his face, Martin blinked, looked towards the peephole and nodded. "Oh my god! Marty!"

He heard the lock disengaging and the door was yanked open. Abigail stepped out and threw her arms around his neck. Martin gently put his arms around her and pushed his face into her hair.

They stood like that for several minutes, neither caring to move. It was Martin who eventually said they should go inside.

Abigail closed and locked the door behind them. Martin waited for her. The moment she turned to him she went in for a kiss, but he blocked her advance, blushing.

"Uh, you seriously might want to hang off until I get hold of a toothbrush."

She smiled and let out a little laugh.

"Morning breath again, huh?"

"Several mornings worth," he told her. "I think my teeth are starting to melt. Then of course there's the hobo chic look I've got going on, which I think is complemented nicely by the unkempt hair and facial fuzz." He shook his head and for a moment thought he was going to cry. He heard it in his voice when he said, "Christ, I'm a mess."

"Then let's get you cleaned up."

"Can I use your computer first?"

He logged into his e-mail account and sent a message to Stephen updating him and saying he'd be back in touch when he could. That done, Abigail took him by the hand and led him upstairs to the bathroom. She undressed him and put him in a hot shower, and as he was cleaning up she took his clothes down and threw them in the washer/dryer. Back upstairs, she waited for him to finish and then dried him and led him through to the bedroom, where she laid him down, undressed and got into the bed beside him. After his time in jail, it was nirvana for Martin.

"Rest now," Abigail told him, snuggling up beside him. "Talk later."

Martin was asleep before he had the chance to respond.

A couple of hours later, Martin awoke to find Abigail's side of the bed empty. The delicious smells wafting through the bedroom door gave a clue as to her whereabouts. He got up and saw his freshly washed and dried clothes over the back of a chair. He dressed and headed for the stairs, changing course at the last minute to enter the bathroom, where he squeezed some toothpaste onto his finger and spread it across his teeth, gums and tongue. A vigorous rinse and he decided his mouth was as good as it was going to get for now. After washing his hands, he went down to the kitchen.

This time it was Martin who went in for the kiss, and Abigail did not resist him. When they came up for air, both were smiling. Abigail said,

"It's ridiculous how much I missed that."

"I'm not sure if that's a compliment or an insult."

"Well that'll give you something to think about while we eat."

Ten minutes later they were sitting down to bacon and eggs. Though the food in jail had been passable, Martin's appetite hadn't been great the last few days. Now a relatively free man, his stomach made its wishes very clear.

"Good lord!" exclaimed Abigail as the rumbling died away. "Didn't they feed you?"

"Yes, but I didn't eat much, something I now intend to put right."

He cleaned his plate, and was more than happy to accept another. Once that was done, he mopped up with a slice of bread and sat back in his chair, grinning and stifling a burp.

"That was superb," he complimented Abigail. "I'd really like to go back to bed now, but we need to talk."

Abigail, who had long since finished eating and was now sipping her coffee, nodded in agreement. They put their dishes in the sink and went into the living room, sitting side by side on the couch. Abigail outlined the last few days for Martin. When she was finished, she was practically bouncing up and down in her seat.

"I'm guessing you're anxious to know why I was released," said Martin.

"Yes!"

"He went after someone else." Abigail stopped bouncing. "He didn't get her," Martin explained. "It was a girl named Cassandra Church. She was attacked walking through Beaumont Park last night. Someone saw what was going on and called the cops, who were on their way there when two people saved the girl when her attacker was about to use a knife on her. She was cut, but not badly. She's shaken up, obviously, but she'll live. The attacker and the good Samaritans fled the scene and Flaghan found her. He then decided he had enough reason to doubt he had the right man in custody, so he released me. I'm not allowed to leave town, but at least I'm no longer behind bars."

"So, did he apologise or anything?"

"No." Abigail rolled her eyes. "He was doing his job, Abi. What they found in the cabin didn't seem to leave any room for doubt, yet Flaghan admitted having some. The anonymous phone call that told him where the bodies were didn't sit well with him, plus he told me that nothing else had been found at the cabin that linked me to the crimes, which in his own words he found odd. Last night's attack was what finally convinced him I should be released, though he made it very clear I'm still a suspect."

"Did he mention if they had any clues as to who the killer really is? Did the people who saved the girl come forward to maybe give a description or something?"

Martin took a breath, held it a moment as he prepared to speak, then let it back out again, blowing it out slowly between his lips.

"What is it?"

"I had another visitor the day I was arrested."

"Who?"

"Do you remember the name of my primary school teacher who started the pen-pal scheme?"

"Of course: Miss Coyle." Martin gave her a sheepish look, raising his eyebrows. "Miss Coyle came to see you? Your old teacher came to see you in jail?" Martin nodded.

"Insane, I know, but that's who it was. I don't know what she told Flaghan she was to me, but she managed to get him to let her and I chat for a few minutes."

"What did she say?"

"Something I've been thinking about on and off for three days and still can't make any sense of."

Martin relayed in as much details as he was able the conversation he'd had with Andrea Coyle. Abigail listened until he was finished, and then asked,

"Do you believe she and her friends saved that girl?"

"Honestly, I don't know." Abigail chewed the inside of her cheek for a few seconds and then said,

"We need to find her."

"What? How?"

"There's no way in hell her being here is a coincidence. She told you herself that there was more to all of this than what she told you that day. I'd say it's pretty damned important that we find her and get the whole story."

"Abi, don't you think that we might be looking for a lunatic? It occurred to me in jail: what if she knew everything she told me about because she made it up? There's even the possibility that she herself is the killer, or linked to him in some way. The man that attacked Cassandra Church might have been one of Coyle's "associates". Plus she said she would see me again soon. She might know by now that I'm out of jail, and to tell the truth I'm not sure how I feel about another visit from her."

"But we have to speak to her, Marty," said Abigail. "What if everything she said was true?" he didn't have an answer for her. "Think about it," she said as she got off the couch. "I have to go and call Beth and Amanda. They'll want to know you've been released."

She took the phone and went upstairs. Martin sat, considering her suggestion. Maybe Abigail was right. Maybe they needed to find her, to hear her out, if only so they would have everything necessary to decide if she was telling the truth or not. This led back to the problem of actually locating her, though Martin still believed that they might not have to, believed that not before long, Miss Coyle would seek them out.

He heard Abigail coming back, then the phone rang and her footsteps paused on the stairs as she answered the call.

"Oh, hi," he heard her say. "Yes, I know." Pause. "Yes." Pause. "Okay. We'll see you when you get here."

She walked back into the lounge and set the phone in its charger, then sat back down beside Martin.

"The girls say they hope you're okay and that they hope to see you soon. Beth's still okay to look after the store, so you and I can go teacher hunting."

"Who's coming over?"

"My aunt and uncle." Martin's mouth formed a little o. "You okay with that?"

"I don't exactly look my best, but I dare say the window for me to make a good first impression on them has already closed. Then had a brick put through it." He shrugged. "No sense putting it off any longer I suppose."

For the next ten minutes he was so unsettled he felt close to ridiculous. When he sat down he fidgeted, when he got up and paced the floor he felt like he wanted to run out the front door and keep running. On several occasions Martin had met the parents or guardians of women he was going out with, but this was different. On those other occasions, Martin had been able to be himself, to be warm and friendly, jocular, maybe even, on a really good day, a little bit charming. That was because none of those encounters had ever really meant anything to him. Yes he wanted the people to like him, wanted them to know he wasn't the kind of guy who would get their daughter knocked up and then pull a disappearing act, but he hadn't been especially concerned that they wouldn't. If they decided they didn't like him, then so what? Things would happen and he would deal with them. Sometimes the opinion of the parents had had an effect on the way the woman had felt, sometimes it hadn't. Sometimes the relationship had gone on a while, sometimes he'd received a phone call and been told "I'm sorry, I just can't be with someone my Mum and Dad don't like." He had always been understanding, had never broken down or whined, asking why they hadn't liked him.

None of those people had been the man and woman who had raised the woman he loved.

Having been told about the conversation Abigail had had with her guardians the day of his arrest Martin doubted their not liking him would be the end of his relationship with Abigail, though this idea did little to calm him. He wasn't sure how he should act when they arrived, what he should say to them. They had told Abigail they trusted her judgement, but that didn't necessarily mean they trusted him, and he wanted them to. Saving any form of good standing with these people was going to be an uphill battle. A hill someone had covered in oil.

He was in the middle of a pacing phase when Abigail asked him,

"I don't suppose telling you to calm down will have any effect whatsoever?"

"Not a bit," he replied.

"How about if I threatened to put my foot up your ass if you don't sit down and stop worrying?"

"I'd sit down, but I wouldn't stop worrying."

"Marty, they're not going to walk in the door and try to lynch you."

He turned to her, about to try to put his fears into words, when the doorbell rang. He visibly flinched and his face went a little paler. Abigail saw this and went to him.

"I'm with you, okay."

He managed a nod and she kissed him and went to answer the door. He heard the pleasant greetings exchanged between Abigail and her aunt and uncle. Some hushed words, and then Abigail came back, followed by Peter and Janine Morton.

"Aunt Janine, Uncle Peter, meet Martin Muir."

Martin stepped forward feeling like he had lead weights on the end of his legs instead of feet. He extended a hand that suddenly felt so damp he wondered if he should blot it on his trouser leg first. He did not, and in turn Peter and Janine half-heartedly shook his hand. As he lowered his arm, Martin knew what he wanted to do.

"Please," he said, indicating the couch. "Take a seat."

Abigail had been about to offer their guests coffee, but she sensed Martin had suddenly developed a plan and was putting it into action. Rather than interrupt, she sat down beside her aunt and uncle.

"I apologise for my appearance; I haven't had a chance to shave yet. I don't even want to imagine what must be going through your minds right now. I've come here from across an ocean to meet your niece, who I know is more like a daughter to you. Then, before we've even had a chance to meet, I'm arrested, something which I'm guessing I don't have to go into detail about. It doesn't paint a good picture of me. I know Abigail has told you how she feels, what she believes, and I know that you've told her you can trust her judgement." He paused, gathered his courage and continued. "But that's not good enough for me. You took her in, you raised her, loved her and now, in your mind, she's going out with man who might very well be a killer. That has to prey on your mind, regardless of what you've said to Abigail, because although you know you can trust her judgement, you can't trust me. Am I right?"

There was silence as he awaited an answer, which eventually came from Peter.

"You are."

Abigail turned to look at her uncle, clearly shocked.

"Abi," Martin said softly. "He was asked a question and he answered it honestly, and I can ask him for no more than that."

As Peter Morton looked apologetically at his niece, Martin looked to Janine. She looked back at him for a moment or two before asking,

"How can we? How can we trust you?"

"Keep going, Janine," said Martin. "Talk to me."

"We don't even know you," the woman went on. "We know what Abigail has told us about you, how she feels about you, but after all that's happened, what are we supposed to think?"

"What do you think?" Martin asked. "Both of you. I need to know."

"Why?" asked Peter.

"Because I need a starting point," Martin explained. "Your view of me had been coloured before you'd even clapped eyes on me, and I can't blame you for that. You have an image of the kind of man I might be stuck in your head, and I need to know how far from who I know I am that image is. Until then I can't start to try to prove to you that I am innocent, that I had nothing to do with the deaths of those women. I need to know that there's a point to trying, or if your minds are already made up."

Peter and Janine looked at one another, and then back at Martin.

"It was a friend of ours who'd heard a rumour that you had been released early this morning," Peter told Martin. "What our friend didn't know was why." Martin nodded.

"A girl was attacked last night." Peter's eyes widened and his wife gasped. "She's alive," Martin added quickly.

"Who was it?" asked Janine.

"Cassandra Church."

"I don't know the name," said Peter. His wife shook her head, indicating she didn't know the victim either.

"It happened late last night. She was saved by…" He glanced briefly at Abigail. "Persons unknown. They intervened, fought with the attacker, and then everyone ran away as the sheriff, who had been called by someone who had seen the girl being chased, showed up. The sheriff decided that I should be released as there was room for doubt that I was guilty. No further evidence has been found at the cabin, and the sheriff also told me that he thought the phone call that told them where to find the missing women was suspicious. However, I am not to leave town until the situation had been resolved."

There was an uneasy silence as the elder Mortons digested what they had been told. Janine was the first to speak.

"Our law states that a man is innocent until proven guilty. I think I can safely speak for both my husband and myself when I say that we'd be lying if we hadn't come here this morning with a certain image of you in our heads. That image was incorrect, I'm glad to say, but I'd also be lying if I told you I didn't have my doubts." Peter nodded and said,

"I was worried that being associated with you might have a detrimental effect on Abigail and her business." His niece muttered under her breath that people and their opinions could kiss her ass and go to hell. "But I have to trust my instincts," Peter continued "And they're telling me that you're not a monster. Now, like my wife, I have my doubts, but my instincts are telling me that there seems to be something out of whack with this whole situation. Did the sheriff say anything to you about how the bod... How the women got into that room in the cabin?"

"No," replied Martin. "I haven't spent a lot of time up there since I arrived though, so the killer had plenty of opportunities to break in."

"Isn't the place alarmed?"

"Yes, but I suppose someone with the right skills could have gotten past it, gone upstairs and picked the lock on the master bedroom."

"But why that cabin?" asked Janine. "Why leave them where you were staying?"

"That we're completely in the dark about," Abigail told her aunt. "Marty had only been in Hannerville a few days."

"No arguments or fights with anybody in town?" Peter asked Martin.

"Not so much as a cross word; everybody I'd met had been very friendly."

"Damn odd," commented Peter.

"I hate to be the one to bring this up," Janine began. "But what if it really is David Brannon?"

Martin caught the pained expression that briefly crossed Peter's face, then he and Abigail exchanged a brief glance. For a moment Martin considered letting Peter and Janine in on what Coyle had told him, but he felt like he had done himself some good during the conversation and so he quickly decided against it. Plus it would only add to the number of questions they had, the answers to which he did not yet have.

"If it is," Abigail said. "Then we will deal with it."

"I'm tempted to tell you that I'll do whatever I can to help catch whoever's responsible for all this," Martin told them. "But that would be a stupid thing to do. Promises like that won't help ease your doubts, and in all truth there's probably not a damn thing I can do to help catch the killer anyway. But there is one promise I will make, and it's one I will keep, come hell or high water. I promise you that whatever it takes, I will take care of Abigail."

He felt like adding something truly grandstanding, like "Even if it costs me my life, I'll do it", but even in his head it sounded like a line from a bad movie, so he left it at what he'd said. Peter and Janine regarded him solemnly for a short time, and then Peter got to his feet. Janine followed suit.

"You've been very honest today, Martin," Peter said. "So I'll be just as frank. You seem genuine enough, but bad men hide behind nice masks. If you cause my niece any harm, I will see that you pay for it, and pay dearly. If you are the man you appear to be, the man Abigail believes you are, then after all this is behind us, I look forward to getting to know you better. Seem fair?" He extended a hand. Martin nodded and they shook on it.

Abigail saw her aunt and uncle to the door. When they were out of sight, Martin collapsed onto the couch and rubbed his face with his hands. He heard Abigail close the front door and eyed her as she came back into the living room, walked across the floor and sat down beside him. She turned and gave him a smile.

"Under the circumstances, I don't really think that could have gone any better. Do you?" Martin shook his head.

"Your uncle didn't knock out any of my teeth, and your aunt didn't open her bag, take out a small gun and shoot me. I'm calling it a win." Abigail chuckled and snuggled up next to him. The two of them sat there for a while. Martin didn't realise Abigail was crying until he felt a tear splash against his hand.

"What's wrong?" he asked, suddenly feeling as though he'd just asked the stupidest question on the planet; he could take his pick of the things that might have brought her to tears and end up being correct. But, having realised she was crying, it was the first, and stupid or not the most important question, that came to mind. Abigail sniffed and shook her head, then let out a little sob. "Abigail?"

"It's just... I can't even talk to Beth and Amanda about it because I'm afraid it would upset them too." Martin realised why she was crying. Three days since the body of one of her closest friends had been found, and Abigail had had no one to talk to about it.

"I'm sorry I wasn't here before," he said softly. "But I'm here now. Talk to me."

Abigail sniffed some more, taking a hankie out of her pocket as she sat up. She blew her nose, then blushed and looked abashedly at Martin.

"Sorry."

"Why? When you have a full bladder, you pee, and when you have a runny nose, you blow it."

She forced a laugh and nodded, scrunching the hankie into a ball in her hand.

"I'm so fed up of euphemisms," she declared. "In the last three days, whenever anyone has talked about the murders, they always try to use other words so that things don't sound as bad. You and my uncle did it today, not ten minutes ago. I've heard people do it in my store, and in the grocery store, even on the street. It's as if they're all afraid to confront it head on in case it shatters their lives, makes it real and calls the killer down upon them next. Or maybe they think that whispering about it in socially acceptable terms makes it okay, that nothing too bad really happened. But it did." Her voice cracked a little on the last word, but she cleared her throat and went on. "Those women died. Someone kidnapped them and hurt them and killed them, and people should be fucking furious about that. Scared, yes, and when they all wake up and find out they're not so safe this morning as they were last night, that the bastard is still out there, they'll be even more scared, but they should be even angrier. Maybe no one they knew died, but someone I knew, someone I loved, did, and every time someone plays it down or hushes it up, it stabs me in the heart because she's gone, Marty. Sophie's gone."

Her voice broke and as the emotion she had held in for three days was set free, she threw herself into the arms of the man she loved. Martin caught her and held her as she buried her face against his chest and cried. He did not pat her back, did not coo to her that it would all be okay; this was not a time for such things. Abigail did not need comforting right now, what she needed was to let it all out, and Martin let her.

When she stopped crying, Martin stroked her hair for a time. When he felt her move he released her and she sat back, her eyes red and puffy, in stark contrast to her pale cheeks. She did her best to make the thoroughly squashed hankie useable again, but it was a lost cause. Martin got up and found a box of tissues, which he brought back, noticing as he passed them to her that the front of his shirt was dotted with dark spots.

"Sorry about that," she said as she took a tissue out of the box and blew her nose again. Another she used to dry her eyes.

"Don't be daft," Martin chided her. Then he glanced back down at the damp splotches. "As long as they're all tears. They're all tears, right? No snot drops?" Abigail laughed and shook her head, dabbing at her eyes. "Good." He smiled at her and then told her, "You really should speak to Beth and Amanda about this. I'd be surprised if they didn't feel the same way."

"I'm just afraid of upsetting them."

"Abi, they're upset already, and they'll need someone they can talk to about it. Preferably someone who's going to understand how they feel, and for each of you there are only two people who fit that bill. I mean if you want to talk to me about it, believe me I will sit and listen, but I had only just met Sophie. She seemed like a wonderful person, but I didn't know her, Abi. Beth knew her, Amanda knew her, and you knew her. They're your friends, you're their friend. Bring them round, get some snacks and drinks, and remember Sophie." They spent some time making up for the past three days of being apart. They watched some TV, but halfway through the show they were watching they ended up having sex on the couch. They managed to get through a movie, though there was a lot of kissing and fondling going on, and then they made lunch. Afterwards they went upstairs to bed and made love.

Just after two in the afternoon. Abigail was in the bathroom. Martin lay naked in bed, a contented smile on his face. Right there and then it was possible for him to convince himself that the last three days hadn't happened, that the world and all its problems were gone. In a sense they were, he but knew that he was enjoying what would eventually prove to be a temporary respite. As if to prove him right, the doorbell rang.

"Marty?" Abigail called.

"I'm on it!" Martin replied, leaping from the bed and snatching his jeans up off the floor. He tugged them on then grabbed his T-shirt, pulling it over his head as he padded barefoot down the stairs. He got to the front door and looked through the peephole, his breath catching in his throat when he saw Andrea Coyle. He heard the toilet flush upstairs and said,

"Just a minute."

Jogging back upstairs, he got to the landing as the bathroom door opened and Abigail poked her head out.

"Who was it?" she asked as he scampered past, going into the bedroom. He came out with her clothes in his arms and dumped them at her feet.

"It's *her,*" he whispered.

"Her who?" asked Abigail.

"Miss Coyle." Abigail's eyebrows shot up in surprise.

"Oh, shit!" She started getting dressed.

"Should we answer?"

"Yes, we should. We need to hear what she has to say, Marty."

With both of them now fully clothed, they went back downstairs. Martin waited for Abigail to answer the door. When she made no move to do so, he looked at her. She nodded towards the door. He frowned and pointed at himself. Abigail nodded emphatically. Martin opened the door.

"Hello again, Martin," Coyle said brightly. "May I come in?"

"Yes," answered Abigail. "Please."

She entered and Martin led them through to the living room. Abigail closed and locked the door and joined them, standing beside Martin and inviting their guest to take a seat and asking her if she would like a drink.

"I think a proper introduction is warranted first," said Coyle, extending her hand. Andrea Coyle."

"Abigail Morton."

"Pleasure to meet you, and thank you; cup of tea would be lovely."

"Cool. Marty?"

"Nothing for me, thanks. You want a hand?"

"No, you stay with Miss Coyle."

Soon Martin and Abigail were on the sofa, with Miss Coyle in the armchair. She sipped at her tea and nibbled on the selection of biscuits Abigail had set out. She and Martin exchanged furtive glances as they waited for Coyle to speak. Eventually, Martin broke the silence.

"Thank you," he said.

"For what?" enquired Coyle.

"For saving that girl last night," clarified Martin. "I'm assuming that was you."

"One of my associates and I, yes," confirmed his old teacher. "When we saw him go after the girl, we phoned the station and then followed. By that point, Corday was in what I suppose you could call hunt mode; he was focussing on who he was after, not who might be after him. We hoped the sheriff would arrive before he caught her - and to give him his due, Flaghan got there very quickly – but when he heard the sirens, Corday apparently decided to simply kill the girl. We knocked him off of her, struggled with him. To say he was furious would be an understatement, as it would be to say that our escaping with nothing but bruises and grazes was lucky. We were armed, but were afraid of hitting the girl in the dark. When she cried out, Corday ran and we did the same." She took another sip of tea and a small smile creased her lips. "We found out you had been released early this morning, but we decided to wait a while before coming round."

Martin and Abigail blushed slightly.

"That reminds me," said Abigail. "How did you get in to see Marty in jail? Who did you tell the sheriff you were?"

"A defence lawyer from the firm who deals with Martin's company's legal affairs who had been sent over as soon as word reached us about your arrest."

"Inventive," responded Martin, nodding his head slowly. "Complete bollocks, but inventive all the same."

"It worked, which was the important thing."

"Marty's told me about the discussion the two of you had when you went to see him," Abigail told Coyle. She paused, pursed her lips a little, then sighed and finished with, "What is going on here?"

Coyle sat forward and sat her cup on the table, then sat up straight and said,

"I'm not going to ask if you both trust me, because we both know you'd be utterly stupid if you did. However, if you'll indulge me, I'd like to ask you both to hold hands and close your eyes for a moment."

Martin and Abigail regarded her with expressions that were equal parts suspicion and confusion. They looked at one another for a moment, and then Abigail reached for Martin's hand. Their fingers laced together and they looked back to Coyle, who had a broad smile on her face. They both closed their eyes. Martin's old teacher spoke some words neither of them recognised, words that seemed to them to be made up nonsense. When Coyle stopped, the pair opened their eyes.

They were not where they had been.

Martin and Abigail stood, hand in hand, in a small square room. The yellowish walls, one of which had a doorway in it covered by a hanging sheet of ragged edged cloth, had rough surfaces. The floor was dirt and the ceiling above them was thatched. In one corner there was a rectangular mat of straw covered by some more of the cloth that hung in the doorway.

"Marty, what the hell is going on?" asked Abigail, a clear note of fear in her voice.

"I have no idea," Martin admitted.

"Have we been hypnotised or something?"

"I don't know."

Abigail reached out and tried to run a hand over the wall, but it passed straight through. She yanked her hand back and stared at it, then at the wall.

"I can't touch that wall, but I know exactly what it feels like, the texture of it." She let go of Martin's hand, knelt down and tried to drag a finger through the dirt. Nothing. "And I know what this floor feels like too. This is so weird." Straightening up, she turned to Martin. "It feels like a really vivid dream."

"How could Miss Coyle cause us to have a shared dream?"

"Those words she was speaking? Maybe she hypnotised us into having the same dream at the same time. Maybe that's why she made us hold hands." She glanced around. "I mean, a trance is a dreamlike state, isn't it?"

"But what is all this about?"

Abigail shrugged.

"Should we go outside?" she asked after a short interval had passed.

"Nothing much else to see in here," Martin replied, heading for the door.

He tried to draw back the curtain, but found that his hand could not grasp it. Frowning, he tried again and got the same result. He looked at Abigail, who shrugged and took his hand again. Together they stepped through the curtain and found themselves in a narrow alleyway, only a few feet across. Glancing in both directions revealed long rows of dwellings like the one they had just exited. A curtain of slightly higher quality than the one behind them covered the doorway of the building opposite. High above them, the sun hung in the bright blue, cloudless sky. Abigail looked up, shielding her eyes with her hand, but Martin stared intently at the doorway in front of him.

"I know the name of the man who lives there," he murmured.

"What did you say, Marty?" asked Abigail, dropping her hand and lowering her gaze.

"I said I know the name of the man who lives in that house. It's Raffikan."

"How could you know that? How do you know there's even someone in there?"

Martin shook his head.

"He's not in there right now." He glanced up. "It's around midday; he's been at work all morning. He makes clothes."

"He's about six feet tall," said Abigail suddenly. "A kindly looking man with a big bushy beard and pale green eyes."

They looked at one another.

"A friendly man," continued Abigail. "When I think about him, I feel cheery." She paused, the serene expression falling from her face, replaced by a look of alarm. "Marty, why am I so sure of these things? Why do I get that feeling thinking about a man I've never known in a place I've ever been before?"

"I don't know," Martin replied, tightening his grip on her hand. "But when I think of him I feel a similar way. We should…"

There was a burst of noise from the end of the alleyway. They both turned to see a group of children, three boys and two girls, all around the age of eleven or twelve, come barrelling round the corner, laughing and shouting. As the children got closer, Martin picked out the face of one of the girls, and his own was suddenly decorated with an ear to ear grin. Beside him, Abigail had locked her gaze onto one of the boys, and she too smiled. Both of them experienced a warm sense of friendship, of comfort.

They came out of their reverie too late to get out of the way of the oncoming kids, which didn't make much of a difference as the kids ran right through them as if they weren't even there. The boy in the lead thrust the curtain aside and bid his friends enter, which they did. When they were all inside, the boy joined them, letting the curtain drop back over the door.

Martin and Abigail stepped back through into the dwelling to find the children seated in a circle. They were apparently about to play a game. As the boy who had led them into the house explained the rules, the adults in the room both realised something. Abigail spoke first.

"What's odd?"

"Everything."

"Fair point, but this one might really blow your mind." He turned to her and she explained. "You can understand what the boy's saying?" Martin nodded. "So can I, but he's not speaking English."

Martin returned his attention to the boy and found that she was quite right. He couldn't even identify the language the child was speaking, yet he understood every word.

"How is that even possible?" he muttered.

They watched as the children played their game. Again their attentions were drawn to the boy and girl they had spotted outside. After a few minutes, Abigail asked Martin if he had singled any of the kids out and he replied that he had, and they identified their respective youngsters.

"His name is Bakari," said Abigail.

"Her's is Mandisa."

"A mutual friend, a boy named Sefu, he introduced them."

"Just this morning," added Martin, nodding. "But they know they like one another already."

The children and the room became still, and then were suddenly and silently blown away, becoming what looked like a storm of multi coloured grains of sand. Martin and Abigail stood inside the maelstrom, watching as one image was swept away and another quickly took its place.

A hilltop, overlooking the outskirts of a city. Hundreds of torches burned, illuminating the buildings. It was easy from this vantage point to pick out the path that led from the city up to the magnificent palace, a brightly lit jewel against the backdrop of the night sky. It sat almost directly across from the hill Martin and Abigail now found themselves on. Looking around, they soon spotted two seventeen or eighteen year olds, who they immediately knew to be older versions of Bakari and Mandisa. They sat side by side on the grass, looking away from the city, out towards the dark expanse of a vast desert. The two teens were lost in their own thoughts, neither speaking. They were sharing a comfortable silence.

Martin and Abigail approached, both feeling slightly nauseous.

"He's thinking that he's not good enough for her," said Martin. "That he'll never be able to buy her a palace like that one." He jerked his head back over his shoulder, indicating the ornate edifice on the opposite hilltop. "He's afraid, and I mean scared out of his mind, that she's going to leave him for someone who can provide a better future for her."

"She's worried that that's exactly what her father is going to force her to do," Abigail took up the narrative. "But she doesn't want that; she wants to be with him. She loves him, adores him, has never so much as considered being with anyone else, even though there have been others who have shown an interest. But she isn't sure if he feels the same way."

"Because he never talks about it, because he's afraid that if he does then all his worst fears will be realised. But he knows that she wants to talk about it, and he's worried that if he doesn't broach the subject he's going to lose her anyway."

Without warning, Abigail let go of his hand and ran back to where they had entered this whatever-the-hell-this-was. Martin went after her, catching up to her as she doubled over and wretched. Nothing came up, but when she was finished she dropped to her knees in the grass, tears running down her face. Martin, pale with worry, crouched behind her and put his arms around her.

"I can feel it, Marty," she sobbed. "What that girl is feeling right now, I can feel and it's horrible. It's not as bad as what I felt when you were in jail, but it's tearing her apart inside. How is it possible that I can feel her feelings?" Martin thought about trying to come up with an explanation for what she was feeling, for what *he* was feeling; he knew, without doubt, that the trembling in his arms and the thunderous beat of his heart were not entirely because of Abigail's distress but were also to do with the inner turmoil of the boy seated behind them. He drew a blank on the explanation side of things, so he briefly considered lying to her to try and calm her down. That idea made him feel worse and so he told her the simple truth.

"I don't know, Abi." He held her tighter. "I don't know."

The torchlights in the city and at the palace ceased to twinkle. The soundless hurricane returned, scattering humble home and royal residence alike. Martin and Abigail soon found themselves huddled together on the floor of a room not unlike the one the children had been playing in, though this one was much larger. Two doorways led out of this room, one with a length of cloth covering it, the other filled by an actual wooden door. Light flickered around the edges of the cloth and Abigail and Martin stood up, walked over and stepped through.

Bakari and Mandisa, appearing now to be in their early thirties, were entwined together, naked, panting and sweaty on the floor in front of an open fire. As Martin and Abigail realised what they had walked in on, the couple on the floor loosed twin moans signalling that odd mix of pleasure and disappointment; orgasm achieved, but the coupling was over, for the time being at least. They disentangled themselves and lay on their backs on the rumpled sheet they had spread out. Martin drank in the sight of Mandisa's nakedness and he felt himself stiffen. Likewise, Abigail's eyes travelled the length of Bakari's lean, muscled form and she felt a distinct tingle at her crotch. Both of them knew that this was not the first time the couple on the floor had been together. They also knew that they were married and had been for some time, the uncertainty of that night on the hilltop during their teenage years long behind them. They were very, very happy together, and had spent many a night in front of this fire, on this very floor, expressing their love or simply giving into the lust that was ebbing away from them at that moment. Martin and Abigail glanced at one another, each giving some serious thought to stepping back into the other room and, assuming it was possible in wherever this was, indulging in a quickie. They both smiled and Martin opened his mouth to say something when Bakari spoke.

"I have a gift for you," he told his wife. Mandisa levered herself up on one elbow and looked at him inquisitively. "Wait here." He rose and exited the room through another cloth draped doorway, returning moments later with something behind his back. He sat down cross legged on the floor, facing his wife, who sat up and favoured him with a light hearted look of suspicion.

"What do you have there?"

Her husband didn't answer, but Martin and Abigail saw quite clearly that in his hands he held a scroll.

"When we were younger," said Bakari. "I wanted to be able to give you a palace. Much time has passed, and you have made me happier than I ever could have dreamed I would be, but I have been unable to give you a palace." Mandisa started to say something, but Bakari stopped her.

"She wants to tell him that she loves their house, that she doesn't need a palace," whispered Abigail, though by now she knew she could be neither seen nor heard. "She only needs to be wherever he is."

"He knows," said Martin. "And he feels the same, but he wants to give her something unique…"

"I wanted to give you something," began Bakari. "Something that no one else had ever had before. A gift that would see our love go on forever."

"Has that old fool of a magician been filling your head with his mad talk of immortality?" Mandisa asked, her tone one of mild rebuke, laced with the threat of a sterner rebuke if she got an answer she didn't like. Bakari chuckled and shook his head.

"Amun is just an old man who likes to tell stories to people in the hope they will buy him a drink. He can do a few simple tricks, but he is no magician." He paused and looked sheepishly at his wife. "But that doesn't mean true magicians don't exist." Before Mandisa could say anything, he went on, heedless of the other people in the room, who moved to a spot where they could view both husband and wife. "Immortality is the right of the gods alone, and such a fate should not be shared by ones such as us. For a human to live forever, to see those you love succumb to death, to witness all you know being torn down or decaying... I can think of few things closer to damnation itself. The gods make all they love and all they know last forever with them, they have that power, we do not. But such was not the power I went looking for."

He produced the scroll from behind his back and handed it to his wife.

"This is what I found," he told her as she unrolled the parchment and frowned at it, not recognising the language. "I know, it is not written in our tongue, but the man I bought it from taught me how to speak it."

"To what end? What do these words mean? What do they do?"

"They will ensure that our love will live on long after our deaths."

"How can that be?"

"The one good and true immortality that a human can wish for is to be remembered after their death. For many this means their children carrying on the family line." At this, Mandisa's face fell and tears sprung to her eyes. She dropped the scroll and turned away from her husband, who, quickly realising that it had been his words that had upset her, went to her and put his arms around her, the couple almost copying the pose Abigail and Martin had been in when they had arrived in the other room.

"She can't have children," said Abigail, her own eyes dampening as she watched, as she felt, Mandisa's anguish. Martin put an arm around her.

"It hurts them both, but that pain is part of the reason he went looking for something to give her, and found the scroll."

"You know what it does?" He nodded.

"Her tears are just starting, and as she always does she's going to blame herself for the fact they will have no children. When she has calmed down, after he has told her over and over again, the same way he has many times before, that it is no one's fault they will have no children to carry their bloodline forward, he'll tell her about the scroll. About how, since they will have no children to remember the love they shared, they will choose two young children. The children will be unrelated, orphans, but his intention is not to adopt. It is to use the scroll to copy his and Mandisa's memories into the children's minds and lock them away. He will then see to it that the children are placed with different families, close by one another. It's his hope that they will grow up and that the love he and his wife share will blossom again. If it does, the memories belonging to him and his wife will be unlocked and the children will be able to recall them as if they were their own. He and Mandisa, their love and their life together, will be remembered and in this way they will live on forever, for the children they choose will eventually do as they intend to, gifting their memories to another pair of children and beginning the cycle again."

The flames in the fire froze. Its crackling, and the gentle sobbing of Mandisa and the soothing words spoken by her husband, ceased. The room and its occupants blew away and when the world solidified again, Martin and Abigail found themselves in a dim space. Lit by only a few candles, they spotted Bakari and Mandisa, each standing at the foot of a cradle, in which lay a sleeping baby. They watched as first Bakari and then Mandisa read from the scroll, speaking the strange words clearly and precisely.

"It sounds like the same language Miss Coyle was speaking," said Martin. Abigail nodded, watching as the couple rolled the scroll up and put it away.

"Do you think it worked?" Mandisa asked her husband. He turned to her and smiled.

"I have faith that it did, my love," he told her. "Only time will tell."

Pause. Dissolve. Abigail and Martin were now in a bedroom, bright light flooding in from a high window. There was a large bed and in it lay the elderly Bakari and Mandisa. On the former's side of the bed, in a simple wooden chair, sat a middle aged man whose name both newcomers to the room knew to be Akhom. He was listening to Bakari speak and writing down what he heard on the parchment he had spread across his lap. Soon the old man stopped, unable to go on. He laid a gnarled hand on Akhom's and smiled at him. The younger man nodded, got up and left the room. Martin and Abigail stepped up to the foot of the bed and gazed at the couple whose life and love they had just fast forwarded through. Both knew the elderly couple were not long for this world, and yet neither was sad. They felt happy, content and serene.

They turned at the sound of footsteps behind them. A couple in their mid-forties entered the room, hand in hand. Martin and Abigail got out of the way when it became apparent the couple meant to stand where they were, though both knew that moving wasn't necessary. A simple reflex reaction. They moved to the side of the bed and listened as the younger couple thanked the elderly couple for the many gifts they had given them. They announced that they had chosen their successors and that the ceremony would be conducted within the next few weeks. Good families had also been chosen. The couple in the bed smiled and nodded and the younger couple, tears in their eyes, exited the room. Martin and Abigail moved back to the foot of the bed, where they stood unspeaking for several moments. It was Abigail who suddenly hissed the words,

"The Traitor."

The scene altered only slightly this time, the daylight fading out, replaced by candlelight. Abigail reached out and gripped Martin's hand and the two of them looked over their shoulders to see a figure, his face wrapped in material so only his wide eyes showed, leaping towards them, a knife clutched in his hand. One name flashed through both their minds: Sefu.

Chapter 38

They opened their eyes slowly, seeing the familiar surroundings of Abigail's living room. Martin turned to look at Abigail, who looked back at him, an uncertain smile on her face. He then looked to Coyle, who was obviously waiting for some questions.

"That wasn't a dream or a trance, was it?" Coyle shook her head. "What we saw… They were memories. Someone else's memories." Coyle nodded.

"The memories of a man and woman who died almost three and a half thousand years ago. A man and woman who sought to immortalise not themselves, but their love for one another. That, and to make better the lives of some less fortunate than themselves."

Without warning, Abigail's eyes rolled back in her head and she slumped to the side, falling away from Martin. He called her name and slid off the couch, kneeling in front of her, shaking her gently. Coyle rose calmly from her chair and stepped over. She checked the younger woman's breathing and pulse and then lifted her feet off the floor and swung them up onto the couch.

"She's fine, Martin. This is quite a common result of the glimpse." She looked at Martin. "Do you know if she keeps any spirits around the house?"

"You want a drink?"

"I was thinking more along the lines that you might like one, a wee whisky or some such to steady your nerves." He shook his head.

"I never really developed a taste for spirits." He rose to stand, swaying a little. "I'll be fine in a minute or two. I just got a fright when she passed out. Then there's this memory business."

"I've got thick skin; I can take whatever insults and accusations you might see fit to throw at me."

"What are you talking about?"

"Right at this moment you might be feeling confused, possibly afraid, or you might be worried that this is all some sort of elaborate trick. You, like many before you, will be experiencing lots of different emotions which will be difficult to handle all at once. Usually these internal emotional clashes result in accusations and insults being thrown at the Guardian. In fact one very unfortunate instance resulted in the Guardian being shot!"

"Guardian? Guardian of what?"

"Of a Bearer."

Martin looked at her blankly for a couple of seconds and then looked at the floor, shaking his head.

"All I know is that I seem to be able to remember things as if I had lived them myself, but I know for a fact I didn't." He looked back up at his old teacher. "I just want you to explain what's going on here."

Coyle smiled and nodded, motioning for him to retake his seat. Martin moved Abigail's feet and sat down, then placed her feet in his lap. Coyle sat back down in her chair.

"The memories you experienced just now have been locked inside your head all of your life," she began. "The words I spoke were an incantation designed to unlock only a few of the complete collection of memories you possess. Most wouldn't believe it if they were simply told about it, but actually being able to experience a few of those memories is something that generally makes a believer out of a person. Though it should be said that what you saw is a long way from being the full story. You saw the children?" Martin nodded. "The hilltop, and the ceremony?" Another nod. "Some of the major points in the lives of Bakari and Mandisa, enough to clue you in on how, and why, this all began. The last thing you saw was a figure with his face hidden, lunging at you with a knife?"

"Yes, and as he did, Abigail said "The Traitor" and I thought of the name Sefu. That was the name of one of the children; the name of the boy who introduced Bakari and Mandisa. But when we saw those two at that point they were old, dying even. Sefu would have been the same age as them, and the guy with the knife was moving way too fast..." He stopped. Coyle gave him a moment and then said,

"I understand. I've read that it's quite difficult to reconcile the world you know and the well rounded, both-feet-on-the-ground kind of person you are with the fact that you're sitting describing things you know so well, people and places that you saw and emotions you felt, and yet they all took place long before even your earliest ancestor drew their first breath." Martin said nothing; he just stared at Abigail's feet. "When you both come round, we'll have a chat."

With that, Coyle sat back in her chair and closed her eyes. Seconds later, Martin passed out.

When he came to, he heard Abigail laughing. For a moment he thought everything had been a dream and that he was on the couch next to Abigail and she was laughing at something on the television. Then he heard Miss Coyle's voice say,

"He tried to eat the play dough!"

Abigail laughed again and Martin pulled his head forward, wincing as something in his neck made a loud cracking noise. He looked at Abigail, who was indeed on the couch beside him, chuckling, and then at Coyle, who had a little smirk on her face.

"Play dough?" he asked. "Why are you talking about play dough?"

"I was telling Abigail about the time you were playing with some when you were in primary one. You made a little cake out of it, squashing together lots of different bits of differently coloured dough. Then you tried to eat it. I got to you just before you could."

"I don't remember trying to eat play dough."

"Technically you didn't because I managed to stop you. How do you feel?"

"Bit groggy."

"I did too," said Abigail. "But it passes pretty quickly." She moved closer to him, kissed him on the cheek and hugged him. He hugged her back. She was right; he was feeling a bit better already. He took a deep breath, blew it out slowly and looked back to his old teacher. She nodded.

"The new memories you both now have are but a tiny fraction of the many lifetimes worth of memories you each have locked away in your brain. What Bakari and Mandisa started has continued throughout history. Their memories were passed to the first two Bearers, the term we use for the chosen recipients of the memories. Those first two eventually passed the memories on, along with their own memories, to the ones they chose. It went on like that, the memories accumulating as time went by. The rules set down by Bakari and Mandisa have always been adhered to: the Bearers are not to be related, to their predecessors or one another, in any way. Anything that develops between them must be allowed to happen on its own, with no interference from the Guardians."

Martin and Abigail both went to ask something, but Coyle stalled them.

"Whatever you want to ask, make sure you remember it later; this could take all day if you keep interrupting." The couple closed their mouths, Martin ending up pouting slightly.

"You still sound like a teacher, I'll give you that."

"And you still get that petulant look about you when you think you've been told off." Martin didn't need to look at Abigail to know she was grinning. He looked at Coyle until she went on.

"I am a Guardian, one of a long and proud lineage that stretches as far back as Bakari and Mandisa. We Guardians are tasked to watch over the Bearers, and eventually to educate and advise them. Only once, and indeed *if*, the Bearers fall in love do we reveal ourselves, and only at that point are we supposed to unlock the memories they hold. We also help them deal with the memories, as initially it can be difficult. Obviously there have been instances where nothing has happened between the Bearers. In that event they are collected and the transferral ceremony is conducted. When it is over, they go back to their lives, none the wiser but with a small stipend to help them along.

"However there was one thing Bakari and Mandisa never foresaw. As a child, the boy Sefu fell in love with Mandisa, but she never saw him as anything other than a friend. Even saying it out loud right now, it sounds like such a cliché, but bear in mind this all happened long before romantic fiction and soap operas turned it into a cliché. Sefu watched as the girl he loved fell for another, one he called his friend. Over time his love turned to hate, and hate born of love is perhaps the most persistent, the most powerful, and the most deadly. He stayed close to the couple, keeping his true feelings a secret. He was actually with Bakari the day he went to the magician he had heard spoken of in the city, the day he purchased the scroll. Bakari did not reveal to his friend what it was for, which made Sefu determined to find out. He went to the magician and beat the truth out of the man, forced him to copy the incantation down on another scroll for him.

"It was not long after this that the city was attacked. Raiders rode in one night and caused chaos. Bakari and Mandisa fled the city together, eventually finding a new home for themselves. Sefu searched in vain for them for many years, but he did not find them. He eventually realised he would not live to see his dream of their love being torn apart come to pass, and so he performed the transferral ceremony himself, imparting his spite, hatred and bitterness to another. He spent the rest of his life teaching this child to hate Bakari and Mandisa, telling the boy that they must never be allowed to be at peace, that his sole purpose in life was to seek them out and destroy them. By the time the boy managed to locate them, they were on the cusp of departing from this world, something the boy helped them do in a most bloodthirsty fashion.

"By that point the transference of their memories had been completed and the new Bearers taken to safety by their Guardians. When the boy found this out, he set off to find the new Couple, and eventually he too chose another to take the memories, and Sefu's hatred was reborn anew.

"It was, for such a long time, the oddest of status quos, and then one was chosen to be given The Traitor's memories. One who was far, far worse than any who had come before him. A young boy named Andrew Corday.

"Though in the past some have chosen their successors because the idea of corrupting a good soul amuses them, darkness is usually inherent in whatever child The Traitor chooses. Indeed, it is something most go looking for, the darkness within them able to seek it out in others, even when they are babies. However the hatred for Bakari and Mandisa, for whosoever now holds their memories, is something that is taught to the new Bearer. Chosen as an infant and raised by his predecessor, Philip Garrett, Andrew Corday took to being taught to hate like a duck to water.

"Most of us are raised to know the difference between right and wrong, that our actions have consequences. But what if you were raised to believe that nothing you did, however heinous, would have any impact on your life? You can do anything you want and any resulting mess – dead bodies, pregnant rape victims – can all be made to vanish with a simple command? What kind of person would that make you?"

Martin and Abigail could offer no answer. Coyle continued.

"When Corday was around fourteen or fifteen, Garrett unlocked The Traitor's memories in Corday's mind. It is not advisable to do so when the Bearer is so young, or when their predecessor is still alive, but it was something that had been done before. However,

Garrett underestimated the monster he had fashioned. I've heard it said that the young Corday was in something akin to a coma for almost a week afterwards, and when he reawakened, he was changed. It was almost as if he hadn't simply accessed the memories, but had assimilated them, taken on aspects of the many men and women who had come before him. He was a colder, more calculating human being. It was a few years later that he struck down his predecessor, literally stabbing him in the back. The murder was not committed simply to gain unfettered access to the man's fortune, which was vast, but also to put his own plan into action.

"Corday had decided that he wanted to end everything. He did not like the idea of spending his life chained to an ancient enmity, but he was unable to ignore his upbringing. He resolved to destroy The Couple. Not just the present Bearers but their Guardians and The Order as well, ensuring that the memories would never be passed on again. Breaking the chain had been tried before, but at no time had any Traitor ever tried to wipe out everything. Corday's fantastic audacity might well have been what allowed him to come so close to achieving his goal. You see he had decided that only when he had broken the chain, and destroyed every link on it, would he be able to live a free life and enjoy his money. He kept with him a cadre of lackeys who obeyed his every order, such was their fear of him even at a young age. The ones he did not need he slaughtered. He then began scouring the world searching for The Couple, slaying anyone connected with them, and those connected with The Traitor. When Corday turned twenty-one he killed his remaining servants, no longer needing them to provide a cover for when he travelled or to access places he couldn't go because of his age.

"By nineteen-seventy nine, the Bearers and their Guardians were in turmoil. We knew that Corday was closing in, but the children had been chosen and we had to make sure the ceremony was performed. Corday struck during the closing moments of the ceremony, as the final words of the incantation were being spoken by Abigail's predecessor. We managed to fend him off long enough for the two of you to be taken to safety. Corday was badly injured, but afterwards many of us had been killed, the man who had taught me in the ways of Guardianship among them. I wanted to mourn him, but I knew that as far as he would have been concerned my first duty was to the children who held the memories. I got together as many of my fellows as I could and we hunted for Corday, but to no avail. I then made a decision that might well have meant Corday would succeed in his ultimate goal of ending what the members of The Order had spent so long protecting and upholding.

"I decided to split the two of you up.

"Adoptive parents had already been chosen for you both, but in the interests of keeping you hidden, new families were chosen for each of you. Martin, you were placed with a family in Scotland, whereas you, Abigail, were brought to America and placed with parents here in Hannerville. A new Guardian was appointed and moved here to watch over you. We kept the operation as quiet as we could, but despite the numbers on both sides having been drastically reduced thanks to Corday, there were still those with sharp ears and big mouths. Having discovered that the ceremony had been performed before his attack, the bastard resurfaced a few years later to engineer the car crash that killed Martin's mother and father. He only found out later that Martin had survived, but by then he was on his way to America to look for you, Abigail. He had a vague location, and so set himself up with a false identity whilst his agents sought you out. The name he gave himself was David Brannon. During his wait for information on your whereabouts, he grew bored, restless, his natural need to inflict pain and suffering on others building and building. Thus began the serial killings that came to an end on the night of October second, nineteen eighty-four.

"Corday was carted off to a hospital for the criminally insane. Since he'd had to take on some help in his search, there was a group who decided to look after his money. They took "looking after" to mean feather their own nest. They did little or nothing to help him during his incarceration at Berrybeck. The Order took more of an interest in him, and we honestly thought he would never walk out of that place. Or perhaps it's more accurate to say we fooled ourselves into thinking that.

"Our intention was to put you, Abigail, with another family, but as we believed Corday no longer a threat, and as you were already with your aunt and uncle, it was decided that things would be left as they were. I took a teaching job at a primary school and a few years passed. I began teaching a very bright little boy named Martin Muir, whose life I had followed with great interest. It was then that I decided to do what I could to ensure the continuation of the chain. I set up the pen-pal scheme, making sure that you two were chosen to write to one another. That was as far as my involvement went, but here we are, all these years later, and the two of you... It makes me so happy to see you together."

She then spoke directly to Abigail.

"I owe you an apology, my dear; I am so sorry. What you went through that night was my fault. I knew where Corday was, what he was doing, and I saw a way to get rid of him once and for all; I leaked your location to someone I knew would pass the information on to him. My intention was to have your Guardian contact the police and have them waiting for Corday when he arrived. I underestimated Corday's need to get to you, underestimated the extent of his madness. By the time the police arrived at the house..."

She let the sentence trail off. A short time passed and she got to her feet. She reached into her pocket and withdrew a small piece of paper. Placing it on the table she said,

"I can be reached at this number, at any time..."

"Don't you dare," said Abigail. Martin and Coyle both looked at her, shocked at the coldness in her tone. Slowly, she looked up at the older woman. "Don't you dare just tell me that pile of bullshit and then leave. What the hell is this? You come in here telling us this crap, putting us in a trance and making us see things, and then you tell me that you're responsible for the deaths of my mother and father, a man and woman who, according to you, weren't really my parents, and then you try to leave. What sort of sick scam is this? And what about Marty? The man and woman he thought were his parents, who died in a car crash, they weren't really his parents either?" She got to her feet and pointed at Coyle. "You are sick, lady, fucking sick. We are in a totally screwed up situation with some sick pervert who's running around killing people, who killed my friend, and you tell us you have information, that you can help us, and this is what you give us! Some love-is-forever fairytale crap with added psychopaths?" Martin rose and stood beside her.

"Abi, calm down." She turned to him.

"No! This is insane! Did you listen to what she told us? She's delusional, Marty."

"I listened to what she said," he said softly. "And I agree with you, it sounds ridiculous. But what we experienced weren't just scenes we were told to see, Abigail. We *felt* what those people were feeling when we saw them. The details we knew, those we could have been told. I don't know if, even under hypnosis, we could have been forced to feel to the degree that we did." Tears began to spill down Abigail's cheeks as she looked at him, her eyes imploring him to be with her on this.

"How can you even think of believing what she told us when it might mean that everything we feel for each other isn't real?"

"What?"

"She's told us that our heads are full of the memories of other people who have been in love. If it was even possible, how could we be sure that what we've got is genuine and not just the lingering memories of someone long dead?"

"Only a few of those memories have been unlocked," Coyle chimed in. "And that was only done here, today, in this room."

"Miss Coyle," said Martin, looking in her direction. He inclined his head a little. "Please." She stopped speaking. Martin looked Abigail in the eye and said, "I don't know if I could ever believe what we've been told. It seems too fantastic, too ridiculous, to be true, yet I can't shake the idea that it just might be real. But given what you just said, whether or not I believe Miss Coyle isn't my biggest concern right now. I'm not sure if she's on the level, or if she's a bloody crackpot, but one thing I am perfectly sure of is how I feel about you. Those feelings are mine and no one else's. They were not given to me; they developed over the course of a life in which you have been the one constant. The gamble I took asking you if I could come and see you was the biggest I've ever taken, and it scared me to death because if it had all gone wrong then I'd have lost you. The idea of my life without you in it, even if only via letter, made me feel sick, lost. I love you. *I* love you. Not someone from hundreds or thousands of years ago, me. Martin Muir loves Abigail Morton, and that fact is down to no one but you. Not some love-struck bint from Ancient Egypt or wherever the hell they lived, but you, Abi.

"The only reason I could even start to take Miss Coyle's story seriously is that I have faith that unbelievable things can sometimes happen in this world. The fact that it's already happened to me once, when you told me you loved me, makes it a little difficult to believe it could happen to me again, but thanks to you I'm at least willing to consider taking another gamble. Plus if what she's told us is true, then there's every possibility that she can help us get the bastard who killed Sophie. For that reason alone I'd like to hear the rest of what she has to say."

Tears rolled down Abigail's cheeks. She couldn't believe she was thinking of Coyle's story in terms of it being real, but she was telling herself that if those memories had only been unlocked today then they couldn't have had any bearing on her life before, which meant that what she felt for Marty was perfectly real.

Is it? What if these memories bleed into yours over time? What if one morning you wake up and see him and realise that he's not who you thought he was? That he's not the handsome, charming and thoughtful man you've developed feelings for over all these years, but that those qualities have all been superimposed on him, coming originally from someone else's memories of someone they loved. Maybe he's really a complete schmuck who could be sucked in by the dumbest of stories.

Wiping tears out of her eyes, she looked at the man who had only recently shared her bed, but whose good nature and kind heart, whose wit, charm, wisdom and faults and foibles had been a cherished part of her life. A life in which he had been the one constant.

She threw her arms around his neck and held onto him as tightly as she could. He held her just as tightly, almost lifting her off the floor. They eventually released one another and Abigail moved to stand beside Martin, holding on to his hands. Staring at Coyle, she asked Martin,

"I'm not convinced this woman isn't a complete maniac, but assuming she's telling the truth, how do we know she's not in on this with Corday?"

Martin too regarded his old teacher, though with a little more warmth in his expression than did his girlfriend.

"No, I don't think so."

"Reason?"

"If she was on his side, she could have killed me a long time ago."

"Seems like sound reasoning. All right, lady, you're in no danger of being kicked out, or knocked out, right now. We're all going to sit back down and talk some more. When we're finished talking I will make one of two calls: a judgement call that you are telling the truth, or a call for an ambulance after I've kicked your ass. Okay?"

"Agreed," said Coyle. "But for what it's worth to you right now, I want to stress the fact that what you and Martin share is true. There has been no interference of any kind, from any one, in your relationship."

"What about these memories?" asked Abigail as she took her seat. "Can they seep out?"

"Before being unlocked? No."

"You said the ceremony that was held was interrupted, that my predecessor didn't finish the incantation. Might that have had some sort of effect on…" Her voice grew quiet, only just above a whisper as she concluded with the words, "My memory?"

She turned to find Martin staring at her with wide eyes.

"What is it?" asked Coyle.

"Nothing," Abigail said quickly, whipping her head round. No way was she willing to reveal her secret to this woman. She might never be, but her curiosity was finally piqued. All of her research had never yielded another case of a memory condition like the one she suffered from, so perhaps its extraordinary nature had an extraordinary origin. "So, could it have had an effect?"

"I don't know."

"You don't know?"

"No. Corday's interruption of your transferral ceremony was something that had never happened before."

"All that time and no one carrying The Traitor's memories had ever gate-crashed a ceremony?" asked Abigail, clearly incredulous.

"Oh, one or two had been interrupted before, but on those occasions the new Bearers did not survive, and the current Couple fled to perform the ceremony again at a later date. Yours was the first wherein the opposite occurred. Therefore there is no frame of reference as to whether or not the fact the incantation was not completed would have had an effect on your memory."

"Give us an opinion," Martin requested. Coyle thought it over.

"It might have, but I can't be sure."

"Is there any way to find out?" asked Abigail.

"I could check The Order's records to find out if anything similar is mentioned. Perhaps track down a few people knowledgeable in the field, ask their opinion."

Abigail began to ask another question, but Martin jumped in ahead of her. He knew that she wanted to reveal as little to Coyle as she could, whilst at the same time getting as much information as possible about something which might well explain her memory problems. Knowing how Abigail felt about her condition, he feared she may reveal more than she meant to in her attempt to garner new information, something which would annoy and upset her.

"We saw The Traitor attack the old couple in bed, and I thought of the name Sefu just as the figure attacked. But if the ceremony had already been performed by that time, how could their memory of that attack have been transferred?"

"When the incantation is read over a child, a link is made between the old and new Bearers. The memories of past Bearers are transferred right away, but the present Bearers own memories stay with them until they die. Death severs the link, but not before that lifetime of memories has been passed on."

Abigail, knowing why Martin had talked over her and knowing that he was probably right in his thinking that she would have given away too much by asking too many questions on the same subject, decided to ask a question on a different topic.

"Who were my real parents?"

"I understand that you both must have a lot of questions like that one, and under normal circumstances I would be more than happy to sit for as long as you liked answering them for you. These are not normal circumstances. Once the problem of Corday has been dealt with, you have my promise that I will answer any and all questions, but we need to start working out how we're going to deal with him. We thwarted him and he told us we would pay, and he is not a man who makes idle threats. I don't imagine his revenge would be limited to my associates and I. Abigail, everyone you care about in this town is in grave danger and they must all be warned. How we're going to do that without them asking too many questions we can't answer I'm not sure, but they must be told something to put them on alert. Martin, I know you have no family back home, but you might want to send your friends a message. Again we can work out the wording and deal with the questions later."

Martin and Abigail said nothing, did nothing. Coyle could read in their expressions disbelief, bewilderment and mistrust. She understood, and her heart went out to the two of them. The truth was usually enough to deal with, but with such a threat hanging over their heads, and the knowledge that that threat was also hanging over the heads of their loved ones, Coyle feared it might be too much. But sometimes the Bearers needed to draw strength from those whose duty it was to guide and protect them.

She only hoped she had such strength left in her.

Chapter 39

The messages had been sent, the calls made.

Martin had again used Abigail's computer to log into his e-mail account to send the same message to Stephen, Trevor, Dougie and James. He had kept it vague, saying that he had run into a little bother here in Hannerville and that if anyone came asking about him his friends should deny all knowledge. He also told them to be careful and not to trust strangers. When he had read it out to Abigail and Miss Coyle – he couldn't get used to the idea of referring to her by her first name, even though she had requested he do so twice now – it had sounded like the words of someone suffering from delusional paranoia. Martin was concerned that his friends would worry about his state of mind, try to contact him somehow and then, when they couldn't, maybe make their way over here. Martin would most likely have done the same in their position. His message, written in the hope of informing and reassuring them, might end up dragging them into the situation he and Abigail were in. However, no matter how he reworded it, it still sounded like he was losing his mind. Eventually, an exasperated Martin had just sent the damn thing, adding at the end that he was fine in both body and mind and would explain it all to them when he saw them.

Abigail also had a problem with not telling her family and friends the truth. A large part of that problem was that neither she nor Martin was particularly convinced of the truth as it had been explained to them by Coyle. Abigail called her aunt and uncle, then Beth and Amanda, telling them that she wanted them to take extra care, to watch out for one another, to not go anywhere alone or speak to anyone they didn't know. Due to the people she was contacting knowing that there was a very real threat in town, they all took her concern to heart and she elicited promises from each of them that they would heed her words.

Now the three of them sat once again in the living room, Martin and Abigail together on the couch, Coyle in the armchair.

"Now what?" asked Abigail.

"I think it might be an idea to introduce you to my associates," said Coyle.

Martin and Abigail both agreed to this and set about getting ready to go. As they did that, Coyle made a phone call. Soon they were getting into Coyle's car, Abigail riding shotgun, Martin in the back. They had been driving for only a few minutes when Abigail asked,

"So, the Guardians are something like bodyguards?"

"Something along those lines," the older woman replied, then fell silent.

"Are you going to elaborate on that any?" Martin asked.

"The first Guardian was employed to do two things, the first of which was to make a record of the last few hours of Bakari and Mandisa's lives. His second task was to protect and guide the Bearers. It soon became apparent to him that he would be unable to fulfil this last task on his own, such was the drive behind The Traitor. He took on an apprentice, trained him, and eventually the two of them cultivated a network of contacts, informants, procurers and the like. At the same time their ranks swelled, more taken on and trained so that the Bearers could be discreetly protected wherever they went. Thus The Order was born.

"By the time Corday began his hunt there were hundreds of men and women all over the world who were connected to The Order. When word got out of Corday and his intentions, a lot of them went into hiding. That devil cut down any of our people that he came across, and I dare say that had he not ended up in Berrybeck he would have continued his vendetta until none remained.

"In the years since that wonderful day when the evil bastard was locked away, The Order has been rebuilt. Wherever you two go in the world after this is all over, you can be guaranteed a safe haven."

Neither Abigail nor Martin knew quite how to respond to that statement, so instead Martin brought up something he had heard earlier.

"You mentioned something before; a Guardian?"

"Each Bearer has a Guardian, someone who will be there during the transferral ceremony. They will be the one who reveals to the Bearer the gifts that have been given to them, and they will also perform the unlocking ceremony. To their charge they will be a teacher, a confidant, a protector, and a friend."

"So, you're our Guardian?"

"I am Martin's Guardian, dear," Coyle clarified. "However given the circumstances it was decided that I would be the one who approached both of you. One of the people we are on our way to meet is your Guardian, Abigail, and she has waited a very long time to say hello to you."

"It's someone I might have seen on the street?"

"Indeed, a someone who has been keeping an eye out for you all your life, but who was sworn never to interfere. Many times she has contacted me, expressing her wish to be to you what a Guardian can be to a Bearer, but always I reminded her that until the time when it seemed either that you two would fulfil our greatest hopes, or it became apparent that that was never going to come to pass, we must keep our distance and our silence."

"Marty, do you feel as creeped out by this as I do?"

"A little. The idea that there's been someone watching us all our lives is an odd one, but that they've been doing so for our benefit balances it out. Just. I think."

They made the rest of the journey in silence. On the edge of town, Coyle pulled into a driveway, parking behind a car that was already there. Abigail got out first, looking at the pleasant little dwelling before admiring the neatly mown lawn and the well-tended flower beds that bordered it. When Martin had joined her, Coyle led them up the path to the front door, where she rang the doorbell. It was quickly answered, the door being pulled open to reveal a woman who looked to be only slightly younger than Coyle, with a slightly friendlier, more open face and a little more meat on her bones. Her hair, in contrast to Coyle's shoulder length, straight dark hair, was a small mass of wild blonde curls and her dress sense was a touch less severe. Abigail could not remember ever having seen her before. The woman smiled at Coyle and stepped back, inviting them in.

"Martin, Abigail," began Coyle when they were standing in the hallway, the front door closed. "This is Sandra Logan, Abigail's Guardian."

Sandra stepped forward and shook Martin's hand. Martin smiled and said hello. The woman then moved on to the person she was obviously most anxious to meet. Abigail offered her hand and Logan took it and shook it gently.

"I have to be honest," she said, a slight trace of her native Scottish accent detectable beneath the American one she had picked up over time. "I was nervous that I was going to get a bit too excited when I met you. That I would act like a star-struck little girl and frighten you by babbling on about what a pleasure it is to finally meet you. How am I doing keeping that in check?" Abigail smiled.

"You're doing great." Sandra nodded.

"Good." She smiled. "It is a pleasure to finally meet you though." Releasing Abigail's hand, she gestured them through a door into the living room, where a young man sat on the couch. He rose as they entered and Coyle introduced him.

"This is Matthew Sabbard." The young man stepped forward and shook hands with Martin and Abigail.

"Nice to meet you both," he told them, both of them catching his French accent.

Sandra told everyone to take a seat and then asked them if they would like a drink. Only Coyle declined. Once she had come back with what the others had asked for, the five of them sat for a few minutes.

"You've been told a few things this morning that have been difficult to get your head around," said Sandra, finally breaking the silence. Martin nodded.

"That's one way of putting it."

"It's left us both a little freaked out," Abigail admitted. Sandra nodded and took a sip of her coffee.

"Completely normal," she said. "I imagine finding out that someone has been watching over you, even in a benign manner, all your life would be one that would shake even the hardiest of souls. Please don't take this as a complaint, but to be perfectly honest the job isn't one I've relished every moment of. I was committed to making sure no harm came to you from The Traitor's forces, and if they had I would have intervened, but there have been times when all I've wanted to do was give you a hug." She noted the questioning look on Abigail's face. "Had anyone from Corday's camp shown up in town looking to cause you harm, I would have simply found them and... changed their minds. Until the man himself showed up, no one ever did, and so it was the most commonplace of things that caused upset in your life. Bad grades, boys, losing a job, break-up's... the little trials faced by everyone, and ones which I could not help you with. Holding back was not easy, and on several occasions I thought of trying to help you in small ways. That was when I would call Andrea." She looked to Coyle with a respectful smile. "A colleague and a friend, and a source of strength for many years now." She looked to Martin. "You may not have known it, you may not even think it now, but you were fortunate to have this woman keeping an eye on you. She may look all prim and proper, but last night The Traitor himself found out that she can still dish out an ass kicking when it's called for. I was quite proud of a few of the knocks I got in myself."

"Oh," exclaimed Martin, clearly surprised. He then clammed up and stared intently into his cup of tea.

"What?" asked Coyle. Martin told her it was nothing, but she insisted he tell them.

"It's just... uh... When we met Matthew I assumed that he had been the one who had gone with you last night." The trio grinned and Martin felt the colour rise in his cheeks. He looked to Sandra and told her, "Sorry."

"Don't worry about it. If I don't look like I can swing a punch and do some damage then I must be doing something right." Her smile morphed into a wicked little grin. "Just in case I wasn't as capable as I thought, I had a taser with me. I was happy to punch that bastard, but I'd have been just as happy to put a few volts through his balls."

Abigail burst out laughing.

The conversation was contained mostly to idle chit-chat for a while as they got used to one another's company. It was Martin who changed tack first, asking for details on the circumstances that led to Coyle, Logan and Sabbard becoming members of The Order.

"The three of us were recruited," Coyle replied. "I was in my early twenties, holidaying in Madrid in Spain with a few of my friends. Charles Velnot, the Guardian of Martin's predecessor and the leader of The Order, was there too, along with the Guardian of Abigail's predecessor. They were both accompanying their charges on a sight-seeing trip. I met the Bearers first, in the bar of the hotel we were all staying at. Velnot became suspicious of me, wondering if I might be an operative of The Traitor. He wasn't a suspicious man by nature; that's just the mind-set Guardians develop after a while. He followed me for a time until he was certain I was not a threat, but as he did so he began to get a feeling about me. He decided that I might make a good Guardian and, once he had thoroughly checked my background, he approached me and offered me a job. I just about laughed in his face, at first thinking he was trying to chat me up, but as I lay in my hotel room thinking about it that night, I became intrigued by his offer, by the suddenness and the sincerity of it. I began to think that perhaps he wasn't some sleazy pick up artist and that maybe his offer had been genuine.

"I found him the following day and told him that I would like to accept this offer. I believed for almost a year that I was an attaché to two very prominent and powerful business people, a man and wife who owned a big multinational company. I travelled the world, learned all manner of things, and bit by bit, and without my knowledge, I was inducted into the ranks of The Order. By the time the truth was told to me, I had no trouble believing it, even before I was shown proof. After that, Velnot trained me personally. He was a good man, one into whose shoes I had to step when Corday cut him down at your transferral ceremony. I was greatly uncertain of my ability to be his replacement, especially considering the state of things at that time.

"I like to think I did my best, but there is one thing I wish I could go back and change. I wish I could go back and utilise the option of sending someone into Berrybeck to put an end to Corday once and for all."

"Why didn't you?" asked Martin.

"What time I was afforded by Corday's incarceration I used to make sure you two were safe, and then I started getting the organisation designed to help and support you back into some semblance of working order. By the time that had been achieved, Corday had still not attempted an escape. I foolishly allowed myself to believe he might never try, and was therefore reluctant to attempt an assassination, just in case it somehow set things off again. An error, one I now regret more than I can say. One compounded by my own damn complacency."

"Don't you dare sit there and criticize yourself, lady," Sandra chastened Coyle. "You stepped up and took charge. As a chosen Guardian that was your duty, but I don't think many would have volunteered should you have decided to turn and run. Your successes far outweigh your failures."

Coyle gave the woman a grateful smile.

"How did you become a Guardian?" Abigail asked Sandra.

"I was recruited as a translator. As Andrea said, your predecessors were into big business and that took them all over the world. I'm good with languages and so I went where they went. Andrea and I became friends because she was always there, being taught how to be a Guardian, though neither of us knew it. I remember the night she called me and told me what had happened at the ceremony; that Alan and Jill were both dead. I was heartbroken. But she made sure I had plenty to do to keep my mind occupied."

"Sandra is as much responsible for the fact there is still an Order as I am," commented Coyle. "When your original Guardian passed away only a few months after Corday attacked you in your home, Sandra was my first and only choice to replace her."

"From translator to Guardian," chuckled Sandra. "Hell of a leg up the corporate ladder, though not an easy decision. I knew I didn't have the proper training, and from being around Andrea so much I knew that being a Guardian is a somewhat lonely position to occupy, especially when the circumstances seem to suggest that all hope is lost for the Bearers to get together. But she talked me into it, has talked me through it all these years, and here we are."

Silence again descended until Matthew realised that Abigail and Martin were looking at him, obviously waiting for his story.

"Oh, sorry," he apologised. "No such grand associations for me, I'm afraid. I was a bad kid, living in a suburb of Paris and getting myself into a lot of trouble. The only skills I possessed were house breaking and running like hell. A lady whose house I had broken into, she caught me and took me down with a single punch to the face. When I woke, she had me tied to a chair and was asking me about my family. I told her I was an orphan. She left me tied to that chair in her basement, scared out of my mind. When she came back she told me she had checked me out and that I had been telling the truth. Then she asked me if I wanted to work for her. I couldn't believe it. I asked her what it was she wanted me to do and she told me that she could use a kid who was quick witted and quick on his feet. I replied that since she had captured me with such ease it seemed apparent I wasn't quick witted or quick footed enough. She laughed and said I was young, I was still learning, but I was an obviously gifted amateur. I became an operative for The Order."

"Doing what?" enquired Martin. Matthew glanced at Coyle, who nodded, before responding.

"My specialist field eventually became what I suppose you could call espionage. There are people out there, members of neither our camp nor Corday's, who have heard stories or rumours, or have read in books, of The Couple and The Traitor and their long history. Many have been so enamoured of what they have discovered that they have dug deeper. Part of what I do is throw them off the track, make sure what is secret stays that way."

"How do you do that?" asked Abigail.

"And what do you do if someone you try to induct into The Order decides that it's all crap and wants to walk away?" was Martin's question.

"Questions for another time," Coyle said. "Right now, we all need to be thinking about what we're going to do next."

"My stuff," Martin stated, drawing confused looks from everyone. "I need my stuff, particularly my clothes and my laptop. It's all up at the cabin. The police are finished with it and I need to get it back."

"I'll take you up there." Coyle offered. Martin nodded his thanks, but added,

"We need to go get someone from the sheriff's office first; I'm not allowed to go up there alone." Coyle asked Martin if he had the sheriff's number. "He gave me his card... Shit, I left it at Abigail's house."

"No problem," chirped Sandra, who vanished from the room and returned a minute later. "Phone book," she smiled as she handed Martin a slip of paper with a number on it. "Old fashioned, but still very reliable."

Martin dialled the number and the call was promptly answered. He gave his name and was put straight through.

"Mr Muir," came the sheriff's deep voice. "I didn't expect to be hearing from you quite so soon."

"Sheriff, is someone free at the moment? I'd like to go up to the cabin to collect my things."

"I'm afraid I don't have anyone to spare right now, Mr Muir. Is it urgent?"

"I can't say it is, I'd just like to get my stuff out of there." There was a pause on the other end of the line. Then:

"Give me twenty minutes and then make your way here; I'll take you up. Have to be quick about it though."

"I will be. Thank you, sheriff."

He hung up and filled the others in on the side of the conversation they hadn't heard. Coyle nodded.

"I'll take you to meet Sheriff Flaghan, and then I'll go with you to the cabin. He thinks I'm your legal representative, so he shouldn't have a problem with that. Abigail can stay here with Sandra and Matthew and..."

235

"Why can't she come with us?"

"There's no need for her to."

"Not a need as such, no, but…"

"But you don't want her staying here with a couple of people you just met?" ventured Matthew.

"I'm sorry, but yes. I mean you both seem like decent people, but you, Matthew, have already confessed to being a thief." Matthew nodded.

"That story I told you, I was twelve when that happened. I'm twenty-five now. I can assure you my criminal days are far behind me."

"But we've only got your word on that."

"And mine," Sandra chimed in.

"Fine, but we've only just met you too."

"Martin," Coyle said. "Do you remember what you said to Abigail earlier? When she asked you why you didn't think I was in league with Corday?" Martin tried, couldn't. Abigail did. She looked at him and said,

"You told me that if she had wanted to kill you, she could have done so a long time ago. I think she's trying to say the same applies to Sandra and me." She looked to Coyle for confirmation and Martin's former teacher smiled and nodded.

"I can understand your reluctance, Martin, and I know that it will be very difficult for both of you, but you must trust us. We're on your side. Whilst we're gone, Abigail will be safer here than anywhere else in town."

Martin looked to Abigail. She looked back at him, raised her eyebrows and one corner of her mouth and said,

"When your situation is this screwed up, I suppose at some point you're going to have to trust somebody."

Chapter 40

Fifteen minutes later, Martin and Abigail hugged as he prepared to leave with Coyle. He made sure his old teacher had given Abigail her number, and that Abigail had put it into her phone's memory. He told her that when he got his own phone from the cabin he would give her a call to let her know they were on their way back. As Coyle exited Sandra's house, Martin hugged Abigail again and promised her he'd see her soon. He wanted to whisper in her ear that if she thought at any time that she was in danger, she should run screaming into the street, or get a knife and start stabbing. He released her and followed Coyle, nodding a farewell to Sandra and Matthew as he went. He wanted to say something to them, something cool and calm but menacing: "Hurt her and I'll hunt you down and tear you open so you can watch the crows eat your intestines while you die," or something along those lines. Fortunately he said nothing, but promised himself that if they did do anything to Abigail when he was gone, he would exact his revenge in the most brutal manner he could think of.

On his way to Coyle's car, Martin told himself that it was something of an empty promise, as he was not a violent man. He countered that by admitting to himself that no, he was not a violent man, but if you flick the right switch even a placid man will turn on you. Someone hurting Abigail was his switch. If they flicked it, he'd go from Mr Nice Guy to the nastiest bastard they had ever seen. Corday would have nothing on him.

They got into the car and Coyle started the engine and pulled away. A few minutes later she said,

"Penny for your thoughts?"

"Sorry?"

"You look like you were giving something some serious thought."

"Mm. I was just thinking that all that separates a civilised man from an animal are checks and balances. If the scales tip the wrong way, even a nice guy like me could turn into someone capable of dishing out some vicious beatings."

"Is that your subtle way of saying that if anything happens to Abigail you're going to come after myself, Sandra and Matthew?"

"I don't like making threats, Miss Coyle. Tell truth, personality wise I'm probably not that much different from the boy you knew. Yes, my sense of humour is probably a little dirtier now, but I'm still not the kind of person who goes around hurling insults, starting fights and throwing punches. The only time I've ever been in what could charitably be called a fight was a couple of years after being in your class. You remember a wee boy named Charlie Brant?"

"A year or two younger than you, and almost the polar opposite personality wise. Short child, pudgy, scrunched up little face. His hair always looked like it had been cut using a sharpened piece of flint."

"That's him. You remember Craig Fulston?"

"Chubby, greasy haired lad. A friend of yours if I recall correctly."

"You do. One day during break, Brant took Craig's specs and snapped them. I was wandering around the playground when Craig came running round the corner, crying and snivelling. He ran past me, and I tried to ask him what was wrong. I got no answer. Then Brant came round the corner, clapped eyes on me and strode up with that wee evil smile that always seemed to be on his face. He stopped in front of me and said he'd heard I wanted to fight him. Now in all probability it was complete bollocks…"

He clamped his lips together, then remembered that he was no longer a schoolboy, and Miss Coyle was no longer his teacher.

"He might have actually heard it somewhere, but I doubt it; he was just looking to start something. My first instinct was to say he'd got it wrong and walk away. I didn't want to get into trouble over the likes of him, but then I looked at my friend, tears streaming down his face and snot running down over his lips. Craig was a quiet boy, a bit dim, but not deserving of what had been done to him, and I decided I was going to flatten that little shit Brant. So I turned back to him and I told him he was quite right.

"The words were barely out of my mouth but he took a swing at me, and I don't think I've ever reacted quicker in my life. I dodged back and then lashed out, caught him a cracker right across the jaw. He spun and I moved in, grabbed him around the throat with one arm and started smacking him in the face with my fist. They weren't hard blows because I didn't have a bloody clue what I was doing. He fought back, struggling, kicking, the little sod even tried to bite me at one point. Eventually I had him on his knees. I was standing behind him, one hand across his jaw, one across the middle of his face, and I was pulling in opposite directions. I swear I could feel his nose bone starting to bend and his jaw bone starting to shift.

"My father…" He paused again, decided not to amend that to "My second adoptive father," as it sounded bitter and the man he was speaking of deserved better than that. "He told me once that the real winner of a fight is the man who walks away first. I remembered those words that day. They saved Charlie Brant from a possible broken nose and broken jaw, and saved me from who knows what kind of trouble. I let him go and I walked away, and in all the years since I haven't thrown a single punch. I took a lot of stick in high school from idiots who got their laughs teasing and annoying people, and my teachers always told me they weren't worth the trouble I'd get into if I threw the first punch. I always nodded and told them I knew that, so I never lashed out, though I wanted to, plenty of times. It wasn't just that I didn't want to get into trouble, it's that it's not in my nature." He turned to look at his old teacher. "Having said that, if anyone tries to harm Abigail, I will lash out at them like a mad bastard."

"Understood, Martin," Coyle said, smiling. He asked her what the smile was about. "I'm proud of you," she answered. "I have no real right to be, I know, since I was merely an observer of your upbringing and not a part of it, but you are a fine young man. Good mannered, kind hearted, with your own business that you've worked very hard to build. You've got your friends and now you're here and you're with Abigail, and you're obviously very much in love and willing to do whatever it takes to keep her safe. Your parents would be very, very proud, and rightly so."

"Did you know them?"

"I met them when you were given to them. They had been carefully chosen and they seemed like really nice people. I never saw them again after that night. I did attend their funeral though. A silly thing to do."

"Why?"

"Because when I saw you I wanted so much to go to you, comfort you, do anything I could to help you through your grief."

"You called Sandra for support?" Coyle shook her head.

"No, I fought my feelings and I won, but I promised myself to stay away from then on, and I kept that promise. Until all this of course."

"What has your life been like?" Martin asked, surprised at his own question. He couldn't take it back, and so he waited either for the silence to take hold or to be told to sod off and that it was none of his business.

"Why do you ask that?"

"What you said just now about fighting your feelings; you sounded lonely. Is that what The Order did for you? Took you and made you someone who could have no one to lean on because she was the boss and had to set an example?"

"Being a Guardian does not preclude relationships or even marriage and having children, Martin. Yes, my position was a difficult weight to bear at times, but I was not lonely. There have been personal relationships over the years, and had I met the right person I might well have gotten married, but it was just something that never came up." She turned briefly to look at him, then returned her attention to the road and said, "I am proud of what I've achieved with The Order. We were in chaos when I suddenly found myself in the top job. I've overseen the rebuilding of a veritable underground empire that exists to support, maintain and continue something truly amazing. It may not have been the path I would have chosen, but I have been happy, Martin. I am happy. That you and Abigail have become a couple only makes me more so.

"If Corday wasn't still drawing breath, I'd be on cloud nine." Her former pupil nodded.

"I just didn't like the idea of someone foregoing their own life for my sake."

"I understand," she said. "And I assure you that anything I may have missed in my life was my own fault."

A short time later, as they opened the front door of the sheriff's office, they heard an excited sounding voice, a voice which at that moment fell to a whisper and said, "I have to go, Collette, someone's coming in. I'll call you back."

Doreen Spellner looked up as they walked towards the counter, and the practiced smile she was building up to froze on her lips when she saw Martin.

"Good afternoon," he said. "We've got an appointment with Sheriff Flaghan."

"Uh, oh, yes, of course. Just a moment, please."

She lifted one of the three phones in front of her and dialled. A brief pause followed, then she spoke, informing the sheriff his visitors had arrived. She put the phone down and smiled at them.

"The sheriff will be with you in a minute or two," she informed them. Then addressing Martin, she asked, "So have you been okay since you were released?"

Martin did not like gossips. For the purposes of their own entertainment they spread stories and rumours, which most of the time were false. Even when they weren't, matters beyond their own lives were none of their damn business. They felt like it was their duty – their right - to make sure everyone was informed about what everyone else was doing, as long as no one knew what they themselves got up to behind closed doors. Even in these days of smart phones and the internet, the average gossip, never the type to check their facts, could do more damage to a reputation than any secretly recorded conversation, private photograph or horny honeymoon video uploaded online. They were probably quicker at it too. Since his release, Martin had been informed of Doreen Spellner's favourite pastime. Abigail had told him that it was probably due to stories Spellner had started that her store had lately been frequented by people more interested in getting a look at the murderer's girlfriend than buying a book. Martin therefore had more reason than usual to dislike this gossip, so he sure as hell was not about to bite the baited line she'd just tossed out.

"I've been fine, Mrs Spellner," he said. "Thanks for asking." He leaned on the counter. "How have you been?"

"Me? Oh, you know, just, uh, getting along. So, you haven't been anywhere... nice?"

"Nice enough just to be out of that cell," he responded. "Say, Mrs Spellner, where do you live?"

The woman's eyes widened and she visibly paled at his enquiry.

"Why would you want to know that?" she stammered. He shrugged.

"Just idle curiosity. Want to learn a bit more about the town, keep myself occupied, you know." He waved his splay fingered hands at her. "Idle hands and all that." She nodded, smiling. He heard a door opening; the sheriff coming to meet them. "Mrs Spellner, there's an old Scottish term that applies to you." He leaned forward a bit further and, in a far deeper voice and thicker accent than normal, told her, "Yer a beaky auld craw."

Flaghan walked into the reception area, putting his hat on. He paused when he noticed Miss Coyle.

"Hello again, Sheriff Flaghan," she greeted him. "I hope it's all right if I tag along."

"Not a problem, ma'am," he replied. Looking to Martin he nodded a hello, then turned to his receptionist. "Doreen, are you all right?"

"Fine," she replied, her voice a little higher than normal. Martin's words had made no sense to her, but his delivery had made clear they were not complimentary. She cleared her throat and repeated herself. Flaghan frowned, but nodded.

"You know how to reach me. I shouldn't be gone long."

He walked to the door and held it open, gesturing for Coyle and Martin to go ahead of him, each thanking him as they passed. The trio made their way to the car park. On the way, Martin asked the sheriff about Cassandra Church.

"She's as well as can be expected," was his reply. "Going to take her a little time to get over it, but she's got her family around her so she'll get there. You brought your own car?"

"Yes, mine," Coyle replied.

"You want to ride with me or follow me up there?"

Martin looked uncertainly at the rear of the cruiser, recalling with a sick feeling the last time he'd been seated there.

"I think we'll take our car, thank you, sheriff," he said.

"Understood."

They each went to their vehicles and set off for Jackpot Road.

"We go any higher up this bloody hill and I'm going to get a nosebleed!"

"Bit of a ridiculous road, isn't it."

"A *bit*? What on earth possessed you to rent a cabin all the way up here?"

"It was the only place left in town because of the celebrations. The view from the place is beautiful though." He stopped, his mind drifting from the gorgeous vista visible from the hilltop to the horrors that had been discovered in the master bedroom. Abigail had described it to him, so although he had never actually seen it, his imagination had no trouble recreating the scene for him. His stomach roiled. "I don't know if I'll be able to go in," he admitted.

"Can't blame you for feeling like that," Coyle said. "If you let me know where your things are, I'll go in and get them for you."

"We'll see," he said quietly.

Only a couple of minutes later the sheriff's car pulled to the side and parked in front of the cabin. Martin looked up at the façade and felt his stomach tighten, but he had decided that he was going to go in there and get his stuff back. It just felt like something he had to do.

Coyle pulled in beside the cruiser and everyone got out, congregating a few yards from the steps leading to the front door. Coyle looked out at the lake, nodding in appreciation. Martin and Flaghan were both staring at the front door as though they were expecting it to open it and for the ghosts of the three victims to emerge and come floating towards them, wailing that it was their fault they had died. Neither man knew it, but both believed that even if such a thing happened, they would deserve the condemnation.

The idea of being visited by three angry ghosts shook Martin a little more than it did the sheriff. Flaghan knew it was a ridiculous idea, self-recrimination brought up by his guilt. Martin however had learned today that the world may contain things beyond what he considered normal. If his mind really did contain the memories of other people from centuries ago, memories that could be transferred and unlocked by means of an incantation, was it really that big a stretch to think that ghosts might exist too? Not figurative ghosts, not a haunting of the mind by an unwanted yet persistent memory, but an actual supernatural entity? He caught himself shivering.

"Don't we need the owners to be here?" asked Coyle.

"Why?" enquired Flaghan.

"I would assume they would have changed the code on the security system, or taken other such measures." The sheriff shook his head.

"They can't touch the place until the investigation is over. The code is the same." He turned to Martin, saw he expression on his face. "You okay to do this?" It took Martin a moment or two to realise he'd been spoken to.

"What?" he blurted, his head jerking towards the sheriff. "Oh, yes. Yes, let's go."

They approached the front door, Coyle keeping a close eye on Martin, worried that given all he had been told today, this may prove too much for him. The sheriff punched in the code and opened the front door, stepped inside. Martin, after only a brief hesitation, followed him. Coyle entered last, opening the door wide and leaving it that way.

"Miss Coyle, if you'd wait right here," said Flaghan. She nodded and the sheriff looked to Martin and gestured to the door on the right. Martin nodded, glanced briefly up the stairs, and then entered the room.

Half expecting to find another body lying on the bed he'd been using, Martin let out the breath he'd been holding when all he saw lying on top of the covers were his belongings. He went to the cupboard where he'd put his suitcase, retrieved it, sat it on the bed, opened it and began cramming everything into it. The only thing he left out was his mobile.

"I promised Abigail I'd call her to let her know I was on my way back," he explained to Flaghan, who nodded but did not move, staying in the doorway where he could keep an eye on both Martin and Coyle. Martin turned away, found Abigail's number in his phonebook, and hit the call button. She answered after one ring.

"Marty?"

"Yeah, it's me. Is everything okay?"

"Everything's fine. You're at the cabin?"

"Yes. I've got all my stuff packed, so we're just about to leave. Should be back in about twenty minutes or so."

"Good. I'll see you soon. I love you."

Her declaration blew away his fears and unease, and suddenly he was himself again.

"See, now, I can't go saying that back to you because the sheriff's listening, and I don't want to sound like a sissy. But I can't play it cool because then you'll be annoyed at me. You've put me in a really bad spot, Abi." She chuckled.

"Just tell me you love me, dipshit." He grinned.

"I love you."

"Good. Now get your ass back here quick."

"I'll see you soon."

He hung up, shoved his mobile into his pocket, grabbed his suitcase and he and Flaghan went back into the foyer.

"Got everything?" Coyle asked him.

"All packed." He looked to the sheriff. "We good to go?"

Flaghan nodded and stepped towards the door. Martin made to follow him, but his eyes swept over the lounge area and he paused. Despite the horrors of what had been discovered in the master bedroom, that lounge was where he had told Abigail for the first time that he loved her. The place where she had told him she loved him too. Martin thought to himself that if all this sending your memories on down the line to someone else was real, then whoever got his would be onto a winner with that one. That memory could carry a wounded soul over any heartache, brighten the darkest night and warm the coldest of hearts. At least he thought it could. He knew for a fact that it made him feel like there was nothing life could throw at him that he couldn't handle, because if it seemed to be getting too much all he had to do was think of that night. It was proof that dreams sometimes came true. Fair enough, this dream had come with a few unexpected problems, but as Martin remembered that first moment when his lips touched Abigail's, he believed that even if he had known then what he knew now, he wouldn't have changed a thing.

He thought to himself that there had surely been past links in this chain of memories who had felt the same. People who recalled with crystal clarity the first kiss with someone they truly loved. Martin found himself becoming intrigued by the idea of being able to recall those memories.

From behind him there was a yell, a thump, a thud, a short pause and the flat bang of a gunshot. Martin jumped, dropping his suitcase as he turned towards the door. Framed in the doorway he saw a pair of feet and Miss Coyle, her bag dropped to lie beside the feet, taking aim with a gleaming revolver. She loosed off another shot as Martin ran towards her.

"What the hell happened?" he cried, reaching the door and looking down to see the sheriff lying there on his back, his eyes closed, blood seeping from a wound at his temple. Next to him lay a large rock.

"Corday!" breathed Coyle, clearly shocked. Martin noticed her arm trembling as she lowered the gun. "The sheriff walked out, Corday charged, hit him with that rock. I went for my gun, and as the bastard turned towards me I shot at him. I missed. He ran and I took another shot, but I missed again. I'm not used to using a gun."

"Where did he go?"

"He ran towards the back of the cabin. Martin, wait!"

"Look after the sheriff," he called over his shoulder as he vaulted the railing at the far end, landed, and took off after Corday.

From the rear of the cabin there was only one way Corday could go, and that was the stairs leading down to the short stretch of tarmacked walkway, which led either to a field or to the other stairs that led to the shingle beach. Martin leapt through the long grass and reached the head of the stairs, catching sight of his quarry, already halfway down. One hand hovering over the railing, Martin descended as fast as he dared. He kept his eyes on Corday, watching to see which direction the man would go.

Left. The stairs. The beach.

As he continued to descend, he asked himself exactly what he hoped to achieve with this pursuit. Andrew Corday was a stone cold killer, a madman capable of terrible things, and Martin Muir was a man who had recently confessed to never having thrown a proper punch. Regardless, he had meant what he'd told Coyle earlier: inexperienced fighter or not, anyone who meant Abigail harm would see a side of him that had often begged for release, but which he'd always kept caged. Corday had just attacked a good man with a rock, sneakily too, like a damned coward. Doubtless if Miss Coyle hadn't had her gun, he would have had a go at her, and then he would most likely have turned his attention to Martin himself. After that he would have gone after Abigail. That might not happen today, but unless he was stopped Corday would eventually attack, and that would not stand.

He was out of breath by the time he reached the bottom of the stairs, and wishing he had spent a little more time in the gym. Even so he kept running, reaching the head of the first of the staircases leading to the beach. There was Corday below, still with a good lead. Martin started making his way down, aware that this staircase was even more treacherous than the last, and would only get worse. As he went, he wondered exactly where Corday was planning on going. Over the huge boulders bordering both sides of the beach he was heading for lay other small shingle beaches, and on the other sides of those were impassable tangles of trees and bushes.

Shouldn't you go back then? Call the police, let them come down and take care of him?

He discounted that idea. Just because he didn't think there was a way off the beach didn't mean Corday didn't have one. There was no time to wait for the police.

Martin's heart leapt into his throat as he felt his foot slide out from under him. His hand shot out and grabbed the chain that was strung between posts set at regular intervals beside the stairs. His other foot slid out and he dropped, his backside slamming down onto the stair. His arm jerked and the chain shook and rattled. Ignoring the stinging in his buttocks and the throbbing in his shoulder, he got to his feet and carried on, concentrating on nothing but the stairs and his determination to get to the bottom alive and whole.

By the time he was stepping through the gate and onto the metal gangway, he realised he had not seen in which direction Corday had gone. Remembering his first venture down to the beach, he carefully made his way along the metal walkway, getting to the side and dropping down onto the stones as soon as he could. As he landed, he turned sharply, almost overbalancing, suddenly certain that Corday was about to attack from the space underneath the gangway. He wasn't there. Turning back, Martin stood still and listened, but heard nothing except his own panting breaths, the birds and the gentle lapping of the water.

Taking a few deep breaths, he advanced across the beach towards the boulders, looking towards the back of the area as he went, in case Corday had hidden there amidst the foliage. If he was he was doing a damn good job of it. Martin's gaze flicked up to the cabin, then back to the boulders in front of him. If Corday was waiting on the other side, it would be child's play for him to pick Martin off as he climbed into view. When he reached the border, Martin knelt down and lifted the largest rock he could find, and then began to climb. He found a good perch and, holding his breath, he jumped up onto the top of the barrier. He quickly scanned for a target, but saw no one. Again suddenly convinced the attack was going to come from behind, he swivelled to look over his shoulder, but saw no one.

That was when Corday skittered out from a hollow at the base of the other side of the wall. Pulling himself up using the boulders, he slammed into Martin, who let out a cry of surprise and anger as he fell backwards, Corday above him. It took only seconds before Martin landed on the large, flat boulder that protruded out a little over the water, but in that short space of time he had a stroke of luck. Reflexively, he brought up the hand holding the rock and smashed it into Corday's temple. With an outraged bellow Corday fell off him and so Martin's painful landing was not made worse by having the weight of another fully grown man land on him.

Keeping his mind off his earlier pains had been relatively simple, as he had been able to turn his attention to something else. Now, even though he knew there was a threat to his life that required his immediate focus, Martin was stunned into immobility by the sharp pains in his skull, his spine and his elbows. He did manage to turn his head to the side where, through blurry eyes, he saw Corday, his eyes closed, one with a splotch of red beside it, the impact point of the rock, the lucky strike that had spared Martin from greater injury. Corday was moving, but sluggishly, perhaps in worse shape than Martin was. But as Martin looked, the eyes opened and locked onto him. The sluggish movements took on a greater purpose and Martin realised that Corday was readying himself to strike again. He fought to conquer the various areas of hurt over his body, to shift himself, to prepare for the attack or, better yet, to attack first himself. Could he do it though? Yes, he would be defending himself, but...

This man is a sick, twisted fucker. He hunted those women, killed them. He killed Sophie. If he gets up first, he will kill you and then he will go for Abi.

At that thought, the purest of furies flooded through him, providing Martin with a very effective, though temporary, anaesthetic. He clenched and unclenched his hands, then forced his legs to bend, forced his arms to bend, to lever him up into a sitting position. From there a spin put him on all fours and seconds later he got to his feet. Corday was also in motion, matching Martin's recovery almost step for step.

Taking a deep breath, Martin clenched the fingers of his right hand into a white knuckled fist and broke into a dead run for his opponent, who was standing on seemingly unsteady legs, staring at the ground.

Martin swung the first real punch of his life, and Corday's head suddenly snapped up, his eyes wide and bright and very alert. His arm rose, deflecting the punch. His other shot out, the strike catching Martin right in the gut. The air vacated his body in a single forced exhalation and he doubled over, staggering back, his hands clutching his midsection. His right knee buckled and he performed a strange and graceless genuflection, one that sent a fresh lance of pain up through his knee.

Corday let out a low, throaty chuckle.

"Did you really think you were going to get the better of me, Muir?" he asked, stepping forward. "You thought sheer grim determination would save your hide, did you? Maybe you were counting on a little luck, eh. Well tough shit! You have to make your own luck in this world. For instance, those lovely little playthings wouldn't have fallen into my lap through luck. No, I had to go out and make those opportunities happen."

The words registered, but Martin was too busy trying to will the pain away to pay attention. But then, as he moved to stand above Martin, Corday said perhaps the worst thing he could have said.

"I'm going to spread the contents of your skull all over this rock, and then I'm going to pay Abigail a little visit. Oh, the things I'm going to do to her, Muir. I'd describe them to you, but you probably wouldn't know what most of them were." He let out another chuckle. "Let's just say I'm going to greatly expand her horizons... and her pussy... and her asshole... and her mouth, all with my great big cock."

He chuckled again, but his own words had tickled him so much it turned into an outright laugh. He lifted his head and laughed away, staring out over Martin's head. This meant he did not realise Martin had got his breath back. Nor did not see the hand drop from Martin's stomach. He did not see it clench. His first inclination that something was amiss was when Martin Muir threw the second proper punch of his life, and this time nothing got in the way. Martin pushed himself upwards with one leg, thrusting his bent arm up as he rose. The punch connected spectacularly with Corday's exposed jaw, snapping his head back and almost lifting him off his feet. He staggered back and Martin stepped back, pain blazing in his bruised knuckles. Corday was just starting to get his senses back when Martin played the man's words back in his head. With an inarticulate howl of rage, he charged, ducking down and slamming into Corday, hoisting the stunned son of a bitch onto his shoulder. At the edge of the boulder he stopped and released his cargo, but as he did so his cargo's clutching fingers snagged the shoulder of his shirt. The contact was brief, but lasted long enough to yank Martin forward. Realising what was going to happen, he stepped off the edge.

The trip was brief, the arrival far less damaging for Martin than for Corday. They landed a few feet apart, Martin on his feet, Corday on his back. The jarring impact reawakened all the little points of pain and discomfort all over Martin's body. His recently regained breath gasped out of him and for a few moments he stood, mouth open but no air going in our out.

During those few moments, and those that followed it during which Martin remembered how to breathe, Corday snarled, rolled to the side and got to his feet, growling.

Martin saw, and was stunned at the man's ability to shake off what must have been a physically agonising landing.

Strength and endurance of the insane, or is his want to see my skull caved in driving him the way my anger is driving me?

"That fucking *hurt,* you asshole!"

He breathed through his nostrils, snorting like an enraged bull. Martin saw the sheer, unremitting madness in his eyes and knew there was no way he could win this. There was also no way he could escape; Corday stood between him and the gangway, and any attempt to pass him would be easily headed off. Clambering over the rocks behind him would only present his back to Corday, as would going into the water. Martin told himself he would not give up though, not until the choice was taken out of his hands. Until then he would use everything at his disposal – teeth, knees, fists, forehead, feet and every dirty, low down fighting move the Marquess of Queensberry would disapprove of – to do as much damage as he could to this warped excuse for a human being. Taking a deep breath, he stood as straight as he could and advanced.

"You've got bigger balls than I gave you credit for," sneered Corday. "But you can't be under any illusions about how this is going to end."

"I'm not."

Corday actually seemed surprised by this, but the look, which somehow didn't sit right on his face, quickly melted away, replaced by cold hatred.

He quickly bent down, snatched a large rock from the ground, and stood. Hefting it in his hand, he stepped towards Martin.

There was a bang and a puff of dust spat up just in front of Corday's foot. The noise echoed up and down the hill and Martin and Corday both looked up to where Martin could just make out the figure of Sheriff Flaghan standing on the cabin's porch, a rifle braced against his shoulder.

"Oh, *fuck off!*" yelled Corday, as another bang heralded another puff of dust, this one nearer to him. Seconds later, another shot just missed him.

The rock that Martin threw at him did not. It hit him square in the crotch, which was, amazingly enough, exactly where Martin had intended it to go. Corday bent forward, dropping his own projectile and cursing Martin to hell and back. Martin picked up another rock and advanced, fully intending to bring it down onto the back of Corday's skull. However another rifle shot jerked Corday out of his pain induced paralysis and he staggered backwards, almost tripping over his own feet. Flaghan kept shooting and Corday eventually turned and ran as best he could for the boulders. Martin staggered after him, the rock still clutched in his hand, his mind still marvelling at how quickly this man could recover from injuries that would leave a normal man crippled.

Simple answer to that: he's not normal. Far from it.

Corday reached the boulders and started to climb. Another shot from the sheriff ricocheted off one of the larger rocks, close to Corday's hand, eliciting a short stream of curses. Martin stopped walking, reared back and threw the rock he held. It clattered against its bigger brothers just to Corday's side. More curses, and then he was over the top. Moments later Martin reached the foot of the wall and almost started to climb, but then he heard the splash, followed by more splashing. Corday had gone into the lake and was swimming away.

Martin turned and leaned against the rocks, suddenly very queasy and very dizzy. He leaned forward, braced his hands on his thighs, and threw up.

"What in the hell were you thinking?"

Martin had just arrived back at the cabin, after a very slow and painful walk back up the stairs from the beach. A clearly angry Sherrif Flaghan had met him at the door and greeted him with the question, which he repeated when an answer wasn't immediately forthcoming.

"I wasn't thinking," Martin said finally.

"Something we can all agree on," commented Coyle. Martin shot her a sour look. "Don't give me that, laddie. What you did was reckless as hell, and if the sheriff hadn't come to the chances are good that your brains would be getting picked at by the birds by now."

"I know! I just saw what he'd done and I got angry, so I chased him."

"And just who the hell was he?" asked the sheriff.

"It was…" Martin realised at the last moment that he couldn't give Flaghan Corday's name. "The bastard who set me up, the one who killed Sophie and those other women."

"How do you work that out?"

"He told me, down on the beach. He said he wanted to kill me and Abigail."

"You recognise him?"

"Never see him before."

"He happen to give you a name, or mention why he's so determined to kill you and your girlfriend?" Martin sat down on the front steps and shook his head, so he didn't see the suspicious look the sheriff was giving him. "He told you down on the beach he was the man who set you up, so why did you take off after him before you knew who he was?"

"I did know who he was." Flaghan raised an eyebrow. "Who else would have cause to attack me but the man who, for god knows what reason, tried to frame me for three murders?"

"The very large bump on my head indicates I was the one he attacked, Mr Muir."

"Yes, sheriff," said Coyle. "However, with you unconscious, the man turned on me and asked me where Martin was. He threatened to kill me if I didn't tell him. I pretended to go for a gun in my handbag and he fled." Martin continued with,

"And having heard everything from inside I came out and, infuriated, took off after him. I chased him down to the beach and fought with him and he got the upper hand, and that was where you stepped in. Thanks for that, by the way."

"Welcome," said Flaghan. "Though truth be told I was looking to get him for blindsiding me with a rock. If I hadn't been mildly concussed, I might even have hit the fucker." He raised his fingers to the spot where he had been hit, then thought better of it and dropped his hand. "I've called the station to report this. Both of you are going to have to come down to make statements and give a description of the guy. I'll have it sent to a sketch artist and see what he can come up with. I'll also have a couple of my men come up and have a good look around. If this guy has been hanging around up here he might have left something behind that could be useful to us."

"Here's hoping they don't somehow manage to recover those bullets," murmured Coyle when she and Martin got back into her car.

"Where did you get a gun from anyway?"

"You don't need to know. If I'd had a bit more experience with the damn thing this situation might have been ended at that cabin today." She paused. "I doubt they'll find the bullets; their search probably won't extend out into the trees where my shots ended up. If they do find them I'll say I forgot to mention it because of the shock" Another pause. "I panicked," she admitted. "That was the first time I've ever fired a gun, but he was right there in front of me. I shouldn't have missed, but I did because I panicked. I looked into his eyes, Martin."

"So did I. Like nothing I've ever seen before, and something I hope I never see again."

"Well I hope your hope might prevent you from doing something as foolish as taking off after a mad man again. I'm finding it very difficult not to give you a good slap up the back of the head. Honestly, Martin, what were you thinking?"

"I've already said, I wasn't thinking. I acted, I didn't think. The sheriff was out cold and the man who wants me and Abigail dead was within reach, so I went after him. That he could snap my neck didn't cross my mind until the point where I thought that was exactly what he was going to do. I felt so guilty at that moment, Miss Coyle. I took after him intending to fight him to the death, but if he had killed me, Abi would have been alone."

"Not totally alone," his old teacher corrected him.

"But without me," he clarified. "She loves me, and if I died it would hurt her so much, just the same way as her being hurt would destroy me. That's why I went after Corday without thinking: he wants to hurt her and I will not stand for that. But I didn't understand. This man is soulless. He's completely over the edge, down into the abyss. How do you defend someone from something like that? How do you defeat something like that?"

"He's not a something Martin, he's a person, and we'll beat him the same way we would defeat anyone of his ilk: any way we can."

Chapter 41

After Martin and Coyle left, Abigail sat in an armchair for ten minutes, flicking back and forth through a magazine she had found. The silence became uncomfortable very quickly. After a short time Matthew excused himself, and eventually Abigail threw down the magazine and stared at her Guardian. Sandra stared straight back at her, smiling.

"This feels weird."

"In what way?"

"Well, you're my Guardian and I don't have a clue what the hell that is, really."

"Feel free to ask whatever questions you have, Abigail," Sandra told her.

"Where do I even begin?" Abigail asked out loud, though it was clearly a rhetorical question. "Uh, well, I know how you got to be my Guardian, but what does that entail exactly?"

"In a nutshell, it's about being a teacher and a guide to your charge, though most are called to take on those roles a lot earlier than Andrea and I have. But until now my duty has always been the same: to watch over you."

"How?"

"You mean did I follow you around making notes about where you went, and plant hidden cameras in your house? No, dear, though I must admit that in the early days I did feel like a bit of a stalker, being there unseen in the background of your life, surreptitiously watching you. But it was my task to make sure you were safe. That duty still stands, but I'm now also able to fulfil the role of teacher, to make sure you understand the wonderful thing you're part of. At least I will be once this situation is resolved. I understand that you barely know me, but I would also like you to know that whenever you need someone to talk to, I am here. After all, speaking to your friends and family about everything you've learned recently, about anything connected to it, might be somewhat difficult without making them think you've lost your mind. You have Martin, of course, but sometimes a person needs someone other than their love to talk to. In your Guardian you have an attentive pair of ears from which no subject is taboo."

"How much do you know about me?"

"I know that you are a determined woman, one with a good head on her shoulders. I know your business means the world to you, as do your friends and family. Your relationship with Martin, even before he came to Hannerville, was a cherished part of your life. Oh, I also know that you like animals but don't want a pet."

"Have you kept tabs on my sex life?" Sandra chuckled.

"No, Abigail, I haven't. Your private life has always been your own. My job was to observe and intervene if necessary, not to pry. What I know about you I have gleaned over the years. Little bits of information picked up here and there."

The two of them chatted for a while, Abigail discovering that her Guardian was a very easy person to talk to. Though Sandra had spoken of being a teacher, that afternoon it was actually Abigail who was doing the teaching, clueing the woman in on things she had witnessed the start of, but had never learned of the resolution to. Sandra was most eager to learn about an incident from Abigail's early teens.

"I was walking by the high school that day, not actually on one of my observational outings but coming back from the grocery store. I saw the boy sneaking up behind you, something in his hands. Then he dropped it down the back of your top. You squealed and he ran off with his friends, all of them laughing, back into the school. Seconds later you ran inside too." Abigail was nodding.

"Jerry Tobler, the little shit. It was a frog he dropped down my top. He took it from one of the science labs. I ran inside with this slimy little lump in the small of my back, squirming around. It felt disgusting. In the hallway I yanked up my top and the thing fell out, but I yanked it up so high that I accidentally gave Jerry and his buddies a look at my bra. Schmucks were all so damn stunned they didn't budge as I got myself calmed down, walked up and kicked Jerry right in his little nards. Twerp actually had the nerve to ask me out a few months later. I had to fight back the urge to kick him in the crotch again."

"Remind me never to piss you off," Matthew's voice came from behind her. She looked over her shoulder, smiling.

"Damn straight; I can kick a lot harder now." He walked over to the seat he had been sitting in earlier, holding up his hands as he sat down.

"More than willing to take your word for it."

"So, what is it you're doing here, Matthew?"

"I'm sorry?"

"Well, Andrea is here because she's Martin's Guardian. Sandra is my Guardian. You said earlier your area of expertise was in making sure all this stuff about Guardians and Traitors is kept a secret; how did you end up being here on the front line?" Matthew nodded.

"I was delivering a report to Andrea when she found out that Corday was heading back to Hannerville. She wanted to get here quickly and didn't have time to do a proper selection on who to bring. That Lucas and I were available is really the only reason we were chosen."

"Lucas?" Matthew looked to Sandra.

"He went up against Corday. He didn't survive."

"I'm so sorry."

"Though none of us knew him well, his death affected us all."

"Myself a little more than Andrea and Sandra," Matthew admitted. Abigail turned to him. His eyes met hers and she saw the fear in them. "I was unprepared. Unprepared for how cold he would be, how harsh, how damnably clever. I got scared, but I got past it. I gave my word to do whatever was necessary, and I never break my word." He took a breath and shrugged off the sombre mood threatening to overtake him. "Besides, I'm hoping that doing whatever is necessary means getting even with this guy for the dent he's put in my pride."

"In a way I feel kind of sorry for those chosen to receive The Traitor's memories."

Abigail and Matthew swivelled their heads to look at Sandra, both wearing expressions of utter astonishment. She looked from one to the other, realising they had misunderstood her.

"Oh, don't get me wrong, Corday deserves to fry for everything he's done. There can be no forgiveness, no mercy; he's got to go. What I meant was that although none of the Bearers are given a choice about receiving the memories, the Bearers for The Couple do not have their lives interfered with, the memories unlocked only if they fall in love with one another, and only then to enrich their lives. The Traitor's Bearers are usually brought up being taught how to hate, how to torment and kill. It's true that they're chosen because their predecessor senses something inherently bad in them, just as many of The Couple's Bearers have been chosen because their predecessors felt a kinship with them, a link between good and decent souls if you like, but that doesn't mean they would have turned out bad if left alone. Their natural development is often subverted by the one who chose them, to ensure the drive to seek out and destroy The Couple is maintained, or even inflamed. Just as I will teach you, Abigail, so they are taught, from a far earlier age, about what has happened through the many years that have gone by, with The Traitor always made to look like the wronged party. Who was Mandisa that she should not have loved Sefu, who loved her so much more than Bakari ever could? Who was Bakari to think he could simply steal away Sefu's one true love? That kind of thing, all of it presented as truth, though really nothing more than falsehoods, reinforced every time they have been told. These children have grown up being taught that no one could ever love them and that it is their destiny to be alone, their duty to hate those, not just The Couple, who do find someone to share their lives with.

"I would pity anyone brought up in such a fashion, but there can be no doubt as to the fate that awaits Andrew Corday. For many years we allowed ourselves to think, some of us maybe even to believe, that he had gone away for good. That he had given up and would be content to stay in Berrybeck until he died." She sighed. "More fool us."

Chapter 42

"What's Doctor Glenster doing here?" muttered Martin when he saw the man get out of his car as he and Coyle pulled into the car park.

Coyle pulled the car into a space and turned off the engine, by which time Sheriff Flaghan was shaking hands with Glenster. Martin and his Guardian got out and approached them.

"Mr Muir," Glenster said, giving Martin a nod and extending his hand.

"Nice to see you again, Mr Glenster." They shook hands, and Martin caught the man's questioning glance towards Coyle. "This is my legal representative, Andrea Coyle. Miss Coyle, this is Philip Glenster." The two shook hands. "Why are you here? Is everything all right?"

"My doing," said Flaghan. "I called Phil on my way back, asked him to meet us here and give us a quick once over, just in case."

Martin nodded and the four of them went inside, Martin pointedly ignoring the receptionist as he passed by her desk.

They went directly to Flaghan's office, where the town's former doctor examined the sheriff and pronounced him a little beat up but no more. He did caution the sheriff that should he experience any problems with his vision or equilibrium that he should seek medical help immediately, but some pain killers and rest should see him right as rain. His exam over, Flaghan announced that he was going to go and call up some of his men to go and check over the cabin and the surrounding area.

"So, what condition are you in, Martin?" Glenster asked as the door closed.

"I can't speak for him physically," said Coyle. "But given the stunt he pulled, I believe there's a mental issue that needs to be addressed." Martin glowered at her, and Glenster chuckled.

"I'm afraid I can't help with that, but if you'd like to point where you're hurting I'll see if there's anything you need to worry about."

Martin pointed out the various aches and pains all over his body, answering the questions Glenster asked as the doctor examined each of the bruised areas on Martin's arms, back, chest and legs. When he was finished he took a look at Martin's head, probing different areas of the skull and asking if anywhere was particularly tender.

"Other than a small lump at the back of your head, you seem fine. I'd maybe put some ointment on those bruises but, as with the sheriff, some painkillers and rest and you should be fine. Maybe lay off playing the hero for a little while," he added with a wry grin.

"Don't feel much like a hero," Martin said.

"I'd say you saved the sheriff and Miss Coyle from a very dangerous situation," Glenster told him. "Going after their attacker wasn't the brightest idea you've ever had, but I think you know that." He pursed his lips. "In fact given that there is a possibility the man you chased was David Brannon, going after him was next door to suicidal. Can you describe him to me?"

Martin nodded and gave the doctor a description of the man he had fought with, knowing that it was exactly who Glenster thought it was, and also knowing that the man would not recognise the description. On the plus side they had now officially seen the man who had committed the murders. As far as the law was concerned this man's guilt on that score was not a certainty – they only had Martin's assertion to go on - but he was guilty of attacking the sheriff, and so a description would be circulated of Corday as he looked now.

Glenster shook his head as Martin finished describing Corday.

"That doesn't sound like him. At least that's not what he looked like back then." He looked suddenly pensive. "I can't say for sure what he looked like when he escaped from

Berrybeck. He was in there for a long, long time; who knows how much he might have changed physically. Also there's nothing to say he hasn't managed to change his appearance since his escape." He looked at Martin. "We can rule out nothing at this point, something that will stand until he's apprehended." Martin nodded.

"With a description being put around town, someone will see him, call the sheriff. He'll be brought in soon enough."

"Hopefully soon enough to avoid further deaths," Glenster said grimly. There was a short silence before he looked up, forced a smile and told them, "I'd best be getting home. Tell Abigail I said hello."

"I will. Thank you, Mr Glenster."

The man nodded at him, then smiled and nodded at Coyle and then left.

"Nice fellow," remarked Coyle. "Terribly frightened."

"He has a good reason to be scared." Coyle nodded.

"It might well be the case that had the good doctor not intervened that night, Abigail might not have made it." Martin almost asked how she knew about what had happened, then stopped himself. Doubtless she had access to more information on what had transpired that night than anyone else. "It almost cost him his life," she went on. "The wound Corday inflicted was not deep enough to damage the internal organs, but the blood loss almost did for him."

The two of them were quiet for the minute or so before Flaghan came back and asked Coyle to wait whilst he took Martin to make his statement. Martin stuck to the story he had originally given, managing to overcome his discomfiture by reminding himself that he wasn't lying to an officer of the law, just not giving him the full story. After he had finished, Flaghan asked him to give as detailed a description as possible of the man he had fought with. Martin did so, and was then taken back to Flaghan's office, where he waited while the sheriff interviewed Miss Coyle.

While he waited, he wondered exactly how he was going to tell Abigail what he had done, and whether or not another examination from Philip Glenster might be required afterwards.

Only the fact that there was precious little left in one piece was preventing Corday from taking out his anger on his house. That, and the possibility of someone calling the police to complain about the noise again.

Instead he sat huddled on the living room floor, stripped naked, his soaked clothes lying in a pile in the corner, the blanket from his bed wrapped around him. He had the heating on, and was sitting close to a grate, but the chill had seeped into his bones and was reluctant to leave.

He simply couldn't fathom how it had all gone so terribly wrong. He had been waiting for them at Abigail's house when Coyle had shown up. Corday had had no doubts that she had gone there to reveal the truth to them. Since he hadn't seen her thrown out on her ass, she must have convinced the pair that there was some credence to her story. When they had come out he had given consideration to mowing them down in the street, but he wanted to look into their eyes as the life left them, so he followed them to another house instead. When Coyle and Muir had come out by themselves he had been curious and followed them first to the sheriff's department, and from there to the cabin. Deciding that this was a wonderful opportunity to take out three birds with one stone, he had picked up a large stone from the ground, snuck up, charged, and nailed that dickhead sheriff with it. Coyle was next in line. Unfortunately he'd had no idea the bitch was packing heat! His plan shot to shit in an instant, only her terrible aim had spared him from ending up the same way. He had fled, and that uppity little bastard from bonnie Scotland had chased him! Corday had been flabbergasted to realise the fucker had been at his heels. The only silver lining had been the fact that Muir had been apparently unaware he was rushing after a man who was more than capable of killing him. And he had been so close on that beach. He had seen it in Muir's eyes: the guy had been beaten. He had known there was no way he was going to survive.

Then that asshole cop had opened up with his rifle. Adding insult to injury, that cowardly little bastard Muir had nailed him in the balls with a rock! Cheap fucking shot! With no option but to retreat, Corday had climbed out of sight of the sheriff, realising too late he had climbed over onto another small beach from which there were only two exits: back the way he had come or into the freezing waters of the lake. Choice number one was a no go, so before he had time to think about it, he had thrown himself into the water and swam for it.

The swim had nearly killed him, so cold was the water. He only just made it to shore, and even then working up the energy to get back to town had been a mammoth task. He had walked along the road and a car had stopped, a concerned citizen asking if he could be of any help. Corday had spun him a story about trying to change a tyre beside the lake. The thing had gotten away from him and he'd chased it into the water. The man had offered him a lift, which Corday had accepted. On the way back, a trip to the hospital had been suggested as Corday looked to be, in the man's words, "Colder than a witch's tit," but Corday had waved off his concern, saying he just needed to get dry and warm. He had the man drop him off a block away from his house.

During the short walk back to his house he had reflected on the loss of his car. It wasn't as though he had a strong connection to the vehicle, but during that sometimes seemingly endless journey home, he would have dearly loved to have had it. As it was he'd left it sitting in the driveway of one of the places neighbouring the cabin. It was only a matter of time before someone reported it as having been abandoned and the cops found it. It was possible he could get back out there and reclaim it before that happened, but he didn't hold out much hope. The problem was he would need a car to get out of town once matters had been taken care of.

As he again tried to stop himself shivering, Corday decided to go and buy a new car later that afternoon. He also decided that it would end the night of the Hanner Carnival. That night, come hell or high water, all scores would be settled and he would be leaving this wretched little town for good.

The idea of this whole mess being put to rights, allowing him to get on with living his life, spread a warm glow through him that the air gushing from the grate couldn't hope to match. To drive out of this shitty little town with the blood of so many still warm on his hands would be the realisation of a dream, a fantasy made flesh.

Torn and bloodied flesh.

"I'll deal with you later," was Abigail's somewhat chilling initial response to being told that Martin had chased down and fought with a mad man. She then all but commanded that he and Coyle sit down and tell her, Sandra and Matthew what had happened at the cabin. When the story had been told, Matthew was the first one to speak.

"I do believe that what you did was foolish in the extreme, but I also believe that it was not as unthinking as you make out. You thought to end Corday before he could cause Abigail any further harm?" Martin nodded.

"Anger started me running," he told them. "Thinking that I could put an end to that bastard then and there kept me going. It wasn't until I was face to face with him that I realised how big a mistake I had made. I thought it was too late to do anything about it by that point; he had me cornered. But I picked up that rock and I..."

Without warning Abigail leapt from her seat and ran for the stairs. Moments later a door slammed. Martin got to his feet and followed her.

Putting his ear to the first door he came to, Martin heard the gentle sobbing. Taking a deep breath he opened the door and stepped inside to find Abigail standing at the window. She had her arms wrapped around her and her shoulders were rising and falling. Martin felt like the world's biggest arsehole. Closing the door behind him, he took a few tentative steps towards her.

"I hope the first words out of your mouth aren't going to be "What's the matter?" because if they are we have a problem."

"No, I know why you're upset, and you have every right to be. You're probably also entitled to a better explanation, but I'm not sure if there's much of one to give other than what I said downstairs. I wanted to keep him away from you, and I saw what I thought was a chance to do that. I honestly had no idea what I was chasing until I looked into his eyes. I honestly thought that was it, that I was finished. Two things struck me at that moment: the determination to damage him as much as possible before it was over, and an almost incapacitating guilt over how much my death would hurt you."

"Do you have any idea how much it hurts just hearing you talk about your own death like that? The idea that you could have died today makes me want to throw up, Marty. The fact that you willingly chased after the person who could have killed you makes we want to kick your ass! That bastard has already murdered my parents and my friend, and today he could have gotten you too." She turned to face him, her arms dropping to her sides, her hands clenched into fists. Light glinted off the moisture in her eyes, but what snared Martin's attention was the anger he saw in them. He realised she was furious, and as she advanced towards him, he almost stepped back. But he decided that if taking a swing at him was what she needed, then that was what she was going to be allowed. She stopped in front of him, looking up into his eyes.

"You have no idea how much I want to punch you right now, just so you might remember in the future to not attempt throwing your life away. The only things stopping me are the fact that you've already been knocked around once today, and the fact that, pissed off as I am at you, I can't help but consider that what you did was for my benefit." She unclenched her fists, reached up, gripped his head between her hands and pulled it down towards her. "Understand this, Marty; it makes me very happy and very proud to know that you are willing to fight for me, maybe even to die for me. But in the future you should bear in mind that having you not chasing after a lunatic and instead having you remain by my side makes me much, much happier. I'd rather love a living man than worship the memory of a dead one."

Martin could find no words, and wasn't certain he could have spoken any he might have thought of, and so he just nodded.

"Okay?" she asked, fresh tears springing to her eyes. "I need you to hear me here, Marty, I need to know you're on board. I need to know that if you're thinking of what's best for me, then you're doing your best to get back to me." Martin nodded again and croaked out, "I get it."

"You get it?"

"I do."

She released his head, put her arms around him and held him. Martin hugged her, breathed in the smell of her hair, felt the press of her breasts against his chest. That the simple pleasure of holding her might be taken away from him by Corday brought forth the thought that he had been right in what he had done earlier. Doing so in the future, in defiance of Abigail's wishes, and therefore running the risk of angering her, of hurting her, possibly of losing her, might not be an option as long as he remembered this moment.

"Just so as you know," Abigail said quietly. "Once you're healed up, I'm still going to punch you."

When they went back downstairs it was suggested to them that they stay at Sandra's until the present situation had been sorted out. As unsure as they were about everything that was going on in their lives right now, Martin and Abigail both knew that Corday was most assuredly a threat, and both saw the sense in not being where he might easily find them.

Sandra drove them both to Abigail's house, where Abigail quickly packed a bag with clothes, toiletries and her journal. Back at Sandra's they were both shown to a room that had been prepared for them. It was early evening by this time, and not long after Sandra announced that they would be ordering dinner soon. That neither of them felt particularly hungry changed when they caught the aroma of the food when it was delivered. They both cleaned their plates, and although it was still early, Coyle suggested they go to their room and get some rest.

"Shouldn't we be discussing things?" asked Abigail.

"Coming up with some sort of strategy?" added Martin.

"And we will," said Coyle. "But after everything else the pair of you have been through today, I'm wary of going into all that right now. I think a little time is called for, for thought, reflection, rest... whatever. The three of us will rotate guard duty through the night, so try not to concern yourselves. You're safe here."

Martin and Abigail thanked them all and went upstairs. They lay on the bed for a while, just holding one another, and then Abigail announced that she felt she had better write in her journal as she felt like she might fall asleep at any time.

Once the entry had been made, they got into bed and put on the TV. Neither could concentrate on the programme they chose, however, as their own thoughts tilted and whirled through their minds.

"I feel like we should be talking about this," said Martin after a while. "But I just can't seem to get my head together."

"I know what you mean," said Abigail. "So many things have happened." She paused. "Maybe we should just get some rest."

"I agree."

"Do me a favour first?"

"What?"

"Wedge that chair under the door handle."

Martin got out of bed and did as asked, then got back in beside her. They switched out the light and were soon asleep.

It turned out to be a very long sleep, as it was close to lunchtime the following day before either of them stirred.

"You've got to be kidding," muttered Martin when he saw the time.

"Oh, man," murmured Abigail. "Why didn't someone wake us?"

They went downstairs and found Andrea, Sandra and Matthew in the living room. Abigail put her question to them.

"We thought it better to let you sleep as long as you needed to," said Coyle. "It isn't unusual for the Bearers to sleep for a lot longer than usual after the first few memories have been unlocked. It takes a toll on the mind, leaving them far more tired than they realise. The same thing often happens when all of the memories are unlocked, but that's not something you need to consider just now."

"Can I get you anything to eat?" asked Sandra.

An hour or so later, after they had eaten a hearty brunch, Martin and Abigail sat down on the couch beside Coyle and Abigail asked,

"I take it you guys have been discussing the situation?"

"We have," answered Coyle."

"So what do we do now?"

"Well, Matthew and Sandra both believe that we should stay here and allow the police to put things in motion. They have a description of Corday, and so a sketch will be produced and distributed. He will not leave town and so it seems like only a matter of time before he is hunted down like the animal he is. Were we discussing anyone other than Andrew Corday I would agree with that assessment."

"He won't allow himself to be caught," Martin said. "He's fighting his own cause and it's one he believes in fanatically. He'll take whatever steps are necessary to get what he wants without running the risk of being caught. If he is seen, or someone catches up with him, take it from someone who's been there: Corday will not let them stop him." Coyle nodded.

"So what's your idea?" Abigail asked her.

"In short, I want to go after the bastard and put a bullet in his head."

"You're going a little gung-ho all of a sudden, aren't you? Given what happened yesterday…"

"Abigail, Martin hit the nail on the head with what he just said. Corday will not stop until he has what he wants. Until he is dead, neither you, nor Martin, nor anyone either of you are close to will be safe. We mistakenly believed that the threat Corday posed had been nullified, that his time in incarceration had relieved him of his goals. We were wrong. He simply spent years biding his time until the conditions were right for him to get out. Now that he is, do you honestly believe that anything will deter him?" Abigail held up her hands.

"Don't get me wrong, I am all for you blowing this fucker's brains out. What I'm saying is that given his plans yesterday obviously went wrong, he's going to be pissed off. Maybe going looking for him isn't the best idea right now."

"He's not going to simmer down. No time to go after him will be a good one, and I do not believe that waiting for him to strike again is a viable option."

"How would we find him?" asked Martin. "Even if Flaghan's men do find something up at the cabin that leads them to him, they're not going to share it with us."

Sandra, sensing the way the wind was blowing, answered him.

"We know where his house is."

"He has a house?" blurted Martin. "Why haven't you sent the sheriff there…"

"No point," explained Matthew, who had also realised how this conversation was going to pan out. "The house was bought legally, and there is no way he is keeping anything there that could possibly link him to anything." Coyle took up the thread.

"During his spree back in the early eighties, Corday had a place in the woods where he took his victims, a run-down shack. We believe some warped sense of nostalgia may have led him to set up something similar in the woods around Hannerville. On a few occasions, before he knew we were here, we followed him out towards the woods at the east end of town. Even then he took no chances, and made his route so damn complex that we always lost him. We even tried searching the woods out that way for somewhere, but we never found anything."

"You were looking in the wrong place," said Abigail. All eyes turned to her. "He may not have known you were tailing him, but he still didn't want anyone knowing where he was really going. The reason you always lost him was because after heading out to the east side of town, he doubled back and made his way to the west. The old shacks are out in the western woods."

"You mean the old settlers shacks?" asked Martin. Abigail looked at him and nodded.

"The ones I wrote you about years ago, the ones my friends and I used to go to." She turned to the others. "Arthur Hanner founded Hannerville in the early nineteen hundreds, after opening up the Hanner Mining Company. Some of the miners built themselves little places out in the woods for them and their families to live in. Through time some of them moved into better accommodations in the town proper and the shacks were abandoned. A lot of people thought that when the mines closed the town would dry up and blow away, but the people living here loved the place so much they stayed on. As more and more people came, some of them chose to live in the miners old shacks until they could afford somewhere better.

"By the time I was in my early teens, those few shacks that remained standing were strictly off limits because of the fact they could collapse at any moment. All the kids had heard stories about nasty things that had happened to the people who used to live in those places – men murdering their families and stuff like that – but to be honest we were never sure if the stories were true, or just stuff our parents made up to make sure we stayed away. If that was their intention, it backfired big-time. Going out to the shacks was almost a rite of passage for the kids in town. Groups of us would go out there and someone would always be dared to go in. I remember the day I went up there with my friends. We found beer bottles and used condoms all over the place." She smiled and let out a little laugh. "Beth said it was the place the older kids went to play hookie and get some nookie.

"I was the one they dared to go into one of the shacks that day.

"I know it's going to sound like I'm playing it tough, but I wasn't really that bothered about doing it. Yeah, the place looked like a strong breeze might push it over, but I wasn't worried about being hacked to pieces by a bloodthirsty zombie miner. It became a slightly different story once I was actually inside though. Much as I kept telling myself that there was nothing to be afraid of except maybe a critter pissed that I had invaded its hidey hole, the atmosphere in the place was chilling. I felt my flesh crawl, and the little hairs stand up on the back of my neck. I quickly became convinced that if I turned around really fast I'd see that long dead miner, coming at me with his pick axe. I barely held in a scream as I ran out of the place. I haven't been out there since."

She looked towards Coyle.

"If Corday found one of those shacks, and decided the place was stable enough, it would be perfect for him."

Coyle pursed her lips and made a clucking noise with her tongue.

"Sly bastard that he is. Abigail, could you give us directions to where these shacks are?"

"They're scattered all through the woods, but I can give you directions to the ones nearest to town."

"Excellent."

"They're still some way out into the woods though."

"Ideal for him," commented Matthew. Abigail got out of her seat and went to look for some paper and a pen.

"What's your plan?" Martin enquired.

"My plan," began Coyle. "Is to take Matthew and follow Abigail's directions to these shacks, see if we can maybe sneak up on Corday and put a stop to him for good. If not that, then maybe we can find his shack and either destroy it or place another anonymous call to the police, tell them where to find it. Either way I want to make sure he can't use it again."

"A dangerous play," commented Matthew, getting to his feet. "I'll go grab us some equipment."

"Thank you, Matthew."

"Are you sure you don't want me to go with you, Andrea?" asked Sandra. Shaking her head, Coyle replied,

"No, I need you to stay here with Martin and Abigail. If something goes wrong and we don't come back, and you don't hear from us, assume the worst. Lock yourself in this house and contact the Glasgow office, get them to send others. Bring in an outside specialist if you have to." Martin's eyes widened in surprise.

"If calling for backup is an option, why don't we do it now?"

"At the moment Corday doesn't see us as a threat, but the moment he realises we've called in reinforcements, he will do the same. I do not want to turn this little town into a battleground; enough innocent people have already perished." Martin nodded his understanding.

A few minutes later Abigail and Matthew returned, the former with a sheet of paper, the latter with a backpack. Abigail handed Andrea the directions.

"As I said, it's been a long time since I was anywhere near there. The layout may have changed a little, but following those should get you there."

"Thank you."

Abigail sat down beside Martin and cuddled up to him. He put his arm around her and kissed the top of her head, watching as Coyle asked Matthew what he was bringing. Opening the backpack, he pulled out a torch.

"We've got plenty of daylight left," he told her. "But just in case. There is a second torch in here too. We have Abigail's directions to some of the shacks, but there's no guarantee those are the right ones, so we might be in for a bit of a trek, so I threw in some bottles of water and some biscuits, couple of pairs of gloves. I don't have a compass but…" He took his mobile from his trouser pocket, pressed a few buttons and turned it around for the others to see. On the screen was a display showing a compass. "This should suffice if one is required." He pocketed the phone and stuck a hand into the backpack. "In terms of weapons I have a kitchen knife I just took from Sandra's kitchen drawer, and my pistol. You might want to reload your revolver, by the way."

Coyle nodded and left the room.

Chapter 43

There was still a hint of the path Abigail and her friends had once used to reach the area of the woods where the shacks stood, but that hint was all Coyle and Matthew were getting. Also every so often the undergrowth would completely obscure what remained of the path, leaving them with nothing but hope that they were still heading in the right direction.

Neither of the two of them had spoken much since leaving Sandra's house. At first it had been because both of them were too preoccupied with thoughts of what they might find out here in the woods out by the western end of town. Now it was because they couldn't spare the breath to talk; the path, such as it was, had been uphill from the get go. Not only that, but due to the tangles of bushes and low lying plants and tree roots, they could not walk in the normal way, instead having to lift their knees high, stepping where the rampant greenery dictated they could safely place their feet. It was exhausting, and after half an hour of it, Coyle breathlessly said that they should rest.

Finding a relatively clear spot, they sat down, Matthew slinging his pack off his back, sitting it on the ground and taking out a bottle of water, which he handed to Coyle. He reached in for another bottle, withdrew it, opened it and took a gulp.

"Oh, that tastes good," he sighed. Glancing back into the bag, he said, "I should have brought a machete instead of a kitchen knife."

"Would have been handy for getting through the woods, and for taking care of Corday. Unfortunately bloody great knives aren't something Sandra keeps around the house." Matthew chuckled, then his expression grew concerned.

"Are you going to be all right, Andrea? This is some difficult terrain, and we might have to trudge through it for a long while before we find anything."

"Wondering if the old bird is up to it, are you," smirked Coyle.

"I have absolutely no idea what your fitness level is like," he admitted. "But I do believe you will push yourself to find what we're looking for, to find Corday and deal with him, even when you know you shouldn't force yourself to go any further."

"Thank you for your concern, I appreciate it. To be honest I'm a little out of shape, and I know it. However, as you say, I will press on, though not to the detriment of my physical wellbeing. I've waited a long time to be able to impart to Martin the knowledge I have to give him, and I'd like to get the chance to do so. I will therefore do my best to ensure that I myself am not the reason I don't get said chance."

She took another swig, twisted the cap back onto the bottle, tossed it back into the backpack and got to her feet.

"Ready?"

Matthew smiled, put his own bottle back in the pack, stood and put the pack on.

"Let's go."

Fifteen minutes later the two of them had to put on gloves to use the vegetation as handholds to make their way up a steep incline. Matthew went first, and as she made her way behind him, Andrea lifted her head and her eyes fell upon Matthew's backside. Ingrained training made her look for the tell-tale signs that he might be about to look over his shoulder and catch her in the act. Safe for the moment, she admired the tight curve of his buttocks as they strained against the material of his trousers with every step he took. She graded them A+ and smiled. It had been quite some time since she had been with a man, but it seemed there was still a fire in the furnace. Maybe not the blaze of years gone by, evidently she was not yet done with thoughts of sex. It hadn't been something that had ever crossed her mind before, but now that it did she dropped her gaze from Matthew's backside and watched for possible obstacles as she thought about her body. When she had told Matthew she was out of shape, she had been referring to her endurance in terms of exercise, not her physical form, which, she thought with some degree of pleasure, was still in pretty good condition. And they said sex was one of the best forms of cardio vascular exercise, didn't they. An unbidden image flashed through her mind: her and Matthew, writhing semi naked on the ground, him on top, between her legs, thrusting as she sank her fingernails into those tight buttocks of his.

She shook her head. That kind of thing was not what she should be concentrating on at this precise moment. Though the picture was easily dismissed, the idea of indulging in a sexual relationship was not. It was quickly becoming something she was going to do, and as the idea solidified in her mind, she once again found herself staring at the posterior of the younger man ahead of her. The question of choice would not be an easy one for her. She did not interact with many people beyond those linked to The Order, though that in itself offered a great deal of men of all ages. It was reasonable to assume that one of them might be willing to help her satisfy her sexual urges. However from painful experience, Andrea knew that such relationships – even those of a no strings nature – could be dangerous and uncertain ground.

The idea also occurred to her that it might not be something completely without strings that she was looking for. Might a little romance not bring an extra something to her life?

It was here the Guardian truly rebuked herself and demanded that she focus on the task at hand. It was possible that Martin and Abigail's pairing, and her proximity of late to the two of them, was having an effect on her, but here and now was not the time to be thinking about it. She had obligations and their being fulfilled was more important than anything else. Andrea put all sexual and romantic thoughts to the back of her mind, promising herself that she would return to them when the current situation was resolved.

Assuming she survived said resolution.

Another twenty minutes passed. They reached the top of an incline and had a brief rest before starting off again. Neither of them mentioned it, but both were becoming worried that they had already passed by the destination given in Abigail's directions, that they had wandered too far off course, or that the shacks had collapsed and been swallowed by the wood. They had some light left, and they had the torches, but even using them it was not a good idea to go blundering through the woods, unsure if they were even on the right track.

Andrea glanced at her watch and prepared to tell Matthew that they would have to set themselves a deadline for when to turn back when he hissed out a single word.

"There!"

They both stopped and she followed his pointing finger to a clearing up ahead. The squat shapes of four dwellings, at least two of which canted badly to one side, could be made out. Andrea and Matthew quietly made their way to the edge of the clearing. They concealed themselves behind a large tree and observed the area for a few minutes. They detected no sounds or movement made by anything other than birds and woodland critters.

"What do you think?" whispered Matthew.

"I think he isn't here," she whispered back. "There have been no reports of any other women going missing from town, so he has no real reason to be here. Of course just because we haven't heard of any further kidnappings doesn't mean there haven't been any." She pursed her lips and her brow furrowed as she thought it through. "There's also a chance that the sick bastard might just make the trip up here to bask in the memory of past kills. But he feels safe up here, has no reason to be overly cautious." She looked at her companion. "We'll give it another couple of minutes and, if there are no signs he's around, we'll go and check." Matthew nodded and the two of them waited.

Andrea ruminated on the fact that they might still have to make the trip back with nothing to show for having come all the way out here. They had followed the directions and found the shacks, but there were no guarantees that one of these shacks had been the one Corday had used, if indeed he had used a shack at all.

The couple of minutes were over and there had been nothing to suggest there was anyone other than themselves present. Matthew asked her if she wanted her gun.

"Yes," she said uncertainly. "But since I've proved that in broad daylight, and at close range, I'm next to useless with the damn thing, it'll be for emergencies only." She asked for a torch and he handed one to her. She took the wide end in her hand and slapped the solid metal body of the device into her palm. "This I know how to use."

She took the gun, checked that the safety was on, and then put it in the pocket of her jacket. She watched as Matthew performed similar checks on his firearm.

"Ready," he announced.

"All right," she said, aware that her heart rate had increased. "We'll go to the far left first. We're looking for any indications that this is the place we're looking for."

"What kind of indications?"

"We'll know them if we see them. Now stay sharp. If you believe anyone is approaching, get back here quickly and quietly. No shooting unless you know you're shooting at the right man, and you're sure you're not going to miss. Understood?"

"Understood."

They made their way to the first shack. The ground leading to the laughable excuse for a front door showed no signs of having been disturbed by anything other than small paws for some time. A quick check around the outside of the decrepit structure also yielded nothing. Matthew looked through one of the gaping holes that had once presumably been filled with glass, but saw nothing of interest.

All of Andrea's fears about their having had a wasted journey vanished the moment she saw the ground around the second shack. There were clear drag marks in the dirt, and at least one clear footprint. They scrutinised the exterior of the shack, noting that boards had been placed over two of the windows. A quick check of the other two shacks showed that the second was the only one with the windows covered. Matthew examined the boards, informing Andrea that the wood was old but the nails holding them in place were new. He took out a torch and shone the light through a small gap, pressed his eye to another. After a few seconds he stood back, shaking his head.

"Can't see much."

"I can smell something though." She shone her torch at the wood under the window. It was criss-crossed with scratch marks. "Something was trying to get at whatever is making that smell. Looking for an easy meal I expect, though the bulk of what they were after is long gone. Let's make a check of the outside for wires or anything that might suggest some kind of security system, or even some kind of booby trap."

"You think he might have gone to that much trouble?"

"I don't know, but I'm taking no chances."

They made a circuit of the shack, going in opposite directions from one another to ensure a thorough search, but neither of them spotted anything that suggested an alarm or any other kind of deterrent. Meeting back at the window, Andrea told Matthew,

"I want you to stay out here."

"Why?"

"Your eyes and ears are better than mine; you'll have a better chance of hearing or seeing anyone coming. Plus I don't know what it's going to be like in there, but I doubt it'll be pretty, and you're not used to that sort of thing."

"You are?"

"No, but this is how it's going to be."

Without another word she took the torch from him, walked over to the door and gave it a gentle shove. It stayed put. She pushed harder, and this time the door opened a little. A third push was required before it opened far enough for her to get inside. She wanted to make a thorough search of the place, but deciding that they might not have the time for that, she made her way to the door she guessed accessed the first room with a covered window. This door opened easily enough, and she stepped inside.

The first breath she drew made her gorge want to rise, but she fought it down. The first thing the torch beam picked out was nearly her undoing. Andrea felt her legs wobble. She braced herself against the wall and closed her eyes, wanting to take a deep breath but fearful that inhaling so much of the air in here in one go really would make her sick. She took shallow breaths through her mouth and got herself under control. Pushing herself away from the wall, she stepped into the room and looked around.

There was nothing else in the room except the table and dried blood. It was on the floor, the walls, the table, as well as the four sets of shackles bolted to the table-top. At one end of the table Andrea also noticed several long strands of hair.

She made her way out into the hallway and went quickly to the next room. Here she found the bed, shackles at each corner, a small patch of dried blood roughly in the centre, smaller specks to the left and right at the top. Though there was far less blood here than in the other room, what she saw made her furious. Andrea's grip on the torch tightened and at that moment she wished more than anything that Andrew Corday was here in front of her right now. If it were so, nothing on earth would stop her from smashing his fucking skull in with the torch she held. She'd bring it down on his head until there was nothing left but mush, and then she'd piss on his remains before leaving them here to rot. Such was her fury that her thoughts spun out of control, and she imagined tracking down and eradicating all that remained of Corday's network of allies, putting an end to The Traitor once and for all.

When she came back to herself, she continued to look around the room, but found nothing other than a filthy towel. She checked the rest of the cabin but found nothing of interest. Andrea made her way back outside, where Matthew asked her what she had found. She handed the torch back to him and in a flat voice told him,

"This is where he brought them. He raped them and then he killed them." She walked away from the shack, stopped, turned back. "There might be evidence in there that could exonerate Martin, and for that reason alone I will leave it standing for the time being. But when this is all over and done with, I am going to come back here and burn this cursed little hovel to the ground. My wish is that I'll be able to put Corday in there first, still alive, with his arms and legs broken."

She turned away and headed into the woods. Matthew closed his eyes, murmuring a quick and quiet prayer before following her.

Chapter 44

About an hour after Coyle and Matthew left, Abigail, lying on the couch with her head in Martin's lap, fell asleep. Martin waited for ten minutes before gently lifting her head and getting off the couch, putting a cushion beneath her head before setting it back down. Abigail stirred and mumbled something, but quickly stilled and returned to whatever it was she was dreaming about. Martin hoped it was something pleasant. She deserved it given what reality had thrown at her in the last few days.

He stretched and then wandered out into the hallway. From there he went into the kitchen, where Sandra was examining the contents of the cupboards. She turned as he entered, smiled, and then said,

"My cupboards are kind of bare. I think we may be ordering in tonight."

Martin could think of nothing to say, so he just nodded. Sandra closed the cupboard door and approached him.

"You okay? You're not worried about Andrea and Matthew, are you?"

"No. Well, not yet. They haven't been gone that long, though I'm sure they can look after themselves if they run into trouble."

"You're worried about Abigail?"

"Very," he confirmed. "Specifically I'm worried about how all of this is going to affect her. She's a strong woman, but some of what's happened this last week or so, what with poor Sophie being killed, and being told about the memories and The Order and all that." He shrugged. "Everyone has their breaking point, and some people can put up with a lot before they go a bit loopy, but not everyone gets told there are several lifetimes worth of memories locked inside their head, and that some lunatic is out to kill them because of those memories."

"Those memories, and everything that goes with them, are a blessing, Martin. Unfortunately, they come with a price."

"But not one that Abigail and I agreed to pay."

"None of the ones chosen ever agreed to pay a price, Martin, but please bear in mind that a situation like yours and Abigail's has never occurred before. Normally all of this would have been revealed to you, for one reason or another, many years ago, in a safe and secure location. But after what Corday did at your ceremony we realised just how terrible a threat he was, how far he was willing to go. We did what we could, what we thought was right, and we'll continue to do so until he's caught or killed."

"You really think this could end with his being killed?"

"It's one of several possibilities."

"You think you could kill him?"

"Given what he's done, what he could do if left unchecked, I believe I could." Martin nodded.

"I believe I could too," he said.

"Taking someone's life is not something to be spoken of lightly, Martin."

"I'm perfectly serious. He's a murderer, and I truly believe he would follow me and Abigail to the ends of the earth to kill us. I won't have her live the rest of her life looking over her shoulder, fearful of everyone around her. She deserves far better than that."

Sandra grinned and nodded.

"I agree, but I doubt if she could meet a better man than you, Martin."

"Everyone has their good and bad points," he said, slightly abashed. "There will be better men than me out there, there will be worse. All I know for certain is that there are damn few who are as lucky. Everything that's happened to me recently, from being accused of murder, to being put in jail, to being beaten up and coming damn close to being bludgeoned to death, all of it was worth it. It was worth it because outside of all of that stuff there was Abigail. We may not have agreed to pay the price for our relationship, but as far as I'm concerned it's more than worth it."

"I've seen the way she looks at you when you're not looking," Sandra told him. "I'm certain she feels the same way." Martin smiled, and then thought of something.

"Do you have internet access?"

"Oh, yes. Wireless and everything. Feel free to use my computer."

"No, that's fine, thanks; I have my laptop. I need to check my e-mails."

He went back to the living room, going behind the couch where he had dumped his belongings earlier. Quietly, he opened his case and retrieved his laptop and charger. A few minutes later, after acquiring the password to connect to Sandra's wireless router, he logged in to his e-mail account and checked to see if any of his friends had replied. None of them had, but one e-mail had been received, from an address that he recognised only vaguely. It wasn't until he scrolled down and saw several old e-mails from the same address that he realised who it was: the owner of the cabin. With no small amount of apprehension, he opened the e-mail.

It made for a short, but depressing, read.

The owner started off by informing Martin in very colourful terms what she thought of him, and then told him that she intended to sue him for everything he had for desecrating her beautiful cabin. She ended her missive by assuring him that this was no empty threat, that she could not possibly live there, nor rent the place out, given what had happened there, and that she and her lawyer fully believed she should be compensated for the loss.

Martin thought briefly about replying to her, but realised that there was no way he could explain the truth of the situation to her. Instead he decided that this latest kick in the teeth was one best dealt with later, after other, more serious, problems had been dealt with. He shut down the laptop and sat it on the floor beside the chair, wincing at the various pains this action produced. Sitting up straight, he relaxed and stared at Abigail. He was wondering if it would be possible to lie down on the couch beside her without waking her when he dozed off.

Just over an hour later, he opened his eyes and lifted his chin from his chest, hissing as his neck cracked and pain lanced up and down his spine and across his shoulders. Looking across at the couch, he saw Abigail begin to wake. Martin stood up, wincing again as numerous joints popped, and crossed to the couch.

"Hello, sleepyhead," he said, smiling down at Abigail. She blinked and looked up, focussed on him, and returned the smile.

"What time is it?"

"A little before five."

"Have they come back yet?"

"I don't know."

Abigail pushed herself into a sitting position and wiped at her eyes.

"Let's go find out," she said, holding out her hands. Martin took them and helped her up off the couch. They hugged and then went out into the hallway. "Sandra?"

"Yes?" came the reply from upstairs. Hurried footfalls followed and she appeared at the top of the stairs, concern on her face. "Is everything all right?"

"Yeah, we were just wondering if Andrea and Matthew were back yet."

"Not yet," they were told as Sandra started down the stairs. "I'm trying to decide if I should be worried or not."

No sooner were the words out of her mouth than the front door opened and Andrea entered, Matthew behind her. Neither of them said a word. Andrea went straight to the living room, and Matthew closed the front door and followed her. Martin, Abigail and Sandra looked at one another, shrugged, and then entered the living room to find the two sitting side by side on the couch, their heads bowed. Moments passed as the three of them tried to work out if the obvious dark mood hanging over the pair was the result of failure or success.

"Did you find it?" Martin asked eventually. Coyle lifted her head.

"We found it."

"Did anything happen?" This from Abigail.

"I went inside," Coyle replied. "Suffice it to say that it was utterly horrific. I wanted to destroy the place, but I didn't. It may help Martin in the future; there's a good chance Corday's fingerprints or DNA are in there. But I've made myself a promise that someday I will go back there and burn it to the ground, and that's a promise I intend to keep."

"You're upset," stated Sandra. Coyle shifted her gaze to look at her old friend, and shook her head.

"I am furious beyond anything I've ever known. With Corday, and with myself. I should never have assumed that he would remain in Berrybeck until…"

"Are you, or are you not, my Guardian?"

Struck by the uncharacteristically harsh tone of Martin's voice, Coyle looked at him with surprise. His expression surprised her more: furrowed brow and eyebrows slanting in towards the bridge of his nose. He was angry. He repeated the question and she nodded.

"You are supposed to help me, guide me, advise me, and presumably, you're supposed to pay close attention to anything I say?"

"Yes," she confirmed uncertainly, wondering where he was going with this.

"Then do not start down the road of blaming yourself for all this. We do not have the bloody time for you to get maudlin over what you perceive to be your own failures. You're a Guardian, so act like it. Later, you can have a complete and utter breakdown, but right now I need you to keep your head together, because I am relying on you to get Abigail and me out of this and ensure we live long and happy lives together."

Not having taken a breath, he wheezed the last word out and then sucked in air, but he did not take his gaze from his old teacher, who stared at him, eyebrows raised. When they came down a little, she asked,

"How do you know that I was going to blame myself?"

"Look me in the eye and tell me you weren't," he challenged her. A ghost of a smile crossed her lips. She nodded slowly a couple of times.

"You're quite right, of course, Martin. Thank you. I cannot afford the luxury of guilt right now, but if I get out of this alive, you owe me a couple of months of sessions with a good psychiatrist."

"If I can't find one, I'll get myself a degree and counsel you myself," he responded. "Now we know where he's been killing these women. What do we do with that information?"

Coyle regarded her former pupil for a few moments, marvelling that the young innocent boy she had helped with his mathematics problems all those years ago had become the fine man she saw now. It was possible that the memories of having been his teacher were the cause of the slight irritation she felt now at the way he had spoken to her. However, his words had been well meant. He had seen she was headed down a dark road, the wrong road, and he had blocked her way.

"Please," she said, indicating the other chairs. "The three of you take a seat."

Abigail, Martin and Sandra all sat down.

"As far as the shack in the woods is concerned," Coyle began. "The sooner we get the authorities out there, the better. One of us will make an anonymous call giving the directions. Sandra I think would be best; there's a slim chance Abigail's voice might be recognised by whoever takes the call. Matthew's, Martin's and my own accents are all too distinctive.

"When Corday realises that his… *lair* has been found, which will happen either when he goes up there himself and finds that someone forced their way in, or when word spreads around town about what the police will find when they get there, he will be incensed. He's already angry now, having been stopped from getting that girl in the park and from doing away with myself, Martin and the sheriff, so losing the shack might just push him over the edge. Now that's a good thing and a bad thing."

"Good because he won't be thinking straight," Abigail broke in. "Which in turn might make him slip up, maybe get him caught."

"Quite right, Abigail," Coyle told her.

"Bad," said Sandra quietly. "Because he might just throw caution to the winds and attack, not caring if he gets caught or not."

"Unfortunately, that's also correct," Coyle confirmed. "The worst of it is that we simply don't know, and have no way to predict, which it will be. That's assuming it is one of those scenarios; he might do something completely unexpected."

Silence descended for a few minutes, and then Martin spoke, saying two words which confused everyone else in the room.

"The carnival." The others exchanged puzzled glances.

"What about it?" asked Abigail.

"That's where we get him," said Martin, clearly expecting this to be explanation enough. The perplexed faces around him were proof to the contrary. "Corday will realise who told the police where the shack was and, as we've said, he's going to be pissed off, but he's not going to lose control; he's going to give it some thought. I think he'll decide that the best place to get us will be at the celebrations. Big crowd, lots of cover; he'll think it'll be child's play.

"But we'll be watching for him, waiting for him, and in whatever way possible we get the bastard."

"Are you nuts?" blurted Abigail. "You want us to set ourselves up as bait?" He turned to face her.

"Abi, purely because of who we are, we're already bait to him. We're the ones he wants, and he will follow us wherever we go until he gets us. Isn't it better that we're the ones laying the trap?"

"It's not much of a trap, Martin," commented Matthew.

"I know it's not. I know I sound like a character in a bad horror film, the one where the audience all say "Oh, he's a dick! You just know his plan is going to go horribly wrong!" I've watched enough of those movies, criticised those very characters, but we've got to bring this to an end."

"But if we do as you've suggested, we can't guarantee whose end it will be," Sandra pointed out.

"We can't guarantee that anyway," said Abigail softly. "Maybe the police will find something up at the cabin that gets Marty off the hook, and maybe after that they decide he can leave town. So we run, and Corday follows us. We lose him, we're safe for a while, he finds us again, we run again. And over and over and over. That's no kind of life. It's sure as hell not the life I want to have with Marty, always looking over our shoulders, never able to relax.

"The carnival works for him because it affords him cover, allows him to blend into the crowd. But by now pretty much everyone in town will know what he looks like because of the posters. We'll all be looking out for him, and he'll be looking out for, Marty and I especially. One of you guys will watch each of us, and the other can be a floating point, watching for Corday."

"And when we see him?" asked Matthew.

"Your second option is to find a cop and point Corday out, and your third is to cause a fuss and draw attention to him."

"What's the first option?" asked Andrea.

"If at all possible," said Martin in a low voice. "Kill him."

There was a brief silence, and then Abigail turned to him.

"Marty, I don't know if I could..." He took her hand and said,

"You won't have to worry about it. You'll be with me, and if we spot him, I'll take care of it. I'm not trying to be macho or anything, but if we get the chance to end this bastard, we can't pass it up."

"You really think you could kill a man?"

"In cold blood, Matthew, no, I don't think I could. But this man means to kill me. More importantly he means to kill Abigail. If I get the chance to permanently remove that threat, I will take it."

"You need to be sure about this, Martin," Coyle told him. "And to be honest, I don't know if you could..."

"None of us here are like him," Abigail interjected. "Despite who we're talking about killing, no one in this room can really say they'd do it, even if the opportunity arose. But let's not kid ourselves; it's him or us."

Martin gazed at her, again amazed by her strength. She turned to look at him and smiled, and he knew that there was nothing he would not do for her. Killing someone like Corday would be a small price to pay for the time he would spend with her. Martin thought for a moment that it was possible committing such an act against someone like Corday wouldn't even trouble his conscience, but decided that that was something he'd have to wait and see about.

"How do we know he's going to decide we'll be at the carnival?" asked Sandra.

"We don't," said Coyle honestly. "But he wants this ended as much as we do, and although he won't know for sure that we'll be there, he's got to know it'll be his best chance." She paused, drew in a deep breath. "Okay, so we have a plan. I can't say I'm thrilled with it, but unless we can come up with something better..."

"Why can't we just give him to the police?" Everyone turned to look at Matthew. "I mean it. This plan may be all we have, but that doesn't mean it's a good one. There are god alone knows how many variables we can't take into account, any number of things that could go wrong that might result in one or more of us not coming back alive, and even if we all do, there's no guarantee that we'll have accomplished what we set out to do. But we know where this guy lives, and we know where his little shack is out there in the woods. Why don't we just give the police what we know and let them deal with it? It's not as though he's going to spill the beans about The Order, and even if he did they'd just think he was mad. His Brannon identity still holds up. He changed his face, but he can't have changed his fingerprints or his DNA. We hand him to the cops, give them the location of the shack, and watch it all fall into place. We can even smile and wave at the bastard as he's carted off."

"Matthew," said Sandra. "You said yourself that there are a number of things we can't know, can't anticipate. We also can't be sure that there is anything in that shack that ties Corday to it. We know he didn't expect anyone to find it, but he may have taken precautions just the same. And we know he won't have anything lying around that house that incriminates him. If we give his address and the location of the shack to the sheriff and his men, they may investigate and turn up nothing that proves Corday is guilty."

"Sandra is right, Matthew," said Coyle. "Letting them know the location of the shack is one thing. They know the victims weren't killed at the cabin. Tests will confirm that that shack is where those poor women died. Hopefully there will also be something that takes Martin out of the frame and puts Corday in it, but we can't hang our hopes on that possibility.

Direct action is needed, dangerous though it may be. And to tell you the truth, I'd rather see Corday dead than in prison, that way no one will ever have to worry about him again."

"There is one thing," Sandra began reluctantly. Coyle, clearly tired, turned to look at her. "Um, say Corday does come at one of us and we do manage to put a stop to him. How do we deal with the police? I mean, you, Matthew and I will all have guns, so we get close enough, we can shoot him. Now, in my case, I am a US citizen, my gun is legal and I can say I had it on me for protection because of the murders, but if it's you or Matthew who does the deed…"

"We may have to deal with the consequences of that later," was Coyle's response.

"Speaking of guns," said Abigail. "Do you have any spares you could give me and Marty?"

"No," Coyle told her. "But to be honest I'm not sure I want you two running around with guns anyway. One of us ending up in trouble with the law is one thing, but after all this I want you and Martin to be able to go on with your lives unimpeded, which means neither one of you going to prison."

"We could get them stun guns," suggested Matthew. "Tasers. Something tells me if there's anywhere near here that sells such things, they're going to be doing a booming business in the next day or two." Coyle nodded her agreement.

Doreen Spellner was packing up. She had received a text message from a "friend" of hers who had told their circle that she had some juicy information regarding the recent murders, and invited them all round to hear it. Normally Doreen would have been excited by this, but given her position within the sheriff's department, she would have learned of any new developments - any real, bona fide, true developments – in the case, and so she was certain that her "friend" was just trying to score points. Points she was looking forward to wiping off the board by proclaiming whatever she was told to be complete hogwash, and that if such information were real, it would have already been mentioned somewhere within her place of work and so have been picked up by her bat-like ears.

She glanced at the clock and realised that she was already a few minutes late in leaving, meaning she would likely be late for the meeting. She started to shut down her computer and then heard her phone vibrating in her drawer. She took it out and answered the call.

"Hi, Marie. Yes, I got the message. Oh, honey, she's talking bull; we both know that if anything had broken in the case, yours truly would have heard about it first."

Doreen took the time to reassure her friend that when it came to hot gossip in Hannerville, Spellner was still the one to beat. The minutes ticked by and Doreen realised this was going to be a lengthy conversation. As her friend talked, Doreen packed up, and was just rising from her seat when the phone on her desk rang. She thought about not answering it, then decided that she had better.

"Marie, hang on a second honey, I just have to answer the phone."

She sat her mobile on her desk and answered the landline.

"Hello, sheriff's department."

A hushed voice informed Doreen that it had some information regarding the murders. It then quickly began to relate that information. Doreen asked who was speaking, but the voice simply kept going. Doreen listened to what was said, scrabbling around her desk for a pen and some paper. By the time she had located those items, the caller had hung up. Doreen put the phone down and quickly scribbled down what she could recall of the information. It wasn't the first of such calls to have come in today, providing a possible location for the killer. Doreen had made mental notes of all the information she had taken down and passed on, but nothing had come of any of it, or else she would have heard. This latest information was likely to be just as much of a dead end as the others, not really worth bothering the sheriff about so late in the day. Besides, the voice calling her name from her mobile phone reminded her that she had a meeting to attend, and a liar to take down a peg or two.

She put the note in her desk drawer, and stuck a note to her screen to remind her to pass the information on first thing tomorrow morning. She got up, grabbed her phone and assured her friend that she was on her way.

"Job done," said Sandra as she came back into the lounge.

"What did they say?" asked Martin.

"It was that Spellner woman I spoke to," she told him. "Or spoke at rather. I just gave her the information and hung up."

"Good," said Coyle, yawning and stretching. "I suggest we all get a little rest for an hour or two. Then we'll get together and get things organised for tomorrow night."

Chapter 45

Long before he walked into the mayor's office, Flaghan became convinced he was on a fool's errand. Be that as it may, he also knew he had to give it a shot.

"Sheriff," Mayor Harold Ashby greeted him a little coldly. Obviously still smarting from having had to accept the release of their only suspect, the mayor was displeased with the lack of progress made in finding the killer. That was one of the reasons the sheriff was sure his words were going to fall on deaf ears. "Take a seat."

Flaghan closed the door, crossed the room and eased himself into a chair.

"Any news to report at all on the case?" asked Ashby, though he must surely have known there was not, or else Flaghan would have called instead of coming to see him in person. The sheriff shook his head.

"We're doing what we can, sir, but the case is why I've come to see you." Ashby raised his eyebrows in query. "I'd like you to consider cancelling the carnival."

To his surprise, the mayor did not burst out laughing at the idea. He actually seemed to be mulling it over, and for a few moments Flaghan thought that this visit might not turn out to be a waste of time after all.

"I'd be lying if I said I hadn't thought about it, Mark." The mayor took a deep breath and let it out slowly. "But it can't be done. The carnival means too much to the town. It's cost us a small fortune and we have to recoup that, and you know yourself that the vast majority of that money will be made the night of the carnival itself."

"You're right, I do know that, but..." The mayor held up his hands.

"Mark, please, I know you're thinking that I'm a stuffed shirt more concerned with the town's finances than with the townspeople's safety, but I assure you that's not the case." He clasped his hands together and rested them in his lap. "I'll be at the carnival, my wife and my children will be at the carnival, as will my friends, just as we've been every year of our lives. Every hotel in town is booked solid, crowded out by people from neighbouring towns and counties who come here every year to be with friends or family, or just because we always put on a world class party. Hell, Mark, the Hanner Carnival is bigger than Christmas to some people in Hannerville. Folks are already scared and depressed; cancelling the festival now would only make matters worse."

"But a massive outdoor party is the perfect hunting ground for this bastard. We're serving up victims on a plate."

"Have you organised the usual extra manpower?"

"And then some, but more cops on the street is no guarantee that this sick fucker won't try something."

"I heard someone mention earlier something about a sketch?"

Mentally cursing his receptionist, Flaghan recounted for the mayor what had happened when he had taken Muir and Coyle up to the cabin. When he was finished, Ashby gave his considered opinion on the man who was most likely their killer.

"Ballsy son of a bitch, isn't he. Attacking the sheriff in broad daylight. And Muir took off after this guy?" Flaghan nodded.

"Idiot could have gotten himself killed. Was nothing but dumb luck I regained consciousness. Just dumb bad luck I was too dazed to shoot straight."

"Well, you saved a man's life, so there's some consolation. Maybe this Muir isn't the monster we thought he was." His gaze dropped to his desktop, and a pensive expression crossed his face. When he looked back up he said, "Or maybe it was all a setup to throw us off the track."

"I don't believe so; I saw the state Muir was in afterwards. He was shaken, badly. Impulse made him go after that guy, and I think when he thought back on it he realised just how stupid he'd been. Plus I saw part of their fight, and it was no put on. Muir took some knocks. Even then, whilst I was trying to aim straight, he threw a rock and caught the killer right in the balls with it. How the fucker managed to clamber over those rocks and swim away I'll never know."

"You searched the place for clues?"

"Yeah. Nothing of interest."

"Shame. Anyway, you got two good descriptions and a sketch was made up?"

"Yes. I've got men putting notices up all over town right now."

"Excellent," Ashby said with a smile. "So people know who to look out for."

"They're not going to be looking out for anyone, mayor," the sheriff argued. "They're going to be out for a good time."

"Everyone knows what's happened," Ashby said in a placating manner, every inch the politician now. "They all know about the horror that has visited this little town of ours. Yes, they're looking for the chance to forget about it for a while, to let their hair down and have a party, but they will be vigilant all the same. We have to assume the killer will find out about the sketch on the notices, and that he'll realise he will have every pair of eyes in this town looking out for him. Do you really think that, knowing that, he'd chance venturing out into a big party?"

"Mayor, we can't possibly predict what this guy will do."

"No, but we know what the town will do," Ashby said with conviction, determined to win over his audience of one. "It will pull together. The carnival does that; it brings them together. I believe that in the midst of tragedy, *because* of tragedy, that bond will be made stronger. I'd even be willing to bet that, if we organised a poll and asked people to vote to keep or cancel the festival, they'd vote to keep it. They need it to prove to themselves that they can go on. They need it to prove to this killer that he cannot break them."

Flaghan felt like telling him to shut up and get down off his god damn soap box, but he also realised the mayor was right. He didn't like it, but he couldn't deny it. To some, a huge party being held in light of recent events might seem disrespectful, but the victims had lived here all their days, had most likely attended this carnival every year with their families and friends. The sheriff considered the mayor's idea of a poll, and found himself thinking that the most vocal opponents of cancelling the carnival might well be the families and friends of the victims. The carnival was normal, and a good dose of normal couldn't be bad.

Still, Flaghan was ill at ease with the idea of the killer mingling with the crowd, a piranha in a river full of little fish.

"I understand," he said finally, rising from his chair. He extended a hand, which the mayor shook. "Thanks for your time, mayor." He tried to release the mayor's hand, but the mayor tightened his grip. Surprised, Flaghan looked at their joined hands, and then at the mayor, who was staring at him intently. In a hushed tone he said,

"I love this town, Mark, make no mistake about that. What happened to those girls, the idea that it could have been one of my own daughters, chills me to the fucking bone. Now you can tell anyone you like about what I'm going to say to you, and although I think most would agree with me, I will deny it with my dying breath.

"If this man shows up at the festival and he is caught, he will be tried, he will be convicted and he will serve his time in prison, which is all well and just." The mayor leaned forward and lowered his voice further. "But if it comes to it, he could just as easily serve his time in hell."

Slightly stunned by the possible meaning of the mayor's words, Flaghan nodded and Ashby released his hand. The sheriff turned and walked out of the office and out of the building, heading for his cruiser. He got in, put the key in the ignition, but then just sat behind the wheel for a minute or two. Again he was forced to concede that Ashby was probably right, that most people would prefer to see the killer on a slab than in a cell. Had the mayor been telling him to execute the killer if he got the chance? Flaghan shook his head. Ashby was a good man; his words had probably come from a place of fear for his family, for his town. He was angry at what had happened, and people said things they didn't mean when they were angry. Then again there had been that "if it comes to it" part, and the fact that Ashby had said he would deny having said anything if ever asked. Starting the engine, the sheriff decided that the mayor had been wasting his breath.

Mark Flaghan would have had no qualms about putting this animal down this afternoon if he'd been able. Likewise, if it came to it during the carnival, or at any time in the future for that matter, he would not hesitate to pull the trigger.

Chapter 46

Martin and Abigail were resting in their room when Mayor Ashby's belief about how the citizens of Hannerville felt about the Hanner Carnival bit Abigail right on the ass.

As they lay watching but not really seeing the sit-com episode that was on, her phone rang. Digging it out of her pocket, she checked the display to see who was calling.

"It's Beth," she told Martin, who reached for the remote and turned the TV volume down. Abigail thanked him and answered the call.

"Hey, hon," said Beth. "How you doing?"

"I'm fine. I was going to call later to make sure everything was going all right at the store."

"It's all good, Abigail. Everything is under control. Business could be better, mind you, but it could be worse too."

"Hey, get your own insightful phrases about running a store and stop using mine." Her friend laughed.

"I was just calling to find out what your plans are for tomorrow night."

I'm going to go out to the festival to put into action a half assed plan to catch a raving lunatic!

It pained her to lie to her friend, but she told herself that needs must.

"I don't think I'm going to go this year. What with everything that's happened, plus the fact they still haven't caught this guy yet..."

"Abigail, tell me you're joking."

"What?"

"I can't believe that you're willing to lie down to this bastard!"

"I'm sorry?"

"This festival has been a part of our lives since birth. We were carried around it as babies, we went as kids, ate too much candy and yelled to go on every ride, and we went as teenagers and made out with guys on the big wheel. Every year of our adult lives we have gone to that festival and had a good time together: you, me, Amanda and Sophie. Remember the year the power went out? Everybody just hooked up generators and lit candles and kept going. The year it rained? We looked up at the clouds, laughed in their face and kept on going."

"But this is different, Beth," Abigail said, hoping the emotion that was threatening tears was not also detectible in her voice. "This guy, he's a maniac. And Sophie..."

"Yes, she is," said Beth, her emotions very clear. Abigail's tears began as her friend continued. "She is dead and gone, but she will not be forgotten. She was so excited about you and Marty getting together that she barely mentioned it this year, but any other year Sophie would have always been going on about the carnival. What time are we going? What are we wearing? The girl got stiff nipples just thinking about riding that god damn roller coaster!" She sobbed. "Whoever this guy is, whoever this stinking, rotten, sick, demented bastard is who took her away from us, he can go and suck the devil's dick in hell! There is no way I am not going to that party this year. I may not have a good time. In fact it's pretty much a foregone conclusion that I'm just going to wander around blubbing and screwing up everyone else's good time, but I'm still going. I'm going for Sophie. I'm going to drink too much booze and eat too many burgers and hot dogs, and ride that coaster till I throw up, and I'm going to pretend that dippy little girl is right there with me. Dangerous? Very likely. Stupid? Almost definitely, but I am going to be there."

She stopped and Abigail, the tears running slowly down her cheeks, listened to her friend putting down the phone, blowing her nose and trying to calm herself. Abigail focussed, running through her head the various ways in which she could convince her friend to not go to the carnival. Short of knocking her out and tying her to a chair, there were none.

And why shouldn't she go? asked an aggravated voice in Abigail's head. *She's right: Sophie loved the carnival, and as her friends we should be there this year if for no other reason than to say goodbye to her.*

But it's not that simple. I know who's going to be there, what he wants to do. He'll use anyone, go through anyone, to get to me, but I can't explain that to Beth. She's going to go no matter what, so maybe it's better if she's with me. If I see Corday coming I can get her out of the way, and if not, I'll be so near at hand the fucker will make straight for me.

She heard the receiver at the other end being picked up.

"It's not stupid," she said before Beth could say anything. "You're right, we should be there."

"You sure," Beth sniffed. "I came across a little strong there, hon. I don't want you to feel pressured or anything."

"I don't. One thing though."

"What's that?"

"I'm bringing Marty with me."

"Oh, that's cool. Sophie really liked him. If she were still here she'd have wanted him there with us. Amanda and I will come get you guys around four tomorrow afternoon?"

"Okay." She remembered where she was and realised the difficulty she would have in explaining why she wasn't staying at her house. "Oh, no, wait, Beth. I think Marty was planning on taking me out for dinner, so we'll just meet you guys at the store at four."

"That's fine. We'll see you then, hon."

"See you soon."

Martin had guessed at the nature of the conversation, but before he could even begin asking questions, Abigail was making another call.

"Uncle Peter? Hi. How are you?" She listened for a few moments. "And Aunt Janine, she's okay? Good. Listen, are you guys planning on going to the celebrations tomorrow night?" Her face twisted with anguish as she listened to the reply. "Me? Uh, yeah, the girls are going, and Marty's coming along too. Yeah, that's about what Beth said too." Pause as she listened to her uncle speak. "I am a little concerned; I think most are, but as you say, the town isn't going to let this guy win. Okay, well, we're going to all meet at the store... Yes, my store. We're all going to meet around four o'clock, so we'll see you and Aunt Janine there, yeah? Okay, good. See you tomorrow, Uncle Peter. Bye."

She hung up and started to rise, wiping the last of the tears from her face.

"Where are you going?" Martin asked, concerned.

"We need to talk to Andrea and the others," she told him. "We need to revise our plans for tomorrow night."

"Abi, wait," Martin caught her arm and eased her back down. "Tell me what was said."

"It's not going to work, Marty," she said, her voice cracking and becoming a choked sob as she spoke his name. "When we were discussing it last night, it didn't even dawn on me that Beth and Amanda might want to go. I thought they would give it a miss because of what happened, but that's the reason they're going." Martin nodded thoughtfully.

"I remember you mentioning a few times that Sophie always got really excited when carnival time came round."

"Beth sees going this year as a kind of tribute, and she isn't put off by the thought that there might be a killer in the middle of it all. Uncle Peter and Aunt Janine think the same; they think that if no one goes then it would be like letting the killer win, and they're not about to do that. According to what he said, most of their friends feel the same way." She drew in a shuddering breath. "None of them understand what he is, Marty. They think whoever killed Sophie and those other women will run away in the face of a town united. They don't get what this bastard is really after. Oh, Christ, it's awful to say it, but I thought I could go through with this when I didn't really know any of the people who might be hurt. But my friends and family are going to be there, Marty. If they're off in the crowd he can get to them before we know it, and if they're beside us they might get hurt when he comes for us. We don't have enough people who know what we're up against to make this work."

She broke down and threw herself into his arms, pressing her face against his chest as she cried. Martin held her gently, his head bowed, her hair brushing his face. He closed his eyes and tried to think of something to say that could comfort her, but unfortunately she was right. When with him and Abigail, Beth, Amanda and Abigail's aunt and uncle would be in the crosshairs, liable to be hurt during any attack Corday made. Separated from them, they would be easy prey. That it was perhaps the only assurance he could offer did not make it any easier to say.

"Abi," he whispered. "Am I right in thinking that there's nothing we could say to them that would make them change their minds about going?" Amidst the sobs he made out a nod. "Then all we can do is hope, because if they're determined to go, they're going to be in danger whether they're with us or not. All we can do is hope that we get Corday before he gets anyone else."

She made no reply and he fell silent, holding her a little tighter than before. He wondered if perhaps she was right, and that they should call the whole thing off. It was tempting, but he knew that if everyone else was going, Abigail would be there too, and if she was there, he would be there by her side. The plan wouldn't change at all really; there would just be a few more unwitting players on the field now.

Abigail eventually stopped crying. Martin stroked her hair and waited to hear what she had to say.

"No fucking around tomorrow night," she said suddenly. "We go to this thing, we find Corday and we deal with him, quickly and quietly. I will be damned if that bastard is getting near anyone else I love."

Not long after, Martin, Abigail, Andrea, Sandra and Matthew all sat around the table. Abigail had told everyone about the phone call and they had all said much the same as Martin. After that silence had fallen, and had held sway for a good five minutes now. It was fairly obvious from everyone's manner that the rest Coyle had suggested earlier had not come easy, if indeed it had come at all. Eventually Abigail said,

"Can we address the elephant in the room and admit we're all scared shitless?"

There was a visible relaxing in the posture of everyone there. Shoulders slumped and heads lowered slightly, insincere grins faded and fidgeting ceased.

"Thank you, Abigail," Coyle said sincerely. "You're quite right, we are all scared, and we should be. I don't have a cure for fear, but I do know that stewing in it won't do any of us any good. All we can do is try to find a way to deal with it. If it makes any of you feel any better, I believe we are safe here. Corday might well know about this house, but I don't believe he'd risk attacking us here, not on our turf."

"I'm reluctant to bring this up," began Sandra. "But it occurred to me: what do we do if we don't get Corday at the carnival? What if we don't find him at all, or if we find him but he escapes?"

"That had occurred to me as well," Matthew said, nodding. "There is a slim chance that, given the potential size of the crowd tomorrow night, he won't find us and we won't find him."

"That being the case, I don't think we'll have any choice but to attack him at his house," Coyle told them. "Last ditch attempt to take him down. I hope it doesn't come to that because such an undertaking holds the possibility of ending up a terrible mess."

"How so?" asked Martin

"Because I'd have to call in reinforcements. I've resisted the temptation to call in other members of The Order, as well as some outside contractors, but if we don't get him tomorrow night, I will call them in. We go to his house, we tear it to shreds, him along with it, and we all leave before anyone realises what's happened. It'll be a mystery that will never be solved, but it will take care of our problem."

"So why is that our backup plan?" Abigail asked. "How could it turn into a mess?"

"We could attack and Corday might not be there. If he is he might evade capture or death. If, for whatever reason, he is not caught or killed, he'll call in his own back-up and turn this town into a war zone. As I said I've resisted calling for any other help in the hope of avoiding that, but if tomorrow night doesn't go as I hope…"

She let the sentence trail off, shrugged, lifted her mug and sipped her tea.

Martin regarded her for a few moments, realising how tired she looked. It was difficult for him to imagine the stress she was under. He didn't really have a clue what her job, if it could be called that, with The Order entailed, but from what he'd heard he doubted it was anything like this.

"Could everyone give Miss Coyle and I a minute or two please," he said before he had even realised he was going to. The others looked at one another and then got up from the table. Martin turned to Abigail and gave her a reassuring smile. "Won't be long, I promise."

Andrea sat back in her chair and regarded her former pupil with curiosity. He looked right back at her, his expression vague.

"Is it safe to say that the Guardians of the Bearers are the top of the tree when it comes to The Order?"

"I suppose if you had to pick someone who was in charge it would be the Guardians, yes."

"And so when you ended up in charge of The Order things were a mess, but then you got it all straightened out and it all ran like clockwork for a very long time. You didn't have a great deal to worry about. Now there's a big, nasty spanner in the works and you feel like it's your job to deal with it."

"It is," Coyle stated matter-of-factly. Martin nodded.

"Maybe so, Miss Coyle, but you've already admitted that this kind of thing isn't in your usual remit. You're obviously tired, probably stressed and…"

Coyle opened her mouth to tell him that she was absolutely fine, but then Martin finished his sentence with,

"… I'm worried about you."

She closed her mouth, and in her mind's eyes she suddenly saw two Martin Muir's sitting across from her. One was the young boy she had taught all those years ago, and the other the man he had become. For the first time in god alone knew how many years, she felt tears prickle the corners of her eyes. She could think of nothing to say.

"I get the impression that a Guardian is supposed to be solid, unflappable, the person to whom a Bearer can turn when they need someone to lend them strength. But who does the Guardian turn to, Miss Coyle? In times like this, when it's all on your shoulders, who are you supposed to look to for help, for guidance, for reassurance? Yourself? You do that often enough and you'll either become completely cut off from everyone else, or you'll drive yourself mad."

"I've had Sandra to talk to."

"As a friend, yes, but not as counsel in circumstances like this. You've taken on something that's almost military in its makeup, and you are not a military leader. You're making plans, deciding on tactics, trying to rally your troops, but that's not something you're used to doing. Look me right in the eye right now and tell me you're not feeling the strain."

She did not. She could not, not without lying, and she would not lie to Martin. He nodded.

"Thank you for not bullshitting me. You're not alone in this, Miss Coyle. I won't let you be, because when all this is over and done with, I'm going to need you to sit me down and explain, in great detail, why Abi and I have had to go through all of this. To be honest I still don't quite understand it, or know if I believe what I think I do understand. You'll have your work cut out for you when that conversation comes, but for now you have a job to do, and you're doing it as well as anyone could. I thank you for that. But you've got to realise that you cannot keep pushing yourself indefinitely. At some point you're going to hit the wall. That means Abi and I will be left with Sandra and Matthew to help us. Now I mean no disrespect to them by that; they both seem very capable of taking care of us, teaching us, but who do you think they draw the vast majority of their strength from?"

He paused a moment and then concluded.

"I don't know if you're bound by an oath or something to do anything I tell you to do. If you are then this is an order. If not, then it's some good advice from a friend: get some rest, proper rest, several hours of it. Try to sleep. If you can't, exercise until you're so bloody tired you can't keep your eyes open. Or watch the most boring show you can find on TV. Just rest. Recharge."

Coyle was quiet for a long moment, and then she said,

"I'm not bound by anything to automatically do whatever anyone tells me to do." She rose from her chair and walked around to stand beside Martin's. He looked up and she looked down at him, smiling warmly. "But, just as soon as Matthew is on his way to pick up what we need for tomorrow night, I will heed the advice of a friend." She leaned down and kissed him on the cheek. "Thank you, Martin."

She went back to her seat and sat down, then called out, telling the others that they could come back in. Abigail, Sandra and Matthew filed back in and took their seats. They made a show of sipping their lukewarm drinks and appearing nonplussed about having been asked to leave. Martin's eyes flitted from one to the other, and the only one who met his gaze was Abigail, who looked at him with adoration written all over her face.

"So you all listened in then," he said. The response was a chorus of very unconvincing murmurs. Martin chuckled and shook his head.

"You're a good guy," Matthew told him. Martin nodded in acknowledgement of the compliment, and then Andrea started going over the plan.

Half an hour later, with Matthew off to the nearest mall to collect some supplies, Martin sat on the couch, trying to concentrate on the film they were watching. But his thoughts kept veering back towards the subject of tomorrow night. He knew that if he allowed them to do so, he would go over and over it in his mind and eventually call a halt to the whole thing. Despite knowing that it was as good a shot as they were ever going to get at Corday (and vice versa, though he didn't like acknowledging that), part of Martin wanted to just take Abigail, pack their stuff into a car and take off. If the law wanted to pursue him, fine. If their Guardians wanted to chase them, fine. If Corday came looking for them, murder weapon in hand, fuck it, they'd find a way to deal with it. Anything seemed preferable to sitting on this couch, in this nice little house, waiting for time to pass until they went out to see whether or not they could kill Corday before he killed all of them.

Abigail came back from the bathroom and lay down on the couch, her head on his leg. She asked him if she had missed anything important and he told her no. She nodded and watched the film.

Martin looked down at her, willing his memory to record in great detail every aspect of the moment. The quiet of the house, the smell of Sandra's living room, the weight of Abigail's head on his leg, the cadence of her breathing, each line and curve of her face, the placement of every hair on her head. He studied the way her hands lay, clasped gently together at her midsection, the way her legs were drawn up slightly. He breathed in the scent of her shampoo, and the slightly fainter aroma of her perfume. His eyes widened a little as he realised he still hadn't asked what kind it was she used, and he told himself to remember to ask her. It seemed he was asking a lot of his memory, but given all the things he had forgotten over the years, he reasoned there was plenty of space in there to store one question plus this tiny section of his life so that in the future he could recall everything about it with complete clarity.

Tomorrow night, if it dawns on me that I don't have long left to live, this is where I'll come back to. Not to any of our firsts, like letters, pictures, meeting, kissing and loving, but to here. I'll come back here and remember that I've never felt like this about anybody else in my life, and that if this is where I am at the end of it, then I'll be as happy as I've ever been in my life, just watching you.

Martin swallowed the lump in his throat and realised that only now was he considering that he might not make it back. He felt tears and realised he was not about to cry over thoughts of his death, but over thoughts of being parted from Abigail. Blinking the tears away, he took in a deep breath and let it out, ignoring the gentle tremor in his chest as he exhaled. If his death was what it took to save Abigail, he told himself, then that's what it would take. He just hoped that if it came to the point where he had to lay down his life, he managed to hold his nerve and be noble about it. Martin quickly became convinced that it would be better to not be here at all than to live with the knowledge that his inaction had led to Abigail being hurt, or worse.

Matthew was not gone long. Just over an hour after he left, the front door opened and he walked in, a bag in each hand.

In the lounge they all sat down and Coyle asked Matthew if he had managed to find everything. He nodded and reached out, pulled the nearest bag to him, opened it and reached inside.

"Ah ah ah," Sandra said, lifting a finger. "Before we get into inventorying everything, I think we should get some dinner organised."

"I agree," Abigail told them, placing the flat of one hand on her stomach.

"So do I," said Martin. Abigail slapped him on the shoulder. "What was that for?"

"It was for those of us who can't sit on our asses and eat what we want without worrying about gaining weight."

"I second that," Sandra said, grinning.

"Motion carried," Coyle announced, raising a hand. The three women chuckled. Martin looked to Matthew for support. He was answered with a mock scowl.

"Don't look at me; I work for my six pack."

"Martin doesn't have a six pack," Abigail began, barely restraining her sniggers. "He's got a little keg!"

She laughed out loud, followed closely by Coyle, Sandra and Matthew. Martin pulled a sour face and directed it at each of them in turn.

"Bunch of Benedict Arnolds, that's what you lot are. Turning on a man just because he's not vain and image obsessed. For shame."

"So I can eat till I get huge and it won't bother you?" Abigail asked.

"As long as you're healthy, sweetheart," he told her, sounding sincere. Then he gave her a wicked grin and said, "And large enough that you can't chase me when you find out about all the hot skinny chicks I've been with whilst you've been turning yourself into Abi the Hut!"

Abigail's mouth dropped open as she feigned shock, which was obvious from the fact the she was clearly trying to hold back a smile. She picked up a cushion and smacked Martin with it and everyone chuckled.

It was all slightly forced, but it was better than nothing.

After dinner, they congregated in the living room again and Matthew showed them what he had bought. The others watched as he removed item after item from the bags, including walkie-talkies, compact stun sticks (the place had been out of stun guns, but the guy behind the counter has assured Matthew that the smaller devices still packed a wallop), small torches, batteries and boxes of ammunition for Andrea and Sandra's guns. It was as he set these on the floor that he began to rummage through the empty bags, clearly looking for something. When asked what it was, he asked everyone to wait a minute and he went outside. Returning wearing a scowl a few moments later, he explained that he had gone and forgotten to pick up a box of ammunition for his own gun.

"I thought it might have fallen out of the bag and into the car," he said. "But there is no sign of it."

"How much ammunition do you have left?" Coyle asked him.

"Just what's in the clip that's in the gun right now. In fact the only reason I have the gun with me at all is that I had it on me before we left to come to Hannerville. I'd rather venture out tomorrow night knowing I've got plenty of spare ammunition in case I need it." He threw his hands in the air. "Nothing else for it; I'll have to go back to the mall."

Telling them that he would not be gone long, he departed and the others set about sorting through the equipment he'd unpacked. The stun sticks were put on to charge and the instructions studied. The walkie-talkies were examined and toyed with until they got the hang of the basics. At one point Martin asked why use walkie-talkies and not their personal phones. He said that it would be handier if they had to call the authorities. Plus they could use Bluetooth headsets.

"The hands free option would be nice," said Sandra. "But there are a couple of problems with using the phones. They need to be dialled for one thing. We could avoid that by conference calling and leaving the line open, but then all of us would be a constant voice in one another's ears. It would be confusing, distracting, and there will be enough distractions tomorrow night. With the walkie-talkies you just push the button and speak. As for contacting the authorities, there will be deputies everywhere tomorrow night."

"But won't the people we're meeting think it's odd that we're walking around with walkie-talkies?"

"We'll tell them it's a security precaution," said Coyle. "It's not much of a lie."

When they were finished, they all realised that they had been busying themselves for almost an hour and a half, but Matthew had not yet returned.

Coyle assured them that this was no cause for concern. In an effort to prove this she called Matthew, but there was no answer.

Thirty minutes passed, and this time it was Martin who suggested they deal with the elephant in the room.

"Corday may have gone after him?"

"But why?" Abigail questioned him. "Why now? If Corday had been watching, surely he would have made a play when Matthew went out earlier. After all, there's no way he could have known Matthew would have to go back out because he'd forgotten something."

"Good point," said Sandra. Coyle agreed, but added,

"There is also the possibility that Matthew has simply been held up by something else. There might have been an accident on the road, or maybe he decided to pick up some extra stuff at the mall."

"You don't think he might have called to let us know?"

"Perhaps," Coyle conceded. "But I have to agree with Abigail about the likelihood of it having been an attack from Corday." She paced about for a few moments and then told them, "I'll just have to go and look for him."

That was when the doorbell rang.

Sandra actually gasped out loud at the sound, as all four of them looked in the direction of the door. Abigail looked at Martin, who looked at her and shrugged before turning to Coyle. The Guardian did not shift her gaze, staring at the doorway as if she could somehow see beyond it, focus on the front door and see through it to the porch, to who had rung the bell. A long minute passed but the bell did not ring a second time.

Martin glanced around the room and made a decision. Getting to his feet, he went to where the stun sticks were charging. Though not yet fully charged, he decided that they should have enough juice in them by now to be of some use.

"Wait," commanded Abigail as he headed for the door. She followed his footsteps, lifting another of the defensive weapons and joining him.

"Safety in numbers," stated Coyle, nodding to Sandra. They each grabbed a stun stick and the quartet made their way to the front door with Martin in the lead. He reached the front door and looked through the peephole. Seeing no one, he turned to the others and shrugged. Coyle nodded towards the door handle. Martin nodded and motioned for them to stand back. He reached out, grabbed the handle, yanked the door open and jumped back, stun stick held out like a rapier.

A figure lay on the porch, curled into a ball, their back to the group. Though the face wasn't visible, none of them were in any doubt as to who it was. Martin cursed, and behind him heard Sandra choke back a cry. He held out a hand to stop anyone from going to aid Matthew and stepped forward, going to one side of the door and then the next. Seeing no one, he gingerly stepped up to Matthew and, moving from the waist up, lunged out and back. He did so again looking in the opposite direction. Nothing happened. He told the others to keep an eye out and, as they gathered around the doorway, he knelt down, hooked his hands under Matthew's arms and dragged him into the hallway. Matthew moaned and, as his legs slid across the threshold, gave out a high pitched yell of pain. As soon as he was inside, everyone retreated from the door and Abigail closed it over.

She, Coyle and Sandra stood over Martin as he gently lowered Matthew's shoulders to the ground. All four of them got their first good look at the man's face, and they felt sick. The Frenchman was barely recognisable beneath a patchwork of bruises and lacerations. His lips were swollen and burst in one place, his nostrils rimed with dried blood and snot. His nose was reddened, and one eye had been so badly battered it was closed over completely. They also noticed a blood speckled patch of his scalp where a handful of hair had been torn out.

"We need to get him to the hospital," said Martin, standing up. No one else moved or said anything. "Hey! Come on! The man's been beaten, very likely has injuries we can't see. Given the noise he made as I brought him in there's almost definitely something wrong with at least one of his legs. Staring at him isn't going to help him."

"Who takes him?" asked Abigail.

"We all go," Martin said decisively. "From now until Corday's dead, we go nowhere alone, not even to the bloody bathroom! Miss Coyle, you'll have to drive." Coyle continued to stare down at Matthew's ruined face. "Andrea," Martin said softly. She looked up at him. "Please go and get your car keys; we need to get him to where someone can help him." Coyle nodded and did as asked. When she came back, he said, "We don't know if this fucker is still out there, so Miss Coyle, you're going to go out to the car, get in and get it started. If anyone comes at you, we attack. Once you're in the car, have a look around. If all seems clear, I'll lift Matthew and carry him out, and Abigail and Sandra, you two can flank me, at the ready with your stun sticks. We get Matthew into the back seat, we pile in and take off."

"Sounds simple enough," murmured Sandra.

"It's as half arsed as it gets, but if you have a better idea, we'll go with that." Sandra looked at him blankly.

"What if he attacks?" asked Abigail.

"Jab your stun stick into his eyeball and push the button," said Martin. "Everybody ready? No? Good, then let's not give ourselves any more time to think about it. Miss Coyle."

Corday watched them from the shadows at the side of a house across the street, a smirk on his face. As the little shit that had had the gall to attempt to attack him in his own home was dragged into the house, Corday looked down at his hands, at the darker areas where the blood had dried on his knuckles. When it had dawned on him what had been going on, he had seen red. The young man had been easily disarmed and laid out on the floor. Corday had surprised himself with the initial ferocity of his attack, ruining the man's face. He pulled back a little, deciding to do damage but let him live, let him serve as a warning to the others, both a needle to inject fear and a sponge to soak up the last of their hope.

He noticed movement and looked up to see Coyle run out to the car, head turning left and right, obviously expecting an attack. She reached the car, got in, got it started. That seemed to be the signal for the rest to join her. That prick Muir came out carrying the battered Frenchman, Abigail and that other bitch covering him all the way. Muir reached the car and Abigail opened the door. As Martin bundled his burden into the back seat, the Frenchman loosed a brief but high pitched scream. Once they were all inside, Coyle reversed out of the drive and took off like a shot, tyres screeching.

He waited until the rear lights vanished around a corner, and then looked back to the house. Corday thought about perhaps burning it down while they were gone, but decided there had been enough excitement for one night.

After all, he didn't want to spoil his appetite for tomorrow night.

The four of them sat in the waiting area. Martin, still slightly shaken by the scream Matthew had let out as he had been put into the car, sat with his head leaning against Abigail's shoulder. He thought back to the drive here, during which he had sat in the back seat with his arm around Matthew's shoulder. He had spoken to him constantly, every so often nudging Matthew's head off his shoulder and telling him he needed to stay awake. He'd had no idea if that was the case, but in films and on TV when a person was badly injured, they tried to keep them awake, lest they fall asleep and never wake up again, and so Martin had done the same. All the while, as he had spouted whatever came into his head, he hoped he had not caused the man greater injury as he had put him into the car.

When they had reached the hospital, Abigail had been opening the door even before Miss Coyle had stopped the car. She'd run inside, returning moments later with three orderlies, two of them pushing a gurney. Matthew had been removed from the car and Sandra had accompanied him as he had been wheeled inside. Abigail and Martin had stayed with Coyle as she had parked the car, then the three of them had made their way to the waiting area to find Sandra filling out forms. Matthew had been whisked away so his injuries could be assessed and she had sat down to fill in the small sheaf of forms given to her by the nurse at reception.

That had been an hour ago. The forms had been completed and handed back, coffees had been bought from the nearby machine and consumed, weak attempts at idle conversation made and abandoned. Now they just waited for news, hoping for the best, hoping they were adequately prepared for the worst. Also, in the darkest recesses of their minds, they waited for their theories to be proven wrong, for Corday to appear here and now, his plan to flush them out having worked perfectly.

Martin sighed, sat up and leaned his head in the opposite way from the one it had been lying in, stretching out the muscles. Looking over he found Abigail staring at him, and he saw the worry in her eyes. He wanted to tell her that he thought Matthew would be fine, but in truth he didn't. If the man's body had been beaten as badly as his face, the damage inflicted upon his insides must have been considerable. Not to mention the possibility of brain damage.

"I'm sure the doctors will do their best," he said, giving in to his need to say something.

"Will it be enough?" asked Coyle, her voice low, conspiratorial, despite there only being two other people around, over on the other side of the waiting area, both engrossed in their own conversation.

"We'll have to hope so," said Sandra. For a moment Martin thought she was going to cry, but she held herself together. "Did you see his face? How could someone do that to another person?"

"It's difficult for us to understand," Abigail answered her. "Because that's not how our minds work. Corday can beat a person to a pulp with the same ease with which you or I would swat a fly."

"He's a twisted bastard, pure and simple," spat Coyle. "He followed that young man, attacked him and beat him, and then left him on the doorstep like so much waste. I don't like to think of myself as a violent person, but so help me if I get the chance I'm going to do that fucker damage before I send him on to whatever awaits him beyond this life."

She rose from her seat and headed for the bathroom. Sandra went after her. Martin thought about making a humorous observation regarding women never going to the bathroom alone, but thought better of it. This wasn't the time or the place for jocularity, regardless of how well intentioned.

"You've made me really proud of you today," Abigail told him.

"Me? What did I do?"

"What you said to Miss Coyle earlier today, and how you reacted when we found Matthew. You were looking out for her needs when you told her to rest, and when you saw Matthew, you knew what had to be done and you made it happen."

"Thank you," he smiled at her. Leaning over, he kissed her neck, just behind her ear, then whispered, "I didn't do it alone."

She reached over, took his hand and squeezed it. He squeezed back.

Andrea and Sandra returned a few minutes later, just ahead of the doctor, who walked into the waiting area and asked for Miss Logan. Sandra stood and started making her way over. Martin and Abigail made to follow suit, but Coyle prevented them with a shake of her head.

"Miss Logan?" Sandra nodded. "I'm Doctor Jameson. The young gentleman you brought in..?"

"We don't know his name," Sandra informed him when she realised that was what he was waiting for her to give him. Jameson nodded.

282

"The beating he took did a bit of damage, though a lot of it is on the surface. Internally it's mostly bones: three broken ribs, one cracked rib, his left leg is broken in two places and his right forearm is also broken. The x-rays revealed no major damage to the skull or his brain. He's out right now, but in time he should make a full recovery." He consulted his watch. "I have another patient I need to check on right now, but I wanted you to know how he was doing. Oh, and we've had to contact the sheriff's office. We've been asked to report all incidents of this nature, so a deputy will be here shortly. I realise this is an inconvenience, but I'm afraid you'll have to wait to answer his questions."

"But I don't know the young man," stammered Sandra. Jameson nodded.

"I realise that, but you will have to let the deputy know the details of how you found him."

He turned and rushed off down the corridor. Sandra went back to her seat and filled the others in.

"Damn it to hell," cursed Coyle. "I can't let you two go back to the house on your own, but I don't want to leave you here by yourself, Sandra." She blew out a frustrated breath. "Couldn't you leave your details with the receptionist and ask her to get the deputy to contact you."

"He'd probably come out to the house," said Sandra. "If he sees Martin and word gets back to the sheriff that he was involved in this, some questions might be asked that we might find difficult to answer." Coyle nodded, reluctantly agreeing with the assessment.

"All right. Abigail, Martin, we'll take a taxi back to the house. Sandra," she continued. "You do not move from this waiting area until the deputy arrives. As soon as he has taken your statement, you come home. You call before you leave, and you leave the call on loudspeaker till you get back. Okay?"

"Understood."

"All right. Martin will come back in with the car keys once we've retrieved the stun sticks." Sandra nodded and the other three got up and headed for the exit.

When they arrived back at Sandra's, they went through the house looking for signs of forced entry. They each had a weapon at the ready, though Coyle had opted for her gun, deciding lethal force would be preferable should Corday be lying in wait.

A tense ten minutes passed, but they found no evidence that anyone had broken in, and no one jumped out at them from behind any doors, though each expected just such an occurrence at every door they passed. After all the doors and windows had been checked, they sat in the living room, anxiously waiting for Sandra to call. None of them could relax. At various times each one of them, too fidgety to stay seated, rose and paced around the room, much to the unspoken chagrin of the other two.

Fifty slow minutes passed in this manner, during which time they all became more and more fearful that Sandra would not call. When Coyle's phone rang, all three jumped. Martin and Abigail stared at Coyle as she answered. She then put her phone on loudspeaker and sat it down on the table. The three of them listened to Sandra give a running commentary of her journey. As she described pulling into the street, Andrea, her gun in hand, moved to the window and looked out.

"She's back."

Martin got out of his chair, picked up his stun stick and made his way to the front door, closely followed by Abigail. He watched through the peephole as Sandra got out of the car and came towards the door, his hand on the handle in case he had to rush out to her aid. She reached the door, which he opened for her, closing it quickly as soon as she was inside.

Back in the living room, they all sat down and Sandra told them what had transpired after they left the hospital.

"The deputy arrived not long after you three left. The receptionist showed us into a little room and he sat me down, took out his notebook and asked me to recount what had happened, start to finish. I gave him the same story I gave to the medics when I arrived at the hospital, telling him that you, Andrea, were an old friend of mine from way back and that you were here visiting. I told him Abigail was here because I had ordered a book from her store, and that she had come in to update me on my order. He was on the ball; right away he asked why Abigail hadn't just called. I told him that she had been on her way by and had decided to pop in to tell me in person. Told him that kind of service was why your store was such a success.

"Anyway, I stuck to the truth as much as I could, only leaving out Martin's having been here. I explained his presence at the hospital by saying he was Abigail's boyfriend and that she had called him as we took Matthew to the hospital. I said she was badly shaken and asked him to meet her there. He asked where you all were and I said that you had all gone home, adding that there was nothing any of you could tell him that I hadn't already told him about. I added that if it was necessary to talk to him then he shouldn't have trouble finding you all." Coyle nodded her approval.

"You did well, Sandra. Well done."

"Just before he left I asked the deputy what the next step was. He didn't go into detail, but said they would try getting a match on Matthew's fingerprints or DNA."

"That will get them nowhere," threw in Coyle.

"Beyond that, as Matthew had no identification on him, they have to wait for someone to report him missing. I asked if someone would be keeping an eye on him, but he said the sheriff's office would simply be contacted when Matthew woke up."

"You're worried Corday might go to the hospital to… finish what he started," said Abigail. Sandra nodded.

"I know our theories regarding what Corday might and might not do haven't panned out so far tonight," Martin said. "But surely if he had wanted Matthew dead, he'd have left a corpse on the doorstep and not a battered body."

"I think it's clear we cannot hope to know what that man might do," Coyle said gravely. "But I think, I hope, that Matthew is as safe as he can be for the time being. Now, what we…" In a timid voice, Sandra cut her off with,

"I did something else before I came back." She squirmed uncomfortably under everyone's questioning gaze. "I asked if it would be possible for me to see Matthew before I left. Told them I just wanted to look in on him. They let me in for a few minutes. I took his hand and he opened his eyes. He asked for some water, so I gave him a sip from a cup that was sitting on the bedside table. It took everything he had, but he gave me a brief account of what happened.

"Corday didn't come after Matthew. Matthew went after Corday and it went terribly wrong." Before anyone could ask anything, she went on. "Matthew's been unsure of our plan since we came up with it. He decided that he was going to do something so that none of us had to put our necks on the line. He made up the story about having to go back to pick up something he had forgotten at the mall, instead going to Corday's house. He was going to sneak in, shoot him, and sneak back out, but Corday got the drop on him. He didn't try to get any information from him, he just beat him until he lost consciousness. The next thing he knew, he was being dragged in the door here." She looked to Andrea. "He asked me to tell you he's sorry."

Chapter 47

Martin and Abigail sat side by side on the edge of the bed, holding hands.

"It feels like we should be talking about stuff," she said softly. "Like we should be discussing what we're going to do after this is all over." She raised her free hand, balled it into a fist and thumped it down. "Damn it, this isn't the way it should be at all. We shouldn't be discussing what we'll do when this is over; it shouldn't be fucking happening in the first damn place. What kind of a sick world brings us together, makes us happy, and then throws something like Corday at us? It sucks! It fucking sucks! Maybe Matthew had the right idea. Maybe we should all just storm his house, burn him out and gun him down in the street. Son of a bitch doesn't deserve any better than that."

"I'm frightened too," Martin said without looking up. She looked at him, half smiling. "Is it that obvious?"

"It is to me," he said, continuing to look at his shoes. "Part of me wants to get up on the roof and scream at fate to go fuck itself with a live hand grenade, but I don't know that I believe in fate. Every relationship goes through trials and tribulations. Maybe Corday is one of ours."

"He's a bit more than a trial or a tribulation, Marty." Martin nodded.

"True, but he's something we've got to get past all the same. If you start thinking about it in terms of fate, then what's the point in fighting him? If fate is so determined to destroy what we have that it drops something like Corday in our laps, why would it stop if we beat him? It'll just keep chucking stuff at us till we're worn down enough to call it a day." He shook his head thoughtfully. "No, fate isn't at fault here. This is just how it is."

"You don't think we were fated to be together? You know, the memories and all that." He looked up and turned to face her. He reached out and she turned slightly to him, giving him her other hand.

"Fate had nothing to do with me falling in love with you," he told her. "*You* were the only reason I fell in love with you. A million different little things I picked up on from your letters over the years built a profile of a woman I'd never met, but who I finally realised had my heart in her hand. Maybe I was too close, or just bloody stupid, I don't know. Was it fate that I never settled down with any of the other women I dated, or that Stephen finally got me to face up to how I felt? No. Those women realised they were in your shadow, and quite rightly they didn't like it, and so the relationships fell apart. Stephen realised I was too ignorant, or too scared or stupid to admit that I had found someone I loved. Someone I knew so well, who knew me, someone I wanted to be with, to hold." He lifted her hands to his lips, kissed the back of each in turn. "Fate didn't make me get on a plane and come here to see you, Abigail Morton. The person you are, the person you have always been and always will be, brought me here. Fate is what people claim brought them together when they're afraid their relationship is on unsteady ground. I won't lie; I am as scared right now as I have ever been in my life, even more so than on the day I met you, but I'm not scared about how steady our relationship is. It's been built over years, put together brick by brick by you and me, and it is solid, right down to its foundations.

"My fear is that something will happen to you. I'll do whatever it takes to make sure it doesn't, and I can only hope that's enough. Our big, bad wolf doesn't need to huff and puff. This fucker is a wrecking ball, but he's not fated to destroy us, Abi. Fate is fate, unchangeable, whereas the outcome to our situation is far from certain. If it's within my power to ensure the end of this sees you alive and well and living on, it'll be done, whatever the cost."

"You can't say that," she scolded him, blinking back tears. "You can't tell me you hope I live even if it means you might not. You think I could just go on if something happened to you? Just pick up and carry on from where I was before you were here?"

"Aww, you went and interrupted my big speech," he whined playfully. She released one of his hands and punched him on the shoulder.

"Dick!" she half laughed, half sobbed."

"Oh, don't punch that, please." They both chuckled. "You're the only person who could possibly know how much it means to me to hear you say what you just said. That I could mean so much to you that the idea of life without me is so bad? Makes me feel all big and manly. It also makes me feel like a complete idiot." Her features contorted into a mask of confusion. "When I think of how much time I wasted not being by your side, I want to go back in time and kick myself right up the arse! But I am determined to make up for that time, Abi, and if a man like Corday has to die to make sure that happens, then he's fucked."

She let go of his hands, stood up, stepped closer, and sat down on his lap, wrapping her arms around him. He put his arms around her waist, laid his head against her chest, closed his eyes and breathed in her scent.

"You're mine," she said. "And no one, not some chick with bigger boobs or some demented mother fucker with a grudge, is going to take you away from me."

"The chick with bigger boobs might have a shot." She squeezed hard. "Urgh! Kidding! Kidding!" She eased up. "Besides, your boobs look enormous from where I am."

"You're screwing up a tender moment here, butt crack!" He pushed her back a little, looked up into her eyes.

"Here's one to replace it with then."

He reached up, took her head in his hands, and brought her lips down to his. He felt warm moisture dribble down his cheek and for a moment wasn't sure if the tear belonged to him or Abigail. As they broke contact, he realised it was hers.

"Hey, come on, no tears. You need to man... uh, woman up. I need an Amazon backing me up tomorrow night, not a teenage girl who just found out her favourite boy band split up." Abigail sniffed.

"You're right," she said. "But afterwards, I get to cry my eyes out, okay."

"Deal."

"There's something else I want to do too."

"What's that?"

"I want to ask Andrea and Sandra about my memory."

"Okay."

"I just... Oh, honey, we can sit here and fight the darkness all around with words all we want, but the truth of it is that we might not..."

"No, we might not, but we're not going to say it out loud. If I get to be chicken shit about anything, it's saying it out loud." She nodded emphatically, understanding completely; she was glad he'd cut her off as she hadn't been sure she could have finished the sentence.

"I want you to go and lock the door," she told him. Martin did as bid, turning round only a second before Abigail pounced on him. She pressed her lips to his so hard that the back of his head bounced off the door. Her hands flew to his belt and started to unbuckle it, a move which ignited his own desire. He fumbled only briefly with the button of her jeans before managing to undo it, then he tugged down the zipper. He felt Abigail's hand work its way inside his jeans, caressing his already rigid member. He gasped into her mouth and then grabbed her wrist, forcibly removing her hand. She broke the kiss and opened her mouth to ask what was happening, but did not get the chance. Martin grabbed her by the shoulders and spun, reversing their places, putting her against the door. He dropped to his knees, his fingers already hooked into the waistband of her jeans, drawing them down as he went, exposing her cotton underpants. Even as he helped her step out of the jeans, he pushed his face into her crotch, felt the wetness there, the heat. The smell of her was intoxicating. He ran his hands up the back of her smooth legs as he nibbled at her through the thin material, eliciting gasps. When he clutched her buttocks she let out a quiet little squeal of pleasure. Leaving one hand on her behind, he brought the other to the front, yanked the underpants out of his way and, even as her hands were pressed to the back of his head, he dove in. Abigail's squeal as she felt his tongue run over her most intimate area was very loud, and neither of them gave a damn.

There was an urgency to it all that neither of them had ever experienced before in their lives. Both of them knew the cause, but it was forgotten as the rest of their clothes were removed and a variety of positions were assumed on the floor at the foot of the bed. It wasn't love, it wasn't even sex, it was a declaration to whatever forces, be they those of fate or luck, to go and burn in hell. Tomorrow would come and it would bring with it events that were beyond their control, but here, now, tonight, was theirs and if there was to be no day for them after tomorrow, then tonight would forever bear their stamp.

For all their fervour, their releases were hard fought for. Though neither was consciously aware of it, they did not want this to end, for in the very back of their minds was the thought that such a night might never happen again. Soon both their bodies were slick with sweat, which in many places mingled with trails of saliva. Their resolve to hold onto the here and now was so strong that their limbs became sore, their muscles ached, and every erogenous zone became overworked and tender.

Martin was sitting on the floor, his back against the bottom of the bed. His hands gently held on to Abigail's buttocks as she sat in his lap, bouncing up and down in a fast, steady rhythm. Her hands were clasped behind his head, pressing his face into her cleavage. He moved his hands so he could fondle her breasts, occasionally turning his face to the side and pushing a nipple into his mouth to suck on it, nip it gently with his teeth. This made Abigail go faster and both realised at the same moment that they were nearing the end. Keeping her hips moving, Abigail leaned back slightly, grasped the sides of Martin's head and tilted it up so they were looking into one another's eyes.

"With me, okay," she panted.

"Are you sure?" She nodded.

"Please." He nodded. She could have asked for every drop of blood in his body and he'd have nodded. Not just at that moment, but at any time, for any reason, and he would have nodded.

She leaned forward and kissed him, wrapping her arms around his neck and increasing her tempo. He gripped her waist and began to buck his hips in time with hers. Moments later their bodies shuddered as their climaxes tore through them. Abigail tightened her grip on Martin, and he put his arms around her and held her against him, feeling her breasts press against his upper chest. It occurred to him that every nerve ending in his body was hyper-stimulated, as he imagined he could feel every point of contact his body made with hers. For a few all too brief moments that seemed to stretch into eternity, there was nothing else that existed for either of them except the other.

But nothing so intense can truly last for eternity, for if it did, poor human minds would soon wander down paths that lead to nothing good.

As the intensity dialled down they both began to tremble. They released one another and Abigail leaned back, propping herself up by placing her hands on Martin's damp chest. They looked into one other's eyes again, but were silent.

Nothing needed to be said.

A short time later, after they had both showered and after Abigail had written in her journal, they lay beside one another in bed, Abigail's head on Martin's chest. The lights were out and the house was quiet. Both thought the other asleep, but both of them were awake.

Martin could not keep himself from worrying about what might happen to Abigail, her friends and her family. He wanted to be able to guarantee her, and himself, that nothing would befall them, but he could not and that fact would not leave him alone. The threat to them was one man, just one man, but such a man as he had never come across before. If this all turned out as he hoped it would, his greatest hope thereafter would be that he never came across such a man again. He tried telling himself that he would do everything he could to make sure everyone was safe, and that no more could be asked, or had been asked, of him.

It didn't work.

Almost as if sensing that worrying about her friends and family was already being taken care of, Abigail kept sleep at bay wondering if she would ever find herself in this position again. Here she was, after what was without doubt the most incredible sexual experience of her life (no matter how she had worded it or how detailed she had tried to make it, her recording of the act in her journal did not do it justice), lying beside the man she loved, warm and safe, and worried that it might be the last time. It was fucking unfair! They had only just got together and now it was in danger of being torn away from them. Was it selfish of her to expect to be happy for the rest of her life when so many would go through theirs never knowing the kind of excitement and joy a relationship like hers and Martin's could bring? Was she a bad person because she felt she deserved some measure of contentment given what she'd been through in her life? Many people kept a diary, a journal, in which they recorded their thoughts, but how many of them had to do so as diligently as she, lest certain memories be lost forever? It had been damnably hard at times, but she'd had no choice and so she had made sure those damn books had been written in every damn night.

Or had she?

Her train of thought threatened to derail itself as an old ghost rose up to haunt her: the possibility that she had forgotten on some nights to write in her journal and, because of that, simply didn't recall that she had forgotten.

Her ire, however, would not be so easily set aside and eventually it settled upon a target. In the minutes before sheer tiredness carried her off, Abigail resolved to make sure that after tomorrow, Andrew Corday would never again cast a shadow over her life with Martin.

Chapter 48

The day of the Hanner Carnival dawned bright and cold, a slight breeze ruffling the bunting that had been strung up all over town.

During the morning, the various workmen employed by the town went about finalising everything. The many rides were checked and re-checked and run through tests to ensure they were safe for the many revellers who would board them that night. The parade route through the town was inspected and any litter or possible problems were sorted out. For the seventh year in a row, a very nice lady by the name of Tracy Merrin, sixty-three, nearly gave herself a coronary. She was the town's official carnival organiser, and every year she ran herself ragged making sure the Hanner Carnival went off without a hitch. Every year she promised herself, and her long suffering husband, Tom, that this was the last year. Then, every year, the mayor himself would contact her and request she return to do her customary excellent job of setting the whole thing up. Loathe to think of someone else running, and most likely ruining, what she had come to think of as her carnival, Tracy always broke her promise. Tom had gotten used to it by now; seeing her walk into the room with that embarrassed look on her face to announce she had accepted the mayor's offer to organise the damn thing once again was for him almost as much of a tradition as the carnival itself.

At nine o'clock Sheriff Flaghan gathered his officers together. They all stood at ease as the sheriff gave them the usual spiel about keeping the peace during the day, and more importantly during the night when a lot of people would start the heavy drinking and hard-core partying. He encouraged them to be tough but fair, to keep an eye out for the repeat offenders, and to make damn sure he did not find out any one of them had a bottle of anything more alcoholic than cola in their hand at any time.

Normally this was where his little speech would end, but this year, as they all knew, he had another matter to address. He removed his hat, ran a hand through his hair, took a deep breath and said,

"We have a stone cold killer somewhere in this town. Everyone here knows it, I know it, and more to the point the townspeople know it. Now we thought we had him in custody, but it turned out that was not the case. He is still out there, and we have a description of him. The posters are up all over town, there are lots of them lying around the station. If you haven't seen one, get one and commit the sketch to memory. If you have seen one, get another one and make sure you have the image on it locked in your minds. I had hoped that today might be postponed in order to give us time to nab this bastard, but hope didn't get me very far. Mayor Ashby thinks the citizens of Hannerville will band together, look out for one another, protect each other. I think that is a wonderful sentiment, and I believe that many will go out tonight believing that they will do just that. But that isn't their job; it's ours, ladies and gentlemen. The day of the Hanner Carnival is a long one every year, but this year it's going to seem even longer because I need every one of you to be giving it everything you've got until the last person is off home safe to bed, or locked up in a cell to sleep it off, as has been the case in years gone by.

"Vigilance, people. No slacking, no goofing off, and you treat everything seriously. Someone tells you they saw someone acting suspiciously, you check it out. If you think you see this guy, you radio for backup, and I expect whoever is in the vicinity to get to where they're needed as fast as you can. If it comes down to a chase, you are permitted to shoot to wound. If it is at all possible I want this guy taken alive. Only when it becomes clear that you have no other choice do you shoot to kill. I'm counting on you all to use your brains and your good judgement out there today and tonight, people." Flaghan surveyed the grave expressions around the room. "Have I been in any way unclear?" A few dozen heads were shaken. "Good. Dismissed."

In the Glenster household, Philip had been awake since seven. Just after eight, Anne found him sitting at the kitchen table, a mug of cold coffee in front of him as he stared out of the window. They, like many others, had discussed not going to the festivities at all. And, also like many others, they had decided to go. Both of them had lived in Hannerville all of their days, and in the past only the most severe illness or injury had prevented them from attending the carnival. They, like so many others, were determined that the cloud which hung over their town would not keep them away. The friends they had spoken to over the last couple of days had agreed completely with them, and so there would be a sizeable group around them tonight.

But that didn't mean the retired doctor and his wife weren't concerned, weren't afraid, for others, as well as themselves.

In Sandra Logan's house, everyone slept late, none of them having gotten to sleep any earlier than four a.m. As the Glenster's sat quietly in their living room, as the deputies deployed all across town, and as Sheriff Flaghan paid a visit to someone he hoped to have a quick word with, Martin, Abigail, Andrea and Sandra all rose from their beds and congregated in the living room. They were all bleary eyed, and two of them were slightly embarrassed, hoping that no one had heard their activities the previous night. The other two had heard, of course, but were discreet, giving nothing away. Breakfast was made and they all sat down to eat. Afterwards, whilst Andrea, Martin and Abigail washed the dishes, Sandra called the hospital to enquire about Matthew. All she was told was that his condition had improved slightly and that they still had no idea who he was, information she relayed to the others. After getting washed and dressed, they all once again found themselves together in the living room, settling down for what was going to be a long, unsettled afternoon.

As they were doing that, Matthew was receiving a visitor.

Having been in and out of consciousness all night, Matthew was drowsy but awake enough to realise someone had opened the door to his room. He turned his head slowly, opening his eyes to see a blurry shadow standing there. That it was not any of his friends he knew straight away. The certainty that it was Corday come to finish him off solidified in his foggy mind just as quickly. Feeling weaker than he ever had in his life – a state caused jointly by his injuries and the medication he had been given to help with the pain – Matthew reached out with one hand for the alarm button. The shadow stepped into the room and closed the door, quickly approached the bed, reached out with one large hand and gently took his wrist.

"No need for that, sir," said a deep voice he didn't recognise. Matthew blinked away tears and willed his vision to focus. He eventually found himself looking up at the concerned face of Sheriff Mark Flaghan. The fear that had briefly powered him fled, and when the sheriff released his wrist, his arm flopped back down onto the bed.

"I apologise if I frightened you," said his visitor. "I'm Sheriff Mark Flaghan. I read the report about what happened to you, decided to come down and see if you were perhaps up to answering a few questions."

Matthew knew he had two options: play the sympathy card and get the sheriff to leave, or answer his questions as best he could. He chose the latter, nodding weakly and motioning for the sheriff to give him some water. Flaghan took the plastic cup from the nightstand and held it while Matthew caught the straw between his lips and took a few sips. He nodded and the sheriff withdrew the cup, putting it back on the nightstand. Matthew swallowed, winced and croaked,

"Thank you, sheriff." Flaghan's eyebrows rose.

"You're French?" Matthew nodded. "I wasn't expecting that."

"I do not mean to be rude, sheriff, but I am very tired and will not be able to talk for long."

"I understand. Can you please tell me your name?" Knowing there was no harm in it, Matthew answered him honestly. "And can you tell me why you're here in Hannerville?"

"I had always wanted to visit the States," Matthew said, again being completely honest. Then the fibbing started. "But I had always put it off for some reason or other. Eventually I got annoyed at myself, thinking I would be putting it off till I was an old man. I got a map of the US, stuck a pin in it to pick a state, then got a map of that state and stuck another pin in it to pick a town. Hannerville was the closest place to where my pin pointed."

Flaghan jotted down his every word, and when he finished writing he said,

"I am very sorry for what happened to you here in our town. I want you to know that my men and I will do everything we can to catch whoever did this to you."

"Thank you."

The sheriff then asked Matthew to tell him what happened, in as much detail as he could. Matthew told him he had been out for a walk, naming the street he had been on. He said that he stopped outside a house to tie his shoelace. He even recalled the house number. He said that he had heard a door close somewhere, and then footsteps, and then a few moments later he had been set upon by someone who had wrestled him to the ground and beat him until he was unconscious. The next thing he knew, he was in hospital. The sheriff asked if Matthew had gotten a look at his attacker at all, and was told that he had, but only briefly. Could he describe the man? Matthew did, giving a description that wasn't too detailed, but which would match the face on the posters stuck up around the town.

His intention realised and his strength waning fast, Matthew started to drowse again. Flaghan finished scribbling notes and asked one last question: was there anyone Matthew wanted informed about what had happened. Matthew managed a shake of his head before he lost consciousness.

The sheriff jotted down a couple of questions he wanted to ask on his next visit and left.

Throughout the morning and afternoon, in most of the households throughout town, parents called their children, from infants to teenagers to twenty somethings, into various rooms and told them to make sure they took extra care this year. Given the gender of all the previous victims, many a father and mother fussed over their daughters, making them promise to make sure they had a phone on them at all times, making sure they had seen one of the posters the police had put up, and begging them not to do anything foolish, like get so drunk they didn't know who they were talking to or what they were doing. The very young would enquire as to why these warnings were being given, and the parents would explain it to them as they saw fit, which varied from toned down versions of the truth to outright lies designed to safeguard the child from the real world, and from nightmares, if only for a little while. The teenagers rolled their eyes and sighed that they were grown up enough to take care of themselves and that, as usual, their parents were getting worked up over nothing. For many however this was a knee jerk reaction, and only when they had returned to their bedrooms did they give it any in-depth thought. Most decided to heed the advice they had been given. Others, believing it would never happen to them, laughed it off with their friends over phone calls, video calls and text messages. The grown up children thanked their parents for the advice and made sure their parents were going to take care as well.

For one unfortunate girl though, it was already too late.

Last night.

17 year old Lucy Berendon was having a fight with her parents, Mitch and Jenna, neither of whom was particularly fond of their eldest child's boyfriend, 21 year old Scott Connley. At nine o'clock at night, Lucy had announced out of the blue that she was going out to meet him. Her parents had told her there was no way in hell she was going anywhere to meet anyone. Lucy instantly took umbrage. Her opening salvo had been that they were controlling, her mother responding by telling her that they were just looking out for her. Lucy played her "I'm an adult" card and her father told her that as old as she may be, as long as she lived in his house she'd abide by his rules. With her trump card already played, Lucy resorted to veiled threats, yelling at her father that if that was the case then maybe she wouldn't be living in his house much longer.

This was not the first such argument between Lucy, Mitch and Jenna. In the past the differences of opinion had been about things like too much in the way of make-up and not enough in the way of clothing, and all the previous times Lucy had mentioned moving out, her father had confronted her with the truth: she was too used to the good life at home to be bothered with things like earning her own money (her parents were fed up to the back teeth telling her to go and at least look for a job) or doing her own laundry. The idea of her own space in which she could do as she pleased thrilled her. The idea of having to be responsible and grown up so she could afford and maintain that place did not.

However, never before had they argued about her simply leaving the house at this time of night when there had been three murders committed and the killer still on the loose. Determined to make his daughter see sense, Mitch skipped his usual response to Lucy's idle threat and asked "Is your dipshit boyfriend worth going out and getting raped and murdered for?"

A stunned silence descended upon the Berendon family living room. Mitch did not regret asking the question, only how anger had made him word it. Even his wife, who had been driven to distraction by her daughter many times, was aghast, staring at him with her mouth hanging open, her eyes wide. The two younger Berendon children, Archie, seven, and Louise, twelve, both looked at their father with shocked expressions. Louise had some inkling of what her father was talking about, but little Archie, sitting with an action figure in his hand, was really just mimicking his mother and sisters.

Mitch's anger refused to let him apologise. After all, as harshly as it had been put, he was making sense. There was a fucking killer out there, and she wanted to walk out of the house at this time of night to go and see that dumb fuck? Kid had a moustache and goatee that looked like he'd shaved a cat's ass and stuck the hair to his face! For that she wanted to risk running into the killer! No, no way was he saying sorry to anyone tonight. Once again, Lucy was the one who had started the fucking argument. Once again, the quiet of their home had been torn asunder because Lucy just didn't want to realise there were people who still had a say in how she lived her life, whether she liked it or not. Lucy, his cherished daughter who was just going through the phase of being an ass that most teenagers went through, just didn't get that there were people who loved her and didn't want to see her hurt.

Had that sentiment been put into words, a lot of heartache might have been avoided. As it was Mitch, his anger fuelled by the knowledge that he wasn't quite getting things right here, yelled into the silence.

"Is that what you want? Because that's what might be out there waiting for you!"

Lucy, tears in her eyes, turned and stormed upstairs. Mitch watcher her go, then hung his head. In the quiet, everyone heard Archie ask why his mommy was crying. His sister told him that she was upset because Lucy had caused another fight.

"It wasn't just Lucy," Jenna croaked, speaking to her son and daughter but looking at her husband.

"No," Mitch said quietly, lifting his head. Relieved to find that his anger seemed to have departed along with his eldest child, he met his wife's stare. "No, it wasn't just Lucy, but where would you rather she was tonight, Jenna: up there, or out there?"

Lucy had inherited several things from her father, and the only one of those he wasn't entirely happy about was his temper. Where intense regret cooled his down in the immediate aftermath of the latest confrontation, hers only got worse.

She sat in her room, on her bed, seething, tears streaming down her face, appalled at the unfairness of it all. She knew about the murders, knew there was a sick pervert out there, but in her opinion there was no way something like that could happen to her. If some sicko came up to her and tried to do anything, she'd kick his ass, and she'd still be kicking it when the cops arrived to arrest the fucker. But of course her fuckwit parents just didn't get that she could take care of herself, whatever the situation.

A small voice at the back of her mind told her that they were looking out for her, which was what parents were supposed to do. This voice told her that every teenager at some point felt like their parents were trying to control their lives too much, but that the things they said came from a place of concern. Certainly she knew a couple of girls who could do with a lot more paternal care, girls who had gotten into drink and drugs at a very early age. Sure, Lucy had swigged from a bottle of beer or puffed on a joint on occasion, but she knew better than to get too into shit like that. Hell, these days the only way she could let Scott touch her was if she'd had some booze or some weed. Though her parent's disapproval had played a big part in her staying with him as long as she had, his lack of hygiene and his pathetic attempts at being a lover were beginning to get on her nerves. She reflected briefly on her father's question and decided that no, Scott was not worth the risk.

But that was beside the fucking point.

Whether he was worth the risk or not, going out when she wanted and why she wanted should be her decision, not her mother and father's. At that point Lucy Berendon decided that her dad's attempt to scare her into submission would not succeed.

She text Scott and told him she'd be a little late. He text back telling her to hurry, saying that he was hungry for her, his version of a seduction line, one that made her roll her eyes. Sneaking out of the house was something she had done a few times before, but she decided that tonight's great escape would require extra caution. She lay in her room listening, trying to work out who was doing what. She glanced at the clock on her bedside table to see that it was just after ten. She knew that her mother would soon put the kids to bed before going to bed herself. Chances were good that her dad would plant his fat ass in a chair and watch some TV with a beer in his hand before coming upstairs.

Sure enough, not long after, Jenna had come upstairs with Archie and Louise, watched them as they brushed their teeth, and then put them to bed. Lucy had heard her mother pause outside her door, probably listening, probably going to knock, stick her head in and ask if everything was okay. Stupid question; of course things weren't okay. But Jenna did not knock, did not ask the stupid question. Instead she let out a long breath, shook her head and went to bed. The part of Lucy that hated fighting with her parents was saddened by this, but the part of her that felt she was the most unjustly treated young woman in the whole damn world rejoiced. *That's right,* Mom, it said. *No need to check on me. I'm just fine. In fact I'm ready to take on the fucking world!*

To her surprise, it was only fifteen minutes later that she heard her father come upstairs. That part of her that was still very much a little girl, that wanted to be stopped before she could do something stupid, got its hopes up that he would knock on her door, come in, apologise and make it all okay. He did not. He didn't even pause outside her door and think about coming in. He just went into his room, closing the door softly. *Too damn stubborn to admit you're wrong, you asshole!* Lucy silently scorned him. That her own stubbornness had been partly to blame for the situation occurred to her, but did not fit in with how she wanted things to be, and so was ignored.

She waited a further fifteen minutes. She knew she didn't have to hurry: whatever get-together Scott wanted to take her to was sure to last into the early hours. She'd just have to make sure she got back before anyone else got out of bed. Certain that everyone was asleep, Lucy climbed off her bed and went to her door. Slowly, she pushed the handle down, opened it a little, waited to hear if there was any noise, and then opened it a little more, enough for her to squeeze out. Thankfully there was only one door she would have to creep by in order to reach the stairs: Archie's. Lucy knew her little brother slept deep, but still took a great deal of care to be quiet, literally tip-toeing past his bedroom door, onto which was taped a sheet of A4 paper with "Archie's Room" scrawled across it in various colours of crayon. Lucy smiled warmly as she recalled seeing the boy working on it at the table, the tip of his tongue sticking out of the corner of his mouth as he'd worked, a crayon clutched in his fist.

Eventually she reached the front door, unlocking it with the duplicate key she'd had cut a few months before. Though she always presented the very soul of teenage rebellion to her parents, every time she looked at that key she felt a tingle of fear. Lucy was certain that if her parents ever found out she had been conniving and duplicitous enough to have it made, they would actually kick her out. It was one thing to threaten it, another thing if she chose to make good on that threat, but being booted out would be so fucking embarrassing, not to mention shitty. It was just a fucking key, for god sakes, what would the big deal be? Wasn't she old enough to have her own door key? Wasn't she responsible enough?

Clearly not, she answered herself, for once turning the full withering bluntness she usually reserved for her father on herself. *You had to steal Mom's keys to get the copy made, and you've only ever used it to sneak out when they've pissed you off and said you couldn't go.* That almost stopped her, but soon the righteous teenage angst flooded back and she snuck out, locking the front door behind her.

As she turned and stepped onto the grass to muffle her footsteps, she realised she should have brought a jacket as it was chilly out. Shrugging, she took her phone out of her pocket and dialled Scott's number.

"Babe," he answered. "You coming or what?"

"Where are you?" she whispered.

"We're outside the gate to Beaumont Park."

"I'm on my way."

She hung up, put her phone back in her pocket and started walking. It occurred to her that not only should she have brought a jacket, she should have brought money too, as doubtless someone would be going to a store for booze. With Scott's friends it was usually a case of if you hadn't chipped in for the booze you stayed sober, but if her boyfriend wanted to get his hands on her goodies tonight, he was going to have to pay her way.

Lucy was only a few blocks from the park, trying to enjoy the euphoria of disobeying orders even as it vied for contention with the guilt she'd feel if her parents woke up and found her gone, when Corday grabbed her.

After having watched the little group of fools take their battered friend away in the car, Corday had decided that he needed to let off a little steam. There was only one way he could think of to do that, and so, unwilling to wander around, he had gone straight to where he was sure an opportunity would present itself. He had driven to a spot near Tarker's Bar, parked his car and then hung around in the shadows across from the bar's entrance, waiting for some sweet young lady to make the mistake of venturing out into the night alone. It seemed however that his own recent successes were working against him, as every viable prospect who exited the bar and walked off did so in the company of others. No doubt they had made sure they would be accompanied all the way home, or they had some form of weapon in their handbags. As impatient as he eventually became, Corday deemed the risks too great. Frustrated and annoyed, he went back to his car and began to make his way home, only to notice a very pretty young thing walking alone, heading in the direction of Beaumont Park.

Corday smiled, revealing teeth. *There's always one,* he reminded himself cheerily as he turned the car around.

Lucy Berendon had noticed the car pass by, but paid it no heed, walking alone in the dark having had little effect on her belief that if anyone tried anything she could successfully defend herself. She didn't notice the driver pull a U turn and come back down the street towards her. When the car passed her again, she tried to work out if it was the same one she had seen only a minute ago. As she did, Corday stopped, leapt out, clamped a hand over her mouth, stuck the needle in her arm and pressed the plunger. When the full dose had been administered, he removed the needle, pocketed it, and bundled the already woozy girl into the back seat of his car, copping a rough feel of her breast as he did so. He searched her, found her phone and dashed it to pieces against the pavement. He already had an erection by the time he got back behind the wheel and sped off.

Corday knew of a different path to the shack, one that was a little less arduous than the track Matthew and Coyle had used, particularly for someone often burdened by the dead weight of another person. The headband torch lit his way and his exhilaration put speed in his stride, so although he was sweaty and wheezing a little by the time he reached his destination, he was nonetheless in good spirits.

Until he noticed that he'd had a visitor.

Seeing the open door, Corday lowered the girl to the ground and went inside, finding other doors open that should have been closed. He went back outside, telling himself that this intrusion was simply one more reason for him to make Muir and the rest suffer tomorrow night. But his burning indignation at the violation of his sanctuary would not be laid to rest so easily. Grabbing the girl by the wrists, he dragged her into the shack, to the room where the others had been before her. He turned on the lantern and left her on the bed whilst he quickly undressed. Naked, he roughly tore the girls clothes from her and fell upon her, unleashing his wrath on her, wishing she were awake to feel the full force of it.

Eventually she was, and Corday spent the night in the shack.

So it was that the killer he desperately wanted to find was not at home the following morning when Sheriff Flaghan pulled up outside the address the hospitalised Frenchman had given him.

Closing the car door, Flaghan looked up and down the street, but there was no one else around. He peered at the house and then directed his gaze to the ground, looking for any sign of the attack that had happened here last night, specifically blood drops. There had been no rain since last night, but he found nothing. Frowning, he looked back towards the house.

Something was nagging at the back of his mind, something about this house. It took him a minute or two, but Flaghan eventually worked out what it was, but he wanted to make sure. He unclipped his radio from his belt.

"Sheriff to base. Doreen, you there?"

"I'm here, sheriff," came the swift reply.

"Doreen, what was the address of that disturbance call Jack went out to a night or two ago?"

"Just a second, sheriff. Here we go: 23 Coopers Way."

"Thanks, Doreen."

He replaced the radio and looked at the front of number 23 Coopers Way. Parchett had been out here because a neighbour had reported a disturbance. He had spoken briefly to his deputy about it; some guy whose wife had left him had gotten drunk and started smashing the place up. A Mr Ganthrup? Gandrap? Something along those lines. Might it be that the man had gotten drunk again and this time set about taking his grievances out on an innocent pedestrian? One way to find out.

Flaghan strode up the path to the front door, rapping it hard three times and standing back to wait. No one answered. He tried again, and when no one answered this time he took to calling through the letterbox. Still no one answered the door. The sheriff walked around the side of the house to the back yard, trying to peer in a couple of windows as he went but was prevented from doing so by the curtains closed over every one.

The back yard was unremarkable. The windows that all looked out onto it were either curtained or had blinds up at them. He tried knocking on the back door, but again received no answer. He turned and surveyed the lawn, and something occurred to him. Hadn't Parchett mentioned that this guy was dirty and bleeding because he had torn apart a rose bush? From what Flaghan could see there was no rose bush in evidence, torn apart or otherwise. No sign that one had recently existed either. Odd.

After trying the back door handle and finding the door locked, he walked back to the front of the house only to find the front door locked too. He had no good cause to go forcing entry, but he did want to find and have a word with Mr Whatever-his-name-was.

His hand was already reaching for the radio when it blared to life.

"Dispatch to Sheriff Flaghan."

"I'm here. What's up?"

"We have a disturbance reported at 87 Richton Street. I figured given what today is you might want to check it out."

"I'm on my way."

He saw the fight as he pulled up. Parking and getting out, Flaghan heard the words "Bastard son of yours knows where my daughter is!" There and then he got a sinking feeling in his insides. He quickly approached the front yard of number 87, where a small crowd had gathered to watch two men take swings at one another. Two women stood by, one shocked, the other obviously distressed. On the ground between them sat a young man, bleeding profusely from his nose.

"Hey!" yelled the sheriff as he reached them. Both men continued fighting. He reached out and grabbed each one of them by the shoulder and forced them apart, stepping between them as they tried to engage in further combat. Moments later, both men realised who it was that had stopped them and one of them backed off. The other did not. He shoved his face in Flaghan's - who smelled his sour breath and sweat - and pointed over Flaghan's shoulder.

"That fucker won't tell me where my daughter is!" Slowly and evenly, Flaghan told the man to calm down. The man did not heed him. "I want that rat bastard to tell me where my Lucy is!"

"Sir," said Flaghan, keeping his voice calm but putting a little more force into it. "I need you to calm down and explain to me what's going on here."

"He's a fucking nut job!" cried a voice behind him. "Come's up here, starts beating up my son. Fucking jerk thinks he's…"

"Enough," stated the sheriff, looking over his shoulder. "I've got a lot on my plate today, so the quicker I get this cleared up, the better." He glanced at the gawkers. "Get yourselves off home. Now."

The small crowd quickly dispersed. Flaghan moved so he could keep an eye on everybody left: two sets of parents, one with a slightly injured son between them. Flaghan took their names and asked Mr Berendon to explain exactly why he had decided to risk an assault charge.

"We woke up this morning and our daughter, Lucy, was gone. She tried to leave the house last night but we wouldn't let her. I have no idea how she got out, but she must have waited until we were all in bed. She was coming out to meet this prick…" The father of the prick, Jack Connley, reddened and opened his mouth to speak. Flaghan silenced him with a glance. "So he better tell me where she is," Mitch Berendon concluded.

"I don't know where she is," moaned the Connley's son, still trying to stem the flow of blood from his nose.

"Did she come to meet you last night?" asked Flaghan.

"She called me to ask where I was," the boy told him. "Said she was on her way, but she never arrived. I figured she'd either changed her mind or been caught sneaking out."

That sinking feeling in Flaghan's gut intensified. This was shaping up to be really, really bad.

"Does your daughter have a cell phone?" he asked the Berendons.

"We've tried calling," answered the wife, Jenna, her voice high and ready to break. "But there's been no answer."

"I told her!" exploded Mitch. "I fucking told her she wasn't allowed out, not with that psycho out there."

"You're treating her like a kid was why she felt she had to sneak out," commented Scott, picking the wrong time to become an amateur psychologist. Mitch Berendon moved with speed, shoving Jack out of the way, swiping Scott's hand away from his nose and slamming his fist into it. Scott's nose breaking was clearly heard by all. His mother gasped and went pale, and even Jenna Berendon looked shocked. Flaghan stepped towards Mitch as Jack came in to attack, but something he saw stopped him cold. For a moment the sheriff thought Berendon had pulled a weapon of some sort, but the man just stood above the prone boy, pointing down at him.

"She snuck out to see you, you sack of shit, and now she might be dead. My little girl might be dead." His voice cracked, but he went on. "And regardless of what anyone tells you from this day forward, that's on you. You are responsible."

Flaghan laid a hand on the man's shoulder, felt the muscle tense and prepared to defend himself. Berendon turned to face him, and the sheriff caught a brief glimpse of what had made Connley reconsider taking a swing. The fire in Mitch's eyes was fuelled by rage, fear and guilt, and it made him look like he might be capable of anything. But when he saw the sheriff standing there, the fire dimmed and his shoulders slumped. Flaghan dropped his hand and stepped back as the man began to weep. Jenna, crying herself, moved in and put her arms around him. Her husband embraced her, buried his face in her hair and wailed. Both Mrs Connley and her son were also crying, Jack beside them, looking like he'd just stared death in the face.

With a heavy heart, Flaghan reached for his radio to put in the call to begin organising the search.

A few minutes later, the conversation between Flaghan and Deputy Parchett ended and the deputy sat his radio on the desk and shook his head. Christ, another one. Not confirmed, but there wasn't a single person in town who wouldn't jump to the conclusion that Lucy Berendon would not be found alive. Wearily he got to his feet, just as the office door burst open to reveal Doreen Spellner, her face ashen, a piece of paper clutched in her hand.

Flaghan was escorting the Berendons back to their car when his radio squawked. He apologised and moved away to answer it.

"Flaghan here."

"Sheriff," said Parchett, his voice tense. "I've just been handed a piece of paper, a note about a call that came in late yesterday afternoon. It was an anonymous call saying that the killer has been using one of the old shacks out in the woods. The caller gave directions."

"Why the hell are we just finding out about this?" growled the sheriff.

"Doreen… She took the message just as she was leaving. She got a call and she forgot, sheriff." In his head, Flaghan threw a stream of invective at his receptionist.

"I'll deal with her later," he said. "Give me the directions."

Chapter 49

Thirty minutes later, Flaghan and two of his deputies, Colts and Reeves, made their way up through the woods. Flaghan had his notebook in his hands, following the directions he had scribbled down as Parchett had read them from the note Doreen had taken the night before.

He was still mad as hell at Doreen Spellner. He kept trying to put it to the back of his mind, but it just kept sneaking up on him. He wasn't entirely sure what he intended to do about it, but he had a gut feeling that it would depend largely on what he found at wherever the directions led him. Flaghan told himself over and over that it was probably some asshole teenagers having a laugh at sending the sheriff way out into the woods. But if it wasn't, if the missing Berendon girl had been kidnapped last night and this information was accurate and the killer was using one of the old shacks out here, the delay might have cost Lucy Berendon her life. There was no way he could allow Doreen to keep her job if things turned out that way. There was no way he would be able to trust her again. In fact he wasn't sure if trusting her again was an option as things stood now.

Of course, much as he dwelled on that, he spared some time to berate himself. Yes, Spellner had fucked up, but what of his own oversight? When it had been determined that the women had not been murdered where they had been found, he should have done more to determine where the murders had taken place. He tried to tell himself that he'd had no reason to investigate the shacks in the woods. Nothing had pointed to them any more than anywhere else in town. However, regardless of the fact that the ones still standing were scattered throughout the hills and searching them all would have taken more time and manpower than he had available to him, and irrespective of the idea that bringing the victims way out here and then taking them all the way back to town seemed like a big risk for the killer to have taken, Flaghan told himself he should have looked into it. A little more diligence on his part might well have prevented the taking of innocent lives.

A decision had been reached before he was even aware there was a decision to be made. If the girl was not found alive, he was going to resign as sheriff, maybe even retire from law enforcement altogether. He imagined others might tell him that he was being hasty, that it was too big a decision to be made without a great deal more thought, that it was a knee jerk reaction to this situation. But he felt that he had let down the people it was his job to protect.

As they reached the top of the slope, Mark Flaghan told himself that there was one thing he would do before he stepped down, if that was what it was going to come to. He promised himself, and the memories of Janice Mallory, Charlotte Webster and Sophie Thomas that he would find the person responsible for their deaths and see to it that they were made to pay.

They paused at the top of the slope to catch their breath.

"Sheriff," said Reeves, pointing through the trees. Flaghan looked and saw the clearing, and the shacks.

Corday was about finished with the girl. She had stopped being a source of amusement hours ago, every sound from her having ceased. He stood at the door, still naked, having deemed getting dressed again before he was ready to leave pointless. His skin was dotted here and there with her blood, and there would probably be a lot more before he left, but his clothes would cover it when he made his way back into town. He intended to get back to his house and clean up before resting for a while – his exertions since last night had left him greatly fatigued, though not entirely satisfied – before getting ready for tonight.

He stared down at the girl, whose eyes were closed? Sleeping? Unconscious? Dead already? Who knew, and who cared. She had served her purpose as well as she was able. His eyes roamed from her lacerated thighs to her crotch, to her navel, coming to rest on her bloodied and bitten breasts. He felt his member start to stiffen and thought that he might have her one last time before he left, but decided against it.

Stepping over to the side of the bed, he reached down and picked the blood stained knife up off the floor. He leaned over the bed, placing the point of the knife at her throat, then using it to trace a line down her torso. Adjusting his wrist, he brushed the flat of the blade through her pubic hair.

"Our time together is over," he cooed.

He was about to start dragging the blade back up towards her throat when he heard a very clear, sharp snapping noise from outside. Corday looked to the window, his mind taking only a second to process the information his ears had delivered. A dry branch being stepped on. Someone in the woods. Someone he'd need to take care of.

He was so focussed on watching the window and listening for any other sounds that he did not see Lucy Berendon's eyes snap open, her sleep having been a ruse she hoped would deter him from hurting her any more. The poor girl hadn't held out much hope it would work. After all, her falling unconscious hadn't stopped him; she had regained consciousness at times during her captivity to find herself face down on the bed, him on top of her, thrusting into her. But she had heard the sound outside just as clearly as her captor had, but her mind processed it slightly differently: a dry branch being stepped on. Someone in the woods.

Someone who could save her!

She took a deep breath, and with every bit of strength left in her abused and injured body, she screamed for help.

Flaghan was still glaring wide eyed at Reeves, who had momentarily forgotten to watch his step and had stood on the branch.

Moments later, a female's scream sounded from inside the shack.

The sheriff took off towards the clearing, drawing his service revolver as he went. Bursting out from the trees he paused, zeroing in on the shack with the covered windows. Reeves and Colts were on either side of him now. He looked to Colts, mouthed to him to shout out to whoever was in the shack.

"To anyone in the shack," bellowed the deputy. "We are deputies of the Sevier County Sheriff's Department. Come out now!"

As soon as Colts started speaking, Flaghan charged towards the shack. He reached the front door and kicked it in, bellowing out for anyone in the place to stay where they were. He rounded a corner just in time to see a naked figure vanish through a doorway. He shouted out again as he made his way down the short corridor. He looked left, out through a back door, to see a man running into the woods. He looked right and saw a naked, bloodied girl cuffed to a bed, her eyes squeezed shut. Flaghan swivelled left, brought his sidearm to bear and fired. He knew immediately that he had not hit his target; he was in a bad position from which to aim with any accuracy. He fired again, and again, stopping when he realised he could no longer see his target, and that all his shots were doing was making the girl scream. He yelled to his deputies that the bastard was making a run for it. He told Reeves to take care of the girl and for Colts to come around and join him at the back, then he headed out the door.

They had to jump as much as run to avoid tripping in the dense vegetation, and their quarry had managed to get a decent head start. The chase had not long begun when Flaghan tried taking a shot on the run, but it went wide of the mark. Colts also took a chance, but had no more luck. The sheriff even tried shouting out for the man to freeze but, as expected, the order was not heeded.

At one point they found themselves running through a particularly dense cluster of trees. It was here that Flaghan's broad shoulders proved a problem, as he misjudged the distance between two broad trunks and his right shoulder collided with one, slamming him off balance. He spun to the side and knew he was going to go down. Before Colts had the chance to slow down to help him, Flaghan told him to keep after the bastard, then he was on the ground, cursing, panting, wincing at the pain in his shoulder and gratified to hear the sound of his deputy continuing pursuit. After a few moments of recuperation, the sheriff pushed himself up, hocked, spat and followed.

He could still see Colts up ahead, and further ahead still the suspect, though in truth Flaghan no longer thought of him as the suspect; this was their killer. All three of them seemed to be approaching the end of the treeline. Flaghan forced himself to go faster. All he needed was one clear shot, and if the bastard found himself suddenly on open ground, he would either halt or he'd take a round in the back.

The figure some way ahead of Colts suddenly vanished with a cry. Both the sheriff and his deputy thought the same thing: he had tripped and fallen. Then Flaghan saw Colts vanish with a similar cry.

"Sheriff!" screamed the deputy. "Be careful! There's no ground after the trees!"

Flaghan stopped where the trees ended and saw that the ground continued for only a few feet before there was a sheer drop off. He saw the mark in the dirt where his deputy had tried to skid to a halt, then spotted Colts fingers gripping the ledge. He looked around and then rushed forwards, kneeling down and reaching out for his deputy's arm. He had just gotten a hold of it when he heard noises from off to the side and looked to see the killer appear further along the ridge. Flaghan took aim and emptied his revolver, but knew he had not hit his target. Dropping the gun, he reached over with his now free hand, grabbing Colts and dragging the man back up.

"Your gun?" he demanded of his deputy as the man lay on his back, chest rising and falling rapidly. Colts shook his head.

"Dropped it when I fell," he said apologetically.

Flaghan snatched his own sidearm off the ground, jumped to his feet and took off. He moved back inside the treeline, opening and emptying the barrel of his revolver as he went. He paused for precious seconds to reload and then continued, peering between the trees to try and spot his target. He saw no hint of naked flesh but kept running, dodging, jumping, angry at having been duped, at having been led to that precipice. The bastard obviously knew the area well, and his fall had been staged, a plot to make them run harder, thinking him injured, and it had worked perfectly. It was nothing short of a miracle that Colts had lived.

He suddenly felt a pressure across his shoulder blades and realised he had made another foolish mistake. As pain spread out across his back, he pitched forwards, almost losing his grip on his gun. More pain, his head this time. The sheriff staggered forward and thrust his gun under his left arm and pulled the trigger. He heard a cry just before he hit the ground. He got his knees under him, shook his head to clear away some of the encroaching fug. Pushing with his free hand, he rolled himself over onto his back in time to see the killer lope away into the trees, his right hand clasped against the side of his head. Shaking his head again, the sheriff aimed and fired until the hammer fell on an empty chamber.

When it finally registered that his gun was empty, he allowed his arm to drop. A sudden wave of nausea washed over him and he leaned to one side, retching but not being sick. It took a minute or two before he felt able to get to his feet, at which point he looked down and saw the large branch he'd been clubbed with. Peering through the trees with blurry eyes, he saw no sign of the killer. He knew giving chase would be pointless, but he wasn't happy about it. Far from it. Unclipping his radio from his belt, he put a call through to dispatch, outlining the situation and asking for a call to be put out to every officer around

Hannerville to keep their eyes peeled, and to listen for any mention of a naked man being spotted. That done, he contacted Reeves and asked for a report. The deputy had found the keys to the cuffs and released the girl, though she was still in shock and crying, asking repeatedly for her parents. Flaghan outlined what had happened and warned Reeves to be alert as it was possible the bastard would head back their way. If that happened, Reeves was to shoot on sight. In the meantime he was to radio for paramedics, report the girl's condition and give them the location of their cruiser.

Frustrated and in pain, Flaghan started back to where he had left Colts, calling him on his radio as he went. Colts replied, asking if the man had been apprehended or brought down.

"Negative," the sheriff told him miserably. "I'll explain later. Head back to the shack and wait there with Reeves till I get back."

It felt like a long trudge before the shack was in view again. Flaghan walked around to the front and saw the door lying open. He called out to his men and Reeves appeared at the door, minus his shirt. He caught his boss's frown.

"I couldn't find anything else to cover her with," he explained. "I didn't think it would be a good idea to use the bastard's clothes." Flaghan nodded his understanding.

"Good man." Reeves nodded at the commendation. "How is she?"

"Still sobbing, though that's understandable given what he must have done to her." He coloured slightly. "Before I covered her up I couldn't help but notice the mess the poor girl is in. Sheriff, I had a look around in there in case there was someone else there. There was no one, but there is another room, with a table... Jesus Christ, Sheriff, I've never seen anything like it."

Flaghan nodded again and walked inside, went to the room. As Reeves had said, it was something out of a nightmare. The sheriff's stomach gurgled. He closed the door over and went into the room with the bed. The girl sat on the floor, her back against the wall, legs drawn up against her chest, hers arms wrapped round them, Reeves shirt draped over her. He knelt down a slight distance from her and said,

"Miss, I'm Sheriff Flaghan. Can you tell me your name?"

"I want my mom and dad," she managed, the statement broken into individual words by her sobs.

"I understand that, honey," Flaghan responded, keeping his voice low, calm, friendly. "My deputies and I are going to get you back to town as quickly as we can, and if you can give me your name we'll make sure you parents are waiting for you when we get there."

She looked at him and the pain and fear he saw in her eyes made him want to weep. Eventually she told him,

"My name is Lucy Berendon." Flaghan nodded and smiled.

"Lucy, you're not going to be able to walk back to where our car is parked, and at the moment we have nothing to carry you on. There might be a way to rig something but to be honest I want you travelling in as much comfort as we can manage, so Deputy Colts and I are going to stay here with you, and Deputy Reeves there is going to go back to our car. By the time he gets there, some paramedics will be waiting for him who will have been told about the situation, and they'll come up here with a board that we can carry you down to the ambulance on. That sound okay?" The girl nodded and Flaghan looked up at Reeves. "Get there carefully, but get there quick." Reeves gave a curt nod and headed out. Flaghan's attention was drawn back to the girl when she asked quietly,

"What if the man comes back?"

"Lucy," he said. "We are going to wait right here until my deputy comes back with the paramedics. Now this room has two ways in and out: the door and the window. The window is boarded up, so I am going to stand at that door, and if that bas... if that *man* dares to show his face, I am going to shoot him."

Roughly seventy five minutes later, two paramedics bore Lucy Berendon into the woods on a stretcher. Reeves went ahead of them, and Colts was behind.

Flaghan briefed the small team of officers he had ordered up to the shack to go through everything with a fine tooth comb. He wanted every hair and fibre and speck of dirt bagged and tagged. Unfortunately there would be some corruption of the scene, he told them, but any traces he, Colts and Reeves had left behind could be easily identified and separated out later. He requested a full report as quickly as possible, and then he started out after the group taking Lucy Berendon back to her family.

He paused at the edge of the wood, looking back at the place where three women had met their gruesome ends.

As he turned and walked into the trees, Sheriff Flaghan decided that he would really like a word with all the shy, well informed people hanging around Hannerville these days.

Chapter 50

Abigail, Martin, Sandra and Andrea sat in the living room, each of them trying to relax and failing miserably. It had been like this for the last couple of hours, and Abigail had had enough.

"If we're going to have to sit here for another couple of hours like this," she said exasperatedly. "I'm going to have a breakdown or something. And lord help the person who suggests playing a board game."

The other three looked at one another, Martin shrugging and telling Abigail,

"Open to suggestions."

Abigail opened her mouth and realised that, other than once again go over what they had to do tonight, she couldn't think of anything. Inspiration struck when she glanced in the direction of the Guardians.

"Tell us about the others."

"Others?" enquired Coyle.

"Yes, the Bearers who came before us. You must have an idea of the history of all this stuff, and there must be some stories to be told."

"Well, yes," Sandra confirmed uncertainly. "But you'll get first-hand accounts of all that when the unlocking ceremony is performed and…"

"Sandra," said Abigail sternly, holding up a hand. "We all know that there's every chance that ceremony will never take place. I for one would like a little insight into these memories I might, or might not, get to experience."

Sandra looked somewhat aggrieved at Abigail's bluntness, though she knew the younger woman was quite correct in her assessment. She looked to Andrea, who nodded and said,

"As you are both aware, this all began back in Ancient Egypt with a man and a woman who loved one another very deeply, to the point where the man decided that the greatest gift he could bestow upon his beloved was that their love be remembered forever more. He tracked down a man known to have certain abilities and who was known for writing words that could accomplish marvellous things. You also know about the other player in the story, the man whose friendship and love turned to hate, and who also got hold of the powerful incantation.

"The trail is somewhat long and complex after those chosen to hold Bakari and Mandisa's memories fled Egypt to escape Sefu's Bearer. It would take some time to go through it all, and to be honest I don't recall everything that has been recorded."

"But you recall some things," Abigail pressed her. "There must be a story that you've heard or read that caught your imagination."

Coyle gave it some thought and eventually a small smile bent the corners of her mouth upwards.

"There is one I remember reading about that thrilled me." She looked at Martin and Abigail, whose expressions told her to go on. "Sometime around seventeen fifty-two, the chosen Bearers, Captain Michelle Fontaine and her First Mate, Eduard LeMarche…"

"The woman was the captain?" asked Martin, earning himself disapproving looks from the three women in the room. "Oh, shit, no, I didn't mean it like that," he hastily defended himself. "I meant wasn't it unusual for a woman to hold that kind of position back then?"

"It was rare, yes, but not entirely unheard of," clarified Coyle. "After having spent several years on land trying to avoid The Traitor, LeMarche suggested a life at sea, thinking it might be a good way to avoid the odious man out to kill them, one Pierre Argler. Unfortunately LeMarche found that he had no head for the intricacies of nautical navigation.

Fontaine, on the other hand, was a natural, and so became captain of the ship they purchased together. They very quickly settled into a life of adventure on the high seas. However, they did manage to get themselves into all sorts of scrapes involving pirates and buried treasures." She chuckled, warming to her tale. "They didn't become privateers themselves of course; financially they were better off than many kings and queens of the era, but they both loved life at sea. Their pursuit of treasure was simply for the thrill of it. Of course there were many dedicated pirates of the day who knew of them, and who hated them for what they did with any loot they found, which was to give it to orphanages and other such philanthropic endeavours. Thus they made a fair few enemies, but they also fostered a lot of friendships, albeit with some unsavoury characters. The cost of those friendships was a guaranteed share in any treasure found, prior to it being put to good use. For Fontaine and LeMarche it was a worthwhile expense, but on more than one occasion they were forced to show their, shall we say, *sterner* sides, when a supposed ally decided to take more than their agreed share.

"However, they could not outrun the determined Argler forever. Eventually he caught up with them, and by the time he did he had put together a crew of bastards, every one of them as vicious as he was himself. One day they boarded the ship, cutting down crewman after crewman until Fontaine and LeMarche appeared on deck. Fontaine could use a pistol, but was better with a blade, just as LeMarche could handle a sword, but was a dead shot with a flintlock. They cut a swathe through the attackers until Fontaine, realising her crew was in danger of being wiped out, ordered them to fall back behind her and LeMarche. She knew the invaders would not risk going through her and her lover; she knew Argler would want them all to himself.

"She was correct. The deck, awash with blood and bodies, fell silent, and into the quiet, Fontaine screamed her demand that Argler, the cowardly bastard, show himself. He stepped out from the crowd of men he had ordered to attack their ship and smiled at them, complimenting them on trying to prevent further bloodshed, but telling them that before the day was out, their entire crew would be dead. LeMarche called out, saying that the fight was between the three of them, which Argler responded to by saying that whoever was with them was against him. He hated the two of them, and so he hated those who stood with them, and so they would all die. Fontaine demanded that he stop blethering and fight. Then she turned to her lover and told him to promise that whatever happened, he would not interfere. If this was to be her end, she would meet it with the strength and dignity she had always displayed in life. LeMarche reluctantly agreed and they shared what they both knew might be their final kiss, and then she went out to fight, almost tripping on one of the many corpses littering the deck. Argler is said to have called out mockingly that she could barely stand amidst the dead let alone duel, and that she should have some of her men clear the deck. Fontaine's response was to tell him that if he didn't like the state of the venue, which was his own doing, he could fuck off. Enraged at being spoken to like that by a woman, Argler drew his sword and charged.

"It was not a long fight. Every spectator was silent, the only sounds those of the sea and clashing steel. Eventually Argler resorted to underhand tactics, delivering an attack with his sword that caused Fontaine to raise both arms, leaving her stomach an easy target. He punched her and she staggered back, breathless. She raised her weapon to block his next attack. She succeeded but could not hold on to her sword, which was knocked from her grasp. Argler reached out and fondled her, but she looked him in the eye and told him that that was as close as he would ever get to her, in this life or any other. He shoved her backwards and she fell over a dead body, her hand sliding underneath another corpse and finding what would be her salvation.

"Well, that and her opponent's propensity for being a complete arsehole!

"Argler took a few moments to gloat, smiling and nodding to his men, who egged him on, telling him to kill the bitch. One or two of the more detestable men stated that they would be more than happy to have their way with Fontaine even if she were run through and bleeding to death. Argler pointed at LeMarche and told him he was next, and then he raised his sword above his head, intending to cleave Fontaine's head in two.

"That was when Fontaine lunged forward, and clasped in her hand was the dagger she had found under the corpse. The blade was not long, but it was sharp, and did a wonderful job of putting a long, deep slash across Argler's stomach. For a moment he was too stunned to do anything, and she used that moment to get her legs underneath her. Crying out, she thrust upwards, putting the blade of the dagger through his jaw. The blade sliced through his tongue and embedded itself in the roof of his mouth.

"As his sword fell from his hands and he began to stumble backwards, Fontaine stood tall, and told him that her final attack had been for the men who had died there that day, condemned by Argler's vile tongue.

"She turned away from the fallen man and addressed his crew, telling them that their captain was dead, and that they had better get the hell off her ship and sail away. She added that if there were any praying men among them, they might want to do so in the hope that their ship wouldn't be fired upon and sunk. One of the men stepped forward and said that many of them had not agreed with Argler's plan as there had been no profit in it. He said they would leave if Fontaine promised not to fire on them. She told them that they would leave, either alive and on their ship, or dead, carried away by the sea.

"Argler's crew left, the loss of their captain, not to mention the manner of that loss, having reduced their bloodlust to angry sneers, dirty looks and mouthed curses.

"Argler's had already passed on the memories, of course, but Fontaine and LeMarche were never bothered by The Traitor again."

"Kick ass," breathed Abigail, a small smile on her face.

"Yeah," agreed Martin. "Formidable lady."

"One of many," Sandra told him. "One I read about whom I admired a great deal was…"

The phone rang. Having been eager to tell her story, Sandra tutted as she rose from her seat to answer the call.

"Hello?"

"Sandra, have you heard?"

"Heard what?" she asked, recognising the voice of her friend Winnie

"You haven't. He took another girl. A seventeen year old girl."

"Oh, no! When?"

"Sometime last night. But she's alive. The sheriff and a couple of his men found the bastard up at one of the old shacks this morning, stopped him from killing the girl."

"Did they get him?"

"No, he got away. Ran naked into the woods, so I was told."

"The girl?"

"Taken to hospital. Seems she's in a bad way, but she'll live. Berendon's her name, Lucy Berendon. Ring any bells?"

"No. So, one of the old shacks. How did the sheriff know to go way out there?"

"I heard that an anonymous phone call was made to the sheriff's office last night, but it wasn't delivered until this morning. Whoever didn't deliver that message is in for some trouble. I think Doreen Spellner might be out of a job pretty soon," Winnie added with relish. "I just heard about all this, and I thought you'd want to know."

"Yeah. Uh, thanks for calling, Winnie. I'll talk to you again soon."

She hung up and turned to find Martin, Abigail and Andrea on their feet, concerned expressions on their faces.

"That was Winnie Eggleton," she told them. "She's one of Doreen Spellner's circle, meaning she's handy to know for someone who likes to be kept up to date about what's going on around town; I only ever hear from her when there's something she considers scandalous going on. Corday took another girl last night, a teenager named Lucy Berendon, but she's alive. Sheriff Flaghan got to the shack this morning and rescued her."

"Corday?" asked Andrea.

"Fled, naked, into the woods apparently."

Martin's brow was deeply furrowed.

"Why didn't the sheriff go up there yesterday after we called?" he asked, though the question didn't seem directed at any one in particular. "If the girl was taken last night, she's been at the shack since then, so if he had gone last night, she might have been spared whatever she went through. That was why we called, to make the place unusable for Corday. Why did Flaghan wait till today?"

"From what Winnie said, it seems as though the sheriff didn't get the message until today. She intimated that Doreen Spellner had something to do with it."

"That stupid fucking bitch!" shouted Martin, his cheeks reddening with anger. "She should have passed the message on as soon as it was delivered. *Damn it!* That poor wee lassie when through what she went through because what? Because Doreen bloody Spellner couldn't wait to get home last night so she could start spreading some more gossip?"

"Marty," said Abigail softly. "Calm down."

"But that was why we called," he said. "So this wouldn't happen again. But because of that mean minded old cow, it happened. You can bet she wasn't the one who started putting this story about. No, she'll be really fucking quiet for a while now, the witch."

"Martin," said Coyle, her voice stern but not overly so. "Despite her ordeal, the girl is alive. Now we did what we could, and had no control over what happened. If Spellner was to blame, then whoever must deal with that will hopefully do so, but that is not our concern.

"All we need to concentrate on is ending this tonight."

Chapter 51

At 4:10pm that afternoon, the town square was bustling. It was shoving room only as the crowd awaited the arrival of the first of the parade floats. Despite the harrowing story that had been circulating all day, the crowd was in the mood for revelry, though many were a little edgier than usual, keeping a much closer eye on their loved ones than they might normally.

That applied to no one more so than Abigail.

Before leaving Sandra's house, the four of them had made sure that their stun sticks were fully charged. Sandra and Andrea were also carrying guns in their handbags. A quick check of the walkie-talkies proved they were working perfectly, so after a round of hugs and good lucks, the four of them had left.

Andrea and Sandra had gone directly to the town square to join the crowd and begin looking for Corday. Martin and Abigail had gone to Pages and Pages where they had met up with Beth, Amanda and Abigail's Uncle Peter and Aunt Janine. After the greetings had been exchanged, and brief discussions were had on the walkie-talkies (which Uncle Peter said were a really good idea), and on the story of the day, the group had made their way to the square to find it packed.

"Told you this guy wouldn't scare people into hiding," said Beth. Abigail smiled and nodded, doing her best to appear at ease as she looked around trying to spot Corday. As she looked from person to person, the hopelessness of the task quickly became apparent and she felt her stomach start to churn as her anxieties over the disastrous possibilities of tonight played through her mind.

Martin was just beside Abigail, her hand in his, his eyes also roaming the crowd. He was also painfully aware of how badly this could all end, but his blood was up. After everything that had happened, even after facing Corday down once before and almost being killed, Martin wanted to face the man again. He was so angry, wanted so badly to see the man punished, that he hoped for a confrontation, even though he knew such a hope was almost insane. However, as he took in the sheer size of the crowd, he wondered if it would be possible to spot any one person. On the plus side, that meant Corday would have just as hard a time finding them.

Martin and Abigail's walkie-talkies clicked, the signal that they were being contacted. Martin made an excuse about someone who'd had the same idea being on a similar frequency and dropped back a few steps.

"Martin here," he said, momentarily feeling like a child playing at being a spy.

"Martin," said Andrea. "Anything happening?"

"No, not yet."

"Where are you all?"

"We just entered the square. We're just across from the grocery store. Where are you and Sandra?"

"I'm not sure where Sandra is right now," came the reply. "But I'm close by the gazebo where Mayor Ashby is due to make his speech just after the parade. I haven't seen *him* so far."

"Neither have we, but this crowd is bloody massive. We could be here for hours and never find him, and vice versa."

"Keep your group together as much as possible," she advised. "Make contact if you see or hear anything."

Then she was gone. Martin thought that the conversation should have ended with "Over", as all such communications seemed to in films and on TV. Then he noticed how far away the others were getting. He stood up and made his way quickly to them, again taking Abigail's hand. She looked at him and he leaned in.

"Miss Coyle's near the gazebo in the centre of the square. She's not sure where Sandra is but neither of them has spotted him yet."

They shifted their heads so she could speak into his ear.

"Given the size of this crowd, we might not find him, and he might not find us. To be honest, I'm not sure if I want either to happen; there are so many people, and we have no way of keeping the others safe."

All Martin could do was nod.

They found a spot and stopped to wait for the parade.

A few minutes later, a marching band struck up, the first few notes drawing a calamitous cheer from the crowd. The parade began, the high school marching band making their way into the square, closely followed by the first float, which commemorated Hannerville founder Arthur Hanner. Several students and teachers rode the float, each one depicting Hanner at various points in his life. The second float was in celebration of the high school basketball team, the young men clad in their uniforms smiling and waving to the crowd.

The third float drew another huge cheer from the crowd. On this one rode little Susie Wickers, who had earlier in the day been crowned Little Miss Hannerville. The next float in line also got a big cheer. This one was The Queen of the Parade, a flower bedecked float featuring a raised dais on which sat a throne of gold, actually an old wingback chair spray painted the required colour. Upon this paste jewel encrusted wonder sat the high school senior who had been voted to become Queen of the Parade, a young woman by the name of Sandy Possen. Clad in a beautiful dress handmade by her mother, and wearing the tiara that came with the title, Sandy beamed at the adoring crowd, waving to all, every so often losing a little of her stately composure when she saw one of her friends.

The final float, one quickly put together after Mayor Ashby had insisted be built especially for this year's parade, was about community spirit. As the float entered the square, the team who had worked tirelessly to get it ready in time all stood linked arm in arm beneath a large banner that read "Together we can do anything". As the assembly clapped and cheered, the people on the float unhooked themselves from one another and reached down into sacks at their feet, removing handfuls of sweets and tossing them into the crowd.

Sheriff Mark Flaghan found it in very bad taste.

He had known of Ashby's intention, had tried to talk him out of it, but the man had been determined, and so there was the float. And the crowd seemed to love it, one man yelling and hollering that the message delivered by the float was "Damn straight!" Another called out "Yes we can!" as the float went by, following the others and the band as they all made their circuit of the square. When that circuit was completed, the marching band paused and fell silent, as did the floats, their drivers shutting down their engines. The noise of the crowd fell to a hushed murmur, only to reignite as Mayor Ashby appeared on the gazebo, smiling and waving at them.

Any other year, Flaghan thought to himself. *Any other year and that band, and those floats, and the vast majority of this crowd would already be on their way to Beaumont Park for the carnival. But not this year. This year they're all far too interested in what he has to say.*

Ashby waved and smiled for a while, then he flicked a switch and a moment of feedback from the PA system made everyone wince.

"Good evening!" said Ashby, his voice amplified by the numerous speakers set up around the square. "First of all I want to thank all the students and teachers from Hannerville High who have, once again, provided us with some fantastic music and some truly wonderful floats this year." The crowd whooped and applauded. "And how about another big round of applause for Miss Sandy Possen, this year's Queen of the Parade." The crowd duly showed

309

their appreciation, someone managing to be heard calling out "I love you, Sandy!" above the din. Ashby waited for the hubbub to settle down before continuing.

"Yes, as in years gone by, our students and all those who helped with the floats have done us proud, my friends." His smiled straightened out a little, and he allowed a sombre note to enter his voice. "But perhaps more importantly, Hannerville, you have done yourselves proud this year. There has been a dark cloud hanging over us these past few days, days which have seen the senseless taking of innocent lives. I dare say few of you have failed to notice the posters up all over town, showing the face of the man we believe is responsible for these heinous crimes.

"I'm sure you've all heard the rumours that another young woman was taken last night, and those rumours are true. However, it gives me great pleasure to tell you, ladies and gentlemen, that young woman was saved by our law enforcement officers. Acting on information received, Sheriff Mark Flaghan and his deputies raided one of the old shacks out in the woods, and they found the young woman alive. They also have the perpetrator on the run, and it is only a matter of time before he is caught, before he will be made to pay for what he has done."

The largest cheer so far burst forth from the crowd, drowning out their own applause. Flaghan shifted uncomfortably as several people looked in his direction, smiling and giving him the thumbs up. One or two people who were a little closer clapped him on the shoulder. He grinned and nodded, wondering how it was that these people didn't read between the lines and come after him with torches and pitchforks. Where Ashby had stated that Flaghan and his men had "the perpetrator on the run," the sheriff had heard, "Flaghan fucked up and let the bastard get away!"

"There is much evil in this world, and we here in Hannerville were as likely to encounter it as people living anywhere, and so we have, my friends. But evil does not always triumph. Two young women have now been snatched back from this man's hands, two lives saved, and no one will tell me that doesn't count for something." He paused as the crowd made known their agreement. "By coming here tonight, each and every one of you have made a statement. You have stated that you will not be cowed. You have let this evil man know that you will all stand tall, and stand together."

With his last word he slammed his hand down on the rail of the gazebo, a sure sign that his speech was over, and the cue for the crowd to once again launch into rapturous celebration.

Flaghan felt a little sick. Ashby was a born politician: he had not spoken one word of a lie, and had managed to whip the crowd into a veritable frenzy, yet he had left out a few key facts. Cassandra Church, the girl attacked in Beaumont Park, was still trying to deal with the fright she had suffered that night. As bad as that experience had been for her, it was nothing compared to what that bastard had done to Lucy Berendon. Flaghan felt ever queasier as he recalled the doctor's report on Lucy's condition. The girl would be lucky if she didn't spend the rest of her life afraid to leave the house, afraid of men, afraid of just about everything. There was also the fact that her family were in pieces, particularly her father. They had all been there to meet Lucy when she arrived at the hospital, though the girl had been rushed through so quickly all they caught was a glimpse of her face, and even that had been enough to reduce them to tears. Flaghan had waited until the doctor had come out with a brief preliminary report on Lucy's injuries, her condition and her chances of a full recovery (one thing that was for certain was that so much damage had been done that she would never have children of her own), at which point her father had all but collapsed. Knowing that any apologies or condolences from him would be unwelcome, Flaghan had left them to their grief. His first order of business after leaving the hospital was to check in with his deputies to ask if anything had been seen or heard of the killer.

The answer had been no, and that was the other little bit of information Ashby hadn't bothered sharing with the crowd. Yes, the man had been running the last time he'd been seen, but he hadn't been seen since. Chances were good the rat bastard was somewhere in this crowd, hence the reason there was a cop on just about every corner, and many other places besides.

"Ladies and gentlemen," came Ashby's voice, drowning out the sheriff's own thoughts. "It is time for us to follow the band to Beaumont Park, where the carnival awaits."

The crowd loosed a final cheer and the band started up again, leading the mighty procession in the direction of the park.

Flaghan watched the crowd disperse until there were only a few stragglers left behind in the square. As they milled about, he started to follow the crowd, but at that moment a quick, panicked voice issued from his radio. Flaghan turned away from the curious stares of those nearby and answered.

"Sheriff, this is Deputy Berby."

"What's the matter, Berby?"

"I just came across an elderly lady running down the street, screaming her head off! She says she's found her friends dead."

"Who and where?"

"I can't get anything out of her; she's hysterical. All I know for sure is that she came running from the direction of Keebler Street."

Flaghan froze.

"Keebler Street? You're certain?"

"Yes, sir."

"See if you can find out where the woman lives and get her home."

"But what about..?"

"I'll check it out."

Flaghan contacted Jack Parchett to let him know where he was going, then he clipped the radio back to his belt and ran for his car.

Martin and Abigail had their work cut out for them keeping close to the others during the walk to Beaumont Park. Things didn't look as though they would get much better when they arrived at the densely packed carnival ground. Realising that there was a good possibility that someone would break away at some point, Abigail gathered Beth, Amanda and her aunt and uncle around her before they passed through the park gates.

"All right, I'm not going to lie; I'm on edge tonight, and we all know why. I had hoped to be able to keep an eye on all of you tonight, but that's probably not going to be possible when we get in there. If you do have to go somewhere, let me know." She looked at each of them in turn as she said, "I want you all to promise me that you will be careful in there tonight, and on your way home. I also want you to send me a text message when you get home, to let me know you got there safely. Okay?"

To their credit, no one accused her of overreacting. Her aunt and uncle said they would do as she asked, and Beth and Amanda hugged her and said they would seldom be far from her side. The little group then entered Beaumont Park together.

They had been there only ten minutes when Martin was contacted by Coyle. He fell back a little again and answered her, reporting his and Abigail's position and being told that Coyle was close by the big wheel. Sandra was somewhere by the main entrance, hoping to spot Corday as he entered the park. So far they hadn't seen him. Martin almost mentioned that it was unlikely Corday would come in the front way, and would most likely sneak in from the rear of the park, but he did not. There was no way they could effectively patrol a crowd like this, so they were doing what they could. Pointing out the inadequacies of their approach wouldn't help matters. He signed off, telling Coyle he would report in again in fifteen minutes, unless circumstances dictated they should contact one another sooner. Martin then caught up with the others.

He was glad of the cacophony as he was sure that if it had been quiet, the sounds his stomach was making would have been clearly heard by all in the vicinity. He just wanted to catch sight of Corday, or for Corday to come for him, anything to put an end to this waiting. At the same time, he didn't want either of those things to happen. He wanted this to wait until tomorrow, or some other day when they would be less vulnerable. Martin almost made himself chuckle with that one. Until Corday was caught or killed, preferably killed, they would always be vulnerable. But he could feel his nerves fraying, feel the stress building, and every time he glanced at Abigail he could see it in her eyes too. Trying to keep an eye on the others was a problem they didn't need.

Keep it together! he scalded himself as he began to feel beads of sweat run down his back under his shirt. Abigail's uncle asked if anyone wanted some cotton candy, and as Martin smiled and shook his head, his stomach gurgled like a drain. From the corner of his eye he saw Abigail look up at him.

"Are you okay?" she said, leaning in towards him.

"I'll be fine," he told her, hoping he was telling the truth. "It's just nerves."

"Me too," she said, squeezing his hand. He squeezed back, and then for the hundredth time looked around at the faces surrounding them. How would the attack come? Would one of the people he was looking at suddenly turn and rush at them? Would he suddenly be struck from behind? Or would he turn at some point and discover that Beth or Amanda were no longer there?

As his eyes continued to rove across the crowd, he wondered,

Where are you, you bastard?

Chapter 52

Flaghan got out of his cruiser, slammed the door shut and, ignoring the curious faces at a few windows across the road, started up the garden path towards the front door of 75 Keebler Street.

The address of Philip and Anne Glenster.

All the way here he had told himself that just because someone had been found in the vicinity shouting about their dead friends did not mean anything had happened to Phil and his wife. No matter how many times he had told himself that, the cold knot in his stomach only got worse.

Seeing the front door of the house sitting ajar made it worse still.

The sheriff drew his revolver, stood to one side and nudged the door open with his foot. He called for Philip and Anne and received no reply. Then he detected a familiar scent, one he had caught up at the shack earlier today: blood. This time it was stronger, fresher. Flaghan entered the house, calling out who he was, that he was armed, and that anyone in the property should announce themselves and come out. No one did.

With his heartbeat a thunderous drumroll, he made his way to the living room, where he found the owners of the house.

Two chairs had been placed back to back in the middle of the room. Philip Glenster was tied to one, his wife to the other. Their throats had been slit, the fronts of their clothes stained to a dark maroon. Their heads were lowered, their chins touching their chests. In their last moments, the two of them had managed to bend their wrists at such an angle that they could grip one another's fingers. The knife used to kill them lay on the floor at Philip Glenster's feet.

The smell in the room caught in the back of Flaghan's throat and he felt his gorge rise. He fought it down, and also fought the tears that sprang to his eyes as he beheld the fate of two people who had only ever done good things with their lives. He felt his bottom lip begin to quiver and commanded it to stop. He backed away, closed the door and then conducted a quick inspection of the rest of the house. Whoever had done this was long gone, the only evidence of their having been there being a bloodied knife, a jumble of Philip's clothes all over the bedroom floor, the watery bloodstains in the shower and the bodies of two good people. After slaughtering the couple, the bastard had actually taken the time to wash up and raid Philip's wardrobe for a change of clothes. It made Flaghan sick.

Why them? he wondered sadly. *Of all the people, why them?*

After making the necessary calls, he ended up back at the living room door, but couldn't make himself open it. He told himself there was no need for him to go in there. Better that he didn't in fact; the specialists were on their way and all he could do was mess up the scene.

He went outside, took a deep breath of fresh air, and went to the nearest front door to start making enquiries.

Abigail's aunt and uncle were the first ones to split off from the group; they noticed a few of their friends in the crowd and went off to talk to them. Before they left, Abigail, realising she had no real excuse to stop them going, reminded them of their promise and they reassured her they had not forgotten.

A few minutes later, as they neared the line for the big wheel, Beth gathered Abigail, Amanda and Martin into a huddle.

"Marty, there's something us girls have to do tonight, and I don't want you to take this personally, but we need to do it ourselves."

"Okay." Martin said a little uncertainly. He didn't like the idea, but as Abigail had experienced with her aunt and uncle, he had no way of getting around it. At least not without raising some questions neither he nor Abigail could answer. He glanced at her, and she gave him a half smile and a brief nod.

"I also need you to do us a favour," continued Beth. He nodded for her to go on. "While we get into the line for the wheel, can you go get us a slushie?"

"Just one?"

"Please. Blue."

"Will do," he said, perplexed.

Abigail, Beth and Amanda joined the line and Martin, ill at ease, quickly made his way to the nearest concession stand, where he purchased a cup of the bright blue iced drink. He returned to find the others close to the front of the line. Handing the drink to Beth, he told them he would be waiting for them when they got off the ride. Beth gave him a kiss on one cheek, Amanda kissed the other. Abigail thanked him with a look and a kiss on the lips. He saw the bright lights of the carnival sparkling in her eyes and realised she was on the verge of tears. Whatever they were doing, it could only be because of one person.

Sophie.

Abigail didn't like the idea of Martin being left on his own in the midst of the crowd, but what the three of them were doing needed to be done. As she took her seat between Amanda and Beth in the carriage, she found Martin and gave him a wave. He raised his hand in response, then pointed to himself, and then at the ground. *I'll be right here.* She smiled and nodded, and then the carriage moved forward, lifting them only slightly before stopping so the next carriage could be filled.

Beth waited until they were almost at the top of the clock before handing the slushie to Amanda and reaching into her jacket, producing a small flask and three shot glasses. She half-filled the shot glasses from the slushie cup, topping them off with a clear liquid poured from the flask. Abigail knew the liquid was vodka. Adding it to the slushie, Beth had created three shots of Sophie's favourite drink. As they reached the apex of the climb, each held a shot glass in hand.

"We've been here before," she said. "Though usually this car would be a little more crowded. Tonight we say goodbye to Sophie." Abigail felt the first tear trickle down her cheek. Just from the sound of Beth's voice, Abigail knew she was also crying, and she had no doubt that Amanda would be too. "We say goodbye here, on her favourite fairground ride, and with a little glass of her favourite drink to keep us warm because, as she told us so long ago…"

"It can freeze the titty nipples off you up here!"

The three of them said it in unison and laughed, the laughter quickly turning to sobs. It had been something Sophie had said many years ago, when nature had decided she should be bestowed with a bosom. Sophie had been so overjoyed that she brought her new assets into the conversation whenever she could. That year at the carnival, as their carriage had come to the highest point of its journey, she had announced the effect the cold might have on her prized breasts. The others had almost fallen out of the carriage laughing at how she had phrased it, and every year since, whenever they had rode the big wheel, the three of them had quoted her words back at her. It had been Sophie who had first snuck a little flask of vodka onto the ride so they could mix it with the slushie, laughingly telling them they might get off the ride with their nipples attached if they had something to keep them warm. The others were not slow in asking exactly how an iced drink was supposed to keep you warm, at which point Sophie had threatened not to give them any vodka. They had quickly capitulated to her superior wisdom.

"This one's for you, honey," Amanda said, her voice thick with emotion. She held her glass high and the others followed her example. "Gone too soon."

They chased the lumps in their throats back down with the shots of the biting concoction. Beth refilled the glasses, but they each waited.

As the wheel turned, Amanda asked,

"Remember the night we were up here and she told us she had lost her virginity?"

"Oh, god, yeah," breathed Beth. "We hadn't seen her that stoked since she got boobs."

"And she hadn't been that nervous since the day she broke her mother's ornamental china teapot," added Abigail. "She was convinced she was going to get pregnant."

"Then there was the year she got her first car," recalled Beth.

"She wouldn't go anywhere that didn't have a drive-thru," chuckled Abigail.

They had time to share a few more memories before they reached the top again, where they downed their shots. Knowing they had one more time to go round, Beth again refilled their glasses. This time as they went round, they were quiet, remembering their friend. At the top once again, the three of them, crying fresh tears, raised their glasses, said their own silent goodbyes, and downed their drinks. Beth gathered in the glasses and put them away in her jacket, then she sat the slushie cup, a little under half full, in the corner of the seat, and nudged Abigail, who looked round as Beth rested her head against her shoulder. Taking the hint, Abigail opened her arms to her friends, pulling them in tight. Beth and Amanda reached out across Abigail to clutch each other's arms and the three of them slowly descended, crying for their lost friend.

Martin was there to meet them as they disembarked. Abigail walked straight to him and threw her arms around him. He hugged her, kissed the top of her head, then started as he felt other arms embrace him. He looked left and right to find Beth and Amanda standing on either side, their arms around him and Abigail. Smiling warmly, Martin extricated his arms from the huddle and did his best to hug all three of them.

They stayed like that for a short time, then separated and set off through the crowd. When they passed a small row of portable toilets, Beth told them that she needed to pee. Amanda said she did too and the two of them headed off.

"We'll wait for you here," Abigail called after them.

"How are you?" Martin asked her. She shrugged.

"Feeling a little played out," she admitted. "Ragged around the edges."

"Do you think you're going to be okay?"

"I have no idea, but we'll find out. You hear anything from Andrea or Sandra?" He shook his head.

"I contacted them, but they had nothing to report. Andrea's starting to think we might have got it wrong, that Corday isn't going to make his move tonight. She thinks the twisted bastard is going to try to drag this out a little further."

"Part of me hopes she's right... another hopes she's wrong."

"I know what you mean."

He put his arm around her and they waited for Beth and Amanda to come back. As Abigail's two friends walked towards them, they heard someone shouting somewhere in the crowd. Martin and Abigail both tensed, wondering if this was the sign they had been waiting for, the sign they had been dreading. The notification that Corday was about to make his move.

However they soon discovered that their enemy wasn't about to do anything; he had already done it.

Although Sheriff Flaghan now had other officers canvassing the street (he had been able to free up a few since the vast majority of the party crowd was now concentrated in one area with an easily guardable entrance and exit) for anyone who might have seen anything, he was still going door to door himself. Had in fact just raised his hand to knock on another door when a voice barked at him from his radio. It was the dispatch officer on duty back at the station.

"Sheriff, we just got a call from the hospital. The French guy who was admitted last night is dead."

"What? I spoke to him earlier today. He was beaten up, but he was recovering."

"He didn't die from his injuries, sheriff," the officer announced grimly. "The man was murdered. Nurse found him with a pillow over his face. Not only that, but someone also reported their car as having been stolen from the hospital parking lot."

"God damn it," Flaghan spat. "What the hell is going on in this town tonight?"

"Sheriff?"

"Rhetorical question. Give Jack Parchett a call, get him over there to take some statements. Get a description of the car out. I'll notify the crime scene people they have another place to visit once they've finished at the Glenster house. Tell Jack to update me as soon as he's able."

"Will do, sheriff."

Shaking his head, Flaghan made to return the radio to its holster, but before he could the dispatch officer came back on.

"Sheriff, one more to add to the list; we just received word that a fire has broken out in town."

"Where?"

"The bookstore."

"Pages and Pages?"

"Yes, sir."

"Have the fire service been called?"

"Yes, sir."

"I'm going to go take a look."

He notified the nearest deputy of where he was going, and then jogged to his car. If it had been anywhere other than the bookstore he might not have been so quick to attend, but that it was Abigail Morton's bookstore set off an alarm bell somewhere in the back of his mind. The sheriff wondered if perhaps he was just making connections where there weren't any, but he nonetheless got behind the wheel, started the engine and drove away.

Word spread quickly through the crowd, soon reaching the area where Martin, Abigail, Amanda and Beth stood.

"Hey, the bookstore is on fire!" they heard someone yelling, and all eyes turned to where a thin column of smoke could be seen rising into the night sky. Before Martin could even turn to her, Abigail had shot away, dodging her way through the crowd, heading for the front gate. He ran after her, aware that Amanda and Beth were following. He collided with one or two people, apologising even as he continued running after Abigail, who seemed to be navigating the milling mass with ease. He lifted the walkie-talkie to his mouth. Just before he spoke he bumped into someone, knocking their drink out of their hand. He felt something splash against his upper arm and shoulder, then felt the chill as the liquid soaked through his clothes. He heard someone shout out in anger, but he was already talking.

"Miss Coyle! Sandra! Are you there?"

"We've heard. Martin, you know what this is."

316

"It's a ploy to draw us out," he said. "And it's working. Abigail isn't going to let her livelihood burn down without trying to save it."

"We're on our way," Sandra told him.

He stuck the walkie-talkie in his pocket and ran. Soon he was within sight of the main gate, and moments later Martin exited Beaumont Park. With no one to get in his way, he managed to catch up to Abigail. He tried to grab her shoulder, but she shrugged it off and sped up. Behind him he heard Beth and Amanda calling to them, but Abigail did not slow down.

Not until a few minutes later, when she turned onto the street her store was on to see flames writhing out from the shattered front window. Her run slowed to a jog as she approached the burning store. Realising there was nothing she could do, her jog slowed to a trot, and then she finally stopped and stared, close enough to the fire that the heat quickly dried the tears coursing down her cheeks. Martin stopped beside her, a little out of breath. Amanda and Beth weren't far behind him. They all watched as the flames consumed the store. Others ran on to the street, some just curious, others because they feared for their own businesses which were situated close to Pages and Pages. They had good reason; the fire was raging out of control.

Above the roar of the fire they could hear sirens, but no one was under any illusions. Though they might arrive in time to spare the buildings to either side of Abigail's store, Pages and Pages was beyond hope. Martin looked at Abigail's stricken face. He saw her lips move, but he did not hear what she said. He leaned in close and asked her to repeat it.

"He did this," she said flatly, her voice barely above a whisper.

Suddenly aware of how exposed they were, Martin looked up and around. Most of the other people were some distance away, and none of them were looking in their direction: all eyes were on the fire. Then Martin spotted one man waking quickly towards them, paying no heed to the nearby conflagration that everyone else seemed unable to look away from. His attention was focussed on Martin. The man was definitely not Corday – he was taller and bulkier than the man Martin had fought on the shingle beach – but Martin could not help but think this man meant him harm. He was soon proved correct.

"You knocked my girlfriend's drink out of her hand, you fucking asshole!" the man shouted as he reached Martin. His large hand shot out and he grabbed a fistful of the front of Martin's shirt.

"What?" blurted Martin, uncomprehending, until he remembered the still damp patch on his arm. So it had been this guy's girlfriend's drink he had spilled. His first thought was to apologise, but before he could open his mouth to do so, another thought made itself known. A much louder, angrier thought: *who the fuck does this dickhead think he is?* Martin had bumped into other people as he had departed the carnival, and none of them had seen fit to come charging after him, shouting and grabbing, clearly threatening him. Martin's eyes darted to the side and he saw Amanda and Beth looking at what was unfolding with wide eyes. Abigail was still looking at the inferno her beloved store had become. Hadn't she been through enough? What did this moron have to gain by this little display of drunken machismo? Now that Martin was so close, the stale smell of booze on the man's breath was inescapable. Maybe it was just the booze, or maybe the guy was the kind to take offense at every little thing. Truth be told, Martin Muir didn't give a shit.

He brought his arms up, bracing himself by grabbing the man by the shoulders. Then he threw his head back and, with all the force he could manage, brought it forward, driving his forehead right into the middle of the man's face. There was a wet snap as the man's nose caved in. He let Martin go and fell to his knees, mewling, his hands cupped in front of his face.

There was a sudden shriek from somewhere and everyone looked to where a woman had just rounded the corner. She cried out "Baby!" as she started running towards the man kneeling in front of Martin. As she got closer, she yelled, "What did you do to my baby, you bastard!" Martin realised that she now meant to attack him. His earlier anger had subsided, but even if it hadn't, Martin would not have hit a woman. As he tried to think of a way to calm her down, Beth stepped forward. Without a word, she met the woman and delivered a punch that threw her to the side and off her feet. Sprawling on the ground, the woman let out a cry.

"Get your ass up, get your dipshit boyfriend on his feet, and go the fuck home!" Beth shouted at her. "Cause if you don't, I will beat you till you're good looking!"

Normally the woman, whose name was Brenda Garthouse and who was usually what could best be described as timid, would have heeded the advice Beth had given. Unfortunately she had consumed just as much alcohol as her long term boyfriend, one Cody Barden. Her cry as she had fallen had been more of surprise than pain, because Brenda was particularly good at two things in life: taking a punch (usually from Cody) and hiding bruises with expertly applied makeup. Her pickled brain told that receiving threats and punches from the man she loved was one thing, but taking them from some uppity bitch in the street was just not on. Getting to her feet, she let loose an inarticulate cry of rage and threw herself at Beth.

Martin gawped as the two women fought, unable to believe what was happening. He was suddenly struck with great force in his midsection, and felt his feet leave the ground as he was shoved backwards. He disbelief intensified as he realised the man who had been kneeling in front of him now had him balanced on one shoulder and was carrying him! Moments later the breath was suddenly forced from him. His attacker backed off and watched him slide down the wall he had slammed him into, a sneer of satisfaction on his face. Martin gasped for breath.

The roar of the fire and wail of the siren were suddenly competing for supremacy as the fire engine turned the corner onto the street and slowed, the firemen already leaping out and preparing to do battle before the large vehicle had completely stopped. At the opposite end of the street, another vehicle, a car, careened around the corner and accelerated towards the burning store. Martin noticed both these things in a vague way, the bulk of his attention concentrated on the sight of the underside of Cody Barden's boot as the man lifted his leg into the air, clearly intending to stamp on Martin's face. Martin threw himself to the side and Barden kicked the wall. Then above the clamour Martin heard a harsh voice bark "Hey!" and looked up to see and deputy grab Barden as he prepared to attack again. Barden growled and swore, but the officer propelled him to one side, away from Martin, who looked over to where Abigail and Amanda still stood. The former was still watching the fire, whilst the latter looked on as another officer broke up the vicious scuffle between Beth and Brenda.

Martin heard the deputy who had pulled Barden away from him say "Stay there and do not move," and then his view was obscured as the lawman hunkered down in front of him.

"How badly are you hurt?"

Martin was still having trouble getting his breath, but he was very aware of the car that was still speeding towards the scene. With what little air he could get, he croaked out,

"Help me up."

"I think it's best if you stay there for the time being," replied the deputy. "Just till we work out how bad your injuries are."

"Hey!" complained Barden. "What I did to him wasn't as bad as what the fucker did to me! You see the mess he made of my face?"

The officer stood up and turned to speak to the man. Martin saw the car still barrelling down the street. He got one good breath into his lungs and bellowed,

"ABIGAIL!"

Abigail turned towards the sound of his voice, just as the car's tyres squealed as they skidded across the road surface. In between where the brakes were applied and where the car eventually stopped were Amanda, Beth, the deputy and Brenda. Amanda was thrown to the side, but the other three were right in the path of the car. Beth went up and over the vehicle, landing behind it and rolling to a stop. The officer and Brenda were pitched forward, ahead of the car, the two of them landing in a tangled heap of limbs.

Martin started to get to his feet on his own as Corday quickly got out of the car, smashed his fist against an astonished Abigail's jaw, dazing her, and then opened the back door and threw her inside. He was getting back in as Martin started to stagger forwards. The deputy who had come to his aid put a hand on his shoulder to stop him going any further, but Martin shrugged it off and continued his painful staggering jog towards the car, which pulled out and went around the bodies on the ground in front of it – Corday didn't want to risk running over them in case it slowed him down - then accelerated as it passed the fire engine. The deputy decided whatever Martin was doing wasn't as important as helping those now lying on the ground. He got on his radio for medical assistance as he jogged to where his fallen comrade lay, bundled together with Brenda Garthouse. Moments later, his animosity towards the prick who was still lumbering after the car forgotten, Brenda's boyfriend was kneeling beside her, begging her to move.

Martin told himself to ignore the pain, to push through the fog clouding his brain, and to get after the car. He took a couple of strides, and then, grimacing against the discomfort, started running. Much to his dismay, his first perfectly clear thought was that there was no way he was going to catch up with the car. Tears of frustration and fury sprang to his eyes and he tried to speed up, even as the car approached the corner.

He heard an engine revving, and suddenly there was another squeal of tyres as a car pulled up beside him. The passenger window was down and Sandra Logan stuck her head out and yelled at him to get in the back. Martin complied. Seated behind the wheel, Andrea Coyle put her foot down, and took off after Corday and Abigail.

Chapter 53

Abigail's mind reeled. Her store – dear god, her store! – had been torched. She wasn't aware of how long she had stood there, unable to do anything but watch it burn. Her mind had gone back to the first day she had opened it, to some of the special events she had held, to the time she and her friends had spent in there, chatting when it was quiet, or having lunch. Seeing the smouldering pages of books coming drifting out from the flames, scattering all over the place, had been too much.

She had been aware of people around her, things happening, but her mind had been too numb to give it much thought. It had been Martin's voice that had brought her back. She recalled turning and being confused, wondering where he had gone, then she had spotted him, over on the other side of the street, a police officer and some big, pissed off looking guy standing beside him. Then the car had screeched to a halt and it had hit... Sweet Jesus, it had hit Amanda and Beth! Then someone had gotten out and hit her and...

An atomic fury ignited inside her that burned away everything else as surely as the fire set by the bastard in the driver's seat had burned away her business. With utter disregard for the consequences, Abigail sat, reached into the front of the car and clawed at the face of the driver, who yelled out in surprise and pain. She began battering at Corday with her fists. He kept one hand on the wheel and attempted to defend himself. The car swerved all over the road, narrowly avoiding collisions with parked cars and lampposts. Eventually Corday roared and jabbed backwards with his elbow. She turned her head to the side and the blow caught her on the temple. Bright lights flashed behind her eyelids and she fell back against the seat, dimly aware that Corday was spitting curses and promising her she would pay.

"Are you all right?" asked Sandra, looking to her right at Martin, who was sitting on the edge of the back seat, a hand gripping the front headrests, his head poking through the gap between.

"Just aches and pains, and I'll have a fair few bumps and bruises tomorrow."

"What happened?" asked Andrea.

"On our way out of the park, I knocked some woman's drink out of her hand. Her arsehole boyfriend followed me to the store and had a go at me."

"Is that a speck of blood on your forehead?" Sandra enquired, peering at the small dark mark on his skin.

"Most likely his," Martin told her. "I got a little angry and I head-butted him. Then his girlfriend shows up, and she gets set to have a go at me too. Beth sorted her out, and then the two of them got into it. Meanwhile the boyfriend slams into me, picks me up and smashes me against a wall. I saw the bastard coming down the street in his car and all I could do was call out Abi's name, but it was too late. Beth and Amanda... they were run over. Christ, I hope they're okay. Then Corday got out of the car. Abigail was too surprised to do anything and..."

"She seems to be doing something now," commented Coyle. They all watched as the car some way ahead of them began veering all over the road. This lasted several seconds before the car began going in a straight line again. However the incident had allowed them to close the gap a little.

"You have your guns: can't we try shooting out his tyres?"

"We try that, we run the risk of hitting Abigail," said Sandra.

"What are we going to do?" Martin asked Coyle.

"Follow him to wherever he's going."

"He'll try to lose us." Coyle nodded, her lips pressed together in a thin, straight line.

"He'll try," she said.

Even if he hadn't known where he was heading, it wouldn't have been hard for Sheriff Flaghan to work it out; a thick, undulating column of smoke indicated where the burning building was. He wondered how badly the premises surrounding the bookstore had been damaged, and hoped that the firemen would be able to get the flames under control before they completely lost any other buildings. Judging by the smoke, Abigail Morton's store was a lost cause.

His mind turned again to the various occurrences of the evening: the murder of the Glensters and the Frenchman, a car stolen, and now a fire. Was the man who had murdered those women responsible for all that as well? If so, why had his targets suddenly changed? He had taken some of Philip Glenster's clothes, but that house would not have been the first he would have come to after coming down out of the woods, so why go there? As for the French fellow, could he perhaps have had some connection to the killer? Had he maybe been an accomplice turned into a loose end that had to be tied up? Or had whoever beat the man up the previous night come back to finish the job? Were the Frenchman's murderer and the car thief one and the same person?

Flaghan shook his head. He was used to things being a little more on the active side come the night of the Hanner Carnival, but this was ridiculous. A few moments later, it became even more so.

There was a car chase going on!

Two cars came tearing down the street, streaking past him. Flaghan caught the registration number of the first car, which did not have its headlights on. He caught a quick glimpse of the man behind the wheel, recognising the face adorning dozens of posters up all over town. Martin Muir and his lawyer, Miss Coyle, with another woman riding shotgun, were all in the second car. The sheriff executed a slightly shaky one hundred and eighty degree turn, hit his lights and siren, and took off after them.

Gripping the steering wheel with his right hand, the sheriff reached for the dashboard radio with his free hand. Putting a call through to dispatch, he asked for the registration number of the car stolen from the hospital car park. It matched the one on the first car. Flaghan reported what was going on and asked for any available patrols to make their way to his location. Before he ended the conversation, the dispatcher informed him of yet another odd happening, this one at the site of the fire.

"Some people got into a tussle, then some crazy son of a b... Sorry, someone comes driving down the street, knocks over four people, including one of ours, then punches some woman, throws her into the car and takes off."

"Thanks," Flaghan signed off tersely. He set the radio back in its cradle and, with both hands back gripping the wheel, put his foot down.

Oddly enough, the drivers of both cars being pursued by Sheriff Flaghan responded in exactly the same way to the sound of the siren: both looked in their rear view mirrors and muttered a curse under their breath.

Corday's thoughts were racing almost as fast as the car he was driving. He needed to work out which was the best route to use to lose those who were after him. The trouble was that one thought kept upsetting his concentration: I've got her! He could scarcely believe that after all this time he finally had Abigail Morton in his possession. Even now, as she lay in the back seat, awake but only just, he could smell her perfume. He imagined taking a deep sniff of it directly from her skin and was instantly erect. His mind tried to wander down avenues of pleasing thought, but the incessant noise of the siren prevented it from doing so.

His plan to get her out into the open had worked a treat, as he had known it would. However he hadn't counted on being followed by one car, let alone two.

The chase saw the three vehicles racing through town. In some cases the one in front missed mowing down civilians by only the very narrowest of margins, the driver telling himself he had to be more careful; hitting people would slow him down, and possibly cause him to lose control of the vehicle.

Corday's pursuers were concentrating so much on keeping up that they only noticed they were heading out of Hannerville as they raced across the bridge. Martin, still perched between the seats of Coyle's car, adrenaline still staving off the worst of the pain caused by the injuries he had sustained, wondered if Corday was going where he thought he was going. His suspicions were confirmed as the car ahead suddenly made a hard right hand turn onto Jackpot Road.

"There's no way back down from here except the way you go up," Martin said, almost to himself. "What the hell is he doing?"

Neither the driver nor the other passenger could offer any answer, and so both remained quiet.

A couple of minutes later, after the cars had navigated the steep straights and tight bends of Jackpot Road, Martin realised they were on the final stretch, the section of road that led up to the cabin. Still uncertain of what Corday had planned, he watched the vehicle ahead, which was still running without its lights on. The road opened up and he saw the cabin, a silhouette against the dark sky. Coyle slowed down, also wary of whatever was coming next.

There was a sudden noise and Corday's car went into a spin. Martin wondered if the maniac had lost control, but quickly realised he had not. As the car ahead spun to face them, its high beams burst into life, flooding the interior of their car with blinding light. Everyone, including the driver, shut their eyes. Hearing the revving of the engine and realising Corday meant to ram them, Coyle yanked the wheel to the right, feeling the brief impact with the other car. She hit the brakes and brought them to a shuddering stop.

Sheriff Flaghan saw what had happened up ahead, saw the car coming at him. For an instant he thought about just ramming the fucker, but he couldn't risk injuring, or possibly killing, Abigail Morton. He spun the wheel, putting his car half on and half off the narrow road and applying the brakes. He was jolted forward in his seat as he hit a tree, the impact causing him to stall the cruiser. The stolen car scraped past him, two wing mirrors meeting and both being torn off. The sheriff looked out of his windscreen to see Muir's car spring forward and turn to follow. The rear end fishtailed wildly for a moment or two before it straightened out and the car took off back down the hill. He restarted his cruiser and tried to reverse, but one of his rear tyres dug itself into the mud. There was no way forward for him to try and rock the car out of the rut, and so, growling with anger, he quickly unbuckled his seatbelt and got out to see what he could do.

Martin marvelled at Miss Coyle's driving, unsure he could have been as calm if he were in the driving seat. He was almost certain there was no way he could have handled the car the way she was handling it. It seemed teaching was not the only skill his old teacher possessed.

Ahead of them, Corday's brake lights flashed as he eased his vehicle into a hairpin bend. Despite slowing down, he still took the corner at speed. As Coyle approached the same corner, Martin felt their car accelerate. His first instinct was to ask what she was doing, but having trusted her thus far, questioning her now seemed pointless. Nonetheless, his heart rate increased as they neared the bend. He looked to Sandra, and saw that she was gripping the sides of her seat. Martin tightened his grip on the headrests as Coyle wrenched the wheel to the left with one hand, and yanked on the handbrake with the other. The tyres screeched, sending up plumes of smoke, as the car drifted around the bend, hitting the straight with almost no loss of speed. Martin's heart hit the back of his throat, and his stomach almost rose with it.

"Bloody hell!" he gasped. "Where and when did you learn how to do that?"

"Here and now," she replied "That closed the distance between us, but we have to put an end to this or he's just going to keep driving until one of us crashes." She took a quick look at the dashboard. "Or runs out of fuel."

"Bump him off the road?" Sandra suggested.

"Not up here," Coyle said, shaking her head. "And not at this speed."

"Abi cold get hurt," stated Martin.

"Martin, if we don't end this and he gets away, she will most definitely get hurt. Running him off the road might be the only way we're going to stop him, but I don't want to run him off this road; I'd rather wait till there's slightly less hazardous terrain on either side."

"We can't..." Martin began, but Sandra cut him off.

"Ask yourself this, Martin: what would Abigail want us to do?"

Even as he told himself to carefully consider the question, Martin knew the answer. There was no way Abigail would choose an option that might leave her at the mercy of the madman driving the car she was in. Swallowing hard, Martin turned to Coyle and told her, "Do it."

As Corday turned off Jackpot Road and headed back towards town, Abigail came back to her senses. Momentarily confused, she quickly recalled the events that had brought her here and felt her hands clench into fists. Before she launched another attack on the driver, however, she was distracted by the sound of squealing tyres. She pushed herself up and looked out of the back window to see another car behind them. Andrea was driving, Sandra was in the passenger seat, and in between she could see Marty, his expression grave. Her heart lifted at the very sight of him and she waved briefly before stopping, not wanting to give away to Corday that she was up and about. However the movement was enough to get her noticed by the trio in the car behind. Martin's lips curved upwards in a small smile. Abigail watched as the three of them exchanged words, but she couldn't work out what they were talking about until Martin looked up at her.

He pointed to Andrea, then made a fist and smacked it into his other hand, and then pointed at her.

Abigail got the message, nodded, and then sat up and put on her seatbelt. So secured, she lifted one arm and gave the thumbs up. Her movements did not go unnoticed by the driver.

"What are you doing back there?"

Abigail didn't answer, and Corday looked in his rear view mirror.

"Shit!"

The interior of the car got brighter and brighter as the car behind them closed in, and then slammed into the back of them. Abigail was pushed against her restraint before being thrown back into her seat, the impact shocking her, even though she had been expecting it. Corday swore through clenched teeth as the car swerved all over the road. He had just regained some control when they were hit again. Abigail realised that he was slowing down, and wondered if she might be able to unbuckle her belt and leap from the car. It was the kind of thing that always worked well in films and television programs, but she got the feeling that it might not go as smoothly if tried in real life. Besides, Corday was speeding up again. She leaned over and looked between the seats, out through the windscreen, and saw they were approaching the bridge. The interior was getting brighter again, and she sat back, awaiting the next collision.

It didn't come.

Corday suddenly pulled the wheel to the right and hit the brakes, slowing the car down, but not stopping it completely. In a blink, the car behind them was beside them, and Corday swung the wheel back to the left, broadsiding the other vehicle. Sparks flew as metal met metal, and then Abigail suddenly realised what the bastard was attempting.

She looked out in time to see the car with Martin, Andrea and Sandra inside veer off the road, heading straight for the gulley.

Chapter 54

There was no chance of stopping in time, but Coyle tried. As rubber slid over grass and mud, Martin, who had sat back and buckled himself in before they had started ramming Corday's car, bellowed in frustration as he watched that same vehicle speed across the bridge.

Then the world tilted forwards and came to a sudden, complete and bone jarring halt.

He heard a siren and opened his eyes to find the interior of the car awash with alternating red and blue light. His hand reached for the button that would undo the belt buckle, and then stopped as he realised that the belt was the only thing holding him in place. It all came back to him in a rush and Martin lifted his legs and planted his feet against the seatback in front of him; Sandra's seat. He pressed the button and the belt retracted, leaving him crouched there on legs that weren't broken, but which nonetheless felt like they might give way at any moment.

Tilting his head, Martin looked at the figure suspended behind the wheel. Miss Coyle appeared unconscious, her head and upper body resting on the deployed air bag, but he could see she was breathing.

As he tried to determine Sandra's condition, the door beside him was tugged open and Sheriff Flaghan appeared. Martin jumped back in surprise.

"Muir, are you hurt?" asked the sheriff.

"No. Miss Coyle is out, but she's breathing. Please, check on Sandra."

Flaghan moved out of view. Martin had time to wonder how much time had passed since the crash before the sheriff was back.

"She's unconscious, but breathing. I've had a look around the underside of the car and there doesn't appear to be any fuel leaking. They seem fine. I'll get them out in a minute or two."

"How long since we crashed?"

"I don't know," replied Flaghan, helping Martin out of the car. He steadied him on the slope, and then as the two of them made their way to where the sheriff had parked his cruiser, he continued. "I don't think it's been any more than a couple of minutes though. I had to gather some branches and shove them under my rear tyres to get some traction to get back onto the road. When I got back down the hill, I had to guess at which way you had all gone. I drove back towards town, saw the ass end of your car sticking out of the gulley, and stopped." He looked at Martin, who was propped against his car, looking like he might be sick. "You want to explain to me what the hell has been happening? Why you, your lawyer and some other lady were chasing someone in a stolen car?"

"Abigail was in that car," Martin told him. He almost used Corday's name, but stopped himself just in time. "The murderer was driving. He took her." His throat tightened and he fought back tears. "And now they're gone."

"I know; I've got my people looking out for the car," he told Martin. "We'll find it."

Martin was about to respond when they heard a cry for help.

"That's Sandra," said Martin, taking a step towards the crashed car. Flaghan grabbed his arm.

"You stay here," he said, his tone brooking no argument. Martin, who was still woozy, nodded, and the sheriff ran to Sandra's aid.

Hot, bitter tears stung Martin's eyes as he wondered where Abigail might be. He leaned forward and wretched, pounding the heel of one fist against his thigh. He had failed her. All those things he had said, the promises he had made, and he had failed her. He wanted to do something, but what was there to do? He had no idea where Corday might have driven to after causing them to crash. He might have taken Abi somewhere in town, or he might have driven on to somewhere else. It didn't really matter; local or otherwise, his destination was unknown. It was all well and good for the sheriff to say he had people looking for the car, but it wasn't someone he loved who was in danger. It wasn't someone he loved who might already be…

Unwilling and unable to finish the thought, Martin took a deep breath, held it, and then let it out slowly from between pressed, slightly trembling, lips.

He's in town, he told himself. *The bastard has hung around here all this time because he wanted to finish this where he started it, so he's not going to go elsewhere now. He's going to want to go somewhere that he feels has some relevance, somewhere with some sort of connection to Abigail. The shack is out. He might have taken her to Pages and Pages if he hadn't torched it. Where else? Where have you taken her, you son of a bitch?*

A very clear and simple answer occurred to him. He had no idea if it was right or wrong, but checking it out was far preferable to standing here stewing in his own impotent rage.

Ignoring his numerous aches and pains, Martin took off, running as fast as he could over the bridge. He was halfway across when he heard Flaghan bellowing his name.

He ignored that too.

After seeing Martin's car go off the road, Abigail had looked at the man in the driver's seat and actually snarled. Her one and only wish at that moment was to cause him as much physical pain as she possibly could. She lunged forward, only to be restrained by her belt and forced back into her seat, making a choked noise of surprise. Corday chuckled.

"I'd rather not," he said. "But if you force me to, I will use this." He waved his left hand over his right shoulder, showing her the gun he now held. "I might not be able to get a great shot, but I'm sure I could still hit you."

Abigail, whose hands had been fumbling with the belt release, stopped and stared daggers at the back of his head. Her head was full of wonderful images like reaching her hands around both sides of his head, finding his eyes and blinding him, or grabbing that gun and putting a bullet in his back, and then another, and another. The possibility that if she attacked he would fire kept her in her seat. As long as she was unhurt, she might have a chance to get out of this. If she ended up with a gunshot wound, her chances would drop drastically. If it was a particularly lucky shot, they might drop to zero. She decided to bide her time.

She closed her eyes and took some long, slow breaths in and out of her mouth. Abigail wondered if Martin, Andrea and Sandra had survived. The idea of either or both of the Guardians having been killed saddened her, but a tear escaped from beneath one closed lid at the idea of Martin not getting out of that car alive. It hadn't been a particularly nasty crash – it wasn't as if the car had exploded into a fireball or anything – but who knew what damage might have been caused by the jolt they would all have taken when the car stopped. It tore at her heart to think that Martin might be gone, might not be coming to help her. Abigail had no doubt that, had he survived and was capable of doing so, Martin would be coming after her.

But what could they hope to do, what kind of victory could they hope to achieve, against an enemy like the human looking *thing* driving this car?

"They're odd things, aren't they?" Corday said. "The choices we make in life," he clarified. "For instance, take your French friend. If he hadn't decided to come sniffing around my house, I wouldn't have had to beat him to a pulp, and take his gun." He waggled the firearm over his shoulder again. "If he had decided not to take me on himself, he might still be around." Abigail almost commented that Matthew, though injured, was very much alive, but then she remembered who she was talking to. The import of Corday's last comment struck her, and she bit back the question, the answer to which would confirm her suspicions. Of course, Corday didn't need the question to be asked to give her an answer. "I paid him a little visit in the hospital. He was surprised to see me to, to say the least. He put up so feeble a fight when I put the pillow over his face that I almost felt sorry for him."

Abigail clenched her fists, digging her nails into the flesh of her palms. She clenched her teeth, refusing to rise to the bait. Her expression betrayed her however, and Corday saw it when he glanced in his rear view mirror. Grinning, he went on.

"After you and I are finished playing, I have to get out of here, and I can't say I'll be sorry to bid this little piss puddle of a town goodbye. I am sorry about not having had the chance to play with a couple more of your friends though. Mind you, if I thought Beth and Amanda would be half as much fun as little Sophie was, I might be compelled to stick around. Or maybe come back for a visit sometime. What do you think, Abigail? Are Beth and Amanda worth sticking around for or popping back in the future?"

He looked in the rear view mirror again, this time to see Abigail looking back at him. There was no evident emotion on her face now, nor in her voice as she said to him,

"I'm going to fucking kill you."

"That's the spirit," he said cheerfully.

Not long after, he pulled in to the kerb and shut off the engine. Turning to look at her, he said,

"We're going to get out now, and go for a quick, and very quiet, walk. I dare say you've got some ideas about trying to escape or call for help, but be warned that if you attempt either of those things, I'll shoot you. You give me any kind of trouble and I will put a bullet in your gut and leave you to bleed to death in the street, for your beloved bastard Martin to find you. Do you understand?"

Abigail nodded and Corday told her to get rid of anything she was carrying. She took out the walkie-talkie and left it on the seat. After a moment's hesitation she took out the stun stick and sat it down beside the walkie-talkie. Corday got out, opened the back door and waited for her. As soon as she was out he grabbed her arm and pulled her close to him, jamming the gun between them, burying the muzzle in her side. She cringed as he pressed his face into her hair and inhaled. He pushed her forward and they set off down the street.

She wondered if someone might see them and become suspicious, maybe call the police, but it didn't seem likely. To the unknowing bystander, they would just look like a couple out and about or maybe on their way back from the carnival. They might wonder why she looked so dejected, but would probably come up with some explanation, like they'd had an argument or something. There would therefore be no reason for said bystander to become suspicious or get involved. Abigail wondered if she might be able to catch someone's eye and plead with them, make them see she was not with this man willingly, but there was no one around. It wasn't that late; most would still be at Beaumont Park having a good time. She told herself it might be just as well; if she did attract attention, it was a good bet Corday would shoot them, and she didn't want that on her conscience.

Putting aside all notion of seeking assistance or trying to flee, Abigail took a good look at the neighbourhood they were walking through. She quickly realised where they were, and where they were going, and her heart almost stopped dead as she asked herself a question.

Does he know?

Ten minutes after Corday and Abigail had abandoned the stolen car, Martin huffed and puffed as he jogged on to the street where the house was. It had taken him a little time to get here; he had been able to recall the address from the newspaper article, but the actual location had been unknown to him. He had taken a chance and gone to a street only a couple of blocks away from the square, approaching someone and asking them for directions. He had specifically chosen someone who looked like they'd had a few beers, someone who hopefully wouldn't notice how dishevelled and nervous he was and become alarmed. The man had barely given him a second glance; he had just said "Sure, buddy," and given him directions.

His pounding footsteps sounded insanely loud, echoing up and down the still, quiet street. Martin slowed as he neared the address he sought.

Part of him had been expecting to come across a dilapidated husk of a building, with boards covering the glassless windows, rubbish strewn across a weed infested garden, maybe even a sign saying "Keep Out" hanging on the front door, the paint on which would be chipped and peeling. It would be an abandoned place that looked and felt like something truly terrible had happened there. What he found was a place that was well maintained and almost certainly occupied.

The house in which Abigail's parents, Ross and Alice Morton, had been murdered by Andrew Corday almost three decades ago was in darkness. Not even the porch light was on. Sweating, partly because of exertion, partly because of fear, Martin examined each curtained window for some sign that he was being watched. As he did so, he cursed himself, thinking that he should have snuck up to the house from the side, instead of walking right up the front and staring at it. There seemed to be no movement however, and so he quickly made his way up the path to the front door. Glancing at the manicured lawn on either side, he wondered what might have become of whoever lived here now. Their deaths would have meant nothing to Corday if killing them meant he got the ending he wanted. To Martin's mind, this would be where Corday would want to bring Abigail; back to where they first met. In his twisted mind there would be a certain symmetry to it, something almost poetic.

Standing at the front door, Martin tried to decide how to enter the house. Ideally there would be a way to gain access without being detected, thus giving himself an edge, but Martin doubted if anything about this situation would turn out to be ideal.

Call the bloody sheriff! he told himself. *There's no way you can manage this by yourself. Get some people here who know what they're doing.*

His phone was in his pocket; making the call would take only a few seconds. But how long would the sheriff and his deputies take to get there? What would happen in the interim? Martin's stomach flipped and he closed his eyes tight, willing away the oncoming barrage of horrible thoughts. No, something had to be done now. Moving to the window, he closed one eye and peeked between the curtains, hoping to get some idea of who was where inside the house. All he could see through the thin gap was darkness.

What if I called through the letterbox that I was here to give myself up? Exchange myself for Abigail?

Martin drew back from the window, giving some serious thought to the idea. There was no element of surprise to it, but then given that he wasn't accustomed to breaking and entering, the element of surprise was a non-starter anyway. Surrendering to Corday would at least get him inside the house. After all, Corday wanted both of them, not just Abigail.

"Who the hell are you?"

Spinning round in surprise, Martin found himself confronted by a group of kids who looked to be in their mid-teens. The one who had spoken to him, a stocky boy with a smattering of acne across his chin, stepped forward.

"Why are you trying to peek into my house, mister?"

Martin took a step towards the boy, and he and his friends stepped back, one of them looking like he was about to run away. Martin stopped and raised his hands.

"Easy, boys," he said in a hushed voice. "I'm not going to hurt you." Addressing the speaker, he asked, "Who else lives here with you?"

"My Mom and Dad, and my sisters. Now what were you doing looking in the window?"

"What's your name?"

"You don't need to know my name, but you do need to tell me what you're up to before I call the police." Martin nodded, wondering how he was going to explain this.

"Listen, I think that someone…"

That was as far as he got before he heard a key turn in the lock on the front door. His head whipped to the side, his eyes zeroing in on the door handle as it moved down. He didn't even have time to cry out to the boys, to tell them to run, as he was sure Corday would hurt them, if not kill them outright.

"Bryan, what the hell is going on?" asked the man who stepped out onto the doorstep, looking from the group of boys to Martin. "Who are you?"

"Dad," said the stocky boy, walking over to join his father, followed closely by his friends. Pointing to Martin, Bryan said, "We caught this guy looking in the window."

Even in the dim light, Martin saw the colour bloom in the man's cheeks. Snapped out of his confusion, he raised his hands and approached.

"Sir, is everything all right?"

"No," growled the man. "You want to tell me why you were spying on my family?"

"I… I thought something might have happened to whoever lives here. I was trying to see… You're all okay?"

"We're fine," said the man, obviously still angry, but now a little curious as well. "Why would you think something was wrong?"

Martin shook his head, lost for words. The man might have been coerced into lying, told to go outside and see what the fuss was, informed that if he did anything but get rid of whoever was there the other members of his family would be slaughtered. But Martin did not think that was correct. The man's annoyance when he had appeared at the door had seemed genuine, his anger the same. If he was acting, he was damn good at it. The conclusion was inescapable.

They weren't here.

Martin was struck by two realisations, the first of which was that having to do away with an entire family was a task that might have caused all sorts of problems for Corday. One of the family members might have put up a fight (this man, who was waiting impatiently for an answer, definitely looked like he would not go down without one). Corday himself may even have been injured in the fracas; Martin didn't doubt Abigail would have had a go at him if given half the chance. As he was only one man, and given how many of them there apparently were living in the house, it was conceivable that one of them might have escaped the attack and called for help, or in all the confusion, Abigail herself might have gotten away, something Martin felt sure Corday would not risk. The second realisation was that there was only one other place left that Corday might have taken her.

"I'm very sorry," he said, then he turned around and ran off, praying he wasn't too late.

Abigail sat tied to a chair at the back of her own lounge, well away from the window. A twisted dish cloth was tied around her face, gagging her. She struggled futilely against the rope which bound her wrists and ankles, close to crying with frustration.

When her fears about their destination had been confirmed, she came perilously close to deciding to yank her arm out of his grip and make a run for it. The most likely outcome was that she would have been shot in the back, but that seemed preferable to what might happen inside the house if Corday knew about her journals. She had been told that he had been in town for some time, but regardless of how long he had been around, she could think of no way he could have found out about her memory problem, or of the importance of the journals. She had decided to wait.

"Everything is all set up and ready to go," he had told her gleefully as they had approached the front door. "After I left the hospital I made a stop off at your friend's place, where you've been holed up. Found your keys in no time. I thought about torching your friend's place too, but I decided to leave it, at least for the time being. If I get the chance, and if they're still alive, I might wait until she and that bitch Coyle are back there, then I'll burn it down. Getting rid of them would be worth hanging around for. Anyway, I picked up some stuff and dropped it off here before going to your store. Now, I'm going to let you go for a moment. You know what'll happen if you try anything."

She'd had to fight to stay where she was when she felt him release his grip, but she had managed it. Corday had taken her keys out of his pocket, opened the door and pushed her inside. Keeping her covered with the gun, he had closed and locked the door, then got her to get together everything he needed to tie her up. Presently he was upstairs doing something. She could hear him thudding around, and as long as she knew he was up there, she was going to keep trying to get loose.

The knots were tight, and the rope chafed her skin. It seemed a hopeless task, but she kept at it, the physical activity freeing her mind to make the connection.

She was tied to a chair in the lounge, and he was upstairs ransacking her house (*Please don't let him go into the attic. He might not know what those journals mean to me, but please don't let him find them*), a similar set of circumstances to the night he had murdered her parents. For some sick reason, he was doing his best to recreate that night! Assuming she was correct, Abigail wondered why Philip Glenster had not been brought here. He was the only other person who had been there who was still alive, and he had played an important role; if Corday was so determined to recreate that night, but this time have it end as he had originally planned, why not bring the doctor here? A dreadful idea entered Abigail's mind and she forced herself to concentrate on the ropes.

It only took a few minutes of fruitless twisting and writhing before her mind went to work again.

She wondered what would happen if, by some miracle, she survived the night, but didn't get the chance to write everything down. Say she got knocked out, or fell unconscious for some reason. When she woke, everything that had happened would be lost to her. She told herself that might not be such a bad thing, and immediately an angry voice yelled in her head that yes, it would be a bad thing. She had already re-written her own history once. She had been a child and she'd had her reasons, and she had made peace with that. She was an adult now, and she would never do such a thing again. She argued with herself that if everyone had her condition, then they would often rid themselves of unwanted memories. Before she could offer any kind of rebuttal, she heard footsteps coming down the stairs.

Corday walked into the lounge, a big smile on his face. He stood in front of her, and reached into his trouser pocket, from which he produced a pair of her panties. Holding them between thumb and forefinger, he waved them about.

"A little souvenir from your underwear drawer," he explained. "To help me remember you in years to come." He stuffed the item back into his pocket, whilst simultaneously removing something else from his other trouser pocket. It was another pair of her panties. "These ones are from your dirty laundry hamper," he told her. He turned the garment inside out and pressed the crotch against his face, inhaling deeply. Beneath the gag, Abigail's upper lip curled in disgust. "Oh!" exclaimed Corday. "That smell might not last long, but while it does it will definitely get me off!" He stuffed the panties back into his pocket, guffawing at his own crude humour. As he approached her, Abigail couldn't help but notice that he was aroused. He stood right in front of her chair and reached out to touch her. She closed her eyes and pulled her head back, but it could only go so far. Soon his fingers were running through her hair.

"Now you might think that with all the fun I've had recently, I'd be all out of ideas on how to show a woman a good time. Let me assure you that that is not the case. I'm going to do things to you you've never even fucking heard of. It won't be like all the same old, same old fucking you've been doing with that little shit Muir. Oh no, I'm going to open your eyes to a whole new world of pain, Abigail. I'd guess that maybe about halfway through, you're going to wish that old prick Glenster hadn't come to your rescue the night your parents died."

He snarled, his hand shifting from her hair to her chest, roughly grabbing her breast. She squealed against the gag and threw herself back in the chair, the force enough to send it and her toppling backwards. Abigail's eyes opened wide as she realised what was going to happen, then squeezed closed again as she braced for the impact. The chair slammed against the carpeted floor, and a spasm of pain lanced up and down her spine. Her head rebounded, a shower of sparks igniting behind the closed lids of her eyes.

Corday moved around and crouched down beside her. As she moaned and continued to try to evade him, he reached out and fondled her breasts.

"I always get what I want, Abigail. If you try to stop me getting what I want, you get hurt even more."

He grabbed a handful of her hair and stood up, pulling her and the chair upright. The pain caused her to yell against the gag, but on the plus side it cleared her woozy head. The front legs of the chair thumped against the floor. Her head hanging down, her chin touching her chest, Abigail felt something that hadn't been there before: the chair now had a slight wobble to it.

"Now," Corday said, stepping back in front of her and taking the gun out of his jacket pocket. "I am going to take that gag out of your mouth and replace it with something else." Abigail lifted her head to see his free hand go to the zipper of his trousers. "If you make a peep during the transition, I'll shoot you in the kneecap. If I even think you're going to use your teeth, I'll shoot you in the kneecap before performing some amateur dentistry using the butt of this gun."

Abigail, a cold ball of utter dread forming instantly in her stomach, drew in a breath and prepared to scream her head off as soon as the opportunity arose. Corday began to drag the zipper down.

The doorbell rang.

Cursing, Corday yanked his zipper back up and spun to face the front of the room. Abigail breathed out through her nose, hoping her first thought regarding who was at her door was wrong.

It wasn't.

"Corday," came Martin's voice a few moments later as he shouted through the letterbox. Abigail was torn between being elated that he was all right, and heartbroken that he was here. "I'm offering you a trade: me for Abigail." Corday half turned, looking down at her in disbelief.

"He's fucking kidding, right?" Chuckling and shaking his head, Corday walked across the room and out to the hallway. The moment he was out of sight, Abigail started struggling.

Corday yanked the front door open and saw Muir standing there, looking a little worse for wear. Corday drew his attention to the gun that was being discreetly aimed at him. Muir just nodded.

"You're an idiot," Corday said disgustedly. "What the hell made you think this little ploy would work?"

"Take me, and let her go," said the clearly deluded man on the doorstep.

331

"I intend to have a great deal of fun tonight, and it isn't going to be with you. You I'd just as soon shoot, or open your throat, and leave you to die."

"And what if I cause a fuss?" asked Martin. "Start shouting and screaming here on the doorstep."

"I shoot you once and drag you inside before anyone knows what's happening, or where. I then leave you to bleed to death, and whilst you're doing that you can listen to me screwing Abigail."

"You make me sick."

"You think I give a shit about your opinion of me, boy? To be honest I'm wondering why I haven't just shot you already. After all, it seems to me that you've really left me with no other choice. I can't let you go, so I have to bring you inside. Now, my sexual proclivities might be a little off centre, but I don't like being watched while I fuck. On the other hand, I don't want to leave you unattended, because then you might decide to interrupt us. My only recourse is to shoot you, so if you'd be so kind as to…"

He was cut off by a crash from the lounge. Instinctively, Corday looked over his shoulder, and Martin seized his chance. He moved his right hand slightly, allowing the stun stick to slide down from inside his sleeve. Gripping it tightly, he lunged forward, pushing the button as he pressed the end of the device against the exposed flesh of Corday's neck. An incapacitating charge jolted through Corday, stiffening his limbs. His finger involuntarily tightened on the trigger and the gun discharged, the bullet embedding itself in the floor. Moments later his limbs went limp and he fell forward. Martin dodged out of the way and let him hit the ground. He then dragged Corday all the way outside before stepping inside, closing and locking the door.

He found Abigail tied to an upended chair, crying fiercely. Her eyes went wide as he moved into view and she called his name through the cloth gag, which he quickly removed.

"Are you all right?"

"I thought he'd shot you," she sobbed. Martin shook his head.

"I stunned him and he fired the gun," he told her. "Missed by a mile," he added, hoping it sounded reassuring. From the way Abigail continued to cry, he guessed not. He repeated his question.

"Mostly." She calmed down enough to explain. "I tipped the chair over earlier and when he straightened it back up I felt one of the legs was wobbling. I thought I might get it to break, maybe loosen these ropes, but when it tipped over just the back leg broke off. I couldn't get loose and then I heard the gunshot…" Her eyes brimmed over with tears again and he knelt down and kissed her.

"I'm fine. Let me get these ropes."

As he tried to loosen the tight knots, Abigail asked about Andrea and Sandra. Martin explained that they had survived the crash, but that they had been unconscious when he had last seen them. He then cursed, unable to loosen the ropes attaching Abigail to the chair.

"I'm going to get a knife from the kitchen."

He ran to the kitchen, checking that the back door was locked whilst he was there. From the cutlery drawer he grabbed a cheese knife with a serrated edge and two sharp tines on the front end, and then ran back to Abigail. It was more difficult than he would have thought to get through the ropes, but he managed eventually. He helped Abigail to her feet and she embraced him. Martin dropped the knife and hugged her back. He didn't want to let her go, but a screaming voice in his head reminded him they weren't safe yet.

"We have to go," he whispered. "I don't know how long that bastard will stay down."

They released one another, and Abigail looked up into his eyes.

"We can't go," she said softly.

"Why not?"

"My journals," was her simple reply.

"Does he know about..?"

"I don't think so. He hasn't mentioned them, but we can't leave them here, Marty. I think on top of everything else he's a borderline pyromaniac: he set fires at Berrybeck, he torched my store and he mentioned earlier that he was going to burn Sandra's house down. If we leave, he might just burn my house down out of spite, and if those journals burn, Marty, I don't know what's going to happen to me." Martin gave it some thought.

"All right," he said before long. "Go up to your room and find the two biggest bags or suitcases you have, then go up to the attic and start cramming as many of the journals as you can into them. Go."

She nodded. Just as she started to run for the stairs, Martin called her name. She turned to see him bend down to pick up the knife he'd dropped. He held it out to her handle first. Without hesitation she took it and tucked it into her belt, then she went upstairs. Martin went to the front door, where he knelt down to peek through the letter box. Corday lay where he'd been left. *I hope your rotten heart exploded in your chest.* He turned and jogged upstairs to find Abigail exiting her room with a large holdall in each hand. He took them from her and she set about opening the hatch to the attic, Martin wondered exactly how much time they had. How long would it take to fill the bags? Would they be able to get safely away laden down with such weight? If they left, might Corday not forego torching the house in favour of chasing them? Probably not, especially since the bastard didn't have to chase them; he still had a gun on him. Martin cursed himself for not having relieved Corday of the weapon, but his thoughts quickly returned to the subject of loading the bags. There were a lot of books in that cabinet up there, however it was obvious Abigail would not leave without them, and so there was really no choice.

The ladder extended and Abigail quickly climbed into the attic, switching on the light as she went. Martin passed the bags up to her and then followed.

They were halfway to the large, blanket draped cabinet when they heard the garage door open. They both froze for a moment, then Abigail turned to look at Martin.

"Go start packing the journals," he told her. She continued on to the cabinet and he strode over to the window. Unlocking and opening it, he gripped the frame and boosted himself up, locking his arms straight so that he could look out. The slant of the roof prevented him from seeing much at first, other than light spilling out from the open garage. Then came footsteps, and suddenly a shadow blocked some of the light from the garage. For a fleeting instant, Martin thought about clambering out and jumping from the roof onto Corday's head. Instead he kept watching, unable to see anything of his enemy. He heard more footsteps though, enough to suggest that Corday had walked from the garage to the front door.

Martin lowered himself back down to the floor, turning to see that Abigail had uncovered, unlocked and opened the ornate cabinet. Having started at the top, she was hastily grabbing handfuls of the volumes and putting them into the bags.

"Keep packing," Martin said as he started towards the hatch.

"What are you going to do?"

"To see what that fucker's up to," he said gravely. He felt he should add something more, some sort of reassurance. Likewise, Abigail felt that some sort of encouragement was warranted. Neither could think of anything, and so they shared a look that said everything, and then both resumed their tasks.

Martin reached the hatch and descended quickly, still asking himself what he was planning on doing. He was no closer to an answer by the time he reached the top of the stairs, where he stopped in his tracks upon seeing the black plastic nozzle sticking through the letterbox, disgorging a small torrent of fuel. A simple, and very possibly suicidal, plan formed in his head and he took the stairs two at a time. As he landed, he drew the stun stick from his pocket, a quick press of the button proving there was no juice left in the thing. With it still being the only weapon to hand, he transferred it to his left hand, using his right to unlock and open the door in rapid succession.

The petrol can was yanked from Corday's grasp, the nozzle jammed tightly in the letterbox. He looked up in surprise, which he quickly overcame. His hand went into his pocket for the gun, and Martin struck with the stun stick, bringing it down in a stabbing motion, the two electrodes on the tip painfully jabbing into Corday's forehead. The man yelled and fell back, and Martin grabbed the handle of the petrol can and tried to dislodge it. It took a couple of tugs to free it, and just after he did, he noticed Corday getting to his feet, the gun in his hand. Martin did the first thing that came to mind: he sloshed a load of fuel over Corday.

The Traitor gasped and closed his eyes, preventing any of the noxious liquid from going into them, but inadvertently taking some in his mouth. He spat it out, choking, and opened his eyes to see Martin swing the petrol can. The can hit his hand and he lost his grip on the gun, which skittered across the walkway, coming to a halt just outside the garage. Martin raised the can so he could smash it down on Corday's head, but before he could Corday roared an inarticulate sound of rage and rushed at him. For the second time that night, Martin was winded as someone slammed a shoulder into his midsection and lifted him off his feet. Corday carried him into the house, but slipped in the puddle of fuel he had created. As the pair crashed to the floor, Martin let go of the petrol can so he could use both hands to defend himself. The can spun away, spitting out fuel as it went.

Corday got to his knees, sitting astride Martin, and battered at him mercilessly, punching him wherever he could. Martin knew if it carried on this way he was dead, so he bucked and blocked, attacking when he got the chance. Corday landed a lucky hit, and in the next moment Martin felt blood run into his eye. He raised his arms and some of the fuel he was lying in found its way into the open wound. Letting out a cry of pain, Martin shoved himself forward, slamming his forehead into Corday's jaw. It gave him a moment of reprieve in which he literally grabbed Corday's testicles and squeezed. Corday howled, his hands going to Martin's wrist. With his free hand, Martin punched the fucker right in the throat. Gagging, Corday fell sideways and Martin scrambled away to the foot of the stairs.

Corday got to his feet, spitting curses. He glowered at Martin for a moment or two, then he took a zippo lighter out of his pocket. He raised it above his head, a triumphant little smile on his face. Martin, also on his feet now, and finding every breath a painful effort, stood on the bottom stair. He asked himself what his chances were of reaching Corday before he could use the lighter, and decided they were bad. Even if they had been good, the chances of him having been able to put up much more of a fight were not.

"Even you're not crazy enough to do that," he said. "You're dripping with fuel."

"Maybe so, you little prick, but I'm also standing at the door. I light this, I drop it, and I step backwards, closing the door behind me as I exit. Then I stand across the street as you and the bitch upstairs burn."

His smile turned into a sneer as he used his thumb to open the lighter and work the wheel. The flame flickered into life, a single little spark leaping from the flame to land on Corday's shoulder, where it caused the fuel soaked material to burst into flame. Corday bawled as he dropped the still lit lighter and whirled in a circle, batting at the flames, not realising he was twirling into the house rather than out the door. Martin turned and ran upstairs as quickly as he was able. He had only gone three steps when the lighter hit the floor, igniting the fuel. A trail of flame shot off to the left and right and a blazing column rose, almost engulfing Corday. Martin did not see this, though he felt the blast of heat hit his back as he lumbered upstairs.

Corday only narrowly avoided being roasted by the surge of flame. He twirled out of the way just in time, tumbling onto the first few stairs. His jacket, however, was still a problem. Giving up trying to stop the fire spreading, he shrugged off the garment before it could set fire to anything else he was wearing. Only after he had thrown it into the quickly growing conflagration in front of him, and made sure nothing else about his person was on fire, did he look around and realise what had happened.

The fire now surrounded the foot of the stairs, completely cutting him off from the door, or any other viable escape route. Had he been dry he might have chanced leaping through the flames, but with parts of his attire still soaked with accelerant, he didn't think it was a good idea.

He had been trapped by the fire he had started. The irony almost made him smile, but the curve of his lips quickly reversed itself, and he grimaced at the thought of the two upstairs. He consoled himself with the thought that if he had no way out, then neither did they. He hadn't intended to be quite so damn close when they burned to death, but he decided that as he was here, he might as well have a little fun before he had to go.

Martin clambered up the ladder into the attic, calling for Abigail. She looked up from where she was still stuffing journals into a bag and saw the flickering light coming up through the hatch. Then Martin appeared, blood running down his face. Abigail gasped, rose and ran over to him, feeling the heat get stronger as she got closer.

"What happened?" she asked, taking his arm and keeping him steady as he came up the last few steps.

"Fire," he replied. "We have to get out of here."

"Downstairs?" He shook his head.

"No way; the flames are thick, and they're all around the foot of the stairs." He looked towards the skylight. "We're going to have to go out that way." She nodded, and the two started back towards the cabinet. "Many left to pack?"

"Not many."

"Yoohoo!" shouted a voice from below. It was followed by a cough, then: "The big bad wolf is coming to say goodbye, kiddies!"

They stopped and turned, seeing a wisp of smoke drift up through the hatch, closely followed by the top of Corday's head. Abigail swore, then released Martin's arm and ran full tilt towards the hatch. Corday's head and shoulders rose above floor level and she drew her foot back. He saw her coming and so managed to avoid what would have been a bone cracking kick had it connected. With one hand he grabbed her ankle and pulled her leg out from under her and she went down hard on her back. Corday kept hold of her ankle as he continued to climb. Martin was making his way over, but Abigail, a little out of breath and running on fury, pulled the bread knife from her belt and drew its serrated edge across the back of Corday's hand. He hissed in pain and released her, allowing her to crab crawl backwards to where Martin helped her to her feet.

"You rotten, stinking, whore!" screamed Corday as he stepped off the ladder and into the attic. "I'm going to gut you with that knife and..." His eyes shifted. "And leave you two lovebirds here to burn whilst I escape out that window." He smiled and advanced on them as the smoke rising from below grew thicker.

Abigail and Martin stood side by side, he with nothing but his fists, Abigail brandishing the knife. They looked at one another, and again needed no words to communicate what they were thinking. Silently, they rushed at Corday.

Taken by surprise, Corday focussed on Abigail as she had the weapon, but his strike at her meant he could not block the solid fist to the jaw that Martin delivered. Reeling backwards, Corday snarled and lashed out at Martin, only to yell in pain as Abigail slashed at his leg with the knife. As his leg buckled, he looked like he was about to go down, and Abigail came at him again with the knife. Corday dodged, grabbed her arm, slapped her with his other hand and then used her to yank himself to his feet. He grabbed her by the shoulders and shoved her backwards, sending her stumbling into a pile of boxes.

Martin grabbed a handful of Corday's hair, pulled his head back and punched him in the side. The blow wasn't particularly powerful, but it still hurt. Corday twisted in Martin's grip and Martin felt a handful of hair tear itself out. Corday swung a punch at his stomach and Martin jumped backwards, not fast enough to avoid the attack entirely, but enough to make sure it didn't do as much damage as it might have done. Corday came at him and he continued to move backwards, aware that he was moving towards the cabinet, and the bags of books. He looked over Corday's shoulder and saw the dancing light being thrown through the open hatch was much stronger now, the fire downstairs raging out of control. Even as he thought this, he realised that his injuries were not the only things making it difficult to breathe in the attic; the smoke was gathering, getting thicker. Martin knew he couldn't retreat much further, but he also knew he didn't have the strength in him to force Corday back very far, certainly not as far as the hatch.

Corday suddenly gasped in pain and threw out his chest as Abigail came up behind him and elbowed him in the kidneys. He looked over his shoulder at her, baring teeth. Martin saw what he was going to do, but wasn't quick enough to stop him. Corday rounded on her, punching her square in the face. Her nose burst and blood flowed, and he kneed her in the stomach. She staggered backwards as Martin leapt on Corday's back. Grabbing one shoulder with one hand, Martin slammed his elbow down at the point where Corday's neck met his shoulder. Corday, already slightly stooped, took a shambling step forwards, but then gathered himself, straightened and prepared to throw himself backwards. Martin wrapped an arm around Corday's throat, lowered his legs to the ground and used Corday's momentum to pivot him around, actually lifting him clear of the floor as he did so. But Corday jammed his feet against the floor as he landed, and at the same time reached back, grabbed Martin's shoulder and pulled him forward as he bent at the waist. Martin was thrown over Corday. His flailing legs smashed into the open doors of the glass front cabinet, shattering them, and he landing on the holdalls Abigail had been packing, feeling small shards of glass bite into his back. Corday kept a hold of his arm and twisted it painfully, using it to keep Martin where he was as he started kicking him in the ribs. Martin grunted with each kick, unsure if the sirens he could hear were in his head or somewhere outside.

Corday stopped kicking him and Martin told himself to get up, to attack, but he had nothing left. He could only watch as Corday moved to stand over him, a foot on either side of Martin's waist. Wreathed in smoke as he was, Corday, now more than ever, looked like something out of a nightmare.

"I'd really like to take my time with you," he said, his voice hoarse. He hocked and turned his head to spit. "But I'm afraid that's not an option. So I'll just have to make this quick."

Martin realised that, in addition to the small pieces of glass, he could also feel an intense heat seeping through the floor. He struggled to move as Corday knelt down and lifted a large piece of glass from the floor.

As he straightened up, he came face to face with Abigail.

As Corday's eyes met hers, and went wide as he read her intent, Abigail stabbed him. One hand wrapped around the handle of the knife, she used her other hand to power the blade forward, embedding it between his ribs right up to the hilt. She didn't know if she had hit his heart, but she didn't care. Corday was pushed backwards by the sheer force of her attack, and as he collided heavily with the large cabinet that for years had housed her journals, she knelt down and did what she could to pull Martin back. He did as much as he could, pushing weakly with his legs, and with her help managed to struggle to his feet. He put an arm around her shoulders and she wrapped an arm around his waist. Together they watched as Corday bounced off the cabinet and fell forward. He landed on his front, amidst the bags and a few scattered journals, the blade being driven deeper still as the handle met the floor. Their eyes were on him, and so they did not see the cabinet rock slowly backwards, and then forwards. Corday looked up at them, a trickle of blood escaping from between his lips.

"I'll remember this," he managed.

Then they both noticed the cabinet. Abigail gasped and tried to rush forward, but Martin held her back. The huge piece of furniture overbalanced, crashing down on top of Corday. The floor, weakened from below by the fire, gave way, and the cabinet, the holdalls and Corday all fell into the inferno below. Martin barely heard Abigail's ear splitting scream over the roar of the fire as it shot up into the attic. Abigail collapsed to the floor, and Martin, suddenly without support, went down with her. When he scrambled to his knees, he saw that her eyes were closed. He looked helplessly at her, and then at the hole in the floor, the flames pushing up through it drying his eyes, preventing him from weeping. He shook her, receiving no response, and he coughed out a sob as he begged her to wake up.

The sirens, much louder now, mingled with the crackling of the fire. He looked up and saw that they had fallen underneath the skylight. Rising on legs that felt like the bones inside had been replaced by jelly, Martin reached up and grabbed the frame, but knew he would not be able to pull himself up to call for help. Instead he stood on tiptoes, putting his mouth as close to the aperture as possible. With everything he had left, he bellowed two words into the night.

"HELP US!"

Then his mind and body stalled, and he collapsed to the floor beside his beloved Abigail.

Chapter 55

Martin sat beside Abigail's hospital bed, his head in his hands, crying.

His shout had been heard by the firemen, who had been able to get him and Abigail out of the house safely. They then managed to extinguish the fire, but the house, like Abigail's store, was beyond help. The two of them had been taken to hospital, where Martin had regained consciousness a few hours later to find a deputy sitting beside his bed. The young woman had asked him how he felt and he found his throat was too dry for him to speak. After she had helped him take a sip of water, he had asked about Abigail. The deputy had refrained from answering, and had instead gone to fetch Sheriff Flaghan.

Upon entering the room, Flaghan had asked the same question as his colleague, and had received the same response.

"She hasn't woken up yet," had been the sheriff's succinct report on Abigail's condition. "Other than a few cuts and bruises she's physically fine. The doctors are confused about why she hasn't regained consciousness yet. I sympathise with you, Mr Muir, I truly do, but I need a few answers from you about what the hell happened tonight."

In a dull monotone, Martin had given the sheriff a version of events that was close to the truth. He and Abigail had been at the carnival and word had reached them that the store was on fire. They had made their way there, he had been attacked by a disgruntled citizen, and the killer, whom Martin recognised from their earlier encounter, had run down four people and kidnapped Abigail. His lawyer, who had also been at the carnival with a friend, had heard about the fire at the store and come to see if there was anything they could do. They had witnessed the kidnapping, and after picking him up they had pursued the killer. The rest the sheriff already knew.

Flaghan had gone on about how he thought Martin might have learned something from his first encounter with the killer. Martin had stared at the wall, saying nothing. Eventually the sheriff had sighed and asked how Martin had known to go to Abigail's house, and also what had happened there. Martin had replied that he hadn't been sure that was where Abigail had been taken, but it was the only place he could think of, and he had turned out to be right. With regards to events at the house prior to the blaze, he again stuck as closely to the truth as he could, only omitting the real reason Abigail was unconscious. Flaghan again told him he had been stupid not to have called the police, and this time Martin responded.

"I didn't have fucking time! She was trapped in there with a murderer, sheriff, and there was no way I was going to arse about outside waiting for you lot. I have no regrets about what I did. The one regret I do have is that the soulless son of a bitch that has put the woman I love in a hospital bed didn't die a slower and more painful death. He got off too fucking lightly!"

"I agree with you there," Flaghan had told him. Martin had shot him a quizzical look. "It seems this bastard was responsible not just for the previous murders, but for the killings of Philip and Anne Glenster, as well as a French traveller who was brought in here last night. Also the officer the fucker ran down died due to massive trauma to the head. The other hit and run victims all survived, though each had a broken bone or two."

The news of the death of the old doctor and his wife, and someone who could only have been Matthew, barely touched Martin, whose capacity for grief had already been stretched beyond its limits. However he had felt a little guilty that he hadn't thought to ask after Beth and Amanda, and he offered his condolences to the sheriff. He had told Martin he should get some rest. He had added that there would probably be more questions, but he had enough to be going on with.

No sooner had Martin been left alone than he had more company, this time in the form of Andrea Coyle and Sandra Logan. Bad as he felt, their appearance drew a smile from him. He asked what had happened after he had departed the scene of the crash.

"We came to, and the sheriff helped us out of the car," Coyle had told him. "He was mightily annoyed at you for running off. Our explanation of what had happened didn't appease him much."

"The two of us wanted to go looking for you," Sandra had added. "But the sheriff was adamant our first stop was to be here at the hospital. We were brought here in an ambulance, and were still here by the time they brought you and Abigail in."

Martin asked to see her. Sandra looked hesitant, but Coyle nodded and helped him out of bed and then helped him put on a robe. With her on one side and Sandra on the other, they made their way to where Abigail lay on a bed in a small room of her own. A wheeled monitor station sat by her bed, the various screens and graphs giving a constant readout of her vital signs. Martin didn't have a clue what any of it meant, but he took the monotonous beeps and clicks to be a good thing.

Then he had laid eyes on Abigail.

Lying on her back, her arms above the covers, her chest rising and falling in a perfectly natural rhythm, her closed eyes and the memory of the shriek she had let out when the journals had burned had taken his legs out from under him. Coyle had caught him as he had collapsed, and Sandra had grabbed a chair for him.

And in that chair he sat now, Coyle and Sandra behind him. After several minutes he collected himself and spoke.

"Corday poured fuel everywhere, then set fire to it. Abi and I were in the attic. She had packed her journals into bags and we were going to try and get out through the skylight, but then he came up. We fought. He was going to kill me. She stabbed him. He hit the cabinet and fell to the floor, then the cabinet came down, took him and the journals down into the flames. She screamed and fell to the floor. I tried to wake her up, but I couldn't. I shouted out the window. Next thing, I woke up in the hospital.

"She knew this would happen if anything happened to those journals," he said. "She wrote in one of them years ago about the murder of her parents, but remembering hurt too much, so she destroyed the page and doing so wiped the memory away. She re-wrote what had happened so she wouldn't have to deal with how they actually died. Miss Coyle, is there anything you can do to bring her back?"

"Martin," said Coyle softly. "What are you talking about?"

It dawned on him then that they didn't know. Martin explained and repeated his question.

"I honestly don't know, Martin" Coyle replied. "But I will find out. I promise you."

She and Sandra remained there for another thirty minutes, and then she suggested he return to his bed.

"I'm staying here," were his first and last words on the subject. Andrea and Sandra offered no argument and left, telling him they would be back later.

Over the course of the next couple of hours, several doctors and nurses came in and told him he should go back to his bed and get some rest. He gave all of them the same three word response he'd given Miss Coyle. He told them that they could drag him kicking and screaming back to his room, or knock him out and wheel him there, but they would have to chain him to the bed to prevent him coming back to Abigail. Eventually they left him alone, and he sat holding her hand until he fell asleep.

He was awoken in the early hours of the morning by the door opening. Turning round, he saw Beth and Amanda standing in the doorway, the former on crutches, one leg in a cast, the latter with her arm in a sling. Martin rose and went to them as they entered the room. He hugged them both and they immediately started crying. He wept along with them before offering Beth his seat. They asked what happened, and he gave them a brief version of events. They asked why Abigail had been targeted, and he lied and told them he didn't know.

"Do they know if she'll wake up?" Amanda asked.

"I haven't spoken to a doctor about it," he told her, biting back a bitter comment about how she would never wake up because everything she was, every memory she had ever had, was nothing more than ashes now. Her mind was a complete blank. The woman he loved was gone forever. He said not one word of this, but the thought alone was enough to make him want to break down, and he came within a hair's breadth of telling the happy lie that he was sure she would wake up, that she was just unconscious and not in a coma or anything.

"We can't lose her too," sniffed Beth.

She and Amanda spent some time talking to Abigail, pleading with her to wake up. They left with a promise to return soon.

Martin sat back down in his chair, took Abigail's hand and laid his head on the bed beside her. After a few minutes, he had fallen back to sleep.

It was only a short time later that the door opened again and Abigail's aunt and uncle entered. Martin rose from his chair, but found that he did not know what to say to them. There was an awkward silence for a few moments, and then Peter Morton extended his hand.

"The sheriff told us about what you did, how you went after her when that son of a bitch took her."

Martin nodded and shook the man's hand. When they had finished, Janine stepped forward and gave Martin a hug, thanking him for saving Abigail. As she stepped back, dabbing at her eyes with a tissue, she asked if there had been any change.

"No," said Martin. "I've been here since I woke up, but she hasn't moved."

"She will," stated Peter, nodding. "She's a strong girl. Whatever is wrong with her, she just needs time to kick its ass, then she'll come back to us."

As Abigail's friends had done, her aunt and uncle sat and spoke to her for a while before leaving, saying they would be back again the following day.

Martin opened his eyes only to squeeze them shut again against the glare of the morning sun streaming through the window. He looked at Abigail and could discern no change, not that he had expected any.

Hadn't expected, but the intense heartache he felt revealed that he had been hoping. He was still holding her hand, and he raised it to his lips, kissing the back of it gently.

"I can't just accept that you're gone, Abi. There has to be something of you still there; you're too strong a person for there not to be. So I want you to listen to me: I need you to come back to me. I need you to come back because if you don't, I will spend the rest of my life sitting in this uncomfortable chair, and you don't want that because I will eventually start to bitch about it. I need you to come back because... because it's just not fair, Abi. We were there. We beat the odds. No more letters, no more picturing things and sharing memories. It was all going to be new from now on, Abi. You and me, making memories, seeing it all together, no need for letters... Abi, please... I can't tell you how much I need you to come back to me... please."

He stared at her, willing her to open her eyes, but she did not.

Then an idea struck him. Unfortunately it required Miss Coyle and Sandra, and he had no way of reaching them. Even if he did find a phone, he had no idea what Sandra's number was. Waiting for them to arrive was torture, and when Sandra walked through the door just after midday, he all but pounced on her.

"My laptop," he said, bypassing a greeting entirely.

"I need you or Miss Coyle to bring me my laptop." He looked over Sandra's shoulder. "Where is Miss Coyle?"

"She's flown back to Scotland to look into the possibility of the messy conclusion to Abigail's transferral ceremony having something to do with her memory issues, and consequently her not waking up. She said she would be back as soon as she could."

"Good. Can you get me my laptop? Please? It's in our room at your house."

"Of course, Martin. I'll go back and get it right now. But, why do you want it?"

"I can't sit here and do nothing, and there's something on there I can use to help me do something. I doubt if it will do any good, but I want to do it anyway."

Sandra nodded and left again. She returned within half an hour with his laptop, and a bag with some clothes and toiletries in it. He took them and thanked her.

"Can I ask what your idea is?"

"On here," he said, booting up his machine. "I have copies of every letter Abigail has ever sent to me. She kept all my replies, but they... They were in the house as well, so they're gone, but I'll tell her what I can remember of what I said."

"You're hoping she'll hear you and it will jog her memory."

"I'm not getting my hopes up, but at least I'll be doing something."

After saying a quick hello and goodbye to Abigail, Sandra gave Martin a note of her phone number. He thanked her, kissed her on the cheek, and said he would call if he needed to update her on anything. When she was gone, he sat down in his chair and explained his idea to Abigail. Then he began.

"Dear Martin, my name is Abigail Morton and I am 9 years old. I live in the town of Hannerville in..."

Over the course of three days, he ate and slept in the chair, moving only to wash and use the facilities. After reading one of Abigail's letters he would pause, doing his best to recall what had been in his reply. He was surprised at how much came back to him as he related a life that had been shared long before they had ever met one another in person.

After the three days, he wasn't even halfway through the letters, and there had been no apparent change in Abigail's condition. Nonetheless, he read on, determined to read them all. It occurred to him at one point that he was reading them more for himself now than for Abigail, clinging to what might well be all that was left of her. Martin told himself if that was so, then he'd read and re-read these letters until he went blind, and then he'd have someone read them to him, just as he was reading them to her now. If that was the only way to keep her with him, then that's what he would do.

On the afternoon of the fourth day, Andrea and Sandra entered the room to find him asleep, his head bowed forward, his laptop switched on and balanced precariously on his knees. Andrea stood beside him and whispered his name. Martin awoke with such a start that his laptop began to slide. He grabbed it, sat it on the bed, got to his feet and asked if Miss Coyle had found anything out.

"I've spoken to someone who is as close to a specialist in this kind of thing as it's possible to get. He came to the conclusion that the interruption of the transferral ceremony is the most likely cause of Abigail's memory issues. He believes that although Abigail had to write things down to remember them, those memories must still have been getting stored in her brain. He believes they are simply locked away. The analogy he used was that the journals were like backup copies, but the originals as still stored in the hard drive of Abigail's brain. He thinks that performing the unlocking might, in addition to unlocking the memories of past Bearers, unlock her own."

"Is this something that could hurt her?" asked Martin.

"I have to be honest, Martin," said Coyle gravely. "These are uncharted waters; I honestly have no idea what might happen." Martin looked at Abigail. Days had passed and she hadn't so much as twitched. If she stayed like that, how long before someone decided she would never wake up? What then?

"Okay," he said. "Do we need candles and robes and whatnot?"

"Nothing of the sort," said Sandra. "That kind of thing is just ceremonial set dressing, though normally there would be a bit of reverence to this."

"All that's really needed is the incantation," said Coyle. "And I have that in here." She tapped the tip of her right index finger against her temple.

Sandra was stationed outside the door to make sure no one walked in. Just in case, they also locked the door. Andrea asked Martin to stand back, and then she positioned herself beside Abigail's bed and placed a hand on her forehead. She began speaking in the same language Martin had caught a snippet of the night he and Abigail had been shown some of the memories hidden away in their minds. He kept his eyes on Abigail as Coyle spoke the incantation. In a minute or two it was done, but there had been no change. Martin tried to hide his disappointment as he approached the bed, but he was sure that if his old teacher looked at him now she would see it written all over his face.

"There have never been circumstances like these before," she murmured. "It might take a little time."

They waited for several minutes, during which Andrea let Sandra back into the room. Martin saw his disappointment mirrored on her face when she saw that Abigail was still unconscious. He sat back down in his chair and took Abigail's hand, and they all waited for almost half an hour. Abigail did not stir.

"What if we wait overnight," suggested Sandra. "Just to be sure."

The others agreed with this and the Guardians departed, leaving Martin to look over Abigail. He sat the entire night, intently watching her for any sign that she might be coming round. He clutched her hand and silently urged her again and again to come back to him. He wasn't even aware that he was falling asleep until he woke up the following morning, his hand still clasping hers.

Abigail was still unconscious.

"Damn it to hell!" spat Coyle when she came in twenty minutes later. "I hoped that would be enough." Her words gave Martin the impression there was something he was missing.

"What do you mean?" he asked. "What else is there?"

"The specialist I spoke to has studied the incantations and their properties for years. He told me of a process that might be of some use to us, but it's dangerous. It would be under normal circumstances, but now that the other memories have been unlocked, it will be even more so, both to Abigail and to whoever tried to help her."

"That'll be me," Martin declared, gazing at Abigail. He looked at Coyle. "What do I have to do?"

"For a start you have to prepare," he was informed. "And you can't do that here. You'll have to come back to Sandra's house. I'll contact the specialist and get him to come over, help you prepare." She saw him get ready to argue and pre-empted it. "No ifs, ands or buts, Martin. Sandra and I will wait for you in the hall." He closed his mouth, and a heartbeat later nodded. The Guardians exited and Martin spoke to Abigail.

"I'm only leaving because it might be the only way to get you back. I'll return as soon as I can, Abi. I love you." He stood, leaned over and kissed her lips, and then quickly left the room.

Somewhere in the depths of her mind, amidst a cacophony of others, Abigail Morton's voice called out six words.

"Marty, I'm here! Please, help me!"

Printed in Great Britain
by Amazon.co.uk, Ltd.,
Marston Gate.